EXTRAORDINARY ACCLAIM FOR
MICHAEL CONNELLY AND
THE REVERSAL

THE #1 *NEW YORK TIMES* BESTSELLER
A *LIBRARY JOURNAL* BEST THRILLER OF THE YEAR
A *MIAMI HERALD* TOP TEN CRIME FICTION OF THE YEAR

"Brilliant...It's always good to see Bosch back in action—and even better reading Connelly's new work...Grade: A."
— *Cleveland Plain Dealer*

"Connelly executes the subtle sleight of hand that makes each of his books so much more than the sum of its parts...He writes true-to-life fiction about true crime. What makes his crime stories ring most true is that they're never really over." — Janet Maslin, *New York Times*

"A crackling good read, smart and emotionally satisfying...THE REVERSAL confirms Connelly's status as a cultural institution in this city...His books are rich in the details and meanings of seismic events that have formed the rough contours of L.A. law and order."
— *Los Angeles Times*

"Connelly is a master." — *New York Times Book Review*

"Another splendid legal thriller." — *San Diego Union-Tribune*

"A searing novel that works as a legal thriller, a police procedural, and an intimate tale about the vagaries of family." — *Miami Herald*

"Connelly may be our most versatile crime writer. His Harry Bosch series has taken the hard-boiled cop novel to a new level of complexity... Reading this book is like watching a master craftsman, slowly and carefully, brick by brick, build something that holds together exquisitely, form and function in perfect alignment."
— *Booklist* (starred review)

"A masterful writer...I'd be willing to bet that in the long run, Bosch ends up as a permanent part of the American literary pantheon, right up there with Huck Finn and Jay Gatsby and Philip Marlowe."

—*Chicago Tribune*

"Michael Connelly is the most talented of crime writers."

—*The New Yorker*

"Grabs you with the first paragraph...The package is wrapped up in Connelly's prose, which is so smooth that it looks easy. Only after the book has accelerated through its unexpected climax and the characters are winding down in preparation to fight another day does it become clear that the work's success is no accident, but the product of a master fully in command of his craft."

—*Denver Post*

"Connelly is a master of mixing realistic details of police work and courtroom procedure with the private feelings and personal lives of his protagonists, and of building suspense even as he evokes the somber poetry inherent in battling the dark side."

—*Wall Street Journal*

"Fascinating...Just when you think you know exactly where [Connelly] is headed he flips on his blinker and makes a U turn. That is what makes him such an exciting writer and one we love to read."

—*Huffington Post*

"Michael Connelly's books about these guys, separately or together, are always rewarding, and this one—with its cast-iron plot and vivid figures—is among his best."

—*Seattle Times*

"Plot, nuance, characters, dialogue—as usual, Connelly delivers it all, and brilliantly."

—*BookPage*

"What are the odds of an author, after publishing twenty novels, producing two stunning back-to-back books? In the world of contemporary noirish crime fiction, there's only one writer who can pull that sort of darkness out of a hat: Michael Connelly."

— *Toronto Globe and Mail*

"[A] genius thriller...must-read...Like a great meal, the preparation is often as marvelous as the finished product...What makes Connelly the master of his craft is that he is constantly reinventing himself and his characters."

— TheDailyBeast.com

"Connelly is, quite simply, the best of the best."

— *Philadelphia Inquirer*

"Breathtaking tension...Connelly is one of the best contemporary writers of crime fiction, and in THE REVERSAL he's at the top of his form...an irresistible read to the very end."

— *St. Petersburg Times*

"[Bosch is] one of the most compelling heroes of modern crime fiction."

— Associated Press

"Connelly has been writing about Bosch since his 1992 Edgar-winning *The Black Echo*, yet he still finds new depths to his constantly evolving character. With Mickey now in the mix, Connelly continues to show why he is one of the best—and most consistent—living crime writers."

— *South Florida Sun-Sentinel*

"Connelly weaves a tale that solidifies his reputation as the master of the modern crime thriller...[It] constantly surprises and has keen character insight."

— *Library Journal*

"The best mystery writer in the world."

— *GQ*

THE
REVERSAL

A NOVEL

MICHAEL
CONNELLY

GRAND CENTRAL
PUBLISHING

NEW YORK   BOSTON

Copyright © 2010 by Hieronymus, Inc.
Preview of *Wrong Side of Goodbye* copyright © 2016 by Hieronymus, Inc.

Grand Central Publishing
Hachette Book Group
1290 Avenue of the Americas
New York, NY 10104
grandcentralpublishing.com
twitter.com/grandcentralpub

Originally published in hardcover and ebook by Little, Brown and Company in October 2010.
First trade paperback edition: November 2013
Reissued: August 2016

Grand Central Publishing is a division of Hachette Book Group, Inc.
The Grand Central Publishing name and logo are trademarks of Hachette Book Group, Inc.

The publisher is not responsible for websites (or their content) that are not owned by the publisher.

The Hachette Speakers Bureau provides a wide range of authors for speaking events. To find out more, go to www.hachettespeakersbureau.com or call (866) 376-6591.

LCCN 2010021820

ISBNs: 978-1-4555-3650-4 (pbk. reissue), 978-0-316-06946-5 (ebook)

Printed in the United States of America

RRD-C

10 9 8 7 6 5 4 3 2 1

To Shannon Byrne
with many thanks

THE
REVERSAL

PART ONE

—The Perp Walk

One

Tuesday, February 9, 1:43 P.M.

The last time I'd eaten at the Water Grill I sat across the table from a client who had coldly and calculatedly murdered his wife and her lover, shooting both of them in the face. He had engaged my services to not only defend him at trial but fully exonerate him and restore his good name in the public eye. This time I was sitting with someone with whom I needed to be even more careful. I was dining with Gabriel Williams, the district attorney of Los Angeles County.

It was a crisp afternoon in midwinter. I sat with Williams and his trusted chief of staff — read political advisor — Joe Ridell. The meal had been set for 1:30 P.M., when most courthouse lawyers would be safely back in the CCB, and the DA would not be advertising his dalliance with a member of the dark side. Meaning me, Mickey Haller, defender of the damned.

The Water Grill was a nice place for a downtown lunch. Good food and atmosphere, good separation between tables for private conversation, and a wine list hard to top in all of downtown. It was the kind of place where you kept your suit jacket on and the waiter put a black napkin across your lap so you needn't be bothered with doing it yourself. The prosecution team ordered martinis at the county taxpayers' expense and I stuck with the free water the restaurant was pouring. It took Williams two gulps of gin and one olive before he got to the reason we were hiding in plain sight.

"Mickey, I have a proposition for you."

I nodded. Ridell had already said as much when he had called that morning to set up the lunch. I had agreed to the meet and then had gone to work on the phone myself, trying to gather any inside information I could on what the proposition would be. Not even my first ex-wife, who worked in the district attorney's employ, knew what was up.

"I'm all ears," I said. "It's not every day that the DA himself wants to give you a proposition. I know it can't be in regard to any of my clients—they wouldn't merit much attention from the guy at the top. And at the moment I'm only carrying a few cases anyway. Times are slow."

"Well, you're right," Williams said. "This is not about any of your clients. I have a case I would like you to take on."

I nodded again. I understood now. They all hate the defense attorney until they need the defense attorney. I didn't know if Williams had any children but he would have known through due diligence that I didn't do juvy work. So I was guessing it had to be his wife. Probably a shoplifting grab or a DUI he was trying to keep under wraps.

"Who got popped?" I asked.

Williams looked at Ridell and they shared a smile.

"No, nothing like that," Williams said. "My proposition is this. I would like to hire you, Mickey. I want you to come work at the DA's office."

Of all the ideas that had been rattling around in my head since I had taken Ridell's call, being hired as a prosecutor wasn't one of them. I'd been a card-carrying member of the criminal defense bar for more than twenty years. During that time I'd grown a suspicion and distrust of prosecutors and police that might not have equaled that of the gangbangers down in Nickerson Gardens but was at least at a level that would seem to exclude me from ever joining their ranks. Plain and simple, they wouldn't want me and I wouldn't want them. Except for that ex-wife I mentioned and a half brother who was an LAPD detective, I wouldn't turn my back on any of them. Especially Williams. He was a politician first and a prosecutor second. That made him even more dangerous. Though briefly a prosecutor early in his legal career, he spent two decades as a civil rights attorney before running for the DA post as an outsider and riding into office on a tide of anti-police and -prosecutor sentiment. I was employing full caution at the fancy lunch from the moment the napkin went across my lap.

"Work for you?" I asked. "Doing what exactly?"

"As a special prosecutor. A onetime deal. I want you to handle the Jason Jessup case."

I looked at him for a long moment. First I thought I would laugh out loud. This was some sort of cleverly orchestrated joke. But then I understood that couldn't be the case. They don't take you out to the Water Grill just to make a joke.

"You want me to prosecute Jessup? From what I hear there's nothing to prosecute. That case is a duck without wings. The only thing left to do is shoot it and eat it."

Williams shook his head in a manner that seemed intended to convince himself of something, not me.

"Next Tuesday is the anniversary of the murder," he said. "I'm going to announce that we intend to retry Jessup. And I would like you standing next to me at the press conference."

I leaned back in my seat and looked at them. I've spent a good part of my adult life looking across courtrooms and trying to read juries, judges, witnesses and prosecutors. I think I've gotten pretty good at it. But at that table I couldn't read Williams or his sidekick sitting three feet away from me.

Jason Jessup was a convicted child killer who had spent nearly twenty-four years in prison until a month earlier, when the California Supreme Court reversed his conviction and sent the case back to Los

Angeles County for either retrial or a dismissal of the charges. The reversal came after a two-decade-long legal battle staged primarily from Jessup's cell and with his own pen. Authoring appeals, motions, complaints and whatever legal challenges he could research, the self-styled lawyer made no headway with state and federal courts but did finally win the attention of an organization of lawyers known as the Genetic Justice Project. They took over his cause and his case and eventually won an order for genetic testing of semen found on the dress of the child Jessup had been convicted of strangling.

Jessup had been convicted before DNA analysis was used in criminal trials. The analysis performed these many years later determined that the semen found on the dress had not come from Jessup but from another unknown individual. Though the courts had repeatedly upheld Jessup's conviction, this new information tipped the scales in Jessup's favor. The state's supreme court cited the DNA findings and other inconsistencies in the evidence and trial record and reversed the case.

This was pretty much the extent of my knowledge of the Jessup case, and it was largely information gathered from newspaper stories and courthouse scuttlebutt. While I had not read the court's complete order, I had read parts of it in the *Los Angeles Times* and knew it was a blistering decision that echoed many of Jessup's long-held claims of innocence as well as police and prosecutorial misconduct in the case. As a defense attorney, I can't say I wasn't pleased to see the DA's office raked over the media coals with the ruling. Call it underdog schadenfreude. It didn't really matter that it wasn't my case or that the current regime in the DA's office had nothing to do with the case back in 1986, there are so few victories from the defense side of the bar that there is always a sense of communal joy in the success of others and the defeat of the establishment.

The supreme court's ruling was announced the week before, starting a sixty-day clock during which the DA would have to retry or discharge Jessup. It seemed that not a day had gone by since the ruling that Jessup was not in the news. He gave multiple interviews by phone and in person at San Quentin, proclaiming his innocence and pot-shotting the police and prosecutors who put him there. In his plight, he had garnered the support of several Hollywood celebrities and professional athletes and had already launched a civil claim against both the city and county, seeking millions of dollars in damages for the many long years during which he was falsely incarcerated. In this day of nonstop media cycles, he had a never-ending forum and was using it to elevate himself to folk hero status. When he finally walked out of prison, he, too, would be a celebrity.

Knowing as little as I did about the case in the details, I was of the impression that he was an innocent man who had been subjected to a quarter century of torture and that he deserved whatever he could get for it. I did, however, know enough about the case to understand that with the DNA evidence cutting Jessup's way, the case was a loser and the idea of retrying Jessup seemed to be an exercise in political masochism unlikely to come from the brain trust of Williams and Ridell.

Unless...

"What do you know that I don't know?" I asked. "And that the *Los Angeles Times* doesn't know."

Williams smiled smugly and leaned forward across the table to deliver his answer.

"All Jessup established with the help of the GJP is that his DNA was not on the victim's dress," he said. "As the petitioner, it was not up to him to establish who it did come from."

"So you ran it through the data banks."

Williams nodded.

"We did. And we got a hit."

He offered nothing else.

"Well, who was it?"

"I'm not going to reveal that to you unless you come aboard on the case. Otherwise, I need to keep it confidential. But I will say that I believe our findings lead to a trial tactic that could neutralize the

DNA question, leaving the rest of the case—and the evidence—pretty much intact. DNA was not needed to convict him the first time. We won't need it now. As in nineteen eighty-six, we believe Jessup is guilty of this crime and I would be delinquent in my duties if I did not attempt to prosecute him, no matter the chances of conviction, the potential political fallout and the public perception of the case."

Spoken as if he were looking at the cameras and not at me.

"Then why don't you prosecute him?" I asked. "Why come to me? You have three hundred able lawyers working for you. I can think of one you've got stuck up in the Van Nuys office who would take this case in a heartbeat. Why come to me?"

"Because this prosecution can't come from within the DA's office. I am sure you have read or heard the allegations. There's a taint on this case and it doesn't matter that there isn't one goddamn lawyer working for me who was around back then. I still need to bring in an outsider, an independent to take it to court. Somebody—"

"That's what the attorney general's office is for," I said. "You need an independent counsel, you go to him."

Now I was just poking him in the eye and everybody at the table knew it. There was no way Gabriel Williams was going to ask the state AG to come in on the case. That would cross the razor-wire line of politics. The AG post was an elected office in California and was seen by every political pundit in town as Williams's next stop on his way to the governor's mansion or some other lofty political plateau. The last thing Williams would be willing to do was hand a potential political rival a case that could be used against him, no matter how old it was. In politics, in the courtroom, in life, you don't give your opponent the club with which he can turn around and clobber you.

"We're not going to the AG with this one," Williams said in a matter-of-fact manner. "That's why I want you, Mickey. You're a well-known and respected criminal defense attorney. I think the public will trust you to be independent in this matter and will therefore trust and accept the conviction you'll win in this case."

While I was staring at Williams a waiter came to the table to take our order. Without ever breaking eye contact with me, Williams told him to go away.

"I haven't been paying a lot of attention to this," I said. "Who's Jessup's defense attorney? I would find it difficult to go up against a colleague I know well."

"Right now all he's got is the GJP lawyer and his civil litigator. He hasn't hired defense counsel because quite frankly he's expecting us to drop this whole thing."

I nodded, another hurdle cleared for the moment.

"But he's got a surprise coming," Williams said. "We're going to bring him down here and retry him. He did it, Mickey, and that's all you really need to know. There's a little girl who's still dead, and that's all any prosecutor needs to know. Take the case. Do something for your community and for yourself. Who knows, you might even like it and want to stay on. If so, we'll definitely entertain the possibility."

I dropped my eyes to the linen tablecloth and thought about his last words. For a moment, I involuntarily conjured the image of my daughter sitting in a courtroom and watching me stand for the People instead of the accused. Williams kept talking, unaware that I had already come to a decision.

"Obviously, I can't pay you your rate, but if you take this on, I don't think you'll be doing it for the money anyway. I can give you an office and a secretary. And I can give you whatever science and forensics you need. The very best of every —"

"I don't want an office in the DA's office. I would need to be independent of that. I have to be completely autonomous. No more lunches. We make the announcement and then you leave me alone. I decide how to proceed with the case."

"Fine. Use your own office, just as long as you don't store evidence there. And, of course, you make your own decisions."

"And if I do this, I pick second chair and my own investigator out of the LAPD. People I can trust."

"In or outside my office for your second?"

"I would need someone inside."

"Then I assume we're talking about your ex-wife."

"That's right—if she'll take it. And if somehow we get a conviction out of this thing, you pull her out of Van Nuys and put her downtown in Major Crimes, where she belongs."

"That's easier said than—"

"That's the deal. Take it or leave it."

Williams glanced at Ridell and I saw the supposed sidekick give an almost imperceptible nod of approval.

"All right," Williams said, turning back to me. "Then I guess I'll take it. You win and she's in. We have a deal."

He reached his hand across the table and I shook it. He smiled but I didn't.

"Mickey Haller for the People," he said. "Has a nice ring to it."

For the People. It should have made me feel good. It should have made me feel like I was part of something that was noble and right. But all I had was the bad feeling that I had crossed some sort of line within myself.

"Wonderful," I said.

TWO

Friday, February 12, 10:00 A.M.

Harry Bosch stepped up to the front counter of the District Attorney's Office on the eighteenth floor of the Criminal Courts Building. He gave his name and said he had a ten A.M. appointment with District Attorney Gabriel Williams.

"Actually, your meeting is in conference room A," said the receptionist after checking a computer screen in front of her. "You go through the door, turn right and go to the end of the hall. Right again and conference room A is on the left. It's marked on the door. They're expecting you."

The door in the paneled-wood wall behind her buzzed free and Bosch went through, wondering about the fact that *they* were waiting for him. Since he had received the summons from the DA's secretary the afternoon before, Bosch had been unable to determine what it was about. Secrecy was expected from the DA's Office but usually some information trickled out. He hadn't even known he would be meeting with more than one person until now.

Following the prescribed trail, Bosch came to the door marked CONFERENCE ROOM A, knocked once and heard a female voice say, "Come in."

He entered and saw a woman seated by herself at an eight-chaired table, a spread of documents, files, photos and a laptop computer in front of her. She looked vaguely familiar but he could not place her. She was attractive with dark, curling hair framing her face. She had sharp eyes that followed him as he entered, and a pleasant, almost curious smile. Like she knew something he didn't. She wore the standard female prosecutor's power suit in navy blue. Harry might not have been able to place her but he assumed she was a DDA.

"Detective Bosch?"

"That's me."

"Come in, have a seat."

Bosch pulled out a chair and sat across from her. On the table he saw a crime scene photograph of a child's body in an open Dumpster. It was a girl and she was wearing a blue dress with long sleeves. Her feet were bare and she was lying on a pile of construction debris and other trash. The white edges of the photo were yellowed. It was an old print.

The woman moved a file over the picture and then offered her hand across the table.

"I don't think we've ever met," she said. "My name is Maggie McPherson."

Bosch recognized the name but he couldn't remember from where or what case.

"I'm a deputy district attorney," she continued, "and I'm going to be second chair on the Jason Jessup prosecution. First chair—"

"Jason Jessup?" Bosch asked. "You're going to take it to trial?"

"Yes, we are. We'll be announcing it next week and I need to ask you to keep it confidential until then. I am sorry that our first chair is late coming to our meet—"

The door opened and Bosch turned. Mickey Haller stepped into the room. Bosch did a double take. Not because he didn't recognize Haller. They were half brothers and he easily knew him on sight. But seeing Haller in the DA's office was one of those images that didn't quite make sense. Haller was a criminal defense attorney. He fit in at the DA's office about as well as a cat did at the dog pound.

"I know," Haller said. "You're thinking, What in the hell is this?"

Smiling, Haller moved to McPherson's side of the table and started pulling out a chair. Then Bosch remembered how he knew McPherson's name.

"You two...," Bosch said. "You were married, right?"

"That's right," Haller said. "Eight wonderful years."

"And what, she's prosecuting Jessup and you're defending him? Isn't that a conflict of interest?"

Haller's smile became a broad grin.

"It would only be a conflict if we were opposing each other, Harry. But we're not. We're prosecuting him. Together. I'm first chair. Maggie's second. And we want you to be our investigator."

Bosch was completely confused.

"Wait a minute. You're not a prosecutor. This doesn't—"

"I'm an appointed independent prosecutor, Harry. It's all legit. I wouldn't be sitting here if it weren't. We're going after Jessup and we want you to help us."

"From what I heard, this case is beyond help. Unless you're telling me Jessup rigged the DNA test."

"No, we're not telling you that," McPherson said. "We did our own testing and matching. His results were correct. It wasn't his DNA on the victim's dress."

"But that doesn't mean we've lost the case," Haller quickly added.

Bosch looked from McPherson to Haller and then back again. He was clearly missing something.

"Then whose DNA was it?" he asked.

McPherson glanced sideways at Haller before answering.

"Her stepfather's," she said. "He's dead now but we believe there is an explanation for why his semen was found on his stepdaughter's dress."

Haller leaned urgently across the table.

"An explanation that still leaves room to reconvict Jessup of the girl's murder."

Bosch thought for a moment and the image of his own daughter flashed in his mind. He knew there were certain kinds of evil in the world that had to be contained, no matter the hardship. A child killer was at the top of that list.

"Okay," he said. "I'm in."

Three

The DA's Office had a press conference room that had not been updated since the days they'd used it to hold briefings on the Charles Manson case. Its faded wood-paneled walls and drooping flags in the corner had been the backdrop of a thousand press briefings and they gave all proceedings there a threadbare appearance that belied the true power and might of the office. The state prosecutor was never the underdog in any undertaking, yet it appeared that the office did not have the money for even a fresh coat of paint.

The setting, however, served the announcement on the Jessup decision well. For possibly the first time in these hallowed halls of justice, the prosecution would indeed be the underdog. The decision to retry Jason Jessup was fraught with peril and the realistic likelihood of failure. As I stood at the front of the room next to Gabriel Williams and before a phalanx of video cameras, bright lights and reporters, it finally dawned on me what a terrible mistake I had made. My decision to take on the case in hopes of currying favor with my daughter, ex-wife and myself was going to be met with disastrous consequences. I was going to go down in flames.

It was a rare moment to witness firsthand. The media had gathered to report the end of the story. The DA's Office would assuredly announce that Jason Jessup would not be subjected to a retrial. The DA might not offer an apology but would at the very least say the evidence was not there. That there was no case against this man who had been incarcerated for so long. The case would be closed and in the eyes of the law as well as the public Jessup would finally be a free and innocent man.

The media is rarely fooled in complete numbers and usually doesn't react well when it happens. But there was no doubt that Williams had punked them all. We had moved stealthily in the last week, putting together the team and reviewing the evidence that was still available. Not a word had leaked, which must've been a first in the halls of the CCB. While I could see the first inkling of suspicion creasing the brows of the reporters who recognized me as we entered, it was Williams who delivered the knockout punch when he wasted no time in stepping before a lectern festooned with microphones and digital recorders.

"On a Sunday morning twenty-four years ago today, twelve-year-old Melissa Landy was taken from her yard in Hancock Park and brutally murdered. An investigation quickly led to a suspect named Jason Jessup. He was arrested, convicted at trial and sentenced to life in prison without parole. That conviction was reversed two weeks ago by the state supreme court and remanded to my office. I am here to announce that the Los Angeles County District Attorney's Office will retry Jason Jessup in the death of Melissa Landy. The charges of abduction and murder stand. This office intends once again to prosecute Mr. Jessup to the fullest extent of the law."

He paused to add appropriate gravity to the announcement.

"As you know, the supreme court found that irregularities occurred during the first prosecution — which, of course, occurred more than two decades before the current administration. To avoid political conflicts and any future appearance of impropriety on the part of this office, I have appointed an independent special prosecutor to handle the case. Many of you know of the man standing here to my right. Michael Haller has been a defense counselor of some note in Los Angeles for two decades. He is a fair-minded and respected member of the bar. He has accepted the appointment and has assumed responsibility for the case as of today. It has been the policy of this department not to try cases in the media. However, Mr. Haller and I are willing to answer a few questions as long as they don't tread on the specifics and evidence of the case."

There was a booming chorus of voices calling questions out at us. Williams raised his hands for calm in the room.

"One at a time, people. Let's start with you."

He pointed to a woman sitting in the first row. I could not remember her name but I knew she worked for the *Times*. Williams knew his priorities.

"Kate Salters from the *Times*," she said helpfully. "Can you tell us how you came to the decision to prosecute Jason Jessup again after DNA evidence cleared him of the crime?"

Before coming into the room, Williams had told me that he would handle the announcement and all questions unless specifically addressed to me. He made it clear that this was going to be his show. But I decided to make it clear from the outset that it was going to be my case.

"I'll answer that," I said as I leaned toward the lectern and the microphones. "The DNA test conducted by the Genetic Justice Project only concluded that the bodily fluid found on the victim's clothing did not come from Jason Jessup. It did not clear him of involvement in the crime. There is a difference. The DNA test only provides additional information for a jury to consider."

I straightened back up and caught Williams giving me a don't-fuck-with-me stare.

"Whose DNA was it?" someone called out.

Williams quickly leaned forward to answer.

"We're not answering questions about evidence at this time."

"Mickey, why are you taking the case?"

The question came from the back of the room, from behind the lights, and I could not see the owner of the voice. I moved back to the microphones, angling my body so Williams had to step back.

"Good question," I said. "It's certainly unusual for me to be on the other side of the aisle, so to speak. But I think this is the case to cross over for. I'm an officer of the court and a proud member of the California bar. We take an oath to seek justice and fairness while upholding the Constitution and laws of this nation and state. One of the duties of a lawyer is to take a just cause without personal consideration to himself. This is such a cause. Someone has to speak for Melissa Landy. I have reviewed the evidence in this case and I think I'm on the right side of this one. The measure is proof beyond a reasonable doubt. I think that such proof exists here."

Williams moved in and put a hand on my arm to gently move me off the microphone stand.

"We do not want to go any further than that in regard to the evidence," he said quickly.

"Jessup's already spent twenty-four years in prison," Salters said. "Anything less than a conviction for first-degree murder and he will probably walk on time served. Mr. Williams, is it really worth the expense and effort of retrying this man?"

Before she was finished asking the question, I knew she and Williams had a deal working. She lobbed softballs and he hit them out of the park, looking good and righteous on the eleven o'clock news and in the morning paper. Her end of the deal would come with inside scoops on the evidence and trial strategy. I decided in that moment that it was *my case, my trial, my deal.*

"None of that matters," I said loudly from my position to the side.

All eyes turned to me. Even Williams turned.

"Can you talk into the microphones, Mickey?"

It was the same voice from behind the line of lights. He knew to call me Mickey. I once again moved to the microphones, boxing Williams out like a power forward going for the rebound.

"The murder of a child is a crime that must be prosecuted to the full extent of the law, no matter what the possibilities or risks are. There is no guarantee of victory here. But that was not part of the decision. The measure is reasonable doubt and I believe we surpass that. We believe that the totality of evidence shows that this man committed this horrible crime and it doesn't matter how much time has gone by or how long he has been incarcerated. He must be prosecuted.

"I have a daughter only a little older than Melissa was.... You know, people forget that in the original trial, the state sought the death penalty but the jury recommended against it and the judge imposed a life sentence. That was then and this is now. We will once again be seeking the death penalty on this case."

Williams put his hand on my shoulder and pulled me away from the microphones.

"Uh, let's not get ahead of ourselves here," he said quickly. "My office has not yet made a determination in regard to whether we will be seeking the death penalty. That will come at a later time. But Mr. Haller makes a very valid and sad point. There can be no worse crime in our society than the murder of a child. We must do all that is within our power and our reach to seek justice for Melissa Landy. Thank you for being here today."

"Wait a minute," called a reporter from one of the middle seats. "What about Jessup? When will he be brought here for trial?"

Williams put his hands on both sides of the lectern in a casual move designed to keep me from the microphones.

"Earlier this morning Mr. Jessup was taken into custody by the Los Angeles police and is being transported from San Quentin. He will be booked into the downtown jail and the case will proceed. His conviction was reversed but the charges against him remain in place. We have nothing further at this time."

Williams stepped back and signaled me toward the door. He waited until I started moving and was clear of the microphones. He then followed, coming up behind me and whispering into my ear as we went through the door.

"You do that again and I'll fire you on the spot."

I turned to look back at him while I walked.

"Do what? Answer one of your setup questions?"

We moved into the hallway. Ridell was waiting there with the office's media spokesman, a guy named Fernandez. But Williams turned me down the hall away from them. He was still whispering when he spoke.

"You went off the script. Do it again and we're done."

I stopped and turned and Williams almost walked into me.

"Look, I'm not your puppet," I said. "I'm an independent contractor, remember? You treat me otherwise and you're going to be holding this hot potato without an oven mitt."

Williams just glared at me. I obviously wasn't getting through.

"And what was this shit about the death penalty?" he asked. "We haven't even gotten there and you didn't have the go-ahead to say it."

He was bigger than me, taller. He had used his body to crowd my space and back me up against the wall.

"It will get back to Jessup and keep him thinking," I said. "And if we're lucky, he comes in for a deal and this whole thing goes away, including the civil action. It'll save you all that money. That's really what this is about, right? The money. We get a conviction and he's got no civil case. You and the city save a few million bucks."

"That's got nothing to do with this. This is about justice and you still should have told me what you were doing. You don't sandbag your own boss."

The physical intimidation got old real fast. I put my palm on his chest and backed him off me.

"Yeah, well, you're not my boss. I don't have a boss."

"Is that right? Like I said, I could fire your ass right here right now."

I pointed down the hall to the door to the press conference room.

"Yeah, that'll look good. Firing the independent prosecutor *you* just hired. Didn't Nixon do that during the Watergate mess? Worked real well for him. Why don't we go back in and tell them? I'm sure there are still a few cameras in there."

Williams hesitated, realizing his predicament. I had backed him against the wall without even moving. He would look like a complete and unelectable fool if he fired me, and he knew it. He leaned in closer and his whisper dropped lower as he used the oldest threat in the mano a mano handbook. I was ready for it.

"Do not fuck with me, Haller."

"Then don't fuck with my case. This isn't a campaign stop and it's not about money. This is murder, boss. You want me to get a conviction, then get out of my way."

I threw him the bone of calling him boss. Williams pressed his mouth into a tight line and stared at me for a long moment.

"Just so we understand each other," he finally said.

I nodded.

"Yeah, I think we do."

"Before you talk to the media about this case, you get it approved by my office first. Understand?"

"Got it."

He turned and headed down the hall. His entourage followed. I remained in the hallway and watched them go. The truth was, there was nothing in the law that I objected to more than the death penalty. It was not that I had ever had a client executed or even tried such a case. It was simply a belief in the idea that an enlightened society did not kill its own.

But somehow that didn't stop me from using the threat of the death penalty as an edge in the case. As I stood there alone in the hallway, I thought that maybe that made me a better prosecutor than I had imagined I could be.

Four

It usually was the best moment of a case. The drive downtown with a suspect handcuffed in the backseat. There was nothing better. Sure there was the eventual payoff of a conviction down the line. Being in the courtroom when the verdict is read — watching the reality shock and then deaden the eyes of the convicted. But the drive in was always better, more immediate and personal. It was always the moment Bosch savored. The chase was over and the case was about to morph from the relentless momentum of the investigation to the measured pace of the prosecution.

But this time was different. It had been a long two days and Bosch wasn't savoring anything. He and his partner, David Chu, had driven up to Corta Madera the day before, checking into a motel off the 101 and spending the night. In the morning they drove over to San Quentin, presented a court order that transferred custody of Jason Jessup to them, and then collected their prisoner for the drive back to Los Angeles. Seven hours each way with a partner who talked too much. Seven hours on the return with a suspect who didn't talk enough.

They were now at the top of the San Fernando Valley and an hour from the City Jail in downtown L.A. Bosch's back hurt from so many hours behind the wheel. His right calf muscle ached from applying pressure to the gas pedal. The city car did not have cruise control.

Chu had offered to drive but Bosch had said no. Chu religiously stuck to the speed limit, even on the freeway. Bosch would take the backache over an extra hour on the freeway and the anxiety it would create.

All of this aside, he drove in uneasy silence, brooding about a case that seemed to be proceeding backwards. He had been on it for only a few days, hadn't had the opportunity to even become acquainted with all the facts, and here he was with the suspect hooked up and in the backseat. To Bosch it felt like the arrest was coming first and the investigation wouldn't really start until after Jessup was booked.

He checked his watch and knew the scheduled press conference must be over by now. The plan was for him to meet with Haller and McPherson at four to continue kicking around the case. But by the time Jessup was booked he would be late. He also needed to go by LAPD archives to pick up two boxes that were waiting for him.

"Harry, what's wrong?"

Bosch glanced at Chu.

"Nothing's wrong."

He wasn't going to talk in front of the suspect. Besides, he and Chu had been partnered for less than a year. It was a little soon for Chu to be making reads off of Bosch's demeanor. Harry didn't want him to know that he had accurately deduced that he was uncomfortable.

Jessup spoke from the backseat, his first words since asking for a bathroom break outside of Stockton.

"What's wrong is that he doesn't have a case. What's wrong is that he knows this whole thing is bullshit and he doesn't want to be part of it."

Bosch checked Jessup in the rearview mirror. He was slightly hunched forward because his hands were cuffed and locked to a chain that went to a set of shackles around his ankles. His head was shaved, a routine prison practice among men hoping to intimidate others. Bosch guessed that with Jessup it had probably worked.

"I thought you didn't want to talk, Jessup. You invoked."

"Yeah, that's right. I'll just shut the fuck up and wait for my lawyer."

"He's in San Francisco, I wouldn't hold my breath."

"He's calling somebody. The GJP's got people all over the country. We were ready for this."

"Really? You were ready? You mean you packed your cell up because you thought you were being transferred? Or was it because you thought you were going home?"

Jessup didn't have an answer for that one.

Bosch merged onto the 101, which would take them through the Cahuenga Pass and into Hollywood before they reached downtown.

"How'd you get hooked up with the Genetic Justice Project, Jessup?" he asked, trying once again to get something going. "You go to them or they come to you?"

"Website, man. I sent in my appeal and they saw the bullshit going on in my case. They took it over and here I am. You people are totally fucked if you think you're going to win this. I was railroaded by you motherfuckers once before. Ain't gonna happen again. In two months, this'll all be over. I've been in twenty-four years. What's two more months? Just makes my book rights more valuable. I guess I should be thanking you and the district attorney for that."

Bosch glanced at the mirror again. Normally, he would love a talkative suspect. Most times they talked themselves right into prison. But Jessup was too smart and too cagey. He chose his words carefully, stayed away from talking about the crime itself, and wouldn't be making a mistake that Bosch could use.

In the mirror now, Bosch could see Jessup staring out the window. No telling what he was thinking about. His eyes looked dead. Bosch could see the top of a prison ink tattoo on his neck, just breaking the collar line. It looked like part of a word but he couldn't tell for sure.

"Welcome to L.A., Jessup," Chu said without turning around. "Guess it's been a while, huh?"

"Fuck you, you chink motherfucker," Jessup retorted. "This'll all be over soon and then I'll be out and on the beach. I'm going to get a longboard and ride some tasty waves."

"Don't count on it, killer," Chu said. "You're going down. We got you by the balls."

Bosch knew Chu was trying to provoke a response, a slip of the tongue. But he was coming off as an amateur and Jessup was too wise for him.

Harry grew tired of the back-and-forth, even after six hours of almost complete silence. He turned on the car's radio and caught the tail end of a report on the DA's press conference. He turned it up so Jessup would hear, and Chu would keep quiet.

"Williams and Haller refused to comment on the evidence but indicated they were not as impressed with the DNA analysis as the state's supreme court was. Haller acknowledged that the DNA found on the victim's dress did not come from Jessup. But he said the findings did not clear him of involvement in the crime. Haller is a well-known defense attorney and will be prosecuting a murder case for the first time. It did not sound this morning as though he has any hesitation. 'We will once again be seeking the death penalty on this case.' "

Bosch flicked the volume down and checked the mirror. Jessup was still looking out the window.

"How about that, Jessup? He's going for the Jesus juice."

Jessup responded tiredly.

"Asshole's posturing. Besides, they don't execute anybody in this state anymore. You know what *death row* means? It means you get a cell all to yourself and you control what's on the TV. It means better access to phone, food and visitors. Fuck it, I hope he does go for it, man. But it won't matter. This is bullshit. This whole thing is bullshit. It's all about the money."

The last line floated out there for a long moment before Bosch finally bit.

"What money?"

"My money. You watch, man, they'll come at me with a deal. My lawyer told me. They'll want me to take a deal and plead to time served so they don't have to pay me the money. That's all this fucking is and you two are just the deliverymen. Fuckin' FedEx."

Bosch was silent. He wondered if it could be true. Jessup was suing the city and county for millions. Could it be that the retrial was simply a political move designed to save money? Both government entities were self-insured. Juries loved hitting faceless corporations and bureaucracies with obscenely large judgments. A jury believing prosecutors and police had corruptly imprisoned an innocent man for twenty-four years would be beyond generous. A hit from an eight-figure judgment could be devastating to both city and county coffers, even if they were splitting the bill.

But if they jammed Jessup and maneuvered him into a deal in which he acknowledged guilt to gain his freedom, then the lawsuit would go away. So would all the book and movie money he was counting on.

"Makes a lot of sense, doesn't it?" Jessup said.

Bosch checked the mirror and realized that now Jessup was studying him. He turned his eyes back to the road. He felt his phone vibrate and pulled it out of his jacket.

"You want me to take it, Harry?" Chu asked.

A reminder that it was illegal to talk on a phone while driving an automobile. Bosch ignored him and took the call. It was Lieutenant Gandle.

"Harry, you close?"

"Getting off the one-oh-one."

"Good. I just wanted to give you a heads-up. They're lining up at intake. Comb your hair."

"Got it, but maybe I'll give my partner the airtime."

Bosch glanced over at Chu but didn't explain.

"Either way," Gandle said. "What's next?"

"He invoked so we just book him. Then I have to go back to the war room and meet with the prosecutors. I've got questions."

"Harry, do they have this guy or not?"

Bosch checked Jessup in the mirror. He was back to looking out the window.

"I don't know, Lieutenant. When I know, you'll know."

A few minutes later they pulled into the rear lot of the jail. There were several television cameras and their operators lined up on a ramp leading to the intake door. Chu sat up straight.

"Perp walk, Harry."

"Yeah. You take him in."

"Let's both do it."

"Nah, I'll hang back."

"You sure?"

"I'm sure. Just don't forget my cuffs."

"Okay, Harry."

The lot was clogged with media vans with their transmitters cranked to full height. But they had left the space in front of the ramp open. Bosch pulled in and parked.

"Okay, you ready back there, Jessup?" Chu asked. "Time to sell tickets."

Jessup didn't respond. Chu opened the door and got out, then opened the rear door for Jessup.

Bosch watched the ensuing spectacle from the confines of the car.

Five

One of the very best things about having previously been married to Maggie McPherson was that I never had to face her in court. The marital split created a conflict of interest that saved me professional defeat and humiliation at her hands on more than one occasion. She was truly the best prosecutor I'd ever seen step into the well and they didn't call her Maggie McFierce for no reason.

Now, for the first time, we would be on the same team in court, sitting side by side at the same table. But what had seemed like such a good idea—not to mention such a positive potential payoff for Maggie—was already manifesting itself as something jagged and rusty. Maggie was having issues with being second chair. And for good reason. She was a professional prosecutor. From drug dealers and petty thieves to rapists and murderers, she had put dozens of criminals behind bars. I had appeared in dozens of trials myself but never as a prosecutor. Maggie would have to play backup to a novice and that realization wasn't sitting well with her.

We sat in conference room A with the case files spread out before us on the big table. Though Williams had said I could run the case from my own independent office, the truth was, that wasn't practical at the moment. I didn't have an office outside my home. I primarily used the backseat of my Lincoln Town Car as my office and that wouldn't do for *The People versus Jason Jessup*. I had my case manager setting up a temporary office in downtown but we were at least a few days away from that. So temporarily there we sat, eyes down and tensions up.

"Maggie," I said, "when it comes to prosecuting bad guys, I will readily admit that I couldn't carry your lunch. But the thing is, when it comes to politics *and* prosecuting bad guys, the powers that be have put me in the first chair. That's the way it is and we can either accept it or not. I took this job and asked for you. If you don't think we—"

"I just don't like the idea of carrying your briefcase through this whole thing," Maggie said.

"You won't be. Look, press conferences and outward appearances are one thing, but I fully assume that we'll be working as a tag team. You'll be conducting just as much of the investigation as I will be, probably more. The trial should be no different. We'll come up with a strategy and choreograph it together. But you have to give me a little credit. I know my way around a courtroom. I'll just be sitting at the other table this time."

"That's where you're wrong, Mickey. On the defense side you have a responsibility to one person. Your client. When you are a prosecutor, you represent the people and that is a lot more responsibility. That's why they call it the *burden of proof*."

"Whatever. If you're saying I shouldn't be doing this, then I'm not the guy you should be complaining to. Go down the hall and talk to your boss. But if he kicks me off the case, you get kicked as well, and then you go back to Van Nuys for the rest of your career. Is that what you want?"

She didn't answer and that was an answer in itself.

"Okay, then," I said. "Let's just try to get through this without pulling each other's hair out, okay? Remember, I'm not here to count convictions and advance my career. For me, it's one and done. So we both want the same thing. Yes, you will have to help me. But you will also be helping—"

My phone started vibrating. I had left it out on the table. I didn't recognize the number on the screen but took the call, just to get away from the conversation with Maggie.

"Haller."

"Hey, Mick, how'd I do?"

"Who is this?"

"Sticks."

Sticks was a freelance videographer who fed footage to the local news channels and sometimes even the bigs. I had known him so long I didn't even remember his real name.

"How'd you do at what, Sticks? I'm busy here."

"At the press conference. I set you up, man."

I realized that it had been Sticks behind the lights, throwing the questions to me.

"Oh, yeah, yeah, you did good. Thanks for that."

"Now you're going to take care of me on the case, right? Give me the heads-up if there's something for me, right? Something exclusive."

"Yeah, no need to worry, Sticks. I got you covered. But I gotta go."

I ended the call and put the phone back on the table. Maggie was typing something into her laptop. It looked like the momentary discontent had passed and I was hesitant to touch it again.

"That was a guy who works for the news stations. He might be useful to us at some point."

"We don't want to do anything underhanded. The prosecution is held to a much higher standard of ethics than the defense."

I shook my head. I couldn't win.

"That's bullshit and I am not talking about doing anything un—"

The door opened and Harry Bosch stepped in, pushing the door with his back because he was carrying two large boxes in his hands.

"Sorry, I'm late," he said.

He put the boxes down on the table. I could tell the larger one was a carton from evidence archives. I guessed that the smaller one contained the police file on the original investigation.

"It took them three days to find the murder box. It was on the 'eighty-five aisle instead of 'eighty-six."

He looked at me and then at Maggie and then back at me.

"So what'd I miss? War break out in the war room?"

"We were talking about prosecutorial tactics and it turns out we have opposing views."

"Imagine that."

He took the chair at the end of the table. I could tell he was going to have more to say. He lifted the top off the murder box and pulled out three accordion files and put them on the table. He then moved the box to the floor.

"You know, Mick, while we're airing out our differences...I think before you pulled me into this little soap opera, you should've told me a few things up front."

"Like what, Harry?"

"Like that this whole goddamn thing is about money and not murder."

"What are you talking about? What money?"

Bosch just stared at me without responding.

"You're talking about Jessup's lawsuit?" I asked.

"That's right," he said. "I had an interesting discussion with Jessup today on the drive down. Got me thinking and it crossed my mind that if we jam this guy into a deal, the lawsuit against the city and county goes away because a guy who admits to murder isn't going to be able to sue and claim he was railroaded. So I guess what I want to know is what we're really doing here. Are we trying to put a murder suspect on trial or are we just trying to save the city and county a few million bucks?"

I noticed Maggie's posture straighten as she considered the same thing.

"You gotta be kidding me," she said. "If that—"

"Hold on, hold on," I interjected. "Let's be cool about this. I don't think that's the case here, okay? It's not that I haven't thought about it but Williams didn't say one word about going for a dispo on this case. He told me to take it to trial. In fact, he assumes it will go to trial for the same reason you just mentioned. Jessup will never take a dispo for time served or anything else because there is no pot of gold in that. No book, no movie, no payout from the city. If he wants the money, he's got to go to trial and win."

Maggie nodded slowly as if weighing a valid supposition. Bosch didn't seem appeased at all.

"But how would you know what Williams is up to?" he asked. "You're an outsider. They could've brought you in, wound you up and pointed you in the right direction and then sat back to watch you go."

"He's right," Maggie added. "Jessup doesn't even have a defense attorney. As soon as he does he'll start talking deal."

I raised my hands in a calming gesture.

"Look, at the press conference today. I threw out that we were going for the death penalty. I just did that to see how Williams would react. He didn't expect it and afterward he pressed me in the hallway. He told me that it wasn't a decision I got to make. I told him it was just strategy, that I wanted Jessup to start thinking about a deal. And it gave Williams pause. He didn't see it. If he was thinking of a deal just to blow up the civil action, I would have been able to read it. I'm good at reading people."

I could tell I still hadn't quite won Bosch over.

"Remember last year, with the two men from Hong Kong who wanted your ass on the next plane to China? I read them right and I played them right."

In his eyes I saw Bosch relent. That China story was a reminder that he owed me one and I was collecting.

"Okay," he said. "So what do we do?"

"We assume Jessup's going to go to trial. As soon as he lawyers up, we'll know for sure. But we start preparing for it now, because if I was going to represent him, I would refuse to waive speedy trial. I would try to jam the prosecution on time to prepare and make the people put up or shut up."

I checked the date on my watch.

"If I'm right, that gives us forty-eight days till trial. We've got a lot of work to do between now and then."

We looked at one another and sat in silence for a few moments before I threw the lead to Maggie.

"Maggie has spent the better part of the last week with the prosecution file on this. Harry, I know what you just brought in will have a lot of overlap. But why don't we start here by having Mags go through the case as presented at trial in 'eighty-six? I think that will give us a good starting point of looking at what we need to do this time out."

Bosch nodded his approval and I signaled for Maggie to begin. She pulled her laptop over in front of her.

"Okay, a couple of basics first. Because it was a death penalty case, jury selection was the longest part of the trial. Almost three weeks. The trial itself lasted seven days and then there were three days of deliberation on the initial verdicts, then the death penalty phase went another two weeks. But seven days of testimony and arguments — that to me is fast for a capital murder case. It was pretty cut-and-dried. And the defense... well, there wasn't much of a defense."

She looked at me as if I were responsible for the poor defense of the accused, even though I hadn't even gotten out of law school by 'eighty-six.

"Who was his lawyer?" I asked.

"Charles Barnard," she said. "I checked with the California bar. He won't be handling the retrial. He's listed as deceased as of 'ninety-four. The prosecutor, Gary Lintz, is also long gone."

"Don't remember either of them. Who was the judge?"

"Walter Sackville. He's long retired but I do remember him. He was tough."

"I had a few cases with him," Bosch added. "He wouldn't take any shit from either side."

"Go on," I said.

"Okay, so the prosecution's story was this. The Landy family—that was our victim, Melissa, who was twelve, her thirteen-year-old sister, Sarah, mother, Regina, and stepfather, Kensington—lived on Windsor Boulevard in Hancock Park. The home was about a block north of Wilshire and in the vicinity of the Trinity United Church of God, which on Sundays back then drew about six thousand people to its two morning services. People parked their cars all over Hancock Park to go to the church. That is, until the residents there got tired of their neighborhood being overrun every Sunday with traffic and parking issues and went to City Hall about it. They got the neighborhood turned into a residential parking zone during weekend hours. You had to have a sticker to park on the streets, including Windsor. This opened the door to city-contracted tow truck operators patrolling the neighborhood like sharks on Sunday morning. Any cars without the proper resident sticker on the windshield were fair game. They got towed. Which finally brings us to Jason Jessup, our suspect."

"He drove a tow truck," I said.

"Exactly. He was a driver for a city contractor named Aardvark Towing. Cute name, got them to the front of the listings in the phone book back when people still used phone books."

I glanced at Bosch and could tell by his reaction that he was somebody who still used the phone book instead of the Internet. Maggie didn't notice and continued.

"On the morning in question Jessup was working the Hancock Park patrol. At the Landy house, the family happened to be putting a pool in the backyard. Kensington Landy was a musician who scored films and was doing quite well at the time. So they were putting in a pool and there was a large open hole and giant piles of dirt in the backyard. The parents didn't want the girls playing back there. Thought it was dangerous, plus on this morning the girls were in their church dresses. The house has a large front yard. The stepfather told the girls to play outside for a few minutes before the family was planning to go off to church themselves. The older one, Sarah, was told to watch over Melissa."

"Did they go to Trinity United?" I asked.

"No, they went to Sacred Heart in Beverly Hills. Anyway, the kids were only out there about fifteen minutes. Mother was still upstairs getting ready and the stepfather, who was also supposed to be keeping an eye on the girls, was watching television inside. An overnight sports report on ESPN or whatever they had back then. He forgot about the girls."

Bosch shook his head, and I knew exactly how he felt. It was not in judgment of the father but in understanding of how it could have happened and in the dread of any parent who knows how a small mistake could be so costly.

"At some point, he heard screaming," Maggie continued. "He ran out the front door and found the older girl, Sarah, in the yard. She was screaming that a man took Melissa. The stepfather ran up the street looking for her but there was no sign. Like that, she was gone."

My ex-wife stopped there for a moment to compose herself. Everyone in the room had a young daughter and could understand the shearing of life that happened at that moment for every person in the Landy family.

"Police were called and the response was quick," she continued. "This was Hancock Park, after all. The first bulletins were out in a matter of minutes. Detectives were dispatched right away."

"So this whole thing went down in broad daylight?" Bosch asked.

Maggie nodded.

"It happened about ten-forty. The Landys were going to an eleven o'clock service."

"And nobody else saw this?"

"You gotta remember, this was Hancock Park. A lot of tall hedges, a lot of walls, a lot of privacy. People there are good at keeping the world out. Nobody saw anything. Nobody heard anything until Sarah started screaming, and by then it was too late."

"Was there a wall or a hedge at the Landy house?"

"Six-foot hedges down the north and south property lines but not on the street side. It was theorized at the time that Jessup drove by in his tow truck and saw the girl alone in the yard. Then he acted impulsively."

We sat in silence for a few moments as we thought about the wrenching serendipity of fate. A tow truck goes by a house. The driver sees a girl, alone and vulnerable. All in a moment he figures he can grab her and get away with it.

"So," Bosch finally said, "how did they get him?"

"The responding detectives were on the scene in less than an hour. The lead was named Doral Kloster and his partner was Chad Steiner. I checked. Steiner is dead and Kloster is retired and has late-stage Alzheimer's. He's no use to us now."

"Damn," Bosch said.

"Anyway, they got there quickly and moved quickly. They interviewed Sarah and she described the abductor as being dressed like a garbage man. Further questioning revealed this to mean that he was wearing dirty coveralls like the city garbage crews used. She said she heard the garbage truck in the street but couldn't see it through a bush where she had hidden from her sister during a game of hide-and-seek. Problem is that it was a Sunday. There was no garbage pickup on Sundays. But the stepfather hears this and puts it together, mentions the tow trucks that run up and down the street on Sunday mornings. That becomes their best lead. The detectives get the list of city contractors and they start visiting tow yards.

"There were three contractors who worked the Wilshire corridor. One of them is Aardvark, where they go and are told they have three trucks working in the field. The drivers are called in and Jessup is one of them. The other two guys are named Derek Wilbern and William Clinton — really. They're separated and questioned but nothing comes up suspicious. They run 'em through the box and Jessup and Clinton are clean but Wilbern has an arrest but no conviction on an attempted rape two years before. That would be good enough to get him a ride downtown for a lineup, but the girl is still missing and there's no time for formalities, no time to put together a lineup."

"They probably took him back to the house," Bosch said. "They had no choice. They had to keep things moving."

"That's right. But Kloster knew he was on thin ice. He might get the girl to ID Wilbern but then he'd lose it in court for being unduly suggestive — you know, 'Is this the guy?' So he did the next best thing he could. He took all three drivers in their overalls back to the Landy house. Each was a white man in his twenties. They all wore the company overalls. Kloster broke procedure for the sake of speed, hoping to have a chance to find the girl alive. Sarah Landy's bedroom was on the second floor in the front of the house. Kloster takes the girl up to her room and has her look out the window to the street. Through the venetian blinds. He radios his partner, who has the three guys get out of two patrol cars and stand in the street. But Sarah doesn't ID Wilbern. She points to Jessup and says that's the guy."

Maggie looked through the documents in front of her and checked an investigative chronology before continuing.

"The ID is made at one o'clock. That is really quick work. The girl's only been gone a little over two hours. They start sweating Jessup but he doesn't give up a thing. Denies it all. They are working on him and getting nowhere when the call comes in. A girl's body has been found in a Dumpster behind the El Rey Theatre on Wilshire. That was about ten blocks from Windsor and the Landy house. Cause of death would later be determined to be manual strangulation. She was not raped and there was no semen in the mouth or throat."

Maggie stopped her summary there. She looked at Bosch and then me and solemnly nodded, giving the dead her moment.

Six

Bosch liked watching her and listening to the way she talked. He could tell the case was already under her skin. Maggie McFierce. Of course that was what they called her. More important, it was what she thought about herself. He had been on the case with her for less than a week but he understood this within the first hour of meeting her. She knew the secret. That it wasn't about code and procedure. It wasn't about jurisprudence and strategy. It was about taking that dark thing that you knew was out there in the world and bringing it inside. Making it yours. Forging it over an internal fire into something sharp and strong that you could hold in your hands and fight back with.

Relentlessly.

"Jessup asked for a lawyer and gave no further statement," McPherson said, continuing her summary. "The case was initially built around the older sister's identification and evidence found in Jessup's tow truck. Three strands of the victim's hair found in the seat crack. It was probably where he strangled her."

"There was nothing on the girl?" Bosch asked. "Nothing from Jessup or the truck?"

"Nothing usable in court. The DNA was found on her dress while it was being examined two days later. It was actually the older girl's dress. The younger girl borrowed it that day. One small deposit of semen was found on the front hem. It was typed but of course there was no DNA in criminal prosecutions back then. A blood type was determined and it was A-positive, the second-most popular type among humans, accounting for thirty-four percent of the population. Jessup matched but all it did was include him in the suspect pool. The prosecutor decided not to introduce it at trial because it would've just given the defense the ability to point out to the jury that the donor pool was more than a million men in Los Angeles County alone."

Bosch saw her throw another look at her ex-husband. As if he were responsible for the courtroom obfuscations of all defense attorneys everywhere. Harry was starting to get an idea about why their marriage didn't work out.

"It's amazing how far we've come," Haller said. "Now they make and break cases on the DNA alone."

"Moving on," McPherson said. "The prosecution had the hair evidence and the eyewitness. It also had opportunity—Jessup knew the neighborhood and was working there the morning of the murder. As far as motivation went, their backgrounding of Jessup produced a history of physical abuse by his father and psychopathic behavior. A lot of this came out on the record during the death penalty phase, too. But—and I will say this before you jump on it, Haller—no criminal convictions."

"And you said no sexual assault?" Bosch asked.

"No evidence of penetration or sexual assault. But this was no doubt a sexually motivated crime. The semen aside, it was a classic control crime. The perpetrator seizing momentary control in a world where he felt he controlled very little. He acted impulsively. At the time, the semen found on her dress was a piece of the same puzzle. It was theorized that he killed the girl and then masturbated, cleaning up after himself but leaving one small deposit of semen on the dress by mistake. The stain had the appearance of a transfer deposit. It wasn't a drop. It was a smear."

"The hit we just got on the DNA helps explain that," Haller said.

"Possibly," McPherson responded. "But let's discuss new evidence later. Right now, I'm talking about what they had and what they knew in nineteen eighty-six."

"Fine. Go on."

"That's it on the evidence but not on the prosecution's case. Two months before trial they get a call from the guy who's in the cell next to Jessup at County. He —"

"Jailhouse snitches," Haller said, interrupting. "Never met one who told the truth, never met a prosecutor who didn't use them anyway."

"Can I continue?" McPherson asked indignantly.

"Please do," Haller responded.

"Felix Turner, a repeat drug offender who was in and out of County so often that they made him a jail orderly because he knew the day-to-day operations as well as the deputies. He delivered meals to inmates in high-power lockdown. He tells investigators that Jessup provided him with details that only the killer would know. He was interviewed and he did indeed have details of the crime that were not made public. Like that the victim's shoes were removed, that she was not sexually assaulted, that he had wiped himself off on her dress."

"And so they believed him and made him the star witness," Haller said.

"They believed him and put him on the stand at trial. Not as a star witness. But his testimony was significant. Nevertheless, four years later, the *Times* comes out with a front-page exposé on Felix 'The Burner' Turner, professional jailhouse snitch who had testified for the prosecution in sixteen different cases over a seven-year period, garnering significant reductions in charges and jail time, and other perks like private cells, good jobs and large quantities of cigarettes."

Bosch remembered the scandal. It rocked the DA's office in the early nineties and resulted in changes in the use of jailhouse informants as trial witnesses. It was one of many black eyes local law enforcement suffered in the decade.

"Turner was discredited in the newspaper investigation. It said he used a private investigator on the outside to gather information on crimes and then to feed it to him. As you may remember, it changed how we used information that comes to us through the jails."

"Not enough," Haller said. "It didn't end the entire use of jailhouse snitches and it should have."

"Can we just focus on our case here?" McPherson said, obviously tired of Haller's posturing.

"Sure," Haller said. "Let's focus."

"Okay, well, by the time the *Times* came out with all of this, Jessup had long been convicted and was sitting in San Quentin. He of course launched an appeal citing police and prosecutorial misconduct. It went nowhere fast, with every appellate panel agreeing that while the use of Turner as a witness was egregious, his impact on the jury was not enough to have changed the verdict. The rest of the evidence was more than enough to convict."

"And that was that," Haller said. "They rubber-stamped it."

"An interesting note is that Felix Turner was found murdered in West Hollywood a year after the *Times* exposé," McPherson said. "The case was never solved."

"Had it coming as far as I'm concerned," Haller added.

That brought a pause to the discussion. Bosch used it to steer the meeting back to the evidence and to step in with some questions he had been considering.

"Is the hair evidence still available?"

It took McPherson a moment to drop Felix Turner and go back to the evidence.

"Yes, we still have it," she said. "This case is twenty-four years old but it was always under challenge. That's where Jessup and his jailhouse lawyering actually helped us. He was constantly filing writs and appeals. So the trial evidence was never destroyed. Of course, that eventually allowed him to get the DNA analysis off the swatch cut from the dress, but we still have all trial evidence and will be able to use it. He has claimed since day one that the hair in the truck was planted by the police."

"I don't think his defense at retrial will be much different from what was presented at his first trial and in his appeals," Haller said. "The girl made the wrong ID in a prejudicial setting, and from then on it was a rush to judgment. Facing a monumental lack of physical evidence, the police planted hair from the victim in his tow truck. It didn't play so well before a jury in 'eighty-six, but that was before Rodney King and the riots in 'ninety-two, the O.J. Simpson case, the Rampart scandal and all the other controversies that have engulfed the police department since. It's probably going to play really well now."

"So then, what are our chances?" Bosch asked.

Haller looked across the table at McPherson before answering.

"Based on what we know so far," he said, "I think I'd have a better chance if I were on the other side of the aisle on this one."

Bosch saw McPherson's eyes grow dark.

"Well then, maybe you should cross back over."

Haller shook his head.

"No, I made a deal. It may have been a bad deal but I'm sticking to it. Besides, it's not often I get to be on the side of might and right. I could get used to that — even in a losing cause."

He smiled at his ex-wife but she didn't return the sentiment.

"What about the sister?" Bosch asked.

McPherson swung her gaze toward him.

"The witness? That's our second problem. If she's alive, then she's thirty-seven now. Finding her is the problem. No help from the parents. Her real father died when she was seven. Her mother committed suicide on her sister's grave three years after the murder. And the stepfather drank himself into liver failure and died while waiting for a transplant six years ago. I had one of the investigators here do a quick rundown on her on the computer and Sarah Landy's trail drops off in

San Francisco about the same time her stepfather died. That same year she also cleared a probation tail for a controlled substance conviction. Records show she's been married and divorced twice, arrested multiple times for drugs and petty crimes. And then, like I said, she dropped off the grid. She either died or cleaned up her act. Even if she changed names, her prints would have left a trail if she'd been popped again in the past six years. But there's nothing."

"I don't think we have much of a case if we don't have her," Haller said. "We're going to need a real live person to point the finger across twenty-four years and say he did it."

"I agree," McPherson said. "She's key. The jury will need to hear the woman tell them that as a girl she did not make a mistake. That she was sure then and she is sure now. If we can't find her and get her to do that, then we have the victim's hair to go with and that's about it. They'll have the DNA and that will trump everything."

"And we will go down in flames," Haller said.

McPherson didn't respond, but she didn't have to.

"Don't worry," Bosch said. "I'll find her."

The two lawyers looked at him. It wasn't a time for empty rah-rah speeches. He meant it.

"If she's alive," he said, "I'll find her."

"Good," Haller said. "That'll be your first priority."

Bosch took out his key chain and opened the small penknife attached to it. He used it to cut the red seal on the evidence box. He had no idea what would be in the box. The evidence that had been introduced at trial twenty-four years earlier was still in the possession of the DA's Office. This box would contain other evidence that was gathered but not presented at trial.

Bosch put on a set of latex gloves from his pocket and then opened the box. On top was a paper bag that contained the victim's dress. It was a surprise. He had assumed that the dress had been introduced at trial, if only for the sympathetic response it would get from the jurors.

Opening the bag brought a musty smell to the room. He lifted the dress out, holding it up by the shoulders. All three of them were silent. Bosch was holding up a dress that a little girl had been wearing when she was murdered. It was blue with a darker blue bow in the front. A six-inch square had been cut out of the front hem, the location of the semen stain.

"Why is this here?" Bosch asked. "Wouldn't they have presented this at trial?"

Haller said nothing. McPherson leaned forward and looked closely at the dress as she considered a response.

"I think … they didn't show it because of the cutout. Showing the dress would let the defense ask about the cutout. That would lead to the blood-typing. The prosecution chose not to get into it during the presentation of the evidence. They probably relied on crime scene photos that showed the girl in the dress. They left it to the defense to introduce it and they never did."

Bosch folded the dress and put it down on the table. Also in the box was a pair of black patent leather shoes. They seemed very small and sad to him. There was a second paper bag, which contained the victim's underwear and socks. An accompanying lab report stated that the items had been checked for bodily fluids as well as hair and fiber evidence but no such evidence had been found.

At the bottom of the box was a plastic bag containing a silver necklace with a charm on it. He looked at it through the plastic and identified the figure on the charm as Winnie the Pooh. There was also a bag containing a bracelet of aqua-blue beads on an elastic string.

"That's it," he said.

"We should have forensics take a fresh look at it all," McPherson said. "You never know. Technology has advanced quite a bit in twenty-four years."

"I'll get it done," Bosch said.

"By the way," McPherson asked, "where were the shoes found? They're not on the victim's feet in the crime scene photos."

Bosch looked at the property report that was taped to the inside of the box's top.

"According to this they were found underneath the body. They must've come off in the truck, maybe when she was strangled. The killer threw them into the Dumpster first, then dropped in her body."

The images conjured by the items in the box had brought a decidedly somber mood to the prosecution team. Bosch started to carefully return everything to the box. He put the envelope containing the necklace in last.

"How old was your daughter when she left Winnie the Pooh behind?" he asked.

Haller and McPherson looked at each other. Haller deferred.

"Five or six," McPherson said. "Why?"

"Mine, too, I think. But this twelve-year-old had it on her necklace. I wonder why."

"Maybe because of where it came from," Haller said. "Hayley — our daughter — still wears a bracelet I got for her about five years ago."

McPherson looked at him as if challenging the assertion.

"Not all the time," Haller said quickly. "But on occasion. Sometimes when I pick her up. Maybe the necklace came from her real father before he died."

A low chime came from McPherson's computer and she checked her e-mail. She studied the screen for a few moments before speaking.

"This is from John Rivas, who handles afternoon arraignments in Department one hundred. Jessup's now got a criminal defense attorney and John's working on getting Jessup on the docket for a bail hearing. He's coming over on the last bus from City Jail."

"Who's the lawyer?" Haller asked.

"You'll love this. Clever Clive Royce is taking the case pro bono. It's a referral from the GJP."

Bosch knew the name. Royce was a high-profile guy who was a media darling who never missed a chance to stand in front of a camera and say all the things he wasn't allowed to say in court.

"Of course he's taking it pro bono," Haller said. "He'll make it up on the back end. Sound bites and headlines, that's all Clive cares about."

"I've never gone up against him," McPherson said. "I can't wait."

"Is Jessup actually on the docket?"

"Not yet. But Royce is talking to the clerk. Rivas wants to know if we want him to handle it. He'll oppose bail."

"No, we'll take it," Haller said. "Let's go."

McPherson closed her computer at the same time Bosch put the top back on the evidence box.

"You want to come?" Haller asked him. "Get a look at the enemy?"

"I just spent seven hours with him, remember?"

"I don't think he was talking about Jessup," McPherson said.

Bosch nodded.

"No, I'll pass," he said. "I'm going to take this stuff over to SID and get to work on tracking down our witness. I'll let you know when I find her."

Seven

Tuesday, February 16, 5:30 P.M.

Department 100 was the largest courtroom in the CCB and reserved for morning and evening arraignment court, the twin intake points of the local justice system. All those charged with crimes had to be brought before a judge within twenty-four hours, and in the CCB this required a large courtroom with a large gallery section where the families and friends of the accused could sit. The courtroom was used for first appearances after arrest, when the loved ones were still naive about the lengthy, devastating and difficult journey the defendant was embarking upon. At arraignment, it was not unusual to have mom, dad, wife, sister-in-law, aunt, uncle and even a neighbor or two in the courtroom in a show of support for the defendant and outrage at his arrest. In another eighteen months, when the case would grind to a finale at sentencing, the defendant would be lucky to have even dear old mom still in attendance.

The other side of the gate was usually just as crowded, with lawyers of all stripes. Grizzled veterans, bored public defenders, slick cartel reps, wary prosecutors and media hounds all mingled in the well or stood against the glass partition surrounding the prisoner pen and whispered to their clients.

Presiding over this anthill was Judge Malcolm Firestone, who sat with his head down and his sharp shoulders jutting up and closer to his ears with each passing year. His black robe gave them the appearance of folded wings and the overall image was one of Firestone as a vulture waiting impatiently to dine on the bloody detritus of the justice system.

Firestone handled the evening arraignment docket, which started at three P.M. and went as far into the night as the list of detainees required. Consequently, he was a jurist who liked to keep things moving. You had to act fast in one hundred or risk being run over and left behind. In here, justice was an assembly line with a conveyor belt that never stopped turning. Firestone wanted to get home. The lawyers wanted to get home. Everybody wanted to get home.

I entered the courtroom with Maggie and immediately saw the cameras being set up in a six-foot corral to the left side, across the courtroom from the glass pen that housed defendants brought in six at a time. Without the glare of spotlights this time, I saw my friend Sticks setting the legs of the tool that provided his nickname, his tripod. He saw me and gave me a nod and I returned it.

Maggie tapped me on the arm and pointed toward a man seated at the prosecution table with three other lawyers.

"That's Rivas on the end."

"Okay. You go talk to him while I check in with the clerk."

"You don't have to check in, Haller. You're a prosecutor, remember?"

"Oh, cool. I forgot."

We headed over to the prosecution table and Maggie introduced me to Rivas. The prosecutor was a baby lawyer, probably no more than a few years out of a top-ranked law school. My guess was that he was biding his time, playing office politics and waiting to make a move up the ladder and out of the hellhole of arraignment court. It didn't help that I had come from across the aisle to grab the golden ring of the office's current caseload. By his body language I registered his wariness. I was at the wrong table. I was the fox in the henhouse.

And I knew that before the hearing was over, I was going to confirm his suspicions.

After the perfunctory handshake, I looked around for Clive Royce and found him seated against the railing, conferring with a young woman who was probably his associate. They were leaning toward each other, looking into an open folder with a thick sheaf of documents in it. I approached with my hand out.

"Clive 'The Barrister' Royce, how's it hanging, old chap?"

He looked up and a smile immediately creased his well-tanned face. Like a perfect gentleman, he stood up before accepting my hand.

"Mickey, how are you? I'm sorry it looks like we're going to be opposing counsel on this one."

I knew he was sorry but not too sorry. Royce had built his career on picking winners. He would not risk going pro bono and stepping into a heavy media case if he didn't think it would amount to free advertising and another victory. He was in it to win it and behind the smile was a set of sharp teeth.

"Me, too. And I am sure you will make me regret the day I crossed the aisle."

"Well, I guess we're both fulfilling our public duty, yes? You helping out the district attorney and me taking on Jessup on the cuff."

Royce still carried an English accent even though he had lived more than half his fifty years in the United States. It gave him an aura of culture and distinction that belied his practice of defending people accused of heinous crimes. He wore a three-piece suit with a barely discernible chalk line in the gabardine. His bald pate was well tanned and smooth, his beard dyed black and groomed to the very last hair.

"That's one way of looking at it," I said.

"Oh, where are my manners? Mickey, this is my associate Denise Graydon. She'll be assisting me in the defense of Mr. Jessup."

Graydon stood up and shook my hand firmly.

"Nice to meet you," I said.

I looked around to see if Maggie was standing nearby and could be introduced but she was huddled with Rivas at the prosecution table.

"Well," I said to Royce. "Did you get your client on the docket?"

"I did indeed. He'll be first in the group after this one. I've already gone back and visited and we'll be ready to make a motion for bail. I was wondering, though, since we have a few minutes, could we step out into the corridor for a word?"

"Sure, Clive. Let's do it now."

Royce told his associate to wait in the courtroom and retrieve us when the next group of defendants was brought into the glass cage. I followed Royce through the gate and down the aisle between the crowded rows of the gallery. We went through the mantrap and into the hallway.

"You want to get a cup of tea?" Royce asked.

"I don't think there's time. What's up, Clive?"

Royce folded his arms and got serious.

"I must tell you, Mick, that I am not out to embarrass you. You are a friend and colleague in the defense bar. But you have gotten yourself into a no-win situation here, yes? What are we going to do about it?"

I smiled and glanced up and down the crowded hallway. Nobody was paying attention to us.

"Are you saying that your client wants to plead this out?"

"On the contrary. There will be no plea negotiation on this matter. The district attorney has made the wrong choice and it's very clear what maneuver he is undertaking here and how he is using you as a pawn in the process. I must put you on notice that if you insist on taking Jason Jessup to trial, then you are going to embarrass yourself. As a professional courtesy, I just thought I needed to tell you this."

Before I could answer, Graydon came out of the courtroom and headed quickly toward us.

"Somebody in the first group is not ready, so Jessup's been moved up and was just brought out."

"We'll be in straightaway," Royce said.

She hesitated and then realized her boss wanted her to go back into the courtroom. She went back through the doors and Royce turned his attention back to me. I spoke before he could.

"I appreciate your courtesy and concern, Clive. But if your client wants a trial, he'll get a trial. We'll be ready and we'll see who gets embarrassed and who goes back to prison."

"Brilliant, then. I look forward to the contest."

I followed him back inside. Court was in session and on my way down the aisle I saw Lorna Taylor, my office manager and second ex-wife, sitting at the end of one of the crowded rows. I leaned over to whisper.

"Hey, what are you doing here?"

"I had to come see the big moment."

"How did you even know? I just found out fifteen minutes ago."

"I guess so did KNX. I was already down here to look at office space and heard it on the radio that Jessup was going to appear in court. So I came."

"Well, thanks for being here, Lorna. How is the search going? I really need to get out of this building. Soon."

"I have three more showings after this. That'll be enough. I'll let you know my final choices tomorrow, okay?"

"Yeah, that's—"

I heard Jessup's name called by the clerk.

"Look, I gotta get in there. We'll talk later."

"Go get 'em, Mickey!"

I found an empty seat waiting for me next to Maggie at the prosecution table. Rivas had moved to the row of seats against the gate. Royce had moved to the glass cage, where he was whispering to his client. Jessup was wearing an orange jumpsuit—the jail uniform—and looked calm and subdued. He was nodding to everything Royce whispered in his ear. He somehow seemed younger than I had thought he would. I guess I expected all of those years in prison to have taken their toll. I knew he was forty-eight but he looked no older than forty. He didn't even have a jailhouse pallor. His skin was pale but it looked healthy, especially next to the overtanned Royce.

"Where did you go?" Maggie whispered to me. "I thought I was going to have to handle this myself."

"I was just outside conferring with defense counsel. Do you have the charges handy? In case I have to read them into the record."

"You won't have to enter the charges. All you have to do is stand up and say that you believe Jessup is a flight risk and a danger to the community. He—"

"But I don't believe he's a flight risk. His lawyer just told me they're ready to go and that they're not interested in a disposition. He wants the money and the only way he'll get it is to stick around and go to trial—and win."

"So?"

She seemed astonished and looked down at the files stacked in front of her.

"Mags, your philosophy is to argue everything and give no quarter. I don't think that's going to work here. I have a strategy and—"

She turned and leaned in closer to me.

"Then I'll just leave you and your strategy and your bald buddy from the defense bar to it."

She pushed back her chair and got up, grabbing her briefcase from the floor.

"Maggie..."

She charged through the gate and headed toward the rear door of the courtroom. I watched her go, knowing that while I didn't like the result, I had needed to set the lines of our prosecutorial relationship.

Jessup's name was called and Royce identified himself for the record. I then stood and said the words I never expected I would say.

"Michael Haller for the People."

Even Judge Firestone looked up from his perch, peering at me over a pair of reading glasses. Probably for the first time in weeks something out of the ordinary had occurred in his courtroom. A dyed-in-the-wool defense attorney had stood for the People.

"Well, gentlemen, this is an arraignment court and I have a note here saying you want to talk about bail."

Jessup was charged twenty-four years ago with murder and abduction. When the supreme court reversed his conviction it did not throw out the charges. That had been left to the DA's Office. So he still stood accused of the crimes and his not-guilty plea of twenty-four years ago remained in place. The case now had to be assigned to a courtroom and a judge for trial. A motion to discuss bail would usually be delayed until that point, except that Jessup, through Royce, was pushing the issue forward by coming to Firestone.

"Your Honor," Royce said, "my client was already arraigned twenty-four years ago. What we would like to do today is discuss a motion for bail and to move this case along to trial. Mr. Jessup has waited a long time for his freedom and for justice. He has no intention of waiving his right to a speedy trial."

I knew it was the move Royce would make, because it was the move I would have made. Every person accused of a crime is guaranteed a speedy trial. Most often trials are delayed at the defense's request or acquiescence as both sides want time to prepare. As a pressure tactic, Royce was not going to suspend the speedy-trial statute. With a case and evidence twenty-four years old, not to mention a primary witness whose whereabouts were at the moment unknown, it was not only prudent but a no-brainer to put the prosecution on the clock. When the supreme court reversed the conviction, that clock started ticking. The People had sixty days from that point to bring Jessup to trial. Twelve of them had already gone by.

"I can move the case to the clerk for assignment," Firestone said. "And I would prefer that the assigned judge handle the question of bail."

Royce composed his thoughts for a moment before responding. In doing so he turned his body slightly so the cameras would have a better angle on him.

"Your Honor, my client has been falsely incarcerated for twenty-four years. And those aren't just my words, that's the opinion of the state supreme court. Now they have pulled him out of prison and brought him down here so he can face trial once again. This is all part of an ongoing scheme that has nothing to do with justice, and everything to do with money and politics. It's about avoiding responsibility for corruptly taking a man's freedom. To put this over until another hearing on another day would continue the travesty of justice that has beset Jason Jessup for more than two decades."

"Very well."

Firestone still seemed put out and annoyed. The assembly line had thrown a gear. He had a docket that had probably started with more than seventy-five names on it and a desire to get through them in time to get home for dinner before eight. Royce was going to slow things down immeasurably with his request for a full debate on whether Jessup should be allowed his release while awaiting trial. But Firestone, like Royce, was about to get the surprise of the day. If he didn't make it home in time for dinner, it wouldn't be because of me.

Royce asked the judge for an OR, meaning Jessup would have to put up no money as bail and simply be released on his own recognizance. This was just his opener. He fully expected there to be a financial figure attached to Jessup's freedom, if he was successful at all. Murder suspects didn't get OR'ed. In the rare instance when bail was granted in a murder case, it usually came with a steep price tag. Whether Jessup could raise the money through his supporters or from the book and movie deals he was supposedly negotiating was not germane to the discussion.

Royce closed his request by arguing that Jessup should not be considered a flight risk for the very same reason I had outlined to Maggie. He had no interest in running. His only interest was in fighting to clear his name after twenty-four years of wrongful imprisonment.

"Mr. Jessup has no other purpose at this time than to stay put and prove once and for all that he is innocent and that he has paid a nightmarish price for the mistakes and misconduct of this District Attorney's Office."

The whole time Royce spoke I watched Jessup in the glass cage. He knew the cameras were on him and he maintained a pose of rightful indignation. Despite his efforts, he could not disguise the anger and hate in his eyes. Twenty-four years in prison had made that permanent.

Firestone finished writing a note and then asked for my response. I stood and waited until the judge looked up at me.

"Go ahead, Mr. Haller," he prompted.

"Judge, providing that Mr. Jessup can show documentation of residence, the state does not oppose bail at this time."

Firestone stared at me for a long moment as he computed that my response was diametrically opposite to what he thought it would be. The hushed sounds of the courtroom seemed to get even lower as the impact of my response was understood by every lawyer in the room.

"Did I get that right, Mr. Haller?" Firestone said. "You are not objecting to an OR release in a murder case?"

"That is correct, Your Honor. We are fully expecting Mr. Jessup to show for trial. There's no money in it for him if he doesn't."

"Your Honor!" Royce cried. "I object to Mr. Haller infecting the record with such prejudicial pap directed solely at the media in attendance. My client has no other purpose at this point than—"

"I understand, Mr. Royce," Firestone interjected. "But I think you did a fair amount of playing to the cameras yourself. Let's just leave it at that. Without objection from the prosecution, I am releasing Mr. Jessup on his own recognizance once he provides the clerk with documentation of residence. Mr. Jessup is not to leave Los Angeles County without permission of the court to which his case is assigned."

Firestone then referred the case to the clerk of the court's office for reassignment to another department for trial. We were now finally out of Judge Firestone's orbit. He could restart the assembly line and get home for dinner. I picked up the files Maggie had left behind and left the table. Royce was back at the seat at the railing, dumping files into a leather briefcase. His young associate was helping him.

"How did it feel, Mick?" he asked me.

"What, being a prosecutor?"

"Yes, crossing the aisle."

"Not too much different, to tell you the truth. It was all procedure today."

"You will be raked over the coals for letting my client walk out of here."

"Fuck 'em if they can't take a joke. Just make sure he stays clean, Clive. If he doesn't, then my ass really will be thrown on the fire. And so will his."

"No problem there. We'll take care of him. He's the least of your worries, you know."

"How's that, Clive?"

"You don't have much in the way of evidence, can't find your main witness, and the DNA is a case killer. You're captain of the *Titanic*, Mickey, and Gabriel Williams put you there. Makes me wonder what he's got on you."

Out of all that he said, I only wondered about one thing. How did he know about the missing witness? I, of course, didn't ask him or respond to his jab about what the DA might have on me. I played it like all the overconfident prosecutors I had ever gone up against.

"Tell your client to enjoy himself while he's out there, Clive. Because as soon as the verdict comes in, he's going back inside."

Royce smiled as he snapped his case closed. He changed the subject.

"When can we talk about discovery?"

"We can talk about it whenever you like. I'll start putting a file together in the morning."

"Good. Let's talk soon, Mick, yes?"

"Like I said, anytime, Clive."

He headed over to the court deputy's desk, most likely to see about his client's release. I pushed through the gate and connected with Lorna and we left the courtroom together. Waiting for me outside was a small gathering of reporters and cameras. The reporters shouted questions about my not objecting to bail and I told them no comment and walked on by. They waited in place for Royce to come out next.

"I don't know, Mickey," Lorna confided. "How do you think the DA is going to respond to the no bail?"

Just as she asked it my phone started beeping in my pocket. I realized I had forgotten to turn it off in the courtroom. That was an error that could have proven costly, depending on Firestone's view of electronic interruptions while court was in session.

Looking at the screen, I said to Lorna, "I don't know but I think I'm about to find out."

I held up the phone so she could see that the caller ID said LADA.

"You take it. I'm going to run. Be careful, Mickey."

She kissed me on the cheek and headed off to the elevator alcove. I connected to the call. I had guessed right. It was Gabriel Williams.

"Haller, what the hell are you doing?"

"What do you mean?"

"One of my people said you allowed Jessup to walk on an OR."

"That's right."

"Then I'll ask again, What the hell are you doing?"

"Look, I—"

"No, you look. I don't know if you were just giving one of your buddies in the defense bar what he wanted or you are just stupid, but you *never* let a murderer walk. You understand me? Now, I want you to go back in there and ask for a new hearing on bail."

"No, I'm not going to do that."

There was a hard silence for at least ten seconds before Williams came back.

"Did I just hear you right, Haller?"

"I don't know what you heard, Williams, but I'm not going back for a rehearing. You have to understand something. You gave me a bag of shit for a case and I have to do the best I can with it. What evidence we do have is twenty-four years old. We have a big hole blown in the side of the case with the DNA and we have an eyewitness we can't find. So that tells me I have to do whatever I can do to make this case."

"And what's that got to do with letting this man out of jail?"

"Don't you see, man? Jessup has been in prison for twenty-four years. It was no finishing school. Whatever he was when he went in? He's worse now. If he's on the outside, he'll fuck up. And if he fucks up, that only helps us."

"So in other words, you are putting the general public at risk while this guy is out there."

"No, because you are going to talk to the LAPD and get them to watch this guy. So nobody gets hurt and they are able to step in and grab him the minute he acts out."

Another silence followed but this time I could hear muffled voices and I figured that Williams was talking it over with his advisor, Joe Ridell. When his voice came back to me, it was stern but had lost the tone of outrage.

"Okay, this is what I want you to do. When you want to make a move like this, you come to me first. You understand?"

"That's not going to happen. You wanted an independent prosecutor. That's what you've got. Take it or leave it."

There was a pause and then he hung up without further word. I closed my phone and watched for a few moments as Clive Royce exited the courtroom and waded into the crowd of reporters and cameras. Like a seasoned expert, he waited a moment for everyone to get their positions set and their lenses focused. He then proceeded with the first of what would be many impromptu but carefully scripted press briefings.

"I think the District Attorney's Office is running scared," he began.

It was what I knew he would say. I didn't need to listen to the rest. I walked away.

Eight

Some people don't want to be found. They take measures. They drag the branch behind them to confuse the trail. Some people are just running and they don't care what they leave in their wake. What's important is that the past is behind them and that they keep moving away from it.

Once he back-checked the DA investigator's work, it took Bosch only two hours to find a current name and address for their missing witness, Melissa Landy's older sister, Sarah. She hadn't dragged a branch. She had used the things that were close and just kept moving. The DA's investigator who lost the trail in San Francisco had not looked backwards for clues. That was his mistake. He had looked forward and he'd found an empty trail.

Bosch had started as his predecessor had, typing the name Sarah Landy and birth date April 14, 1972, into the computer. The department's various search engines provided myriad points of impact with law enforcement and society.

First there were arrests on drug charges in 1989 and 1990 — handled discreetly and sympathetically by the Division of Children's Services. But she was beyond the reach and understanding of DYS for similar charges in late 1991 and two more times in 1992. There was probation and a period of rehabilitation and this was followed by a few years during which she left no digital fingerprints at all. Another search site provided Bosch with a series of addresses for her in Los Angeles in the early nineties. Harry recognized these as marginal neighborhoods where rents were probably low and drugs close by and easy to acquire. Sarah's illegal substance of choice was crystal meth, a drug that burned away brain cells by the billions.

The trail on Sarah Landy, the girl who had hidden behind the bushes and watched her younger sister get taken by a killer, ended there.

Bosch opened the first file he had retrieved from the murder box and looked at the witness information sheet for Sarah. He found her Social Security number and fed that along with the DOB into the search engine. This gave him two new names: Sarah Edwards, beginning in 1991, and Sarah Witten in 1997. With women changes of last names only were usually an indicator of marriage, and the DA's investigator had reported finding records of two marriages.

Under the name Sarah Edwards, the arrests continued, including two pops for property crimes and a tag for soliciting for prostitution. But the arrests were spread far enough apart and perhaps her story was sad enough that once again she never saw any jail time.

Bosch clicked through the mug shots for these arrests. They showed a young woman with changing hairstyles and colors but the unwavering look of hurt and defiance in her eyes. One mug shot showed a deep purple bruise under her left eye and open sores along her jawline. The photos seemed to tell the story best. A downward spiral of drugs and crime. An internal wound that never healed, a guilt never assuaged.

Under the name Sarah Witten, the arrests didn't change, only the location. She had probably realized she was wearing thin on the prosecutors and judges who had repeatedly given her breaks — most likely after reading the summary of her life contained in the presentencing investigations. She moved north to San Francisco and once again had frequent encounters with the law. Drugs and petty crime, charges that often go hand in hand. Bosch checked the mug shots and saw a woman who looked old beyond her years. She looked like she was forty before she was yet thirty.

In 2003 she did her first significant jail time when she was sentenced to six months in San Mateo County Jail after pleading guilty to a possession charge. The records showed that she served four months in jail followed by a lockdown rehab program. It was the last marker on the system for her. No one with any of her names or Social Security number had been arrested since or applied for a driver's license in any of the fifty states.

Bosch tried a few other digital maneuvers he had learned while working in the Open-Unsolved Unit, where Internet tracing was raised to an art form, but could not pick up the trail. Sarah was gone.

Putting the computer aside, Bosch took up the files from the murder box. He started scanning the documents, looking for clues that might help him track her. He got more than a clue when he found a photocopy of Sarah's birth certificate. It was then that he remembered that she had been living with her mother and stepfather at the time of her sister's murder.

The birth name on the certificate was Sarah Ann Gleason. He entered it into the computer along with her birth date. He found no criminal history under the name but he did find a Washington State driver's license that had been established six years earlier and renewed just two months before. He pulled up the photo and it was a match. But barely. Bosch studied it for a long time. He would have sworn that Sarah Ann Gleason was getting younger.

His guess was that she had left the hard life behind. She had found something that made her change. Maybe she had taken the cure. Maybe she had a child. But something had changed her life for the better.

Bosch next ran her name through another search engine and got utility and satellite hookups under her name. The addresses matched the one on her driver's license. Bosch was sure he had found her. Port Townsend. He went onto Google and typed it in. Soon he was looking at a map of the Olympic Peninsula in the northwest corner of Washington. Sarah Landy had changed her name three times and had run to the farthest tip of the continental United States, but he had found her.

The phone rang as he was reaching for it. It was Lieutenant Stephen Wright, commander of the LAPD's Special Investigation Section.

"I just wanted you to know that as of fifteen minutes ago we're fully deployed on Jessup. The full unit's involved and we'll get you surveillance logs each morning. If you need anything else or want to ride along at any point, you call me."

"Thank you, Lieutenant. I will."

"Let's hope something happens."

"That would be nice."

Bosch disconnected. And made the call to Maggie McPherson.

"Couple things. First, SIS is in place now on Jessup. You can let Gabriel Williams know."

He thought he heard a small chuckle before she responded.

"Ironic, huh?"

"Yeah. Maybe they'll end up killing Jessup and we won't have to worry about a trial."

The Special Investigation Section was an elite surveillance squad that had existed for more than forty years despite a kill rate higher than that of any other unit in the department, including SWAT. The SIS was used to clandestinely watch apex predators — individuals suspected in violent crimes who would not cease until caught in the act and stopped by the police. Masters of surveillance, SIS officers waited to observe suspects committing new crimes before moving in to make arrests, often with fatal consequences.

The irony McPherson mentioned was that Gabriel Williams was a civil rights attorney before running for and winning the DA's post.

He had sued the department over SIS shootings on multiple occasions, claiming that the unit's strategies were designed to draw suspects into deadly confrontations with police. He had gone so far as to call the unit a "death squad" while announcing a lawsuit over an SIS shooting that had left four robbers dead outside a Tommy's fast-food franchise. That same death squad was now being used in a gambit that might help win the case against Jessup and further Williams's political rise.

"You'll be informed of his activities?" McPherson asked.

"Every morning I'll get the surveillance log. And they'll call me out if anything good happens."

"Perfect. Was there something else? I'm in a bit of a rush. I'm working on one of my preexisting cases and have a hearing about to start."

"Yeah, I found our witness."

"You're brilliant! Where is she?"

"Up in Washington on the northern tip of the Olympic Peninsula. A place called Port Townsend. She's using her birth name, Sarah Ann Gleason, and it appears that she's been living clean up there for about six years."

"That's good for us."

"Maybe not."

"How so?"

"It looks to me like most of her life has been spent trying to get away from what happened that Sunday in Hancock Park. If she's finally gotten past it and is living the clean life up there in Port Townsend, she might not be interested in picking at old scabs, if you know what I mean."

"Not even for her sister?"

"Maybe not. We're talking about twenty-four years ago."

McPherson was quiet for a long moment and then finally responded.

"That's a cynical view of the world, Harry. When are you planning on going up there?"

"As soon as I can. But I have to make arrangements for my daughter. She stayed with a friend when I went up to get Jessup at San Quentin. It didn't turn out so good and now I have to hit the road again."

"Sorry to hear that. I want to go up with you."

"I think I can handle it."

"I know you can handle it. But it might be good to have a woman and a prosecutor with you. More and more, I think she's going to be the key to this whole thing and she's going to be my witness. Our approach to her will be very important."

"I've been approaching witnesses for about thirty years. I think I—"

"Let me have the travel office here make the arrangements. That way we can go up together. Talk out the strategy."

Bosch paused. He knew he wasn't going to be able to change her mind.

"Whatever you say."

"Good. I'll tell Mickey and contact travel. We'll book a morning flight. I'm clear tomorrow. Is that too soon for you? I'd hate to wait on this till next week."

"I'll make it work."

Bosch had had a third reason to call her but now decided to hold back. Her taking over the trip to Washington made him gun-shy about discussing his investigative moves.

They hung up and he was left drumming his fingers on the edge of his desk as he contemplated what he would say to Rachel Walling.

After a few moments he pulled out his cell phone and used it to make the call. He had Walling's number in its memory. To his surprise, she answered right away. He had envisioned her seeing his name on the ID and letting him go to the message. They'd had a relationship that was long over but still left a trail of intense feelings.

"Hello, Harry."

"Hello, Rachel. How are you?"

"I'm fine. And you?"

"Pretty good. I'm calling about a case."

"Of course. Harry Bosch never goes through channels. He goes direct."

"There are no channels for this. And you know I call you because I trust you and more than anything else respect your opinion. I go through channels and I get some profiler in Quantico who's just a voice on the phone. And not only that, he doesn't call me back with anything for two months. What would you do if you were me?"

"Oh . . . probably the same thing."

"Besides that, I don't want the bureau's official involvement. I am just looking for your opinion and advice, Rachel."

"What's the case?"

"I think you're going to like it. It's a twenty-four-year-old murder of a twelve-year-old girl. A guy went down for it back then and now we have to retry him. I was thinking a profile of the crime might be helpful to the prosecutor."

"Is this that Jessup case that's in the news?"

"That's right."

He knew she would be interested. He could hear it in her voice.

"All right, well, bring by whatever you've got. How much time are you giving me? I've got my regular job, you know."

"No hurry this time. Not like with that Echo Park thing. I'll probably be out of town tomorrow. Maybe longer. I think you can have a few days with the file. You still in the same place above the Million Dollar Theater?"

"That's it."

"Okay, I'll drop the box by."

"I'll be here."

Nine

The holding cell next to Department 124 on the thirteenth floor of the CCB was empty except for my client Cassius Clay Montgomery. He sat morosely on the bench in the corner and didn't get up when he saw me come back.

"Sorry I'm late."

He didn't say anything. He didn't acknowledge my presence.

"Come on, Cash. It's not like you'd be going anywhere. What's it matter if you were waiting here or back in County?"

"They got TV in County, man," he said, looking up at me.

"Okay, so you missed *Oprah*. Can you come over here so I don't have to shout our business across the room?"

He got up and came over to the bars. I stood on the other side, beyond the red line marking the three-foot threshold.

"Doesn't matter if you shout our business. There ain't nobody left to hear it."

"I told you, I'm sorry. I've been having a busy day."

"Yeah, and I guess I'm just a no-count nigger when it comes to being on TV and turnin' into the man."

"What's that supposed to mean?"

"I saw you on the news, dog. Now you a prosecutor? What kinda shit is that?"

I nodded. Obviously, my client was more concerned with me being a turncoat than with waiting until the last hearing of the day.

"Look, all I can tell you is that I took the job reluctantly. I am not a prosecutor. I am a defense attorney. I'm your defense attorney. But every now and then they come to you and they want something. And it's hard to say no."

"So what happens to me?"

"Nothing happens to you. I'm still your lawyer, Cash. And we have a big decision to make here. This hearing is going to be short and sweet. It's to set a trial date and that's it. But Mr. Hellman, the prosecutor, says the offer he made to you is good only until today. If we tell Judge Champagne we're ready to go to trial today, then the deal disappears and we go to trial. Have you thought about it some more?"

Montgomery leaned his head in between two bars and didn't speak. I realized he couldn't pull the trigger on a decision. He was forty-seven and had already spent nine years of his life in prison. He was charged with armed robbery and assault with great bodily injury and was looking at a big fall.

According to the police, Montgomery had posed as a buyer at a drive-through drug market in the Rodia Gardens projects. But instead of paying, he pulled a gun and demanded the dealer's drugs and money roll. The dealer went for the gun and it went off. Now the dealer, a gang member named Darnell Hicks, was in a wheelchair for the rest of his life.

As is usual in the projects, no one cooperated with the investigation. Even the victim said he didn't remember what happened, choosing in his silence to trust that his fellow Crips would handle justice in the matter. But investigators made a case anyway. Picking up my client's car on a video camera at the entrance to the projects, they found the car and matched blood on the door to the victim.

It wasn't a strong case but it was solid enough for us to entertain an offer from the prosecution. If Montgomery took the deal he'd be sentenced to three years in prison and would likely serve two and a half. If he gambled and took a conviction at the end of a trial, then he'd be looking at a mandatory minimum of fifteen years inside. The add-on of GBI and use of a firearm in the commission of a robbery were the killers. And I knew firsthand that Judge Judith Champagne wasn't soft on gun crimes.

I had recommended to my client that he take the deal. It was a no-brainer to me but then I wasn't the one who had to do the time. Montgomery couldn't decide. It wasn't so much about the prison time. It was the fact that the victim, Hicks, was a Crip and the street gang had a long reach into every prison in the state. Even taking the three-year sentence could be a death penalty. Montgomery wasn't sure he would make it.

"I don't know what to tell you," I said. "It's a good offer. The DA doesn't want to go to trial on this. He doesn't want to put a victim on the stand who doesn't want to be there and may hurt the case more than help it. So he's gone as low as he can go. But it's up to you. Your decision. You've had a couple weeks now and this is it. We have to go out there in a couple minutes."

Montgomery tried to shake his head but his forehead was pressed between the two bars.

"What's that mean?" I asked.

"It means shit. Can't we win this case, man? I mean, you a prosecutor now. Can't you get a good word in for me on this?"

"They're two different matters, Cash. I can't do anything like that. You got your choice. Take the three or we go to trial. And like I told you before, we can certainly do some stuff at trial. They've got no weapon and a victim who won't tell the story, but they still got his blood on the door of your car and they got video of you driving it out of Rodia right after the shooting. We can try to play it the way you said it went down. Self-defense. You were there to buy a rock and he saw *your* roll and tried to rip *you* off. The jury might believe it, especially if he won't testify. And they might believe it even if he does testify because I'll make him take the fifth so many times they'll think he's Al Capone before he gets off the stand."

"Who's Al Capone?"

"You're kidding me, right?"

"No, man, who is he?"

"Never mind, Cash. What do you want to do?"

"You're cool if we go to trial?"

"I'm cool with it. It's just that there is that gap, you know?"

"Gap?"

"There is a wide gap between what they're offering you right now and what you could get if we lose at trial. We're talking about a minimum twelve-year swing, Cash. That's a lot of time to gamble with."

Montgomery backed away from the bars. They had left twin impressions on both sides of his forehead. He now gripped the bars in his hands.

"The thing is, three years, fifteen years, I ain't going to make it either way. They got hit men in every prison. But in County, they got the system and ev'rybody is separated and locked up tight. I'm okay there."

I nodded. But the problem was that any sentence over a year had to be served in a state prison. The county system was a holding system for those awaiting trial or sentenced to short terms.

"Okay, then I guess we go to trial."

"I guess we do."

"Sit tight. They'll be coming back for you soon."

I knocked quietly on the courtroom door and the deputy opened it. Court was in session and Judge Champagne was holding a status conference on another case. I saw my prosecutor sitting against the rail and went over to confer. This was the first case I'd had with Philip Hellman and I had found him to be extremely reasonable. I decided to test the limits of that reason one last time.

"So, Mickey, I hear we are now colleagues," he said with a smile.

"Temporarily," I said. "I don't plan to make it a career."

"Good, I don't need the competition. So what are we going to do here?"

"I think we are going to put it over one more time."

"Mickey, come on, I've been very generous. I can't keep—"

"No, you're right. You've been completely generous, Phil, and I appreciate that. My client appreciates that. It's just that he can't take a deal because anything that puts him in a state prison is a death penalty. We both know that the Crips will get him."

"First of all, I don't know that. And second of all, if that's what he thinks, then maybe he shouldn't have tried to rip off the Crips and shoot one of their guys."

I nodded in agreement.

"That's a good point but my client maintains it was self-defense. Your vic drew first. So I guess we go to trial and you've got to ask a jury for justice for a victim who doesn't want it. Who will testify only if you force him to and will then claim he doesn't remember shit."

"Maybe he doesn't. He did get shot, after all."

"Yeah, and maybe the jury will buy that, especially when I bring out his pedigree. I'll ask him what he does for a living for starters. According to what Cisco, my investigator, has found out, he's been selling drugs since he was twelve years old and his mother put him on the street."

"Mickey, we've already been down this road. What do you want? I'm getting ready to just say fuck it, let's go to trial."

"What do I want? I want to make sure you don't fuck up the start of your brilliant career."

"What?"

"Look, man, you are a young prosecutor. Remember what you just said about not wanting the competition? Well, another thing you don't want is to risk putting a loss on your ledger. Not this early in the game. You just want this to go away. So here's what I want. A year in County and restitution. You can name your price on restitution."

"Are you kidding me?"

He said it too loud and drew a look from the judge. He then spoke very quietly.

"Are you fucking kidding me?"

"Not really. It's a good solution when you think about it, Phil. It works for everybody."

"Yeah, and what's Judge Judy going to say when I present this? The victim is in a wheelchair for life. She won't sign off on this."

"We ask to go back to chambers and we both sell it to her. We tell her that Montgomery wants to go to trial and claim self-defense and that the state has real reservations because of the victim's lack of cooperation and status as a high-ranking member of a criminal organization. She was a prosecutor before she was a judge. She'll understand this. And she'll probably have more sympathy for Montgomery than she does for your drug-dealing victim."

Hellman thought for a long moment. The hearing before Champagne ended and she instructed the courtroom deputy to bring Montgomery out. It was the last case of the day.

"Now or never, Phil," I prompted.

"Okay, let's do it," he finally said.

Hellman stood up and moved to the prosecution table.

"Your Honor," he intoned, "before we bring the defendant out, could counsel discuss this case in chambers?"

Champagne, a veteran judge who had seen everything at least three times, creased her brow.

"On the record, gentlemen?"

"That's probably not necessary," Hellman said. "We would like to discuss the terms of a disposition in the case."

"Then by all means. Let's go."

The judge stepped down from the bench and headed back toward her chambers. Hellman and I started to follow. As we got to the gate next to the clerk's pod, I leaned forward to whisper to the young prosecutor.

"Montgomery gets credit for time served, right?"

Hellman stopped in his tracks and turned back to me.

"You've got to be —"

"Just kidding," I quickly said.

I held my hands up in surrender. Hellman frowned and then turned back around and headed toward the judge's chambers. I had thought it was worth a try.

Ten

It was a silent breakfast. Madeline Bosch poked at her cereal with her spoon but managed to put very little of it into her stomach. Bosch knew that his daughter wasn't upset because he was going away for the night. And she wasn't upset because she wasn't going. He believed she had come to enjoy the breaks his infrequent travels gave her. The reason she was upset was the arrangements he had made for her care while he was gone. She was fourteen going on twenty-four and her first choice would have been to simply be left alone to fend for herself. Her second choice would have been to stay with her best friend up the street, and her last choice would have been to have Mrs. Bambrough from the school stay at the house with her.

Bosch knew she was perfectly capable of fending for herself but he wasn't there yet. They had been living together for only a few months and it had been only those few months since she had lost her mother. He just wasn't ready to turn her loose, no matter how fervently she insisted she was ready.

He finally put down his spoon and spoke.

"Look, Maddie, it's a school night and last time when you stayed with Rory you both stayed up all night, slept through most of your classes and had your parents and all your teachers mad at both of you."

"I told you we wouldn't do that again."

"I just think we need to wait on that a little bit. I'll tell Mrs. Bambrough that it's all right if Rory comes over, just not till midnight. You guys can do your homework together or something."

"Like she's really going to want to come here when I'm being watched by the assistant principal. Thanks for that, Dad."

Bosch had to concentrate on not laughing. This issue seemed so simple compared with what she had faced in October after coming to live with him. She still had regular therapy sessions and they seemed to go a long way toward helping her cope with her mother's death. Bosch would take a dispute over child care over those other deeper issues any day.

He checked his watch. It was time to go.

"If you're done playing with your food you can put your bowl in the sink. We have to get going."

"*Finished,* Dad. You should use the correct word."

"Sorry about that. Are you *finished* playing with your cereal?"

"Yes."

"Good. Let's go."

He got up from the table and went back to his room to grab his overnight bag off the bed. He was traveling light, expecting the trip to last one night at the most. If they got lucky, they might even catch a late flight home tonight.

When he came back out, Maddie was standing by the door, her backpack over one shoulder.

"Ready?"

"No, I'm just standing here for my health."

He walked up to her and kissed the top of her head before she could move away from him. She tried, though.

"Gotcha."

"Daaaad!"

He locked the door behind them and put his bag in the backseat of the Mustang.

"You have your key, right?"

"Yes!"

"Just making sure."

"Can we go? I don't want to be late."

They drove down the hill in silence after that. When they got to the school, he saw Sue Bambrough working the drop-off lane, getting the slow-moving kids out of the cars and into the school, keeping things moving.

"You know the routine, Mads. Call me, text me, vid me, let me know you're doing okay."

"I'll get out here."

She opened the door early, before they got to where the assistant principal was stationed. Maddie got out and then reached back in to grab her bag. Bosch waited for it, the sign that everything was really okay.

"Be safe, Dad."

There it was.

"You, too, baby."

She closed the door. He lowered the window and drove down to Sue Bambrough. She leaned into the open window.

"Hey, Sue. She's a little upset but she'll get over it by the end of the day. I told her that Aurora Smith could come by but not to make it late. Who knows, maybe they'll do some homework."

"She'll be fine, Harry."

"I left the check on the kitchen counter and there's some cash there for anything you guys'll need."

"Thanks, Harry. Just let me know if you think it will be more than one night. No problem on my end."

Bosch checked the rearview. He wanted to ask a question but didn't want to hold people up.

"What is it, Harry?"

"Uh, to say you're done doing something, is that wrong? You know, bad English?"

Sue tried to hide a smile.

"If she's correcting you, that's the natural course of things. Don't take it personally. We drill it into them here. They go home and want to drill somebody else. It would be proper to say you *finished* doing something. But I know what you meant."

Bosch nodded. Somebody in the line behind him tapped the horn — Bosch assumed it was a man hurrying to make drop-off and then get to work. He waved his thanks to Sue and pulled out.

Maggie McFierce had called Bosch the night before and told him that there was nothing out of Burbank, so they were taking a direct flight out of LAX. That meant it would be a brutal drive in morning traffic. Bosch lived on a hillside right above the Hollywood Freeway but it was the one freeway that wouldn't help him get to the airport. Instead, he took Highland down into Hollywood and then cut over to La Cienega. It bottlenecked through the oil fields near Baldwin Hills and he lost his cushion of time. He took La Tijera from there and when he got to the airport he was forced to park in one of the expensive garages close in because he didn't have time to ride a shuttle bus in from an economy lot.

After filling out the Law Enforcement Officer forms at the counter and being walked through security by a TSA agent, he finally got to the gate while the plane was in the final stages of loading its passengers. He looked for McPherson but didn't see her and assumed she was already on the plane.

He boarded and went through the required meet-and-greet, stepping into the cockpit, showing his badge and shaking the hands of the flight crew. He then made his way toward the back of the plane. He and McPherson had exit-row seats across the aisle from each other. She was already in place, a tall Starbucks cup in hand. She had obviously arrived early for the flight.

"Thought you weren't going to make it," she said.

"It was close. How'd you get here so early? You have a daughter just like me."

"I dropped her with Mickey last night."

Bosch nodded.

"Exit row, nice. Who's your travel agent?"

"We've got a good one. That's why I wanted to handle it. We'll send LAPD the bill for you."

"Yeah, good luck with that."

Bosch had put his bag in an overhead compartment so he would have room to extend his legs. After he sat down and buckled in, he saw that McPherson had shoved two thick files into the seat pocket in front of her. He had nothing out to prep with. His files were in his bag but he didn't feel like getting them out. He pulled his notebook out of his back pocket and was about to lean across the aisle to ask McPherson a question when a flight attendant came down the aisle and stooped down to whisper to him.

"You're the detective, right?"

"Uh, yes. Is there a—"

Before he could finish the Dirty Harry line, the flight attendant informed him that they were upgrading him to an unclaimed seat in the first-class section.

"Oh, that's nice of you and the captain, but I don't think I can do that."

"There's no charge. It's—"

"No, it's not that. See, I'm with this lady here and she's my boss and I—I mean we—need to talk and go over our investigation. She's a prosecutor, actually."

The attendant took a moment to track his explanation and then nodded and said she'd go back to the front of the plane and inform the powers that be.

"And I thought chivalry was dead," McPherson said. "You gave up a first-class seat to sit with me."

"Actually, I should've told her to give it to you. That would have been real chivalry."

"Uh-oh, here she comes back."

Bosch looked up the aisle. The same smiling attendant was headed back to them.

"We're moving some people around and we have room for you both. Come on up."

They got up and headed forward, Bosch grabbing his bag out of the overhead and following McPherson. She looked back at him, smiled and said, "My tarnished knight."

"Right," Bosch said.

The seats were side by side in the first row. McPherson took the window. Soon after they were resituated, the plane took off for its three-hour flight to Seattle.

"So," McPherson said, "Mickey told me our daughter has never met your daughter."

Bosch nodded.

"Yeah, I guess we need to change that."

"Definitely. I hear they're the same age and you guys compared photos and they even look alike."

"Well, her mother sort of looked like you. Same coloring."

And fire, Bosch thought. He pulled out his phone and turned it on. He showed her a photo of Maddie.

"That's remarkable," McPherson said. "They could be sisters."

Bosch looked at his daughter's photo as he spoke.

"It's just been a tough year for her. She lost her mother and moved across an ocean. Left all her friends behind. I've been kind of letting her move at her own pace."

"All the more reason she should know her family here."

Bosch just nodded. In the past year he had fended off numerous calls from his half brother seeking to get their daughters together. He wasn't sure if his hesitation was about the potential relationship between the two cousins or the two half brothers.

Sensing that angle of conversation was at an end, McPherson unfolded her table and pulled out her files. Bosch turned his phone off and put it away.

"So we're going to work?" he asked.

"A little. I want to be prepared."

"How much do you want to tell her up front? I was thinking we just talk about the ID. Confirm it and see if she's willing to testify again."

"And not bring up the DNA?"

"Right. That could turn a yes into a no."

"But shouldn't she know everything she's going to be getting into?"

"Eventually, yes. It's been a long time. I did the trace. She hit some hard times and rough spots but it looks like she might've come out okay. I guess we'll see when we get up there."

"Let's play it by ear, then. I think if it feels right, we need to tell her everything."

"You make the call."

"The one thing that's good is that she'll only have to do it once. We don't have to go through a preliminary hearing or a grand jury. Jessup was held over for trial in 'eighty-six and that is not what the supreme court reversed. So we just go directly to trial. We'll need her one time and that will be it."

"That's good. And you'll be handling her."

"Yes."

Bosch nodded. The assumption was that she was a better prosecutor than Haller. After all, it was Haller's first case. Harry was happy to hear she would be handling the most important witness at trial.

"What about me? Which one of you will take me?"

"I don't think that's been decided. Mickey anticipates that Jessup will actually testify. I know he's waiting for that. But we haven't talked about who will take you. My guess is that you'll be doing a lot of read-backs to the jury of sworn testimony from the first trial."

She closed the file and it looked like that was it for work.

They spent the rest of the flight small-talking about their daughters and looking through the magazines in their seat pockets. The plane landed early at SeaTac and they picked up a rental car and started north. Bosch did the driving. The car came equipped with a GPS system but the DA travel assistant had also provided McPherson with a full package of directions to Port Townsend. They drove up to Seattle and then took a ferry across Puget Sound. They left the car and went up for coffee on the concessions deck, finding an open table next to a set of windows. Bosch was staring out the window when McPherson surprised him with an observation.

"You're not happy, are you, Harry?"

Bosch looked at her and shrugged.

"It's a weird case. Twenty-four years old and we start with the bad guy already in prison and we take him out. It doesn't make me unhappy, it's just kind of strange, you know?"

She had a half smile on her face.

"I wasn't talking about the case. I was talking about you. You're not a happy man."

Bosch looked down at the coffee he held on the table with two hands. Not because of the ferry's movement, but because he was cold and the coffee was warming him inside and out.

"Oh," he said.

A long silence opened up between them. He wasn't sure what he should reveal to this woman. He had known her for only a week and she was making observations about him.

"I don't really have time to be happy right now," he finally said.

"Mickey told me what he felt he could about Hong Kong and what happened with your daughter."

Bosch nodded. But he knew Maggie didn't know the whole story. Nobody did except for Madeline and him.

"Yeah," he said. "She caught some bad breaks there. That's the thing, I guess. I think if I can make my daughter happy, then I'll be happy. But I am not sure when that will be."

He brought his eyes up to hers and saw only sympathy. He smiled.

"Yeah, we should get the two cousins together," he said, moving on.

"Absolutely," she said.

Eleven

Thursday, February 18, 1:30 P.M.

The *Los Angeles Times* carried a lengthy story on Jason Jessup's first day of freedom in twenty-four years. The reporter and photographer met him at dawn on Venice Beach, where the forty-eight-year-old tried his hand at his boyhood pastime of surfing. On the first few sets, he was shaky on a borrowed longboard but soon he was up and riding the break. A photo of Jessup standing upright on the board and riding a curl with his arms outstretched, his face turned up to the sky, was the centerpiece photo on the newspaper's front page. The photo showed off what two decades of lifting prison iron will do. Jessup's body was roped with muscle. He looked lean and mean.

From the beach the next stop was an In-N-Out franchise in Westwood for hamburgers and French fries with all the catsup he wanted. After lunch Jessup went to Clive Royce's storefront office in downtown, where he attended a two-hour meeting with the battery of attorneys representing him in both criminal and civil matters. This meeting was not open to the *Times*.

Jessup rounded out the afternoon by watching a movie called *Shutter Island* at the Chinese theater in Hollywood. He bought a tub of buttered popcorn large enough to feed a family of four and ate every puffed kernel. He then returned to Venice, where he had a room in an apartment near the beach courtesy of a high-school surfing buddy. The day ended at a beach barbecue with a handful of supporters who had never wavered in their belief in his innocence.

I sat at my desk studying the color photos of Jessup that graced two inside pages of the A section. The paper was going all-out on the story, as it had all along, surely smelling the journalistic honors to be gathered at the end of Jessup's journey to complete freedom. Springing an innocent man from prison was the ultimate newspaper story and the *Times* was desperately trying to take credit for Jessup's release.

The largest photo showed Jessup's unabashed delight at the red plastic tray sitting in front of him at a table at In-N-Out. The tray contained a fully loaded double-double with fries smothered in catsup and melted cheese. The caption said

Why Is This Man Smiling? **12:05 — Jessup eats his first Double-Double in 24 years. "I've been thinking about this forever!"**

The other photos carried similarly lighthearted captions below shots of Jessup at the movies with his bucket of popcorn, hoisting a beer at the barbecue and hugging his high-school pal, walking through a glass door that said ROYCE AND ASSOCIATES, ATTORNEYS-AT-LAW. There was no indication in the tone of the article or photos that Jason Jessup was a man who happened to still be accused of murdering a twelve-year-old girl.

The story was about Jessup relishing his freedom while being unable to plan his future until his "legal issues" were resolved. It was a nice turn of phrase, I thought, calling abduction and murder charges and a pending trial merely legal issues.

I had the paper spread wide on the desk Lorna had rented for me in my new office on Broadway. We were on the second floor of the Bradbury Building and only three blocks from the CCB.

"I think you need to put something up on the walls."

I looked up. It was Clive Royce. He had walked through the reception room unannounced because I had sent Lorna over to Philippe's to get us lunch. Royce gestured to the empty walls of the temporary office. I flipped the newspaper closed and held up the front page.

"I just ordered a twenty-by-twenty shot of Jesus on the surfboard here. I'm going to hang him on the wall."

Royce stepped up to the desk and took the paper, studying the photo on the front as if for the first time, which we both knew was not the case. Royce had been deeply involved in the generation of the story, the payoff being the photo of the office door with his firm's name on the glass.

"Yes, they did a good job with it, didn't they?"

He handed it back.

"I guess so, if you like your killers happy-go-lucky."

Royce didn't respond, so I continued.

"I know what you're doing, Clive, because I would do it, too. But as soon as we get a judge, I'm going to ask him to stop you. I'm not going to let you taint the jury pool."

Royce frowned as if I had suggested something completely untoward.

"It's a free press, Mick. You can't control the media. The man just got out of prison, and like it or not, it's a news story."

"Right, and you can give exclusives in exchange for display. Display that might plant a seed in a potential juror's mind. What do you have planned for today? Jessup co-hosting the morning show on Channel Five? Or is he judging the chili cook-off at the state fair?"

"As a matter of fact, NPR wanted to hang with him today but I showed restraint. I said no. Make sure you tell the judge that as well."

"Wow, you actually said no to NPR? Was that because most people who listen to NPR are the kind of people who can get out of jury duty, or because you got something better lined up?"

Royce frowned again, looking as though I had impaled him with an integrity spear. He looked around, grabbed the chair from Maggie's desk and pulled it over so he could sit in front of mine. Once he was seated with his legs crossed and had arranged his suit properly he spoke.

"Now, tell me, Mick, does your boss think that housing you in a separate building is really going to make people think you are acting independently of his direction? You're having us on, right?"

I smiled at him. His effort to get under my skin was not going to work.

"Let me state once again for the record, Clive, that I have no boss in this matter. I am working independently of Gabriel Williams."

I gestured to the room.

"I'm here, not in the courthouse, and all decisions on this case will be made from this desk. But at the moment my decisions aren't that important. It's you who has the decision, Clive."

"And what would that be? A disposition, Mick?"

"That's right. Today's special, good until five o'clock only. Your boy pleads guilty, I'll come down off the death penalty and we both roll the dice with the judge on sentencing. You never know, Jessup could walk away with time served."

Royce smiled cordially and shook his head.

"I am sure that would make the powers that be in this town happy, but I'm afraid I must disappoint you, Mick. My client remains absolutely uninterested in a plea. And that is not going to change. I was actually hoping that by now you would have seen the uselessness of going to trial and would simply drop the charges. You can't win this thing, Mick. The state has to bend over on this one and you unfortunately are the fool who volunteered to take it in the arse."

"Well, I guess we'll see, won't we?"

"We will indeed."

I opened the desk's center drawer and removed a green plastic case containing a computer disc. I slid it across the desk to him.

"I wasn't expecting you to come by for it yourself, Clive. Thought you'd send an investigator or a clerk. You gotta bunch of them working for you, don't you? Along with that full-time publicist."

Royce slowly collected the disc. The plastic case was marked DEFENSE DISCOVERY I.

"Well, aren't we snarky today? Seems that only two weeks ago you were one of us, Mick. A lowly member of the defense bar."

I nodded my contrition. He had nailed me there.

"Sorry, Clive. Perhaps the power of the office is getting to me."

"Apology accepted."

"And sorry to waste your time coming over here. As I told you on the phone, that's got everything we have up until this morning. Mostly the old files and reports. I won't play discovery games with you, Clive. I've been on the wrong end of that too many times to count. So when I get it, you get it. But right now that's all I've got."

Royce tapped the disc case on the edge of the desk.

"No witness list?"

"There is but as of now it's essentially the same list from the trial in 'eighty-six. I've added my investigator and subtracted a few names — the parents, other people no longer alive."

"No doubt Felix Turner has been redacted."

I smiled like the Cheshire cat.

"Thankfully you won't get the chance to bring him up at trial."

"Yes, a pity. I would have loved the opportunity to shove him up the state's ass."

I nodded, noting that Royce had come off the English colloquialisms and was hitting me with pure Americana now. It was a symptom of his frustration over Turner, and as a longtime counsel for the defense I certainly felt it. In the retrial, there would be no mention of any aspect of the first trial. The new jurors would have no knowledge of what had transpired before. And that meant the state's use of the fraudulent jailhouse informant — no matter how grievous a prosecutorial sin — would not hurt the current prosecution.

I decided to move on.

"I should have another disc for you by the end of the week."

"Yes, I can't wait to see what you come up with."

Sarcasm noted.

"Just remember one thing, Clive. Discovery is a two-way street. You go beyond thirty days and we'll go see the judge."

The rules of evidence required that each side complete its discovery exchange no later than thirty days before the start of trial. Missing this deadline could lead to sanctions and open the door to a trial delay as the judge would grant the offended party more time to prepare.

"Yes, well, as you can imagine, we weren't expecting the turn of events that has transpired here," Royce said. "Consequently, our defense is in its infancy. But I won't play games with you either, Mick. A disc will be along to you in short order—provided that we have any discovery to give."

I knew that as a practical matter the defense usually had little in the way of discovery to give unless the plan was to mount an extensive defense. But I sounded the warning because I was leery of Royce. In a case this old, he might try to dig up an alibi witness or something else out of left field. I wanted to know about it before it came up in court.

"I appreciate that," I said.

Over his shoulder I saw Lorna enter the office. She was carrying two brown bags, one of which contained my French dip sandwich.

"Oh, I didn't realize..."

Royce turned around in his seat.

"Ah, the lovely Lorna. How are you, my darling?"

"Hello, Clive. I see you got the disc."

"Indeed. Thank you, Lorna."

I had noticed that Royce's English accent and formal parlance became more pronounced at times, especially in front of attractive women. I wondered if that was a conscious thing or not.

"I have two sandwiches here, Clive," Lorna said. "Would you like one?"

It was the wrong time for Lorna to be magnanimous.

"I think he was just about to leave," I said quickly.

"Yes, love, I must go. But thank you for the most gracious offer."

"I'll be out here if you need me, Mickey."

Lorna went back to the reception room, closing the door behind her. Royce turned back to me and spoke in a low voice.

"You know you should never have let that one go, Mick. She was the keeper. And now, joining forces with the first Mrs. Haller to deprive an innocent man of his long-deserved freedom, there is something incestuous about the whole thing, isn't there?"

I just looked at him for a long moment.

"Is there anything else, Clive?"

He held up the disc.

"I think this should do it for today."

"Good. I have to get back to work."

I walked him out through reception and closed the door after him. I turned and looked at Lorna.

"Feels weird, doesn't it?" she said. "Being on this side of it—the prosecution side."

"It does."

She held up one of the sandwich bags.

"Can I ask you something?" I said. "Whose sandwich were you going to give him, yours or mine?"

She looked at me with a straight face, then a smile of guilt leaked out.

"I was being polite, okay? I thought you and I could share."

I shook my head.

"Don't be giving my French dip sandwich to anybody. Especially a defense lawyer."

I snatched the bag from her hand.

"Thank you, love," I said in my best British accent.

She laughed and I headed back into my office to eat.

Twelve

After driving off the ferry at Port Townsend, Bosch and McPherson followed directions from the rental car's GPS to the address on Sarah Ann Gleason's driver's license. The trail led them through the small Victorian sea village and then out into a more rural area of large and isolated properties. Gleason's house was a small clapboard house that failed to keep the nearby town's Victorian theme. The detective and the prosecutor stood on the porch and knocked but got no response.

"Maybe she's at work or something," McPherson said.

"Could be."

"We could go back into town and get rooms, then come back after five."

Bosch checked his watch. He realized that school was just over and Maddie was probably heading home with Sue Bambrough. He guessed that his daughter was giving the assistant principal the silent treatment.

He stepped off the porch and started walking toward the corner of the house.

"Where are you going?"

"To check the back. Hold on."

But as soon as Bosch turned the corner he could see that a hundred yards beyond the house there was another structure. It was a windowless barn or garage. What stood out was that it had a chimney. He could see heat waves but no smoke rising from the two black pipes that extended over the roofline. There were two cars and a van parked in front of the closed garage doors.

Bosch stood there watching for so long that McPherson finally came around the corner as well.

"What's taking — ?"

Bosch held up his hand to silence her, then pointed toward the outbuilding.

"What is it?" McPherson whispered.

Before Bosch could answer, one of the garage doors slid open a few feet and a figure stepped out. It looked like a young man or a teenager. He was wearing a full-length black apron over his clothes. He took off heavy elbow-length gloves so he could light a cigarette.

"Shit," McPherson whispered, answering her own question.

Bosch stepped back to the corner of the house to use it as a blind. He pulled McPherson with him.

"All her arrests — her drug of choice was meth," he whispered.

"Great," McPherson whispered back. "Our main witness is a meth cook."

The young smoker turned when apparently called from within the barn. He threw down his cigarette, stepped on it, and went back inside. He yanked the door closed behind him but it slid to a stop six inches before closing.

"Let's go," Bosch said.

He started to move but McPherson put her hand on his arm.

"Wait, what are you talking about? We need to call Port Townsend police and get some backup, don't we?"

Bosch looked at her a moment without responding.

"I saw the police station when we went through town," McPherson said, as if to assure him that backup was waiting and willing.

"If we call for backup they're not going to be very cooperative, since we didn't bother to check in when we got to town in the first place," Bosch said. "They'll arrest her and then we have a main witness awaiting trial on drug charges. How do you think that will work with Jessup's jury?"

She didn't answer.

"Tell you what," he said. "You hold back here and I'll go check it out. Three vehicles, probably three cooks. If I can't handle it, we call backup."

"They're probably armed, Harry. You—"

"They're probably not armed. I'll check it out and if it looks like a situation we'll call Port Townsend."

"I don't like this."

"It could work to our favor."

"What? How?"

"Think about it. Watch for my signal. If something goes wrong, get in the car and get out of here."

He held up the car keys and she reluctantly took them. He could tell she was thinking about what he had said. The advantage. If they caught their witness in a compromising situation, it could give them the leverage they needed to assure her cooperation and testimony.

Bosch left McPherson there and headed on foot down the crushed-shell drive to the barn. He didn't attempt to hide in case they had a lookout. He put his hands in his pocket to try to convey he was no threat, somebody just lost and looking for directions.

The crushed shell made it impossible for him to make a completely silent approach. But as he got closer he heard loud music coming from the barn. It was rock and roll but he could not identify it. Something heavy on the guitar and with a pounding beat. It had a retro feel to it, like he had heard the song a long time ago, maybe in Vietnam.

Bosch was twenty feet from the partially opened door when it moved open another two feet and the same young man stepped out again. Seeing him closer, Bosch pegged his age at twenty-one or so. In the moment he stepped out Bosch realized he should have expected that he'd be back out to finish his interrupted smoke. Now it was too late and the smoker saw him.

But the young man didn't hesitate or sound an alarm of any sort. He looked at Bosch curiously as he started tapping a cigarette out of a soft pack. He was sweating profusely.

"You parked up at the house?" he asked.

Bosch stopped ten feet from him and took his hands out of his pockets. He didn't look back toward the house, choosing instead to keep his eyes on the kid.

"Uh, yes, is that a problem?" he asked.

"No, but most people just drive on down to the barn. Sarah usually tells them to."

"Oh, I didn't get that message. Is Sarah here?"

"Yeah, inside. Go on in."

"You sure?"

"Yeah, we're almost done for the day."

Bosch was getting the idea that he had walked into something that was not what he thought it was. He now glanced back and saw McPherson peering around the corner of the house. This wasn't the best way to do this but he turned and headed toward the open door.

The heat hit him the moment he entered. The inside of the barn was like an oven and for good reason. The first thing Bosch saw was the open door of a huge furnace that was glowing orange with flames.

Standing eight feet from the heat source was another young man and an older woman. They also wore full-length aprons and heavy gloves. The man was using a pair of iron tongs to hold steady a large piece of molten glass attached to the end of an iron pipe. The woman was shaping it with a wooden block and a pair of pliers.

They were glassmakers, not drug cooks. The woman wore a welder's mask over her face as protection. Bosch could not identify her but he was pretty sure he was looking at Sarah Ann Gleason.

Bosch stepped back through the door and signaled to McPherson. He gave the okay sign but was unsure she would be able to identify it from the distance. He waved her in.

"What's going on, man?" the smoker asked.

"That's Sarah Gleason in there, you said?" Bosch responded.

"Yeah, that's her."

"I need to talk to her."

"You're going to have to wait until she's set the piece. She can't stop while it's soft. We've been working it for almost four hours."

"How much longer?"

"Maybe an hour. You can probably talk to her while she's working. You want a piece made?"

"That's okay, I think we can wait."

McPherson drove up in the rental car and got out. Bosch opened the door for her and explained quietly that they had read wrong what they had seen. He told her the barn was a glassmaking studio. He told her how he wanted to play it until they could get Gleason into a private setting. McPherson shook her head and smiled.

"What if we had gone in there with backup?"

"I guess we would've broken some glass."

"And had one pissed-off witness."

She got out of the car and Bosch reached in for the file he had put on the dashboard. He put it inside his jacket and under his arm so he could carry it unseen.

They entered the studio and Gleason was waiting for them, with her gloves off and her mask folded up to reveal her face. She had obviously been told by the smoker that they were potential customers and Bosch initially did nothing to dissuade her of that interpretation. He didn't want to reveal their true business until they were alone with her.

"I'm Harry and this is Maggie. Sorry to barge in like this."

"Oh, no problem. We like it when people get a chance to see what we do. In fact, we're right in the middle of a project right now and need to get back to it. You're welcome to stay and watch and I can tell you a little bit about what we're doing."

"That would be great."

"You just have to stay back. We're dealing with very hot material here."

"Not a problem."

"Where are you from? Seattle?"

"No, actually we're all the way up from California. We're pretty far from home."

If the mention of her native state caused Gleason any concern, she didn't show it. She pulled the mask back down over a smile, put her gloves on and went back to work. Over the next forty minutes Bosch and McPherson watched Gleason and her two assistants finish the glass piece. Gleason provided a steady narration as she worked, explaining that the three members of her team had different duties. One of the young men was a blower and the other was a blocker. Gleason was the gaffer, the one in charge. The piece they were sculpting was a four-foot-long grape leaf that would be part of a larger piece commissioned to hang in the lobby of a business in Seattle called Rainier Wine.

Gleason also filled in some of her recent history. She said she started her own studio only two years ago after spending three years apprenticing with a glass artist in Seattle. It was useful information to Bosch. Both hearing her talk about herself and watching her work the soft glass. *Gathering color,* as she called it. Using heavy tools to manipulate something beautiful and fragile and glowing with red-hot danger all at the same time.

The heat from the furnace was stifling and both Bosch and McPherson took off their jackets. Gleason said the oven burned at 2,300 degrees and Bosch marveled at how the artists could spend so many hours working so close to the source. The glory hole, the small opening into which they repeatedly passed the sculpture to reheat and add layers, glowed like the gateway to Hell.

When the day's work was completed and the piece was placed in the finishing kiln, Gleason asked the assistants to clean up the studio before heading home. She then invited Bosch and McPherson to wait for her in the office while she got cleaned up herself.

The office doubled as a break room. It was sparely furnished with a table and four chairs, a filing cabinet, a storage locker and a small kitchenette. There was a binder on the table containing plastic sleeves with photos of glass pieces made previously in the studio. McPherson studied these and seemed taken with several. Bosch took out the file he had been carrying inside his jacket and put it down on the table ready to go.

"It must be nice to be able to make something out of nothing," McPherson said. "I wish I could."

Bosch tried to think of a response but before he could come up with anything the door opened and Sarah Gleason entered. The bulky mask, apron and gloves were gone and she was smaller than Bosch had expected. She barely crested five feet and he doubted there were more than ninety pounds on her tiny frame. He knew that childhood trauma sometimes stunted growth. So it was no wonder Sarah Gleason looked like a woman in a child's body.

Her auburn hair was down now instead of tied into a knot behind her head. It framed a weary face with dark blue eyes. She wore blue jeans, clogs and a black T-shirt that said *Death Cab* on it. She headed directly to the refrigerator.

"Can I get you something? Don't have any alcohol in here but if you need something cold . . ."

Bosch and McPherson passed. Harry noticed she had left the door to the office open. He could hear someone sweeping in the studio. He stepped over and closed it.

Gleason turned from the refrigerator with a bottle of water. She saw Bosch closing the door and a look of apprehension immediately crossed her face. Bosch raised one hand in a calming gesture as he pulled his badge with the other.

"Ms. Gleason, everything is okay. We're from Los Angeles and just need to speak privately with you."

He opened his badge wallet and held it up to her.

"What is this?"

"My name is Harry Bosch and this is Maggie McPherson. She is a prosecutor with the L.A. County District Attorney's Office."

"Why did you lie?" she said angrily. "You said you wanted a piece made."

"No, actually we didn't. Your assistant, the blocker, just assumed that. We never said why we were here."

Her guard was clearly up and Bosch thought they had blown their approach and with that the opportunity to secure her as a witness. But then Gleason stepped forward and grabbed the badge wallet out of his hand. She studied it and the facing ID card. It was an unusual move, taking the badge from him. No more than the fifth time that had ever happened to Bosch in his long career as a cop. He saw her eyes hold on the ID card and he knew she had noticed the discrepancy between what he had said his name was and what was on the ID.

"You said *Harry* Bosch?"

"Harry for short."

"Hieronymus Bosch. You're named after the artist?"

Bosch nodded.

"My mother liked the paintings."

"Well, I like them, too. I think he knew something about inner demons. Is that why your mother liked him?"

"I think so, yeah."

She handed the badge wallet back to him and Bosch sensed a calmness come over her. The moment of anxiety and apprehension had passed, thanks to the painter whose name Bosch carried.

"What do you want with me? I haven't been to L.A. in more than ten years."

Bosch noted that if she was telling the truth, then she had not returned when her stepfather was ill and dying.

"We just want to talk," he said. "Can we sit down?"

"Talk about what?"

"Your sister."

"My sister? I don't — look, you need to tell me what this is —"

"You don't know, do you?"

"Know what?"

"Sit down and we'll tell you."

Finally, she moved to the lunch table and took a seat. She pulled a soft pack of cigarettes out of her pocket and lit one.

"Sorry," she said. "It's my one remaining addiction. And you two showing up like this — I need a smoke."

For the next ten minutes Bosch and McPherson traded off the story and walked her through the short version of Jason Jessup's journey to freedom. Gleason showed almost no reaction to the news. No tears, no outrage. And she didn't ask questions about the DNA test that had sprung him from prison. She only explained that she had no contact with anyone in California, owned no television and never read newspapers. She said they were distractions from work as well as from her recovery from addiction.

"We're going to retry him, Sarah," McPherson said. "And we're here because we're going to need your help."

Bosch could see Sarah turn inward, to start to measure the impact of what they were telling her.

"It was so long ago," she finally responded. "Can't you just use what I said from the first trial?"

McPherson shook her head.

"We can't, Sarah. The new jury can't even know there was an earlier trial because that could influence how they weigh the evidence. It would prejudice them against the defendant and a guilty verdict wouldn't stand. So in situations where witnesses from the first trial are dead or mentally incompetent, we read their earlier testimony into the trial record without telling the jury where it's from. But where that's not the case, like with you, we need the person to come to court and testify."

It wasn't clear whether Gleason had even registered McPherson's response. She sat staring at something far away. Even as she spoke, her eyes didn't come off their distant focus.

"I've spent my whole life since then trying to forget about that day. I tried different things to make me forget. I used drugs to make a big bubble with me in the middle of it. I made . . . Never mind, the point is, I don't think I'm going to be much help to you."

Before McPherson could respond, Bosch stepped in.

"I'll tell you what," he said. "Let's just talk here for a few minutes about what you can remember, okay? And if it's not going to work, then it won't work. You were a victim, Sarah, and we don't want to victimize you all over again."

He waited a moment for Gleason to respond but she sat mute, staring at the water bottle in front of her on the table.

"Let's start with that day," Bosch said. "I don't need you at this point to go through the horrible moments of your sister's abduction, but do you remember making the identification of Jason Jessup for the police?"

She slowly nodded.

"I remember looking through the window. Upstairs. They opened the blinds a little bit so I could look out. They weren't supposed to be able to see me. The men. He was the one with the hat. They made him take it off and that's when I saw it was him. I remember that."

Bosch was encouraged by the detail of the hat. He didn't recall seeing that in the case records or hearing it in McPherson's summary but the fact that Gleason remembered it was a good sign.

"What kind of hat was he wearing?" he asked.

"A baseball cap," Gleason said. "It was blue."

"A Dodgers cap?"

"I'm not sure. I don't think I knew back then either."

Bosch nodded and moved in.

"Do you think if I showed you a photo lineup, you would be able to identify the man who took your sister?"

"You mean the way he looks now? I doubt it."

"No, not now," McPherson said. "What we would need to do in trial is confirm the identification you made back then. We would show you photos from back then."

Gleason hesitated and then nodded.

"Sure. Through everything I've done to myself over the years, I've never been able to forget that man's face."

"Well, let's see."

While Bosch opened the file on the table, Gleason lit a new cigarette off the end of her old one.

The file contained a lineup of six black-and-white booking photos of men of the same age, build and coloring. A 1986 photo of Jessup was included in the spread. Harry knew that this was the make-or-break moment of the case.

The photos were displayed in two rows of three. Jessup's shot was in the middle window on the bottom row. The five hole. It had always been the lucky spot for Bosch.

"Take your time," he said.

Gleason drank some water and then put the bottle to the side. She leaned over the table, bringing her face within twelve inches of the photos. It didn't take her long. She pointed to the photo of Jessup without hesitation.

"I wish I could forget him," she said. "But I can't. He's always there in the back of my mind. In the shadows."

"Do you have any doubt about the photo you have chosen?" Bosch asked.

Gleason leaned down and looked again, then shook her head.

"No. He was the man."

Bosch glanced at McPherson, who made a slight nod. It was a good ID and they had handled it right. The only thing that was missing was a show of emotion on Gleason's part. But maybe twenty-four years had drained her of everything. Harry took out a pen and handed it to Gleason.

"Would you put your initials and the date below the photo you chose, please?"

"Why?"

"It confirms your ID. It just helps make it more solid when it comes up in court."

Bosch noted that she had not asked if she had chosen the right photo. She didn't have to and that was a secondary confirmation of her recall. Another good sign. After she handed the pen back to Bosch he closed the file and slid it to the side. He glanced at McPherson again. Now came the hard part. By prior agreement, Maggie was going to make the call here on whether to bring up the DNA now or to wait until Gleason was more firmly onboard as a witness.

McPherson decided not to wait.

"Sarah, there is a second issue to discuss now. We told you about the DNA that allowed this man to get this new trial and what we hope is only his temporary freedom."

"Yes."

"We took the DNA profile and checked it against the California data bank. We got a match. The semen on the dress your sister was wearing came from your stepfather."

Bosch watched Sarah closely. Not even a flicker of surprise showed on her face or in her eyes. This information was not news to her.

"In two thousand four the state started taking DNA swabs from all suspects in felony arrests. That same year your father was arrested for a felony hit-and-run with injuries. He ran a stop sign and hit—"

"Stepfather."

"Excuse me?"

"You said 'your father.' He wasn't my father. He was my step-father."

"My mistake. I'm sorry. The bottom line is Kensington Landy's DNA was in the data bank and it's a match with the sample from the dress. What could not be determined is how long that sample was on the dress at the time of its discovery. It could have been deposited on the dress the day of the murder or the week before or maybe even a month before."

Sarah started flying on autopilot. She was there but not there. Her eyes were fixed on a distance that was far beyond the room they were in.

"We have a theory, Sarah. The autopsy that was conducted on your sister determined that she had not been sexually abused by her killer or anyone else prior to that day. We also know the dress she wore happened to be yours and Melissa was borrowing it that morning because she liked it."

McPherson paused but Sarah said nothing.

"When we get to trial we're going to have to explain the semen found on the dress. If we can't explain it, the assumption will be that it came from the killer and that killer was your stepfather. We will lose the case and Jessup, the real killer, will walk away free. I'm sure you don't want that, do you, Sarah? There are some people out there who think twenty-four years in prison is enough time served for the murder of a twelve-year-old girl. They don't know why we're doing this. But I want you to know that I don't think that, Sarah. Not by a long shot."

Sarah Gleason didn't answer at first. Bosch expected tears but none came and he began to wonder if her emotions had been cauterized by the traumas and depravities of her life. Or maybe she simply had an internal toughness that her diminutive stature camouflaged. Either way, when she finally responded, it was in a flat, emotionless voice that belied the heartfelt words she spoke.

"You know what I always thought?" she said.

McPherson leaned forward.

"What, Sarah?"

"That that man killed three people that day. My sister, then my mother...and then me. None of us got away."

There was a long moment of silence. McPherson slowly reached out and put her hand on Gleason's arm, a gesture of comfort where no comfort could exist.

"I'm sorry, Sarah," McPherson whispered.

"Okay," Gleason said. "I'll tell you everything."

Thirteen

Thursday, February 18, 8:15 P.M.

My daughter was already missing her mother's cooking—and she'd only been gone one day. I was dropping her half-eaten sandwich into the garbage and wondering how the hell I could've messed up a grilled cheese when my cell phone's ring interrupted. It was Maggie checking in from the road.

"Tell me something good," I said by way of greeting.

"You get to spend the evening with our beautiful daughter."

"Yes, that's something good. Except she doesn't like my cooking. Now tell me something else that's good."

"Our primary witness is good to go. She'll testify."

"She made the ID?"

"She did."

"She told you about the DNA and it fits with our theory?"

"She did and it does."

"And she'll come down here and testify to all of it at the trial?"

"She will."

I felt a twelve-volt charge go through my body.

"That's actually a lot of good things, Maggie. Is there any down-side?"

"Well…"

I felt the wind go out of the sails. I was about to learn that Sarah was still a drug addict or there was some other issue that would prevent me from using her at trial.

"Well, what?"

"Well, there are going to be challenges to her testimony, of course, but she's pretty solid. She's a survivor and it shows. There's really only one thing missing: emotions. She's been through a lot in her life and she basically seems to be a bit burned out—emotionally. No tears, no laughter, just straight down the middle."

"We can work on that. We can coach her."

"Yeah, well, we just have to be careful with that. I am not saying she isn't fine the way she is. I'm just saying that she's sort of a flat line. Everything else is good. I think you're going to like her and I think she'll help us put Jessup back in prison."

"That's fantastic, Maggie. Really. And you're still all right handling her at trial, right?"

"I've got her."

"Royce will attack her on the meth—memory loss and all of that. Her lifestyle . . . you'll have to be ready for anything and everything."

"I will be. That leaves you with Bosch and Jessup. You still think he'll testify?"

"Jessup? Yes, he's got to. Clive knows he can't do that to a jury, not after twenty-four years. So, yes, I've got him and I've got Bosch."

"At least with Harry you don't have to worry about any baggage."

"That Clive knows about yet."

"And what's that supposed to mean?"

"It means don't underestimate Clever Clive Royce. See, that's what you prosecutors always do. You get overconfident and it makes you vulnerable."

"Thank you, F. Lee Bailey. I'll keep that in mind."

"How was Bosch today?"

"He was Bosch. What happened on your end?"

I checked through the door of the kitchen. Hayley was sitting on the couch with her homework spread out on the coffee table.

"Well, for one thing, we've got a judge. Breitman, Department one-twelve."

Maggie considered the case assignment for a moment before responding.

"I would call that a no-win for either side. She's straight down the middle. Never a prosecutor, never a defense attorney. Just a good, solid civil trial lawyer. I think neither side gets an advantage with her."

"Wow, a judge who's going to be impartial and fair. Imagine that."

She didn't respond.

"She set the first status conference in chambers. Wednesday morning at eight before court starts. You read anything into that?"

This meant the judge wanted to meet the lawyers and discuss the case in chambers, starting things off informally and away from the lens of the media.

"I think that's good. She's probably going to set the rules with media and procedure. It sounds to me like she's going to run a tight ship."

"That was what I was thinking. You're free Wednesday to be there?"

"I'll have to check my calendar but I think so. I'm trying to clear everything except for this."

"I gave Royce the first bit of discovery today. It was mostly composed of material from the first trial."

"You know you could have held off on that until the thirty-day marker."

"Yeah, but what's the point?"

"The point is strategy. The earlier you give it to him, the more time he has to be ready for it. He's trying to put the squeeze on us by not waiving speedy trial. You should put the squeeze right back on him by not showing our hand until we have to. Thirty days before trial."

"I'll remember that with the next round. But this was pretty basic stuff."

"Was Sarah Gleason on the witness list?"

"Yes, but under the name Sarah Landy—as it was in 'eighty-six. And I gave the office as the address. Clive doesn't know we found her."

"We need to keep it that way until we have to reveal it. I don't want her harassed or feeling threatened."

"What did you tell her about coming down for the trial?"

"I told her she would probably be needed for two days in trial. Plus the travel."

"And that's not going to be a problem?"

"Well...she runs her own business and has been at it only a couple years. She has one big, ongoing project but otherwise said that things are slow. My guess is we can get her down when we need her."

"Are you still in Port Townsend?"

"Yes, we just got finished with her about an hour ago. We grabbed dinner and checked in at a hotel. It's been a long day."

"And you're coming back tomorrow?"

"We were planning on it. But our flight's not till two. We have to take a ferry—it's a journey just to the airport."

"Okay, call me in the morning before you leave. Just in case I think of something involving the witness."

"Okay."

"Did either of you take notes?"

"No, we thought it might freeze her."

"Did you record it?"

"No, same reason."

"Good. I want to keep as much of this out of discovery as possible. Tell Bosch not to write anything up. We can copy Royce on the six-pack she made the ID off of, but that's it."

"Right. I'll tell Harry."

"When, tonight or tomorrow?"

"What's that supposed to mean?"

"Nothing, never mind. Anything else?"

"Yes."

I braced for it. My petty jealousy had slipped out for one small moment.

"I would like to say good night to my daughter now."

"Oh," I said, relief bursting through my body. "I'll put her on."

I took the phone out to Hayley.

"It's your mother."

PART TWO

—The Labyrinth

Fourteen

Tuesday, February 23, 8:45 P.M.

Each of them worked in silence. Bosch at one end of the dining room table, his daughter at the other. He with the first batch of SIS surveillance logs, she with her homework, her school books and laptop computer spread out in front of her. They were close in proximity but not in much else. The Jessup case had become all-encompassing with Bosch tracing old witnesses and trying to find new ones. He had spent little time with her in recent days. Like her parents, Maddie was good at holding grudges and had not let go of the perceived slight of having been left for a night in the care of an assistant school principal. She was giving Harry the silent treatment and already at fourteen she was an expert at it.

The SIS logs were another frustration to Bosch. Not because of what they contained but because of their delay in reaching him. They had been sent through bureaucratic channels, from the SIS office to the RHD office and then to Bosch's supervisor, where they had sat in an in basket for three days before finally being dropped on Bosch's desk. The result was he had logs from the first three days of the surveillance of Jason Jessup and he was looking at them three to six days after the fact. That process was too slow and Bosch was going to have to do something about it.

The logs were terse accounts of the surveillance subject's movements by date, time and location. Most entries carried only a single line of description. The logs came with an accompanying set of photos as well, but most of the shots were taken at a significant distance so the followers could avoid detection. These were grainy images of Jessup as he moved about the city as a free man.

Bosch read through the reports and quickly surmised that Jessup was already leading separate public and private lives. By day his movements were in concert with the media as he very publicly reacquainted himself with life outside a prison cell. It was about learning to drive again, to choose off a menu, to go for a three-mile run without having to make a turn. But by night a different Jessup emerged. Unaware that he was still being watched by eyes and cameras, he went out cruising alone in his borrowed car. He went to all corners of the city. He went to bars, strip clubs, a prostitute's trick pad.

Of all his activities, one was most curious to Bosch. On his fourth night of freedom, Jessup had driven up to Mulholland Drive, the winding road atop the crest of the Santa Monica Mountains, which cut the city in half. Day or night, Mulholland offered some of the best views of the city. It was no surprise that Jessup would go up there. There were overlooks that offered north and south views of the shimmering lights of the city. They could be invigorating and even majestic. Bosch had gone to these spots himself in the past.

But Jessup didn't go to any of the overlooks. He pulled his car off the road near the entrance to Franklin Canyon Park. He got out and then entered the closed park, sneaking around a gate.

This caused a surveillance issue for the SIS team because the park was empty and the watchers were at risk of being seen if they got too close. The report here was briefer than most entries in the log:

02/20/10—01:12. Subject entered Franklin
Canyon Park. Observed at picnic table

```
area, northeast corner, blind man
trailhead.

02/20/10—02:34. Subject leaves park,
proceeds west on Mulholland to 405
freeway and then south.
```

After that, Jessup returned to the apartment where he was living in Venice and stayed in for the rest of the night.

There was a printout of an infrared photograph taken of Jessup in the park. It showed him sitting at a picnic table in the dark. Just sitting there.

Bosch put the photo print down on the table and looked at his daughter. She was left-handed like he was. It looked like she was writing out a math problem on a work sheet.

"What?"

She had her mother's radar.

"Uh, are you online there?"

"Yes, what do you need?"

"Can you pull up a map of Franklin Canyon Park? It's off of Mulholland Drive."

"Let me finish this."

He waited patiently for her to complete her computations on a mathematical problem he knew would be light-years beyond his understanding. For the past four months he had lived in fear that his daughter would ask him for help with her homework. She had passed by his skills and knowledge long ago. He was useless in this area and had tried to concentrate on mentoring her in other areas, observation and self-protection chief among them.

"Okay."

She put her pencil down and pulled her computer front and center. Bosch checked his watch. It was almost nine.

"Here."

Maddie slid the computer down the table, turning the screen toward him.

The park was larger than Bosch had thought, running south of Mulholland and west of Coldwater Canyon Boulevard. A key in the corner of the map said it was 605 acres. Bosch hadn't realized that there was such a large public reserve in this prime section of the Hollywood Hills. He noticed that the map had several of the hiking trails and picnic areas marked. The picnic area in the northeast section was off of Blinderman Trail. He assumed it had been misspelled in the SIS log as "blind man trailhead."

"What is it?"

Harry looked at his daughter. It was her first attempt at conversation in two days. He decided not to miss it.

"Well, we've been watching this guy. The Special Investigations Section. They're the department's surveillance experts and they're watching this guy who just got out of prison. He killed a little girl a long time ago. And for some reason he went to this park and just sat there at a picnic table."

"So? Isn't that what people do at parks?"

"Well, this was in the middle of the night. The park was closed and he snuck in...and then he sort of just sat there."

"Did he grow up near the park? Maybe he's checking out the places where he grew up."

"I don't think so. We have him growing up out in Riverside County. He used to come to L.A. to surf but I haven't found any connection to Mulholland."

Bosch studied the map once more and noticed there was an upper and lower entrance to the park. Jessup had gone in through the upper entrance. This would have been out of his way unless that picnic area and Blinderman Trail were specific destinations for him.

He slid the computer back to his daughter. And checked his watch again.

"Are you almost done your work?"

"*Finished,* Dad. Are you almost finished? Or you could say 'done *with.*'"

"Sorry. Are you almost finished?"

"I have one more math problem."

"Good. I have to make a quick call."

Lieutenant Wright's cell number was on the surveillance log. Bosch expected him to be home and annoyed with the intrusion but decided to make the call anyway. He got up and walked into the living room so he would not disturb Maddie on her last problem. He punched the number into his cell.

"Wright, SIS."

"Lieutenant, it's Harry Bosch."

"What's up, Bosch?"

He didn't sound annoyed.

"Sorry to intrude on you at home. I just wanted—"

"I'm not at home, Bosch. I'm with your guy."

Bosch was surprised.

"Is something wrong?"

"No, the night shift is just more interesting."

"Where is he right now?"

"We're with him at a bar on Venice Beach called the Townhouse. You know it?"

"I've been there. Is he alone?"

"Yes and no. He came alone but he got recognized. He can't buy a drink in there and probably has his pick of the skanks. Like I said, more interesting at night. Are you calling to check up on us?"

"Not really. I just have a couple of things I need to ask. I'm looking at the logs and the first thing is, how can I get them sooner? I'm looking at stuff from three days ago or longer. The other thing is Franklin Canyon Park. What can you tell me about his stop there?"

"Which one?"

"He's been there twice?"

"Actually, three times. He's gone there the last two nights after the first stop four days ago."

This information was very intriguing to Bosch, mostly because he had no idea what it meant.

"What did he do the last two times?"

Maddie got up from the dining room table and came into the living room. She sat on the couch and listened to Bosch's side of the conversation.

"The same thing he did the first night," Wright said. "He sneaks in there and goes to the same picnic area. He just sits there, like he's waiting for something."

"For what?"

"You tell me, Bosch."

"I wish I could. Did he go at the same time each night?"

"Give or take a half hour or so."

"Does he go in through the Mulholland entrance each time?"

"That's right. He sneaks in and picks up the same trail that takes him to the picnic area."

"I wonder why he doesn't go in the other entrance. It would be easier for him to get to."

"Maybe he likes driving on Mulholland and seeing the lights."

That was a good point and Bosch needed to consider it.

"Lieutenant, can you have your people call me the next time he goes there? I don't care what time it is."

"I can have them call you but you're not going to be able to get in there and get close. It's too risky. We don't want to expose the surveillance."

"I understand, but have them call me. I just want to know. Now, what about these logs? Is there a way for me to get them a little quicker?"

"You can come by SIS and pick one up every morning if you want. As you probably noticed, the logs run six P.M. to six P.M. Each daily log is posted by seven the following morning."

"Okay, LT, I'll do that. Thanks for the info."

"Have a good one."

Bosch closed the phone, wondering about Jessup in Franklin Canyon and what he was doing on his visits there.

"What did he say?" Maddie asked.

Bosch hesitated, wondering for the hundredth time whether he should be telling her as much as he did about his cases.

"He said my guy's gone back to that park the last two nights. Each time, he just sits there and waits."

"For what?"

"Nobody knows."

"Maybe he just wants to be somewhere where he's completely by himself and away from everybody."

"Maybe."

But Bosch doubted it. He believed there was a plan to almost everything Jessup did. Bosch just had to figure out what it was.

"I'm finished with my homework," Maddie said. "You want to watch *Lost?*"

They had been slowly going through the DVDs of the television show, catching up on five years' worth of episodes. The show was about several people who survived a plane crash on an uncharted island in the South Pacific. Bosch had trouble keeping track of things from show to show but watched because his daughter had been completely taken in by the story.

He had no time to watch television right now.

"Okay, one episode," he said. "Then you have to go to bed and I have to get back to work."

She smiled. This made her happy and for the moment Bosch's grammatical and parental transgressions seemed forgotten.

"Set it up," Bosch said. "And be prepared to remind me what's happening."

Five hours later, Bosch was on a jet that was shaking with wild turbulence. His daughter was sitting across the aisle from him rather than in the open seat next to him. They reached across the aisle to each other to hold hands but the bouncing of the plane kept knocking them apart. He couldn't grab her hand.

Just as he turned in his seat to see the tail section break off and fall away, he was awakened by a buzzing sound. He reached to the bed table and grabbed his phone. He struggled to find his voice as he answered.

"This is Bosch."

"This is Shipley, SIS. I was told to call."

"Jessup's at the park?"

"He's in a park, yeah, but tonight it's a different one."

"Where?"

"Fryman Canyon off Mulholland."

Bosch knew Fryman Canyon. It was about ten minutes away from Franklin Canyon.

"What's he doing?"

"He's just sort of walking on one of the trails. Just like at the other park. He walks the trail and then he sits down. He doesn't do anything after that. He just sits for a while and then leaves."

"Okay."

Bosch looked at the glowing numbers on the clock. It was two o'clock exactly.

"Are you coming out?" Shipley asked.

Bosch thought about his daughter asleep in her bedroom. He knew he could leave and be back before she woke up.

"Uh...no, I have my daughter here and I can't leave her."

"Suit yourself."

"When does your shift end?"

"About seven."

"Can you call me then?"

"If you want."

"I'd like you to call me every morning when you are getting off. To tell me where he's been."

"Uh…all right, I guess. Can I ask you something? This guy killed a girl, right?"

"That's right."

"And you're sure about that? I mean, no doubt, right?"

Bosch thought about the interview with Sarah Gleason.

"I have no doubt."

"Okay, well, that's good to know."

Bosch understood what he was saying. He was looking for assurance. If circumstances dictated the use of deadly force against Jessup, it was good to know who and what they would be shooting at. Nothing else needed to be said about it.

"Thanks, Shipley," Bosch said. "I'll talk to you later."

Bosch disconnected and put his head back on the pillow. He remembered the dream about the plane. About reaching out to his daughter but being unable to grab her hand.

Fifteen

J udge Diane Breitman welcomed us into her chambers and offered
a pot of coffee and a plate of shortbread cookies, an unusual move
for a criminal courts judge. In attendance were myself and my second
chair, Maggie McPherson, and Clive Royce, who was without his second but not without his temerity. He asked the judge if he could have
hot tea instead.

"Well, this is nice," the judge said once we were all seated in front
of her desk, cups and saucers in hand. "I have not had the opportunity
to see any of you practice in my courtroom. So I thought it would be
good for us to start out a bit informally in chambers. We can always
step out into the courtroom to go on the record if necessary."

She smiled and none of the rest of us responded.

"Let me start by saying that I have a deep respect for the decorum
of the courtroom," Breitman continued. "And I insist that the lawyers
who practice before me do as well. I am expecting this trial to be a
spirited contest of the evidence and facts of the case. But I won't stand
for any acting out or crossing of the lines of courtesy and jurisprudence. I hope that is clearly understood."

"Yes, Your Honor," Maggie responded while Royce and I nodded.

"Good, now let's talk about media coverage. The media is going to be hovering over this case like the helicopters that followed O.J. down the freeway. That is clearly a given. I have requests here from three local network affiliates, a documentary filmmaker and *Dateline NBC*. They all want to film the trial in its entirety. While I see no problem with that, as long as proper protections of the jury are put in place, my concern is in the extracurricular activity that is bound to occur outside the courtroom. Do any of you have any thoughts in this regard?"

I waited a beat and when no one spoke up, I did.

"Judge, I think because of the nature of this case — a retrial of a case twenty-four years old — there has already been too much media attention and we're going to have a difficult time seating twelve people and two alternates who aren't aware of the case through the filter of the media. I mean, we've had the accused surfing on the front page of the *Times* and sitting courtside at the Lakers. How are we going to get an impartial jury out of this? The media, with no lack of help from Mr. Royce, is presenting this guy as this poor, persecuted innocent man and they don't have the slightest idea what the evidence is against him."

"Your Honor, I object," Royce said.

"You can't object," I said. "This isn't a court hearing."

"You *used* to be a defense attorney, Mick. Whatever happened to innocent until proven guilty?"

"He already has been."

"In a trial the top court in this state termed a travesty. Is that what you want to stand on?"

"Listen, Clive, I'm an attorney and *innocent until proven guilty* is a measure you apply in court, not on *Larry King Live*."

"We haven't been on *Larry King Live* — yet."

"See what I mean, Judge? He wants to —"

"Gentlemen, please!" Breitman said.

She waited a moment until she was certain our debate had subsided.

"This is a classic situation where we need to balance the public's right to know with safeguards that will provide us an untainted jury, an unimpeded trial and a just result."

"But, Your Honor," Royce said quickly, "we can't forbid the media to examine this case. Freedom of the press is the cornerstone of American democracy. And, further, I draw your attention to the very ruling that granted this retrial. The court found serious deficiencies in the evidence and castigated the District Attorney's Office for the corrupt manner in which it has prosecuted my client. Now you are going to prohibit the media from looking at this?"

"Oh, please," Maggie said dismissively. "We're not talking about prohibiting the media from looking at anything, and your lofty defense of the freedom of the press aside, that's not what this is about. You are clearly trying to influence voir dire with your pretrial manipulation of the media."

"That is absolutely untrue!" Royce howled. "I have responded to media requests, yes. But I am not trying to influence anything. Your Honor, this is an—"

There was a sharp crack from the judge's desk. She had grabbed a gavel from a decorative pen set and brought it down hard on the wood surface.

"Let's cool down here," Breitman said. "And let's hold off on the personal attacks. As I indicated before, there has to be a happy medium. I am not inclined to muzzle the press, but I will issue a gag order against the lawyers in my court if I believe they are not acting in a manner that is responsible to the case at hand. I am going to start off by leaving each of you to determine what is reasonable and responsible interaction with the media. But I will warn you now that the consequences for a transgression in this area will be swift and possibly detrimental to one's cause. No warnings. You cross the line and that's it."

She paused and waited for a comeback. No one said anything. She placed the gavel back in its special holder next to the gold pen. Her voice returned to its friendly tone.

"Good," she said. "I think that's understood, then."

She said she wanted to move on to other matters germane to the trial and her first stop was the trial date. She wanted to know if both sides would be ready to proceed to trial as scheduled, less than six weeks away. Royce said once again that his client would not waive the speedy trial statute.

"The defense will be ready to go on April fifth, provided that the prosecution doesn't continue to play games with discovery."

I shook my head. I couldn't win with this guy. I had gone out of my way to get the discovery pipeline going, but he had decided to take a shot at making me look like a cheater in front of the judge.

"Games?" I said. "Judge, I've already turned over to Mr. Royce an initial discovery file. But as you know, it's a two-way street and the prosecution has received nothing in return from him."

"He turned over the discovery file from the first trial, Judge Breit-man, complete with a nineteen eighty-six witness list. It completely subverts the spirit and the rules of discovery."

Breitman looked at me and I could see that Royce had success-fully scored a hit.

"Is this true, Mr. Haller?" she asked.

"Hardly, Your Honor, the witness list was both subtracted from and added to. Additionally, I turned over —"

"One name," Royce interjected. "He added one name and it was his own investigator. Big deal, like I didn't know his investigator might be a witness."

"Well, that's the only new name I have at the moment."

Maggie jumped into the fray with both feet.

"Your Honor, the prosecution is duty-bound to turn over all dis-covery materials thirty days prior to trial. By my count we are still forty days out. Mr. Royce is complaining about a good-faith effort on the part of the prosecution to provide him with discovery material before it even has to. It seems that no good deed goes unpunished with Mr. Royce."

The judge held up her hand to stop commentary while she looked at the calendar hanging on the wall to the left of her desk.

"I think Ms. McPherson makes a good point," she said. "Your complaint is premature, Mr. Royce. All discovery materials are due to both sides by this Friday, March fifth. If you have a problem then, we will take this up again."

"Yes, Your Honor," Royce said meekly.

I wanted to reach over, raise Maggie's hand in the air and shake it in victory but I didn't think that would be appropriate. Still, it felt good to win at least one point against Royce.

After discussion of a few more routine pretrial issues, the meeting ended and we walked out through the judge's courtroom. I stopped there to talk small talk with the judge's clerk. I didn't really know her that well but I didn't want to walk out of the courtroom with Royce. I was afraid I might lose my temper, which would be exactly what he'd want.

After he went through the double doors at the back of the courtroom I cut off the conversation and headed out with Maggie at my side.

"You kicked his ass, Maggie McFierce," I said to her. "Verbally."

"Doesn't matter unless we kick it at trial."

"Don't worry, we will. I want you to take over discovery fulfillment. Go ahead and do what you prosecutors do. Haystack everything. Give him so much material he'll never see what and who's important."

She smiled as she turned and used her back to push through the door.

"Now you're getting it."

"I hope so."

"What about Sarah? He's got to figure we found her and if he's smart he won't wait for discovery. He probably has his own guy looking. She can be found. Harry proved that."

"There's not a whole lot we can do about it. Speaking of Harry, where is he this morning?"

"He called me and said he had some things to check out. He'll be around later. You didn't really answer my question about Sarah. What should —?"

"Tell her that she might have another visitor, somebody working for the defense, but that she doesn't have to talk to anybody unless she wants to."

We headed out into the hallway and then went left toward the elevator bank.

"If she doesn't talk to them, Royce will complain to the judge. She's the key witness, Mickey."

"So? The judge won't be able to make her talk if she doesn't want to talk. Meantime, Royce loses prep time. He wants to play games like he did with the judge in there, then we'll play games, too. In fact, how about this? We put every convict Jessup ever shared a prison cell with on the witness list. That should keep his investigators out of the way for a while."

A broad smile broke across Maggie's face.

"You really *are* getting it, aren't you?"

We squeezed onto the crowded elevator. Maggie and I were close enough to kiss. I looked down into her eyes as I spoke.

"That's because I don't want to lose."

Sixteen

Wednesday, February 24, 8:45 A.M.

After school drop-off Bosch turned his car around and headed back up Woodrow Wilson, past his house, and to what those in the neighborhood called the upper crossing with Mulholland Drive. Both Mulholland and Woodrow Wilson were long and winding mountain roads. They intersected twice, at the bottom and top of the mountain, thus the local description of upper and lower crossings.

At the top of the mountain Bosch turned right onto Mulholland and followed it until it crossed Laurel Canyon Boulevard. He then pulled off the road to make a call on his cell. He punched in the number Shipley had given him for the SIS dispatch sergeant. His name was Willman and he would know the current status of any SIS surveillance. At any given time, SIS could be working four or five unrelated cases. Each was given a code name in order to keep them in order and so that the real names of suspects did not ever go out over the radio. Bosch knew that the Jessup surveillance had been termed Operation Retro because it involved an old case and a retrial.

"This is Bosch, RHD. I'm lead on the Retro case. I want to get a location on the suspect because I'm about to pull into one of his favorite haunts. I want to make sure I don't run into him."

"Hold one."

Bosch could hear the phone being put down, then a radio conversation in which the duty sergeant asked for Jessup's location. The response was garbled with static by the time it reached Bosch over the phone. He waited for the sergeant's official response.

"Retro is in pocket right now," he promptly reported to Bosch. "They think he's catching Zs."

In pocket meant he was at home.

"Then I'm clear," Bosch said. "Thank you, Sergeant."

"Any time."

Bosch closed the phone and pulled the car back onto Mulholland. A few curves later he reached Fryman Canyon Park and turned in. Bosch had talked to Shipley early that morning as he was passing surveillance off to the day team. He reported that Jessup had once again visited both Franklin and Fryman canyons. Bosch was becoming consumed with curiosity about what Jessup was up to and this was only increased by the report that Jessup had also driven by the house on Windsor where the Landy family had once lived.

Fryman was a rugged, inclined park with steep trails and a flat-surface parking and observation area on top and just off Mulholland. Bosch had been there before on cases and was familiar with its expanse. He pulled to a stop with his car pointing north and the view of the San Fernando Valley spread before him. The air was pretty clear and the vista stretched all the way across the valley to the San Gabriel Mountains. The brutal week of storms that had ended January had cleared the skies out and the smog was only now climbing back into the valley's bowl.

After a few minutes Bosch got out and walked over to the bench where Shipley had told him Jessup had sat for twenty minutes while looking out at the lights below. Bosch sat down and checked his watch. He had an eleven o'clock appointment with a witness. That gave him more than an hour.

Sitting where Jessup had sat brought no vibe or insight into what the suspect was doing on his frequent visits to the mountainside parks. Bosch decided to move on down Mulholland to Franklin Canyon.

But Franklin Canyon Park offered him the same thing, a large natural respite in the midst of a teeming city. Bosch found the picnic area Shipley and the SIS reports had described but once again didn't understand the pull the park had for Jessup. He found the terminus of Blinderman Trail and walked it until his legs started to hurt because of the incline. He turned around and headed back to the parking and picnic area, still puzzled by Jessup's activities.

On his return Bosch passed a large old sycamore that the trail had been routed around. He noticed a buildup of a grayish-white material at the base of the tree between two fingers of exposed roots. He looked closer and realized it was wax. Somebody had burned a candle.

There were signs all over the park warning against smoking or the use of matches, as fire was the park's greatest threat. But somebody had lit a candle at the base of the tree.

Bosch wanted to call Shipley to ask if Jessup could have lit a candle while in the park the night before, but knew it was the wrong move. Shipley had just come off a night of surveillance and was probably in his bed asleep. Harry would wait for the evening to make the call.

He looked around the tree for any other signs that Jessup had possibly been in the area. It looked like an animal had burrowed recently in a few spots under the tree. But otherwise there was no sign of activity.

As he came off the trail and into the clearing where the picnic area was located, Bosch saw a city parks ranger looking into a trash can from which he had removed the top. Harry approached him.

"Officer?"

The man whipped around, still holding the top of the trash can away from his body.

"Yes, sir!"

"Sorry, I didn't mean to sneak up on you. I was...I was walking up on that trail and there's a big tree there—I think a sycamore—

and it looks like somebody burned a candle down at its base. I was wondering—"

"Where?"

"Up on Blinderman Trail."

"Show me."

"Actually, I'm not going to go all the way back up there. I don't have the right shoes. It's the big tree in the middle of the trail. I'm sure you can find it."

"You can't light fires in the park!"

The ranger put the top back on the trash can, banging it loudly to underline his statement.

"I know. That's why I was reporting it. But I wanted to ask you, is there anything special about that tree that would make somebody do that?"

"Every tree is special here. The whole park is special."

"Yes, I get that. Can you just tell—"

"Can I see some ID, please?"

"Excuse me?"

"ID. I want to see some ID. A man in a shirt and tie walking the trails with 'the wrong shoes' is a little bit suspicious to me."

Bosch shook his head and pulled out his badge wallet.

"Yeah, here's my ID."

He opened it and held it out and gave the ranger a few moments to study it. Bosch saw the nameplate on his uniform said Brorein.

"Okay?" Bosch said. "Can we get to my questions now, Officer Brorein?"

"I'm a city ranger, not an officer," Brorein said. "Is this part of an investigation?"

"No, it's part of a situation where you just answer my questions about the tree up on that trail."

Bosch pointed in the direction he had come from.

"You get it now?" he asked.

Brorein shook his head.

"I'm sorry but you're on my turf here and it's my obligation to —"

"No, pal, you're actually on my turf. But thanks for all the help. I'll make a note of it in the report."

Bosch walked away from him and headed back toward the parking clearing. Brorein called after him.

"As far as I know, there's nothing special about that tree. It's just a tree, Detective Borsh."

Bosch waved without looking back. He added poor reading skills to the list of things he didn't like about Brorein.

Seventeen

My successes as a defense attorney invariably came when the prosecution was unprepared for and surprised by my moves. The entire government grinds along on routine. Prosecuting violators of the government's laws is no different. As a newly minted prosecutor I took this to heart and vowed not to succumb to the comfort and dangers of routine. I promised myself that I would be more than ready for clever Clive Royce's moves. I would anticipate them. I would know them before Royce did. And I would be like a sniper in a tree, waiting to skillfully pick them off from a distance, one by one.

This promise brought Maggie McFierce and me together in my new office for frequent strategy sessions. And on this afternoon the discussion was focused on what would be the centerpiece of our opponent's pretrial defense. We knew Royce would be filing a motion to dismiss the case. That was a given. What we were discussing were the grounds on which he would make the motion. I wanted to be ready for each one. It is said that in war the sniper ambushes an enemy patrol by first taking out the commander, the radioman and the medic. If he accomplishes this, the remaining members of the patrol panic and scatter. This was what I hoped to quickly do when Royce filed his motion. I wanted to move swiftly and thoroughly with demoralizing arguments and answers that would put the defendant on strong notice that he was in trouble. If I panicked Jessup, I might not even have to go to trial. I might get a disposition. A plea. And a plea was a conviction. That was as good as a win on this side of the aisle.

"I think one thing he's going to argue is that the charges are no longer valid without a preliminary hearing," Maggie said. "This will give him two bites out of the apple. He'll first ask the judge to dismiss but at the very least to order a new prelim."

"But the verdict of the trial was what was reversed," I said. "It goes back to the trial and we have a new trial. The prelim is not what was challenged."

"Well, that's what we'll argue."

"Good, you get to handle that one. What else?"

"I'm not going to keep throwing out angles if you keep giving them back to me to be prepared for. That's the third one you've given me and by my scorecard you've only taken one."

"Okay, I'll take the next one sight unseen. What do you have?"

Maggie smiled and I realized I had just walked into my own ambush. But before she could pull the trigger, the office door opened and Bosch entered without knocking.

"Saved by the bell," I said. "Harry, what's up?"

"I've got a witness I think you two should hear. I think he's going to be good for us and they didn't use him in the first trial."

"Who?" Maggie asked.

"Bill Clinton," Bosch said.

I didn't recognize the name as belonging to anyone associated with the case. But Maggie, with her command of case detail, brought it together.

"One of the tow truck drivers who worked with Jessup."

Bosch pointed at her.

"Right. He worked with Jessup back then at Aardvark Towing. Now he owns an auto repair shop on LaBrea near Olympic. It's called Presidential Motors."

"Of course it is," I said. "What does he do for us as a witness?"

Bosch pointed toward the door.

"I got him sitting out there with Lorna. Why don't I bring him in and he can tell you himself?"

I looked at Maggie, and seeing no objection, I told Bosch to bring Clinton in. Before stepping out Bosch lowered his voice and reported that he had run Clinton through the crime databases and he had come up clean. He had no criminal record.

"Nothing," Bosch said. "Not even an unpaid parking ticket."

"Good," Maggie said. "Now let's see what he has to say."

Bosch went out to the reception room and came back with a short man in his midfifties who was wearing blue work pants and a shirt with an oval patch above the breast pocket. It said Bill. His hair was neatly combed and he didn't wear glasses. I saw grease under his fingernails but figured that could be remedied before he ever appeared in front of a jury.

Bosch pulled a chair away from the wall and placed it in the middle of the room and facing my desk.

"Why don't you sit down here, Mr. Clinton, and we'll ask you some questions," he said.

Bosch then nodded to me, passing the lead.

"First of all, Mr. Clinton, thank you for agreeing to come in and talk to us today."

Clinton nodded.

"That's okay. Things are kind of slow at the shop right now."

"What kind of work do you do at the shop? Is there a specialty?"

"Yeah, we do restoration. Mostly British cars. Triumphs, MGs, Jags, collectibles like that."

"I see. What's a Triumph TR Two-Fifty go for these days?"

Clinton looked up at me, surprised by my apparent knowledge of one of the cars he specialized in.

"Depends on the shape. I sold a beauty last year for twenty-five. I put almost twelve into the restoration. That and a lot of man-hours."

I nodded.

"I had one in high school. Wish I'd never sold it."

"They only made them for one year. 'Sixty-eight. Makes it one of the most collectible."

I nodded. We had just covered everything I knew about the car. I just liked it because of its wooden dashboard and the drop top. I used to cruise up to Malibu in it on weekends, hang out on the surf beaches even though I didn't know how to surf.

"Well, let's jump from 'sixty-eight to 'eighty-six, okay?"

Clinton shrugged.

"Fine by me."

"If you don't mind, Ms. McPherson is going to take notes."

Clinton shrugged again.

"So then, let's start. How well do you remember the day that Melissa Landy was murdered?"

Clinton spread his hands.

"Well, see, I remember it real well because of what happened. That little girl getting killed and it turning out I was working with the guy who did it."

"Must've been pretty traumatic."

"Yeah, it was for a while there."

"And then you put it out of your mind?"

"No, not exactly...but I stopped thinking about it all the time. I started my business and everything."

I nodded. Clinton seemed genuine enough and honest. It was a start. I looked at Bosch. I knew he had pulled some nugget from Clinton that he believed was gold. I wanted him to take over.

"Bill," Bosch said. "Tell them a little about what was going on with Aardvark at the time. About how business was bad."

Clinton nodded.

"Yeah, well, back then we weren't doing so hot. What happened was they passed a law that nobody could park on the side streets off of Wilshire without a resident sticker, you know? Anybody else, we got to tow. So we would go in the neighborhoods on a Sunday morning and hook up cars right and left on account of the church services. In the beginning. Mr. Korish was the owner and we were getting so many cars that he hired another driver and even started paying us for our overtime. It was fun because there were a couple other companies with the same contract, so we were all competing for tows. It was like keeping score and we were a team."

Clinton looked at Bosch to see if he was telling the right story. Harry nodded and told him to keep going.

"So then it all kind of went bad. The people started getting wise and they stopped parking over there. Somebody said the church was even making announcements: 'Don't park north of Wilshire.' So we went from having too much to do to not enough. So Mr. Korish said he had to cut back on costs and one of us was going to have to go, and maybe even two of us. He said he was going to watch our performance levels and make his decision based on that."

"When did he tell you this in relation to the day of the murder?" Bosch asked.

"It was right before. Because all three of us were still there. See, he didn't fire anybody yet."

Taking over the questioning, I asked him what the new edict did to the competition among tow truck drivers.

"Well, it made it rough, you know. We were all friends and then all of a sudden we didn't like each other because we wanted to keep our jobs."

"How was Jason Jessup to work with then?"

"Well, Jason was real cutthroat."

"The pressure got to him?"

"Yeah, because he was in last place. Mr. Korish put up a tote board to keep track of the tows and he was last place."

"And he wasn't happy about it?"

"No, not happy. He became a real prick to work with, excuse my French."

"Do you remember how he acted on the day of the murder?"

"A little bit. Like I told Detective Bosch, he started claiming streets. Like saying Windsor was all his. And Las Palmas and Lucerne. Like that. And me and Derek — he was the other driver — we told him there were no rules like that. And he said, 'Fine, try hooking a car on one of those streets and see what happens.'"

"He threatened you."

"Yeah, you could say that. Definitely."

"Do you remember specifically that Windsor was one of the streets he claimed was his?"

"Yes, I do. He claimed Windsor."

This was all good information. It would go to the state of mind of the defendant. It would be a challenge getting it on the record if there wasn't additional corroboration from Wilbern or Korish, if either was still alive and available.

"Did he ever act on that threat in any way?" Maggie asked.

"No," Clinton said. "But that was the same day as the girl. So he got arrested and that was that. I can't say I was too upset about seeing him go. Turned out Mr. Korish then laid off Derek 'cause he lied about not having a record. I was the last man standing. I worked there another four years — till I saved up the money to start my place."

A regular American success story. I waited to see if Maggie had a follow but she didn't. I did.

"Mr. Clinton, did you ever talk about any of this with the police or prosecutors twenty-four years ago?"

Clinton shook his head.

"Not really. I mean I spoke to the detective who was in charge back then. He asked me questions. But I wasn't ever brought to court or anything like that."

Because they didn't need you back then, I thought. But I'm going to need you now.

"What makes you so sure that this threat from Jessup occurred on the day of the murder?"

"I just know it was that day. I remember that day because it's not every day that a guy you're working with gets arrested for murder."

He nodded as if to underscore the point.

I looked at Bosch to see if we had missed anything. Bosch took the cue and took back the lead.

"Bill, tell them what you told me about being in the police car with Jessup. On the way to Windsor."

Clinton nodded. He could be led easily and I took that as another good sign.

"Well, what happened was they really thought that Derek was the guy. The police did. He had a criminal record and lied about it and they found out. So that made him suspect numero uno. So they put Derek in the back of one patrol car and then me and Jason in another."

"Did they say where they were taking you?"

"They said they had additional questions, so we thought we were going to the police station. There were two officers in the car with us and we heard them talking about all of us being in a lineup. Jason asked them about it and they said it was no big thing, they just wanted guys in overalls because they wanted to see if a witness could pick out Derek."

Clinton stopped there and looked expectantly from Bosch to me and then to Maggie.

"So what happened?" I asked.

"Well, first Jason told the two cops that they couldn't just take us and put us in a lineup like that. They just said that they were following orders. So we go over to Windsor and pull up in front of a house. The cops got out and went and talked to the lead detective, who was standing there with some other detectives. Jason and I were watching out the windows but didn't see any witness or anything. Then the detective in charge goes inside the house and doesn't come back out. We don't know what's going on, and then Jason says to me he wants to borrow my hat."

"Your hat?" Maggie asked.

"Yeah, my Dodgers hat. I was wearing it like I always did and Jason said he needed to borrow it because he recognizes one of the other cops that was already standing there at the house when we pulled up. He said that he got in a fight with the guy over a tow and if he sees him there's going to be trouble. He goes on like that and says, let me have your hat."

"What did you do?" I asked.

"Well, I didn't think it was a big deal on account of I didn't know what I knew later, you know what I mean? So I gave him my hat and he put it on. Then when the cops came back to get us out of the car, they didn't seem to notice that the hat was switched. They made us get out of the car and we had to go over and stand next to Derek. We were standing there and then one of the cops gets a call on the radio — I remember that — and he turns and tells Jason to take off the hat. He did and then a few minutes later they're all of a sudden surrounding Jason and putting the cuffs on him, and it wasn't Derek, it was him."

I looked from Clinton to Bosch and then to Maggie. I could see in her expression that the hat story was significant.

"You know the funny thing?" Clinton asked.

"No, what?" I said.

"I never got that hat back."

He smiled and I smiled back.

"Well, we'll have to get you a new hat when this is all said and done. Now let me ask you the key question. What you have told us here, are you willing to testify to all of it at Jason Jessup's trial?"

Clinton seemed to think about it for a few seconds before nodding.

"Yeah, I could do that," he said.

I stood up and came around the desk, extending my hand.

"Then it looks like we've got ourselves a witness. Many thanks to you, Mr. Clinton."

We shook hands and then I gestured to Bosch.

"Harry, I should have asked you, did we cover everything?"

Bosch stood up as well.

"I think so. For now. I'll take Mr. Clinton back to his shop."

"Excellent. Thank you again, Mr. Clinton."

Clinton stood up.

"Please call me Bill."

"We will, I promise. We'll call you Bill and we'll call you as a witness."

Everybody laughed in that phony way and then Bosch shepherded Clinton out of the office. I went back to my desk and sat down.

"So tell me about the hat," I said to Maggie.

"It's a good connection," she said. "When we interviewed Sarah she remembered that Kloster radioed from the bedroom down to the street and had them make Jessup take off his hat. That was when she made the ID. Harry then looked through the case file and found a property list from Jessup's arrest. The Dodgers hat was on there. We're still trying to track his property — hard to do after twenty-four years. But it might have gone up to San Quentin. Either way, if we don't have the hat, we have the list."

I nodded. This was good on a number of levels. It showed witnesses independently corroborating each other, put a crack in any sort of defense contention that memories cannot be trusted after so many years and, last but not least, showed state of mind of the defendant. Jessup knew he was somehow in danger of being identified. Someone had seen him abduct the girl.

"All right, good," I said. "What do you think about the initial stuff, about how there was competition between them and somebody was going to get laid off? Maybe two of them."

"Again, it's good state-of-mind material. Jessup was under pressure and he acted out. Maybe this whole thing was about that. Maybe we should put a shrink on the witness list."

I nodded.

"Did you tell Bosch to find and interview Clinton?"

She shook her head.

"He did it on his own. He's good at this."

"I know. I just wish he'd tell me a little more about what he's up to."

Eighteen

Thursday, February 25, 11 A.M.

Rachel Walling wanted to meet at an office in one of the glass towers in downtown. Bosch went to the address and took the elevator up to the thirty-fourth floor. The door to the offices of Franco, Becerra & Itzuris, attorneys-at-law, was locked and he had to knock. Rachel answered promptly and invited him into a luxurious suite of offices that was empty of lawyers, clerks and anybody else. She led him to the firm's boardroom, where he saw the box and files he had given her the week before on a large oval table. They entered and he walked over to the floor-to-ceiling windows that looked out over downtown.

Bosch couldn't remember being up so high in downtown. He could see all the way to Dodger Stadium and beyond. He checked out the civic center and saw the glass-sided PAB sitting next to the *Los Angeles Times* building. His eyes then scanned toward Echo Park and he remembered a day there with Rachel Walling. They had been a team then, in more ways than one. But now that seemed so long ago.

"What is this place?" he said, still staring out and with his back to her. "Where is everybody?"

"There isn't anybody. We just used this in a money-laundering sting. So it's been empty. Half of this building is empty. The economy.

This was a real law office but it went out of business. So we just sort of borrowed it. The management was happy for the government subsidy."

"They were washing money from drugs? Guns?"

"You know I can't say, Harry. I am sure you'll read about it in a few months. You'll put it together then."

Bosch nodded as he remembered the firm's name on the door. Franco, Becerra & Itzuris: FBI. Clever.

"I wonder if management will tell the next tenants that this place was used by the bureau to take down some bad people. Friends of those bad people could come looking."

She didn't respond to that. She just invited him to sit down at the table. He did, taking a good look at her as she sat across from him. Her hair was down, which was unusual. He had seen her that way before but not while she was on duty. The dark ringlets framed her face and helped direct attention to her dark eyes.

"The firm's refrigerator is empty or I'd offer you something to drink."

"I'm fine."

She opened the box and started taking out the files he had given her.

"Rachel, I really appreciate this," Bosch said. "I hope it didn't disrupt your life too much."

"The work, no. I enjoyed it. But you, Harry, you coming back into my life was a disruption."

Bosch wasn't expecting that.

"What do you mean?"

"I'm in a relationship and I'd told him about you. About the single-bullet theory, all of that. So he wasn't happy that I've been spending my nights off working this up for you."

Bosch wasn't sure about how to respond. Rachel Walling always hid deeper messages in the things she said. He wasn't sure if there was more to be considered than what she had just said out loud.

"I'm sorry," he finally said. "Did you tell him it was only work, that I just wanted your professional opinion? That I went to you because I can trust you and you're the best at this?"

"He knows I'm the best at it, but it doesn't matter. Let's just do this."

She opened a file.

"My ex-wife is dead," he said. "She was killed last year in Hong Kong."

He wasn't sure why he'd blurted it out like that. She looked up at him sharply and he knew she hadn't known.

"Oh my God, I'm so sorry."

Bosch just nodded, deciding not to tell her the details.

"What about your daughter?"

"She lives with me now. She's doing okay but it's been pretty tough on her. It's only been four months."

She nodded and then seemed to lose her grounding as she took in what had just been said.

"What about you? I assume it's been rough for you, too."

He nodded but couldn't think of the right words. He had his daughter fully in his life now, but at a terrible cost. He realized that he had brought the subject up but couldn't talk about it.

"Look," he said, "that was weird. I don't know why I just laid that on you. You mentioned the single bullet and I remember I told you about her. We can talk about it some other time. I mean, if you want. Let's just get to the case now. Is that okay?"

"Yes, sure. I was just thinking about your daughter. To lose her mother and then have to move so far from the place she knows. I mean, I know living with you will be fine, but it's...quite an adjustment."

"Yeah, but they say kids are resilient because they actually are. She's got a lot of friends already and is doing well in school. It's been a major adjustment for both of us but I think she'll come out okay."

"And how will you come out?"

Bosch held her eyes for a moment before answering.

"I've already come out ahead. I have my daughter with me and she's the best thing in my life."

"That's good, Harry."

"It is."

She broke eye contact and finished removing the files and photos from the box. Bosch could see the transformation. She was now all business, an FBI profiler ready to report her findings. He reached into his pocket and pulled out his notebook. It was in a folding leather case with a detective shield embossed on the cover. He opened it and got ready to write.

"I want to start with the photos," she said.

"Fine."

She spread out four photos of Melissa Landy's body in the Dumpster, turning them to face him. She then added two photos from the autopsy in a row above these. Photos of a dead child were never easy to look at for Bosch. But these were particularly difficult. He stared for a long moment before coming to the realization that the clutch in his gut was due to the setting of the body in a Dumpster. For the girl to be disposed of like that seemed almost like a statement about the victim and an added insult to those who loved her.

"The Dumpster," he said. "You think that was chosen as a statement?"

Walling paused as if considering it for the first time.

"I'm actually going at it from a different standpoint. I think that it was an almost spontaneous choice. That it wasn't part of a plan. He needed a place to dump the body where he wouldn't be seen and it wouldn't be immediately found. He knew about that Dumpster behind that theater and he used it. It was a convenience, not a statement."

Bosch nodded. He leaned forward and wrote a note on his pad to remind himself to go back to Clinton and ask about the Dumpster. The El Rey was in the Wilshire corridor the Aardvark drivers worked. It might have been familiar to them.

"Sorry, I didn't mean to start things off in the wrong direction," he said as he wrote.

"That's okay. The reason I wanted to start with the photos of the girl is that I believe that this crime may have been misunderstood from the very beginning."

"Misunderstood?"

"Well, it appears that the original investigators took the crime scene at face value and looked at it as the result of the suspect's kill plan. In other words, Jessup grabbed this girl, and his plan was to strangle her and leave her in the Dumpster. This is evidenced by the profile that was drawn up of the crime and submitted to the FBI and the California Department of Justice for comparison to other crimes on record."

She opened a file and pulled out the lengthy profile and submission forms prepared by Detective Kloster twenty-four years earlier.

"Detective Kloster was looking for similar crimes that he might be able to attach Jessup to. He got zero hits and that was the end of that."

Bosch had spent several days studying the original case file and knew everything that Walling was telling him. But he let her run with it without interruption because he had a feeling she would take him somewhere new. That was her beauty and art. It didn't matter that the FBI didn't recognize it and use her to the best of her abilities. He always would.

"I think what happened was that this case had a faulty profile from the beginning. Add to that the fact that back then the data banks were obviously not as sophisticated or as inclusive as they are now. This whole angle was misdirected and wrong and so no wonder they hit a dead end with it."

Bosch nodded and wrote a quick note.

"You tried to rebuild the profile?" he asked.

"As much as I could. And the starting point is right here. The photos. Take a look at her injuries."

Bosch leaned across the table and over the first row of photographs. He actually didn't see injuries to the girl. She had been dropped haphazardly into the almost full trash bin. There must have been stage building or a renovation project going on inside the theater, because the bin contained mostly construction refuse. Sawdust, paint buckets, small pieces of cut and broken wood. There were small cuts of wallboard and torn plastic sheeting. Melissa Landy was faceup near one of the corners of the Dumpster. Bosch didn't see a drop of blood on her or her dress.

"What injuries are we talking about?" he asked.

Walling stood up in order to lean over. She used the point of a pen to outline the places she wanted Bosch to look on each of the photos. She circled discolorations on the victim's neck.

"Her neck injuries," she said. "If you look you see the oval-shaped bruising on the right side of the neck, and on the other side you have a larger corresponding bruise. This evidence makes it clear that she was choked to death with one hand."

She used the pen to illustrate what she was saying.

"The thumb here on her right side and the four fingers on the left. One-handed. Now, why one-handed?"

She sat back down and Bosch leaned back away from the photos himself. The idea that Melissa had been strangled with one hand was not new to Bosch. It was in Kloster's original profile of the murder.

"Twenty-four years ago, it was suggested that Jessup strangled the girl with his right hand while he masturbated with his left. This theory was built on one thing — the semen collected from the victim's dress. It was deposited by someone with the same blood type as Jessup and so it was assumed to have come from him. You follow all of this?"

"I'm with you."

"Okay, so the problem is, we now know that the semen didn't come from Jessup and so the basic profile or theory of the crime in nineteen eighty-six is wrong. It is further demonstrated as being wrong because Jessup is right-handed according to a sample of his writing in the files, and studies have shown that with right-handers masturbation is almost always carried out by the dominant hand."

"They've done studies on that?"

"You'd be surprised. I sure was when I went online to look for this."

"I knew there was something wrong with the Internet."

She smiled but was not a bit embarrassed by the subject matter of their discussion. It was all in a day's work.

"They've done studies on everything, including which hand people use to wipe their butts. I actually found it to be fascinating reading. But the point here is that they had this wrong from the beginning. This murder did not occur during a sex act. Now let me show you a few other photos."

She reached across the table and slid all of the photos together in one stack and then put them to the side. She then spread out photos taken of the inside of the tow truck Jessup was driving on the day of the murder. The truck actually had a name, which was stenciled on the dashboard.

"Okay, so on the day in question, Jessup was driving Matilda," Walling said.

Bosch studied the three photos she had spread out. The cab of the tow truck was in neat order. Thomas Brothers maps — no GPS back then — were neatly stacked on top of the dashboard and a small stuffed animal that Bosch presumed was an aardvark hung from the rearview mirror. A cup holder on the center console held a Big Gulp from 7-Eleven and a sticker on the glove compartment door read *Grass or Ass — Nobody Rides for Free.*

With her trusty pen, Walling circled a spot on one of the photos. It was a police scanner mounted under the dashboard.

"Did anybody consider what this means?"

Bosch shrugged.

"Back then, I don't know. What's it mean now?"

"Okay, Jessup worked for Aardvark, which was a towing company licensed by the city. However, it wasn't the only one. There was competition among tow companies. The drivers listened to scanners, picking up police calls about accidents and parking infractions. It gave them the jump on the competition, right? Except that every tow truck had a scanner and everybody was listening and trying to get the jump on everyone else."

"Right. So what's it mean?"

"Well, let's look at the abduction first. It is pretty clear from the witness testimony and everything else that this was not a crime of great planning and patience. This was an impulse crime. That much they've had right from the beginning. We can talk about the motivating factors at length in a little while, but suffice it to say, something caused Jessup to act out in an almost uncontrollable way."

"I think I might have motivating factors covered," Bosch said.

"Good, I'm eager to hear about it. But for now, we will assume that some sort of internal pressure led Jessup to act on an undeniable impulse and he grabbed the girl. He took her back to the truck and took off. He obviously didn't know about the sister hiding in the bushes and that she would sound the alarm. So he completes the abduction and drives away, but within minutes he hears the report about the abduction on the police scanner he has in the truck. That brings home to him the reality of what he's done and what his predicament is. He never imagined things would move so fast. He more or less comes to his senses. He realizes he must abandon his plan now and move into preservation mode. He needs to kill the girl to eliminate her as a witness and then hide her body in order to prevent his arrest."

Bosch nodded as he understood her theory.

"So what you're saying is, the crime that occurred was not the crime that he intended."

"Correct. He abandoned the true plan."

"So when Kloster went to the bureau looking for similars, he was looking for the wrong thing."

"Right again."

"But could there actually have been a plan? You just said yourself that it was a crime of compulsion. He saw an opportunity and within a few seconds acted on it. What plan could there have been?"

"Actually, it is more than likely that he had a complex and complete plan. Killers like these have a paraphilia — a set construct of the perfect psychosexual experience. They fantasize about it in great detail. And as you can expect, it often involves torture and murder. The paraphilia is part of their daily fantasy life and it builds to the point where the desire becomes the urge which eventually becomes a compulsion to act out. When they do cross that line and act out, the abduction of the victim may be completely unplanned and improvisational, but the killing sequence is not. The victim is unfortunately dropped into a set construct that has played over and over in the killer's mind."

Bosch looked at his notebook and realized he had stopped taking notes.

"Okay, but you're saying that didn't happen here," he said. "He abandoned the plan. He heard the abduction report on the scanner, and that took him from fantasy to reality. He realized that they could be closing in on him. He killed her and dumped her, hoping to avoid detection."

"Exactly. And therefore, as you just noted, when investigators attempted to compare elements of this murder to others', they were comparing apples and oranges. They found nothing that matched and believed that this was a onetime crime of opportunity and compulsion. I don't think it was."

Bosch looked up from the photos to Rachel's eyes.

"You think he did this before."

"I think the idea that he had acted out before in this way is compelling. It would not surprise me if you were to find that he was involved in other abductions."

"You're talking about more than twenty-four years ago."

"I know. And since there was no linking of Jessup to known unsolved murders, we are probably talking about missing children and runaways. Cases where there was never a crime scene established. The girls were never found."

Bosch thought of Jessup's middle-of-the-night visits to the parks along Mulholland Drive. He thought he might now know why Jessup would light a candle at the base of a tree.

Then a more stunning and scary thought pushed through.

"Do you think a guy like this would use those crimes from so long ago to feed his fantasy now?"

"Of course he would. He's been in prison, what other choice did he have?"

Bosch felt an urgency take hold inside. An urgency that came with the growing certainty that they weren't dealing with an isolated instance of murder. If Walling's theory was correct, and he had no reason to doubt it, Jessup was a repeater. And though he had been on ice for twenty-four years, he was now roaming the city freely. It would not be long now before he became vulnerable to the pressures and urges that had driven him to deadly action before.

Bosch came to a fast resolve. The next time Jessup was seized by the pressures of his life and overcome by the compulsion to kill, Bosch was going to be there to destroy him.

His eyes refocused and he realized Rachel was looking at him oddly.

"Thank you for all of this, Rachel," he said. "I think I need to go."

Nineteen

It was only a hearing on pretrial motions but the courtroom was packed. Lots of courthouse gadflies and media, and a fair number of trial lawyers were sitting in as well. I sat at the prosecution table with Maggie and we were going over our arguments once again. All issues before Judge Breitman had already been argued and submitted on paper. This would be when the judge could ask further questions and then announce her rulings. I had a growing sense of anxiety. The motions submitted by Clive Royce were all pretty routine and Maggie and I had submitted solid responses. We were also ready with oral arguments to back them, but a hearing like this was also a time for the unexpected. On more than one occasion I had sandbagged the prosecution in a pretrial hearing. And sometimes the case is won or lost before the trial begins with a ruling in one of these hearings.

I leaned back and looked behind us and then took a quick glance around the courtroom. I gave a phony smile and nod to a lawyer I saw in the spectator section, then turned back to Maggie.

"Where's Bosch?" I asked.

"I don't think he's going to be here."

"Why not? He's completely disappeared in the last week."

"He's been working on something. He called yesterday and asked if he had to be here for this and I said he didn't."

"He'd better be working on something related to Jessup."

"He tells me it is and that he's going to bring it to us soon."

"That's nice of him. The trial starts in four weeks."

I wondered why Bosch had chosen to call her instead of me, the lead prosecutor. I realized that this made me upset with Maggie as well as Bosch.

"Listen, I don't know what happened between you two on your little trip to Port Townsend, but he should be calling me."

Maggie shook her head as if dealing with a petulant child.

"Look, you don't have to worry. He knows you're the lead prosecutor. He probably figures you are too busy for the day-to-day updates on what he's doing. And I'm going to forget what you said about Port Townsend. This one time. You make another insinuation like that and you and I are going to have a real problem."

"Okay, I'm sorry. It's just that—"

My attention was drawn across the aisle to Jessup, who was sitting at the defense table with Royce. He was staring at me with a smirk on his face and I realized he had been watching Maggie and me, maybe even listening.

"Excuse me a second," I said.

I got up and walked over to the defense table. I leaned over him.

"Can I help you with something, Jessup?"

Before Jessup could say a word his lawyer cut in.

"Don't talk to my client, Mick," Royce said. "If you want to ask him something, then you ask me."

Now Jessup smiled again, emboldened by his attorney's defensive move.

"Just go sit down," Jessup said. "I got nothing to say to you."

Royce held his hand up to quiet him.

"I'll handle this. You be quiet."

"He threatened me. You should complain to the judge."

"I said be quiet and that I would handle this."

Jessup folded his arms and leaned back in his chair.

"Mick, is there a problem here?" Royce asked.

"No, no problem. I just don't like him staring at me."

I walked back to the prosecution table, annoyed with myself for losing my calm. I sat down and looked at the pool camera set up in the jury box. Judge Breitman had approved the filming of the trial and the various hearings leading up to it, but only through the use of a pool camera, which would provide a universal feed that all channels and networks could use.

A few minutes later the judge took the bench and called the hearing to order. One by one we went through the defense motions, and the rulings mostly fell our way without much further argument. The most important one was the routine motion to dismiss for lack of evidence, which the judge rejected with little comment. When Royce asked to be heard, she said that it wasn't necessary to discuss the issue further. It was a solid rebuke and I loved it even though outwardly I acted as though it were routine and boring.

The only ruling the judge wanted to discuss in detail was the oddball request by Royce to allow his client to use makeup during trial to cover the tattoos on his neck and fingers. Royce had argued in his motion that the tattoos were all prison tattoos applied while he was falsely incarcerated for twenty-four years. He said the tattoos could be prejudicial when noticed by jurors. His client intended to cover these with skin-tone makeup and he wanted to bar the prosecution from addressing it in front of the jury.

"I have to admit I have not had a motion like this come before me," the judge said. "I'm inclined to allow it and hold the prosecution from drawing attention to it but I see the prosecution has objected to the motion, saying that it contains insufficient information about the content and history of these tattoos. Can you shed some light on the subject, Mr. Royce?"

Royce stood and addressed the court from his place at the defense table. I looked over and my eyes were drawn to Jessup's hands. I knew the tattoos across his knuckles were Royce's chief concern. The neck markings could largely be covered with a collared shirt, which he would wear with a suit at trial. But the hands were difficult to hide. Across the four digits of each hand he had inked the sentiment FUCK THIS and Royce knew that I would make sure it was seen by jurors. That sentiment was probably the chief impediment to having Jessup testify in his defense, because Royce knew I would find a way either casually or specifically to make sure the jury got his message.

"Your Honor, it is the defense's position that these tattoos were administered to Mr. Jessup's body while he was falsely imprisoned and are a product of that harrowing experience. Prison is a dangerous place, Judge, and inmates take measures to protect themselves. Sometimes it is through tattooing that is designed to be intimidating or to show an association the prisoner might not actually have or believe in. It would certainly be prejudicial for the jury to see, and therefore we ask for relief. This, I might add, is merely a tactic by the prosecution to delay the trial, and the defense firmly stands by its decision to not delay justice in this case."

Maggie stood up quickly. She had handled this motion on paper and therefore it was hers to handle in court.

"Your Honor, may I be heard on the defense's accusation?"

"One moment, Ms. McPherson, I want to be heard myself. Mr. Royce, can you explain your last statement?"

Royce bowed politely.

"Yes, of course, Judge Breitman. The defendant has begun to go through a tattoo removal process. But this takes time and will not be completed by trial. By objecting to our simple request to use makeup, the prosecution is trying to push the trial back until this removal process is completed. It's an effort to subvert the speedy trial statute which since day one the defense, to the prosecution's consternation, has refused to waive."

The judge turned her gaze to Maggie McFierce. It was her turn.

"Your Honor, this is simply a defense fabrication. The state has not once asked for a delay or opposed the defense's request for a speedy trial. In fact, the prosecution is ready for trial. So this statement is outlandish and objectionable. The true objection on the part of the prosecution to this motion is to the idea of the defendant being allowed to disguise himself. A trial is a search for truth, and allowing him to use makeup to cover up who he really is would be an affront to the search for truth. Thank you, Your Honor."

"Judge, may I respond?" Royce, still standing, said immediately.

Breitman paused for a moment while she wrote a few notes from Maggie's brief.

"That won't be necessary, Mr. Royce," she finally said. "I'm going to make a ruling on this and I will allow Mr. Jessup to cover his tattoos. If he chooses to testify on his behalf, the prosecution will not address this issue with him in front of the jury."

"Thank you, Your Honor," Maggie said.

She sat down without showing any outward sign of disappointment. It was just one ruling among many others and most had gone the prosecution's way. This loss was minor at worst.

"Okay," the judge said. "I think we have covered everything. Anything else from counsel at this time?"

"Yes, Your Honor," Royce said as he stood again. "Defense has a new motion we would like to submit."

He stepped away from the defense table and brought copies of the new motion first to the judge and then to us, giving Maggie and me individual copies of a one-page motion. Maggie was a fast reader, a skill she had genetically passed on to our daughter, who was reading two books a week on top of her homework.

"This is bullshit," she whispered before I had even finished reading the title of the document.

But I caught up quickly. Royce was adding a new lawyer to the defense team and the motion was to disqualify Maggie from the prosecution because of a conflict of interest. The new lawyer's name was David Bell.

Maggie quickly turned around to scan the spectator seats. My eyes followed and there was David Bell, sitting at the end of the second row. I knew him on sight because I had seen him with Maggie in the months after our marriage had ended. One time I had come to her apartment to pick up my daughter and Bell had opened the door.

Maggie turned back and started to stand to address the court but I put my hand on her shoulder and held her in place.

"I'm taking this," I said.

"No, wait," she whispered urgently. "Ask for a ten-minute recess. We need to talk about this."

"Exactly what I was going to do."

I stood and addressed the judge.

"Your Honor, like you, we just got this. We can take it with us and submit but we would rather argue it right now. If the court could indulge us with a brief recess, I think we would be ready to respond."

"Fifteen minutes, Mr. Haller? I have another matter holding. I could handle it and come back to you."

"Thank you, Your Honor."

This meant we had to leave the table while another prosecutor handled his business before the judge. We pushed our files and Maggie's laptop to the back of the table to make room, then got up and walked toward the back door of the courtroom. As we passed Bell he raised a hand to get Maggie's attention but she ignored him and walked by.

"You want to go upstairs?" Maggie asked as we came through the double doors. She was suggesting that we go up to the DA's office.

"There isn't time to wait for an elevator."

"We could take the stairs. It's only three flights."

We walked through the door into the building's enclosed stairwell but then I grabbed her arm.

"This is good enough right here," I said. "Tell me what we do about Bell."

"That piece of shit. He's never defended a criminal case, let alone a murder, in his life."

"Yeah, you wouldn't have made the same mistake twice."

She looked pointedly at me.

"What's that supposed to mean?"

"Never mind, bad joke. Let's just stay on point."

She had her arms folded tightly against her chest.

"This is the most underhanded thing I've ever seen. Royce wants me off the case so he goes to Bell. And Bell . . . I can't believe he would do something like this to me."

"Yeah, well, he's probably in it for a dip into the pot of gold at the end of the rainbow. We probably should have seen something like this coming."

It was a defense tactic I had used myself before, but not with such obviousness. If you didn't like the judge or the prosecutor, one way of getting them off the case was to bring someone onto your team who has a conflict of interest with them. Since the defendant is constitutionally guaranteed the defense counsel of his choice, it is usually the judge or prosecutor who must be disqualified from the trial. It was a shrewd move by Royce.

"You see what he's doing, right?" Maggie said. "He is trying to isolate you. He knows I'm the one person you would trust as second chair and he's trying to take that away from you. He knows that without me you are going to lose."

"Thanks for your confidence in me."

"You know what I mean. You've never prosecuted a case. I'm there to help you through it. If he gets me kicked off the table, then who are you going to have? Who would you trust?"

I nodded. She was right.

"Okay, give me the facts. How long were you with Bell?"

"With him? I wasn't. We went out briefly seven years ago. No more than two months and if he says differently he's a liar."

"Is the conflict that you had the relationship or is there something else, something you did or said, something he has knowledge of that creates the conflict?"

"There's nothing. We went out and it just didn't take."

"Who dropped who?"

She paused and looked down at the floor.

"He did."

I nodded.

"Then there's the conflict. He can claim you carry a grudge."

"A woman scorned, is that it? This is such bullshit. You men are—"

"Hold on, Maggie. Hold on. I'm saying that is their argument. I am not agreeing. In fact, I want—"

The door to the stairwell opened and the prosecutor who took our places when we had gotten up for the recess entered and started up the steps. I checked my watch. Only eight minutes had gone by.

"She went back into chambers," he said as he passed. "You guys are fine."

"Thanks."

I waited until I heard his steps on the next landing before continuing in a quiet tone with Maggie.

"Okay, how do I fight this?"

"You tell the judge that this is an obvious attempt to sabotage the prosecution. They've hired an attorney for the sole reason that he had a relationship with me, not because of any skill he brings to the table."

I nodded.

"Okay. What else?"

"I don't know. I can't think...it was remote in time, no strong emotional attachment, no effect on professional judgment or conduct."

"Yeah, yeah, yeah...and what about Bell? Does he have something or know something I have to watch out for?"

She looked at me like I was some sort of traitor.

"Maggie, I need to know so there's no surprise on top of the surprise, okay?"

"Fine, there's nothing. He must really be hard up if he's taking a fee just to knock me off the case."

"Don't worry, two can play this game. Let's go."

We went back into the courtroom and as we went through the gate I nodded to the clerk so she could call the judge back from chambers. Instead of going to the prosecution table, I diverted to the defense side where Royce was sitting next to his client. David Bell was now seated at the table on the other side of Jessup. I leaned over Royce's shoulder and whispered just loud enough that his client would hear.

"Clive, when the judge comes out, I'll give you the chance to withdraw this motion. If you don't, number one, I'm going to embarrass you in front of the camera and it will be digitally preserved forever. And number two, the release-and-remuneration offer I made to your client last week is withdrawn. Permanently."

I watched Jessup's eyebrows rise a few centimeters. He hadn't heard anything about an offer involving money and freedom. This was because I hadn't made one. But now it would be up to Royce to convince his client that he had not withheld anything from him. Good luck with that.

Royce smiled like he was pleased with my comeback. He leaned back casually and tossed his pen on his legal pad. It was a Montblanc with gold trim and that was no way to treat it.

"This is really going to get good, yes, Mick?" he said. "Well, I'll tell you. I'm not withdrawing the motion and I think if you had made me an offer involving release and remuneration I would've remembered it."

So he had called my bluff. He'd still have to convince his client. I saw the judge step out from the door of her chambers and start up the three steps to the bench. I took one more whispered shot at Royce.

"Whatever you paid Bell you wasted."

I stepped over to the prosecution table and remained standing. The judge brought the courtroom to order.

"Okay, back on the record in *California versus Jessup*. Mr. Haller, do you want to respond to the defendant's latest motion or take it on submission."

"Your Honor, the prosecution wishes to respond right now to... this motion."

"Go right ahead, then."

I tried to build a good tone of outrage into my voice.

"Judge, I am as cynical as the next guy but I have to say I am surprised by the defense's tactics here with this motion. In fact, this isn't a motion. This is very plainly an attempt to subvert the trial system by denying the People of Cal—"

"Your Honor," Royce interjected, jumping to his feet, "I strenuously object to the character assassination Mr. Haller is putting on the record and before the media. This is nothing more than grand—"

"Mr. Royce, you will have an opportunity to respond *after* Mr. Haller responds to your motion. Please be seated."

"Yes, Your Honor."

Royce sat down and I tried to remember where I was.

"Go ahead, Mr. Haller."

"Yes, Your Honor, as you know, the prosecution turned over all discovery materials to the defense on Tuesday. What you have before you now is a very disingenuous motion spawned by Mr. Royce's realization of what he will be up against at trial. He thought the state was going to roll over on this case. He now knows that it is not going to do so."

"But what does this have to do with the motion at hand, Mr. Haller?" the judge asked impatiently.

"Everything," I said. "You've heard of judge shopping? Well, Mr. Royce is prosecutor shopping. He knows through his examination of discovery materials that Margaret McPherson is perhaps the most important part of the prosecution team. Rather than take on the evidence at trial, he is attempting to undercut the prosecution by splintering the team that has assembled that evidence. Here we are, just four weeks before trial and he makes a move against my second chair. He has hired an attorney with little to no experience in criminal defense, not to mention defending a murder case. Why would he do that, Judge, other than for the purpose of concocting this supposed conflict of interest?"

"Your Honor?"

Royce was on his feet again.

"Mr. Royce," the judge said, "I told you, you will have your chance."

The warning was very clear in her voice.

"But, Your Honor, I can't —"

"Sit down."

Royce sat down and the judge put her attention back on me.

"Judge, this is a cynical move made by a desperate defense. I would hope that you would not allow him to subvert the intentions of the Constitution."

Like two men on a seesaw, I went down and Royce immediately popped up.

"One moment, Mr. Royce," the judge said, holding up her hand and signaling him back down to his seat. "I want to talk to Mr. Bell."

Now it was Bell's turn to stand up. He was a well-dressed man with sandy hair and a ruddy complexion, but I could see the apprehension in his eyes. Whether he had come to Royce or Royce had come to him, it was clear that he had not anticipated having to stand in front of a judge and explain himself.

"Mr. Bell, I have not had the pleasure of seeing you practice in my courtroom. Do you handle criminal defense, sir?"

"Uh, no, ma'am, not ordinarily. I am a trial attorney and I have been lead counsel in more than thirty trials. I do know my way around a courtroom, Your Honor."

"Well, good for you. How many of those trials were murder trials?"

I felt total exhilaration as I watched what I had set in motion take on its own momentum. Royce looked mortified as he watched his plan shatter like an expensive vase.

"None of them were murder trials per se. But several were wrongful death cases."

"Not the same thing. How many criminal trials do you have under your belt, Mr. Bell?"

"Again, Judge, none were criminal cases."

"What do you bring to the defense of Mr. Jessup?"

"Your Honor, I bring a wealth of trial experience but I don't think that my résumé is on point here. Mr. Jessup is entitled to counsel of his choice and—"

"What exactly is the conflict you have with Ms. McPherson?"

Bell looked perplexed.

"Did you understand the question?" the judge asked.

"Yes, Your Honor, the conflict is that we had an intimate relationship and now we would be opposing each other at trial."

"Were you married?"

"No, Your Honor."

"When was this intimate relationship and how long did it last?"

"It was seven years ago and it lasted about three months."

"Have you had contact with her since then?"

Bell raised his eyes to the ceiling as if looking for an answer. Maggie leaned over and whispered in my ear.

"No, Your Honor," Bell said.

I stood up.

"Your Honor, in the interest of full disclosure, Mr. Bell has sent Ms. McPherson a Christmas card for the past seven years. She has not responded likewise."

There was a murmur of laughter in the courtroom. The judge ignored it and looked down at something in front of her. She looked like she had heard enough.

"Where is the conflict you are worried about, Mr. Bell?"

"Uh, Judge, this is a bit difficult to speak of in open court but I was the one who ended the relationship with Ms. McPherson and my concern is that there could be some lingering animosity there. And that's the conflict."

The judge wasn't buying this and everyone in the courtroom knew it. It was becoming uncomfortable even to watch.

"Ms. McPherson," the judge said.

Maggie pushed back her chair and stood.

"Do you hold any lingering animosity toward Mr. Bell?"

"No, Your Honor, at least not before today. I moved on to better things."

I could hear another low rumble from the seats behind me as Maggie's spear struck home.

"Thank you, Ms. McPherson," the judge said. "You can sit. And so can you, Mr. Bell."

Bell thankfully dropped into his chair. The judge leaned forward and spoke matter-of-factly into the bench's microphone.

"The motion is denied."

Royce stood up immediately.

"Your Honor, I was not heard before the ruling."

"It was your motion, Mr. Royce."

"But I would like to respond to some of the things Mr. Haller said about—"

"Mr. Royce, I've made my ruling on it. I don't see the need for further discussion. Do you?"

Royce realized his defeat could get even worse. He cut his losses.

"Thank you, Your Honor."

He sat down. The judge then ended the hearing and we packed up and headed toward the rear doors. But not as quickly as Royce. He and his client and supposed co-counsel split the courtroom like men who had to catch the last train on a Friday night. And this time Royce didn't bother stopping outside the courtroom to chat with the media.

"Thanks for sticking up for me," Maggie said when we got to the elevators.

I shrugged.

"You stuck up for yourself. Did you really mean that, what you said about moving on from Bell to better things?"

"From him, yes. Definitely."

I looked at her but couldn't read her beyond the spoken line. The elevator doors opened, and there was Harry Bosch waiting to step off.

Twenty

Bosch stepped off the elevator and almost walked right into Haller and McPherson.

"Is it over?" he asked.

"You missed it," Haller said.

Bosch quickly turned and hit one of the bumpers on the elevator doors before it could close.

"Are you going down?"

"That's the plan," Haller said in a tone that didn't hide his annoyance with Bosch. "I thought you weren't coming to the hearing."

"I wasn't. I was coming to get you two."

They rode the elevator down and Bosch convinced them to walk with him a block over to the Police Administration Building. He signed them in as visitors and they went up to the fifth floor, where Robbery-Homicide Division was located.

"This is the first time I've been here," McPherson said. "It's as quiet as an insurance office."

"Yeah, I guess we lost a lot of the charm when we moved," Bosch replied.

The PAB had been in operation for only six months. It had a quiet and sterile quality about it. Most of the building's denizens, including

Bosch, missed the old headquarters, Parker Center, even though it was beyond decrepit.

"I've got a private room over here," he said, pointing to a door on the far side of the squad room.

He used a key to unlock the door and they walked into a large space with a boardroom-style table at center. One wall was glass that looked out on the squad room but Bosch had lowered and closed the blinds for privacy. On the opposite wall was a large whiteboard with a row of photos across the top margin and numerous notes written beneath each shot. The photos were of young girls.

"I've been working on this nonstop for a week," Bosch said. "You probably have been wondering where I disappeared to so I figured it was time to show you what I've got."

McPherson stopped just a few steps inside the door and stared, squinting her eyes and revealing to Bosch her vanity. She needed glasses but he'd never seen her wearing them.

Haller stepped over to the table, where there were several archival case boxes gathered. He slowly pulled out a chair to sit down.

"Maggie," Bosch prompted. "Why don't you sit down?"

McPherson finally broke from her stare and took the chair at the end of the table.

"Is this what I think it is?" she asked. "They all look like Melissa Landy."

"Well," Bosch said. "Let me just go over it and you'll draw your own conclusions."

Bosch stayed on his feet. He moved around the table to the whiteboard. With his back to the board he started to tell the story.

"Okay, I have a friend. She's a former profiler. I've never —"

"For whom?" Haller asked.

"The FBI, but does it matter? What I'm saying is that I've never known anybody who was better at it. So, shortly after I came into this I asked her informally to take a look at the case files and she did. Her conclusions were that back in 'eighty-six this case was read all wrong.

And where the original investigators saw a crime of impulse and opportunity, she saw something different. To keep it short, she saw indications that the person who killed Melissa Landy may have killed before."

"Here we go," Haller said.

"Look, man, I don't know why you're giving me the attitude," Bosch said. "You pulled me in as investigator on this thing and I'm investigating. Why don't you just let me tell you what I know? Then you can do with it whatever you want. You think it's legit, then run with it. You don't, then shitcan it. I will have done my job by bringing it to you."

"I'm not giving you any attitude, Harry. I'm just thinking out loud. Thinking about all the things that can complicate a trial. Complicate discovery. You realize that everything you are telling us has to be turned over to Royce now?"

"Only if you intend to use it."

"What?"

"I thought you'd know the rules of discovery better than me."

"I know the rules. Why did you bring us here for this dog and pony show if you don't think we should use it?"

"Why don't you just let him tell the story," McPherson said. "And then maybe we'll understand."

"Then, go ahead," Haller said. "Anyway, all I said was 'Here we go,' which I think is a pretty common phrase indicating surprise and change of direction. That's all. Continue, Harry. Please."

Bosch glanced back at the board for a moment and then turned back to his audience of two and continued.

"So my friend the profiler thinks Jason Jessup killed before he killed Melissa Landy, and most likely was successful in hiding his involvement in these previous crimes."

"So you went looking," McPherson said.

"I did. Now, remember our original investigator, Kloster, was no slouch. He went looking, too. Only problem was he was using the wrong profile. They had semen on the dress, strangulation and a body dump in an accessible location. That was the profile, so that is what he went looking for and he found no similars, or at least no cases that connected. End of story, end of search. They believed Jessup acted out this one time, was exceedingly disorganized and sloppy, and got caught."

Harry turned and gestured to the row of photographs on the whiteboard behind him.

"So I went a different way. I went looking for girls who were reported missing and never showed up again. Girls reported as runaways as well as possible abductions. Jessup is from Riverside County so I expanded the search to include Riverside and L.A. counties. Since Jessup was twenty-four when he was arrested I went back to when he was eighteen, putting the search limits from nineteen eighty to 'eighty-six. As far as victim profile, I went Caucasian aged twelve to eighteen."

"Why did you go as old as eighteen?" McPherson asked. "Our victim was twelve."

"Rachel said—I mean, the profiler said that sometimes starting out, these people pick from their own peer group. They learn how to kill and then they start to define their targets according to their paraphilias. A paraphilia is—"

"I know what it is," McPherson said. "You did all of this work yourself? Or did this Rachel help you?"

"No, she just worked up the profile. I had some help from my partner pulling all of this together. But it was tough because not all the records are complete, especially on cases that never got above runaway status, and a lot was cleared out. Most of the runaway files from back then are gone."

"They didn't digitize?" McPherson asked.

Bosch shook his head.

"Not in L.A. County. They prioritized when they switched over to computerized records and went back and captured records for major crimes. No runaway cases unless there was the possibility of abduction involved. Riverside County was different. Fewer cases out there so they archived everything digitally. Anyway, for that time period in these two counties, we came up with twenty-nine cases over the six-year period we're looking at. Again, these were unresolved cases. In each the girl disappeared and never came home. We pulled what records we could find and most didn't fit because of witness statements or other issues. But I couldn't rule out these eight."

Bosch turned to the board and looked at the photos of eight smiling girls. All of them long gone over time.

"I'm not saying that Jessup had anything to do with any of these girls dropping off the face of the earth, but he could have. As Maggie already noticed, they all have a resemblance to one another and to Melissa Landy. And by the way, the resemblance extends to body type as well. They're all within ten pounds and two inches of one another and our victim."

Bosch turned back to his audience and saw McPherson and Haller transfixed by the photographs.

"Beneath each photo I've put the particulars," he said. "Physical descriptors, date and location of disappearance, the basic stuff."

"Did Jessup know any of them?" Haller asked. "Is he connected in any way to any of them?"

That was the bottom line, Bosch knew.

"Nothing really solid—I mean, not that I've found so far," he said. "The best connection that we have is this girl."

He turned and pointed to the first photo on the left.

"The first girl. Valerie Schlicter. She disappeared in nineteen eighty-one from the same neighborhood in Riverside that Jessup grew up in. He would've been nineteen and she was seventeen. They both went to Riverside High but because he dropped out early, it doesn't look like they were there at the same time. Anyway, she was counted as a runaway because there were problems in her home. It was a single-parent home. She lived with her mother and a brother and then one day about a month after graduating from high school, she split.

The investigation never rose above a missing persons case, largely because of her age. She turned eighteen a month after she disappeared. In fact, I wouldn't even call it an investigation. They more or less waited to see if she'd come home. She didn't."

"Nothing else?"

Bosch turned back and looked at Haller.

"So far that's it."

"Then discovery is not an issue. There's nothing here. There's no connection between Jessup and any of these girls. The closest one you have is this Riverside girl and she was five years older than Melissa Landy. This whole thing seems like a stretch."

Bosch thought he detected a note of relief in Haller's voice.

"Well," he said, "there's still another part to all of this."

He stepped over to the case boxes at the end of the table and picked up a file. He walked it down and put it in front of McPherson.

"As you know, we've had Jessup under surveillance since he was released."

McPherson opened the file and saw the stack of 8 × 10 surveillance shots of Jessup.

"With Jessup they've learned that there is no routine schedule, so they stick with him twenty-four/seven. And what they're documenting is that he has two remarkably different lives. The public one, which is carried in the media as his so-called journey to freedom. Everything from smiling for the cameras and eating hamburgers to surfing Venice Beach to the talk-show circuit."

"Yes, we're well aware," Haller said. "And most of it orchestrated by his attorney."

"And then there's the private side," Bosch said. "The bar crawls, the late-night cruising and the middle-of-the-night visits."

"Visits where?" McPherson asked.

Bosch went to his last visual aid, a map of the Santa Monica Mountains. He unfolded it on the table in front of them.

"Nine different times since his release Jessup has left the apartment where he stays in Venice and in the middle of the night driven up to Mulholland on top of the mountains. From there he has visited one or two of the canyon parks up there per night. Franklin Canyon is his favorite. He's been there six times. But he also has hit Stone Canyon, Runyon Canyon and the overlook at Fryman Canyon a few times each."

"What's he doing at these places?" McPherson asked.

"Well, first of all, these are public parks that are closed at dusk," Bosch replied. "So he's sneaking in. We're talking two, three o'clock in the morning. He goes in and he just sort of sits. He communes. He lit candles a couple times. Always the same spots in each of the parks. Usually on a trail or by a tree. We don't have photos because it's too dark and we can't risk getting in close. I've gone out with the SIS a couple times this week and watched. It looks like he just sort of meditates."

Bosch circled the four parks on the map. Each was off Mulholland and close to the others.

"Have you talked to your profiler about all this?" Haller asked.

"Yeah, I did, and she was thinking what I was thinking. That he's visiting graves. Communing with the dead . . . his victims."

"Oh, man . . . ," Haller said.

"Yeah," Bosch said.

There was a long pause as Haller and McPherson considered the implications of Bosch's investigation.

"Harry, has anybody done any digging in any of these spots?" McPherson asked.

"No, not yet. We didn't want to go too crazy with the shovels, because he keeps coming back. He'd know something was up and we don't want that yet."

"Right. What about—"

"Cadaver dogs. Yeah, we brought them out there undercover yesterday. We—"

"How do you make a dog go undercover?" Haller asked.

Bosch started to laugh and it eased some of the tension in the room.

"What I mean is, there were two dogs and they weren't brought out in official vehicles and handled by people in uniforms. We tried to make it look like somebody walking their dog, but even that was a problem because the park doesn't allow dogs on these trails. Anyway, we did the best we could and got in and got out. I checked with SIS to make sure Jessup wasn't anywhere near Mulholland when we went in. He was surfing."

"And?" McPherson asked impatiently.

"These dogs are the type that just lie down on the ground when they pick up the scent of human decay. Supposedly they can pick it up through the ground after even a hundred years. Anyway, at three of the four places Jessup's gone in these parks, the dogs didn't react. But at one spot one of the two dogs did."

Bosch watched McPherson swivel in her seat and look at Haller. He looked back at her and there was some sort of silent communication there.

"It should also be noted that this particular dog has a history of being wrong — that is, giving a false positive — about a third of the time," Bosch said. "The other dog didn't react to the same spot."

"Great," Haller said. "So what does that tell us?"

"Well, that's why I invited you over," Bosch said. "We've reached the point where maybe we should start digging. At least in that one spot. But if we do, we run the risk that Jessup will find out and he'll know we've been following him. And if we dig and we find human remains, do we have enough here to charge Jessup?"

McPherson leaned forward while Haller leaned back, clearly deferring to his second chair.

"Well, I see no legal embargo on digging," she finally said. "It's public property and there is nothing that would stop you legally. No need for a search warrant. But do you want to dig right now based on this one dog with what seems like a high false-positive rate, or do we wait until after the trial?"

"Or maybe even during the trial," Haller said.

"The second question is the more difficult," McPherson said. "For the sake of argument, let's say there are remains buried in one or even all of those spots. Yes, Jessup's activities seem to form an awareness of what is below the earth in the places he visits in the middle of the night. But does that prove he's responsible? Hardly. We could charge him, yes, but he could mount a number of defenses based on what we know right now. You agree, Michael?"

Haller leaned forward and nodded.

"Suppose you dig and you find the remains of one of these girls. Even if you can confirm the ID—and that's going to be a big if—you still don't have any evidence connecting her death to Jessup. All you have is his guilty knowledge of the burial spot. That is very significant but is it enough to go into court with? I don't know. I think I'd rather be defense counsel than prosecutor on that one. I think Maggie's right, there are any number of defenses that he could employ to explain his knowledge of the burial sites. He could invent a straw man—somebody else who did the killings and told him about them or forced him to take part in the burials. Jessup's spent twenty-four years in prison. How many other convicts has he been exposed to? Thousands? Tens of thousands? How many of them were murderers? He could lay this whole thing on one of them, say that he heard in prison about these burial spots and he decided to come and pray for the souls of the victims. He could make up anything."

He shook his head again.

"The bottom line is, there are a lot of ways to go with a defense like this. Without any sort of physical evidence connecting him or a witness, I think you would have a problem."

"Maybe there is physical evidence in the graves that connects him," Bosch offered.

"Maybe, but what if there isn't?" Haller shot right back. "You never know, you could also pull a confession out of Jessup. But I doubt that, too."

McPherson took it from there.

"Michael mentioned the big if, the remains. Can they be IDed? Will we be able to establish how long they were in the ground? Remember, Jessup has an ironclad alibi for the last twenty-four years. If you pull up a set of bones and we can't say for sure that they've been down there since at least 'eighty-six, then Jessup would walk."

Haller got up and went to the whiteboard, grabbing a marker off the ledge. In a clear spot he drew two circles side by side.

"Here's what we've got so far. One is our case and one is this whole new thing you've come up with. They're separate. We have the case with the trial about to go and then we have your new investigation. When they're separate like this we're fine. Your investigation has no bearing on our trial, so we can keep the two circles separate. Understand?"

"Sure," Bosch said.

Haller grabbed the eraser off the ledge and wiped the two circles off the board. He then drew two new circles, but this time they overlapped.

"Now if you go out there and start digging and you find bones? This is what happens. Our two circles become connected. And that's when your thing becomes our thing and we have to reveal this to the defense and the whole wide world."

McPherson nodded in agreement.

"So then, what do we do?" Bosch asked. "Drop it?"

"No, we don't drop it," Haller said. "We just be careful and we keep them separate. You know what is universally held as the best trial strategy? Keep it simple, stupid. So let's not complicate things. Let's keep our circles separate and go to trial and get this guy for killing Melissa Landy. And when we're done that, we go up to Mulholland with shovels."

"Done *with*."

"What?"

"When we're done *with* that."

"Whatever, Professor."

Bosch's eyes moved from Haller's connected circles on the board to the row of faces. All his instincts told him that at least some of those girls did not get any older than they were in the photos. They were in the ground and had been buried there by Jason Jessup. He hated the idea of them spending another day in the dirt but knew that they would have to wait a little longer.

"Okay," he said. "I'll keep working it on the side. For now. But there's also one other thing from the profiler that you should know."

"The other shoe drops," McPherson said. "What?"

Haller had returned to his seat. Bosch pulled out a chair and sat down himself.

"She said a killer like Jessup doesn't reform in prison. The dark matter inside doesn't go away. It stays. It waits. It's like a cancer. And it reacts to outside pressures."

"He'll kill again," McPherson said.

Bosch slowly nodded.

"He can visit the graves of his past victims for only so long before he'll feel the need for...fresh inspiration. And if he feels under pressure, the chances are good he'll move in that direction even sooner."

"Then we'd better be ready," Haller said. "I'm the guy who let him out. If you have any doubts about him being covered, then I want to hear them."

"No doubts," Bosch said. "If Jessup makes a move, we'll be on him."

"When are you planning on going out with the SIS again?" McPherson asked.

"Whenever I can. But I've got my daughter, so it's whenever she's on a sleepover or I can get somebody to come in."

"I want to go once."

"Why?"

"I want to see the real Jessup. Not the one in the papers and on TV."

"Well..."

"What?"

"Well, there are no women on the team and they're constantly moving with this guy. There won't be any bathroom breaks. They piss in bottles."

"Don't worry, Harry, I think I can handle it."

"Then I'll set it up."

Twenty-one

I checked my watch when I heard Maggie say hello to Lorna in the reception room. She entered the office and dropped her case on her desk. It was one of those slim and stylish Italian leather laptop totes that she never would have bought for herself. Too expensive and too red. I wanted to know who gave it to her like I wanted to know a lot of things she would never tell me.

But the origin of her red briefcase was the least of my worries. In thirteen days we would start picking jurors in the Jessup case and Clive Royce had finally landed his best pretrial punch. It was an inch thick and sat in front of me on my desk.

"Where have you been?" I said with a clear note of annoyance in my voice. "I called your cell and got no answer."

She came over to my desk, dragging the extra chair with her.

"More like, where were you?"

I glanced at my calendar blotter and saw nothing in the day's square.

"What are you talking about?"

"My phone was turned off because I was at Hayley's honors assembly. They don't like cell phones ringing when they are calling the kids up to get their pins."

"Ah, shit!"

She had told me and copied me on the e-mail. I printed it out and put it on the refrigerator. But not on my desk blotter or into my phone's calendar. I blew it.

"You should've been there, Haller. You would've been proud."

"I know, I know. I messed up."

"It's all right. You'll get other chances. To mess up or stand up."

That hurt. It would've been better if she had chewed my ass out like she used to. But the passive-aggressive approach always got deeper under the skin. And she probably knew that.

"I'll be at the next one," I said. "That's a promise."

She didn't sarcastically say *Sure, Haller,* or *I've heard that one before.* And somehow that made it worse. Instead, she just got down to business.

"What is that?"

She nodded at the document in front of me.

"This is Clive Royce's last best stand. It's a motion to exclude the testimony of Sarah Ann Gleason."

"And of course he drops it off on a Friday afternoon three weeks before trial."

"More like seventeen days."

"My mistake. What's he say?"

I turned the document around and slid it across the desk to her. It was held together with a large black clip.

"He's been working on this one since the start because he knows the case comes down to her. She's our primary witness and without her none of the other evidence matters. Even the hair in the truck is circumstantial. If he takes out Sarah he takes out our case."

"I get that. But how's he trying to get rid of her?"

She started flipping through the pages.

"It was delivered at nine and is eighty-six pages long so I haven't had the time to completely digest it. But it's a two-pronged effort. He's attacking her original identification from when she was a kid. Says the setup was prejudicial. And he—"

"That was already argued, accepted by the trial court and it held up on appeal. He's wasting the court's time."

"He's got a new angle this time. Remember, Kloster's got Alzheimer's and is no good as a witness. He can't tell us about the investigation and he can't defend himself. So this time out Royce alleges that Kloster told Sarah which man to identify. He pointed Jessup out for her."

"And what is his backup? Supposedly only Sarah and Kloster were in the room."

"I don't know. There's no backup but my guess is he's riffing on the radio call Kloster made telling them to make Jessup take off his hat."

"It doesn't matter. The lineup was put together to see if Sarah could identify Derek Wilbern, the other driver. Any argument that he then told her to put the finger on Jessup is ridiculous. That ID came quite unexpectedly but naturally and convincingly. This is nothing to get worked up about. Even without Kloster we'll tear this one up."

I knew she was right but the first attack wasn't really what I was most worried about.

"That's just his opening salvo," I said. "That's nothing compared with part two. He also seeks to exclude her entire testimony based on unreliable memory. He's got her whole drug history laid out in the motion, seemingly down to every chip of meth she ever smoked. He's got arrest records, jail records, witnesses who detail her consumption of drugs, multiple-partner sex and what they term her belief in out-of-body experiences—I guess she forgot to mention that part up in Port Townsend. And to top it all off, he's got experts on memory loss and false memory creation as a by-product of meth addiction. So in all, you know what he's got? He's got us fucked coming and going."

Maggie didn't respond as she was scanning the summary pages at the end of Royce's motion.

"He's got investigators here and up in San Francisco," I added.

"It's thorough and exhaustive, Mags. And you know what? It doesn't even look like he's gone up to Port Townsend to interview her yet. He says he doesn't have to because it doesn't matter what she says now. It can't be relied upon."

"He'll have his experts and we'll have ours on rebuttal," she said calmly. "We expected this part and I've already been lining ours up. At worst, we can turn this into a wash. You know that."

"The experts are only a small part of it."

"We'll be fine," she insisted. "And look at these witnesses. Her ex-husbands and boyfriends. I see Royce conveniently didn't bother to include their own arrest records here. They're all tweakers themselves. We'll make them look like pimps and pedophiles with grudges against her because she left them in the dust when she got straight. She married the first one when she was eighteen and he was twenty-nine. She told us. I'd love to get him in the chair in front of the judge. I really think you are overreacting to this, Haller. We can argue this. We can make him put some of these so-called witnesses in front of the judge and we can knock every one of them out of the box. You're right about one thing, though. This is Royce's last best stand. It's just not going to be good enough."

I shook my head. She was seeing only what was on paper and what could be blocked or parried with our own swords. Not what was not written.

"Look, this is about Sarah. He knows the judge is not going to want to chop our main witness. He knows we'll get by this. But he's putting the judge on notice that this is what he is going to put Sarah through if she takes the stand. Her whole life, every sordid detail, every pipe and dick she ever smoked, she's going to have to sit up there and take it. Then he'll trot out some PhD who'll put pictures of a melted brain on the screen and say this is what meth does. Do we want that for her? Is she strong enough to take it? Maybe we have to go to Royce, offer a deal for time served and some kind of payout from the city. Something everybody can live with."

Maggie flopped the motion onto the desk.

"Are you kidding me? You're running scared because of this?"

"I'm not running scared. I'm being realistic. I didn't go up to Washington. I have no feel for this woman. I don't know if she can stand up to this or not. Besides, we can always take a second bite of the apple with those cases Bosch has been working."

Maggie leaned back in her chair.

"There's no guarantee that anything will come out of those other cases. We have to put everything we have into this one, Haller. I could go back up there and hold Sarah's hand a little bit. Tell her more about what to expect. Get her ready. She already understood it wasn't going to be pretty."

"To put it mildly."

"I think she's strong enough. I think in some weird way she might need it. You know, get it all out there, expiate her sins. It's about redemption with her, Michael. You know about that."

We held each other's eyes for a long moment.

"Anyway, I think she'll be more than strong and the jury will see it," she said. "She's a survivor and everybody likes a survivor."

I nodded.

"You have a way of convincing people, Mags. It's a gift. We both know you should be lead on this, not me."

"Thank you for saying that."

"All right, go up there and get her prepped for this. Next week, maybe. By then we should have a witness schedule and you can tell her when we'll be bringing her down."

"Okay," she said.

"Meantime, how's your weekend looking? We have to put together an answer to this."

I pointed at the defense motion on the desk.

"Well, Harry finally got me a ride-along with the SIS tomorrow night. He's going, too — I think his daughter has a sleepover. Other than that, I'm around."

"Why are you going to spend all that time watching Jessup? The police have that covered."

"Like I said before, I want to see Jessup out there when he doesn't think anyone is watching. I would suggest that you come, too, but you've got Hayley."

"I wouldn't waste the time. But when you see Bosch, can you give him a copy of this motion? We're going to need him to run down some of these witnesses and statements. Not all of them were in Royce's discovery package."

"Yeah, he played it smart. He keeps them off his witness list until they show up here. If the judge shoots down the motion, saying Gleason's credibility is a jury question, he'll come back with an amended witness list, saying, okay, I need to put these people in front of the jury in regard to credibility."

"And she'll allow it or she'll be contradicting her own ruling. Clever Clive. He knows what he's doing."

"Anyway, I'll get a copy to Harry, but I think he's still chasing those old cases."

"Doesn't matter. The trial is the priority. We need complete backgrounds on these people. You want to deal with him or do you want me to?"

In our divvying up of pretrial duties I had given Maggie the responsibility of prepping for defense witnesses. All except Jessup. If he testified, he was still mine.

"I'll talk to him," she said.

She furrowed her brow. It was a habit I'd seen before.

"What?"

"Nothing. I'm just thinking about how to attack this. I think we throw in a motion *in limine,* seeking to limit Royce on the impeachable stuff. We argue that the events of her life in between are not relevant to credibility if her identification of Jessup now matches her identification back then."

I shook my head.

"I would argue that you're infringing on my client's sixth amendment right to cross-examine his accuser. The judge might limit some of this stuff if it's repetitive, but don't count on her disallowing it."

She pursed her lips as she recognized that I was right.

"It's still worth a try," I said. "Everything is worth a try. In fact, I want to drown Royce in paper. Let's hit him back with a phonebook to wade through."

She looked at me and smiled.

"What?"

"I like it when you get all angry and righteous."

"You haven't seen anything yet."

She looked away before it went a step further.

"Where do you want to set up shop this weekend?" she asked. "Remember, you have Hayley. She's not going to like it if we work the entire weekend."

I had to think about that for a moment. Hayley loved museums. To the point that I was tired of going to the same museums over and over. She also loved movies. I would need to check and see if a new movie was out.

"Bring her to my house in the morning and be prepared to work on our response. We can maybe trade off. I'll take her to a movie or something in the afternoon and then you go on and do your thing with the SIS. We'll make it work."

"Okay, that's a deal."

"Or . . ."

"Or what?"

"You could bring her over tonight and we could have a little dinner celebrating our kid making second honors. And we might even get a little work on this done."

"And I stay over, is that what you mean?"

"Sure, if you want."

"You wish, Haller."

"I do."

"By the way, it was first honors. You better have it right when you see her tonight."

I smiled.

"Tonight? You mean that?"

"I think so."

"Then don't worry. I'll have everything right."

Twenty-two

Saturday, March 20, 8:00 P.M.

Because Bosch had mentioned that a prosecutor wanted to join the SIS surveillance, Lieutenant Wright arranged his schedule to work Saturday night and be the driver of the car the visitors were assigned to. The pickup point was in Venice at a public parking lot six blocks off the beach. Bosch met McPherson there and then he put a radio call in to Wright, saying they were ready and waiting. Fifteen minutes later a white SUV entered the lot and drove up to them. Bosch gave McPherson the front seat and he climbed into the back. He wasn't being chivalrous. The long bench seat would allow him to stretch out during the long night of surveillance.

"Steve Wright," the lieutenant said, offering McPherson his hand.

"Maggie McPherson. Thanks for letting me come along."

"No sweat. We always like it when the District Attorney's Office takes an interest. Let's hope tonight is worth your while."

"Where's Jessup now?"

"When I left he was at the Brig on Abbot Kinney. He likes crowded places, which works in our favor. I have a couple guys inside and a few more on the street. We're kind of used to his rhythm now.

He hits a place, waits to be recognized and for people to start buying him drinks, then he moves on—quickly if he isn't recognized."

"I guess I'm more interested in his late-night travels than his drinking habits."

"It's good that he's out drinking," Bosch said from the backseat. "There's a causal relationship. The nights he takes in alcohol are usually the nights he goes up to Mulholland."

Wright nodded in agreement and headed the SUV out of the lot. He was a perfect surveillance man because he didn't look like a cop. In his late fifties with glasses, a thinning hairline and always two or three pens in his shirt pocket, he looked more like an accountant. But he had been with the SIS for more than two decades and had been in on several of the squad's kills. Every five years or so the *Times* did a story on the SIS, usually analyzing its kill record. In the last exposé Bosch remembered reading, the paper had labeled Wright "SIS's unlikely chief gunslinger." While the reporters and editors behind the story probably viewed that as an editorial putdown, Wright wore it like a badge of honor. He had the sobriquet printed below his name on his business card. In quotes, of course.

Wright drove down Abbot Kinney Boulevard and past the Brig, which was located in a two-story building on the east side of the street. He went two blocks down and made a U-turn. He came back up the street and pulled to the curb in front of a fire hydrant a half block from the bar.

The lighted sign outside the Brig depicted a boxer in a ring, his red gloves up and ready. It was an image that seemed at odds with the name of the bar, but Bosch knew the story behind it. As a much younger man he had lived in the neighborhood. He knew the sign with the boxer was put up by a former owner who had bought out the original owners. The new man was a retired fighter and had decorated the interior with a boxing motif. He also put the sign up out front. There was still a mural on the side of the building that depicted the fighter and his wife, but they were long gone now.

"This is Five," Wright said. "What's our status?"

He was talking to the microphone clipped to the sun visor over his head. Bosch knew there was a foot button on the floor that engaged it. The return speaker was under the dash. The radio setup in the cars allowed the surveillance cops to keep their hands free while driving and, more important, helped them maintain their cover. Talking into a handheld rover was a dead giveaway. The SIS was too good for that.

"Three," a voice said over the radio. "Retro is still in the location along with One and Two."

"Roger that," Wright said.

"Retro?" McPherson said.

"Our name for him," Wright said. "Our freqs are pretty far down the bandwidth and on the FCC registry they're listed as DWP channels, but you never know who might be listening. We don't use the names of people or locations on the air."

"Got it."

It wasn't even nine yet. Bosch wasn't expecting Jessup to leave anytime soon, especially if people were buying him drinks. As they settled in, Wright seemed to like McPherson and liked informing her about procedures and the art of high-level surveillance. She might have been bored with it but she never let on.

"See, once we establish a subject's rhythms and routines we can react much better. Take this place, for example. The Brig is one of three or four places Retro hits sort of regularly. We've assigned different guys to different bars so they can go in while he's in the location and be like regulars. The two guys I've got right now in the Brig are the same two guys that always go in there. And two other guys would go into Townhouse when he's there and two others have James Beach. It goes like that. If Retro notices them he'll think it's because he's seen them in there before and they're regulars in the place. Now if he saw the same guy at two different places, he'd start getting suspicious."

"I understand, Lieutenant. Sounds like the smart way to do it."

"Call me Steve."

"Okay, Steve. Can your people inside communicate?"

"Yes, but they're deaf."

"Deaf?"

"We've all got body mikes. You know, like the Secret Service? But we don't put in the earpieces when we're in play inside a place like a bar. Too obvious. So they call in their positions when possible but they don't hear anything coming back unless they pull the receiver up from under their collar and put it in. Unfortunately, it's not like TV where they just put the bean in their ear and there's no wire."

"I see. And do your men actually drink while in a bar on a surveillance?"

"A guy in a place like that ordering a Coke or a glass of water is going to stand out as suspicious. So they order booze. But then they nurse it. Luckily, Retro likes to go to crowded places. Makes it easier to maintain cover."

While the small talk continued in the front seat, Bosch pulled his phone and started what some would consider a conversation of small talk himself. He texted his daughter. Though he knew there were several sets of eyes on the Brig and even inside on Jessup, he looked up and checked the door of the bar every few seconds.

Howzit going? Having fun?

Madeline was staying overnight at her friend Aurora Smith's house. It was only a few blocks from home but Bosch would not be nearby if she needed him. It was several minutes before she grudgingly answered the text. But they had a deal. She must answer his calls and texts, or her freedom — what she called her leash — would be shortened.

Everything's fine. You don't have to check on me.

Yes I do. I'm your father. Don't stay up too late.

K.

And that was it. A child's shorthand in a shorthand relationship. Bosch knew he needed help. There was so much he didn't know. At times they seemed fine and everything appeared to be perfect. Other times he was sure she was going to sneak out the door and run away. Living with his daughter had resulted in his love for her growing more than he thought was possible. Thoughts of her safety as well as hopes for her happy future invaded his mind at all times. His longing to make her life better and take her far past her own history had at times become a physical ache in his chest. Still, he couldn't seem to reach across the aisle. The plane was bouncing and he kept missing.

He put his phone away and checked the front of the Brig again. There was a crowd of smokers standing outside. Just then a voice and the sharp crack of billiard balls colliding in the background came over the radio speaker.

"Coming out. Retro is coming out."

"This seems early," Wright said.

"Does he smoke?" McPherson asked. "Maybe he's just—"

"Not that we've seen."

Bosch kept his eyes on the door and soon it pushed open. A man he recognized even from a distance as Jessup stepped out and headed along the sidewalk. Abbot Kinney slashed in a northwesterly direction across Venice. He was heading that way.

"Where did he park?" Bosch asked.

"He didn't," Wright said. "He only lives a few blocks from here. He walked over."

They watched in silence after that. Jessup walked two blocks on Abbot Kinney, passing a variety of restaurants, coffee shops and galleries. The sidewalk was busy. Almost every place was still open for Saturday-night business. He stepped into a coffee shop called Abbot's Habit. Wright got on the radio and assigned one of his men to enter it but before that could happen, Jessup stepped back out, coffee in hand, and proceeded on foot again.

Wright started the SUV and pulled into traffic going the opposite direction. He made a U-turn when he was two blocks further down and away from Jessup's view, should he happen to turn around. All the while he maintained constant radio contact with the other followers. Jessup had an invisible net around him. Even if he knew it was there he couldn't lose it.

"He's heading home," a radio voice reported. "Might be an early night."

Abbot Kinney, named for the man who built Venice more than a century earlier, became Brooks Avenue, which then intersected with Main Street. Jessup crossed Main and headed down one of the walk streets where automobiles could not travel. Wright was ready for this and directed two of the tail cars over to Pacific Avenue so they could pick him up when he came through.

Wright pulled to a stop at Brooks and Main and waited for the report that Jessup had passed through and was on Pacific. After two minutes he started to get anxious and went to the radio.

"Where is he, people?"

There was no response. No one had Jessup. Wright quickly sent somebody in.

"Two, you go in. Use the twenty-three."

"Got it."

McPherson looked over the seatback at Bosch and then at Wright.

"The twenty-three?"

"We have a variety of tactics we use. We don't describe them on the air."

He pointed through the windshield.

"That's the twenty-three."

Bosch saw a man wearing a red windbreaker and carrying an insulated pizza bag cut across Main and into the walk street named Breeze Avenue. They waited and finally the radio burst to life.

"I'm not seeing him. I walked all the way through and he's not—"

The transmission cut off. Wright said nothing. They waited and then the same voice came back in a whisper.

"I almost walked into him. He came out between two houses. He was pulling up his zipper."

"Okay, did he make you?" Wright asked.

"That's a negative. I asked for directions to Breeze Court and he said this was Breeze Avenue. We're cool. He should be coming through now."

"This is Four. We got him. He's heading toward San Juan."

The fourth car was one of the vehicles Wright had put on Pacific. Jessup was living in an apartment on San Juan Avenue between Speedway and the beach.

Bosch felt the momentary tension in his gut start to ease. Surveillance work was sometimes tough to take. Jessup had ducked between two houses to take a leak and it had caused a near panic.

Wright redirected the teams to the area around San Juan Avenue between Pacific and Speedway. Jessup used a key to enter the second-floor apartment where he was staying and the teams quickly moved into place. It was time to wait again.

Bosch knew from past surveillance gigs that the main attribute a good watcher needed was a comfort with silence. Some people are compelled to fill the void. Harry never was and he doubted anyone in the SIS was. He was curious to see how McPherson would do, now that the surveillance 101 lesson from Wright was over and there was nothing left but to wait and watch.

Bosch pulled his phone to see if he had missed a text from his daughter but it was clear. He decided not to pester her with another check-in and put the phone away. The genius of his giving McPherson the front seat now came into play. He turned and put his legs up and across the seat, stretching himself into a lounging position with his back against the door. McPherson glanced back and smiled in the darkness of the car.

"I thought you were being a gentleman," she said. "You just wanted to stretch out."

Bosch smiled.

"You got me."

Everyone was silent after that. Bosch thought about what McPherson had said while they had waited in the parking lot to be picked up by Wright. First she handed him a copy of the latest defense motion, which he locked in the trunk of his car. She told him he needed to start vetting the witnesses and their statements, looking for ways to turn their threats to the case into advantages for the prosecution. She said she and Haller had worked all day crafting a response to the attempt to disqualify Sarah Ann Gleason from testifying. The judge's ruling on the issue could decide the outcome of the trial.

It always bothered Bosch when he saw justice and the law being manipulated by smart lawyers. His part in the process was pure. He started at a crime scene and followed the evidence to a killer. There were rules along the way but at least the route was clear most of the time. But once things moved into the courthouse, they took on a different shape. Lawyers argued over interpretations and theories and procedures. Nothing seemed to move in a straight line. Justice became a labyrinth.

How could it be, he wondered, that an eyewitness to a horrible crime would not be allowed to testify in court against the accused? He had been a cop more than thirty-five years and he still could not explain how the system worked.

"This is Three. Retro's on the move."

Bosch was jarred out of his thoughts. A few seconds went by and the next report came from another voice.

"He's driving."

Wright took over.

"Okay, we get ready for an auto tail. One, get out to Main and Rose, Two, go down to Pacific and Venice. Everybody else, sit tight until we have his direction."

A few minutes later they had their answer.

"North on Main. Same as usual."

Wright redirected his units and the carefully orchestrated mobile surveillance began moving with Jessup as he took Main Street to Pico and then made his way to the entrance of the 10 Freeway.

Jessup headed east and then merged onto the northbound 405, which was crowded with cars even at the late hour. As expected, he was heading toward the Santa Monica Mountains. The surveillance vehicles ranged from Wright's SUV to a black Mercedes convertible to a Volvo station wagon with two bikes on a rear rack to a pair of generic Japanese sedans. The only thing missing for a surveillance in the Hollywood Hills was a hybrid. The teams employed a surveillance procedure called the *floating box*. Two outriders on either side of the target car, another car up front and one behind, all moving in a choreographed rotation. Wright's SUV was the floater, running backup behind the box.

The whole way Jessup stayed at or below the speed limit. As the freeway rose to the crest of the mountains Bosch looked out his window and saw the Getty Museum rising in the mist at the top like a castle, the sky black behind it.

Anticipating that Jessup was heading to his usual destinations on Mulholland Drive, Wright told two teams to break off from the box and move ahead. He wanted them already up and on Mulholland ahead of Jessup. He wanted a ground team with night vision goggles in Franklin Canyon Park before Jessup went in.

True to form, Jessup took the Mulholland exit and was soon heading east on the winding, two-lane snake that runs the spine of the mountain chain. Wright explained that this was when the surveillance was most vulnerable to exposure.

"You need a bee to properly do this up here but that's not in the budget," he said.

"A bee?" McPherson asked.

"Part of our code. Means helicopter. We could sure use one."

The first surprise of the night came five minutes later when Jessup drove by Franklin Canyon Park without stopping. Wright quickly recalled his ground team from the park as Jessup continued east.

Jessup passed Coldwater Canyon Boulevard without slowing and next drove by the overlook above Fryman Canyon. When he passed through the intersection of Mulholland and Laurel Canyon Boulevard he was taking the surveillance team into new territory.

"What are the chances he's made us?" Bosch asked.

"None," Wright said. "We're too good. He's got something new on his mind."

For the next ten minutes the follow continued east toward the Cahuenga Pass. The command car was well behind the surveillance, and Wright and his two passengers had to rely on radio reports to know what was happening.

One car was moving in front of Jessup while all the rest were behind. The rear cars followed a continual rotation of turning off and moving up so the headlight configurations would keep changing in Jessup's rearview. Finally, a radio report came in that made Bosch move forward in his seat, as if closer proximity to the source of the information would make things clearer.

"There's a stop sign up here and Retro turned north. It's too dark to see the street sign but I had to stay on Mulholland. Too risky. Next up turn left at the stop."

"Roger that. We got the left."

"Wait!" Bosch said urgently. "Tell him to wait."

Wright checked him in the mirror.

"What do you have in mind?" he asked.

"There's only one stop on Mulholland. Woodrow Wilson Drive. I know it. It winds down and reconnects with Mulholland at the light down at Highland. The lead car can pick him up there. But Woodrow Wilson is too tight. If you send a car down there he may know he's being followed."

"You sure?"

"I'm sure. I live on Woodrow Wilson."

Wright thought for a moment and then went on the radio.

"Cancel that left. Where's the Volvo?"

"We're holding up until further command."

"Okay, go on up and make the left on the two wheelers. Watch for oncoming. And watch for our guy."

"Roger that."

Soon Wright's SUV got to the intersection. Bosch saw the Volvo pulled off to the side. The bike rack was empty. Wright pulled over to wait, checking the teams on the radio.

"One, are you in position?"

"That's a roger. We're at the light at the bottom. No sign of Retro yet."

"Three, you up?"

There was no response.

"Okay, everybody hold till we hear."

"What do you mean?" Bosch asked. "What about the bikes?"

"They must've gone down deaf. We'll hear when they—"

"This is Three," a voice said in a whisper. "We came up on him. He'd closed his eyes and went to sleep."

Wright translated for his passengers.

"He killed his lights and stopped moving."

Bosch felt his chest start to tighten.

"Are they sure he's in the car?"

Wright communicated the question over the radio.

"Yeah, we can see him. He's got a candle burning on the dashboard."

"Where exactly are you, Three?"

"About halfway down. We can hear the freeway."

Bosch leaned all the way forward between the two front seats.

"Ask him if he can pick a number off the curb," he said. "Get me an address."

Wright relayed the request and almost a minute went by before the whisper came back.

"It's too dark to see the curbs here without using a flash. But we got a light next to the door of the house he's parked in front of. It's one of those cantilever jobs hanging its ass out over the pass. From here it looks like seventy-two-oh-three."

Bosch slid back and leaned heavily against the seat. McPherson turned to look at him. Wright used the mirror to look back.

"You know that address?" Wright asked.

Bosch nodded in the darkness.

"Yeah," he said. "It's my house."

Twenty-three

Sunday, March 21, 6:40 A.M.

My daughter liked to sleep in on Sundays. Normally I hated losing the time with her. I only had her every other weekend and Wednesdays. But this Sunday was different. I was happy to let her sleep while I got up early to go back to work on the motion to save my chief witness's testimony. I was in the kitchen pouring the first cup of coffee of the day when I heard knocking on my front door. It was still dark out. I checked the peep before opening it and was relieved to see it was my ex-wife with Harry Bosch standing right behind her.

But that relief was short-lived. The moment I turned the knob they pushed in and I could immediately feel a bad energy enter with them.

"We've got a problem," Maggie said.

"What's wrong?" I asked.

"What's wrong is that Jessup camped outside my house this morning," Bosch said. "And I want to know how he found it and what the hell he's doing."

He came up too close to me when he said it. I didn't know which was worse, his breath or the accusatory tone of his words. I wasn't sure what he was thinking but I realized all the bad energy was coming from him.

I stepped back from him.

"Hayley's still asleep. Let me just go close her bedroom door. There's fresh decaf in the kitchen and I can brew some fully leaded if you need it."

I went down the hall and checked on my daughter. She was still down. I closed the door and hoped the voices that were bound to get loud would not wake her.

My two visitors were still standing when I got back to the living room. Neither had gone for coffee. Bosch was silhouetted by the big picture window that looked out upon the city — the view that made me buy the house. I could see streaks of light entering the sky behind his shoulders.

"No coffee?"

They just stared at me.

"Okay, let's sit down and talk about this."

I gestured toward the couch and chairs but Bosch seemed frozen in his stance.

"Come on, let's figure it out."

I walked past them and sat down in the chair by the window. Finally, Bosch started to move. He sat down on the couch next to Hayley's school backpack. Maggie took the other chair. She spoke first.

"I've been trying to convince Harry that we didn't put his home address on the witness list."

"Absolutely not. We gave no personal addresses in discovery. For you, I listed two addresses. Your office and mine. I even gave the general number for the PAB. Didn't even give a direct line."

"Then how did he find my house?" Bosch asked, the accusatory tone still in his voice.

"Look, Harry, you're blaming me for something I had nothing to do with. I don't know how he found your house but it couldn't have been that hard. I mean, come on. Anybody can find anybody on the Internet. You own your house, right? You pay property taxes, have utility accounts, and I bet you're even registered to vote — Republican, I'm sure."

"Independent."

"Fine. The point is, people can find you if they want. Added to that, you have a singular name. All anybody would have to do is punch in—"

"You gave them my full name?"

"I had to. It's what's required and what's been given in discovery for every trial you've ever testified in. It doesn't matter. All Jessup needed was access to the Internet and he could've—"

"Jessup's been in prison for twenty-four years. He knows less about the Internet than I do. He had to have help and I'm betting it came from Royce."

"Look, we don't know that."

Bosch looked pointedly at me, a darkness crossing his eyes.

"You're defending *him* now?"

"No, I'm not defending anybody. I'm just saying we shouldn't rush to any conclusions here. Jessup's got a roommate and is a minor celebrity. Celebrities get people to do things for them, okay? So why don't you calm down and let's back up a little bit. Tell me what happened at your house."

Bosch seemed to take it down a notch but he was still anything but calm. I half expected him to get up and take a swing at a lamp or punch a hole in a wall. Thankfully, Maggie was the one who told the story.

"We were with the SIS, watching him. We thought he was going to go up to one of the parks he's been visiting. Instead, he drove right by them all and kept going on Mulholland. When we got to Harry's street we had to hang back so he wouldn't see us. The SIS has a bike car. Two of them saddled up and rode down. They found Jessup sitting in his car in front of Harry's house."

"Goddamn it!" Bosch said. "I have my daughter living with me. If this prick is—"

"Harry, not so loud and watch what you say," I said. "My daughter's on the other side of that wall. Now, please, go back to the story. What did Jessup do?"

Bosch hesitated. Maggie didn't.

"He just sat there," Maggie said. "For about a half hour. And he lit a candle."

"A candle? In the car?"

"Yeah, on the dashboard."

"What the hell does that mean?"

"Who knows?"

Bosch couldn't remain sitting. He jumped up from the couch and started pacing.

"And after a half hour he drove off and went home," Maggie said. "That was it. We just came from Venice."

Now I stood up and started to pace, but in a pattern clear of Bosch's orbit.

"Okay, let's think about this. Let's think about what he was doing."

"No shit, Sherlock," Bosch said. "That's the question."

I nodded. I had that coming.

"Is there any reason to think that he knows or suspects he's being followed?" I asked.

"No, no way," Bosch said immediately.

"Wait a minute, not so fast on that," Maggie said. "I've been thinking about it. There was a near-miss earlier in the night. You remember, Harry? On Breeze Avenue?"

Bosch nodded. Maggie explained it to me.

"They thought they lost him on a walk street in Venice. The lieutenant sent a guy in with a pizza box. Jessup came out from between two houses after taking a leak. It was a close call."

I spread my hands.

"Well, maybe that was it. Maybe that planted suspicion and he decided to see if he was being followed. You show up outside the lead investigator's house and it's a good way to draw out the flies if you've got them on you."

"You mean like a test?" Bosch asked.

"Exactly. Nobody approached him out there, right?"

"No, we left him alone," Maggie said. "If he had gotten out of his car I think it would've been a different story."

I nodded.

"Okay, so it was either a test or he's got something planned. In that case, it would've been a reconnaissance mission. He wanted to see where you live."

Bosch stopped and stared out the window. The sky was fully lit now.

"But one thing you have to keep in mind is that what he did was not illegal," I said. "It's a public street and the OR put no restrictions on travel within Los Angeles County. So no matter what he was up to, it's a good thing you didn't stop him and reveal yourself."

Bosch stayed at the window, his back to us. I didn't know what he was thinking.

"Harry," I said. "I know your concerns and I agree with them. But we can't let this be a distraction. The trial is coming up quick and we have work to do. If we convict this guy, he goes away forever and it won't matter if he knows where you live."

"So what do I do till then, sit on my front porch every night with a shotgun?"

"The SIS is on him twenty-four/seven, right?" Maggie said. "Do you trust them?"

Bosch didn't answer for a long moment.

"They won't lose him," he finally said.

Maggie looked at me and I could see the concern in her eyes. Each of us had a daughter. It would be hard to put your trust in anybody else, even an elite surveillance squad. I thought for a moment about something I had been considering since the conversation began.

"What about you moving in here? With your daughter. She can use Hayley's room because Hayley's going back to her mother's today. And you can use the office. It's got a sleeper sofa that I've spent more than a few nights on. It's actually comfortable."

Bosch turned from the window and looked at me.

"What, stay here through the whole trial?"

"Why not? Our daughters will finally get a chance to meet when Hayley comes over."

"It's a good idea," Maggie said.

I didn't know if she was referring to the daughters meeting or the idea of Bosch and child staying with me.

"And look, I'm here every night," I said. "If you have to go out with the SIS, I got you covered with your daughter, especially when Hayley's here."

Bosch thought about it for a few moments but then shook his head.

"I can't do that," he said.

"Why not?" I asked.

"Because it's my house. My home. I'm not going to run from this guy. He's going to run from me."

"What about your daughter?" Maggie asked.

"I'll take care of my daughter."

"Harry, think about it," she said. "Think about your daughter. You don't want her in harm's way."

"Look, if Jessup has my address, then he probably has this address, too. Moving in here isn't the answer. It's just . . . just running from him. Maybe that's his test — to see what I do. So I'm not doing anything. I'm not moving. I've got the SIS, and if he comes back and so much as crosses the curb out front, I'll be waiting for him."

"I don't like this," Maggie said.

I thought about what Bosch had said about Jessup having my address.

"Neither do I," I said.

Twenty-four

Bosch didn't need to be in court. In fact, he wouldn't be needed until after jury selection and the actual trial began. But he wanted to get a close look at the man he had been shadowing from a distance with the SIS. He wanted to see if Jessup would show any reaction to seeing him in return. It had been a month and a half since they had spent the long day in the car driving down from San Quentin. Bosch felt the need to get closer than the surveillance allowed him to. It would help him keep the fire burning.

It was billed as a status conference. The judge wanted to deal with all final motions and issues before beginning jury selection the next day and then moving seamlessly into the trial. There were scheduling and jury issues to discuss and each side's list of exhibits were to be handed in as well.

The prosecution team was locked and loaded. In the last two weeks Haller and McPherson had sharpened and streamlined the case, run through mock witness examinations and reconsidered every piece of evidence. They had carefully choreographed the ways in which they would bring the twenty-four-year-old evidence forward. They were ready. The bow had been pulled taut and the arrow was ready to fly.

Even the decision on the death penalty had been made—or rather, announced. Haller had officially withdrawn it, even though Bosch assumed all along that his use of it to threaten Jessup had merely been a pose. He was a defense attorney by nature, and there was no getting him across that line. A conviction on the charges would bring Jessup a sentence of life in prison without the possibility of parole, and that would have to be enough justice for Melissa Landy.

Bosch was ready as well. He had diligently reinvestigated the case and located the witnesses who would be called to testify. All the while, he was still out riding with the SIS as often as possible—nights that his daughter stayed at the homes of friends or with Sue Bambrough, the assistant principal. He was prepared for his part and had helped Haller and McPherson get ready for theirs. Confidence was high and that was another reason for Bosch to be in the courtroom. He wanted to see this thing get started.

Judge Breitman entered and the courtroom was brought to order at a few minutes after nine. Bosch was in a chair against the railing directly behind the prosecution table where Haller and McPherson sat side by side. They had told him to pull the chair up to the table but Harry wanted to hang back. He wanted to be able to watch Jessup from behind, and besides, there was too much anxiety coming from the two prosecutors. The judge was going to make a ruling on whether Sarah Ann Gleason would be allowed to testify against Jessup. As Haller had said the night before, nothing else mattered. If they lost Sarah as a witness, they would surely lose the case.

"On the record with *California versus Jessup* again," the judge said upon taking the bench. "Good morning to all."

After a chorus of good mornings fired back to her, the judge got right down to business.

"Tomorrow we begin jury selection in this case and then we proceed to trial. Therefore today is the day that we're going to clean out the garage, so to speak, so that we can finally bring the car in. Any last motions, any pending motions, anything anybody wants to talk about in regard to exhibits or evidence or anything else, now is the time. We have a number of motions pending and I will get to them first. The prosecution's request to redress the issue of the defendant's use of makeup to cover certain body tattoos is dismissed. We argued that at length already and I do not see the need to go at it further."

Bosch checked Jessup. He was at a sharp angle to him, so he could not see the defendant's face. But he did see Jessup nod his head in approval of the judge's first ruling of the day.

Breitman then went through a housekeeping list of minor motions from both sides. She seemed to want to accommodate all so neither side emerged as a clear favorite. Bosch saw that McPherson was meticulously keeping notes on each decision on a yellow legal pad.

It was all part of the buildup to the ruling of the day. Since Sarah was to be McPherson's witness to question during trial, she had handled the oral arguments on the defense motion two days earlier. Though Bosch had not attended that hearing, Haller had told him that Maggie had held forth for nearly an hour in a well-prepared response to the motion to disqualify. She had then backed it with an eighteen-page written response. The prosecution team was confident in the argument but neither member of the team knew Breitman well enough to be confident in how she would rule.

"Now," the judge said, "we come to the defense motion to disqualify Sarah Ann Gleason as a witness for the prosecution. The question has been argued and submitted by both sides and the court is ready to make a ruling."

"Your Honor, could I be heard?" Royce said, standing up at the defense table.

"Mr. Royce," the judge said, "I don't see the need for further argument. You made the motion and I allowed you to respond to the prosecution's submission. What more needs to be said?"

"Yes, Your Honor."

Royce sat back down, leaving whatever he was going to add to his attack on Sarah Gleason a secret.

"The defense's motion is dismissed," the judge said immediately. "I will be allowing the defense wide latitude in its examination of the prosecution's witness as well as in the production of its own witnesses to address Ms. Gleason's credibility before the jury. But I believe that this witness's credibility and reliability is indeed something that jurors will need to decide."

A momentary silence enveloped the courtroom, as if everyone collectively had drawn in a breath. No response followed from either the prosecution or defense table. It was another down-the-middle ruling, Bosch knew, and both sides were probably pleased to have gotten something. Gleason would be allowed to testify, so the prosecution's case was secured, but the judge was going to let Royce go after her with all he had. It would come down to whether Sarah was strong enough to take it.

"Now, I would like to move on," the judge said. "Let's talk about jury selection and scheduling first, and then we'll get to the exhibits."

The judge proceeded to outline how she wanted voir dire to proceed. Though each side would be allowed to question prospective jurors, she said she would strictly limit the time for each side. She wanted to start a momentum that would carry into the trial. She also limited each side to only twelve peremptory challenges — juror rejections without cause — and said she wanted to pick six alternates because it was her practice to be quick with the hook on jurors who misbehaved, were chronically late or had the audacity to fall asleep during testimony.

"I like a good supply of alternates because we usually need them," she said.

The low number of peremptory challenges and the high number of alternates brought objections from both the prosecution and the defense. The judge grudgingly gave each side two more challenges but warned that she would not allow voir dire to get bogged down.

"I want jury selection completed by the end of the day Friday. If you slow me down, then I will slow you down. I will hold the panel and every lawyer in here until Friday night if I have to. I want opening statements first thing Monday. Any objection to that?"

Both sides seemed properly cowed by the judge. She was clearly exerting command of her own courtroom. She next outlined the trial schedule, stating that testimony would begin each morning at nine sharp and continue until five with a ninety-minute lunch and morning and afternoon breaks of fifteen minutes each.

"That leaves a solid six hours a day of testimony," she said. "Any more and I find the jurors start losing interest. So I keep it to six a day. It will be up to you to be in here and ready to go each morning when I step through the door at nine. Any questions?"

There were none. Breitman then asked each side for estimates on how long their case would take to present. Haller said he would need no more than four days, depending on the length of the cross-examinations of his witnesses. This was already a shot directed at Royce and his plans to attack Sarah Ann Gleason.

For his part, Royce said he needed only two days. The judge then did her own math, adding four and two and coming up with five.

"Well, I'm thinking an hour each for opening statements on Monday morning. I think that means we'll finish Friday afternoon and go right to closing arguments the following Monday."

Neither side objected to her math. The point was clear. Keep it moving. Find ways to cut time. Of course a trial was a fluid thing and there were many unknowns. Neither side would be held to what was said at this hearing, but each lawyer knew that there might be consequences from the judge if they didn't keep a continuous velocity to their presentations.

"Finally, we come to exhibits and electronics," Breitman said. "I trust that everyone has looked over each other's lists. Any objections to these?"

Both Haller and Royce stood up. The judge nodded at Royce.

"You first, Mr. Royce."

"Yes, Judge, the defense has an objection to the prosecution's plans to project numerous images of Melissa Landy's body on the court-room's overhead screens. This practice is not only barbaric but exploitative and prejudicial."

The judge swiveled in her seat and looked at Haller, who was still standing.

"Your Honor, it is the prosecution's duty to produce the body. To show the crime that brings us here. The last thing we want to do is be exploitative or prejudicial. I will grant Mr. Royce that it is a fine line, but we do not plan to step across it."

Royce came back with one more shot.

"This case is twenty-four years old. In nineteen eighty-six there were no overhead screens, none of this Hollywood stuff. I think it infringes on my client's right to a fair trial."

Haller was ready with his own comeback.

"The age of the case has nothing to do with this issue, but the defense is perfectly willing to present these exhibits the way they would've—"

McPherson had grabbed his sleeve to interrupt him. He bent down and she whispered in his ear. He then quickly straightened up.

"Excuse me, Your Honor, I misspoke. The *prosecution* is more than willing to present these exhibits in the manner they would have been presented to the jury in nineteen eighty-six. We would be happy to hand out color photographs to the jurors. But in earlier conversation the court indicated that she did not like this practice."

"Yes, I find that handing these sorts of photos directly to the jurors to be possibly more exploitative and prejudicial," Breitman said. "Is that what you wish, Mr. Royce?"

Royce had walked himself into a jam.

"No, Judge, I would agree with the court on this point. The defense was simply trying to limit the scope and use of these photographs. Mr. Haller lists more than thirty photographs that he wants to put on the big screen. It seems over-the-top. That is all."

"Judge Breitman, these are photographs of the body in the place it was found as well as during autopsy. Each one is—"

"Mr. Haller," the judge intoned, "let me just stop you right there. Crime scene photographs are acceptable, as long as they come with appropriate foundation and testimony. But I see no need to show our jurors this poor girl's autopsy shots. We're not going to do that."

"Yes, Your Honor," Haller said.

He remained standing while Royce sat down with his partial victory. Breitman spoke while writing something.

"And you have an objection to Mr. Royce's exhibit list, Mr. Haller?"

"Yes, Your Honor, the defense has a variety of drug paraphernalia alleged to have once been owned by Ms. Gleason on its exhibit list. It also lists photos and videos of Ms. Gleason. The prosecution has not been given the opportunity to examine these materials but we believe they only go to the point that we will be conceding at trial and eliciting in direct examination of this witness. That is that at one time in her life she used drugs on a regular basis. We do not see the need to show photos of her using drugs or the pipes through which she ingested drugs. It's inflammatory and prejudicial. It is not needed based on the concessions of the prosecution."

Royce stood back up and was ready to go. The judge gave him the floor.

"Judge, these exhibits are vitally important to the defense case. The prosecution of Mr. Jessup hinges on the testimony of a longtime drug addict who cannot be relied upon to remember the truth, let alone tell it. These exhibits will help the jury understand the depth and breadth of this witness's use of illegal substances over a lengthy period of time."

Royce was finished but the judge was silent as she studied the defense exhibit list.

"All right," she finally said, putting the document aside. "You both make cogent arguments. So what we are going to do is take these exhibits one at a time. When the defense would like to proffer an exhibit, we will discuss it first out of earshot of the jury. I'll make a decision then."

The lawyers sat down. Bosch almost shook his head but didn't want to draw the judge's attention. Still, it burned him that she had not slapped the defense down on this one. Twenty-four years after seeing her little sister abducted from the front yard, Sarah Ann Gleason was willing to testify about the awful, nightmarish moment that had changed her life forever. And for her sacrifice and efforts, the judge was actually going to entertain the defense's request to attack her with the glass pipes and accoutrements she had once used to escape what she had been through. It didn't seem fair to Bosch. It didn't seem like anything that approached justice.

The hearing ended soon after that and all parties packed their briefcases and moved through the doors of the courtroom en masse. Bosch hung back and then insinuated himself into the group right behind Jessup. He said nothing but Jessup soon enough felt the presence behind him and turned around.

He smirked when he saw it was Bosch.

"Well, Detective Bosch, are you following me?"

"Should I be?"

"Oh, you never know. How's your investigation going?"

"You'll find out soon enough."

"Yes, I can't—"

"Don't talk to him!"

It was Royce. He had turned and noticed.

"And don't *you* talk to him," he added, pointing a finger at Bosch. "If you continue to harass him, I'll complain to the judge."

Bosch held his hands out in a no-touching gesture.

"We're cool, Counselor. Just making small talk."

"There is no such thing when it comes to the police."

He reached out and put his hand on Jessup's shoulder and shepherded him away from Bosch.

In the hallway outside they moved directly to the waiting huddle of reporters and cameras. Bosch moved past but looked back in time to see Jessup's face change. His eyes went from the steely glare of a predator to the wounded look of a victim.

The reporters quickly gathered around him.

PART THREE

— To Seek a True
and Just Verdict

Twenty-five

Monday, April 5, 9:00 A.M.

I watched the jury file in and take their assigned seats in the box. I watched them closely, keying on their eyes mostly. Checking for how they looked at the defendant. You can learn a lot from that; a furtive glance or a strong judgmental stare.

Jury selection had gone as scheduled. We went through the first panel of ninety prospective jurors in a day but had sat only eleven after most were eliminated because of their media knowledge of the case. The second panel was just as difficult to choose from and it wasn't until Friday evening at five-forty that we had our final eighteen.

I had my jury chart in front of me, and my eyes were jumping between the faces in the box and the names on my Post-its, trying to memorize who was who. I already had a good handle on most of them but I wanted the names to become second nature to me. I wanted to be able to look at them and address them as if they were friends and neighbors.

The judge was on the bench and ready to go at nine sharp. She first asked the attorneys if there was any new or unfinished business to address. Upon learning there was not, she called in the jurors.

"Okay, we are all here," she said. "I want to thank all of the jurors and other parties for being on time. We begin the trial with opening statements from the attorneys. These are not to be construed as evidence but merely—"

The judge stopped, her eyes fixed on the back row of the jury box. A woman had timidly raised her hand. The judge stared for a long moment and then checked her own seating chart before responding.

"Ms. Tucci? Do you have a question?"

I checked my chart. Number ten, Carla Tucci. She was one of the jurors I had not yet committed to memory. A mousy brunette from East Hollywood. She was thirty-two years old, unmarried and she worked as a receptionist at a medical clinic. According to my color-coded chart, I had her down as a juror who could be swayed by stronger personalities on the panel. This was not a bad thing. It just depended on whether those personalities were for a guilty verdict or not.

"I think I saw something I wasn't supposed to see," she said in a frightened voice.

Judge Breitman hung her head for a moment and I knew why. She couldn't get the wheels out of the mud. We were ready to go and now the trial would be delayed before opening statements were even in the record.

"Okay, let's try to take care of this quickly. I want the jury to stay in place. Everyone else stay in place and Ms. Tucci and the attorneys and I will go quickly back to chambers to find out what this is about."

As we got up I checked my jury chart. There were six alternates. I had three of them pegged as pro-prosecution, two in the middle and one siding with the defense. If Tucci was ejected for whatever misconduct she was about to reveal, her replacement would be chosen randomly from the alternates. This meant that I had a better-than-even chance of seeing her replaced with a juror who was partial to the prosecution and only a one in six chance of getting a juror who was pro-defense. As I followed the entourage into chambers I decided that I liked my chances and I would do what I could to have Tucci ejected from the panel.

In chambers, the judge didn't even go behind her desk, perhaps hoping this was only going to be a minor question and delay. We stood in a group in the middle of her office. All except the court reporter, who sat on the edge of a side chair so she could type.

"Okay, on the record," the judge said. "Ms. Tucci, please tell us what you saw and what is bothering you."

The juror looked down at the ground and held her hands in front of her.

"I was riding on the Metro this morning and the man sitting across from me was reading the newspaper. He was holding it up and I saw the front page. I didn't mean to look but I saw a photo of the man on trial and I saw the headline."

The judge nodded.

"You are talking about Jason Jessup, correct?"

"Yes."

"What newspaper?"

"I think it was the *Times*."

"What did the headline say, Ms. Tucci?"

"New trial, old evidence for Jessup."

I hadn't seen the actual *L.A. Times* that morning but had read the story online. Citing an unnamed source close to the prosecution, the story said the case against Jason Jessup was expected to be comprised entirely of evidence from the first trial and leaning heavily on the identification provided by the victim's sister. Kate Salters had the byline on it.

"Did you read the story, Ms. Tucci?" Breitman asked.

"No, Judge, I just saw it for a second and when I saw his picture I looked away. You told us not to read anything about the case. It just kind of popped up in front of me."

The judge nodded thoughtfully.

"Okay, Ms. Tucci, can you step back into the hallway for a moment?"

The juror stepped out and the judge closed the door.

"The headline tells the story, doesn't it?" she said.

She looked at Royce and then me, seeing if either of us was going to make a motion or a suggestion. Royce said nothing. My guess was that he had juror number ten pegged the same way that I did. But he might not have considered the leanings of the six alternates.

"I think the damage is done here, Judge," I said. "She knows there was a previous trial. Anybody with any basic knowledge of the court system knows they don't retry you if you get a not-guilty. So she'll know Jessup went down on a guilty before. As much as that prejudices things in the prosecution's favor, I think to be fair she has to go."

Breitman nodded.

"Mr. Royce?"

"I would agree with Mr. Haller's assessment of the prejudice, not his so-called desire to be fair. He simply wants her off the jury and one of those churchgoing alternates on it."

I smiled and shook my head.

"I won't dignify that with a response. You don't want to kick her off, that's fine with me."

"But it's not counsel's choice," the judge said.

She opened the door and invited the juror back in.

"Ms. Tucci, thank you for your honesty. You can go back to the jury room and gather your things. You are dismissed and can report back to the juror assembly room to check with them."

Tucci hesitated.

"Does that mean —?"

"Yes, unfortunately, you are dismissed. That headline gives you knowledge of the case you should not have. For you to know that Mr. Jessup was previously tried for these crimes is prejudicial. Therefore, I cannot keep you on the jury. You may go now."

"I'm sorry, Judge."

"Yes, so am I."

Tucci left the chambers with her shoulders slumped and with

the hesitant walk of someone who has been accused of a crime. After the door closed, the judge looked at us.

"If nothing else, this will send the right message to the rest of the jury. We're now down to five alternates and we haven't even started. But we now clearly see how the media can impact our trial. I have not read this story but I will. And if I see anyone in this room quoted in it I am going to be very disappointed. There are usually consequences for those who disappoint me."

"Judge," Royce said. "I read the story this morning and no one here is quoted by name but it does attribute information to a source close to the prosecution. I was planning to bring this to your attention."

I shook my head.

"And that's the oldest defense trick in the book. Cut a deal with a reporter to hide behind the story. A source close to the prosecution? He's sitting four feet across the aisle from me. That was probably close enough for the reporter."

"Your Honor!" Royce blurted. "I had nothing to—"

"We're holding up the trial," Breitman said, cutting him off. "Let's get back to court."

We trudged back. As we went back into the courtroom I scanned the gallery and saw Salters, the reporter, in the second row. I quickly looked away, hoping my brief eye contact had not revealed anything. I had been her source. My goal was to manipulate the story—the *scene setter,* as the reporter had called it—into being something that gave the defense false confidence. I hadn't intended it as a means of changing the makeup of the jury.

Back on the bench, the judge wrote something on a pad and then turned and addressed the jury, once again warning the panelists about reading the newspaper or watching television news programs. She then turned to her clerk.

"Audrey, the candy bowl, please."

The clerk then took the bowl of individually wrapped sourballs off the counter in front of her desk, dumped the candy into a drawer, and took the bowl to the judge. The judge tore a page from her notebook, tore it again into six pieces and wrote on each piece.

"I have written the numbers one through six on pieces of paper and I will now randomly select an alternate to take juror number ten's seat on the panel."

She folded the pieces of paper and dropped them into the bowl. She then swirled the bowl in her hand and raised it over her head. With her other hand she withdrew one piece of paper, unfolded it and read it out loud.

"Alternate number six," Breitman said. "Would you please move with any belongings you might have to seat number ten in the jury box. Thank you."

I could do nothing but sit and watch. The new juror number ten was a thirty-six-year-old film and television extra named Philip Kirns. Being an extra probably meant that he was an actor who had not yet been successful. He took jobs as a background extra to make ends meet. That meant that every day, he went to work and stood around and watched those who had made it. This put him on the bitter side of the gulf between the haves and have-nots. And this would make him partial to the defense — the underdog facing off against the Man. I had him down as a red juror and now I was stuck with him.

Maggie whispered into my ear at the prosecution table as we watched Kirns take his new seat.

"I hope you didn't have anything to do with that story, Haller. Because I think we just lost a vote."

I raised my hands in a *not me* gesture but it didn't look like she was buying it.

The judge turned her chair fully toward the jury.

"Finally, I believe we are ready to start," she said. "We begin with the opening statements from the attorneys. These statements are not to be taken as evidence. These statements are merely an opportunity for the prosecution and defense to tell the jury what they expect the evidence will show. It is an outline of what you can expect to see and hear during the trial. And it is incumbent upon counsel to then present evidence and testimony that you will later weigh during deliberations. We start with the prosecution statement. Mr. Haller?"

I stood up and went to the lectern that was positioned between the prosecution table and the jury box. I took no legal pad, 3 × 5 cards or anything else with me. I believed that it was important first to sell myself to the jury, then my case. To do that I could not look away from them. I needed to be direct, open and honest the whole time. Besides, my statement was going to be brief and to the point. I didn't need notes.

I started by introducing myself and then Maggie. I next pointed to Harry Bosch who was seated against the rail behind the prosecution table and introduced him as the case investigator. Then I got down to business.

"We are here today about one thing. To speak for someone who can no longer speak for herself. Twelve-year-old Melissa Landy was abducted from her front yard in nineteen eighty-six. Her body was found just a few hours later, discarded in a Dumpster like a bag of trash. She had been strangled. The man accused of this horrible crime sits there at the defense table."

I pointed the finger of accusation at Jessup, just as I had seen prosecutor after prosecutor point it at my clients over the years. It felt falsely righteous of me to point a finger at anyone, even a murderer. But that didn't stop me. Not only did I point at Jessup but I pointed again and again as I summarized the case, telling the jury of the witnesses I would call and what they would say and show. I moved along quickly, making sure to mention the eyewitness who identified Melissa's abductor and the finding of the victim's hair in Jessup's tow truck. I then brought it around to a big finish.

"Jason Jessup took the life of Melissa Landy," I said. "He grabbed her in the front yard and took her away from her family and this world forever. He put his hand around this beautiful little girl's throat and choked the life out of her. He robbed her of her past and of her future. He robbed her of everything. And the state will prove this to you beyond a reasonable doubt."

I nodded once to underline the promise and then returned to my seat. The judge had told us the day before to be brief in our openers, but even she seemed surprised by my brevity. It took her a moment to realize I was finished. She then told Royce he was up.

As I expected he would, Royce deferred to the second half, meaning he reserved his opening statement until the start of the defense's case. That put the judge's focus back on me.

"Very well, then. Mr. Haller, call your first witness."

I went back to the lectern, this time carrying notes and printouts. I had spent most of the previous week before jury selection preparing the questions I would ask my witnesses. As a defense attorney I am used to cross-examining the state's witnesses and picking at the testimony brought forward by the prosecutor. It's a task quite different from direct examination and building the foundation for the introduction of evidence and exhibits. I fully acknowledge that it is easier to knock something down than to build it in the first place. But in this case I would be the builder and I came prepared.

"The People call William Johnson."

I turned to the back of the courtroom. As I had gone to the lectern Bosch had left the courtroom to retrieve Johnson from a witness waiting room. He now returned with the man in tow. Johnson was small and thin with a dark mahogany complexion. He was fifty-nine but his pure white hair made him look older. Bosch walked him through the gate and then pointed him in the direction of the witness stand. He was quickly sworn in by the court clerk.

I had to admit to myself that I was nervous. I felt what Maggie had tried to describe to me on more than one occasion when we were married. She always called it the *burden of proof.* Not the legal burden. But the psychic burden of knowing that you stood as representative of all the people. I had always dismissed her explanations as self-serving. The prosecutor was always the overdog. The Man. There was no burden in that, at least nothing compared to the burden of the defense attorney, who stands all alone and holds someone's freedom in his hands. I never understood what she was trying to tell me.

Until now.

Now I got it. I felt it. I was about to question my first witness in front of the jury and I was as nervous as I had been at my first trial out of law school.

"Good morning, Mr. Johnson," I said. "How are you, sir?"

"I am good, yes."

"That's good. Can you tell me, sir, what you do for a living?"

"Yes, sir. I am head of operations for the El Rey Theatre on Wilshire Boulevard."

"'Head of operations,' what does that mean?"

"I make sure everything works right and runs—from the stage lights to the toilets, it's all part of my job. Mind you, I have electricians work on the lights and plumbers work on the toilets."

His answer was greeted with polite smiles and modest laughter. He spoke with a slight Caribbean accent but his words were clear and understandable.

"How long have you worked at the El Rey, Mr. Johnson?"

"For going on thirty-six years now. I started in nineteen seventy-four."

"Wow, that's an achievement. Congratulations. Have you been head of operations for all that time?"

"No, I worked my way up. I started as a janitor."

"I would like to draw your attention back to nineteen eighty-six. You were working there then, correct?"

"Yes, sir. I was a janitor back then."

"Okay, and do you remember the date of February sixteenth of that year in particular?"

"Yes, I do."

"It was a Sunday."

"Yes, I remember."

"Can you tell the court why?"

"That was the day I found the body of a little girl in the trash bin out back of the El Rey. That was a terrible day."

I checked the jury. All eyes were on my witness. So far so good.

"I can imagine that being a terrible day, Mr. Johnson. Now, can you tell us what it was that brought you to discover the body of the little girl?"

"We were working on a project in the theater. We were putting new drywall into the ladies' room on account of a leak. So I took a wheelbarrow full of the stuff we had demoed—the old wall and some rotting wood and such—and wheeled it out to put in the Dumpster. I opened the top and there this poor little girl was."

"She was on top of the debris already in the trash bin?"

"That's right."

"Was she covered at all with any trash or debris?"

"No, sir, not at all."

"As if whoever threw her in there had been in a hurry and didn't have time to cover—"

"Objection!"

Royce had jumped to his feet. I knew he would object. But I had almost gotten the whole sentence—and its suggestion—to the jury.

"Mr. Haller is leading the witness and asking for conclusions for which he would have no expertise," Royce said.

I withdrew the question before the judge could sustain the objection. There was no sense in having the judge side with the defense in front of the jury.

"Mr. Johnson, was that the first trip you had made to the trash bin that day?"

"No, sir. I had been out there two times before."

"Before the trip during which you found the body, when had you last been to the trash bin?"

"About ninety minutes before."

"Did you see a body on top of the trash in the bin that time?"

"No, there was no body there."

"So it had to have been placed in that bin in the ninety minutes prior to you finding it, correct?"

"Yes, that's right."

"Okay, Mr. Johnson, if I could draw your attention to the screen."

The courtroom was equipped with two large flat-screen monitors mounted high on the wall opposite the jury box. One screen was slightly angled toward the gallery to allow courtroom observers to see the digital presentations as well. Maggie controlled what appeared on the screens through a PowerPoint program on her laptop computer. She had constructed the presentation over the last two weeks and weekends as we choreographed the prosecution's case. All of the old photos from the case files had been scanned and loaded into the program. She now put up the trial's first photo exhibit. A shot of the trash bin Melissa Landy's body had been found in.

"Does that look like the trash bin in which you found the little girl's body, Mr. Johnson?"

"That's it."

"What makes you so sure, sir?"

"The address — fifty-five fifteen — spray-painted on the side like that. I did that. That's the address. And I can tell that's the back of the El Rey. I've worked there a long time."

"Okay, and is this what you saw when you raised the top and looked inside?"

Maggie moved to the next photo. The courtroom was already quiet but it seemed to me that it grew absolutely silent when the photo of Melissa Landy's body in the trash bin went up on the screens. Under the existing rules of evidence as carved by a recent ruling by the Ninth District, I had to find ways of bringing old evidence and exhibits to the present jury. I could not rely on investigative records. I had to find people who were bridges to the past and Johnson was the first bridge.

Johnson didn't answer my question at first. He just stared like everyone else in the courtroom. Then, unexpectedly, a tear rolled down his dark cheek. It was perfect. If I had been at the defense table I would have viewed it with cynicism. But I knew Johnson's response was heartfelt and it was why I had made him my first witness.

"That's her," he finally said. "That's what I saw."

I nodded as Johnson blessed himself.

"And what did you do when you saw her?"

"We didn't have no cell phones back then, you see. So I ran back inside and I called nine-one-one on the stage phone."

"And the police came quickly?"

"They came real quick, like they were already looking for her."

"One final question, Mr. Johnson. Could you see that trash bin from Wilshire Boulevard?"

Johnson shook his head emphatically.

"No, it was behind the theater and you could only see it if you drove back there and down the little alley."

I hesitated here. I had more to bring out from this witness. Information not presented in the first trial but gathered by Bosch during his reinvestigation. It was information that Royce might not be aware of. I could just ask the question that would draw it out or I could roll the dice and see if the defense opened a door on cross-examination. The information would be the same either way, but it would have greater weight if the jury believed the defense had tried to hide it.

"Thank you, Mr. Johnson," I finally said. "I have no further questions."

The witness was turned over to Royce, who went to the lectern as I sat down.

"Just a few questions," he said. "Did you see who put the victim's body in the bin?"

"No, I did not," Johnson said.

"So when you called nine-one-one you had no idea who did it, is that correct?"

"Correct."

"Before that day, had you ever seen the defendant before?"

"No, I don't think so."

"Thank you."

And that was it. Royce had performed a typical cross of a witness who had little value to the defense. Johnson couldn't identify the murderer, so Royce got that on the record. But he should have just let Johnson pass. By asking if Johnson had ever seen Jessup before the murder, he opened a door. I stood back up so I could go through it.

"Redirect, Mr. Haller?" the judge asked.

"Briefly, Your Honor. Mr. Johnson, back during this period that we're talking about, did you often work on Sundays?"

"No, it was my day off usually. But if we had some special projects I would be told to come in."

Royce objected on the grounds that I was opening up a line of questioning that was outside the scope of his cross-examination. I promised the judge that it was within the scope and that it would become apparent soon. She indulged me and overruled the objection. I went back to Mr. Johnson. I had hoped Royce would object because in a few moments it would look like he had been trying to stop me from getting to information damaging to Jessup.

"You mentioned that the trash bin where you found the body was at the end of an alley. Is there no parking lot behind the El Rey Theatre?"

"There is a parking lot but it does not belong to the El Rey Theatre. We have the alley that gives us access to the back doors and the bins."

"Who does the parking lot belong to?"

"A company that has lots all over the city. It's called City Park."

"Is there a wall or a fence separating this parking lot from the alley?"

Royce stood again.

"Your Honor, this is going on and on and it has nothing to do with what I asked Mr. Johnson."

"Your Honor," I said. "I will get there in two more questions."

"You may answer, Mr. Johnson," Breitman said.

"There is a fence," Johnson said.

"So," I said, "from the El Rey's alley and the location of its trash bin, you can see into the adjoining parking lot, and anyone in the adjoining parking lot could see the trash bin, correct?"

"Yes."

"And prior to the day you discovered the body, did you have occasion to be at work on a Sunday and to notice that the parking lot behind the theater was being used?"

"Yes, like a month previously, I came to work and in the back there were many cars and I saw tow trucks towing them in."

I couldn't help myself. I had to glance over at Royce and Jessup to see if they were squirming yet. I was about to draw the first blood of the trial. They thought Johnson was going to be a noncritical witness, meaning he would establish the murder and its location and nothing else.

They were wrong.

"Did you inquire as to what was going on?" I asked.

"Yes," Johnson said. "I asked what they were doing and one of the drivers said that they were towing cars from the neighborhood down the street and holding them there so people could come and pay and get their cars."

"So it was being used like a temporary holding lot, is that what you mean?"

"Yes."

"And did you know what the name of the towing company was?"

"It was on the trucks. It was called Aardvark Towing."

"You said trucks. You saw more than one truck there?"

"Yeah, there were two or three trucks when I saw them."

"What did you tell them after you were informed what they were doing there?"

"I told my boss and he called City Park to see if they knew about it. He thought there could be an insurance concern, especially with people being mad about being towed and all. And it turned out Aardvark wasn't supposed to be there. It wasn't authorized."

"What happened?"

"They had to stop using the lot and my boss told me to keep an eye out if I worked on weekends to see if they kept using it."

"So they stopped using the lot behind the theater?"

"That's right."

"And this was the same lot from which you could see the trash bin in which you would later find the body of Melissa Landy?"

"Yes, sir."

"When Mr. Royce asked you if you had ever seen the defendant before the day of the murder, you answered that you didn't think so, correct?"

"Correct."

"You don't think so? Why are you not sure?"

"Because I think he could've been one of the Aardvark drivers I saw using that lot. So I can't be sure I didn't see him before."

"Thank you, Mr. Johnson. I have no further questions."

Twenty-six

Monday, April 5, 10:20 A.M.

For the first time since he had been brought into the case Bosch felt as though Melissa Landy was in good hands. He had just watched Mickey Haller score the first points of the trial. He had taken a small piece of the puzzle Bosch had come up with and used it to land the first punch. It wasn't a knockout by any means but it had connected solidly. It was the first step down the path of proving Jason Jessup's familiarity with the parking lot and trash bin behind the El Rey Theatre. Before the trial would end, its importance would be made clear to the jury. But what was even more significant to Bosch at the moment was the way Haller had used the information Harry had provided. He had hung it on the defense, made it look as though it had been their attempt to obfuscate the facts of the case that drew the information out. It was a smooth move and it gave Bosch a big boost in his confidence in Haller as a prosecutor.

He met Johnson at the gate and walked him out of the courtroom to the hallway, where he shook his hand.

"You did real good in there, Mr. Johnson. We can't thank you enough."

"You already have. Convicting that man of killing that little girl."

"Well, we're not quite there yet but that's the plan. Except most people who read the paper think we're going after an innocent man."

"No, you got the right man. I can tell."

Bosch nodded and felt awkward.

"You take care, Mr. Johnson."

"Detective, your music is jazz, right?"

Bosch had already turned to go back to the courtroom. Now he looked back at Johnson.

"How'd you know that?"

"Just a guess. We got jazz acts that come through. New Orleans jazz. You ever want tickets to a show at the El Rey, you look me up."

"Yeah, I'll do that. Thanks."

Bosch pushed through the doors leading back into the courtroom. He was smiling, thinking about Johnson's guess about his music. If he was right about that, then maybe he would be right about the jury convicting Jessup. As he moved down the aisle, he heard the judge telling Haller to call his next witness.

"The state calls Regina Landy."

Bosch knew he was on. This part had been choreographed a week earlier by the judge and over the objection of the defense. Regina Landy was unavailable to testify because she was dead, but she had testified in the first trial and the judge had ruled that her testimony could be read to the current jurors.

Breitman now turned to the jurors to offer the explanation, guarding against revealing any hint that there had been an earlier trial.

"Ladies and gentlemen, the state has called a witness who is no longer available to testify. However, previously she gave sworn testimony that we will read to you today. You are not to consider why this witness is unable to testify or where this previous sworn testimony is from. Your concern is the testimony itself. I should add that I have decided to allow this over the objection of the defense. The U.S. Constitution holds that the accused is entitled to question his accusers.

However, as you will see, this witness was indeed questioned by an attorney who previously represented Mr. Jessup."

She turned back to the court.

"You may proceed, Mr. Haller."

Haller called Bosch to the stand. He was sworn in and then took the seat, pulling the microphone into position. He opened the blue binder he had carried with him and Haller began.

"Detective Bosch, can you tell us a little bit about your experience as a law enforcement officer?"

Bosch turned toward the jury box and moved his eyes over the faces of the jurors as he answered. He did not leave the alternates out.

"I have been a sworn officer for thirty-six years. I have spent more than twenty-five of those years working homicides. I have been the lead investigator in more than two hundred murder investigations in that time."

"And you are the lead investigator on this case?"

"Yes, I am now. I did not take part in the original investigation, however. I came into this case in February of this year."

"Thank you, Detective. We will be talking about your investigation later in the trial. Are you prepared to read the sworn testimony of Regina Landy taken on October seventh, nineteen eighty-six?"

"I am."

"Okay, I will read the questions that were posed at the time by Deputy District Attorney Gary Lintz and defense counsel Charles Barnard and you will read the responses from the witness. We start with direct examination from Mr. Lintz."

Haller paused and studied the transcript in front of him. Bosch wondered if there would be any confusion from his reading the responses of a woman. In deciding to allow the testimony the week before, the judge had disallowed any reference to emotions described as having been exhibited by Regina Landy. Bosch knew from the transcript that she was crying throughout her testimony. But he would not be able to communicate that to the present jurors.

"Here we go," Haller said. "'Mrs. Landy, can you please describe your relationship with the victim, Melissa Landy.'"

"'I am her mother,'" Bosch read. "'She was my daughter...until she was taken away from me.'"

Twenty-seven

Monday, April 5, 1:45 P.M.

The reading of Regina Landy's testimony from the first trial took us right up to lunch. The testimony was needed to establish who the victim was and who had identified her. But without the incumbent emotion of a parent's testimony, the reading by Bosch was largely procedural, and while the first witness of the day brought reason to be hopeful, the second witness was about as anticlimactic as a voice from the grave could possibly be. I imagined that Bosch's reading of Regina Landy's words was confusing to the jurors when they were not provided with any explanation for her absence from the trial of her daughter's alleged killer.

The prosecution team had lunch at Duffy's, which was close enough to the CCB to be convenient but far enough away that we wouldn't have to worry about jurors finding the same place to eat. Nobody was ecstatic about the start of the trial but that was to be expected. I had planned the presentation of evidence like the unfolding of *Scheherazade,* the symphonic suite that starts slow and quiet and builds to an all-encompassing crescendo of sound and music and emotion.

The first day was about the proof of facts. I had to bring forward the body. I had to establish that there was a victim, that she had been taken from her home and later found dead and that she had been murdered. I had hit two of those facts with the first witnesses, and now the afternoon witness, the medical examiner, would complete the proof. The prosecution's case would then shift toward the accused and the evidence that tied him to the crime. That would be when my case would really come to life.

Only Bosch and I came back from lunch. Maggie had gone over to the Checkers Hotel to spend the afternoon with our star witness, Sarah Ann Gleason. Bosch had gone up to Washington on Saturday and flown down with her Sunday morning. She wasn't scheduled to testify until Wednesday morning but I had wanted her close and I had wanted Maggie to spend as much time as possible prepping her for her part in the trial. Maggie had already been up to Washington twice to spend time with her but I believed that any time they could spend together would continue to promote the bond I wanted them to have and the jury to see.

Maggie left us reluctantly. She was concerned that I would make a misstep in court without her there watching over me as my second. I assured her that I could handle the direct examination of a medical examiner and would call her if I ran into trouble. Little did I know how important this witness's testimony would come to be.

The afternoon session got off to a late start while we waited ten minutes for a juror who did not return from lunch on time. Once the panel was assembled and returned to court, Judge Breitman lectured the jurors again on timeliness and ordered them to eat as a group for the remainder of the trial. She also ordered the courtroom deputy to escort them to lunch. This way no one would stray from the pack and no one would be late.

Finished with the lunch business, the judge gruffly ordered me to call my next witness. I nodded to Bosch and he headed to the witness room to retrieve David Eisenbach.

The judge grew impatient as we waited but it took Eisenbach a few minutes longer than most witnesses to make his way into the courtroom and to the witness stand. Eisenbach was seventy-nine years old and walked with a cane. He also carried a pillow with a handle on it, as if he were going to a USC football game at the Coliseum. After being sworn in he placed the pillow on the hard wood of the witness chair and then sat down.

"Dr. Eisenbach," I began, "can you tell the jury what you do for a living?"

"Currently I am semiretired and derive an income from being an autopsy consultant. A *gun for hire,* you lawyers like to call it. I review autopsies for a living and then tell lawyers and juries what the medical examiner did right and did wrong."

"And before you were semiretired, what did you do?"

"I was assistant medical examiner for the county of Los Angeles. Had that job for thirty years."

"As such you conducted autopsies?"

"Yes, sir, I did. In thirty years I conducted over twenty thousand autopsies. That's a lot of dead people."

"That is a lot, Dr. Eisenbach. Do you remember them all?"

"Of course not. I remember a handful off the top of my head. The rest of them I would need my notes to remember."

After receiving permission from the judge I approached the witness stand and put down a forty-page document.

"I draw your attention to the document I have placed before you. Can you identify it?"

"Yes, it's an autopsy protocol dated February eighteenth, nineteen eighty-six. The deceased is listed as Melissa Theresa Landy. My name is also on it. It is one of mine."

"Meaning you conducted the autopsy?"

"Yes, that is what I said."

I followed this with a series of questions that established the autopsy procedures and the general health of the victim prior to death. Royce objected several times to what he termed leading questions. Few of these were sustained by the judge but that was not the point.

Royce had adopted the tactic of attempting to get me out of rhythm by incessantly interrupting, whether such interruptions were valid or not.

Working around these interruptions, Eisenbach was able to testify that Melissa Landy was in perfect health until the moment of her violent death. He said she had not been sexually attacked in any determinable way. He said there was no indication of prior sexual activity — she was a virgin. He said the cause of her death was asphyxiation. He said the evidence of crushed bones in her neck and throat indicated she had been choked by a powerful force — a man's single hand.

Using a laser pointer to mark locations on photographs of the body taken at autopsy, Eisenbach identified a bruise pattern on the victim's neck that was indicative of a one-handed choke hold. With the laser point he delineated a thumb mark on the right side of the girl's neck and the larger, four-finger mark on the left side.

"Doctor, did you make a determination of which hand the killer used to choke the victim to death?"

"Yes, it was quite simple to determine the killer had used the right hand to choke this girl to death."

"Just one hand?"

"That is correct."

"Was there any determination of how this was done? Had the girl been suspended while she was choked?"

"No, the injuries, particularly the crushed bones, indicated that the killer put his hand on her neck and pressed her against a surface that offered resistance."

"Could that have been the seat of a vehicle?"

"Yes."

"How about a man's leg?"

Royce objected, saying the question called for pure speculation. The judge agreed and told me to move on.

"Doctor, you mentioned twenty thousand autopsies. I assume that many of these were homicides involving asphyxiation. Was it unusual to come across a case where only one hand was used to choke a victim to death?"

Royce objected again, this time saying the question asked for an answer outside the witness's expertise. But the judge went my way.

"The man has conducted twenty thousand autopsies," she said. "I'm inclined to think that gives him a lot of expertise. I'm going to allow the question."

"You can answer, Doctor," I said. "Was this unusual?"

"Not necessarily. Many homicides occur during struggles and other circumstances. I've seen it before. If one hand is otherwise occupied, the other must suffice. We are talking about a twelve-year-old girl who weighed ninety-one pounds. She could have been subdued with one hand if the killer needed the left hand for something else."

"Would driving a vehicle fall into that category?"

"Objection," Royce said. "Same argument."

"And same ruling," Breitman said. "You may answer, Doctor."

"Yes," Eisenbach said. "If one hand was being used to maintain control of a vehicle the other hand could be used to choke the victim. That is one possibility."

At this point I believed I had gotten all that there was to get from Eisenbach. I ended direct examination and handed the witness over to Royce. Unfortunately for me, Eisenbach was a witness who had something for everybody. And Royce went after it.

"'One possibility,' is that what you called it, Dr. Eisenbach?"

"Excuse me?"

"You said the scenario Mr. Haller described—one hand on the wheel, one hand on the neck—was one possibility. Is that correct?"

"Yes, that is a possibility."

"But you weren't there, so you can't know for sure. Isn't that right, Doctor?"

"Yes, that is right."

"You said one possibility. What are some of the other possibilities?"

"Well...I wouldn't know. I was responding to the question from the prosecutor."

"How about a cigarette?"

"What?"

"Could the killer have been holding a cigarette in his left hand while he choked the girl with his right?"

"Yes, I suppose so. Yes."

"And how about his penis?"

"His..."

"His penis, Doctor. Could the killer have choked this girl with his right hand while holding his penis with his left?"

"I would have to...yes, that is a possibility, too."

"He could have been masturbating with one hand while he choked her with the other, correct, Doctor?"

"Anything is possible but there is no indication in the autopsy report that supports this."

"What about what is not in the file, Doctor?"

"I'm not aware of anything."

"Is this what you meant about being a hired gun, Doctor? You take the prosecution's side no matter what the facts are?"

"I don't always work for prosecutors."

"I'm happy for you."

I stood up.

"Your Honor, he's badgering the witness with—"

"Mr. Royce," the judge said. "Please keep it civil. And on point."

"Yes, Your Honor. Doctor, of the twenty thousand autopsies you have performed, how many of them were on victims of sexually motivated violence?"

Eisenbach looked across the floor to me, but there was nothing I could do for him. Bosch had taken Maggie's place at the prosecution table. He leaned over to me and whispered.

"What's he doing? Trying to make our case?"

I held up my hand so I would not be distracted from the back-and-forth between Royce and Eisenbach.

"No, he's making their case," I whispered back.

Eisenbach still hadn't answered.

"Doctor," the judge said, "please answer the question."

"I don't have a count but many of them were sexually motivated crimes."

"Was this one?"

"Based on the autopsy findings I could not make that conclusion. But whenever you have a young child, particularly a female, and there is a stranger abduction, then you are almost always —"

"Move to strike the answer as nonresponsive," Royce said, cutting the witness off. "The witness is assuming facts not in evidence."

The judge considered the objection. I stood up, ready to respond but said nothing.

"Doctor, please answer only the question you are asked," the judge said.

"I thought I was," Eisenbach said.

"Then let me be more specific," Royce said. "You found no indications of sexual assault or abuse on the body of Melissa Landy, is that correct, Doctor?"

"That is correct."

"What about on the victim's clothing?"

"The body is my jurisdiction. The clothing is analyzed by forensics."

"Of course."

Royce hesitated and looked down at his notes. I could tell he was trying to decide how far to take something. It was a case of "so far, so good — do I risk going further?"

Finally, he decided.

"Now, Doctor, a moment ago when I objected to your answer, you called this a stranger abduction. What evidence from the autopsy supported that claim?"

Eisenbach thought for a long moment and even looked down at the autopsy report in front of him.

"Doctor?"

"Uh, there is nothing I recall from the autopsy alone that supports this."

"Actually, the autopsy supports a conclusion quite the opposite, doesn't it?"

Eisenbach looked genuinely confused.

"I am not sure what you mean."

"Can I draw your attention to page eight of the autopsy protocol? The preliminary examination of the body."

Royce waited a moment until Eisenbach turned to the page. I did as well but didn't need to. I knew where Royce was going and couldn't stop him. I just needed to be ready to object at the right moment.

"Doctor, the report states that scrapings of the victim's fingernails were negative for blood and tissue. Do you see that on page eight?"

"Yes, I scraped her nails but they were clean."

"This indicates she did not scratch her attacker, her killer. Correct?"

"That would be the indication, yes."

"And this would also indicate that she knew her attack—"

"Objection!"

I was on my feet but not quick enough. Royce had gotten the suggestion out and to the jury.

"Assumes facts not in evidence," I said. "Your Honor, defense counsel is clearly attempting to plant seeds with the jury that do not exist."

"Sustained. Mr. Royce, a warning."

"Yes, Your Honor. The defense has no further questions for this prosecution witness."

Twenty-eight

Bosch knocked on the door of room 804 and looked directly at the peephole. The door was quickly opened by McPherson, who was checking her watch as she stood back to let him enter.

"Why aren't you in court with Mickey?" she asked.

Bosch entered. The room was a suite with a decent view of Grand Avenue and the back of the Biltmore. There was a couch and two chairs, one of them occupied by Sarah Ann Gleason. Bosch nodded his hello.

"Because he doesn't need me there. I'm needed here."

"What's going on?"

"Royce tipped his hand on the defense's case. I need to talk to Sarah about it."

He started toward the couch but McPherson put her hand on his arm and stopped him.

"Wait a minute. Before you talk to Sarah you talk to me. What's going on?"

Bosch nodded. She was right. He looked around but there was no place for private conversation in the suite.

"Let's take a walk."

McPherson went to the coffee table and grabbed a key card.

"We'll be right back, Sarah. Do you need anything?"

"No, I'm fine. I'll be here."

She held up a sketchpad. It would keep her company.

Bosch and McPherson left the room and took the elevator down to the lobby. There was a bar crowded with pre–happy hour drinkers but they found a private spot in a sitting area by the front door.

"Okay, how did Royce tip his hand?" McPherson asked.

"When he was cross-examining Eisenbach, he riffed off of Mickey's question about the killer using only his right hand to choke her."

"Right, while he was driving. He panicked when he heard the call on the police radio and killed her."

"Right, that's the prosecution theory. Well, Royce is already setting up a defense theory. On cross he asked whether it was possible that the killer was choking her with one hand while masturbating with the other."

She was silent as she computed this.

"This is the old prosecution theory," she said. "From the first trial. That it was murder in the commission of a sex act. Mickey and I sort of figured that once Royce got all the discovery material and learned that the DNA came from the stepfather, the defense would play it this way. They're setting up the stepfather as the straw man. They'll say he killed her and the DNA proves it."

McPherson folded her arms as she worked it out further.

"It's good but there are two things wrong with it. Sarah and the hair evidence. So we're missing something. Royce has got to have something or someone who discredits Sarah's ID."

"That's why I'm here. I brought Royce's witness list. These people have been playing hide-and-seek with me and I haven't run them all down. Sarah's got to look at this list and tell me which one I need to focus on."

"How the hell will she know?"

"She's got to. These are her people. Boyfriends, husbands, fellow tweakers. All of them have records. They're the people she hung out with before she got straight. Every address is a last-known and worth-less. Royce has got to be hiding them."

McPherson nodded.

"That's why they call him Clever Clive. Okay, let's talk to her. Let me try first, okay?"

She stood up.

"Wait a minute," Bosch said.

She looked at him.

"What is it?"

"What if the defense theory is the right one?"

"Are you kidding me?"

He didn't answer and she didn't wait long. She headed back toward the elevator. He got up and followed.

They went back to the room. Bosch noticed that Gleason had sketched a tulip on her pad while they had been gone. He sat down on the couch across from her, and McPherson took the chair right next to her.

"Sarah," McPherson said. "We need to talk. We think that some-body you used to know during those lost years we were talking about is going to try to help the defense. We need to figure out who it is and what they are going to say."

"I don't understand," Sarah said. "But I was thirteen years old when this happened to us. What does it matter who my friends were after?"

"It matters because they can testify about things you might have done. Or said."

"What things?"

McPherson shook her head.

"That's what is so frustrating. We don't really know. We only know that today in court the defense made it clear that they are going to try to put the blame for your sister's death on your stepfather."

Sarah raised her hands as if warding off a blow.

"That's crazy. I was there. I saw that man take her!"

"We know that, Sarah. But it's a matter of what is conveyed to the jury and what and who the jurors believe. Now, Detective Bosch has a list of the defense's witnesses. I want you to take a look at it and tell us what the names mean to you."

Bosch pulled the list from his briefcase. He handed it to McPherson, who handed it to Sarah.

"Sorry, all those notes are things I added," Bosch said, "when I was trying to track them down. Just look at the names."

Bosch watched her lips move slightly as she started to read. Then they stopped moving and she just stared at the paper. He saw tears in her eyes.

"Sarah?" McPherson prompted.

"These people," Gleason said in a whisper. "I thought I'd never see them again."

"You may never see them again," McPherson said. "Just because they're on that list, it doesn't mean they'll be called. They pull names out of the records and load up the list to confuse us, Sarah. It's called *haystacking*. They hide the real witnesses, and our investigator — Detective Bosch — wastes his time checking out the wrong people. But there's got to be at least one name on there that counts. Who is it, Sarah? Help us."

She stared at the list without responding.

"Someone who will be able to say you two were close. Who you spent time with and told secrets to."

"I thought a husband couldn't testify against a wife."

"One spouse can't be forced to testify against the other. But what are you talking about, Sarah?"

"This one."

She pointed to a name on the list. Bosch leaned over to read it. Edward Roman. Bosch had traced him to a lockdown rehab center in North Hollywood where Sarah had spent nine months after her last incarceration. The only thing Bosch had guessed was that they'd had contact in group therapy. The last known address provided by Royce was a motel in Van Nuys but Roman was long gone from there. Bosch had gotten no further with it and had dismissed the name as part of Royce's haystack.

"Roman," he said. "You were with him in rehab, right?"

"Yes," Gleason said. "Then we got married."

"When?" McPherson said. "We have no record of that marriage."

"After we got out. He knew a minister. We got married on the beach. But it didn't last very long."

"Did you get divorced?" McPherson asked.

"No...I never really cared. Then when I got straight I just didn't want to go back there. It was one of those things you block out. Like it didn't happen."

McPherson looked at Bosch.

"It might not have been a legal marriage," he said. "There's nothing in the county records."

"Doesn't matter if it was a legal marriage or not," she said. "He is obviously a volunteer witness, so he can testify against her. What matters is what his testimony is going to be. What's he going to say, Sarah?"

Sarah slowly shook her head.

"I don't know."

"Well, what did you tell him about your sister and your stepfather?"

"I don't know. Those years...I can hardly remember anything from back then."

There was a silence and then McPherson asked Sarah to look at the rest of the names on the list. She did and shook her head.

"I don't know who some of these people are. Some people in the life, I just knew them by street names."

"But Edward Roman you know?"

"Yes. We were together."

"How long?"

Gleason shook her head in embarrassment.

"Not long. Inside rehab we thought we were made for each other. Once we were out, it didn't work. It lasted maybe three months. I got arrested again and when I got out of jail, he was gone."

"Is it possible that it wasn't a legitimate marriage?"

Gleason thought for a moment and halfheartedly shrugged.

"Anything is possible, I guess."

"Okay, Sarah, I'm going to step out with Detective Bosch again for a few minutes. I want you to think about Edward Roman. Anything you can remember will be helpful. I'll be right back."

McPherson took the witness list from her and handed it back to Bosch. They left the room but just took a few paces down the hallway before stopping and talking in whispers.

"I guess you'd better find him," she said.

"It won't matter," Bosch said. "If he's Royce's star witness he won't talk to me."

"Then find out everything you can about him. So when the time comes we can destroy him."

"Got it."

Bosch turned and headed down the hall toward the elevators. McPherson called after him. He stopped and looked back.

"Did you mean it?" McPherson asked.

"Mean what?"

"What you said down in the lobby. What you asked. You think twenty-four years ago she made it all up?"

Bosch looked at her for a long moment, then shrugged.

"I don't know."

"Well, what about the hair in the truck? Doesn't that tie her story in?"

Bosch held a hand up empty.

"It's circumstantial. And I wasn't there when they found it."

"What's that supposed to mean?"

"It means sometimes things happen when the victim is a child. And that I wasn't there when they found it."

"Boy, maybe you should be working for the defense."

Bosch dropped his hand to his side.

"I'm sure they've thought of all of this already."

He turned back toward the elevators and headed down the hallway.

Twenty-nine

Tuesday, April 6, 9:00 A.M.

Sometimes the wheels of justice roll smoothly. The second day of trial started exactly as scheduled. The full jury was in the box, the judge was on the bench and Jason Jessup and his attorney were seated at the defense table. I stood and called my first witness of what I hoped would be a productive day for the prosecution. Harry Bosch even had Izzy Gordon in the courtroom ready to go. By five minutes after the hour, she was sworn in and seated. She was a small woman with black-framed glasses that magnified her eyes. My records said she was fifty years old but she looked older.

"Ms. Gordon, can you tell the jury what you do for a living?"

"Yes. I am a forensic technician and crime scene supervisor for the Los Angeles Police Department. I have been so employed in the forensics unit since nineteen eighty-six."

"Were you so employed on February sixteenth of that year?"

"Yes, I was. It was my first day of work."

"And what was your assignment on that day?"

"My job was to learn. I was assigned to a crime scene supervisor and I was to get on-the-job training."

Izzy Gordon was a major find for the prosecution. Two technicians and a supervisor had worked the three separate crime scenes relating to the Melissa Landy case—the home on Windsor, the trash bin behind the El Rey and the tow truck driven by Jessup. Gordon had been assigned to be at the supervisor's side and therefore had been in attendance at all three crime scenes. The supervisor was long since dead and the other techs were retired and unable to offer testimony about all three locations. Finding Gordon allowed me to streamline the introduction of crime scene evidence.

"Who was that supervisor?"

"That was Art Donovan."

"And you got a call out with him that day?"

"Yes, we did. An abduction that turned into a homicide. We ended up going from scene to scene to scene that day. Three related locations."

"Okay, let's take those scenes one at a time."

Over the next ninety minutes I walked Gordon through her Sunday tour of crime scenes on February 16, 1986. Using her as the conduit, I could deliver crime scene photographs, videos and evidence reports. Royce continued his tack of objecting at will in an effort to prevent the unimpeded flow of information to the jury. But he was scoreless and getting under the judge's skin. I could tell, and so I did not complain. I wanted that annoyance to fester. It might come in handy later.

Gordon's testimony was fairly pedestrian as she first discussed the unsuccessful efforts to find shoe prints and other trace evidence on the front lawn of the Landy's house. It turned more dramatic when she recalled being urgently called to a new crime scene—the trash bin behind the El Rey.

"We were called when they found the body. It was handled in whispers because the family was there in the house and we did not want to upset them until it was confirmed that there was a body and that it was the little girl."

"You and Donovan went to the El Rey Theatre?"

"Yes, along with Detective Kloster. We met the assistant medical examiner there. We now had a homicide, so more technicians were called in, too."

The El Rey portion of Gordon's testimony was largely an opportunity for me to show more video footage and photographs of the victim on the overhead screens. If nothing else, I wanted every juror in the box to be incensed by what they saw. I wanted to light the fire of one of the basic instincts. Vengeance.

I counted on Royce to object and he did, but by then he had exhausted his welcome with the judge, and his argument that the images were graphic and cumulatively excessive fell on deaf ears. They were allowed.

Finally, Izzy Gordon brought us to the last crime scene — the tow truck — and she described how she had spotted three long hairs caught in the crack that split the bench seat and pointed them out to Donovan for collection.

"What happened to those hairs?" I asked.

"They were individually bagged and tagged and then taken to the Scientific Investigation Division for comparison and analysis."

Gordon's testimony was smooth and efficient. When I turned her over to the defense, Royce did the best he could. He did not bother to assail the collection of evidence but merely attempted once again to gain a foothold for the defense theory. In doing so he skipped the first two crime scenes and zeroed in on the tow truck.

"Ms. Gordon, when you got to the Aardvark towing yard, were there police officers already there?"

"Yes, of course."

"How many?"

"I didn't count but there were several."

"What about detectives?"

"Yes, there were detectives conducting a search of the whole business under the authority of a search warrant."

"And were these detectives you had seen earlier at the previous crime scenes?"

"I think so, yes. I would assume so but I do not remember specifically."

"But you seem to remember other things specifically. Why don't you remember which detectives you were working with?"

"There were several people working this case. Detective Kloster was the lead investigator but he was dealing with three different locations as well as the girl who was the witness. I don't remember if he was at the tow yard when I first arrived but he was there at some point. I think that if you refer to the crime scene attendance logs, you will be able to determine who was at what scene and when."

"Ah, then we shall do just that."

Royce approached the witness stand and gave Gordon three documents and a pencil. He then returned to the lectern.

"What are those three documents, Ms. Gordon?"

"These are crime scene attendance logs."

"And which scenes are they from?"

"The three I worked in regard to the Landy case."

"Can you please take a moment to study those logs and use the pencil I have given you to circle any name that appears on all three lists."

It took Gordon less than a minute to complete the task.

"Finished?" Royce asked.

"Yes, there are four names."

"Can you tell us?"

"Yes, myself and my supervisor, Art Donovan, and then Detective Kloster and his partner, Chad Steiner."

"You were the only four who were at all three crime scenes that day, correct?"

"That is correct."

Maggie leaned into me and whispered.

"Cross-scene contamination."

I shook my head slightly and whispered back.

"That suggests accidental contamination. I think he's going for intentional planting of evidence."

Maggie nodded and leaned away. Royce asked his next question.

"Being one of only four who were at all four scenes, you had a keen understanding of this crime and what it meant, isn't that correct?"

"I'm not sure what you mean."

"Among police personnel, were emotions high at these crime scenes?"

"Well, everyone was very professional."

"You mean nobody cared that this was a twelve-year-old girl?"

"No, we cared and you could say things were at least tense at the first two scenes. We had the family at one and the dead little girl at the other. I don't really remember things being emotional at the tow yard."

Wrong answer, I thought. She had opened a door for the defense.

"Okay," Royce said, "but you are saying that at the first two scenes the emotions were high, correct?"

I stood up, just to give Royce a dose of his own medicine.

"Objection. Asked and answered already, Your Honor."

"Sustained."

Royce was undaunted.

"Then how did these emotions display themselves?" he asked.

"Well, we talked. Art Donovan told me to keep professional detachment. He said we had to do our best work because this had been just a little girl."

"What about detectives Kloster and Steiner?"

"They said the same thing. That we couldn't leave any stone unturned, that we had to do it for Melissa."

"He called the victim by her name?"

"Yes, I remember that."

"How angry and upset would you say Detective Kloster was?"

I stood and objected.

"Assumes facts not in evidence or testimony."

The judge sustained it and told Royce to move on.

"Ms. Gordon, can you refer to the crime scene attendance logs still in front of you and tell us if the arrival and departure of law enforcement personnel is kept by time?"

"Yes, it is. There are arrival and departure times listed after each name."

"You have previously stated that detectives Kloster and Steiner were the only two investigators besides yourself and your supervisor to appear at all three scenes."

"Yes, they were the lead investigators on the case."

"Did they arrive at each of the scenes before you and Mr. Donovan?"

It took Gordon a moment to confirm the information on the lists.

"Yes, they did."

"So they would have had access to the victim's body before you ever arrived at the El Rey Theatre, correct?"

"I don't know what you mean by 'access' but, yes, they were on scene first."

"And so they would have also had access to the tow truck before you got there and saw the three strands of hair conveniently caught in the seat crack, correct?"

I objected, saying the question required the witness to speculate on things she would not have witnessed and was argumentative because of the use of the word "conveniently." Royce was obviously playing to the jury. The judge told Royce to rephrase the question without taking editorial license.

"The detectives would have had access to the tow truck before you got there and before you were the first to see the three strands of hair lodged in the seat crack, correct?"

Gordon took the hint from my objection and answered the way I wanted her to.

"I don't know because I wasn't there."

Still, Royce had gotten his point across to the jury. He had also gotten the point of his case across to me. It was now fair to assume that the defense would put forth the theory that the police—in the person of Kloster and/or his partner, Steiner — had planted the hair evidence to secure a conviction of Jessup after he had been identified by the thirteen-year-old Sarah. Further to this, the defense would posit that Sarah's wrongful identification of Jessup was intentional and part of the Landy family's effort to hide the fact that Melissa had died either accidentally or intentionally at the hands of her stepfather.

It would be a tough road to take. To be successful it would take at least one person on the jury buying into what amounted to two conspiracies working independently of one another and yet in concert. But I could think of only two defense attorneys in town who could pull it off, and Royce was one of them. I had to be prepared.

"What happened after you noticed the hair on the tow truck's seat, do you remember?" Royce asked the witness.

"I pointed it out to Art because he was doing the actual collection of evidence. I was just there to observe and gather experience."

"Were detectives Kloster and Steiner called over to take a look?"

"Yes, I believe so."

"Do you recall what if anything they did then?"

"I don't recall them doing anything in relation to the hair evidence. It was their case and so they were notified of the evidence find and that was it."

"Were you happy with yourself?"

"I don't think I understand."

"It was your first day on the job — your first case. Were you pleased with yourself after spotting the hair evidence? Were you proud?"

Gordon hesitated before answering, as if trying to figure out if the question was a trap.

"I was pleased that I had contributed, yes."

"And did you ever wonder why you, the rookie, spotted the hair in the seat crack before your supervisor or the two lead investigators?"

Gordon hesitated again and then said no. Royce said he had no further questions. It had been an excellent cross, planting multiple seeds that could later bloom into something larger in the defense case.

I did what I could on redirect, asking Gordon to recite the names of the six uniformed police officers and two other detectives who were listed as arriving ahead of Kloster and Steiner on the crime scene attendance log kept at the location where Melissa Landy's body was found.

"So, hypothetically, if Detective Kloster or Steiner had wanted to take hair from the victim to plant elsewhere, they would have had to do it under the noses of eight other officers or enlist them in allowing them to do it. Is that correct?"

"Yes, it would seem so."

I thanked the witness and sat down. Royce then went back to the lectern for recross.

"Also hypothetically, if Kloster or Steiner wanted to plant hair from the victim at the third crime scene, it would not have been necessary to take it directly from the victim's head if there were other sources for it, correct?"

"I guess not if there were other sources."

"For example, a hairbrush in the victim's home could have provided hair to them, correct?"

"I guess so."

"They were in the victim's home, weren't they?"

"Yes, that was one of the locations where they signed in."

"Nothing further."

Royce had nailed me and I decided not to pursue this any further. Royce would have a comeback no matter what I brought forward from the witness.

Gordon was dismissed and the judge broke for lunch. I told Bosch that he would be on the stand after the break, reading Kloster's testimony into the record. I asked if he wanted to grab lunch together to talk about the defense's theory but he said he couldn't, that he had something to do.

Maggie was heading over to the hotel to have lunch with Sarah Ann Gleason, so that left me on my own.

Or so I thought.

As I headed down the center aisle to the rear door of the courtroom, an attractive woman stepped out of the back row in front of me. She smiled and stepped up to me.

"Mr. Haller, I'm Rachel Walling with the FBI."

At first it didn't compute but then the name caught on a memory prompt somewhere inside.

"Yes, the profiler. You distracted my investigator with your theory that Jason Jessup is a serial killer."

"Well, I hope it was more help than distraction."

"I guess that remains to be seen. What can I do for you, Agent Walling?"

"I was going to ask if you might have time for lunch. But since you consider me a distraction, then maybe I should just..."

"Guess what, Agent Walling. You're in luck. I'm free. Let's have lunch."

I pointed to the door and we headed out.

Thirty

This time it was the judge who was late returning to court. The prosecution and defense teams were seated at the appointed time and ready to go but there was no sign of Breitman. And there had been no indication from the clerk as to whether the delay was because of personal business or some sort of trial issue. Bosch got up from his seat at the railing and approached Haller, tapping him on the back.

"Harry, we're about to start. You ready?"

"I'm ready, but we need to talk."

"What's wrong?"

Bosch turned his body so his back was to the defense table and lowered his voice into a barely audible whisper.

"I went to see the SIS guys at lunch. They showed me some stuff you need to know about."

He was being overly cryptic. But the photos Lieutenant Wright had showed him from the surveillance the night before were troubling. Jessup was up to something and whatever it might be, it was going to go down soon.

Before Haller could respond, the background hubbub of the courtroom ceased as the judge took the bench.

"After court," Haller whispered.

He then turned back to the front of the courtroom and Bosch returned to his seat at the railing. The judge told the deputy to seat the jury and soon everyone was in place.

"I want to apologize," Breitman said. "This delay was my responsibility. I had a personal matter come up and it took far longer than I expected it would. Mr. Haller, please call your next witness."

Haller stood and called for Doral Kloster. Bosch stood and headed for the witness stand while the judge once again explained to the jury that the witness called by the prosecution was unavailable and that prior sworn testimony would be read by Bosch and Haller. Though all of this had been worked out in a pretrial hearing and over the objection of the defense, Royce stood once again and objected.

"Mr. Royce, we've already argued this issue," the judge responded.

"I would ask that the court reconsider its ruling as this form of testimony entirely undercuts Mr. Jessup's Constitutional right to confront his accusers. Detective Kloster was not asked the questions I would want to ask him based on the defense's current view of the case."

"Again, Mr. Royce, this issue has been settled and I do not wish to rehash it in front of the jury."

"But, *Your Honor,* I am being inhibited from presenting a full defense."

"Mr. Royce, I have been very generous in allowing you to posture in front of the jury. My patience is now growing thin. You may sit down."

Royce stared the judge down. Bosch knew what he was doing. Playing to the jury. He wanted them to see him and Jessup as the underdogs. He wanted them to understand that it was not just the prosecution against Jessup but the judge as well. When he had drawn out the stare as long as he dared, he spoke again.

"Judge, I cannot sit down when my client's freedom is at stake. This is an egregious —"

Breitman angrily slammed her hand down, making a sound as loud as a shot.

"We're not going to do this in front of the jury, Mr. Royce. Will the jurors please return to the assembly room."

Wide-eyed and alert to the tension that had engulfed the courtroom, the jurors filed out, to a person glancing back over their shoulders to check the action behind them. The whole time, Royce held his glare on the judge. And Bosch knew it was mostly an act. This was exactly what Royce wanted, for the jury to see him being persecuted and prevented from bringing his case forward. It didn't matter that they would be sequestered in the jury room. They all knew that Royce was about to get slapped down hard by the judge.

Once the door to the jury assembly room was closed, the judge turned back to Royce. In the thirty seconds it had taken the jury to leave the courtroom, she had obviously calmed down.

"Mr. Royce, at the end of the trial we will be holding a contempt hearing during which your actions today will be examined and penalized. Until then, if I ever order you to sit down and you refuse that order, I will have the courtroom deputy forcibly place you in your seat. And it will not matter to me if the jury is present or not. Do you understand?"

"Yes, Your Honor. And I would like to apologize for allowing the emotions of the moment to get the best of me."

"Very well, Mr. Royce. You will now sit down and we'll bring the jury back in."

They held each other's eyes for a long moment until Royce finally and slowly sat down. The judge then told the courtroom deputy to retrieve the jury.

Bosch glanced at the jurors as they returned. They all had their eyes on Royce, and Harry could see the defense attorney's gambit had worked. He saw sympathy in their eyes, as if they all knew that at any moment they might cross the judge and be similarly rebuked. They didn't know what happened while they were behind the closed door, but Royce was like the kid who had been sent to the principal's office and had returned to tell everyone about it at recess.

The judge addressed the jury before continuing the trial.

"I want the members of the jury to understand that in a trial of this nature emotions sometimes run high. Mr. Royce and I have discussed the issue and it is resolved. You are to pay it no mind. So, let's proceed with the reading of prior sworn testimony. Mr. Haller?"

"Yes, Your Honor."

Haller stood and went to the lectern with his printout of Doral Kloster's testimony.

"Detective Bosch, you are still under oath. Do you have the transcript of sworn testimony provided by Detective Doral Kloster on October eighth, nineteen eighty-six?"

"Yes, I do."

Bosch placed the transcript on the stand and took a pair of reading glasses out of his jacket's inside pocket.

"Okay, then once again I will read the questions that were posed to Detective Kloster under oath by Deputy District Attorney Gary Lintz, and you will read the responses from the witness."

After a series of questions used to elicit basic information about Kloster, the testimony moved quickly into the investigation of the murder of Melissa Landy.

"'Now, Detective, you are assigned to the detective squad at Wilshire Division, correct?'"

"'Yes, I am on the Homicide and Major Crimes table.'"

"'And this case did not start out as a homicide.'"

"'No, it did not. My partner and I were called in from home after patrol units were dispatched to the Landy house and a preliminary investigation determined that it appeared to be a stranger abduction. That made it a major crime and we were called out.'"

"'What happened when you got to the Landy house?'"

"'We initially separated the individuals there — the mother, father and Sarah, the sister — and conducted interviews. We then brought the family together and conducted a joint interview. It often works best that way and it did this time. In the joint interview we found our investigative direction.'"

"'Tell us about that. How did you find this direction?'"

"'In the individual interview, Sarah revealed that the girls had been playing a hide-and-seek game and that she was hiding behind some bushes at the front corner of her house. These bushes blocked her view of the street. She said she heard a trash truck and saw a trash-man cross the yard and grab her sister. These events occurred on a Sunday, so we knew there was no city trash pickup. But when I had Sarah recount this story in front of her parents, her father quickly said that on Sunday mornings several tow trucks patrol the neighborhood and that the drivers wear overalls like the city sanitation workers do. And that became our first lead.'"

"'And how did you follow that lead?'"

"'We were able to obtain a list of city-licensed tow truck compa-nies that operated in the Wilshire District. By this time I had called in more detectives and we split the list up. There were only three compa-nies that were operating on that day. Each pair of detectives took one. My partner and I went to a tow yard on La Brea Boulevard that was operated by a business called Aardvark Towing.'"

"'And what happened when you got there?'"

"'We found that they were about to shut down for the day because they essentially worked no-parking zones around churches. By noon they were done. There were three drivers and they were securing things and about to head out when we got there. They all voluntarily agreed to identify themselves and answer our questions. While my partner asked preliminary questions I went back to our car and called their names into central dispatch so they could check them for criminal records.'"

"'Who were these men, Detective Kloster?'"

"'Their names were William Clinton, Jason Jessup and Derek Wilbern.'"

" 'And what was the result of your records search?' "

" 'Only Wilbern had an arrest record. It was an attempted rape with no conviction. The case, as I recall, was four years old.' "

" 'Did this make him a suspect in the Melissa Landy abduction?' "

" 'Yes, it did. He generally fit the description we had gotten from Sarah. He drove a large truck and wore overalls. And he had an arrest record involving a sex crime. That made him a strong suspect in my mind.' "

" 'What did you do next?' "

" 'I returned to my partner and he was still interviewing the men in a group setting. I knew that time was of the essence. This little girl was still missing. She was still out there somewhere and usually in a case like this, the longer the individual is missing, the less chance you have of a good ending.' "

" 'So you made some decisions, didn't you?' "

" 'Yes, I decided that Sarah Landy ought to see Derek Wilbern to see if she could identify him as the abductor.' "

" 'So did you set up a lineup for her to view?' "

" 'No, I didn't.' "

" 'No?' "

" 'No. I didn't feel there was time. I had to keep things moving. We had to try to find that girl. So what I did was ask if the three men would agree to go to a separate location where we could continue the interview. They each said yes.' "

" 'No hesitation?' "

" 'No, none. They agreed.' "

" 'By the way, what happened when the other detectives visited the other towing companies that worked in the Wilshire District?' "

" 'They did not find or interview anyone who rose to the level of suspect.' "

" 'You mean no one with a criminal record?' "

" 'No criminal records and no flags came up during interviews.' "

" 'So you were concentrating on Derek Wilbern?' "

" 'That's right.' "

" 'So when Wilbern and the other two men agreed to be interviewed at another location, what did you do?' "

" 'We called for a couple of patrol cruisers and we put Jessup and Clinton in the back of one car and Wilbern in the back of the other. We then closed and locked the Aardvark tow yard and drove ahead in our car.' "

" 'So you got back to the Landy house first?' "

" 'By design. We had told the patrol officers to take a circuitous route to the Landy house on Windsor so we could get there first. When we arrived back at the house I took Sarah upstairs to her bedroom, which was located at the front and was overlooking the front yard and street. I closed the blinds and had her look through just a crack so she would not be visibly exposed to the tow truck drivers.' "

" 'What happened next?' "

" 'My partner had stayed out front. When the patrol cruisers arrived, I had him take the three men out of the cars and have them stand together on the sidewalk. I asked Sarah if she recognized any of them.' "

" 'Did she?' "

" 'Not at first. But one of the men — Jessup — was wearing a baseball hat and he was looking down, using the brim to guard his face.' "

Bosch flipped over two pages of the testimony at this point. The pages had been X-ed out. They contained several questions about Jessup's demeanor and attempt to use his hat to hide his face. These questions were objected to by Jessup's then-defense counsel, sustained by the trial judge, then resculpted and reasked, and objected to again. In the pretrial hearing, Breitman had agreed with Royce's contention that the current jury should not even hear them. It was one of the only points Royce had won.

Haller picked up the reading at the point the skirmish had ended.

" 'Okay, Detective, why don't you tell the jury what happened next?' "

" 'Sarah asked me if I could ask the man with the hat to remove it.

I radioed my partner and he told Jessup to take off the hat. Almost immediately, Sarah said it was him.'"

"'The man who abducted her sister?'"

"'Yes.'"

"'Wait a minute. You said Derek Wilbern was your suspect.'"

"'Yes, based on his having a record of a prior arrest for a sex crime, I thought he was the most likely suspect.'"

"'Was Sarah sure of her identification?'"

"'I asked her several times to confirm the identification. She did.'"

"'What did you do next?'"

"'I left Sarah in her room and went back downstairs. When I got outside I placed Jason Jessup under arrest, handcuffed him and put him in the back of a patrol car. I told other officers to put Wilbern and Clinton in another car and take them down to Wilshire Division for questioning.'"

"'Did you question Jason Jessup at this point?'"

"'Yes, I did. Again, time was of the essence. I didn't feel that I had the time to take him to Wilshire Division and set up a formal interview. Instead, I got in the car with him, read him the Miranda warning and asked if he would talk to me. He said yes.'"

"'Did you record this?'"

"'No, I did not. Frankly, I forgot. Things were moving so quickly and all I could think about was finding that little girl. I had a recorder in my pocket but I forgot to record this conversation.'"

"'Okay, so you questioned Jessup anyway?'"

"'I asked questions but he gave very few answers. He denied any involvement in the abduction. He acknowledged that he had been on tow patrol in the neighborhood that morning and could have driven by the Landy house but that he did not remember specifically driving on Windsor. I asked him if he remembered seeing the Hollywood sign, because if you are on Windsor you have a straight view of it up the street and on top of the hill. He said he didn't remember seeing the Hollywood sign.'"

"'How long did this questioning go on?'"

"'Not long. Maybe five minutes. We were interrupted.'"

"'By what, Detective?'"

"'My partner knocked on the car's window and I could tell by his face that whatever he had was important. I got out of the car and that's when he told me. They had found her. A girl's body had been found in a Dumpster down on Wilshire.'"

"'That changed everything?'"

"'Yes, everything. I had Jessup transported downtown and booked while I proceeded to the location of the body.'"

"'What did you discover when you got there?'"

"'There was a body of a girl approximately twelve or thirteen years old discarded in the Dumpster. She was unidentified at that time but she appeared to be Melissa Landy. I had her photograph. I was pretty sure it was her.'"

"'And you moved the focus of your investigation to this location?'"

"'Absolutely. My partner and I started conducting interviews while the crime scene people and coroner's people dealt with the body. We soon learned that the parking lot adjacent to the rear yard of the theater had previously been used as a temporary auto storage point by a towing company. We learned that company was Aardvark Towing.'"

"'What did that mean to you?'"

"'To me it meant there was now a second connection between the murder of this girl and Aardvark. We had the lone witness, Sarah Landy, identifying one of the Aardvark drivers as the abductor, and now we had the victim found in a Dumpster next to a parking lot used by Aardvark drivers. To me the case was coming together.'"

"'What was your next step?'"

"'At that point my partner and I split up. He stayed with the crime scene and I went back to Wilshire Division to work on search warrants.'"

"'Search warrants for what?'"

"'One for the entire premises at Aardvark Towing. One for the tow truck Jessup was driving that day. And two more for Jessup's home and personal car.'"

"'And did you receive these search warrants?'"

"'Yes, I did. Judge Richard Pittman was on call and he happened to be playing golf at Wilshire Country Club. I brought him the warrants and he signed them on the ninth hole. We then began the searches, starting at Aardvark.'"

"'Were you present at this search?'"

"'Yes, I was. My partner and I were in charge of it.'"

"'And at some point did you become aware of any particular evidence being found that you deemed important to the case?'"

"'Yes. At one point the forensics team leader, a man named Art Donovan, informed me that they had recovered three hairs that were brown in color and over a foot in length each from the tow truck that Jason Jessup was driving that day.'"

"'Did Donovan tell you specifically where in the truck these hair specimens were found?'"

"'Yes, he said they were caught in the crack between the lower and upper parts of the truck's bench seat.'"

Bosch closed the transcript there. Kloster's testimony continued but they had reached the point where Haller had said he would stop because he would have all he needed on the record.

The judge then asked Royce if he wished to have any of the defense's cross-examination read into the record. Royce stood to respond, holding two paper-clipped documents in his hand.

"For the record, I am reluctant to participate in a procedure I object to but since the court is calling the game, I shall play along. I have two brief read-backs of Detective Kloster's cross-examination. May I give a highlighted printout to Detective Bosch? I think it will make this much easier."

"Very well," the judge said.

The courtroom deputy took one of the documents from Royce and delivered it to Bosch, who quickly scanned it. It was only two pages of testimony transcriptions. Two exchanges were highlighted in yellow. As Bosch read them over, the judge explained to the jury that Royce would read questions posed by Jessup's previous defense attorney, Charles Barnard, while Bosch would continue to read the responses of Detective Doral Kloster.

"You may proceed, Mr. Royce."

"Thank you, Your Honor. Now reading from the transcript, 'Detective, how long was it from when you closed and locked Aardvark Towing and took the three drivers over to Windsor, and returned with the search warrant?'"

"'May I refer to the case chronology?'"

"'You may.'"

"'It was about two hours and thirty-five minutes.'"

"'And when you left Aardvark Towing, how did you secure those premises?'"

"'We closed the garages, and one of the drivers—I believe, Mr. Clinton—had a key to the door. I borrowed it to lock the door.'"

"'Did you return the key to him after?'"

"'No, I asked if I could keep it for the time being and he said that was okay.'"

"'So when you went back with the signed search warrant, you had the key and you simply unlocked the door to enter.'"

"'That is correct.'"

Royce flipped the page on his copy and told Bosch to do likewise.

"Okay, now reading from another point in the cross-examination. 'Detective Kloster, what did you conclude when you were told about the hair specimens found in the tow truck Mr. Jessup had been driving that day?'"

"'Nothing. The specimens had not been identified yet.'"

"'At what later point were they identified?'"

"'Two days later I got a call from SID. A hair-and-fiber tech told me that the hairs had been examined and that they closely matched samples taken from the victim. She said that she could not exclude the victim as a source.' "

" 'So then what did that tell you?' "

" 'That it was likely that Melissa Landy had been in that tow truck.' "

" 'What other evidence in that truck linked the victim to it or Mr. Jessup to the victim?' "

" 'There was no other evidence.' "

" 'No blood or other bodily fluids?' "

" 'No.' "

" 'No fibers from the victim's dress?' "

" 'No.' "

" 'Nothing else?' "

" 'Nothing.' "

" 'With the lack of other corroborating evidence in the truck, did you ever consider that the hair evidence was planted in the truck?' "

" 'Well, I considered it in the way I considered all aspects of the case. But I dismissed it because the witness to the abduction had identified Jessup, and that was the truck he was driving. I didn't think the evidence was planted. I mean, by who? No one was trying to set him up. He was identified by the victim's sister.' "

That ended the read-back. Bosch glanced over at the jury box and saw that it appeared that everyone had remained attentive during what was most likely the most boring stage of the trial.

"Anything further, Mr. Royce?" the judge asked.

"Nothing further, Judge," Royce responded.

"Very well," Breitman said. "I think this brings us to our afternoon break. I will see everyone back in place — and I will admonish myself to be on time — in fifteen minutes."

The courtroom started to clear and Bosch stepped down from the witness stand. He went directly to Haller, who was huddled with McPherson. Bosch butted into their whispered conversation.

"Atwater, right?"

Haller looked up at him.

"Yes, right. Have her ready in fifteen minutes."

"And you have time to talk after court?"

"I'll make time. I had an interesting conversation at lunch, as well. I need to tell you."

Bosch left them and headed out to the hall. He knew the line at the coffee urn in the little concession stand near the elevators would be long and full of jurors from the case. He decided he would hit the stairwell and find coffee on another floor. But first he ducked into the restroom.

As he entered he saw Jessup at one of the sinks. He was leaning over and washing his hands. His eyes were below the mirror line and he didn't realize Bosch was behind him.

Bosch stood still and waited for the moment, thinking about what he would say when he and Jessup locked eyes.

But just as Jessup raised his head and saw Bosch in the mirror, the door to a stall to the left opened and juror number ten stepped out. It was an awkward moment as all three men said nothing.

Finally, Jessup grabbed a paper towel out of the dispenser, dried his hands and tossed it into the wastebasket. He headed to the door while the juror took his place at the sink. Bosch moved silently to a urinal but looked back at Jessup as he was pushing through the door.

Bosch shot him in the back with his finger. Jessup never saw it coming.

Thirty-one

During the break I checked on my next witness and made sure she was good to go. I had a few spare minutes, so I tracked Bosch down in the line at the coffee concession one floor down. Juror number six was two spots in front of him. I took Bosch by the elbow and led him away.

"You can get your coffee later. There's no time to drink it anyway. I wanted you to know that I had lunch with your girlfriend from the bureau."

"What? Who?"

"Agent Walling."

"She's not my girlfriend. Why did she have lunch with you?"

I led him to the stairwell and we headed back upstairs as we talked.

"Well, I think she wanted to have lunch with you but you split out of here too fast so she settled for me. She wanted to give us a warning. She said she's been watching and reading the reports on the trial and she thinks if Jessup is going to blow, it's going to be soon. She said he reacts to pressure and he's probably never been under more than he is right now."

Bosch nodded.

"That's sort of what I wanted to talk to you about before."

He looked around to make sure that no one was in earshot.

"The SIS says Jessup's nighttime activities have increased since the start of the trial. He's going out every night now."

"Has he gone down your street?"

"No, he hasn't been back there or to any of the other spots off Mulholland in a week. But over the last two nights he's done things that are new."

"Like what, Harry?"

"Like on Sunday they followed him down the beach from Venice and he went into the old storage area under the Santa Monica Pier."

"What storage area? What's this mean?"

"It's an old city storage facility but it got flooded by high tides so many times it's locked up and abandoned. Jessup dug underneath one of the old wood sidings and crawled in."

"Why?"

"Who knows? They couldn't go in or they would risk exposing the surveillance. But that's not the real news. The real news is, last night he met with a couple of guys at the Townhouse in Venice and then went out to a car in one of the beach lots. One of the guys took something wrapped in a towel out of the trunk and gave it to him."

"A gun?"

Bosch shrugged.

"Whatever it was, they never saw, but through the car's plates they IDed one of the two guys. Marshall Daniels. He was in San Quentin in the nineties — same time as Jessup."

I was now catching some of the tension and urgency that was coming off Bosch.

"They could've known each other. What was Daniels up there for?"

"Drugs and weapons."

I checked my watch. I needed to be back in court.

"Then we have to assume Jessup has a weapon. We could violate his OR right now for associating with a convicted felon. Do they have pictures of Jessup and Daniels together?"

"They have photos but I am not sure we want to do that."

"If he's got a gun...Do you trust the SIS to stop him before he makes a move or does some damage?"

"I do, but it would help if we knew what the move was."

We stepped out into the hallway and saw no sign of any jurors or anyone else from the trial. Everybody was back in court but me.

"We'll talk about this later. I have to get back into court or the judge will jump on my ass next. I'm not like Royce. I can't afford a contempt hearing just to make a point with the jury. Go get Atwater and bring her in."

I hurried back to Department 112 and rudely pushed around a couple of the courthouse gadflies who were moving slowly through the door. Judge Breitman had not waited for me. I saw everyone but me in place and the jury was being seated. I moved up the aisle and through the gate and slipped into the seat next to Maggie.

"That was close," she whispered. "I think the judge was hoping to even things up by holding *you* in contempt."

"Yeah, well, she may still."

The judge turned away from the jurors and noticed me at the prosecution table.

"Well, thank you for joining us this afternoon, Mr. Haller. Did you have a nice excursion?"

I stood.

"My apologies, Your Honor. I had a personal matter come up and it took far longer than I expected it would."

She opened her mouth to deliver a rebuke but then paused as she realized I had thrown her words from the morning's delay — her delay — right back at her.

"Just call your next witness, Counselor," she said curtly.

I called Lisa Atwater to the stand and glanced to the back of the courtroom to see Bosch leading the DNA lab technician down the aisle to the gate. I checked the clock up on the rear wall. My goal was to use up the rest of the day with Atwater's testimony, bringing her to the nuts and bolts just before we recessed for the day. That might give Royce a whole night to prepare his cross-examination, but I would happily trade that for what I would get out of the deal—every juror going home with knowledge of the unimpeachable evidence that linked Jason Jessup to the murder of Melissa Landy.

As I had asked her to, Atwater had kept her lab coat on when she walked over from the LAPD lab. The light blue jacket gave her a look of competence and professionalism that the rest of her didn't convey. Atwater was very young—only thirty-one—and had blond hair with a pink stripe down one side, modeling her look after a supercool lab tech on one of the TV crime shows. After meeting her for the first time, I tried to get her to think about losing the pink, but she told me she wouldn't give up her individuality. The jurors, she said, would have to accept her for who and what she was.

At least the lab coat wasn't pink.

Atwater identified herself and was sworn in. After she took the witness seat I started asking questions about her educational pedigree and work experience. I spent at least ten more minutes on this than I normally would have, but I kept seeing that ribbon of pink hair and thought I had to do all I could to turn it into a badge of professionalism and accomplishment.

Finally, I got to the crux of her testimony. With me carefully asking the questions, she testified that she had conducted DNA typing and comparison on two completely different evidence samples from the Landy case. I went with the more problematic analysis first.

"Ms. Atwater, can you describe the first DNA assignment you received on the Landy case?"

"Yes, on February fourth I was given a swatch of fabric that had been cut from the dress that the victim had been wearing at the time of her murder."

"Where did you receive this from?"

"It came from the LAPD's Property Division, where it had been kept in controlled evidence storage."

Her answers were carefully rehearsed. She could give no indication that there had been a previous trial in the case or that Jessup had been in prison for the past twenty-four years. To do so would create prejudice against Jessup and trigger a mistrial.

"Why were you sent this swatch of fabric?"

"There was a stain on the fabric that twenty-four years ago had been identified by the LAPD forensics unit as semen. My assignment was to extract DNA and identify it if possible."

"When you examined this swatch, was there any degradation of the genetic material on it?"

"No, sir. It had been properly preserved."

"Okay, so you got this swatch of material from Melissa Landy's dress and you extracted DNA from it. Do I have that right so far?"

"That's right."

"What did you do next?"

"I turned the DNA profile into a code and entered it into the CODIS database."

"What is CODIS?"

"It's the FBI's Combined DNA Index System. Think of it as a national clearinghouse of DNA records. All DNA signatures gathered by law enforcement end up here and are available for comparison."

"So you entered the DNA signature obtained from semen on the dress Melissa Landy wore on the day she was murdered, correct?"

"Correct."

"Did you get a hit?"

"I did. The profile belonged to her stepfather, Kensington Landy."

A courtroom is a big space. There is always a low-level current of sound and energy. You can feel it even if you can't really hear it. People whisper in the gallery, the clerk and deputy handle phone calls, the court reporter touches the keys on her steno machine. But the sound and air went completely out of Department 112 after Lisa Atwater said what she said. I let it ride for a few moments. I knew this would be the lowest point of the case. With that one answer I had, in fact, revealed Jason Jessup's case. But from this point on, it would all be my case. And Melissa Landy's case. I wouldn't forget about her.

"Why was Kensington Landy's DNA in the CODIS database?" I asked.

"Because California has a law that requires all felony arrest suspects to submit a DNA sample. In two thousand four Mr. Landy was arrested for a hit-and-run accident causing injury. Though he eventually pleaded to lesser charges, it was originally charged as a felony, thus triggering the DNA law upon his booking. His DNA was entered into the system."

"Okay. Now getting back to the victim's dress and the semen that was on it. How did you determine that the semen was deposited on the day that Melissa Landy was murdered?"

Atwater seemed confused by the question at first. It was a skilled act.

"I didn't," she said. "It is impossible to know exactly when that deposit was made."

"You mean it could have been on the dress for a week before her death?"

"Yes. There's no way of knowing."

"What about a month?"

"It's possible because there is —"

"What about a year?"

"Again, it is —"

"Objection!"

Royce stood. About time, I thought.

"Your Honor, how long does this have to go on past the point?"

"Withdrawn, Judge. Mr. Royce is right. We're well past the point."

I paused for a moment to underline that Atwater and I would now be moving in a new direction.

"Ms. Atwater, you recently handled a second DNA analysis in regard to the Melissa Landy case, correct?"

"Yes, I did."

"Can you describe what that entailed?"

Before answering she secured the pink band of hair behind her ear.

"Yes, it was a DNA extraction and comparison of hair specimens. Hair from the victim, Melissa Landy, which was contained in a kit taken at the time of her autopsy and hair recovered from a tow truck operated by the defendant, Jason Jessup."

"How many hair specimens are we talking about?"

"Ultimately, one of each. Our objective was to extract nuclear DNA, which is available only in the root of a hair sample. Of the specimens we had, there was only one suitable extraction from the hairs recovered from the tow truck. So we compared DNA from the root of that hair to DNA from a hair sample taken from the autopsy kit."

I walked her through the process, trying to keep the explanations as simple as possible. Just enough to get by, like on TV. I kept one eye on my witness and one on the jury box, making sure everybody was staying plugged in and happy.

Finally, we came out the other end of the techno-genetic tunnel and arrived at Lisa Atwater's conclusions. She put several color-coded charts and graphs up on the screens and thoroughly explained them. But the bottom line was always the same thing; to feel it, jurors had to hear it. The most important thing a witness brings into a courtroom is her word. After all the charts were displayed, it came down to Atwater's words.

I turned and looked back at the clock. I was right on schedule. In less than twenty minutes the judge would recess for the evening. I turned back and moved in for the kill.

"Ms. Atwater, do you have any hesitation or doubt at all about the genetic match you have just testified about?"

"No, none whatsoever."

"Do you believe beyond a doubt that the hair from Melissa Landy is a unique match to the hair specimen obtained from the tow truck the defendant was operating on February sixteenth, nineteen eighty-six?"

"Yes, I do."

"Is there a quantifiable way of illustrating this match?"

"Yes, as I illustrated earlier, we matched nine out of the thirteen genetic markers in the CODIS protocol. The combination of these nine particular genetic markers occurs in one in one-point-six trillion individuals."

"Are you saying it is a one-in-one-point-six-trillion chance that the hair found in the tow truck operated by the defendant belonged to someone other than Melissa Landy?"

"You could say it that way, yes."

"Ms. Atwater, do you happen to know the current population of the world?"

"It's approaching seven billion."

"Thank you, Ms. Atwater. I have no further questions at this time."

I moved to my seat and sat down. Immediately I started stacking files and documents, getting it all ready for the briefcase and the ride home. This day was in the books and I had a long night ahead of me preparing for the next one. The judge didn't seem to begrudge me finishing ten minutes early. She was shutting down herself and sending the jury home.

"We will continue with the cross-examination of this witness tomorrow. I would like to thank all of you for paying such close attention to today's testimony. We will be adjourned until nine o'clock sharp tomorrow morning and I once again admonish you not to watch any news program or—"

"Your Honor?"

I looked up from the files. Royce was on his feet.

"Yes, Mr. Royce?"

"My apologies, Judge Breitman, for interrupting. But by my watch, it is only four-fifty and I know that you prefer to get as much testimony as possible in each day. I would like to cross-examine this witness now."

The judge looked at Atwater, who was still on the witness stand, and then back to Royce.

"Mr. Royce, I would rather you begin your cross tomorrow morning rather than start and then interrupt it after only ten minutes. We don't go past five o'clock with the jury. That is a rule I will not break."

"I understand, Judge. But I am not planning to interrupt it. I will be finished with this witness by five o'clock and then she will not be required to return tomorrow."

The judge stared at Royce for a long moment, a disbelieving look on her face.

"Mr. Royce, Ms. Atwater is one of the prosecution's key witnesses. Are you telling me you only need five minutes for cross-examination?"

"Well, of course it depends on the length of her answers, but I have only a few questions, Your Honor."

"Very well, then. You may proceed. Ms. Atwater, you remain under oath."

Royce moved to the lectern and I was as confused as the judge about the defense's maneuver. I had expected Royce to take most of the next morning on cross. This had to be a trick. He had a DNA expert on his own witness list but I would never give up a shot at the prosecution's witness.

"Ms. Atwater," Royce said, "did all of the testing and typing and extracting you conducted on the hair specimen from the tow truck tell you how the specimen got inside that truck?"

To buy time Atwater asked Royce to repeat the question. But even upon hearing it a second time, she did not answer until the judge intervened.

"Ms. Atwater, can you answer the question?" Breitman asked.

"Uh, yes, I'm sorry. My answer is no, the lab work I conducted had nothing to do with determining how the hair specimen found its way into the tow truck. That was not my responsibility."

"Thank you," Royce said. "So to make it crystal clear, you cannot tell the jury how that hair — which you have capably identified as belonging to the victim — got inside the truck or who put it there, isn't that right?"

I stood.

"Objection. Assumes facts not in evidence."

"Sustained. Would you like to rephrase, Mr. Royce?"

"Thank you, Your Honor. Ms. Atwater, you have no idea — other than what you were perhaps told — how the hair you tested found its way into the tow truck, correct?"

"That would be correct, yes."

"So you can identify the hair as Melissa Landy's but you cannot testify with the same sureness as to how it ended up in the tow truck, correct?"

I stood up again.

"Objection," I said. "Asked and answered."

"I think I will let the witness answer," Breitman said. "Ms. Atwater?"

"Yes, that is correct," Atwater said. "I cannot testify about anything regarding how the hair happened to end up in the truck."

"Then I have no further questions. Thank you."

I turned back and looked at the clock. I had two minutes. If I wanted to get the jury back on track I had to think of something quick.

"Any redirect, Mr. Haller?" the judge asked.

"One moment, Your Honor."

I turned and leaned toward Maggie to whisper.

"What do I do?"

"Nothing," she whispered back. "Let it go or you might make it worse. You made your points. He made his. Yours are more important — you put Melissa inside his truck. Leave it there."

Something told me not to leave it as is but my mind was a blank. I couldn't think of a question derived from Royce's cross that would get the jury off his point and back onto mine.

"Mr. Haller?" the judge said impatiently.

I gave it up.

"No further questions at this time, Your Honor."

"Very well, then, we will adjourn for the day. Court will reconvene at nine A.M. tomorrow and I admonish the jurors not to read newspaper accounts about this trial or view television reports or talk to family or friends about the case. I hope everyone has a good night."

With that the jury stood and began to file out of the box. I casually glanced over at the defense table and saw Royce being congratulated by Jessup. They were all smiles. I felt a hollow in my stomach the size of a baseball. It was as though I had played it to near perfection all day long — for almost six hours of testimony — and then in the last five minutes managed to let the last out in the ninth go right between my legs.

I sat still and waited until Royce and Jessup and everybody else had left the courtroom.

"You coming?" Maggie said from behind me.

"In a minute. How about I meet you back at the office?"

"Let's walk back together."

"I'm not good company, Mags."

"Haller, get over it. You had a great day. *We* had a great day. He was good for five minutes and the jury knows that."

"Okay. I'll meet you there in a little bit."

She gave up and I heard her leave. After a few minutes I reached over to the top file on the stack in front of me and opened it up halfway. A school photo of Melissa Landy was clipped inside the folder. Smiling at the camera. She looked nothing like my daughter but she made me think of Hayley.

I made a silent vow not to let Royce outsmart me again.

A few moments later, someone turned out the lights.

Thirty-two

Bosch stood by the swing set planted in the sand a quarter mile south of the Santa Monica Pier. The black water of the Pacific to his left was alive with the dancing reflection of light and color from the Ferris wheel at the end of the boardwalk. The amusement park had closed fifteen minutes earlier but the light show would go on through the night, an electronic display of ever-changing patterns on the big wheel that was mesmerizing in the cold darkness.

Harry raised his phone and called the SIS dispatcher. He had checked in earlier and set things up.

"It's Bosch again. How's our boy?"

"He appears to be tucked in for the night. You must've worn him out in court today, Bosch. On the way home from the CCB he went to Ralphs to pick up some groceries and then straight home, where he's been ever since. First night in five he hasn't been out and about at this time."

"Yeah, well, don't count on it staying that way. They've got the back door covered, right?"

"And the windows and the car and the bicycle. We got him, Detective. Don't worry."

"Then I won't. You've got my number. Call me if he moves."

"Will do."

Bosch put the phone away and headed toward the pier. The wind was strong off the water and a fine mist of sand stung his face and eyes as he approached the huge structure. The pier was like a beached aircraft carrier. It was long and wide. It had a large parking lot and an assortment of restaurants and souvenir shops on top. At its midpoint it had a full amusement park with a roller coaster and the signature Ferris wheel. And at its furthest extension into the sea it was a traditional fishing pier with a bait shop, management office and yet another restaurant. All of it was supported on a thick forest of wood pilings that started landside and carried seven hundred feet out beyond the wave break and to the cold depths.

Landside, the pilings were enclosed with a wooden siding that created a semi-secure storage facility for the city of Santa Monica. Only semi-secure for two reasons: The storage area was vulnerable to extreme high tides, which came on rare occasion during offshore earthquakes. Also, the pier spanned a hundred yards of beach, which entailed anchoring the wood siding in moist sand. The wood was always in the process of rotting and was easily compromised. The result was that the storage facility had become an unofficial homeless shelter that had to be periodically cleared out by the city.

The SIS observers had reported that Jason Jessup had slipped underneath the south wall the night before and had spent thirty-one minutes inside the storage area.

Bosch reached the pier and started walking its length, looking for the spot in the wood siding where Jessup had crawled under. He carried a mini Maglite and quickly found a depression where the sand had been dug out at the wall's base and partially filled back in. He crouched down, put the light into the hole and determined that it was too small for him to fit through. He put the light down to the side, reached down and started digging like a dog trying to escape the yard.

Soon the hole seemed big enough and he crawled through. He

was dressed for the effort. Old black jeans and work boots, and a long-sleeved T-shirt beneath a plastic raid jacket he wore inside out to hide the luminescent yellow LAPD across the front and back.

He came up inside to a dark, cavernous space with slashes of light filtering down between the planks of the parking lot above. He stood up and brushed the sand off his clothes, then swept the area with the flashlight. It had been made for close-in work, so its beam did little to illuminate the far reaches of the space.

There was a damp smell and the sound of waves crashing through the pilings only twenty-five yards away echoed loudly in the enclosed space. Bosch pointed the light up and saw fungus caked on the pier's crossbeams. He moved forward into the gloom and quickly came upon a boat covered by a tarp. He lifted up a loose end and saw that it was an old lifeguard boat. He moved on and came upon stacks of buoys and then stacks of traffic barricades and mobile barriers, all of them stenciled with CITY OF SANTA MONICA.

He next came to three stacks of scaffolding used for paint and repair projects on the pier. They looked long untouched and were slowly sinking in the sand.

Across the rear was a line of enclosed storage rooms, but the wood sidings had cracked and split over time, making storage in them porous at best.

The doors were unlocked and Bosch went down the line, finding each one empty until the second to the last. Here the door was secured with a shiny new padlock. He put the beam of his light into one of the cracks between the planks of the siding and tried to look in. He saw what appeared to be the edge of a blanket but that was all.

Bosch moved back to the door and knelt down in front of the lock. He held the light with his mouth and extracted two lock picks from his wallet. He went to work on the padlock and quickly determined that it had only four tumblers. He got it open in less than five minutes.

He entered the storage corral and found it largely empty. There was a folded blanket on the ground with a pillow on top of it. Nothing else. The SIS surveillance report had said that the night before, Jessup had walked down the beach carrying a blanket. It did not say that he had left it behind under the pier, and there had been nothing in the report about a pillow.

Harry wasn't even sure he was in the same spot that Jessup had come to. He moved the light over the wall and then up to the underside of the pier, where he held it. He could clearly see the outline of a door. A trapdoor. It was locked from underneath with another new padlock.

Bosch was pretty sure that he was standing beneath the pier's parking lot. He had occasionally heard the sound of vehicles up above as the pier crowd went home. He guessed that the trapdoor had been used as some sort of loading door for materials to be stored. He knew he could grab one of the scaffolds and climb up to examine the second lock but decided not to bother. He retreated from the corral.

As he was relocking the door with the padlock he felt his phone begin to vibrate in his pocket. He quickly pulled it out, expecting to learn from SIS dispatch that Jessup was on the move. But the caller ID told him the call was from his daughter. He opened the phone.

"Hey, Maddie."

"Dad? Are you there?"

Her voice was low and the sound of crashing waves was loud. Bosch yelled.

"I'm here. What's wrong?"

"Well, when are you coming home?"

"Soon, baby. I've got a little bit more work to do."

She dropped her voice even lower and Bosch had to clamp a hand over his other ear to hear her. In the background he could hear the freeway on her end. He knew she was on the rear deck.

"Dad, she's making me do homework that isn't even due until next week."

Bosch had once again left her with Sue Bambrough, the assistant principal.

"So next week you'll be thanking her when everybody else is doing it and you'll be all done."

"Dad, I've been doing homework all night!"

"You want me to tell her to let you take a break?"

His daughter didn't respond and Bosch understood. She had called because she wanted him to know the misery she was suffering. But she didn't want him to do anything about it.

"I'll tell you what," he said. "When I get back I will remind Mrs. Bambrough that you are not in school when you are at home and you don't need to be working the whole time. Okay?"

"I guess. Why can't I just stay at Rory's? This isn't fair."

"Maybe next time. I need to get back to work, Mads. Can we talk about it tomorrow? I want you in bed by the time I get home."

"Whatever."

"Good night, Madeline. Make sure all the doors are locked, including on the deck, and I'll see you tomorrow."

"Good night."

The disapproval in her voice was hard to miss. She disconnected the call ahead of Bosch. He closed his phone and just as he slid it into his pocket he heard a noise, like a banging of metal parts, coming from the direction of the hole he had slid through into the storage area. He immediately killed his flashlight and moved toward the tarp that covered the boat.

Crouching behind the boat, he saw a human figure stand up by the wall and start moving in the darkness without a flashlight. The figure moved without hesitation toward the storage corral with the new lock on it.

There were streetlights over the parking lot above. They sent slivers of illumination down through the cracks formed by retreating planks in the boardwalk. As the figure moved through these, Bosch saw that it was Jessup.

Harry dropped lower and instinctively reached his hand to his belt just to make sure his gun was there. With his other hand he pulled his phone and hit the mute button. He didn't want the SIS dispatcher to suddenly remember to call him to alert him that Jessup was moving.

Bosch noticed that Jessup was carrying a bag that appeared to be heavily weighted. He went directly to the locked storage room and soon swung the door open. He obviously had a key to the padlock.

Jessup stepped back and Bosch saw a slash of light cross his face as he turned and scanned the entire storage area, making sure he was alone. He then went inside the room.

For several seconds, there was no sound or movement, then Jessup reappeared in the doorway. He stepped out and closed the door, relocking it. He then stepped back into the light and did a 180-degree scan of the larger storage area. Bosch lowered his body even further. He guessed that Jessup was suspicious because he had found the hole under the wall freshly dug out.

"Who's there?" he called out.

Bosch didn't move. He didn't even breathe.

"Show yourself!"

Bosch snaked his hand under the raid jacket and closed his hand on his gun's grips. He knew the indications were that Jessup had obtained a weapon. If he made even a feint in Bosch's direction, Harry was going to pull his own weapon and be ready to fire first.

But it never happened. Jessup started moving quickly back to the entrance hole and soon he disappeared in the darkness. Bosch listened but all he could hear was the crashing of the waves. He waited another thirty seconds and then started moving toward the opening in the wall. He didn't turn on the light. He wasn't sure Jessup had actually left.

As he moved around the stack of scaffolding frames, he banged his shin hard on a metal pipe that was extending out from the pile. It sent a sudden burst of pain up his left leg and shifted the balance of metal frames. The top two loudly slid off stack, clattering to the sand. Bosch threw himself to the sand next to the pile and waited.

But Jessup didn't appear. He was gone.

Bosch slowly got up. He was in pain and he was angry. He pulled his phone and called SIS dispatch.

"You were supposed to call me when Jessup moved!" he whispered angrily.

"I know that," said the dispatcher. "He hasn't moved."

"What? Are you — patch me through to whoever's in charge out there."

"I'm sorry, Detective, but that's not how —"

"Look, shithead, Jessup is not *tucked in* for the night. I just saw him. And it almost turned bad. Now let me talk to somebody out there or my next call is to Lieutenant Wright at home."

While he waited Bosch moved to the sidewall so he could get out of the storage area. His leg hurt badly and he was walking with a limp.

In the darkness he couldn't find the spot where he could slip under the wall. Finally, he put the light on, holding it low to the ground. He found the spot but saw that Jessup had pushed sand into the hole, just as he had the night before.

A voice finally came to him over the phone.

"Bosch? This is Jacquez. You claim you just saw our subject?"

"I don't claim I saw him. I did see him. Where are your people?"

"We're sitting on his zero, man. He hasn't left."

Zero was a surveillance subject's home location.

"Bullshit, I just saw him under the Santa Monica pier. Get your people up here. Now."

"We got his zero down tight, Bosch. There's no —"

"Listen, Jackass, Jessup is my case. I know him and he almost just crawled up my ass. Now call your men and find out which one went off post because —"

"I'll get back to you," Jacquez said curtly and the line went dead.

Bosch turned the phone's ringer back on and put it in his pocket. Once again he dropped to his knees and quickly dug out the hole, using his hands as a scoop. He then pushed his body through, half expecting Jessup to be waiting for him when he came up on the other side.

But there was no sign of him. Bosch got up, gazed south down the beach in the direction of Venice and saw no one in the light from the Ferris wheel. He then turned and looked up toward the hotels and apartment buildings that ran along the beach. Several people were on the beach walk that fronted the buildings but he didn't recognize any of the figures as Jessup.

Twenty-five yards up the pier was a set of stairs leading topside and directly to the pier's parking lot. Bosch headed that way, still limping badly. He was halfway up the stairs when his phone rang. It was Jacquez.

"All right, where is he? We're on our way."

"That's the thing. I lost him. I had to hide and I thought you people were on him. I'm going to the top of the pier now. What the hell happened, Jacquez?"

"We had a guy step out to drop a deuce. Said his stomach was giving him trouble. I don't think he'll be in the unit after tonight."

"Jesus Christ!"

Bosch got to the top of the steps and walked out onto the empty parking lot. There was no sign of Jessup.

"Okay, I'm up on the pier. I don't see him. He's in the wind."

"Okay, Bosch, we're two minutes out. We're going to spread. We'll find him. He didn't take the car or the bike, so he's on foot."

"He could've grabbed a cab at any one of the hotels over here. The bottom line is we don't know where—"

Bosch suddenly realized something.

"I gotta go. Call me as soon as you have him, Jacquez. You got that?"

"Got it."

Bosch ended the call and then immediately called his home on the speed dial. He checked his watch and expected Sue Bambrough to answer, since it was after eleven.

But his daughter picked up the call.

"Dad?"

"Hey, baby, why are you still up?"

"Because I had to do all that homework. I wanted a little break before I went to sleep."

"That's fine. Listen, can you put Mrs. Bambrough on the line?"

"Dad, I'm in my bedroom and I'm in my pajamas."

"That's okay. Just go to the door and tell her to pick up the phone in the kitchen. I need to talk to her. And meantime, you have to get dressed. You're leaving the house."

"What? Dad, I have—"

"Madeline, listen to me. This is important. I am going to tell Mrs. Bambrough to take you to her house until I can get there. I want you out of the house."

"Why?"

"You don't need to know that. You just need to do what I ask. Now, please, get Mrs. Bambrough on the phone."

She didn't respond but he heard the door of her room open. Then he heard his daughter say, "It's for you."

A few moments later the extension was picked up in the kitchen.

"Hello?"

"Sue, it's Harry. I need you to do something. I need you to take Maddie to your house. Right now. I will be there in less than an hour to get her."

"I don't understand."

"Sue, listen, we've been watching a guy tonight who knows where I live. And we lost him. Now, there is no reason to panic or to believe he is heading that way but I want to take all precautions. So I want you to take Maddie and get out of the house. Right now. Go to your place and I will see you there. Can you do this, Sue?"

"We're leaving right now."

He liked the strength in her voice and realized it probably came with the territory of being a teacher and assistant principal in the public school system.

"Okay, I'm on my way. Call me back as soon as you get to your place."

But Bosch wasn't really on his way. After the call, he put the phone away and went back down the steps to the beach. He returned to the hole he had dug under the storage area wall. He crawled back under and this time used his flashlight to find his way to the locked storage room. He used his picks again on the padlock and the whole time he worked he was distracted by thoughts of Jessup's escape from the surveillance. Had it just been a coincidence that he had left his apartment at the same time the SIS watcher had left his post, or was he aware of the surveillance and did he break free when he saw the opportunity?

At the moment, there was no way to know.

Finally, he got the lock open, taking longer than he had the first time. He entered the storage room and moved the light to the blanket and pillow on the ground. The bag Jessup had carried was there. It said *Ralphs* on its side. Bosch dropped to his knees and was about to open it when his phone buzzed. It was Jacquez.

"We got him. He's on Nielson at Ocean Park. It looks like he's walking home."

"Then try not to lose him this time, Jacquez. I gotta go."

He disconnected before Jacquez could reply. He quickly called his daughter's cell. She was in the car with Sue Bambrough. Bosch told her they could turn around and go back home. This news was not received with a thankful release of tension. His daughter was left upset and angry over the scare. Bosch couldn't blame her but he couldn't stay on the line.

"I'll be home in less than an hour. We can talk about it then if you're still awake. I'll see you soon."

He disconnected the call and focused on the bag. He opened it without moving it from its spot next to the blanket.

The bag contained a dozen single-serving-size cans of fruit. There were diced peaches in heavy syrup, chopped pineapple and something called fruit medley. Also in the bag was a package of plastic spoons. Bosch stared at the contents for a long moment and then his eyes moved up the wall to the crossbeams and the locked trapdoor above.

"Who are you bringing here, Jessup?" he whispered.

Thirty-three

Wednesday, April 7, 1:05 P.M.

All eyes were on the back of the courtroom. It was time for the main event, and while I had ringside seats, I was still going to be just a spectator like everybody else. That didn't sit very well with me but it was a choice I could live with and trust. The door opened and Harry Bosch led our main witness into the courtroom. Sarah Ann Gleason told us she didn't own any dresses and didn't want to buy one to testify in. She wore black jeans and a purple silk blouse. She looked pretty and she looked confident. We didn't need a dress.

Bosch stayed on her right side and when opening the gate for her positioned his body between her and Jessup, who sat at the defense table, turned like everybody else toward his main accuser's entrance.

Bosch let her go the rest of the way by herself. Maggie McFierce was already at the lectern and she smiled warmly at her witness as she went by. This was Maggie's moment, too, and I read her smile as one of hope for both women.

We'd had a good morning, with testimony from Bill Clinton, the former tow truck driver, and then Bosch taking the case through to lunch. Clinton told his story about the day of the murder and Jessup borrowing his Dodgers cap just before they became part of the impromptu lineup outside the house on Windsor Boulevard. He also testified to the Aardvark drivers' frequent use of and familiarity with the parking lot behind the El Rey Theatre, and Jessup's claim to Windsor Boulevard on the morning of the murder. These were good, solid points for the prosecution, and Clinton gave no quarter to Royce on cross.

Then Bosch took the stand for a third time in the trial. Rather than read previous testimony, this time he testified about his own recent investigation of the case and produced the Dodgers cap — with the initials *BC* under the brim — from property that had been seized from Jessup during his arrest twenty-four years earlier. We were forced to dance around the fact that the hat as well as Jessup's other belongings had been in the property room at San Quentin for the past twenty-four years. To bring that information out would be to reveal that Jessup had previously been convicted of Melissa Landy's murder.

And now Sarah Gleason would be the prosecution's final witness. Through her the case would come together in the emotional crescendo I was counting on. One sister standing for a long-lost sister. I leaned back in my seat to watch my ex-wife — the best prosecutor I had ever encountered — take us home.

Gleason was sworn in and then took her seat on the stand. She was small and required the microphone to be lowered by the courtroom deputy. Maggie cleared her voice and began.

"Good morning, Ms. Gleason. How are you today?"

"I'm doing pretty good."

"Can you please tell the jury a little bit about yourself?"

"Um, I'm thirty-seven years old. Not married. I live in Port Townsend, Washington, and I've been there about seven years now."

"What do you do for a living?"

"I'm a glass artist."

"And what was your relationship to Melissa Landy?"

"She was my younger sister."

"How much younger was she than you?"

"Thirteen months."

Maggie put a photograph of the two sisters up on the overhead screen as a prosecution exhibit. It showed two smiling girls standing in front of a Christmas tree.

"Can you identify this photo?"

"That was me and Melissa at the last Christmas. Right before she was taken."

"So that would be Christmas nineteen eighty-five?"

"Yes."

"I notice that she and you are about the same size."

"Yes, she wasn't really my little sister anymore. She had caught up to me."

"Did you share the same clothes?"

"We shared some things but we also had our favorite things that we didn't share. That could cause a fight."

She smiled and Maggie nodded that she understood.

"Now, you said she was taken. Were you referring to February sixteenth of the following year, the date of your sister's abduction and murder?"

"Yes, I was."

"Okay, Sarah, I know it will be difficult for you but I would like you to tell the jury what you saw and did on that day."

Gleason nodded as if steeling herself for what was ahead. I checked the jury and saw every eye holding on her. I then turned and glanced at the defense table and locked eyes with Jessup. I did not look away. I held his defiant stare and tried to send back my own message. That two women — one asking the questions, the other answering them — were going to take him down.

Finally, it was Jessup who looked away.

"Well, it was a Sunday," Gleason said. "We were going to go to church. My whole family. Melissa and I were in our dresses so my mother told us to go out front."

"Why couldn't you use the backyard?"

"My stepfather was building a pool and there was a lot of mud in the back and a big hole. My mother was worried we might fall down and get our dresses dirty."

"So you went out to the front yard."

"Yes."

"And where were your parents at this time, Sarah?"

"My mother was still upstairs getting ready and my stepfather was in the TV room. He was watching sports."

"Where was the TV room in the house?"

"In the back next to the kitchen."

"Okay, Sarah, I am going to show you a photo called 'People's prosecution exhibit eleven.' Is this the front of the house where you lived on Windsor Boulevard?"

All eyes went to the overhead screen. The yellow-brick house spread across the screen. It was a long shot from the street, showing a deep front yard with ten-foot hedges running down both sides. There was a front porch that ran the width of the house and that was largely hidden behind ornamental vegetation. There was a paved walkway extending from the sidewalk, across the lawn and to the steps of the front porch. I had reviewed our photo exhibits several times in preparation for the trial. But for the first time, I noticed that the walkway had a crack running down the center of its entire length from sidewalk to front steps. It somehow seemed appropriate, considering what had happened at the home.

"Yes, that was our house."

"Tell us what happened that day in the front yard, Sarah."

"Well, we decided to play hide-and-seek while we waited for our parents. I was It first and I found Melissa hiding behind that bush on the right side of the porch."

She pointed to the exhibit photo that was still on the screen. I realized we had forgotten to give Gleason the laser pointer we had prepared her testimony with. I quickly opened Maggie's briefcase and found it. I stood and handed it to her. With the judge's permission, she gave it to the witness.

"Okay, Sarah, could you use the laser to show us?" Maggie asked.

Gleason moved the red laser dot in a circle around a thick bush at the north corner of the front porch.

"So she hid there and you found her?"

"Yes, and then when it was her turn to be It, I decided to hide in the same spot because I didn't think she would look there at first. When she was finished counting she came down the steps and stood in the middle of the yard."

"You could see her from your hiding place?"

"Yes, through the bush I could see her. She was sort of turning in a half circle, looking for me."

"Then what happened?"

"Well, first I heard a truck go by and —"

"Let me just stop you right there, Sarah. You say you heard a truck. You didn't see it?"

"No, not from where I was hiding."

"How do you know that it was a truck?"

"It was very loud and heavy. I could feel it in the ground, like a little earthquake."

"Okay, what happened after you heard the truck?"

"Suddenly I saw a man in the yard . . . and he went right up to my sister and grabbed her by her wrist."

Gleason cast her eyes down and held her hands together on the dais in front of her seat.

"Sarah, did you know this man?"

"No, I did not."

"Had you ever seen him before?"

"No, I had not."

"Did he say anything?"

"Yes, I heard him say, 'You have to come with me.' And my sister said . . . she said, 'Are you sure?' And that was it. I think he said something else but I didn't hear it. He led her away. To the street."

"And you stayed in hiding?"

"Yes, I couldn't... for some reason I couldn't move. I couldn't call for help, I couldn't do anything. I was very scared."

It was one of those solemn moments in the courtroom when there was absolute silence except for the voices of the prosecutor and the witness.

"Did you see or hear anything else, Sarah?"

"I heard a door close and then I heard the truck drive away."

I saw the tears on Sarah Gleason's cheeks. I thought the courtroom deputy had noticed as well because he took a box of tissues from a drawer in his desk and crossed the courtroom with them. But instead of taking them to Sarah he handed the box to juror number two, who had tears on her cheeks as well. This was okay with me. I wanted the tears to stay on Sarah's face.

"Sarah, how long was it before you came out from behind the bush where you were hiding and told your parents that your sister had been taken?"

"I think it was less than a minute but it was too late. She was gone."

The silence that followed that statement was the kind of void that lives can disappear into. Forever.

Maggie spent the next half hour walking Gleason through her memory of what came after. Her stepfather's desperate 9-1-1 call to the police, the interview she gave to the detectives, and then the lineup she viewed from her bedroom window and her identifying Jason Jessup as the man she saw lead her sister away.

Maggie had to be very careful here. We had used sworn testimony of witnesses from the first trial. The record of that entire trial was available to Royce as well, and I knew without a doubt that he had his assistant counsel, who was sitting on the other side of Jessup, comparing everything Sarah Gleason was saying now with the testimony she gave at the first trial. If she changed one nuance of her story, Royce would be all over her on it during his cross-examination, using the discrepancy to try to cast her as a liar.

To me the testimony came off as fresh and not rehearsed. This was a testament to the prep work of the two women. Maggie smoothly and efficiently brought her witness to the vital moment when Sarah reconfirmed her identification of Jessup.

"Was there any doubt at all in your mind when you identified Jason Jessup in nineteen eighty-six as the man who took your sister?"

"No, none at all."

"It has been a long time, Sarah, but I ask you to look around the courtroom and tell the jury whether you see the man who abducted your sister on February sixteenth, nineteen eighty-six?"

"Yes, him."

She spoke without hesitation and pointed her finger at Jessup.

"Would you tell us where he is seated and describe an article of clothing he is wearing?"

"He's sitting next to Mr. Royce and he has a dark blue tie and a light blue shirt."

She paused and looked at Judge Breitman.

"Let the record show that the witness has identified the defendant," she said.

She went right back to Sarah.

"After all these years, do you have any doubt that he is the man who took your sister?"

"None at all."

Maggie turned and looked at the judge.

"Your Honor, it may be a bit early but I think now would be a good time to take the afternoon break. I am going to go in a different direction with this witness at this point."

"Very well," Breitman said. "We will adjourn for fifteen minutes and I will expect to see everyone back here at two-thirty-five. Thank you."

Sarah said she wanted to use the restroom and left the courtroom with Bosch running interference and making sure she would not cross paths with Jessup in the hallway. Maggie sat down at the table and we huddled.

"You have 'em, Maggie. This is what they've been waiting all week to hear and it's better than they thought it was going to be."

She knew I was talking about the jury. She didn't need my approval or encouragement but I had to give it.

"Now comes the hard part," she said. "I hope she holds up."

"She's doing great. And I'm sure Harry's telling her that right now."

Maggie didn't respond. She started flipping through the legal pad that had her notes and the rough script of the examination. Soon she was immersed in the next hour's work.

Thirty-four

Wednesday, April 7, 2:30 P.M.

Bosch had to shoo away the reporters when Sarah Gleason came out of the restroom. Using his body as a shield against the cameras he walked her back to the courtroom.

"Sarah, you're doing really well," he said. "You keep it up and this guy's going right back to where he belongs."

"Thanks, but that was the easy part. It's going to get hard now."

"Don't kid yourself, Sarah. There is no easy part. Just keep thinking about your sister, Melissa. Somebody has to stand up for her. And right now that's you."

As they got to the courtroom door, he realized that she had smoked a cigarette in the restroom. He could smell it on her.

Inside, he walked her down the center aisle and delivered her to Maggie McFierce, who was waiting at the gate. Bosch gave the prosecutor the nod. She was doing really well herself.

"Finish the job," he said.

"We will," Maggie said.

After passing the witness off, Bosch doubled back up the center aisle to the sixth row. He had spotted Rachel Walling sitting in the middle of the row. He now squeezed around several reporters and observers to get to her. The space next to her was open and he sat down.

"Harry."

"Rachel."

"I think the man who was in that space was planning on coming back."

"That's okay. Once court starts, I have to move back up. You should've told me you were coming. Mickey said you were here the other day."

"When I have some time I like to come by. It's a fascinating case so far."

"Well, let's hope the jury thinks it's more than fascinating. I want this guy back in San Quentin so bad I can taste it."

"Mickey told me Jessup was moonlighting. Is that still—"

She lowered her voice to a whisper when she saw Jessup walking down the aisle and back to his seat at the defense table.

"—happening?"

Bosch matched her whisper.

"Yeah, and last night it almost went completely south on us. The SIS lost him."

"Oh, no."

The judge's door opened and she stepped out and headed up to the bench. Everyone stood. Bosch knew he had to get back to the prosecution table in case he was needed.

"But I found him," he whispered. "I have to go, but are you sticking around this afternoon?"

"No, I have to go back to the office. I'm just on a break right now."

"Okay, Rachel, thanks for coming by. I'll talk to you."

As people started sitting back down he worked his way out of the row and then quickly went back down the aisle and through the gate to take a seat in the row of chairs directly behind the prosecution table.

McPherson continued her direct examination of Sarah Ann Gleason. Bosch thought that both prosecutor and witness had been doing an exceptional job so far, but he also knew that they were moving into new territory now and soon everything said before wouldn't matter if what was said now wasn't delivered in a believable and unassailable fashion.

"Sarah," McPherson began, "when did your mother marry Kensington Landy?"

"When I was six."

"Did you like Ken Landy?"

"No, not really. At first things were okay but then everything changed."

"You, in fact, attempted to run away from home just a few months before your sister's death, isn't that right?"

"Yes."

"I show you People's exhibit twelve, a police report dated November thirtieth, nineteen eighty-five. Can you tell the jury what that is?"

McPherson delivered copies of the report to the witness, the judge and the defense table. Bosch had found the report during his record search on the case. It had been a lucky break.

"It's a missing persons report," Gleason said. "My mother reported me missing."

"And did the police find you?"

"No, I just came home. I didn't have anyplace to go."

"Why did you run away, Sarah?"

"Because my stepfather . . . was having sex with me."

McPherson nodded and let the answer hang out there in the courtroom for a long moment. Three days ago Bosch would have expected Royce to jump all over this part of the testimony but now he knew that this played to the defense's case as well. Kensington Landy was the straw man and any testimony that supported that would be welcomed.

"When did this start?" McPherson finally asked.

"The summer before I ran away," Gleason responded. "The summer before Melissa got taken."

"Sarah, I am sorry to put you through these bad memories. You testified earlier that you and Melissa shared some of each other's clothes, correct?"

"Yes."

"The dress she wore on the day she was taken, that was your dress, wasn't it?"

"Yes."

McPherson then introduced the dress as the state's next exhibit and Bosch set it up for display to the jury on a headless manikin he placed in front of the jury box.

"Is this the dress, Sarah?"

"Yes, it is."

"Now, you notice that there is a square of material removed from the bottom front hem of the dress. You see that, Sarah?"

"Yes."

"Do you know why that was removed?"

"Yes, because they found semen on the dress there."

"You mean forensic investigators?"

"Yes."

"Now, is this something you knew back at the time of your sister's death?"

"I know it now. I wasn't told about it back then."

"Do you know who the semen was genetically identified as belonging to?"

"Yes, I was told it came from my stepfather."

"Did that surprise you?"

"No, unfortunately."

"Do you have any explanation for how it could have gotten on your dress?"

Now Royce objected, saying that the question called for speculation. It also called for the witness to diverge from the defense theory, but he didn't mention that. Breitman sustained the objection and McPherson had to find another way of getting there.

"Sarah, prior to your sister borrowing your dress on the morning she was abducted, when was the last time you wore it?"

Royce stood and objected again.

"Same objection. We're speculating about events twenty-four years old and when this witness was only thirteen years old."

"Your Honor," McPherson rejoined, "Mr. Royce was fine with this so-called speculation when it fit with the defense's scheme of things. But now he objects as we get to the heart of the matter. This is not speculation. Ms. Gleason is testifying truthfully about the darkest, saddest days of her life and I don't think —"

"Objection overruled," Breitman said. "The witness may answer."

"Thank you, Your Honor."

As McPherson repeated the question Bosch studied the jury. He wanted to see if they saw what he saw — a defense attorney attempting to stop the forward progression of truth. Bosch had found Sarah Gleason's testimony to be fully convincing up to this point. He wanted to hear what she had to say and his hope was that the jury was in the same boat and would look unkindly upon defense efforts to stop her.

"I wore it two nights before," Gleason said.

"That would have been Friday night, the fourteenth. Valentine's Day."

"Yes."

"Why did you wear the dress?"

"My mother was making a nice dinner for Valentine's Day and my stepfather said we should get dressed up for it."

Gleason was looking down again, losing all eye contact with the jurors.

"Did your stepfather engage in a sexual act with you on that night?"

"Yes."

"Were you wearing the dress at the time?"

"Yes."

"Sarah, do you know if your father ejac—"

"He wasn't my father!"

She yelled it and her voice echoed in the courtroom, reverberating around a hundred people who now knew her darkest secret. Bosch looked at McPherson and saw her checking out the jury's reaction. It was then Bosch knew that the mistake had been intentional.

"I am sorry, Sarah. I meant your stepfather. Do you know, did he ejaculate in the course of this moment with you?"

"Yes, and some of it got on my dress."

McPherson studied her notes, flipping over several pages of her yellow pad. She wanted that last answer to hang out there as long as possible.

"Sarah, who did the laundry at your house?"

"A lady came. Her name was Abby."

"After that Valentine's Day, did you put your dress in the laundry?"

"No, I didn't."

"Why not?"

"Because I was afraid Abby would find it and know what happened. I thought she might tell my mother or call the police."

"Why would that have been a bad thing, Sarah?"

"I...my mother was happy and I didn't want to ruin things for her."

"So what did you do with the dress that night?"

"I cleaned off the spot and hung it in my closet. I didn't know my sister was going to wear it."

"So two days later when she wanted to put it on, what did you say?"

"She already had it on when I saw her. I told her that I wanted to wear it but she said it was too late because it wasn't on my list of clothes I didn't share with her."

"Could you see the stain on the dress?"

"No, I looked and because it was down at the hem I didn't see any stain."

McPherson paused again. Bosch knew from the prep work that

she had covered all the points she wanted to in this line of questioning. She had sufficiently explained the DNA that was the cause of everyone's being here. She now had to take Gleason further down the road of her dark journey. Because if she didn't, Royce certainly would.

"Sarah, did your relationship with your stepfather change after your sister's death?"

"Yes."

"How so?"

"He never touched me again."

"Do you know why? Did you talk to him about it?"

"I don't know why. I never talked to him about it. It just never happened again and he tried to act like it had never happened in the first place."

"But for you, all of this — your stepfather, your sister's death — it took a toll, didn't it?"

"Yes."

"In what way, Sarah?"

"Uh, well, I started getting into drugs and I ran away again. I ran away a lot, actually. I didn't care about sex. It was something I used to get what I needed."

"And were you ever arrested?"

"Yes, a bunch of times."

"For what?"

"Drugs mostly. I got arrested once for soliciting an undercover, too. And for stealing."

"You were arrested six times as a juvenile and five more times as an adult, is that correct?"

"I didn't keep count."

"What drugs were you taking?"

"Crystal meth mostly. But if there was something else available, I would probably take it. That was the way I was."

"Did you ever receive counseling and rehabilitation?"

"A lot of times. It didn't work at first and then it did. I got clean."

"When was that?"

"About seven years ago. When I was thirty."

"You've been clean for seven years?"

"Yes, totally. My life is different now."

"I want to show you People's exhibit thirteen, which is an intake and evaluation form from a private rehab center in Los Angeles called the Pines. Do you remember going there?"

"Yes, my mother sent me there when I was sixteen."

"Was that when you first started getting into trouble?"

"Yes."

McPherson distributed copies of the evaluation form to the judge, clerk and defense table.

"Okay, Sarah, I want to draw your attention to the paragraph I have outlined in yellow in the evaluation section of the intake form. Can you please read it out loud to the jury?"

"Candidate reports PTSD in regard to the murder of her younger sister three years ago. Suffers unresolved guilt associated with murder and also evinces behavior typical of sexual abuse. Full psych and physical evaluation is recommended."

"Thank you, Sarah. Do you know what PTSD means?"

"Posttraumatic stress disorder."

"Did you undergo these recommended evaluations at the Pines?"

"Yes."

"Did discussion of your stepfather's sexual abuse come up?"

"No, because I lied."

"How so?"

"By then I'd had sex with other men, so I never mentioned my stepfather."

"Before revealing what you have today in court, did you ever talk about your stepfather and his having sex with you with anyone?"

"Just you and Detective Bosch. Nobody else."

"Have you been married?"

"Yes."

"More than once?"

"Yes."

"And you didn't even tell your husbands about this?"

"No. It's not the kind of thing you want to tell anybody. You keep it to yourself."

"Thank you, Sarah. I have no further questions."

McPherson took her pad and returned to her seat, where she was greeted with a squeeze on the arm by Haller. It was a gesture designed for the jury to see but by then all eyes were on Royce. It was his turn and Bosch's measure of the room was that Sarah Gleason had everybody riding with her. Any effort by Royce to destroy her ran the strong risk of backfiring against his client.

Royce did the smart thing. He decided to let emotions cool for a night. He stood and told the judge that he reserved the right to recall Gleason as a witness during the defense phase of the trial. In effect he put off her cross-examination. He then retook his seat.

Bosch checked his watch. It was four-fifteen. The judge told Haller to call his next witness but Bosch knew there were no more witnesses. Haller looked at McPherson and in unison they nodded. Haller then stood up.

"Your Honor," he said. "The People rest."

Thirty-five

Wednesday, April 7, 7:20 P.M.

The prosecution team convened for dinner at Casa Haller. I made a thick Bolognese using a store-bought sauce for a base and boiled a box of bow tie pasta. Maggie chipped in with her own recipe for Caesar salad that I had always loved when we were married but hadn't had in years. Bosch and his daughter were the last to arrive, as Harry first took Sarah Ann Gleason back to her hotel room following court and made sure she was secure for the night.

Our daughters were shy upon meeting and embarrassed by how obvious their parents were about watching the long-awaited moment. They instinctively knew to move away from us and convened in the back office, ostensibly to do their homework. Pretty soon after, we started to hear laughter from down the hall.

I put the pasta and sauce into a big bowl and mixed it all together. I then called the girls out first to serve themselves and take their dishes back to the office.

"How's it going back there, anyway?" I asked them while they were making their plates. "Any homework getting done?"

"Dad," Hayley said dismissively, as if my question were a great invasion of privacy.

So I tried the cousin.

"Maddie?"

"Um, I'm almost finished with mine."

Both girls looked at each other and laughed, as if either the question or its answer were cause for great glee. They scurried out of the kitchen then and back to the office.

I put everything out on the table, where the adults were sitting. The last thing I did was make sure the door to the office was closed so the girls would not hear our conversation and we would not hear theirs.

"Well," I said as I passed the pasta to Bosch. "We're finished with our part. Now comes the hard part."

"The defense," Maggie said. "What do we think they have in store for Sarah?"

I thought for a moment before answering and tried my first bow tie. It was good. I was proud of my dish.

"We know they'll throw everything they can at her," I finally said. "She's the case."

Bosch reached inside his jacket and brought out a folded piece of paper. He opened it on the table. I could see that it was the defense's witness list.

"At the end of court today Royce told the judge he would complete the defense's case in one day," he said. "He said he's calling only four witnesses but he's got twenty-three listed on here."

"Well, we knew all along that most of that list was subterfuge," Maggie said. "He was hiding his case."

"Okay, so we have Sarah coming back," I said, holding up one finger. "Then we have Jessup himself. My guess is that Royce knows he has to put him on. That's two. Who else?"

Maggie waited until she finished a mouthful of food before speaking.

"Hey, this is good, Haller. When did you learn to make this?"

"It's a little thing I like to call Newman's Own."

"No, you added to it. You made it better. How come you never cooked like this when we were married?"

"I guess it came out of necessity. Being a single father. What about you, Harry? What do you cook?"

Bosch looked at us both like we were crazy.

"I can fry an egg," he said. "That's about it."

"Let's get back to the trial," Maggie said. "I think Royce has got Jessup and Sarah. Then I think he's got the secret witness we haven't found. The guy from the last rehab center."

"Edward Roman," Bosch said.

"Right. Roman. That makes three and the fourth one could be his investigator or maybe his meth expert but is probably just bullshit. There is no fourth. So much of what Royce does is misdirection. He doesn't want anybody's eyes on the prize. Wants them looking anywhere but right at the truth."

"What about Roman?" I said. "We haven't found him, but have we figured out his testimony?"

"Not by a long shot," Maggie said. "I've gone over and over this with Sarah and she has no idea what he's going to say. She couldn't remember ever talking about her sister with him."

"The summary Royce provided in discovery says he will testify about Sarah's 'revelations' about her childhood," Bosch said. "Nothing more specific than that and, of course, Royce claims he didn't take any notes during the interview."

"Look," I said, "we have his record and we know exactly what kind of guy we're dealing with here. He's going to say whatever Royce wants him to say. It's that simple. Whatever works for the defense. So we should be less concerned by what he says — because we know it will be lies — and more concerned with knocking him out of the box. What do we have that can help us there?"

Maggie and I both looked at Bosch and he was ready for us.

"I think I might have something. I'm going to go see somebody tonight. If it pans out we'll have it in the morning. I'll tell you then."

My frustrations with Bosch's methods of investigation and communication boiled over at that point.

"Harry, come on. We're part of a team here. This secret agent stuff doesn't really work when we're in that courtroom every day with our asses on the line."

Bosch looked down at his plate and I saw the slow burn. His face grew as dark as the sauce.

"*Your* asses on the line?" he said. "I didn't see anywhere in the surveillance reports that Jessup was hanging around outside your house, Haller, so don't tell me about your ass being on the line. Your job is in that courtroom. It's nice and safe and sometimes you win and sometimes you lose. But no matter what happens, you're back in court the next day. You want your ass on the line, try working out there."

He pointed out the window toward the view of the city.

"Hey, guys, let's just calm down here," Maggie said quickly. "Harry, what's the matter? Has Jessup gone back to Woodrow Wilson? Maybe we should just revoke this guy and put him back in lockup."

Bosch shook his head.

"Not to my street. He hasn't been back there since that first night and he hasn't been up to Mulholland in more than a week."

"Then what is it?"

Bosch put his fork down and pushed his plate back.

"We already know there's a good chance that Jessup has a gun from that meeting the SIS saw him have with a convicted gun dealer. They didn't see what he got from the guy, but since it came wrapped in a towel, it doesn't take a lot to figure it out. And then, you want to know what happened last night? Some bright guy on the surveillance decides to leave his post to use the john without telling anybody and Jessup walked right out of the net."

"They lost him?" Maggie asked.

"Yeah, until I found him right before he found me, which might not have turned out so well. And you know what he's up to? He's building a dungeon for somebody and for all I know—"

He leaned forward over the table and finished in an urgent whisper.

"—might be for my kid!"

"Whoa, wait, Harry," Maggie said. "Back up. He's building a dungeon? Where?"

"Under the pier. There's like a storage room. He put a lock on the door and dropped canned food off there last night. Like he's getting it ready for somebody."

"Okay, that's scary," Maggie said. "But your daughter? We don't know that. You said he went by your place only the one time. What makes you think—?"

"Because I can't afford not to think it. You understand?"

She nodded.

"Yes, I do. Then I come back to what I just said. We violate him for associating with a known criminal—the gun dealer—and pull his OR release. There's only a few days left in the trial and he obviously didn't act out or make the mistake we thought he would. Let's be safe and put him back inside until this is over."

"And what if we don't get the conviction?" Bosch said. "What happens then? This guy walks and that'll also be the end of the surveillance. He'll be out there without any eyes on him."

That brought a silence to the table. I stared at Bosch and understood the pressure he was under. The case, the threat to his daughter, and no wife or ex-wife to help him out at home.

Bosch finally broke the uneasy silence.

"Maggie, are you taking Hayley home with you tonight?"

Maggie nodded.

"Yes, when we're finished here."

"Can Maddie stay with you two tonight? She brought a change of clothes in her backpack. I'd come by in the morning in time to take her to school."

The request seemed to take Maggie by surprise, especially since the girls had just met. Bosch pressed her.

"I need to meet somebody tonight and I don't know where it will take me," Bosch said. "It might even lead to Roman. I need to be able to move without worrying about Maddie."

She nodded.

"Okay, that's fine. It sounds like they're becoming fast friends. I just hope they don't stay up all night."

"Thank you, Maggie."

About thirty seconds of silence went by before I spoke.

"Tell us about this dungeon, Harry."

"I was standing in it last night."

"Why the Santa Monica pier?"

"My guess is that it's because of the proximity to what's on top of the pier."

"Prey."

Bosch nodded.

"But what about noise? You're saying this place is directly below the pier?"

"There are ways of controlling human sound. And last night the sound of waves crashing against the pilings under there was so loud you could've screamed all night and nobody would've heard you. You probably wouldn't even hear a gunshot from down there."

Bosch spoke with a certain authority of the dark places of the world and the evil they held. I lost my appetite then and pushed my plate away. I felt dread come inside me.

Dread for Melissa Landy and all the other victims in the world.

Thirty-six

Wednesday, April 7, 11:00 P.M.

Gilbert and Sullivan were waiting for him in a car parked on Lankershim Boulevard near its northern terminus at San Fernando Road. It was a blighted area populated primarily with used-car lots and repair shops. In the midst of all of this low-rent industry was a run-down motel advertising rooms for fifty dollars a week. The motel had no name on display. Just the lighted sign that said MOTEL.

Gilbert and Sullivan were Gilberto Reyes and John Sullivan, a pair of narcs assigned to the Valley Enforcement Team, a street-level drug unit. When Bosch was looking for Edward Roman he put the word out in all such units in the department. His assumption from Roman's record was that he had never gotten away from the life as Sarah Gleason had. There had to be somebody in the department's narco units with a line on him.

It paid off with a call from Reyes. He and his partner didn't have a bead on Roman but they knew him from past interactions on the street and knew where his current trick partner was holed up and apparently awaiting his return. Long-term drug addicts often partnered with a prostitute, offering her protection in exchange for a share of the drugs her earnings bought.

Bosch pulled his car up behind the narcs' UC car and parked. He got out and moved up to their car, getting in the back after checking the seat to make sure it was clean of vomit and any other detritus from the people they had transported lately.

"Detective Bosch, I presume?" said the driver, whom Bosch guessed was Reyes.

"Yeah, how are you guys?"

He offered his fist over the seat and they both gave him a bump while identifying themselves. Bosch had it wrong. The one who looked to be of Latin origin was Sullivan and the one who looked like a bag of white bread was Reyes.

"Gilbert and Sullivan, huh?"

"That's what they called us when we got partnered," Sullivan said. "Kind of stuck."

Bosch nodded. That was enough for the meet-and-greet. Everybody had a nickname and a story to go with it. These guys together didn't add up to how old Bosch was and they probably had no clue who Gilbert and Sullivan were, anyway.

"So you know Eddie Roman?"

"We've had the pleasure," Reyes said. "Just another piece of human shit that floats around out here."

"But like I told you on the phone, we ain't seen him in a month or so," Sullivan added. "So we got you his next best thing. His onion. She's over there in room three."

"What's her name?"

Sullivan laughed and Bosch didn't get it.

"Her name is Sonia Reyes," said Reyes. "No relation."

"That he knows of," Sullivan added.

He burst into laughter, which Bosch ignored.

"Spell it for me," he said.

He took out his notebook and wrote it down.

"And you're sure she's in the room?"

"We're sure," Reyes said.

"Okay, anything else I should know before I go in?"

"No," Reyes said, "but we were planning on goin' in with you. She might get squirrelly with you."

Bosch reached forward and clapped him on the shoulder.

"No, I got this. I don't want a crowd in the room."

Reyes nodded. Message delivered. Bosch did not want any witnesses to what he might need to do here.

"But thanks for the help. It will be noted."

"An important case, huh?" Sullivan said.

Bosch opened the door and got out.

"They all are," he said.

He closed the door, slapped the roof twice and walked away.

The hotel had an eight-foot security fence around it. Bosch had to press a buzzer and hold his badge up to a camera. He was buzzed into the compound but walked right by the office and down a breezeway leading to the rooms.

"Hey!" a voice called from behind.

Bosch turned and saw a man with an unbuttoned shirt leaning out the door of the motel's office.

"Where the fuck you goin', dude?"

"Go back inside and shut the door. This is police business."

"Don't matter, man. I let you in but this is private property. You can't just come through the—"

Bosch started quickly moving back up the breezeway toward the man. The man took his measure and backed down without Bosch saying a word.

"Never mind, man. You're good."

He quickly stepped back inside and closed the door. Bosch turned back and found room three without a further problem. He leaned close to the jamb to see if he could pick up any sound. He heard nothing.

There was a peephole. He put his finger over it and knocked. He waited and then knocked again.

"Sonia, open up. Eddie sent me."

"Who are you?"

The voice was female, ragged and suspicious. Bosch used the universal pass code.

"Doesn't matter. Eddie sent me with somethin' to hold you over till he's done."

No response.

"Okay, Sonia, I'll tell him you weren't interested. I've got someone else who wants it."

He took his finger off the peep and started walking away. Almost immediately the door opened behind him.

"Wait."

Bosch turned back. The door was open six inches. He saw a set of hollow eyes looking out at him, a dim light behind them.

"Let me see."

Bosch looked around.

"What, out here?" he said. "They got cameras all over the place."

"Eddie tol' me not to open the door for strangers. You look like a cop to me."

"Well, maybe I am, but that doesn't change that Eddie sent me."

Bosch started to turn again.

"Like I said, I'll tell him I tried. Have a nice night."

"Okay, okay. You can come in but only to make the drop. Nothing else."

Bosch walked back toward the door. She moved behind it and opened it. He entered and turned to her and saw the gun. It was an old revolver and he saw no bullets in the exposed chambers. Bosch raised his hands chest high. He could tell she was hurting. She'd been waiting too long for somebody, putting blind junkie trust in something that wouldn't pay off.

"That's not necessary, Sonia. Besides, I don't think Eddie left you with any bullets."

"I got one left. You want to try it?"

Probably the one she was saving for herself. She was skin and bones and close to the end of the line. No junkie went the distance.

"Give it to me," she ordered. "Now."

"Okay, take it easy. I have it right here."

He reached his right hand into his coat pocket and pulled out a balled piece of aluminum foil he had taken from a roll in Mickey Haller's kitchen. He held it out to the right of his body and he knew her desperate eyes would follow it. He shot his left hand out and snatched the gun out of her hand. He then stepped forward and roughly shoved her onto the bed.

"Shut up and don't move," he commanded.

"What is—?"

"I said shut up!"

He popped the gun's barrel out and checked it. She had been right. There was one bullet left. He slid it out into his palm and then put it in his pocket. He hooked the gun into his belt. Then he pulled his badge wallet and opened it for her to see.

"You had that right," he said.

"What do you want?"

"We'll get to that."

Bosch moved around the bed, looking about the threadbare room. It smelled like cigarettes and body odor. There were several plastic grocery bags on the floor containing her belongings. Shoes in one, clothing in a few others. On the bed's lone side table was an overloaded ashtray and a glass pipe.

"What are you hurting for, Sonia. Crack? Heroin? Or is it meth?"

She didn't answer.

"I can help you better if I know what you need."

"I don't want your help."

Bosch turned and looked at her. So far things were going exactly as he predicted they would.

"Really?" he said. "Don't need my help? You think Eddie Roman is going to come back for you?"

"He's coming back."

"I got news for you. He's already gone. I'm guessing they got him cleaned up nice and neat and he won't be coming back up here once he does what they want him to do. He'll take the paycheck and when that runs out he'll just find himself a new trick partner."

He paused and looked at her.

"Somebody who still has something somebody would want to buy."

Her eyes took on the distant look of someone who knows the truth when she hears it.

"Leave me alone," she said in a hoarse whisper.

"I know I'm not telling you anything you don't already know. You've been waiting for Eddie longer than you thought you would, huh? How many days you have left on the room?"

He read the answer in her eyes.

"Already past, huh? Probably giving the guy in the office blow-jobs to let you stay. How long's that going to last? Pretty soon he'll just want the money."

"I said go away."

"I will. But you come with me, Sonia. Right now."

"What do you want?"

"I want to know everything you know about Eddie Roman."

PART FOUR

— The Silent Witness

Thirty-seven

Thursday, April 8, 9:01 A.M.

Before the judge called for the jury, Clive Royce stood and asked the court for a directed verdict of acquittal. He argued that the state had failed to live up to its duty in carrying the burden of proof. He said that the evidence presented by the prosecutors failed to cross the threshold of guilt beyond a reasonable doubt. I was ready to stand to argue the state's side, but the judge held up her hand to signal me to stay in place. She then quickly dispensed with Royce's motion.

"Motion denied," Breitman said. "The court holds that the evidence presented by the prosecution is sufficient for the jury to consider. Mr. Royce, are you ready to proceed with the defense?"

"I am, Your Honor."

"Okay, sir, then we will recall the jury now. Will you have an opening statement?"

"A brief one, Your Honor."

"Very well, I am going to hold you to that."

The jurors filed in and took their assigned places. On many of them I saw expressions of anticipation. I took this as a good sign, as if they were wondering how in the hell the defense would be able to dig its way out of all the evidence the state had dumped on it. It was probably all wishful thinking on my part, but I had been studying juries for most of my adult life and I liked what I saw.

After welcoming the jury back, the judge turned the courtroom over to Royce, reminded the jurors that this was an opening statement, not a listing of facts unless backed up later with testimony and evidence. Royce strode with full confidence to the lectern without a note or file in his hand. I knew he had the same philosophy as I did when it came to making opening statements. Look them in the eyes and don't flinch and don't back down from your theory, no matter how far-fetched or unbelievable. Sell it. If they don't think you believe it, they never will.

His strategy of deferring his opener until the start of the defense's case would now pay dividends. He would begin the day and his case by delivering to the jury a statement that didn't have to be true, that could be as outlandish as anything ever heard in the courtroom. As long as he kept the jury riding along, nothing else really mattered.

"Ladies and gentlemen of the jury, good morning. Today begins a new phase of the trial. The defense phase. This is when we start to tell you our side of the story, and believe me, we have another side to almost everything the prosecution has offered you over the past three days.

"I am not going to take a lot of your time here because I am very eager, and Jason Jessup is very eager, to get to the evidence that the prosecution has either failed to find or chosen not to present to you. It doesn't matter which, at this point; the only things that matter are that you hear it and that it allows you to see the full picture of what transpired on Windsor Boulevard on February sixteenth, nineteen eighty-six. I urge you to listen closely, to watch closely. If you do that, you will see the truth emerge."

I looked over at the legal pad on which Maggie had been doodling while Royce spoke. In large letters she had written *WINDBAG!* I thought, She hasn't seen anything yet.

"This case," Royce continued, "is about one thing. A family's darkest secrets. You got only a glimpse of them during the prosecution's presentation. You got the tip of the iceberg from the prosecution, but today you will get the whole iceberg. Today you will get the cold hard truth. That being that Jason Jessup is the true victim here today. The victim of a family's desire to hide their darkest secret."

Maggie leaned toward me and whispered, "Brace yourself."

I nodded. I knew exactly where we were going.

"This trial is about a monster who killed a child. A monster who defiled one young girl and was going to move on to the next when something went wrong and he killed that child. This trial is about the family that was so fearful of that monster that they went along with the plan to cover up the crime and point the finger elsewhere. At an innocent man."

Royce pointed righteously at Jessup as he said this last line. Maggie shook her head in disgust, a calculated move for the jury.

"Jason, would you please stand up?" Royce said.

His client did as instructed and turned fully to the jury, his eyes boldly scanning from face to face, not flinching or looking away.

"Jason Jessup is an innocent man," Royce said with the requisite outrage in his voice. "He was the fall guy. An innocent man caught in an impromptu plan to cover up the worst kind of crime, the taking of a child's life."

Jessup sat down and Royce paused so his words would burn into every juror's conscience. It was highly theatrical and planned that way.

"There are two victims here," he finally said. "Melissa Landy is a victim. She lost her life. Jason Jessup is also a victim because they are trying to take his life. The family conspired against him and then the police followed their lead. They ignored the evidence and planted their own. And now after twenty-four years, after witnesses are gone and memories have dimmed, they've come calling for him..."

Royce cast his head down as if tremendously burdened by the truth. I knew he would now wrap things up.

"Ladies and gentlemen of the jury, we are here for only one

reason. To seek the truth. Before the end of this day, you will know the truth about Windsor Boulevard. You will know that Jason Jessup is an innocent man."

Royce paused again, then thanked the jury and moved back to his seat. In what I was sure was a well-rehearsed moment, Jessup put his arm around his lawyer's shoulders, gave him a squeeze and thanked him.

But the judge gave Royce little time to savor the moment or the slick delivery of his opening statement. She told him to call his first witness. I turned in my seat and saw Bosch standing in the back of the courtroom. He gave me the nod. I had sent him to get Sarah Ann Gleason from the hotel as soon as Royce had informed me upon arriving at court that she would be his first witness.

"The *defense* calls Sarah Ann Gleason to the stand," Royce said, putting the accent on defense in a way that suggested that this was an unexpected turnabout.

Bosch stepped out of the courtroom and quickly returned with Gleason. He walked her down the aisle and through the gate. She went the rest of the way on her own. She again was dressed for court informally, wearing a white peasant blouse and a pair of jeans.

Gleason was reminded by the judge that she was still under oath and turned over to Royce. This time when he went to the lectern he carried a thick file and a legal pad. Probably most of it — the file, at least — was just an attempt to intimidate Gleason, to make her think he had a big fat file on everything she had ever done wrong in life.

"Good morning, Ms. Gleason."

"Good morning."

"Now, you testified yesterday that you were the victim of sexual abuse at the hands of your stepfather, Kensington Landy, is that correct?"

"Yes."

With the first word of her testimony I detected trepidation. She hadn't been allowed to hear Royce's opening statement but we had prepared Gleason for the way we thought the defense case would go.

She was exhibiting fear already and this never played well with the jury. There was little Maggie and I could do. Sarah was up there on her own.

"At what point in your life did this abuse start?"

"When I was twelve."

"And it ended when?"

"When I was thirteen. Right after my sister's death."

"I notice you didn't call it your sister's murder. You called it her death. Is there a reason for that?"

"I'm not sure what you mean."

"Well, your sister was murdered, correct? It wasn't an accident, was it?"

"No, it was murder."

"Then why did you refer to it as her death just a moment ago?"

"I'm not sure."

"Are you confused about what happened to your sister?"

Maggie was on her feet objecting before Gleason could answer.

"Counsel is badgering the witness," she said. "He's more interested in eliciting an emotional response than an answer."

"Your Honor, I simply am trying to learn how and why this witness views this crime the way she does. It goes to state of mind of the witness. I am not interested in eliciting anything other than an answer to the question I asked."

The judge weighed things for a moment before ruling.

"I'm going to allow it. The witness may answer the question."

"I'll repeat it," Royce said. "Ms. Gleason, are you confused about what happened to your sister?"

During the exchange between lawyers and the judge, Gleason had found some resolve. She answered forcefully while hitting Royce with a hard stare of defiance.

"No, I'm not confused about what happened. I was there. She was kidnapped by your client and after that I never saw her again. There is no confusion about that at all."

I wanted to stand and clap. Instead, I just nodded to myself. It was a fine, fine answer. But Royce moved on, acting as though he had not been hit with the tomato.

"There have been times in your life when you were confused, however, correct?"

"About my sister and what happened and who took her? Never."

"I'm talking about times you were incarcerated in mental health facilities and the psych wards of jails and prisons."

Gleason lowered her head in full realization that she would not escape this trial without a full airing of the lost years of her life. I just had to hope she would respond in the way Maggie had told her to.

"After the murder of my sister, many things went wrong in my life," she said.

She then looked up directly at Royce as she continued.

"Yes, I spent some time in those kinds of places. I think, and my counselors agreed, that it was because of what happened to Melissa."

Good answer, I thought. She was fighting.

"We'll get back into that later on," Royce said. "But getting back to your sister, she was twelve at the time of her murder, correct?"

"That's right."

"This would have been the same age you were when your step-father began to sexually abuse you. Am I right?"

"About the same, yes."

"Did you warn your sister about him?"

There was a long pause as Gleason considered her answer. This was because there was no good answer.

"Ms. Gleason?" the judge prompted. "Please answer the question."

"No, I didn't warn her. I was afraid to."

"Afraid of what?" Royce asked.

"Him. As you've already pointed out, I've been through a lot of therapy in my life. I know that it is not unusual for a child to be unable to tell anyone. You get trapped in the behavior. Trapped by fear. I've been told that many times."

"In other words, you go along to get along."

"Sort of. But that is a simplification. It was more—"

"But you did live with a lot of fear in your life back then?"

"Yes, I—"

"Did your stepfather tell you not to tell anyone about what he was doing to you?"

"Yes, he said—"

"Did he threaten you?"

"He said that if I told anyone I would be taken away from my mother and sister. He said he would make sure that the state would think my mother knew about it and they would consider her unfit. They would take Melissa and me away. Then we would get split up because foster homes couldn't always take two at a time."

"Did you believe him?"

"Yes, I was twelve. I believed him."

"And it scared you, didn't it?"

"Yes. I wanted to stay with my fam—"

"Wasn't it that same fear and control that your stepfather had over you that made you go along to get along after he killed your sister?"

Again Maggie jumped up to object, stating that the question was leading and assumed facts not in evidence. The judge agreed and sustained the objection.

Undeterred, Royce went at Gleason relentlessly.

"Isn't it true that you and your mother did and said exactly what your stepfather told you to in the cover-up of Melissa's murder?"

"No, that's not—"

"He told you to say it was a tow truck driver and that you were to pick one of the men the police brought to the house."

"No! He didn't—"

"Objection!"

"There was no hide-and-seek game outside the house, was there? Your sister was murdered inside the house by Kensington Landy. Isn't that true!"

"Your Honor!"

Maggie was now shouting.

"Counsel is badgering the witness with these leading questions. He doesn't want her answers. He just wants to deliver his lies to the jury!"

The judge looked from Maggie to Royce.

"All right, everyone just calm down. The objection is sustained. Mr. Royce, ask the witness one question at a time and allow her the time to answer. And you will not ask leading questions. Need I remind you, you called her as a witness. If you wanted to lead her you should've conducted a cross-examination when you had the opportunity."

Royce put on his best look of contrition. It must've been difficult.

"I apologize for getting carried away, Your Honor," he said. "It won't happen again."

It didn't matter if it happened again. Royce had already gotten his point across. His purpose was not to get an admission from Gleason. In fact, he expected none. His purpose was to get his alternate theory to the jury. In that, he was being very successful.

"Okay, let's move on," Royce said. "You mentioned earlier that you spent a considerable part of your adult life in counseling and drug rehab, not to mention incarceration. Is that correct?"

"To a point," Gleason said. "I have been clean and sober and a —"

"Just answer the question that was asked," Royce quickly interjected.

"Objection," Maggie said. "She is trying to answer the question he asked, but Mr. Royce doesn't like the full answer and is trying to cut her off."

"Let her answer the question, Mr. Royce," Breitman said tiredly. "Go ahead, Ms. Gleason."

"I was just saying that I have been clean for seven years and a productive member of society."

"Thank you, Ms. Gleason."

Royce then led her through a tragic and sordid history, literally going arrest by arrest and revealing all the details of the depravity Sarah wallowed in for so long. Maggie objected often, arguing that it had little to do with Sarah's identification of Jessup, but Breitman allowed most of the questioning to continue.

Finally, Royce wrapped up his examination by setting up his next witness.

"Getting back to the rehabilitation center in North Hollywood, you were there for five months in nineteen ninety-nine, correct?"

"I don't remember exactly when or for how long. You obviously have the records there."

"But you do remember meeting another client, named Edward Roman, known as Eddie?"

"Yes, I do."

"And you got to know him well?"

"Yes."

"How did you meet him?"

"We were in group counseling together."

"How would you describe the relationship you had with Eddie Roman back then?"

"Well, in counseling we sort of realized that we knew some of the same people and liked doing the same things—meaning drugs. So we started hanging out and it continued after we were both released."

"Was this a romantic relationship?"

Gleason laughed in a way that was not supposed to impart humor.

"What passed for romance between two drug addicts," she said. "I think the term is *enablers*. By being together we were enabling each other. But *romance* is not a word I would use. We had sex on occasion—when he was able to. But there was no romance, Mr. Royce."

"But didn't you in fact believe at one point that you two were married?"

"Eddie set something up on the beach with a man he said was a minister. But it wasn't real. It wasn't legal."

"But at the time you thought it was, didn't you?"

"Yes."

"So were you in love with him?"

"No, I wasn't in love with him. I just thought he could protect me."

"So you were married, or at least thought you were. Did you live together?"

"Yes."

"Where?"

"In different motels in the Valley."

"All this time you were together, you must've confided in Eddie, yes?"

"About some things, yes."

"Did you ever confide in him about your sister's murder?"

"I am sure I did. I didn't keep it a secret. I would have talked about it in group therapy in North Hollywood and he was sitting right there."

"Did you ever tell him that your stepfather killed your sister?"

"No, because that didn't happen."

"So if Eddie Roman were to come to this courtroom and testify that you did indeed tell him that, then he would be lying."

"Yes."

"But you have already testified yesterday and today that you have lied to counselors and police. You have stolen and committed many crimes in your life. But you're not lying here. Is that what we are to believe?"

"I'm not lying. You are talking about a period of my life when I did those things. I don't deny that. I was human trash, okay? But I am past that now and have been past it for a long time. I'm not lying now."

"Okay, Ms. Gleason, no further questions."

As Royce returned to his seat, Maggie and I put our heads together and whispered.

"She held up really well," Maggie said. "I think we should let it stand and I'll just hit a couple high notes."

"Sounds good."

"Ms. McPherson?" the judge prompted.

Maggie stood.

"Yes, Your Honor. Just a few questions."

She went to the lectern with her trusty legal pad. She skipped the buildup and got right to the matters she wanted to cover.

"Sarah, this man Eddie Roman and the phony marriage—whose idea was it to get married?"

"Eddie asked me to get married. He said we would work together as a team and share everything, that he would protect me and that we could never be forced to testify against each other if we got arrested."

"And what did working together as a team mean in that circumstance?"

"Well, I...he wanted me to sell myself so we would have money to buy drugs and to have a motel room."

"Did you do that for Eddie?"

"For a little bit of time. And then I got arrested."

"Did Eddie bail you out?"

"No."

"Did he come to court?"

"No."

"Your record shows you pleaded guilty to soliciting and were sentenced to time served, is that correct?"

"Yes."

"How long was that?"

"I think it was thirteen days."

"And was Eddie there waiting when you got out of jail?"

"No."

"Did you ever see him again?"

"No, I didn't."

Maggie checked her notes, flipped up a couple pages and found what she was looking for.

"Okay, Sarah, you mentioned several times during your testimony earlier today that you did not remember specific dates and occurrences that Mr. Royce asked you about during the time you were a drug user. Is that a fair characterization?"

"Yes, that's true."

"During all of those years of drug abuse and counseling and incarceration, were you ever able to forget what happened to your sister, Melissa?"

"No, never. I thought about it every day. I still do."

"Were you ever able to forget about the man who crossed your front yard and grabbed your sister while you watched from the bushes?"

"No, never. I thought about him every day and still do."

"Have you ever had a moment of doubt about the man you identified as your sister's abductor?"

"No."

Maggie turned and pointedly looked at Jessup, who was looking down at a legal pad and writing what were probably meaningless notes. Her eyes held on him and she waited. Just as Jessup looked up to see what was holding up the testimony she asked her last question.

"Never a single doubt, Sarah?"

"No, never."

"Thank you, Sarah. No further questions."

Thirty-eight

The judge followed Sarah Gleason's testimony by announcing the midmorning break. Bosch waited in his seat at the railing until Royce and Jessup got up and started to file out. He then stood and moved against the grain to get to his witness. As he passed by Jessup he clapped him hard on the arm.

"I think your makeup's starting to run, Jason."

He said it with a smile as he went by.

Jessup stopped and turned and was about to respond to the taunt when Royce grabbed him by the other arm and kept him going.

Bosch moved forward to collect Gleason from the witness stand. After parts of two days on the stand, she looked like she was both emotionally and physically drained. Like she might need help just getting up from the chair.

"Sarah, you did great," he told her.

"Thank you. I couldn't tell if anybody believed me."

"They all did, Sarah. They all did."

He walked her back to the prosecution table, where Haller and McPherson had similar reviews of her testimony. McPherson got up out of her seat and hugged her.

"You stood up to Jessup and you stood up for your sister," she said. "You can be proud of that for the rest of your life."

Gleason suddenly burst into tears and held her hand over her eyes. McPherson quickly pulled her back into the hug.

"I know, I know. You've held it together and stayed strong. It's okay to let it go now."

Bosch walked over to the jury box and grabbed the box of tissues. He brought them to Gleason and she wiped away her tears.

"You're almost done," Haller said to her. "You've totally finished testifying so now all we want you to do is sit in court and observe the trial. We want you to sit up here in the front row when Eddie Roman testifies. After that, we can put you on a plane home this afternoon."

"Okay, but why?"

"Because he's going to tell lies about you. And if he is going to do that, then he's going to have to tell them to your face."

"I don't think he's going to have a problem with that. He never did."

"Well, then, the jury will want to see how you react. And how he'll react. And don't worry, we've got something else cooking that'll make Eddie feel some heat."

At that, Haller turned to Bosch.

"You ready with this?"

"Just give me the sign."

"Can I ask something?" Gleason said.

"Sure," Haller said.

"What if I don't want to get on a plane today? What if I want to be here for the verdict? For my sister."

"We would love that, Sarah," Maggie said. "You are welcome and can stay as long as you like."

Bosch stood in the hallway outside the courtroom. He had his phone out and was slowly typing a text to his daughter with one finger. His efforts were interrupted when he received a text. It was from Haller and was only one word.

NOW

He put his phone away and walked to the witness waiting room. Sonia Reyes was slumped in a chair with her head down, two empty coffee cups on the table in front of her.

"Okay, Sonia, rise and shine. We're going to go do this. You okay? You ready?"

She looked up at him with tired eyes.

"That's too many questions, po-liceman."

"Okay, I'll settle for one. How're you feeling?"

"About how I look. You got any more of that stuff they gave me at the clinic?"

"That was it. But I'm going to have someone take you right back there as soon as we're finished here."

"Whatever you say, po-liceman. I don't think I've been up this early since the last time I was in county lockup."

"Yeah, well, it's not that early. Let's go."

He helped her up and they headed toward Department 112. Reyes was what they called a *silent witness*. She wouldn't be testifying in the trial. She was in no condition to. But by walking her down the aisle and putting her in the front row, Bosch would make sure she would be noticed by Edward Roman. The hope was that she'd knock Roman off his game, maybe even make him change it up. They were banking on his not knowing the rules of evidence and therefore not understanding that her appearance in the gallery precluded her from testifying at the trial and exposing his lies.

Harry hit the door with a fist as he pushed it open because he knew it would draw attention inside the court. He then ushered Reyes in and walked her down the aisle. Edward Roman was already on the stand, sworn in and testifying. He wore an ill-fitting suit borrowed from Royce's client closet and was clean-shaven with short, neat hair. He stumbled verbally when he saw Sonia in the courtroom.

"We had group counseling twice..."

"Only twice?" Royce asked, unaware of the distraction in the aisle behind him.

"What?"

"You said you only had group counseling with Sarah Gleason twice?"

"Nah, man, I meant twice a day."

Bosch escorted Reyes to a seat with a reserved sign on it. He then sat down next to her.

"And approximately how long did this last?" Royce asked.

"Each one was fifty minutes, I think," Roman answered, his eyes holding on Reyes in the audience.

"I mean how long were you both in counseling? A month, a year, how long?"

"Oh, it was for five months."

"And did you become lovers while you were in the center?"

Roman lowered his eyes.

"Uh...yeah, that's right."

"How did you manage that? I assume there are rules against that."

"Well, if there's a will, there's always a way, you know? We found time. We found places."

"Did this relationship continue after you two were released from the center?"

"Yes. She got out a couple weeks ahead of me. Then I got out and we hooked up."

"Did you live together?"

"Uh-huh."

"Is that a yes?"

"Yes. Can I ask a question?"

Royce paused. He hadn't expected this.

"No, Mr. Roman," the judge said. "You can't ask a question. You are a witness in these proceedings."

"But how can they bring her in here like that?"

"Who, Mr. Roman?"

Roman pointed out to the gallery and right at Reyes.

"Her."

The judge looked at Reyes and then at Bosch sitting next to her. A look of deep suspicion crossed her face.

"I'm going to ask the jury to step back into the jury room for a few moments. This should not take long."

The jurors filed back into the jury room. The moment the last one in closed the door, the judge zeroed in on Bosch.

"Detective Bosch."

Harry stood up.

"Who is the woman sitting to your left?"

"Your Honor," Haller said. "Can I answer that question?"

"Please do."

"Detective Bosch is sitting with Sonia Reyes, who has agreed to help the prosecution as a witness consultant."

The judge looked from Haller to Reyes and back to Haller.

"You want to run that by me again, Mr. Haller?"

"Judge, Ms. Reyes is acquainted with the witness. Because the defense did not make Mr. Roman available to us prior to his testimony here, we have asked Ms. Reyes to give us advice on how to proceed with our cross-examination."

Haller's explanation had done nothing to change the look of suspicion on Breitman's face.

"Are you paying her for this advice?"

"We have agreed to help her get into a clinic."

"I should hope so."

"Your Honor," Royce said. "May I be heard?"

"Go ahead, Mr. Royce."

"I think it is quite obvious that the prosecution is attempting to intimidate Mr. Roman. This is a gangster move, Judge. Not something I would expect to see from the District Attorney's Office."

"Well, I strongly object to that characterization," Haller said. "It is perfectly acceptable within the canon of courtroom procedure and ethics to hire and use consultants. Mr. Royce employed a jury consultant last week and that was perfectly acceptable. But now that the prosecution has a consultant that he knows will help expose his witness as a liar and someone who preys on women, he objects. With all due respect, I would call that the gangster move."

"Okay, we're not going to debate this now," Breitman said. "I find that the prosecution is certainly within bounds in using Ms. Reyes as a consultant. Let's bring the jury back."

"Thank you, Judge," Haller said as he sat down.

As the jurors filed back into the box, Haller turned and looked back at Bosch. He gave a slight nod and Bosch knew that he was happy. The exchange with the judge could not have worked better in delivering a message to Roman. The message being that we know your game, and come our turn to ask the questions, so will the jury. Roman now had a choice. He could stick with the defense or start playing for the prosecution.

Testimony continued once the jury was back in place. Royce quickly established through Roman that he and Sarah Gleason had a relationship that lasted nearly a year and involved the sharing of personal stories as well as drugs. But when it came to revealing those personal stories, Roman did a cut and run, leaving Royce hanging in the wind.

"Now, did there come a time when she spoke about her sister's murder?"

"A time? There were lots of times. She talked about it a lot, man."

"And did she ever tell you in detail what she called the 'real story' "

"Yes, she did."

"Can you tell the court what she told you?"

Roman hesitated and scratched his chin before answering. Bosch knew this was the moment that his work either paid off or went for naught.

"She told me that they were playing hide-and-seek in the yard and a guy came and grabbed her sister and that she saw the whole thing."

Bosch's eyes made a circuit of the room. First he checked the jurors and it seemed that even they had been expecting Roman to say something else. Then the prosecution table. He saw that McPherson had grabbed Haller by the back of his arm and was squeezing it. And lastly Royce, who was now the one hesitating. He stood at the lectern looking down at his notes, one armed cocked with his fist on his hip like a frustrated teacher who could not draw the correct answer from a student.

"That is the story you heard Sarah Gleason tell in group counseling at the rehabilitation center, correct?" he finally asked.

"That's right."

"But isn't it true that she told you a different version of events — what she called the 'real story' — when you were in more private settings?"

"Uh, no. She pretty much stuck to the same story all the time."

Bosch saw McPherson squeeze Haller's arm again. This was the whole case right here.

Royce was like a man left behind in the water by a dive boat. He was treading water but he was in the open sea and it was only a matter of time before he went down. He tried to do what he could.

"Now, Mr. Roman, on March second of this year, did you not contact my office and offer your services as a witness for the defense?"

"I don't know about the date but I called there, yeah."

"And did you speak to my investigator, Karen Revelle?"

"I spoke to a woman but I can't remember her name."

"And didn't you tell her a story that is quite different from the one you just recounted?"

"But I wasn't under oath or nothin' then."

"That's right, sir, but you did tell Karen a different story, true?"

"I might've. I can't remember."

"Didn't you tell Karen at that time that Ms. Gleason had told you that her stepfather had killed her sister?"

Haller was up with the objection, arguing that not only was Royce leading the witness but that there was no foundation for the question and that counsel was trying to get testimony to the jury that the witness was not willing to give. The judge sustained the objection.

"Your Honor," Royce said, "the defense would like to request a short break to confer with its witness."

Before Haller could object the judge denied the request.

"By this witness's own testimony this morning, you have had since March second to prepare for this moment. We go to lunch in thirty-five minutes. You can confer with him then, Mr. Royce. Ask your next question."

"Thank you, Your Honor."

Royce looked down at his legal pad. From Bosch's angle he could tell he was looking at a blank page.

"Mr. Royce?" the judge prompted.

"Yes, Your Honor, just rechecking a date. Mr. Roman, why did you call my office on March second?"

"Well, I seen something about the case on the TV. In fact, it was you. I seen you talking about it. And I knew something about it from knowing Sarah like I did. So I called up to see if I was needed."

"And then you came to my offices, correct?"

"Yeah, that's right. You sent that lady to pick me up."

"And when you came to my office, you told me a different story than you are telling the jury now, isn't that right?"

"Like I said, I don't remember exactly what I said then. I'm a drug addict, sir. I say a lot of things I don't remember and don't really mean. All I remember is that the woman who came said she'd put me up in a nicer hotel and I had no money for a place at that time. So I sort of said what she told me to say."

Bosch made a fist and bounced it once on his thigh. This was an unmitigated disaster for the defense. He looked over at Jessup to see if he realized how bad things had just turned for him. And Jessup seemed to sense it. He turned and looked back at Bosch, his eyes dark with growing anger and realization. Bosch leaned forward and slowly raised a finger. He dragged it across his throat.

Jessup turned away.

Thirty-nine

I have had many good moments in court. I've stood next to men at the moment they knew that they were going free because of my good work. I have stood in the well in front of a jury and felt the tingle of truth and righteousness roll down my spine. And I have destroyed liars without mercy on the witness stand. These are the moments I live for in my professional life. But few of them measured up to the moment I watched Jason Jessup's defense unravel with the testimony of Edward Roman.

As Roman crashed and burned on the stand, my ex-wife and prosecution partner squeezed my arm to the point of pain. She couldn't help it. She knew it, too. This was not something Royce was going to recover from. A key part of what was already going to be a fragile defense was crumbling before his eyes. It wasn't so much that his witness had pulled a one-eighty on him. It was the jury seeing a defense that was now obviously built upon a liar. The jury would not forgive this. It was over and I believed everyone in the courtroom—from the judge to the gadflies in the back row of the gallery—knew it. Jessup was going down.

I turned and looked back to share the moment with Bosch. After all, the silent witness maneuver had been his idea. And I caught him giving Jessup the throat slash — the internationally recognized sign that it was over.

I looked back to the front of the court.

"Mr. Royce," the judge said. "Are you continuing with this witness?"

"A moment, Your Honor," Royce said.

It was a valid question. Royce had few ways with which to go with Roman at this point. He could cut his losses and simply end the questioning. Or he could ask the judge to declare Roman to be a hostile witness — a move that was always professionally embarrassing when the hostile witness is one you called to the stand. But it was a move that would allow Royce more latitude in asking leading questions that explored what Roman had initially said to the defense investigator and why he was dissembling now. But this was fraught with danger, especially since this initial interview had not been recorded or documented in an effort to hide Roman during the discovery process.

"Mr. Royce!" the judge barked. "I consider the court's time quite valuable. Please ask your next question or I will turn the witness over to Mr. Haller for cross-examination."

Royce nodded to himself as he came to a decision.

"I'm sorry, Your Honor. But no further questions at this time."

Royce walked dejectedly back to his seat and a waiting client who was visibly upset with the turnabout. I stood up and started moving to the lectern even before the judge turned the witness over to me.

"Mr. Roman," I said, "your testimony has been somewhat confusing to me. So let me get this straight. Are you telling this jury that Sarah Ann Gleason did or did not tell you that her stepfather murdered her sister?"

"She didn't. That's just what they wanted me to say."

"Who is 'they,' sir?"

"The defense. The lady investigator and Royce."

"Besides a hotel room, were you to receive anything else if you testified to such a story today?"

"They just said they'd take care of me. That a lot of money was at—"

"Objection!" Royce yelled.

He jumped to his feet.

"Your Honor, the witness is clearly hostile and acting out a vindictive fantasy."

"He's your witness, Mr. Royce. He can answer the question. Go ahead, sir."

"They said there was a lot of money at stake and they would take care of me," Roman said.

It just kept getting better for me and worse for Jessup. But I had to make sure I didn't come off to the jury as gleeful or vindictive myself. I recalibrated and focused on what was important.

"What was the story that Sarah told you all those years ago, Mr. Roman?"

"Like I said, that she was in the yard and she was hiding and she saw the guy who grabbed her sister."

"Did she ever tell you she identified the wrong man?"

"No."

"Did she ever tell you that the police told her who to identify?"

"No."

"Did she ever once tell you that the wrong man was charged with her sister's murder?"

"No."

"No further questions."

I checked the clock as I returned to my seat. We still had twenty minutes before the lunch break. Rather than break early, the judge asked Royce to call his next witness. He called his investigator, Karen Revelle. I knew what he was doing and I was going to be ready.

Revelle was a mannish-looking woman who wore slacks and a sport jacket. She had ex-cop written all over her dour expression. After she was sworn in, Royce got right to the point, probably hoping to stem the flow of blood from his case before the jurors went to lunch.

"What do you do for a living, Ms. Revelle?"

"I am an investigator for the law firm of Royce and Associates."

"You work for me, correct?"

"That is correct."

"On March second of this year, did you conduct a telephone interview with an individual named Edward Roman?"

"I did."

"What did he tell you in that call?"

I stood and objected. I asked the judge if I could discuss my objection at a sidebar conference.

"Come on up," she said.

Maggie and I followed Royce to the side of the bench. The judge told me to state my objection.

"My first objection is that anything this witness states about a conversation with Roman is clearly hearsay and not allowed. But the larger objection is to Mr. Royce trying to impeach his own witness. He's going to use Revelle to impeach Roman, and you can't do that, Judge. It's damn near suborning perjury on Mr. Royce's part, because one of these two people is lying under oath and he called them both!"

"I strongly object to Mr. Haller's last characterization," Royce said, leaning over the sidebar and moving in closer to the judge. "Suborning perjury? I have been practicing law for more than—"

"First of all, back up, Mr. Royce, you're in my space," Breitman said sternly. "And second, you can save your self-serving objection for some other time. Mr. Haller is correct on all counts. If I allow this witness to continue her testimony, you are not only going to go into hearsay but we will have a situation where one of your witnesses has lied under oath. You can't have it both ways and you can't put a liar on the stand. So this is what we're going to do. You are going to get your investigator off the stand, Mr. Haller is going to make a motion to strike what little testimony she has already given and I will agree to that motion. Then we're going to lunch. During that time, you and your client can get together and decide what to do next. But it's looking to me like your options got really limited in the last half hour. That's all."

She didn't wait for any of us to respond. She simply rolled her chair away from the sidebar.

Royce followed the judge's advice and ended his questioning of Revelle. I moved to strike and that was that. A half hour later I was sitting with Maggie and Sarah Gleason at a table at the Water Grill, the place where the case had started for me. We had decided to go high-end because we were celebrating what appeared to be the beginning of the end for Jason Jessup's case, and because the Water Grill was just across the street from Sarah's hotel. The only one missing at the table was Bosch, and he was on his way after dropping our silent witness, Sonia Reyes, at the drug rehab facility at County-USC Medical Center.

"Wow," I said after the three of us were seated. "I don't think I've ever seen anything like that before in a courtroom."

"Me, neither," Maggie said.

"Well, I've been in a few courtrooms but I don't know enough to know what it all means," said Gleason.

"It means the end is near," Maggie said.

"It means the entire defense imploded," I added. "See, the defense's case was sort of simple. Stepfather killed the girl and the family concocted a cover-up. They came up with the story about hide-and-seek and the man on the lawn to throw the authorities off of stepdad. Then sister — that's you — made a false identification of Jessup. Just sort of randomly set him up for a murder he did not commit."

"But what about Melissa's hair in the tow truck?" Gleason asked.

"The defense claims it was planted," I said. "Either in conspiracy or independent of the family's cover-up. The police realized they didn't have much of a case. They had a thirteen-year-old girl's ID of a suspect and almost nothing else. So they took hair from the body or a hairbrush and planted it in the tow truck. After lunch — if Royce is foolish enough to continue this — he will present investigative chronology reports and time logs that will show Detective Kloster had enough access and time to make the plant in the tow truck before a search warrant was obtained and forensics opened the truck."

"But that's crazy," Gleason said.

"Maybe so," Maggie said, "but that was their case and Eddie Roman was the linchpin because he was supposed to testify that you told him your stepfather did it. He was supposed to plant the seed of doubt. That's all it takes, Sarah. One little doubt. Only he took one look at who was in the audience — namely Sonia Reyes — and thought he was in trouble. You see Eddie did the same thing with Sonia as he did with you. Met her, got close and turned her out to keep him in meth. When he saw her in court, he knew he was in trouble. Because he knew if Sonia got on the stand and told the same story about him as you did, then the jury would know what he was — a liar and predator — and wouldn't trust a single thing he said. He also had no idea what Sonia might have told us about crimes they committed together. So he decided up there that his best out was the truth. To screw the defense and make the prosecution happy. He changed his story."

Gleason nodded as she began to understand.

"Do you think Mr. Royce really told him what to say and was going to pay him off for his lies?"

"Of course," Maggie said.

"I don't know," I said quickly. "I've known Clive a long time. I don't think that's how he operates."

"What?" Maggie said. "You think Eddie Roman just made it all up on his own?"

"No, but he spoke to the investigator before he ever got to Clive."

"Plausible denial. You're just being charitable, Haller. They don't call him Clever Clive for no reason."

Sarah seemed to sense that she had pushed us into a zone of contention that had existed long before this trial. She tried to move us on.

"Do you really think it's over?" she asked.

I thought for a moment about it and then nodded.

"I think if I was Clever Clive I'd be thinking of what's best for my client and that would be not to let this go to a verdict. I'd start thinking about a deal. Maybe he'll even call during lunch."

I pulled my phone out and put it down on the table, as if being ready for Royce's call would make it happen. Just as I did so, Bosch showed up and took the seat next to Maggie. I grabbed my water glass and raised it to him.

"Cheers, Harry. Smooth move today. I think Jessup's house of cards is falling down."

Bosch raised a water glass and clinked it off mine.

"Royce was right, you know," he said. "It was a gangster move. Saw it in one of the *Godfather* movies way back."

He then held his water glass up to the two women.

"Anyway, cheers," he said. "You two are the real stars. Great work yesterday and today."

We all clinked glasses but Sarah hesitated.

"What's wrong, Sarah?" I asked. "Don't tell me you're afraid of clinking glass."

I smiled, proud of my own humor.

"It's nothing," she said. "I think it's supposed to be bad luck to toast with water."

"Well," I said, quickly recovering, "it's going to take more than bad luck to change things now."

Bosch switched subjects.

"What happens next?" he asked.

"I was just telling Sarah that I don't think this will go to a jury. Clive has to be thinking disposition. They really don't have any other choice."

Bosch turned serious.

"I know there's money on the line and your boss probably thinks that's the priority," he said, "but this guy has got to go back to prison."

"Absolutely," Maggie said.

"Of course," I added. "And after what happened this morning, we have all the leverage. Jessup has to take what we offer or we—"

My phone started to buzz. The ID screen said UNKNOWN.

"Speak of the devil," Maggie said.

I looked at Sarah.

"You might be on that plane home tonight after all."

I opened the phone and said my name.

"Mickey, District Attorney Williams here. How are you?"

I shook my head at the others. It wasn't Royce.

"I'm doing fine, Gabe. How are you?"

My informality didn't seem to faze him.

"I'm hearing good things out of court this morning."

His statement confirmed what I had thought all along. While Williams had never once showed his face in the courtroom, he had a plant in the gallery watching.

"Well, I hope so. I think we'll know more about which way this will go after lunch."

"Are you considering a disposition?"

"Well, not yet. I haven't heard from opposing counsel, but I assume that we may soon enter into discussions. He's probably talking to his client about it right now. I would be if I were him."

"Well, keep me in the loop on that before you sign off on anything."

I paused as I weighed this last statement. I saw Bosch put his hand inside his jacket and pull out his own phone to take a call.

"Tell you what, Gabe. As independent counsel I prefer to stay independent. I'll inform you of a disposition if and when I have an agreement."

"I want to be part of that conversation," Williams insisted.

I saw some sort of darkness move into Bosch's eyes. Instinctively, I knew it was time to get off my call.

"I'll get back to you on that, Mr. District Attorney. I've got another call coming in here. It could be Clive Royce."

I closed the phone just as Bosch closed his and started to stand up.

"What is it?" Maggie asked.

Bosch's face looked ashen.

"There's been a shooting over at Royce's office. There's four on the floor over there."

"Is Jessup one of them?" I asked.

"No... Jessup's gone."

Forty

Bosch drove and McPherson insisted on riding with him. Haller had split off with Gleason to head back to court. Bosch pulled a card out of his wallet and got Lieutenant Stephen Wright's number off it. He handed the card and his phone to McPherson and told her to punch in the number.

"It's ringing," she said.

He took the phone and got it to his ear just as Wright answered.

"It's Bosch. Tell me your people are on Jessup."

"I wish."

"Damn it! What the hell happened? Why wasn't SIS on him?"

"Hold your horses, Bosch. We *were* on him. That's one of my people on the floor in Royce's office."

That hit like a punch. Bosch hadn't realized a cop was one of the victims.

"Where are you?" he asked Wright.

"On my way there. I'm three minutes out."

"What do you know so far?"

"Not a hell of a lot. We had a light tail on him during court hours. You knew that. One team during court and full coverage before and after. Today they followed him from the courthouse to Royce's office at lunchtime. Jessup and Royce's team walked over. After they were in there a few minutes my guys heard gunshots. They called it in and then went in. One was knocked down, the other pinned down. Jessup went out the back and my guy stayed to try CPR on his partner. He had to let Jessup go."

Bosch shook his head. The thought of his daughter pushed through everything. She was at school for the next ninety minutes. He felt that she would be safe. For now.

"Who else was hit?" he asked.

"As far as I know," Wright said, "it was Royce and his investigator and then another lawyer. A female. They were lucky it was lunchtime. Everybody else in the office was gone."

Bosch didn't see much that was lucky about a quadruple murder and Jessup out there somewhere with a gun. Wright kept talking.

"I'm not going to shed a tear over a couple of defense lawyers but my guy on the floor in there's got two little kids at home, Bosch. This is not a good goddamn thing at all."

Bosch turned onto First, and up ahead he could see the flashing lights. Royce's office was in a storefront on a dead-end street that ran behind the Kyoto Grand Hotel on the edge of Japantown. Easy walking distance to the courthouse.

"Did you get Jessup's car out on a broadcast?"

"Yes, everybody has it. Somebody will see it."

"Where's the rest of your crew?"

"Everybody's heading to the scene."

"No, send them out looking for Jessup. At all the places he's been. The parks, everywhere, even my house. There's no use for them at the scene."

"We'll meet there and I'll send them out."

"You're wasting time, Lieutenant."

"You think I can stop them from coming to the scene first?"

Bosch understood the impossibility of Wright's situation.

"I'm pulling up now," he said. "I'll see you when you get here."

"Two minutes."

Bosch closed the phone. McPherson asked him what Wright had said and he quickly filled her in as he pulled the car to a stop behind a patrol car.

Bosch badged his way under the yellow tape and McPherson did the same. Because the shooting had occurred only twenty-five minutes earlier, the crime scene was largely inhabited by uniformed officers—the first responders—and was chaotic. Bosch found a patrol sergeant issuing orders regarding crime scene protection and went to him.

"Sergeant, Harry Bosch, RHD. Who is taking this investigation?"

"Isn't it you?"

"No, I'm on a related case. But this one won't be mine."

"Then I don't know, Bosch. I was told RHD will handle."

"Okay, then they're still on their way. Who's inside?"

"Couple guys from Central Division. Roche and Stout."

Babysitters, Bosch thought. As soon as RHD moved in, they would be moved out. He pulled his phone and called his lieutenant.

"Gandle."

"Lieutenant, who's taking the four on the floor by the Kyoto?"

"Bosch? Where are you?"

"At the scene. It was my guy from the trial. Jessup."

"Shit, what went wrong?"

"I don't know. Who are you sending and where the hell are they?"

"I'm sending four. Penzler, Kirshbaum, Krikorian and Russell. But they were all at lunch up at Birds. I'm coming over, too, but you don't have to be there, Harry."

"I know. I'm not staying long."

Bosch closed the phone and looked around for McPherson. He had lost her in the confusion of the crime scene. He spotted her crouching down next to a man sitting on the sidewalk curb in front of the bail-bonds shop next door to Royce's office. Bosch recognized him from the night he and McPherson rode on the surveillance of Jessup. There was blood on his hands and shirt from his efforts to save his partner. Bosch went to them.

"...he went to his car when they got back here. For just a minute. Got in and then got out. He then went into the office. Right away we heard shots. We moved and Manny got hit as soon as we opened the door. I got off a couple rounds but I had to try to help Manny..."

"So Jessup must've gotten the gun from his car, right?"

"Must've. They've got the metal detectors at the courthouse. He didn't have it in court today."

"But you never saw it?"

"No, never saw the weapon. If we had seen it, we would've done something."

Bosch left them there and went to the door of Royce and Associates. He got there just as Lieutenant Wright did. Together they entered.

"Oh, my God," Wright said when he saw his man on the floor just inside the front door.

"What was his name?" Bosch asked.

"Manuel Branson. He's got two kids and I have to go tell his wife."

Branson was on his back. He had bullet entry wounds on the left side of his neck and upper left cheek. There had been a lot of blood. The neck shot appeared to have sliced through the carotid artery.

Bosch left Wright there and moved past a reception desk and down a hallway on the right side. There was a wall of glass that looked into a boardroom with doors on both ends. The rest of the victims were in here, along with two detectives who wore gloves and booties and were taking notes on clipboards. Roche and Stout. Bosch stood in the first doorway of the room but did not enter. The two detectives looked at him.

"Who are you?" one asked.

"Bosch, RHD."

"You taking this?"

"Not exactly. I'm on something related. The others are coming."

"Christ, we're only two blocks from the PAB."

"They weren't there. They were at lunch up in Hollywood. But don't worry, they'll get here. It's not like these people are going anywhere."

Bosch looked at the bodies. Clive Royce sat dead in a chair at the head of a long board table. His head was snapped back as if he were looking at the ceiling. There was a bloodless bullet hole in the center of his forehead. Blood from the exit wound at the back of his head had poured down the back of his jacket and chair.

The investigator, Karen Revelle, was on the floor on the other side of the room near the other door. It appeared that she had tried to make a run for it before being hit by gunfire. She was facedown and Bosch could not see where or how many times she had been hit.

Royce's pretty associate counsel, whose name Bosch could not remember, was no longer pretty. Her body was in a seat diagonal to Royce, her upper body down on the table, an entry wound at the back of her head. The bullet had exited below her right eye and destroyed her face. There was always more damage coming out than going in.

"What do you think?" asked one of the Central guys.

"Looks like he came in shooting. Hit these two first and then tagged the other as she made a run for the door. Then backed into the hall and opened up on the SIS guys as they came in."

"Yeah. Looks that way."

"I'm going to check the rest of the place out."

Bosch continued down the hall and looked through open doors into empty offices. There were nameplates on the wall outside the doors and he was reminded that Royce's associate was named Denise Graydon.

The hallway ended at a break room, where there was a kitchenette with a refrigerator and a microwave. There was another communal table here. And an exit door that was three inches ajar.

Bosch used his elbow to push the door open. He stepped into an alley lined with trash bins. He looked both ways and saw a pay parking lot a half block down to his right. He assumed it was the lot where Jessup had parked his car and had gone to retrieve the gun.

He went back inside and this time took a longer look in each of the offices. He knew from experience that he was treading in a gray area here. This was a law office, and whether the lawyers were dead or not, their clients were still entitled to privacy and attorney-client privilege. Bosch touched nothing and opened no drawer or file. He simply moved his eyes over the surface of things, seeing and reading what was in plain sight.

When he was in Revelle's office he was joined by McPherson.

"What are you doing?"

"Just looking."

"We might have a problem going into any of their offices. As an officer of the court I can't—"

"Then wait outside. Like I said, I'm just looking. I am making sure the premises are secure."

"Whatever. I'll be out front. The media's all over the place out there now. It's a circus."

Bosch was leaning over Revelle's desk. He didn't look up.

"Good for them."

McPherson left the room at the same moment Bosch read something off a legal pad that was on top of a stack of files on the side of the desk near the phone.

"Maggie? Come back here."

She returned.

"Take a look at this."

McPherson came around the desk and bent over to read the notes on the top page of the pad. The page was covered with what looked like random notes, phone numbers and names. Some were circled, others scratched out. It looked like a pad Revelle jotted on while on the phone.

"What?" McPherson asked.

Without touching the pad, Bosch pointed to a notation in the bottom right corner. All it said was *Checkers — 804*. But that was enough.

"Shit!" McPherson said. "Sarah isn't even registered under her name. How did Revelle get this?"

"She must've followed us back after court, paid somebody for the room number. We have to assume that Jessup has this information."

Bosch pulled his phone and called Mickey Haller on speed dial.

"It's Bosch. You still have Sarah with you?"

"Yes, she's here in court. We're waiting for the judge."

"Look, don't scare her but she can't go back to the hotel."

"All right. How come?"

"Because there's an indication here that Jessup has that location. We'll be setting up on it."

"What do I do, then?"

"I'll be sending a protection team to the court — for both of you. They'll know what to do."

"They can cover her. I don't need it."

"That'll be your choice. My advice is you take it."

He closed the phone and looked at McPherson.

"I gotta get a protection team over there. I want you to take my car and get my daughter and your daughter and go somewhere safe. You call me then and I'll send a team to you, too."

"My car's two blocks from here. I can just—"

"That'll waste too much time. Take mine and go now. I'll call the school and tell them you're coming for Maddie."

"Okay."

"Thank you. Call me when you have—"

They heard shouting from the front of the office suite. Angry male voices. Bosch knew they came from the friends of Manny Branson. They were seeing their fallen comrade on the floor and getting fueled with outrage and the scent of blood for the hunt.

"Let's go," he said.

They moved back through the suite to the front. Bosch saw Wright standing just outside the front door, consoling two SIS men with angry, tear-streaked faces. Bosch made his way around Branson's body and out the door. He tapped Wright on the elbow.

"I need a moment, Lieutenant."

Wright broke away from his two men and followed. Bosch walked a few yards to where they could speak privately. But he need not have worried about being overheard. In the sky above, there were at least four media choppers circling over the crime scene and laying down a layer of camouflage sound that would make any conversation on the block private.

"I need two of your best men," Bosch said, leaning toward Wright's ear.

"Okay. What do you have going?"

"There's a note on the desk of one of the victims. It's the hotel and room number of our prime witness. We have to assume our shooter has that information. The slaughter inside there indicates he's taking out the people associated with the trial. The people he thinks did him wrong. That's a long list but I think our witness would be at the top of it."

"Got it. You want to set up at the hotel."

Bosch nodded.

"Yeah. One man outside, one inside and me in the room. We wait and see if he shows."

Wright shook his head.

"We use four. Two inside and two outside. But forget waiting in the room, because Jessup will never get by the surveillance. Instead, you and I find a viewpoint up high and set up the command post. That's the right way to do it."

Bosch nodded.

"Okay, let's go."

"Except there's one thing."

"What's that?"

"If I bring you in on this, then you stay back. My people take him down."

Bosch studied him for a moment, trying to read everything hidden in what he was saying.

"There are questions," Bosch said. "About Franklin Canyon and the other places. I need to talk to Jessup."

Wright looked over Bosch's shoulder and back toward the front door of Royce and Associates.

"Detective, one of my best people is dead on the floor in there. I'm not guaranteeing you anything. You understand?"

Bosch paused and then nodded.

"I understand."

Forty-one

Thursday, April 8, 1:50 P.M.

There was more media in the courtroom than there had been at any other point of the trial. The first two rows of the gallery were shoulder-to-shoulder with reporters and cameramen. The rest of the rows were filled with courthouse personnel and lawyers who had heard what had happened to Clive Royce.

Sarah Gleason sat in a row by the courtroom deputy's desk. It was marked as reserved for law enforcement officers but the deputy put her there so the reporters couldn't get to her. Meantime, I sat at the prosecution table waiting for the judge like a man on a desert island. No Maggie. No Bosch. Nobody at the defense table. I was alone.

"Mickey," someone whispered from behind me.

I turned to see Kate Salters from the *Times* leaning across the railing.

"I can't talk now. I have to figure out what to say here."

"But do you think your total destruction of this morning's witness is what could have—?"

I was saved by the judge. Breitman entered the courtroom and bounded up to the bench and took her seat. Salters took hers and the question I wanted to avoid for the rest of my life remained unasked—at least for the moment.

"We are back on the record in *California versus Jessup.* Michael

Haller is present for the People. But the jury is not present, nor is defense counsel or the defendant. I am aware through unconfirmed media reports of what has transpired in the last ninety minutes at Mr. Royce's office. Can you add anything to what I have seen and heard on television, Mr. Haller?"

I stood up to address the court.

"Your Honor, I don't know what they are putting out to the media at the moment, but I can confirm that Mr. Royce and his cocounsel on this case, Ms. Graydon, were shot and killed in their offices at lunchtime. Karen Revelle is also dead, as well as a police officer who responded to the shooting. The suspect in the shooting has been identified as Jason Jessup. He remains at large."

Judging by the murmur from the gallery behind me, those basic facts had probably been speculated upon but not yet confirmed to the media.

"This is, indeed, very sad news," Breitman said.

"Yes, Your Honor," I said. "Very sad."

"But I think at this moment we need to put aside our emotions and act carefully here. The issue is, how do we proceed with this case? I am pretty sure I know the answer to that question but am willing to listen to counsel before ruling. Do you wish to be heard, Mr. Haller?"

"Yes, I do, Judge. I ask the court to recess the trial for the remainder of the day and sequester the jury while we await further information. I also ask that you revoke Mr. Jessup's pretrial release and issue a capias for his arrest."

The judge considered these requests for a long moment before responding.

"I will grant the motion revoking the defendant's release and issue the capias. But I don't see the need to sequester the jury. Regrettably, I see no alternative to a mistrial here, Mr. Haller."

I knew that would be her first thought. I had been considering my response since the moment I had returned to the courthouse.

"The People object to a mistrial, Judge. The law is clear that

Mr. Jessup waives his right to be present at these proceedings by voluntarily absenting himself from them. According to what the defense represented earlier, he was scheduled to be the last witness today. But he has obviously decided not to testify. So, taking all of this into—"

"Mr. Haller, I am going to have to stop you right there. I think you are missing one part of the equation and I am afraid the horse is already out of the barn. You may recall that Deputy Solantz was assigned lunch duty with our jurors after we had the issue of tardiness on Monday."

"Yes."

"Well, lunch for eighteen in downtown Los Angeles is a tall order. Deputy Solantz arranged for the group to travel by bus together and eat each day at Clifton's Cafeteria. There are TVs in the restaurant but Deputy Solantz always keeps them off the local channels. Unfortunately, one TV was on CNN today when the network chose to go live with what was occurring at Mr. Royce's office. Several jurors saw the live report and got the gist of what was happening before Deputy Solantz managed to kill the feed. As you can imagine, Deputy Solantz is not very happy with himself at the moment, and neither am I."

I turned and looked over at the courtroom deputy's desk. Solantz had his eyes down in humiliation. I looked back at the judge and I knew I was dead in the water.

"Needless to say, your suggestion of sequestering the jury was a good one, just a little late. Therefore, and after taking all things into consideration, I find that the jury in this trial has been prejudiced by events which have occurred outside of the court. I intend to declare a mistrial and continue this case until such time as Mr. Jessup has been brought again before this court."

She paused for a moment to see if I had an objection but I had nothing. I knew what she was doing was right and inevitable.

"Let's bring in the jury now," she said.

Soon the jurors were filing into the box, many of them glancing over at the empty defense table.

When everyone was in place, the judge went on the record and turned her chair directly to the jurors. In a subdued tone she addressed them.

"Ladies and gentlemen of the jury, I must inform you that because of factors that are not fully clear to you but will soon become so, I have declared a mistrial in the case of *California versus Jason Jessup*. I do this with great regret because all of us here have invested a great deal of time and effort in these proceedings."

She paused and studied the confused faces in front of her.

"No one likes to invest so much time without seeing the case through to a result. I am sorry for this. But I do thank you for your duty. You were all dependable and for the most part on time every day. I also watched you closely during the testimony and you were all attentive. The court cannot thank you enough. You are dismissed now from this courtroom and discharged from jury duty. You may all go home."

The jurors slowly filed back into the jury room, many taking a last look back at the courtroom. Once they were gone the judge turned back to me.

"Mr. Haller, for what it's worth, I thought you acquitted yourself quite well as a prosecutor. I am sorry it ended this way but you are welcome back to this court anytime and on either side of the aisle."

"Thank you, Judge. I appreciate that. I had a lot of help."

"Then I commend your whole team as well."

With that, the judge stood and left the bench. I sat there for a long time, listening to the gallery clear out behind me and thinking about what Breitman had said at the end. I wondered how and why such a good job in court had resulted in such a horrible thing happening in Clive Royce's office.

"Mr. Haller?"

I turned, expecting it to be a reporter. But it was two uniformed police officers.

"Detective Bosch sent us. We are here to take you and Ms. Gleason into protective custody."

"Only Ms. Gleason and she's right here."

Sarah was waiting on the bench next to Deputy Solantz's desk.

"Sarah, these officers are going to take care of you until Jason Jessup is in custody or..."

I didn't need to finish. Sarah got up and walked over to us.

"So there's no more trial?" she asked.

"Right. The judge declared a mistrial. That means if Jessup is caught, we would have to start over. With a new jury."

She nodded and looked a little dumbfounded. I had seen the look on the faces of many people who venture naively into the justice system. They leave the courthouse wondering what just happened. Sarah Gleason would be no different.

"You should go with these men now, Sarah. We'll be in touch as soon as we know what happens next."

She just nodded and they headed for the door.

I waited a while, alone in the courtroom, and then headed out to the hallway myself. I saw several of the jurors being interviewed by the reporters. I could've watched but at the moment I wasn't interested in what anybody had to say about the case. Not anymore.

Kate Salters saw me and broke away from one of the clusters.

"Mickey, can we talk now?"

"I don't feel like talking. Call me tomorrow."

"The story's today, Mick."

"I don't care."

I pushed by her in the direction of the elevators.

"Where are you going?"

I didn't answer. I got to the elevators and jumped through the open doors of a waiting car. I moved into the rear corner and saw a woman standing by the panel. She asked me the same question as Salters.

"Where are you going?"

"Home," I said.

She pushed the button marked *G* and we went down.

PART FIVE

— The Takedown

Forty-two

Bosch was stationed with Wright in a borrowed office across the street from the Checkers Hotel. It was the command post, and although no one thought Jessup would be stupid enough to walk in the front door of the hotel, the position gave them a good view of the entire property as well as two of the other surveillance positions.

"I don't know," Wright said, staring out the window. "This guy is smart, right?"

"I guess so," Bosch said.

"Then I don't see him making this move, you know? He'd have already been here if he was. He's probably halfway to Mexico by now and we're sitting here watching a hotel."

"Maybe."

"If I were him, I'd get down there and lie low. Try to spend as many days on the beach as I could before they found me and put me back in the Q."

Bosch's phone began to buzz and he saw that it was his daughter.

"I'm going to step out to take this," he said to Wright. "You got it covered here?"

"I've got it."

Bosch answered the phone as he left the office for the hallway.

370 · Michael Connelly

"Hey, Mads. Everything all right?"

"There's a police car outside now."

"Yeah, I know. I sent it there. Just an added precaution."

They had talked an hour earlier after Maggie McPherson had gotten them safely to a friend's home in Porter Ranch. He had told his daughter about Jessup being out there and what had happened at Royce's office. She didn't know about Jessup's nocturnal visit to their house two weeks earlier.

"So they didn't catch that guy yet?"

"We're working on it and I'm in the middle of stuff here. Stay close to Aunt Maggie and stay safe. I'll come get you as soon as this is over."

"Okay. Here, Aunt Maggie wants to talk to you."

McPherson took the phone.

"Harry, what's the latest?"

"Same as before. We're out looking for him and sitting on all the known locations. I'm with Wright at Sarah's hotel."

"Be careful."

"Speaking of that, where's Mickey? He turned down protection."

"He's at home right now but said he's coming up here."

"Okay, sounds good. I'll talk to you later."

"Keep us posted."

"I will."

Bosch closed the phone and went back into the office. Wright was still at the window.

"I think we're wasting our time and should shut this down," he said.

"Why? What's going on?"

"Just came over the radio. They found the car Jessup was using. In Venice. He's nowhere near here, Bosch."

Bosch knew that dumping the car in Venice could merely be a misdirection. Drive out to the beach, leave the car and then double back in a cab to downtown. Nonetheless, he found himself reluctantly agreeing with Wright. They were spinning their wheels here.

"Damn it," he said.

"Don't worry. We'll get him. I'm keeping one team here and one on your house. Everybody else I'm moving down into Venice."

"And the Santa Monica Pier?"

"Already covered. Got a couple teams on the beach and nobody's gone in or out of that location."

Wright went on the SIS band on the radio and started redeploying his men. As Bosch listened he paced the room, trying to figure Jessup out. After a while he stepped back out to the hallway so as not to disturb Wright's radio choreography and called Larry Gandle, his boss at RHD.

"It's Bosch. Just checking in."

"You still at the hotel?"

"Yeah, but we're about to clear and head to the beach. I guess you heard they found the car."

"Yeah, I was just there."

Bosch was surprised. With four victims at Royce's office, he thought Gandle would still be at the murder scene.

"The car's clean," Gandle said. "Jessup still has the weapon."

"Where are you now?" Bosch asked.

"On Speedway," Gandle said. "We just hit the room Jessup was using. Took a while to get the search warrant."

"Anything there?"

"Not so far. This fucking guy, you see him in court wearing a suit and you think . . . I don't know what you think, but the reality was, he was living like an animal."

"What do you mean?"

"There are empty cans all over the place, food still rotting in them. Food rotting on the counter, trash everywhere. He hung blankets over the windows to black it out like a cave. He made it like a prison cell. He was even writing on the walls."

All at once it hit him. Bosch knew who Jessup had prepared the dungeon under the pier for.

"What kind of food?" he asked.

"What?" Gandle asked.

"The canned food. What kind of food?"

"I don't know, fruits and peaches—all kinds of stuff you can get fresh in any store you walk into. But he had it in cans. Like prison."

"Thanks, Lieutenant."

Bosch closed the phone and walked quickly back into the office. Wright was off the radio now.

"Did your people go under the pier and check the storage room or just set up surveillance?"

"It's a loose surveillance."

"Meaning they didn't check it out?"

"They checked the perimeter. There was no sign that anybody went under the wall. So they backed out and set up."

"Jessup's there. They missed him."

"How do you know?"

"I just know. Let's go."

Forty-three

Thursday, April 8, 6:35 P.M.

I stood at the picture window at the end of my living room and looked out at the city with the sun dropping behind it. Jessup was out there someplace. Like a rabid animal he would be hunted, cornered and, I had no doubt, put down. It was the inevitable conclusion to his play.

Jessup was legally to blame but I couldn't help but think about my own culpability in these dark matters. Not in any legal sense, but in a private, internal sense. I had to question whether consciously or not I had set all of this in motion on the day I sat with Gabriel Williams and agreed to cross a line in the courtroom as well as within myself. Maybe by allowing Jessup his freedom I had determined his fate as well as that of Royce and the others. I was a defense attorney, not a prosecutor. I stood for the underdog, not for the state. Maybe I had taken the steps and made the maneuvers so that there would never be a verdict and I would not have to live with it on my record and conscience.

Such were the musings of a guilty man. But they didn't last long. My phone buzzed and I pulled it from my pocket without looking away from my view of the city.

"Haller."

"It's me. I thought you were coming up here."

Maggie McFierce.

"Soon. I'm just finishing up here. Everything all right?"

"For me, yes. But probably not for Jessup. Are you watching the TV news?"

"No, what are they showing?"

"They've evacuated the Santa Monica Pier. Channel Five has a chopper over it. They're not confirming that it's related to Jessup but they said that LAPD's SIS unit sought an okay from SMPD to conduct a fugitive apprehension. They're on the beach moving in."

"The dungeon? Did Jessup grab somebody?"

"If he did, they're not saying."

"Did you call Harry?"

"I just tried but he didn't pick up. I think he's probably down there on the beach."

I broke away from the window and grabbed the television remote off the coffee table. I snapped on the TV and punched in Channel 5.

"I have it on here," I told Maggie.

On the screen was an aerial view of the pier and the surrounding beach. It looked like there were men on the beach and they were advancing on the pier's underside from both the north and south.

"I think you're right," I said. "It's gotta be him. The dungeon he made down there was actually for himself. Like a safe house he could run to."

"Like the prison cell he was used to. I wonder if he knows they're coming in on him. Maybe he hears the helicopters."

"Harry said the waves under there are so loud you couldn't even hear a gunshot."

"Well, we might be about to find that out."

We watched in silence for a few moments before I spoke.

"Maggie, are the girls watching this?"

"God, no! They're playing video games in the other room."

"Good."

They watched in silence. The newscaster's voice echoing over the line as he inanely described what was on the screen. After a while Maggie asked the question that had probably been on her mind all afternoon.

"Did you think it would come to this, Haller?"

"No, did you?"

"No, never. I guess I thought everything would sort of be contained in the courtroom. Like it always is."

"Yeah."

"At least Jessup saved us the indignity of the verdict."

"What do you mean? We had him and he knew it."

"You didn't watch any of the juror interviews, did you?"

"What, on TV?"

"Yeah, juror number ten is on every channel saying he would've voted not guilty."

"You mean Kirns?"

"Yeah, the alternate that got moved into the box. Everybody else interviewed said guilty, guilty, guilty. But Kirns said not guilty, that we hadn't convinced him. He would've hung the jury, Haller, and you know Williams wouldn't have signed on for round two. Jessup would've walked."

I considered this and could only shake my head. Everything was for nothing. All it took was one juror with a grudge against society, and Jessup would've walked. I looked up from the TV screen and out toward the western horizon to the distance, where I knew Santa Monica hugged the edge of the Pacific. I thought I could see the media choppers circling.

"I wonder if Jessup will ever know that," I said.

Forty-four

The sun was dropping low over the Pacific and burning a brilliant green path across the surface. Bosch stood close to Wright on the beach, a hundred yards south of the pier. They were both looking down at the 5 × 5 video screen contained in a front pack strapped to Wright's chest. He was commanding the SIS takedown of Jason Jessup. On the screen was a murky image of the dimly lit storage facility under the pier. Bosch had been given ears but no mike. He could hear the operation's communications but could not contribute to them. Anything he had to say would have to go through Wright.

The voices over the com were hard to hear because of the background sound of waves crashing beneath the pier.

"This is Five, we're in."

"Steady the visual," Wright commanded.

The focus on the video tightened and Bosch could see that the camera was aimed at the individual storage rooms at the rear of the pier facility.

"This one."

He pointed to the door he had seen Jessup go through.

"Okay," Wright said. "Our target is the second door from the right. Repeat, second door from the right. Move in and take positions."

The video moved in a herky-jerky fashion to a new position. Now the camera was even closer.

"Three and Four are—"

The rest was wiped out by the sound of a crashing wave.

"Three and Four, say again," Wright said.

"Three, Four in position."

"Hold until my go. Topside, you ready?"

"Topside ready."

On the upper level of the evacuated pier there was another team, which had placed small explosives at the corners of the trapdoor above the storage corral where they believed Jessup was holed up. On Wright's command the SIS teams would blow the trapdoor and move in from above and below.

Wright wrapped his hand around the mike that ran along his jawline and looked at Bosch.

"You ready for this?"

"Ready."

Wright released his grip and gave the command to his teams.

"Okay, let's give him a chance," he said. "Three, you have the speaker up?"

"That's a go on the speaker. You're hot in three, two...one."

Wright spoke, trying to convince a man hidden in a dark room a hundred yards away to give himself up.

"Jason Jessup. This is Lieutenant Stephen Wright of the Los Angeles Police Department. Your position is surrounded top and bottom. Step out with your hands behind your head, fingers laced. Move forward to the waiting officers. If you deviate from this order you will be shot."

Bosch pulled his earplugs out and listened. He could hear the muffled sound of Wright's words coming from under the pier. There was no doubt that Jessup could hear the order if he was under there.

"You have one minute," Wright said as his final communication to Jessup.

The lieutenant checked his watch and they waited. At the thirty-second mark Wright checked with his men under the pier.

"Anything?"

"This is Three. I got nothing."

"Four, clear."

Wright gave Bosch a wishful look, like he had hoped it wouldn't come to this.

"Okay, on my mark we go. Keep tight and no crossfire. Topside, if you shoot, you make sure you know who you—"

There was movement on the video screen. A door to one of the storage corrals flung open, but not the door they were focused on. The camera made a jerking motion left as it redirected its aim. Bosch saw Jessup emerge from the darkness behind the open door. His arms came up and together as he dropped into a combat pose.

"Gun!" Wright yelled.

The barrage of gunfire that followed lasted no more than ten seconds. But in that time at least four officers under the pier emptied their weapons. The crescendo was punctuated by the unneeded detonation from the topside. By then Bosch had already seen Jessup go down in the gunfire. Like a man in front of a firing squad, his body seemed at first to be held upright by the force of multiple impacts from multiple angles. Then gravity set in and he fell to the sand.

After a few moments of silence, Wright was back on the com.

"Everybody safe? Count off."

All officers under and on top of the pier reported in safe.

"Check the suspect."

In the video Bosch saw two officers approach Jessup's body. One checked for a pulse while the other held his aim on the dead man.

"He's ten-seven."

"Secure the weapon."

"Got it."

Wright killed the video and looked at Bosch.

"And that's that," he said.

"Yeah."

"I'm sorry you didn't get your answers."

"Me, too."

They started walking up the beach to the pier. Wright checked his watch and went on the com, announcing the official time of the shooting as 7:18 P.M.

Bosch looked off across the ocean to his left. The sun was now gone.

PART SIX

—All That Remains

Forty-five

Harry Bosch and I sat on opposite sides of a picnic table, watching the ME's disinterment team dig. They were on the third excavation, working beneath the tree where Jason Jessup had lit a candle in Franklin Canyon.

I didn't have to be there but wanted to be. I was hoping for further evidence of Jason Jessup's villainy, as though that might make it easier to accept what had happened.

But so far, in three excavations, they had found nothing. The team moved slowly, stripping away the dirt one inch at a time and sifting and analyzing every ounce of soil they removed. We had been here all morning and my hope had waned into a cold cynicism about what Jessup had been doing up here on the nights he was followed.

A white canvas sheet had been strung from the tree to two poles planted outside the search zone. This shielded the diggers from the sun as well as from the view of the media helicopters above. Someone had leaked word of the search.

Bosch had the stack of files from the missing persons cases on the table. He was ready to go with records and descriptors of the missing girls should any human remains be found. I had simply come armed with the morning's newspaper and I read the front-page story now for a second time. The report on the events of the day before was the lead story in the *Times* and was accompanied by a color photo of two SIS officers pointing their weapons into the open trapdoor on the Santa Monica Pier. The story was also accompanied by a front-page side-bar story on the SIS. Headline: ANOTHER CASE, ANOTHER SHOOTING, SIS's BLOODY HISTORY.

I had the feeling this would be a story with legs. So far, no one in the media had found out that the SIS knew Jessup had obtained a gun. When that got out—and I was sure it would—there would no doubt be a firestorm of controversy, further investigations and police commission inquiries. The chief question being: Once it was established that it was likely that this man had a weapon, why was he allowed to remain free?

It all made me glad I was no longer even temporarily in the employ of the state. In the bureaucratic arena, those kinds of questions and their answers have the tendency to separate people from their jobs.

I needed not worry about the outcome of such inquiries for my livelihood. I would be returning to my office—the backseat of my Lincoln Town Car. I was going back to being private counsel for the defense. The lines were cleaner there, the mission clearer.

"Is Maggie McFierce coming?" Bosch asked.

I put the paper down on the table.

"No, Williams sent her back to Van Nuys. Her part in the case is over."

"Why isn't Williams moving her downtown?"

"The deal was that we had to get a conviction for her to get downtown. We didn't."

I gestured to the newspaper.

"And we weren't going to get one. This one holdout juror is tell-ing anybody who'll listen that he would've voted not guilty. So I guess you can say Gabriel Williams is a man who keeps his word. Maggie's going nowhere fast."

That's how it worked in the nexus of politics and jurisprudence. And that's why I couldn't wait to go back to defending the damned.

We sat in silence for a while after that and I thought about my ex-wife and how my efforts to help her and promote her had failed so miserably. I wondered if she would begrudge me the effort. I surely hoped not. It would be hard for me to live in a world where Maggie McFierce despised me.

"They found something," Bosch said.

I looked up from my thoughts and focused. One of the diggers was using a pair of tweezers to put something from the dirt into a plastic evidence bag. Soon she stood up and headed toward us with the bag. She was Kathy Kohl, the ME's forensic archaeologist.

She handed Bosch the bag and he held it up to look. I could see that it contained a silver bracelet.

"No bones," Kohl said. "Just that. We're at thirty-two inches down and it's rare that you find a murder interment much further down than that. So this one's looking like the other two. You want us to keep digging?"

Bosch glanced at the bracelet in the bag and looked up at Kohl.

"How about another foot? That going to be a problem?"

"A day in the field beats a day in the lab anytime. You want us to keep digging, we'll keep digging."

"Thanks, Doc."

"You got it."

She went back to the excavation pit and Bosch handed the evidence bag to me to examine. It contained a charm bracelet. There were clots of dirt in the links and its charms. I could make out a tennis racket and an airplane.

"Do you recognize it?" I asked. "From one of the missing girls?"

He gestured to the stack of files on the table.

"No. I don't remember anything about a charm bracelet in the lists."

"It could've just been lost up here by somebody."

"Thirty-two inches down in the dirt?"

"So you think Jessup buried it, then?"

"Maybe. I'd hate to come away from this empty-handed. The guy had to have come up here for a reason. If he didn't bury them here, then maybe this was the kill spot. I don't know."

I handed the bag back to him.

"I think you're being too optimistic, Harry. That's not like you."

"Well, then what the hell do you think Jessup was doing up here all those nights?"

"I think he and Royce were playing us."

"Royce? What are you talking about?"

"We were had, Harry. Face it."

Bosch held the evidence bag up again and shook it to loosen the dirt.

"It was a classic misdirection," I said. "The first rule of a good defense is a good offense. You attack your own case before you ever get to court. You find its weaknesses and if you can't fix them, then you find ways of deflecting attention away from them."

"Okay."

"The biggest weakness to the defense's case was Eddie Roman. Royce was going to put a liar and a drug addict on the stand. He knew that given enough time, you would either find Roman or find out things about him or both. He needed to deflect. Keep you occupied with things outside the case at hand."

"You're saying he knew we were following Jessup?"

"He could've easily guessed it. I put up no real opposition to his request for an OR release. That was unusual and probably got Royce thinking. So he sent Jessup out at night to see if there was a tail. As we already considered before, he probably even sent Jessup to your house to see if he would engage a response and confirm surveillance. When it didn't, when it got no response, Royce probably thought he was wrong and dropped it. After that, Jessup stopped coming up here at night."

"And he probably thought he was in the clear to go build his dungeon under the pier."

"It makes sense. Doesn't it?"

Bosch took a long time to answer. He put his hand on top of the stack of files.

"So what about all these missing girls?" he asked. "It's all just coincidence?"

"I don't know," I said. "We may never know now. All we know is that they're still missing and if Jessup was involved, then that secret probably died with him yesterday."

Bosch stood up, a troubled look on his face. He was still holding the evidence bag.

"I'm sorry, Harry."

"Yeah, me, too."

"Where do you go from here?"

Bosch shrugged.

"The next case. My name goes back into the rotation. What about you?"

I splayed my hands and smiled.

"You know what I do."

"You sure about that? You made a damn good prosecutor."

"Yeah, well, thanks for that, but you gotta do what you gotta do. Besides, they'd never let me back on that side of the aisle. Not after this."

"What do you mean?"

"They're going to need somebody to blame for all of this and it's going to be me. I was the one who let Jessup out. You watch. The cops, the *Times,* even Gabriel Williams will eventually bring it around to me. But that's okay, as long as they leave Maggie alone. I know my place in the world and I'm going to go back to it."

Bosch nodded because there was nothing else to say. He shook the bag with the charm bracelet again and worked it with his fingers, removing more dirt from its surfaces. He then held it up to study closely and I could tell he saw something.

"What is it?"

His face changed. He was keying on one of the charms, rubbing dirt off it through the plastic bag. He then handed it to me.

"Take a look. What is that?"

The charm was still tarnished and dirty. It was a square piece of silver less than a half inch wide. On one side there was a tiny swivel at center and on the other what looked like a bowl or a cup.

"Looks like a teacup on a square plate," I suggested. "I don't know."

"No, turn it over. That's the bottom."

I did and I saw what he saw.

"It's one of those...a mortarboard. A graduation cap and this swivel on the top was for the tassel."

"Yeah. The tassel's missing, probably still in the dirt."

"Okay, so what's it mean?"

Bosch sat back down and quickly started looking through the files.

"You don't remember? The first girl I showed you and Maggie. Valerie Schlicter. She disappeared a month after graduating from Riverside High."

"Okay, so you think..."

Bosch found the file and opened it. It was thin. There were three photos of Valerie Schlicter, including one of her in her graduation cap and gown. He quickly scanned the few documents that were in the file.

"Nothing here about a charm bracelet," he said.

"Because it probably wasn't hers," I said. "This is a long shot, don't you think?"

He acted as though I had said nothing, his mind shutting out any opposing response.

"I'm going to have to go out there. She had a mother and a brother. See who's still around and can look at this thing."

"Harry, you sure you——"

"You think I have a choice?"

He stood back up, took the evidence bag back from me and gathered up the files. I could almost hear the adrenaline buzzing through his veins. A dog with a bone. It was time for Bosch to go. He had a long shot in his hand but it was better than no shot. It would keep him moving.

I got up, too, and followed him to the excavation. He told Kohl that he had to go check out the bracelet. He told her to call him if anything else was found in the hole.

We moved to the gravel parking lot, Bosch walking quickly and not looking back to see if I was still with him. We had driven separately to the dig.

"Hey," I called to him. "Wait up!"

He stopped in the middle of the lot.

"What?"

"Technically, I'm still the prosecutor assigned to Jessup. So before you go rushing off, tell me what the thinking is here. He buried the bracelet here but not her? Does that even make sense?"

"Nothing makes sense until I ID the bracelet. If somebody tells me it was hers, then we try to figure it out. Remember, when Jessup was up here, we couldn't get close to him. It was too risky. So we don't know exactly what he was doing. He could've been looking for this."

"Okay, I can maybe see that."

"I gotta go."

He continued on to his car. It was parked next to my Lincoln. I called after him.

"Let me know, okay?"

He looked back at me when he got to his car.

"Yeah," he said. "I will."

He then dropped into the car and I heard it roar to life. Bosch drove like he walked, pulling out quickly and throwing dust and gravel into the air. A man on a mission. I got in the Lincoln and followed him out of the park and up to Mulholland Drive. After that, I lost him on the curving road ahead.

Acknowledgments

The author wishes to thank several people for their help in the research and writing of this book. They include Asya Muchnick, Michael Pietsch, Pamela Marshall, Bill Massey, Jane Davis, Shannon Byrne, Daniel Daly, Roger Mills, Rick Jackson, Tim Marcia, David Lambkin, Dennis Wojciechowski, John Houghton, Judge Judith Champagne, Terrill Lee Lankford, John Lewin, Jay Stein, Philip Spitzer, and Linda Connelly.

The author also greatly benefited from reading *Defending the Damned: Inside a Dark Corner of the Criminal Justice System* by Kevin Davis.

About the Author

Michael Connelly is the author of twenty-eight previous novels, including #1 *New York Times* bestsellers *The Crossing* and *The Burning Room*. His books, which include the Harry Bosch series and Lincoln Lawyer series, have sold more than sixty million copies worldwide. Connelly is a former newspaper reporter who has won numerous awards for his journalism and his novels and is the executive producer of *Bosch,* starring Titus Welliver. He spends his time in California and Florida.

New job. Same Bosch.

Don't miss THE WRONG SIDE OF GOODBYE.

Available November 2016.

Please turn the page for a preview.

*T*hey charged from the cover of the elephant grass toward the LZ, five of them swarming the slick on both sides, one among them yelling, "Go! Go! Go!"—as if each man needed to be prodded and reminded that these were the most dangerous seconds of their lives.

The rotor wash bent the grass back and blew the marker smoke in all directions. The noise was deafening as the turbine geared up for a heavy liftoff. The door gunners pulled everyone in by their pack straps and the chopper was quickly in the air again, having alighted no longer than a dragonfly on water.

The tree line could be seen through the portside door as the craft rose and started to bank. Then came the muzzle flashes from the banyan trees. Somebody yelled, "Snipers!"—as if the door gunner had to be told what he had out there.

It was an ambush. Three distinct flashpoints, three snipers. They had waited until the helicopter was up and flying fat, an easy target from six hundred feet.

The gunner opened up his M60, sending a barrage of fire into the treetops, shredding them. But the sniper rounds kept coming. The slick had no armor plating, a decision made nine thousand miles away to take speed and maneuverability over the burden of weight and protection.

One shot hit the turbine cowling, a *thock* sound reminding one of the helpless men on board of a fouled-off baseball hitting the hood of a car in the parking lot. Then came the snap of glass shattering as the next round tore through the cockpit. It was a million-to-one shot, hitting both the pilot and copilot at once. The pilot was killed instantly, and the copilot clamped his hands to his neck in an instinctive but helpless move to keep blood inside his body. The helicopter yawed into a clockwise spin and was soon hurtling out of control. It spun away from the trees and across the rice paddies. The men in the back started to yell helplessly. The man who had just had a memory of baseball tried to orient himself. The world outside the slick was spinning. He kept his eyes on a single word imprinted on the metal wall separating the cockpit from the cargo hold. It said ADVANCE. The letter A with a crossbar was an arrow pointed forward.

He kept his eyes on the word even as the screaming intensified and he could feel the craft losing altitude. Seven months backing recon and now on short time. He knew he wasn't going to make it back. This was the end.

The last thing he heard was someone yell "Brace! Brace! Brace!"— as if there was a possibility that anybody on board had a shot at surviving the impact, never mind the fire that would come after. While the others screamed in panic he whispered a name to himself.

"Vibiana..."

He knew he would never see her.

"Vibiana..."

The helicopter dove into one of the rice paddy dikes and exploded into a million metal parts. A moment later the spilled fuel caught fire and burned through the wreckage and spread flames across the surface of the paddy water. Black smoke rose into the air, marking the wreckage like an LZ marker.

The snipers reloaded and waited for the rescue choppers to come next.

ONE

Bosch didn't mind the wait. The view was spectacular. He didn't bother with the waiting room couch. Instead he stood with his face a foot from the glass and took in the view that ranged from rooftops of downtown to the Pacific Ocean. He was fifty-nine floors up in the U.S. Bank Tower, and Creighton was making him wait because it was something he always did going all the way back to his days at Parker Center, where the waiting room only had a low-angle view of the back side of City Hall. Creighton had moved a mere five blocks west since his days with the Los Angeles Police Department, but he certainly had risen far beyond that measure if you were going upward to the lofty heights of the city's financial gods.

Still, view or no view, Bosch didn't know why anyone would keep offices in the tower. The tallest building west of the Mississippi, it had been the target of two foiled terrorist plots previously. That didn't count the ones unknown or still being planned. Bosch imagined there had to be a general uneasiness added to the daily pressures of work for every soul who entered its glass doors each morning. Relief might soon come in the form of the Wilshire Grand, a glass-sheathed spire rising to the sky a few blocks away. When finished it would take the distinction of tallest building west of the Mississippi from the U.S. Bank Tower. It would probably take the target as well.

Bosch loved any opportunity to see his city from up high.

When he was a young detective he would often take extra shifts as a spotter in one of the department's airships just to take a ride above the city and be reminded of its seemingly infinite vastness.

He looked down at the 110 freeway and saw it was backed up all the way down through South-Central. He also noted the number of helipads on the tops of the buildings below him. The helicopter had become the commuter vessel of the elite. He had heard that even some of the higher-contract players on the Lakers took choppers to work at the Staples Center.

The glass was thick enough to cut off the penetration of any sound. The city below was silent. The only thing Bosch heard was the receptionist behind him answering the phone with same greeting over and over: "Trident Security, how can I help you?"

Bosch's eye held on a fast-moving patrol car going south on Figueroa toward L.A. Live. He saw the 01 painted large on the trunk and knew that the car was from Central Division. Soon it was followed in the air by an LAPD airship that moved at a lower altitude than the fifty-ninth floor. Bosch tracked it but was pulled away by a voice from behind.

"Mr. Bosch?"

He turned to see a woman standing in the middle of the waiting room. She wasn't the receptionist.

"I'm Gloria. We spoke on the phone," she said.

"Right, yes," Bosch said. "Mr. Creighton's assistant."

"Yes, nice to meet you. You can come back now."

"Good. Any longer and I was going to jump."

She didn't smile. She led Bosch through a door into a hallway with framed watercolors perfectly spaced on the walls.

"It's impact-resistant glass," she said. "It can take the force of a category 5 hurricane."

"Good to know," Bosch said. "And I was only joking. Your boss had a history of keeping people waiting—back when he was a deputy chief with the police department."

"Oh, really? I haven't noticed it here."

This made no sense to Bosch since she had just fetched him from the waiting room fifteen minutes after the appointed meeting time.

"He must've read it in a management book back when he was climbing the ranks," Bosch said. "You know, keep 'em waiting even if they're on time. Gives you the upper hand when you finally bring them into the room, lets them know you are a busy man."

"I'm not familiar with that business philosophy."

"Probably more of a cop philosophy."

They entered an office suite where there were two separate desk arrangements, one occupied by a man in his twenties wearing a suit and the other empty and most likely belonging to Gloria. They walked between the desks to a door. Gloria opened it and then stepped to the side.

"Go on in," she said. "Can I bring you a bottle of water?"

"No thanks," Bosch said. "I'm fine."

Bosch entered an even larger room with a desk area to the left and an informal seating area on the right with a couple of couches facing each other across a glass-topped coffee table. Creighton was sitting behind his desk—with Bosch it was going to be formal.

It had been more than a decade since Bosch had seen Creighton in person. He could not remember the occasion but assumed it was a squad meeting where Creighton came in and made an announcement concerning the overtime budget or the department's travel protocols. Back then Creighton was the head bean counter—in charge of budgeting for the department among his other management duties. He was known for instituting strict policies on overtime that required detailed explanations to be written on green cards that were subject to supervisor approval. Since that approval or disapproval usually came after the extra hours were already worked, the new system was viewed by the rank and file as an effort to dissuade cops from working overtime or, worse yet, get them to work overtime and then deny authorization or replace it with comp time. It was during this posting that Creighton became universally known as "Cretin" by the rank and file. Though Creighton left the department for the private sector not long after, the "greenies" were still in use.

"Harry, come in," Creighton said. "Sit down."

Bosch moved to the desk. Creighton was a few years older but in good shape. He stood behind the desk with his hand held forward. He wore a gray suit that was tailor-cut to his wiry frame. He looked good. He looked like money. Bosch shook his hand and then sat down in front of the desk. He hadn't gotten dressed up for the appointment. He was in blue jeans, a blue denim shirt, and a charcoal corduroy jacket he'd had for at least twelve years. These days Bosch's work suits from his days with the department were wrapped in plastic. He didn't want to pull one of them out just for a meeting with Cretin.

"Chief, how are you?" he said.

"It's not 'chief' anymore," Creighton said with a laugh. "Those days are long ago. Call me John."

"John then."

"Sorry to keep you waiting out there. I had a client on the phone and, well, the client always comes first. Am I right?"

"Sure, no problem. I enjoyed the view."

The view through the window behind Creighton was in the opposite direction, stretching northeasterly across the Civic Center and to the snow-capped mountains in San Bernardino. But Bosch guessed that the mountains weren't the reason Creighton picked this office. It was the Civic Center. From his desk Creighton looked down on the spire of City Hall, the Police Administration Building, and the Los Angeles Times. Creighton was above them all.

"It is truly spectacular seeing the world from this angle," Creighton said.

Bosch nodded and got down to business.

"So," he said. "What can I do for you...John?"

"Well, first of all, I appreciate you coming in without really knowing why I wished to see you. Gloria told me she had a difficult time convincing you to come in."

"Yeah, well, I'm sorry about that. But like I told her, if this is about a job I'm not interested. I've got a job."

"I've heard. San Fernando. But that's gotta be part time, right?"

He said it with a slightly mocking tone and Bosch remembered a line from a movie he once saw: "If you're not cop, you're little people." It also held that if you worked for a little department you were still little people.

"It keeps me as busy as I want to be," he said. "I also have a private ticket. I pick up stuff from time to time on that."

"All referrals, correct?" Creighton said.

Bosch looked at him a moment.

"Am I supposed to be impressed that you checked me out?" he finally said. "I'm not interested in working here. I don't care what the pay is, I don't care what the cases are."

"Well, let me just ask you something, Harry," Creighton said. "Do you know what we do here?"

For a moment Bosch looked over Creighton's shoulder and out at the mountains before answering.

"I know you are high-level security for those who can afford it," he said.

"Exactly," Creighton said.

He held up three fingers on his right hand in what Bosch assumed was supposed to be a trident.

"Trident Security," Creighton said. "Specializing in financial, technological, and personal security. I started the California branch ten years ago. We have bases here, New York, Boston, Chicago, Miami, London, and Frankfurt. We are about to open in Istanbul. We are a very large operation with thousands of clients and even more connections in the fields of our expertise."

"Good for you," Bosch said.

He had spent about ten minutes on his laptop reading up on Trident before coming in. The upscale security venture was founded in New York in 1996 by a shipping magnate named Dennis Laughton, who had been abducted and ransomed in the Philippines. Laughton first hired a former NYPD police commissioner to be his front man and had followed suit in every city where he opened a base, plucking a local chief or high-ranking commander from the local police department to make a media splash and secure the absolute must-have of local police cooperation. The word was that ten years ago

Laughton had tried to hire L.A.'s police chief but was turned down and then went to Creighton as a second choice.

"I told your assistant I wasn't interested in a job with Trident," Bosch said. "She said it wasn't about that. So why don't you tell me what it is about so we can both get on with our days."

"I can assure you, I am not offering you a job with Trident," Creighton said. "To be honest, we must have full cooperation and respect from the LAPD to do what we do and to handle the delicate matters that involve our clients and the police. If we were to bring you in as a Trident associate there could be a problem."

"You are talking about the LAPD lawsuit."

"Exactly."

For most of the last year Bosch had been in the middle of a protracted lawsuit against the department where he had worked for more than thirty years. He sued because he believed he had been illegally forced into retirement by the department. The case had drawn ill will from the department toward Bosch. It did not seem to matter that during his time with a badge that he had brought more than a hundred murderers to justice. The lawsuit was settled, but the ill will continued from some quarters of the department, mostly the quarter at the top.

"So if you brought me into Trident that would not be good for your relations with the LAPD," Bosch said. "I get that. But you want me for something. What is it?"

Creighton nodded. It was time to get down to it.

"Do you know the name Whitney Vance?" he asked.

Bosch nodded.

"Of course I do," he said.

"Yes, well, he is a client," Creighton said. "As is his company, Advance Engineering."

"Whitney Vance has got to be eighty years old."

"Eighty-five next month. And..."

Creighton opened the top middle drawer of his desk and removed a document. He put it on the desk between them. Bosch could see it was a printed check with an attached receipt. He wasn't wearing his glasses and was unable to read the amount or the other details.

"He wants to speak to you," Creighton finished.

"About what?" Bosch asked.

"I don't know. He said it was a private matter and he specifically asked for you by name. He said he would discuss the matter privately with you. He had this certified check drawn for ten thousand dollars. It is yours to keep for meeting him, whether the appointment leads to further work or not."

Bosch didn't know what to say. At the moment he was flush because of the lawsuit settlement, but he had put most of the money into long-term investment accounts designed to carry him comfortably into old age with a solid stake left over for his daughter. Meantime she still had three years of college and then graduate school tuition ahead of her, and he was on the hook for a good chunk of it. There was no doubt in his mind that 10K could be put to good use.

"When and where is this appointment going to be?" he finally said.

"Tomorrow morning at nine at Mr. Vance's home in Pasadena," Creighton said. "The address is on the check receipt. You might want to dress a little nicer than that."

Bosch ignored the sartorial jab. From an inside jacket pocket he took out his eyeglasses. He put them on as he reached across the desk and took the check. He studied it for a moment. It was made out to his full name, and Bosch wondered how Vance or Creighton knew about that.

There was a perforated line running across the bottom of the check. Below it was the address and appointment time as well as the admonition; "Don't bring a firearm." Bosch folded the check along the perforation line and looked at Creighton as he put it into his jacket.

"I'm going to go to the bank from here," he said. "I'll deposit this and if it clears I'll be there tomorrow."

Creighton smirked.

"That will not be a problem."

Bosch nodded.

"I guess that's it then," he said.

He stood up to go.

"There is one thing, Bosch," Creighton said.

Bosch noted that he had dropped from first name to last name status with Creighton inside of ten minutes.

"What's that?" he asked.

"I have no idea what the old man is going to ask you, but I'm very protective of him," Creighton said. "He is more than a client and I don't want to see him taken for a ride at this point in his life. Whatever the task is he wants you to perform, I want to be in the loop."

"A ride? Unless I missed something, you called me, Creighton. If anybody's being taken for a ride, it will be me. It doesn't matter how much he's paying me."

"I can assure you that's not the case. The only ride is the ride out to Pasadena for which you just received ten thousand dollars."

"Good. I'm going to hold you to that. I'm going to go see the 'old man' tomorrow and see what this is about. But if he becomes my client then that business, whatever it is, will be between him and me. There won't be any loop that includes you unless Vance tells me there is. That's how I work."

Bosch turned toward the door. When he got there he looked back at Creighton.

"Thanks for the view."

He left and closed the door behind him. On the way out he stopped at the receptionist's desk and got his parking receipt validated. He wanted to be sure Creighton ate the thirty bucks for that.

TWO

T he Vance estate was on San Rafael near the Annandale Country Club. It was a neighborhood of old money, homes and estates that had been passed down generations like money in the bank and guarded just like it behind stone walls and black iron fences. It was a far cry from the Hollywood Hills, where the new money went and the rich left their trash cans out on the street all week. There were no for sale signs here. You had to know somebody, maybe even share their blood, to buy in here.

Bosch parked against the curb about a hundred yards from the gate that guarded entrance to the Vance estate. There were spikes ornately disguised as flowers atop it. For a few moments he studied the curve of the driveway beyond the gate as it wound and rose into the cleft of two rolling green hills and then disappeared. There was no sign of any structure, not even a garage. All of that would be well back from the street, buffered by geography, iron, and money. But Bosch knew that Whitney Vance, eighty-four years old, was up there somewhere beyond those money-colored hills waiting for him.

He was twenty minutes early for the appointment and decided to use the time to review several stories he had found on the Internet and printed out that morning. They were all about the man who the day before had paid Bosch ten thousand dollars to pay him a visit.

The general contours of Whitney Vance's life were known to Bosch, as they were most likely known to most Californians. But he still found the details fascinating and even admirable in that Vance was the rare recipient of a rich inheritance who had turned his silver spoon into gold. He was the fourth-generation Pasadena scion of a mining family that extended all the way back to the California gold rush. Gold was what drew Vance's great-grandfather west but not what the family fortune was founded on. Frustrated by the hunt for gold, the great-grandfather established the state's first strip mining operation, extracting millions of tons of iron ore out of the earth in San Bernardino County. Vance's grandfather then followed that with a second strip mine further south in Imperial County, and his father parlayed that success into a steel mill and fabrication plant that helped support the dawning aviation industry. At the time the face of that industry belonged to Howard Hughes, and he counted Nelson Vance as first a contractor and then a partner in many different aviation endeavors. Hughes would become godfather to Nelson Vance's only child.

Whitney Vance was born in 1931 and as a young man apparently set out to blaze a unique path for himself. He initially went off to the University of Southern California to study filmmaking but eventually dropped out and came back to the family fold, transferring to California Institute of Technology in Pasadena, the school "Uncle Howard" had attended. It was Hughes who urged young Whitney to study aeronautical engineering at Caltech.

As with the elders of his family, when it was his turn Vance pushed the family business in new and ever increasingly successful directions, always with a continuing thread to the family's original product: steel. He won numerous government contracts for the manufacture of aircraft parts and mechanisms and founded Advance Engineering, which held the patents on many of them. Couplings that were used for the safe fueling of aircraft were perfected in the family steel mill and are still used today at every airport in the world. Ferrite extracted from the iron ore culled from Vance mining operations was used in the earliest efforts to build aircraft that avoided radar detection. These processes were meticulously patented and protected by Vance and guaranteed his company participation in in the decades-long development of stealth technologies. Vance and his company were part of the so-called military-industrial complex, and the Vietnam War saw their value grow exponentially. Every mission in or out of that country over the entire length of the war involved equipment that came from Advance Engineering. Bosch remembered seeing the company logo—an arrow through the middle of the A—imprinted on the steel walls of every helicopter he had ever flown on in Vietnam.

Bosch was startled by a sharp rap on the window beside him. He looked up to see a uniformed Pasadena patrol officer. He checked the rearview and saw the black and white parked behind him. He realized he had become so engrossed in his reading that he had not even heard the cop car come up on him.

He had to turn on the Cherokee's engine to lower the window. He knew what this was about. A twenty-year-old vehicle in need of paint parked outside the estate of a family that helped build the state of California constituted a suspicious activity. It didn't matter that Bosch was white, his hair was combed, and he was wearing a crisp suit and tie rescued from a plastic storage bag. It had taken less than fifteen minutes for the police to respond to his intrusion into the neighborhood.

"I know how this looks, officer," he began. "But I have an appointment across the street in about five minutes and I was just—"

"That's wonderful," the cop said. "Do you mind stepping out of the car?"

Bosch looked at him for a moment. He saw the nameplate above his breast pocket said Cooper.

"You're kidding, right?" he asked.

"No, sir, I'm not," Cooper said. "Please step out of the car."

Bosch took a deep breath, opened the door, and did as he was told. He raised his hands to shoulder height and said, "I'm a police officer."

Cooper immediately tensed as Bosch knew he would.

"I'm unarmed," Bosch said quickly. "My weapon's in the glove box."

At that moment he was thankful for the edit typed on the check stub telling him to come to the Vance appointment unarmed.

"Let me some ID," Cooper demanded.

Bosch carefully reached into an inside pocket in his suit coat and pulled his badge case. Cooper studied the detective's badge and then the ID.

"This says you're a reserve officer," he said.

"Yep," Bosch said. "Part timer."

"About fifteen miles off your reservation, aren't you? What are you doing here, Detective Bosch?"

He handed the badge case back and Bosch put it away.

"Well, I was trying to tell you," he said. "I have an appointment—which you are going to make me late for—with Mr. Vance, who I'm guessing you know lives right over there."

Bosch pointed toward the black gate.

"Is this appointment police business?" Cooper asked.

"It's actually none of your business," Bosch replied.

They held each other's cold stare for a long moment, neither man blinking. Finally Bosch spoke.

"Mr. Vance is waiting for me," he said. "Guy like that, he'll probably ask why I'm late, and he'll probably do something about it. You got a first name, Cooper?"

Cooper blinked.

"Yeah, it's fuck you," he said. "Have a nice day."

He turned and started back toward the patrol car.

"Thank you, officer," Bosch called after him.

Bosch got back into his car and immediately turned the ignition, then pulled away from the curb. If the old car still had the juice to leave rubber, he would have done so. But the most he could show Cooper, who remained parked at the curb, was a plume of blue smoke from the exhaust pipe.

He pulled into the entrance channel at the gate to the Vance estate and up to a camera and communication box. Almost immediately he was greeted by a voice.

"Yes?"

It was male, young and tiredly arrogant. Bosch leaned out the window even though he knew he probably didn't have to. He spoke loudly even though he didn't have to.

"Harry Bosch to see Mr. Vance. I have an appointment."

After a moment the gate in front of him started to automatically roll open.

"Follow the driveway to the parking apron by the security post," the voice said. "I will meet you there at the metal detector. Leave all weapons and recording devices in the glove compartment of your vehicle."

"Done," Bosch said.

"Drive up," the voice said.

The gate was all the way open now and Bosch drove through. He followed the cobblestone driveway through a finely manicured set of rolling emerald hills until he came to a second fence line and a guard shack. The double-fencing security measures at the estate were similar to those employed at most prisons Bosch had visited— of course, with the opposite intention of keeping people out instead of in.

The second gate rolled open and a uniformed guard stepped out of a booth to signal Bosch through and to the parking apron. As he passed Bosch waved a hand and noticed the Trident Security patch on the shoulder of the guard's navy blue uniform.

After parking Bosch was instructed to place his keys, phone, watch, and belt in a plastic tub and then walk through an airport-style metal detector while two more Trident men watched. They returned everything but the phone, which they explained would be placed in the glove box of his car.

"Anybody else get the irony here?" he asked as he put his belt back on. "You know, the family made their money on metal—now you have to go through a metal detector to get inside the house."

Neither of the guards said anything.

"Okay, I guess it's just me then," Bosch said.

Once he buckled his belt he was passed off to the next level of security, a man in a suit with the requisite earbud and wrist mike and the dead-eyed stare to go with it. He did not say his name. He escorted Bosch wordlessly through the delivery entrance of a massive gray stone mansion that Bosch guessed would rival anything the du Ponts or Vanderbilts had to offer. According to Wikipedia, he was calling on six billion dollars. There was no doubt in Bosch as he entered that this would be the closest to American royalty he would ever get.

He was led to a room paneled in dark wood with dozens of framed eight-by-ten photographs hung in four rows across one wall. There were a couple of couches and a bar at the end of the room. The escort in the suit pointed Bosch to one of the couches.

"Sir, have a seat and Mr. Vance's secretary will come for you when he is ready to see you."

Bosch took a seat on the couch facing the wall of photos.

"Would you like some water?" the suit asked.

"No, I'm fine," Bosch said.

The suit took a position next to the door they had entered through and clasped one wrist with the other hand in a posture that said he was alert and ready for anything.

Bosch used the waiting time to study the photographs. They offered a record of Whitney Vance's life and the people he had met over the course of it. The first photo depicted Howard Hughes and a young teenager he assumed was Vance. They were leaning against the unpainted metal skin of a plane. From there the photos appeared to run left to right in chronological order. They depicted Vance with numerous well-known figures of industry and politics and the media. Bosch couldn't put a name to every person Vance posed with, but from Lyndon Johnson to Larry King he knew who most of them were. In all the photos Vance displayed the same half smile, the corner of his mouth on the left side curled up, as if to communicate to the camera lens that it wasn't his idea to pose for a picture. The face grew older picture to picture, the eyelids more hooded, but the smile was always the same.

In the photo with Larry King, Vance and King were seated across from each other on the TV set where King had conducted interviews on CNN for more than two decades. Bosch could see that there was a book standing up on the counter between them.

He got up and went to the wall to look more closely at the book in the photo. He took a pair of glasses out of his jacket pocket, put them on and leaned in close to read the book's title.

STEALTH: The Making of the Disappearing Plane
By Whitney P. Vance

The title jogged loose a memory and Bosch recalled something about Whitney Vance writing a family history that the critics trashed more for what was left out than left in. His father, Nelson Vance, had been a brutal businessman and controversial political figure in his day. He was said but never proven to be a member of a cabal of wealthy industrialists who were supporters of eugenics— the so-called science of improving the human race through controlled breeding that would eliminate undesirable attributes. After the Nazis employed a similar but perverted doctrine to carry out genocide in World War II, eugenics fell into disfavor and people like Nelson Vance hid their beliefs and affiliations.

His son's book amounted to little more than a vanity project full of hero worship and little mention of the negatives. Whitney Vance had become such a recluse in his later life that the book was merely just a reason to bring him out into public light and ask him about the things left out. Once he had him on live TV, King probably asked Vance little about what was in the book.

"Mr. Bosch?"

Bosch turned from the photo to a woman standing by the entrance to a hallway on the other side of the room. She looked like she was at least seventy years old, and Bosch guessed she was a valued, long-time employee.

"I'm Mr. Vance's secretary, Ida," she said. "He will see you now."

Bosch stood up and followed her into the hallway. They walked for a distance that seemed like a city block before going up a short set of stairs to another hallway, this one traversing a wing of the mansion built on a higher slope of the hill. Finally they arrived at a set of double doors and Ida ushered Bosch into Whitney Vance's home office.

The man Bosch had come to see was sitting behind a desk, his back to an empty fireplace big enough to take shelter in during a tornado. He motioned for Bosch to come forward with a thin hand so white it looked like he was wearing a latex glove.

Bosch stepped up to the desk and Vance pointed to the lone leather chair in front of it. He made no offer to shake Bosch's hand. As he sat, Bosch noticed that Vance was in a wheelchair with electric controls extending from the left armrest. He saw the desk was clear except for a single white piece of paper that was either blank or had its contents facedown on the polished dark wood.

"Mr. Vance," Bosch said. "How are you?"

"I'm old—that's how I am," Vance said. "I have fought like hell to defeat time, but some things can't be beat. It is hard for a man in my position to accept, but I am resigned, Mr. Bosch."

He gestured with that bony, white hand again, taking all of the room in with a sweep.

"All of this will soon be meaningless," he said.

He offered the smile Bosch had seen on the photos in the waiting room, the upward curve on only one side. He believed it might have been caused by nerve damage. Vance couldn't complete a smile. According to the photos Bosch had seen, he never could.

Bosch didn't quite know how to respond to the old man's words. Instead, he pressed on with words he had thought about repeatedly since meeting with Creighton.

"Well, Mr. Vance, I was told you wanted to see me and you have paid me quite of bit of money to be here. It may not be a lot to you but it is to me. What can I do for you, sir?"

Vance cut the smile and nodded.

"A man who gets right to the point," he said. "I like that. I read about you in the newspaper. Last year, I believe. The case with that doctor in Beverly Hills and the shootout. You seemed to me like a man who stands his ground, Mr. Bosch. They put a lot of pressure on you but you stood up to it. I like that. I need that. There's not a lot of that around anymore."

"What do you want me to do?" Bosch asked again.

"I want you to find someone for me," Vance said. "Someone who might not have ever existed."

THREE

A fter intriguing Bosch with his request Vance flipped over the piece of paper on his desk and told Bosch he would have to sign it before they discussed anything further.

"It is a nondisclosure form," he explained. "My lawyer said it is ironclad. Your signature guarantees that you will not reveal the contents of our discussion or your subsequent investigation to anyone but me. Not even an employee of mine, not even someone who says they have come to you on my behalf. Only me, Mr. Bosch. If you sign this document you answer only to me. You report any findings of your investigation only to me. Do you understand?"

"Yes, I understand," Bosch said. "I have no problem signing it."

"Very good then. I have a pen here."

Vance pushed the document across the desk, then opened a drawer and withdrew a pen. It was a fountain pen that felt heavy in Bosch's hand because it was thick and made of what he presumed was real gold. He signed the document without reading it, put the pen down on top of it and pushed both across the desk back to Vance. He put the document in the desk drawer and closed it. He held the pen up for Bosch to study.

"This pen was made with gold my great-great-grandfather prospected in the Sierra Nevada goldfields in eighteen fifty-two," he said. "That was before the competition up there forced him to head south. Before he realized that there was more to be made from iron than gold."

He looked at the pen himself, turning it in his hand.

"It was passed on generation to generation," he said. "I've had it all of my life."

Vance studied the pen as if seeing it for the first time. Bosch said nothing. He wondered if Vance suffered from any sort of diminished mental capacity. He seemed to be wandering. Bosch wondered if the old man's desire to have him find somebody who may never have existed was some sort of figment of a failing mind.

"Mr. Vance?" he asked.

Vance put the pen into the desk drawer and looked at Bosch.

"I have no one to give it to," he said. "No one to give any of this to."

It was true. The biographical data Bosch had looked up said Vance was never married and childless. Several of the summaries he had read suggested obliquely that he was homosexual, but there was never any confirmation of this. Other biographical extracts suggested that he was simply too driven by his work to keep a steady relationship, let alone establish a family. There were a few brief romances reported, primarily with Hollywood starlets of the moment—a date for the cameras that put off speculation. But nothing in more than forty years that Bosch could find.

"Do you have children, Mr. Bosch?" Vance asked.

"A daughter," Bosch answered.

"Where?"

"In school. Chapman University down in Orange County."

"Good school. Is she a film student?"

"Psychology."

Vance leaned back in his chair and looked off at the past.

"I wanted to study film when I was a young man," he said. "The dreams of youth..."

He didn't finish his thought. Bosch realized he would have to give the money back. This was all some kind of derangement and there was no problem and no job and he could not take the money from this man even if it was only an infinitesimal drop in his money bucket. Bosch didn't take money from damaged people, no matter how rich they were.

Vance broke away from his stare into the abyss of memory and looked at Bosch. He nodded, seeming to know Harry's thoughts. He gripped the armrests of his chair and leaned forward.

"I guess I need to tell you what this is about," he said.

Bosch nodded.

"That would be good, yes."

Vance nodded back and for a moment offered the half smile again. He looked down for a moment and then back up at Bosch, his eyes deeply set and shiny behind rimless glasses.

"A long time ago I made a mistake," he said. "I never corrected it, I never looked back. I now want to find out if I had a child. A child I could give my gold pen to."

Bosch stared at him for a long moment, hoping he might continue. But when he did he seemed to have picked up another string of memory.

"When I was eighteen years old I wanted nothing to do with my father's business," Vance said. "I was more interested in being the next Orson Welles. I wanted to make films, not airplane parts. I was full of myself, as young men often are at that age."

Bosch thought of himself at that age. His desire to blaze his own path had led him into the tunnels of Vietnam.

"I insisted on film school," Vance said. "I enrolled at USC in nineteen forty-nine."

Bosch nodded. He knew from his prior reading that Vance would only spend a year at USC before changing paths and transferring to Caltech and furthering the family dynasty. There had been no explanation found in his Internet search. Bosch now believed he was going to find out why.

"I met a girl," Vance said. "A Mexican girl. And soon after she became pregnant. It was the second worst thing that ever happened to me. The first was telling my father."

Vance grew quiet, his eyes down on the desk in front of him. It wasn't difficult to fill in the blanks, but Bosch needed to hear as much of the story from Vance as he could.

"What happened?" he asked.

"He sent people," Vance said. "People to convince her not to have the child. People who would take her to Mexico to take care of it."

"Did she go?"

"If she did, it was not with my father's people. She disappeared from my life and I never saw her again. And I was too much of a coward to go find her. I had given my father all he needed to control me. The potential embarrassment and disgrace. I transferred to Caltech, and that was the end of it."

Vance nodded, as though confirming something for himself.

"It was a different time then...for me and for her."

Vance looked up now and held Bosch's eyes for a long moment before continuing.

"But now I want to know. It's when you reach the end of things that you want to go back...Can you help me, Mr. Bosch?"

Bosch nodded. He believed the pain in Vance's eyes was real.

"I can try," Bosch said. "Do you mind if I ask a few questions and take some notes?"

"Take your notes," Vance said. "But I warn you again that everything about this must remain completely confidential. Lives could be in danger. Every move you make, you must look over your shoulder. I have no doubt that efforts will be made to find out why I wanted to see you and what you are doing for me. I have a cover story for that, which we can get to later. For now, ask your questions."

Bosch pulled a small notebook from the inside pocket of his suit coat. He pulled out a pen. It was made of plastic, not gold. He'd bought it at a drugstore.

"You just said lives could be in danger. Whose lives? Why?"

"Don't be naïve, Mr. Bosch. I am sure you conducted a modicum of research before coming to see me. I have no heirs—at least, known heirs. When I die, control of Advance Engineering will go to a board of directors who will continue to line their pockets with millions while fulfilling government contracts. A valid heir could change all of that. Billions could be at stake. You don't think people and entities would kill for that?"

Bosch nodded. "It's been my experience that people will kill for any reason and no reason at all," he said. "If I find you have heirs, are you sure you want to possibly make them targets?"

"I would give them the choice," Vance said. "I believe I owe that. And I would protect them as well as is possible."

"What was her name? The girl you got pregnant."

"Vibiana Abas. You spell it A-B-A-S."

Bosch wrote it down on his pad.

"You know her birthdate by any chance?"

"I can't remember it."

"She was a student at USC?"

"No, I met her at the EVK. She worked there."

"EVK?"

"The student cafeteria was called Everybody's Kitchen. EVK, for short."

Bosch immediately knew this eliminated the prospect of tracing Vibiana Abas through student records, which were usually very helpful since most schools kept close track of alumni. It meant the search for the woman would most likely be more difficult and more of a long shot.

"You said she was Mexican," he said. "Was she a U.S. citizen?"

"I don't know. I don't think she was. My father—"

He didn't finish.

"Your father what?" Bosch asked.

"I don't know if it was the truth but my father said that that was her plan," Vance said. "To get pregnant so I would have to marry her and she would become a citizen. But my father said a lot of things to me that weren't true, and he believed a lot of things that were...out of step. So I don't know."

Bosch thought about what he had read about Nelson Vance and eugenics. He pressed on.

"By any chance, do you have a photograph of Vibiana?" he asked.

"No," Vance said. "You don't know how many times I've wished for a photograph. That I could just look at her one more time."

"Where did she live?"

"By the school. Just a few blocks away. She walked to work."

"Do you remember the address? The street maybe?"

"No, I don't remember. It was so long ago and I spent so many years trying to block it out. But the truth is I never really loved anybody again after that."

It was the first time Vance mentioned love or gave an indication of how deep the relationship had been. It had been Bosch's experience that when you looked back at a life you used a magnifying glass. Everything was bigger, amplified. A college tryst could become the love of a lifetime in memory. Still, Vance's pain seemed real so many decades after the events he was describing.

"How long were you together with her before all of this happened?" he asked.

"Eight months between the first and last times I ever saw her," Vance said. "Eight months."

"Do you remember when she told you she was pregnant? I mean, what month or time of year?"

"It was at the end of the school year. May. I had started in September the year before. I noticed her right away working at the EVK. I didn't get the courage to talk to her for a couple months."

The old man looked down at the desk, to see a memory from that time.

"What else do you remember?" Bosch prompted. "Did you ever meet her family? Do you remember any names?"

"No, I didn't," Vance said. "She told me her father was very strict and they were Catholic and I was not. You know, like Romeo and Juliet."

"You know what church she went to?"

Vance looked up, his eyes sharp.

"She told me she was named after the church the family attended, where she was baptized. St. Vibiana."

Bosch nodded. The original St. Vibiana's was downtown, just a block from the LAPD headquarters where he used to work. More than a hundred years old, it was badly damaged in the 1994 earthquake. A new church was built nearby and the old structure was donated to the city and preserved. Bosch wasn't sure but he believed it was an event hall and library now. But the connection to Vibiana Abas was a good one. Catholic churches kept records of births and baptisms. He felt this bit of good information countered the bad news that Vibiana had not been a USC student. It also was a strong indication that she might have been a U.S. citizen, whether her parents were or not.

"If the pregnancy was carried to full term, when would the child have been born?" he asked.

It was a delicate question but Bosch needed to narrow the timing down if he was going to wade into records.

"She told me in May," Vance said. "I would say December would be the birth. Maybe January."

Bosch wrote it down.

"How old was she when you knew her?" he asked.

"She was sixteen when we met," Vance said. "I was eighteen."

It was another reason for the reaction of Vance's father. Vibiana was underage. Getting a sixteen-year-old pregnant in 1950 could have gotten Whitney into minor but embarrassing legal trouble.

"Was she in high school?" Bosch asked.

He knew the area around USC. The high school would have been Manual Arts—another shot at traceable records.

"She had dropped out to work," Vance said. "The family needed the money."

"Did she ever say what her father did for a living?" Bosch asked.

"I don't recall."

"Okay, going back to her birthday, you don't remember the date but do you remember ever celebrating it with her during those seven months?"

Vance thought a moment and then shook his head.

"No, I can't remember a birthday occurring," he said.

"And if I have this right, you were together from October to May, so her birthday would have likely been somewhere in June to September. Roughly."

Vance nodded. Narrowing it to five months might help at

some point when Bosch was going through records. Attaching a birth date to the name Vibiana Abas would be a key starting point. He wrote the spread of months down and then looked up at Vance.

"Do you think your father paid her or her family off?" he asked. "So they would keep quiet and just go away?"

"If he did he never told me that," Vance said. "I was the one who went away. An act of cowardice I have always regretted."

"Have you ever looked for her before now? Ever paid anybody else to?"

"No, sadly, I have not. I can't say if anyone else has."

"Meaning what?"

"Meaning that is quite possible such a search was conducted as a preemptive move in preparation for my death."

Bosch nodded and thought about that for a long moment. He then looked down at the few notes he had written down. He felt he had enough to start.

"You said you had a cover story for me?"

"Yes, James Louis Aldridge."

"Who is he?"

"My first roommate. He was dismissed from school in the first semester."

"For academics?"

"No, for something else. Your cover is that I asked you to find my college roommate because I want to make amends for something we both did but he took the blame for. This way, if you are looking at records from that time it will seem plausible."

Bosch nodded.

"It might work. Is it a true story?"

"It is."

"I should probably know what it is you both did."

"You don't need to know that to find him."

Bosch waited a moment but that was all that Vance had to say on the subject. Harry wrote the name down after checking the spelling of Louis with Vance and then closed his notebook.

"Last question—for now. The odds are Vibiana Abas is dead by now. But what if she had the child and I find living heirs, what do you want me to do? Do I make contact?"

"No, absolutely not. You make no contact until you report to me. I'll need thorough confirmation before any approach will be made."

"DNA confirmation?"

Vance nodded and studied Bosch for a long moment before once more going to the desk drawer. He removed a padded white envelope with nothing written on it. He slid it across the desk to Bosch.

"I am trusting you, Mr. Bosch. I have now given you all you need to trick an old man if you want. I trust you won't."

Bosch picked up the envelope. It wasn't sealed. He looked into it and saw a clear glass test tube containing a swab used to collect saliva. It was Vance's DNA sample.

"This is where you could be tricking me, Mr. Vance."

"How so?"

"It would have been better if I had swabbed you, collected this myself."

"You have my word."

"And you have mine."

Vance nodded and there did not seem to be anything else to say.

"I think I have what I need to start."

"Then I have a final question for you, Mr. Bosch."

"Go ahead."

"I'm curious because it wasn't mentioned in the newspaper stories I read about you. But you appear to be the right age. What was your status during the Vietnam War?"

Bosch paused a moment before answering.

"I was over there," he finally said. "Two tours. I probably flew more times on the helicopters you helped build than you ever did."

Vance nodded. "Probably so," he said.

Bosch stood up. "How do I reach you if I have more questions or want to report what I find out?"

"Of course." Vance opened his desk drawer a final time and

removed a business card. He handed it to Bosch with a shaking hand. There was a phone number printed on it, nothing else.

"Call that number and you will get to me. If it's not me then something is wrong. Don't trust who you speak to."

Bosch looked from the number on the card to Vance, sitting in his wheelchair, his papier-mâché skin and wispy hair looking as frail as dried leaves. He wondered if his caution was paranoia or there was a real danger to the information he would be seeking.

"I'll get back to you soon," he said.

"We have not discussed payment for your services," Vance said.

"You've paid me enough already."

"That was only to get you to come here."

"It's more than enough, Mr. Vance. All right if I find my way out? Or will that set off a security breach?"

"As soon as you leave this room they'll know it and come to meet you."

Vance registered Bosch's puzzled look.

"It is only room in the house not under camera," he explained. "There are cameras even in my bedroom to watch over me. But I insisted on privacy here. As soon as you leave, they will come."

Bosch nodded.

"I understand," he said. "Talk to you soon."

He stepped through the door and started down the hallway. Soon enough Bosch was met by the nameless man in the suit and escorted wordlessly through the house and out to his car.

FOUR

Working cold cases had made Bosch proficient in time travel. He knew how to go back into the past to find people. Going back to 1951 would be the farthest and likely the most difficult trek he had ever made, but he believed he was up to it, and that made him excited about the challenge.

The starting point was finding the birthdate of Vibiana Abas, and he believed he knew the best way to accomplish that. Rather than go home after his meeting with Vance, Bosch took the 210 freeway across the northern rim of the Valley and headed toward the city of San Fernando.

Barely bigger than two square miles in size, San Fernando was an island city within the megalopolis of Los Angeles. A hundred years earlier all of the small towns and cities that comprised the San Fernando Valley were annexed into Los Angeles because of one reason. The newly built Los Angeles Aqueduct offered bountiful supplies of water that would keep their rich agricultural fields from drying up and blowing away. One by one they annexed and Los Angeles grew and spread north, eventually taking in the entire sprawl of the San Fernando Valley. All except for the 2.3 square miles of the Valley's namesake, the city of San Fernando. The little town didn't need L.A.'s water. Its ground supplies were more than adequate. It avoided the overture of the big city that now surrounded it and stayed independent.

A hundred years later it remained so. The Valley's agriculture pedigree may have long given way to urban sprawl and urban blight, but the city of San Fernando remained a quaint throwback to small-town sensibilities. Of course, urban issues and crime were unavoidable but nothing the tiny town's tiny police department couldn't routinely take care of.

That is, until the financial crash of 2008. When the banking crisis occurred and economies constricted and spiraled downward around the world, it was only a few years before the tidal wave of financial pain hit tiny San Fernando. Deep budget cuts occurred and then occurred again. Police Chief Anthony Valdez saw his department shrink from thirty-nine sworn officers, including himself, in 2010 to thirty officers by 2016. He saw his detective squad of five investigators shrink to just two—one detective to handle property crimes and one to handle crimes against persons. Valdez saw cases start to pile up unsolved, some not even investigated fully and properly.

Valdez was born and raised in San Fernando but was seasoned as a cop with the LAPD, putting in twenty years and rising to the rank of captain before taking his pension and checking out before landing the top spot at his hometown's department. His connections to the bigger department that surrounded his own ran deep and his solution to the budgetary crisis was to expand SFPD's reserve program and bring in more officers who worked part time hours but who worked for free.

And it was this expansion that led Chief Valdez to Harry Bosch. One of his early assignments when he was with the LAPD had been in a gang suppression unit in the Hollywood Division, where he ran afoul of a lieutenant named Pounds, who filed an internal complaint and unsuccessfully attempted to have Valdez demoted or even fired.

Valdez avoided both and just a few months later he heard about a detective named Bosch who got into an altercation with Pounds himself and ended up throwing him through a plate glass window at Hollywood Station. Valdez always remembered that name, and years later when he read about a now-retired Harry Bosch suing the LAPD for forcing him out of his job on the cold case squad, he picked up the phone.

Valdez couldn't offer Bosch a paycheck, but he could offer him a detective's badge and access to the cell in the old city jail where the files from all the open and unsolved cases were stored. The SFPD's reserve unit had only three requirements: its officers had to maintain their state training standards as law enforcement officers, had to qualify once a month at the department's indoor shooting range, and had to work at least two shifts a month.

It was a no-brainer for Bosch. The LAPD didn't want or need him anymore but the little town up in the Valley certainly did. And there was work to be done and victims waiting for justice. Bosch took the job the moment it was offered. He knew it was the way. It would allow him to continue his life's mission, and there was no paycheck needed for that.

The reserve officer minimums were easily met and surpassed by Bosch. It was rare that he didn't put in at least two shifts a week, let alone a month, in the detective bureau. He was there so often that he was permanently assigned one of the cubicles in the detective bureau that had been left open when the squad was trimmed in the budget crunch.

Most days he was working in the cubicle or across First Street from the police station where the cells of the old city jail were repurposed as storage rooms. The former drunk tank now housed three rows of standing shelves stocked with open case files going back decades.

Because of the statute of limitations on all crimes but murder, the wide majority of these cases would never be solved or even examined by Bosch. There weren't a lot of murders because the city was small, but Bosch was meticulously going through them looking for ways of applying new technologies to old evidence. He also took on a review of all sexual assaults, nonfatal shootings, and GBI cases within the statute of limitations for those crimes.

The job came with no pay but it had a lot of freedom to it. Bosch could set his own hours and could always take time away from it if a paying job came up for him in private investigation. Chief Valdez knew he was asking a lot to have a detective with Bosch's experience working for him for nothing. He never wanted to impinge on Bosch ability to take on a paying job. He just stressed to Bosch that the two could never mix. Harry couldn't use his badge and access as a San Fernando cop to facilitate or further any private investigation.

Murder knows no bounds or city limits. Most of the cases Bosch reviewed and pursued took him into LAPD turf. It was only expected. Two of the big city's police divisions bordered San Fernando, Mission Division on one half and Foothill Division on the other. In four months Bosch had cleared two unsolved gang murders, connecting them through ballistics to murders in L.A. in which the perpetrators were already in prison, and he had connected a third to a pair of suspects already being sought for murder by the larger department.

Additionally, Bosch had used MO and then DNA to connect four sexual assault cases in San Fernando over a five-year period and was in the process of trying to determine if the attacker was responsible for rapes in Los Angeles as well.

Driving the 210 away from Pasadena allowed Bosch to check for a tail. Midday traffic was light and by alternately driving five miles below the speed limit and then taking it up to fifteen above it, he could check the mirrors for vehicles following the same pattern. He wasn't sure how to take Whitney Vance's concerns about the secrecy of Bosch's investigation, but it didn't hurt to be alert to a tail. He didn't see anything on the road behind him. Of course, he knew that his car could have been tagged with a GPS tracker while he was in the mansion with Vance. He would need to check for that later.

In fifteen minutes he had crossed the top of the Valley and was back in L.A. He took the Maclay Street exit and dropped down into San Fernando, where he turned on to First Street. The SFPD was located in a single-story building with white stucco walls and a red barrel tile roof. The population of the tiny town was 90 percent

Latino, and its municipal structures were all designed with a nod to Mexican culture.

Bosch parked in the employee lot and used an electronic key to enter the station through the side door. He nodded to a couple of uniformed cops through the window of the report room and followed the back hallway past the chief's office to the detective bureau.

By LAPD or any standards, the bureau was quite small. It had once consisted of two rooms, but one room had been subleased to the county coroner's office as a satellite office for two of its investigators. Now there were three detective cubicles crammed into one room with a closet-size supervisor's office adjoining.

Bosch's cubicle had five-foot walls that allowed him privacy from three sides. But the fourth side was open to the door of the supervisor's office. The supervisor was a lieutenant named Trevino, who had so far not been convinced that having Bosch on premises was a good thing. He seemed suspicious of Bosch's motives for working so many hours for no pay and kept a careful watch over him. The only thing that alleviated this unwanted attention for Bosch was that Trevino wore two hats in the department, as is often the case with supervisors in small agencies. He ran the detective bureau and was also in charge of interior operations in the station, including the dispatch center, the firing range, and the sixteen-bed jail built to replace the aging facility across the street.

Bosch checked his mail slot upon entering and found a reminder notice that he was overdue qualifying this month on the range. He moved into his cubicle and sat down at his desk.

He checked his back and saw that Trevino's door was closed. This meant that the lieutenant was most likely in another part of the building carrying out one of his other duties. Bosch had settled on an understanding about Trevino's suspicion and lack of welcome to Bosch. He knew that any success Bosch might have in clearing cases could be seen as a failing on Trevino's part. After all, the detective bureau was his domain. Bosch believed that Trevino's fear of Bosch's success might have set the tone of a relationship. And it wasn't helped any when word got around that Bosch had once thrown a detective lieutenant through a plate glass window.

Still, there was nothing Trevino could do about Bosch's placement in the office because he was a Valdez guy and part of the police chief's effort to overcome personnel cuts.

Bosch turned on his computer terminal and waited for it to boot. It had been four days since he was last in the office. He saw that a flyer for a department bowling night had been left on his desk and he immediately transferred this to the recycle bin beneath it. He liked the people he worked with in the new department, but he wasn't much of a bowler.

He sat up straight to look over the partitions and saw that both of the other cubicles were empty. Lourdes, the CAPs investigator, and Sisto, who handled property crimes, were probably out in the field following up on weekend reports.

Once he was logged into the department's computer system, Bosch opened up the law enforcement databases. He got out his notebook and began the search for Vibiana Abas, knowing he was breaking the one rule the police chief had given him; using his SFPD access to supplement a private investigation. It was not only a firing offense at SFPD but also a crime in California to access a law enforcement database for information not pertaining to a police investigation. If Trevino ever decided to audit Bosch's use of the computer there would be a problem. But Bosch figured that would not happen. Trevino would know that if he made a move against Bosch then he was making a move against the police chief, and that was career suicide.

The search for Vibiana Abas was short. There was no listing of her ever having a driver's license in California, no record of her ever committing a crime or even getting a parking ticket. Of course, the digital databases were less complete the further back the search went, but Bosch knew from experience that it was rare not to find any reference to an entered name. It furthered his speculation that Abas had been an illegal immigrant and possibly returned to Mexico in 1950 after becoming pregnant. Abortion was illegal in California back then. She may have crossed the border to have her baby or to have the pregnancy aborted in one of the backroom clinics in Tijuana.

Bosch knew the law on abortion back then because he had been born in 1950 to an unmarried woman. Soon after becoming a cop he had looked up the laws and the options so that he would better understand the choices his mother faced and had made.

What he was not familiar with was the California penal code in 1950. He accessed it next and looked up the codes for sexual assault. He pretty quickly learned that in 1950 under penal code section 261, sexual intercourse with a female under age eighteen was considered a chargeable offense of rape. Consensual relations were not listed as an exclusion to prosecution. The only exclusion offered in the code was if the female was the wife of the offender.

Bosch thought about what Vance had told him about his father believing the pregnancy was a trap set by Abas to force a marriage that would bring her citizenship and money. If that were the case the penal code gave her a solid piece of leverage. But the lack of any record of Abas in California seemed to belie that angle. Rather than use her leverage, Abas had disappeared, possibly back to Mexico.

Immediately Bosch felt like calling Vance on the number he had given, but decided against it. There would probably be more questions, and he would wait until he had an accumulation. He switched the screen and went back to the DMV interface and typed in "James Louis Aldridge," the cover name Vance had given him. Before the results came up he saw Lt. Trevino enter the squad carrying a cup of coffee from Starbucks. Bosch knew there was a franchise located a few blocks away on Truman.

"Harry, I wasn't expecting you in today," he said.

Trevino always greeted him cordially and by his first name.

"I was in the neighborhood," Bosch said. "Thought I'd check email and send out few more alerts on Screen Cutter."

As he spoke he killed the DMV screen and pulled up the email account he had been given by the department. He didn't turn around as Trevino went to the door behind him and unlocked it.

Bosch heard the door open but then felt Trevino's presence behind him in the cubicle.

"In the neighborhood?" Trevino said. "All the way up here?"

"Well, actually, I was in Pasadena seeing somebody and then I just took the Foothill across," Bosch said. "Thought I'd just send out a few emails, then get out of here."

"Your name's not on the board, Harry. You have to sign in to get credit for your hours."

"Sorry, I was only going to be here a few minutes. And I don't have to worry about making my hours. I put in twenty-four last week alone."

There was a duty board by the entrance to the detective bureau in which Bosch had been instructed to sign in and out so Trevino could chart his hours and make sure he hit the reserve officer minimum.

"I still want you signing in and out," Trevino said.

"You got it, LT," Bosch said.

Trevino stepped into his office and Bosch heard the door close. He turned and checked to make sure, then turned back to his terminal and went back to work. He reopened the DMV portal to run Aldridge's name. He soon pulled up a history that showed Aldridge had a California driver's license from 1948 until 2002, at which point it was surrendered when the license holder moved to Florida. He wrote down Aldridge's date of birth and then entered it with his name on a check of the Florida DMV database. This determined that Aldridge had surrendered his license at age eighty in Florida. The last address listed was in a place called the Villages.

After writing down the information, Bosch checked for a website and found that the Villages was a massive retirement community in Sumter County, Florida. Further searching of online records found an address for Aldridge and no indication of a death record or obituary. He had likely surrendered his driver's license because he no longer could or needed to drive, but it appeared that George Louis Aldridge was still alive.

Content that he had sufficiently chased down the name as needed for a possible cover story, Bosch decided to check through the email that had accumulated on the Screen Cutter case. It was the investigation that had consumed most of his time since he had joined the ranks of the San Fernando Police Department.

FIVE

Screen Cutter" was the case name for a serial rapist Bosch had identified among the department's open sexual assault reports. Combing through the files in the old city jail Bosch had found four cases since 2012 that were seemingly related by MO—modus operandi—but previously not seen as connected. The cases shared four suspect behaviors that alone were not unusual but when taken as a whole indicated the strong possibility of one perpetrator at work. In each case the rapist had entered the victim's home through a rear door or window after cutting the screen rather than removing it. All four assaults occurred during the day and within fifty minutes before or after noon. The rapist used the knife to cut the victim's clothes off rather than ordering her to remove them. And finally the rapist used no condom or other method to avoid leaving his DNA behind.

With these commonalities in hand, Bosch had focused an investigation on the four cases and soon learned that while the suspect's semen had been collected in rape kits in three of the four cases, only in one instance had the material actually been analyzed in the L.A. County Sheriff's crime lab and submitted for comparison to state and national DNA databases, where it found no match. Analysis in the two most recent cases had been delayed because of the massive backlog of rape kits submitted to the county lab for examination. In the fourth case, which was actually the first reported rape, DNA was not collected because the victim had showered and douched before calling police to report the assault.

The county lab and the LAPD lab shared the same building at Cal State LA, and Bosch used his connections from his cold case days to put an urgent push on analysis of the two recent cases. While he awaited results he thought would solidly connect the cases he began follow up interviews of the victims. On two of the cases he had to turn over the questioning to Anabella Lourdes, the department's CAPs detective, because the victims preferred to do the interviews in Spanish. It underlined the one drawback for Bosch in working cases in a city where nine out of every ten citizens were Latino and had varying capabilities when it came to English. He spoke Spanish passably, but for an interview with a crime victim where subtle nuances of storytelling might be important, he needed Lourdes, who understood it as a first language.

What emerged from the four victims—three women in their twenties and a now eighteen-year-old—was a story that was equal parts sad and terrifying. These were undoubtedly stranger rapes, and the attacks had left each woman recovering both mentally and physically even as long as four years after the crime. All of them lived in fear of their attacker returning; none had recovered the confidence they once had. One of them had been married and at the time was trying to conceive a child with her husband. The attack changed things in the marriage, and at the time of the follow-up interview the couple was in the midst of divorce proceedings.

After each interview Bosch felt depressed and couldn't help but think about his own daughter and what sort of impact such an assault would have on her. Each time he called her within the hour to check that she was safe and okay, unable to tell her the true reason he was calling.

But the follow-up interviews did more than reopen wounds for the victims. They help focus the investigation and underline the urgent need to identify and arrest the Screen Cutter.

Lt. Trevino had granted Bosch's request to call in a sketch artist from the Sheriff's Department. The drawings that were produced in separate sessions with the victims were remarkably similar and furthered Bosch's suspicion that one man was responsible for all four attacks. It was while interviewing the first victim, who had showered and cleaned herself directly after the attack, that a detail emerged that would later put the investigation on a level of psychological horror Bosch had never encountered before.

The woman explained that she had taken a shower and cleaned herself immediately after the attack out of fear that she would become pregnant. She and her husband at the time were trying to conceive a child. She had an app on her phone that tracked her menstrual cycle and told her the day of the month she was most likely to conceive. She had checked the app the morning of the attack and knew it was her most fertile day. Knowing this left her unwilling to allow the semen of the man who attacked her to be inside her body while she waited for the police to respond and then went to the hospital for medical care and evidence collection.

When Bosch and Lourdes conducted an interview of the second victim, the woman added details that were not in the original case summaries. She said that she was surprised by the attacker, who was waiting inside her apartment when she came home from work for lunch. She then revealed that in the course of the assault she attempted to dissuade the suspect from raping her by lying and saying she was having her menstrual period.

The woman told Bosch and Lourdes that the man replied, "No, you're not."

When pressed as to whether the attacker could have actually known that she was not menstruating, the victim said she kept a calendar in her bedside table where she kept track of her cycle because she and her boyfriend did not use birth control and employed the rhythm method to keep an active sex life while attempting to avoid pregnancy. The attacker could have found the calendar while waiting for her to arrive home. She provided the calendar to the investigators and they noted that on the day of her assault, she was in the most fertile part of her cycle.

Two interviews, two women who tracked their menstrual

cycles, two assaults on the most fertile day of each woman's cycle. It was a coincidence too eerie to be dismissed. Bosch told Lourdes he didn't believe in coincidences.

The final two victims preferred to speak in Spanish, and their interviews were handled by Lourdes. Both victims revealed under questioning that they also kept track of their menstrual cycles. One victim charted her cycle on a laptop calendar because her doctor had told her that her frequent migraine headaches might be tied to the fluctuations of hormones that occurred during her menstrual period. She tracked her cycle to know when to take a prescribed migraine inhibitor.

The last interview was with the eighteen-year-old, who had been sixteen when attacked on a summer day when she was home alone while her parents were at work. The girl reported that at fourteen she had been diagnosed with juvenile diabetes and her menstrual cycle affected her insulin needs. She tracked the cycle on a calendar on the door of the refrigerator so she and her mother could prepare the proper insulin therapy.

Further questioning revealed that the two victims, like the two before them, were attacked during a day in their menstrual cycle when they were most fertile and likely to conceive.

Bosch and Lourdes drew a number of conclusions from the interviews. The rapist had obviously carefully chosen the day of each attack. While charting of each victim's cycle could be found inside her home, the attacker had to have had this information beforehand. This meant he had stalked his victims and likely had been in their homes previously in an effort to determine the day he would come back for the assault. His cutting of the screens on the day of the attack but not during the early reconnaissance was subterfuge—designed to hide the planning of each assault.

The connection between the cases was stunning and soon confirmed when the DNA results came back linking the three cases in which semen had been collected. There was now no doubt that a serial rapist had struck at least four times in four years in tiny San Fernando.

Bosch had no doubt that there were more victims. In San Fernando alone there was an estimated population of five thousand illegal immigrants, many of whom would not call the police if victimized by crime. It was also ridiculous to consider that such a predator would operate only within the bounds of the tiny city. The four known victims were Latinas and shared common physical appearances: long brown hair, dark eyes, and a small build—none of them weighed more than 110 pounds. The two contiguous LAPD geographic divisions had majority Latino populations, and there was no doubt in Bosch's mind that there were more victims to be found there.

Since discovering the connection between the cases he had been spending almost all of his time on the SFPD job making contact with investigators from LAPD's burglary and sexual assault squads throughout the Valley as well as the nearby departments in Burbank, Glendale, and Pasadena. He was interested in any open cases involving screen cutting. So far nothing had come back, but he knew it was a matter of getting detectives interested and looking, maybe getting the message to the right detective who would remember something.

Bosch had also contacted an old friend who had been a senior profiler with the FBI's Behavioral Analysis Unit. Bosch had worked with Jennifer McKay on several different occasions while he was with the LAPD and she was with the bureau. She was now retired from the FBI and working as a professor of forensic psychology at the John Jay College of Criminal Justice in New York. She also kept her hand in profiling as a private consultant. She agreed to look at Bosch's case pro bono, and he sent her a package on the Screen Cutter. He was keenly interested in knowing the motivation and psychology behind the attacks. Why was the Screen Cutter's stalking pattern geared toward determining fertility dates? Was he trying to impregnate his victims? Was that part of the control and terror he drew fulfillment from?

McKay took two weeks to get back to Bosch and her assessment was surprising to him. She concluded that the perpetrator was not choosing the attack dates because he wished to impregnate his

victims. Quite the opposite. The details of the stalking and subsequent attacks revealed a subject with a deep-seated hatred of
women and disgust toward the bodily ritual of bleeding. The day
of the attack is chosen because the victim is considered by him to
be at the most clean part of her cycle. It is the psychologically safest
moment for him to attack.

McKay's profile ended with an ominous warning: "If you dis-
count the idea that the perpetrator's motive is to give life (impregnate) and realize that the attack is urged by hate, then it is clear
this subject has not concluded his evolution as predator. It is only a
matter of time before these rapes become kills."

The warning resulted in Bosch and Lourdes upping their
game and sending out another set of emails to local law enforcement agencies with McKay's assessment and the composite drawing
attached. This was followed up with phone calls from Bosch and
Lourdes in an effort to break through the typical law enforcement
inertia that descends on investigators who have too many cases and
too little time.

The response was close to nothing. One burglary detective
from LAPD's North Hollywood Division reported that he had an
open burglary case involving a screen cutting but there was no rape
involved. The detective said the victim was a male Hispanic, twen-
ty-six years old. Bosch urged the investigator to go back to the case
and the victim to see if he had a wife or girlfriend who may have
been attacked but afraid or embarrassed to report the assault. A
week later the LAPD detective reported back and said there was no
female in the apartment. The case was unconnected.

Bosch was now playing a waiting game. The rapist's DNA was
not in the databanks. He had never been swabbed. He had left no
fingerprints or other evidence behind other than his semen. Bosch
found no other connecting cases in San Fernando or elsewhere. The
debate over whether to go public with the case and ask for the help
of citizens was simmering on the back burner in the office of Chief
Valdez. It was an age-old law enforcement question: Go public and
possibly draw a lead that leads to an arrest? Or go public and pos-

sibly alert the predator, who then changes up his patterns or moves on and visits his terror on an unsuspecting community somewhere else?

There was no right answer and the chief appeared to be waiting, hoping that Bosch would come through and break the case before another victim was attacked. Bosch was happy not to have the decision on his shoulders. This was why the chief made the big bucks and Bosch made none.

Bosch checked his email now and saw he had no new messages in his queue with "Screen Cutter" in the subject line. Disappointed, he shut down the computer. He put his notebook back in his pocket and wondered if Trevino had looked down on it while hovering in the cubicle. It had been opened to the page with James Louis Aldridge's name written on it.

He left the squad room without bothering to say goodbye to Trevino or write his time down on the board at the front door.

SIX

After leaving the station Bosch got on the 5 freeway and back onto the Whitney Vance case. Not coming up with any birth date or other information on Vibiana Abas on the DMV base was disappointing but no more than a temporary setback. Bosch was headed south to Norwalk, where the time travel goldmine was housed: the Los Angeles County Department of Public Health, where he used to spend so much time as a cold case investigator in the Vital Records office that he knew exactly how the clerks liked their coffee. He felt confident he would be able to answer some questions about Vibiana Abas there.

Bosch put a CD in the Jeep's music slot and started listening to a young horn player named Christian Scott. The first track up, "Litany Against Fear," had a relentless sound and drive to it and that's what Bosch felt he needed at the moment. It took him an hour to get down to Norwalk after a slow crawl around the east edge of downtown. He pulled into the lot fronting the seven-story county building and killed the engine while Scott was in the middle of "Naima," which Bosch thought compared favorably with John Handy's classic version record fifty years earlier.

Just as he stepped out of the car his cell phone buzzed and he checked the screen. It said UNKNOWN CALLER but he took it anyway. It was John Creighton and the call was not a surprise.

"So, you saw Mr. Vance?" he asked.

"I did," Bosch answered.

"Well, how did it go?"

"It went fine. He's a nice man."

Bosch was going to make Creighton dig for it. It might be considered passive-aggressive behavior on his part, but he was keeping the wishes of his client in mind.

"Is there anything we can help with?"

"Uh, no, I think I can handle it. Mr. Vance wants it kept confidential so I'll just leave it at that."

There was a long silence before Creighton spoke next.

"Harry," he said, "you and I go way back to the department, and of course Mr. Vance and I go way back as well. As I said yesterday before hiring you, he's an important client of this firm, and if there is anything I need to know regarding his comfort and security, then I need to know it. I was hoping as former brothers in blue you might share with me what is going on. Mr. Vance is an old man, I don't want him taken advantage of."

"By 'taken advantage of,' are you talking about me?" Bosch asked.

"Of course not, Harry. Poor choice of words. What I mean is if the old man is being extorted or otherwise facing any sort of trouble involving the need for a private detective, well we are here and we have enormous resources at our fingertips. We need to be brought in."

Bosch nodded. He expected this sort of play from Creighton, once Vance had warned him.

"Well," he said. "All I can tell you is that first of all, you didn't hire me. You delivered money to me. Mr. Vance hired me and that's who I work for. Mr. Vance was very specific. He told me not to share what I am doing or why I am doing it with anybody. That would include you. If you want me to break from that, I need to call him back and ask for his per—"

"That won't be necessary," Creighton said quickly. "If that is how Mr. Vance wants it, that is fine. Just know, we are here to help if needed."

"Absolutely," Bosch said in an upbeat but phony voice. "I'll call you if needed, John, and thanks for checking in."

He disconnected the call and headed through the parking lot toward the seven-story building that contained the records of all official births and deaths in L.A. County. All records of marriage and divorce were recorded here as well. The building in front of him was massive and rectangular in dimensions. It always reminded Bosch of a giant treasure chest. The information was in there if you knew where to look—or knew somebody who did. For those who didn't, the front steps of the building were where hawkers stood by ready to counsel the uninitiated on how to fill out request forms—all for the price of a few dollars.

Bosch jogged up the steps, ignoring those who came at him asking if he was applying for a fictitious business name or a marriage licenses. He entered and walked past the information booth and then toward the stairs. He knew from experience that waiting for an elevator in the building could suck the will to live out of a person. He took the stairs down to the basement level, where the BDM section of the Register-Recorder's office was located. As he pushed through the glass door there was a shriek from one of the desks lined along the wall on the other side of the public counter. A woman stood up and smiled broadly at Bosch. She was Asian and her name was Flora. She had always been most helpful to Bosch when he had carried a badge.

"Harry Bosch!" she called out.

"Flora!" he called right back.

Along the counter there was a window for law enforcement requests, which were always given priority, and two windows for citizen requests. There was a man standing at one of the citizen windows. Bosch stepped up to the other. Flora was already heading to the law enforcement window.

"No, you come down here," she instructed.

Bosch did as instructed and then leaned over the counter for an awkward embrace.

"I knew you'd come back to us here," Flora said.

"Sooner or later, right?" he said. "But, hey, I'm here as a citizen right now. I don't want to get you in any trouble."

Bosch knew he could pull the San Fernando badge, but he didn't want a move like that to possibly track back to Valdez or Trevino. That would cause trouble he didn't need. Instead, he made a move to go back to the citizen's window, choosing to keep his private and public detective work separate.

"It no trouble," Flora said. "Not for you."

He ended the charade and remained at the LE window.

"Well, this one might take a while," he said. "I don't have all the information and I need to go way, way back."

"Let me try it. What you want?"

Bosch always had to guard against chopping his language the way she did. But his natural inclination was to start leaving out words when he spoke to her. He had caught himself doing it in the past and he tried to avoid it now.

He pulled out his notebook and looked at some of the dates he had written down that morning in Vance's office.

"Looking for a birth record," he said while reading. "Talking about nineteen thirty-three or thirty-four. What do you have going that far back?"

"Not on database," Flora said. "We have fish here only. No hard record any more. Let me see name."

He knew she was talking about records transferred to microfiche in the seventies and never updated to the computerized database. He turned his notebook around so she could see the name and spelling of Vibiana Abas. Bosch hoped that he would catch a break with the unusualness of it. At least it wasn't a common Latino surname like Garcia or Fernandez. There probably weren't too many Vibiana's around either.

"She old," Flora said. "You want death too?"

"I do. But I have no idea when and if she died. Last time I have her alive for sure is May nineteen fifty."

She made a frowning face.

"Ooh, I see, Harry. But we miss you here."

"Thanks, Flora. Where is Paula? She still here?"

Paula was the other clerk he remembered from his frequent forays to the basement while a detective. Locating witnesses and families of victims was a key part of cold case investigation, usually the foundation of any case. The first thing you did was alert the family that the case is back under active investigation. But murder books from old cases rarely contained updates on deaths and marriages and the migration of people. Consequently, Bosch did some of his best detective work in the halls of records and libraries.

"Paula out today," Flora said. "Just me. I write down now and you get coffee. This take time."

Flora wrote down what she needed.

"Do you want a coffee, Flora?" Bosch asked.

"No, you get," she said. "For waiting."

"Then I think I'll just stick around. I filled up this morning and I have stuff to do."

He pulled his phone out and held it up by way of explanation. Flora went back into microfiche archives to hunt. Bosch sat down on one of the plastic seats in an unused microfiche cubicle.

He was thinking about next moves. Depending on what he came up with here, his next move was to St. Vibiana's to see if he could get a look at baptismal records or the main library downtown, where they kept reverse phone directories going back decades.

Bosch pulled up his phone's search app and typed in "USC EVK" to see what might come up. It got a hit right away. The EVK was still operating on the campus and was located in the Harris Residential Hall on Thirty-fifth Street. He pulled the address up on his maps app and was soon looking at an overview of the sprawling campus just south of downtown. Vance had said Vibiana had lived only a few blocks from the EVK and walked to work. The campus ran along Figueroa Street and the Harbor Freeway corridor. This limited the number of residential streets in the area with direct access to the EVK. Bosch started writing them down along with address spans so that he could look up the names of residents in the reverse directories at the library.

It soon occurred to him that he was looking at a 2016 map of the campus and its surroundings. He realized that the Harbor Freeway may not have even existed in 1950 and that would give the neighborhood around USC and completely different makeup. He went back to the search app and pulled up the history of the freeway also known as the 1-10. He soon learned that the freeway, which slashed a eight-lane diagonal across the county from Pasadena down to the harbor, was built in sections in the 1940s and 50s. It was the dawn of the freeway era in L.A., and the 1-10 was the very first project. The section that edged the east side of the USC campus was begun in 1952 and completed two years later, both dates well after the time Whitney Vance attended the school and met Vibiana Abas.

Bosch went back to his mapping and started including streets that in 1949 and 1950 still provided walking access to the northeast corner of campus, where Harris Hall and the EVK were located. Soon he had a list of fourteen streets with three- or four-block stretches he would search in the reverse directories. He would go down the address listings in search of the name Abas.

He was leaning over his phone's small screen, checking the map for side streets he might have missed, when Flora came back from the bowels of the record center. She was carrying one spool for the microfiche machine triumphantly up in her hand and that immediately put a charge in Bosch's bloodstream. Flora had found Vibiana.

"She not born here," Flora said. "Mexico."

This confused Bosch. He stood up and headed to the counter.

"How do you know that?" he asked.

"It say on her death certificate," Flora said. "Loreto."

Flora had pronounced the name wrong but Bosch understood it. He had once traced a murder suspect to Loreto, far down the inner coast of the Baja peninsula. He guessed if he went there now he would find a St. Vibiana's cathedral or church.

"You already found her death certificate?" he asked.

"Not taking long," Flora said. "Only look to nineteen and fifty-one."

Her words sucked the air out of Bosch. Vibiana was not only dead, but dead so long. He had heard her name for the first time less than six hours ago but somehow Bosch had felt a connection to the girl who walked to work at the cafeteria and had wanted to keep her baby. He held his hand out for the microfiche reel. As Flora handed it to him she told him the record number he should look for—51-659. Bosch recognized it as a low number, even for 1951. The 659th death recorded in L.A. County that year. How far into the year could that be? A month? Two?

A fleeting thought came to him. He looked at Flora. Had she read the cause of death when she had found the document?

"She died in childbirth?" he asked.

Flora looked puzzled.

"Uh, no," she said. "But you read. Make sure."

Bosch took the spool and turned back to the machine. He quickly threaded the film through and turned on the projection light. There was an automatic feed controlled with a button. He sped through the documents, stopping every few seconds to check the record number stamped at the top corner. He was all the way into March before he got to 659th death. By then he realized it had not been a death in childbirth. The math didn't work. If she told Vance she was pregnant in May she had probably conceived in April. The following March was too long—eleven months at least—if she even carried the baby to birth.

When he found the document he found that the State of California certificate of death had not changed much over the decades. It might have been the oldest such document he had ever looked at, but he was intimately familiar with it. His eyes dropped down to the section the coroner or attending physician filled in. The cause of death was handwritten: strangulation by ligature (clothesline) due to suicide.

Bosch stared for a long time at the line without moving or breathing. Vibiana had killed herself. No details beyond what he had already read were written. There was just a signature too scribbled to decipher, followed by the printed words Deputy Coroner.

Bosch leaned back and took in air. He felt immense sadness come over him. He didn't know all the details. He had heard only Vance's view of the story—an eighteen-year-old's story filtered through the frail and guilty memory of an eighty-four-year-old. But he knew enough to know that what happened to Vibiana wasn't right. Vance had left her on the wrong side of goodbye, and what happened in May brought about what happened in March. Bosch had a gut feeling that Vibiana's life was taken from her long before she put the rope around her neck.

The death certificate offered details that Bosch wrote down, beginning with Vibiana's birthdate. She had turned seventeen two days before taking her life on March 5, 1951. Her next of kin was listed as her father, Victor Abas. His address was on Hope Street, which had been one of the streets Bosch had written down after studying the map of the USC neighborhood. The street name seemed like a sad irony now.

The lone curiosity on the document was the location of death. There was only an address on North Occidental Boulevard. Bosch knew that Occidental was west of downtown near Echo Park and not close at all to Vibiana's home neighborhood. He opened his phone and typed the address into the search app. It came back as the address of St. Helen's Home for Unwed Mothers. The search provided several websites associated with St. Helen's and a link to a 2008 story in the *Los Angeles Times* marking the one-hundredth anniversary of the facility.

Bosch quickly pulled the link up and started reading the story.

Maternity Home Marks 100th Birthday

By Keisha Russell, Staff Writer

St. Helen's Home for Unwed Mothers is marking its 100th birthday this week with a celebration that honors its evolution from a place of family secrets to a center for family life.

The three-acre complex near Echo Park will be the site of a full week of programs including a family picnic and featuring an address from a woman who more than 50 years ago was forced by family to give up her newborn for adoption at the center.

Just as social mores have changed in the last few decades, so has St. Helen's. Getting prematurely pregnant once resulted in the mother being hidden away, delivering a child in secret and then having that child immediately taken away for adoption...

Bosch stopped reading as he came to understand what had happened sixty-five years ago to Vibiana Abas.

"She had the baby," he whispered. "And they took it away from her."

WATCH IT. READ IT.

The second season of *BOSCH* based on
these bestselling novels by Michael Connelly

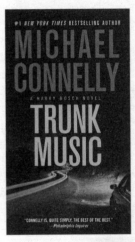
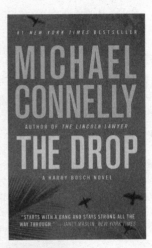

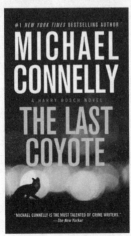

PHENOMENAL PRAISE
FOR *SHADOW WAR*

"*Shadow War* has pace like a catapult, sudden and fierce, and it will hit readers straight between the eyes."
—Ted Bell, *New York Times*
bestselling author of *Patriot*

"Wars produce warriors. Some, like special operator-turned mercenary Tom Locke, find it a curious calling that pulls them into the darkest of nights and most dangerous of places. *Shadow War* brings all of it to life in fascinating detail."
—General Stanley A. McChrystal

"For Black Ops and lots of military action, join Tom Locke for an exciting, wild ride."
—Catherine Coulter, author of *Nemesis*

"I was blown away by Sean McFate's *Shadow War*. A bold, riveting thriller that hurtles readers through a rich, contemporary story full of firefights, grizzled mercenaries, soldiers, gangsters, and spies—along with some of the most fascinating and realistic backroom geopolitical scheming I've ever read in a novel. With well-drawn, fascinating characters and ground-level espionage and combat sure to please fans of Brad Thor, Tom Clancy, and Daniel Silva, *Shadow War* is simply one of the most entertaining and intriguing books I've read in quite some time."
—Mark Greaney, #1 *New York Times*
bestselling author of *Back Blast*

"Step aside, faux thriller writers and armchair warrior storytellers. Ex-mercenary Sean McFate has produced a first novel that's assured, authentic, timely, gritty, and most of all real . . . I enjoyed the hell out of it."

—C.J. Box, *New York Times*
bestselling author of *Off the Grid*

"Intelligent, funny, gritty, Ferrari-paced—at times even electric. *Shadow War* is in the running for best debut of 2016!"

—Ben Coes, *New York Times*
bestselling author of *Eye for an Eye*

"An American James Bond meets the twists and turns of *Homeland.*"

—Adm James Stavridis, USN (Ret),
Supreme Allied Commander at NATO

"A gripping journey inside the world of modern warfare and espionage, and those who enjoy a good military thriller will be hoping that more Tom Locke adventures will follow quickly."   —*Booklist*

"With experience inside the elite 82nd airborne division and work as a private contractor, McFate knows the world of his first thriller intimately . . . The novel provides plenty of drama and a realistic view of political intrigue, and McFate really shines with lines that ring with authenticity. For instance, while sitting at a hotel bar in Kiev, Locke reflects: 'I could sit perfectly at ease at a bar in a strange part of the world and use the reflections in the backsplash to pigeonhole everyone in the room.' A promising debut from an author who clearly knows the realities of the mercenary's trade."   —*Kirkus Reviews*

SHADOWWAR

SHADOWWAR

A Tom Locke Novel

SEAN McFATE
& BRET WITTER

WILLIAM MORROW
An Imprint of HarperCollins*Publishers*

SHADOW WAR. Copyright © 2016 by Sean McFate and Bret Witter. All rights reserved. Printed in the United States of America. No part of this book may be used or reproduced in any manner whatsoever without written permission except in the case of brief quotations embodied in critical articles and reviews. For information, address HarperCollins Publishers, 195 Broadway, New York, NY 10007.

First William Morrow premium printing: May 2017
First William Morrow hardcover printing: May 2016

ISBN 978-0-06-240371-1

Designed by William Ruoto.
Frontispiece courtesy of trekandshoot/Shutterstock.

William Morrow and HarperCollins are registered trademarks of HarperCollins Publishers in the United States of America and other countries.

17 18 19 20 QGM 10 9 8 7 6 5 4 3 2 1

To Ogun, the orisha who looked out for me
when I was raising armies in the field

"It is not the critic who counts; not the man who points out how the strong man stumbles . . . The credit belongs to the man who is actually in the arena, whose face is marred by dust and sweat and blood; who strives valiantly; who errs, who comes short again and again . . . but who does actually strive to do the deeds; who knows great enthusiasms, the great devotions; who spends himself in a worthy cause; who at the best knows in the end the triumph of high achievement, and who at the worst, if he fails, at least fails while daring greatly . . ."

Theodore Roosevelt, 1910

"With lies, you may go forward in the world but you may never go back."

Russian proverb

SHADOWWAR

PROLOGUE

Libya

May 10, 2014

"Target ahead," my team leader, Jimmy Miles, said from the lead car.

"Copy that, Alpha One," I replied into my headset, as the outer wall of the abandoned outpost began to emerge from the desert half a mile away, a dark shadow against a dusty brown hill so slight most people wouldn't have noticed it was there.

I scanned the horizon. Nothing to the east but dunes and distant mountains, the same thing we'd been seeing for the past four hours and two hundred miles. Nothing in front but a dust track in a desert. The hill to the west was maybe fifteen feet at its highest point, rising at a consistent low gradient. It wasn't much more than a tilt of the horizon line, but out here, it could hide an army.

The perfect place for an ambush, I thought, although that didn't mean much. Every building in this rocky corner of the south Sahara was perfect for an ambush, since they were all built in wadis or against small cliffs to escape the wind. Our contacts, the Tuareg, were the legendary bandit-warriors of this harsh world; they knew every foot for five hundred miles. But they didn't have GPS, so you couldn't global-position a meeting. You had to meet them at a spot like this.

This was kinetic country, like the old Wild West: banditos were common and law came out of the barrel of a gun.

"Steady speed," I said. "Eyes open."

The call had come in seventeen hours ago from a new contact in Benghazi. A tribe of Tuareg had two cargo trucks full of weapons, and they wanted to deal.

"Why?"

"They were in Mali last year," the contact said. "They fought the French paratroopers at Gao." I could almost hear the shrug. "Now they need money."

My instinct was to turn the opportunity down. Too many variables. Maybe the contact sensed my hesitation.

"It's not small arms, I assure you," he said. "It's what you want."

Finding AK-47s and rocket-propelled grenade launchers was easy. The world was awash in them, especially Africa. But surface-to-air missiles, anti-tank rockets, 20 mm cannons: those weapons were gold. You laid your hands on them whenever you could.

"When?"

"Tomorrow. Fourteen hundred. Deep southwest,

near the Algerian border. I'll shoot you the coordinates."

The two hundred thousand euros had arrived five hours ago, on a fishing trawler. The boat had probably come from Malta, our primary Mediterranean financial hub since the collapse of the Cypriot banking sector, but that wasn't my concern. What mattered was the courier. He had been late, so now I was late. I had intended to arrive at the rendezvous by noon, two hours early, but . . .

"They're here, Charlie One."

"Copy that, Alpha Two," I said flatly, biting off my frustration at the sight of the off-road trucks. I trusted my team—six Alphas (my team) wearing earpieces, and four local recruits—but I didn't like the Tuareg having the jump. I wouldn't be able to scout the location or position marksmen on surrounding dunes.

This was how the accident happened, I reminded myself.

"Fifteen," Miles said, counting men, as the compound came into view, two crumbling buildings surrounded by a six-foot earthen wall. Sand piled on the west side; the roofs clearly collapsed. It was probably the most habitable permanent structure for a hundred miles.

"Eighteen," said Tingera "Tig" Butuuro, our spotter. "Three against the rise."

Based on the satellite imagery, I had intended to set up between the warehouse and the rise, but the Tuareg were already there. That left my team with the bunkhouse and the earthen wall. At least the

Tuaregs' cargo trucks—two canvas-covered deuce-and-a-halfs that looked like they'd been in use since Indiana Jones slid under a German version eight years before D-Day—would be between us.

"Plan B," Miles said, seeing the same thing. "Use the deuces for cover."

Miles's white Toyota Land Cruiser, obviously stolen from the United Nations and bought by me ten days ago on the black market in Tripoli, left the road and swung wide, giving him a better view into the Tuareg position. Our other two identical vehicles, also bought on the black market, followed.

"Twenty," Tig said, still counting men.

"Twenty-two."

"Jesus," I muttered, as the two Tuareg sentries stood up to announce their positions. At least the deuce-and-a-halfs were facing our convoy. That meant the Tuareg were planning for us to drive them away, as agreed. Or maybe it didn't mean anything.

"Lock and load," I said, as we approached firing range. "Stay frosty."

Manners were important to the Tuaregs. This was a planned meeting; it had to be approached with respect and trust. That meant guns pointed down. Out here, respect meant security . . . if you crossed a line, quite literally, the knives came out.

"Roger that, Charlie One," Miles replied.

I didn't need to tell him anything else. I was the mission leader, but Miles, as always, was in tactical command. He chose the men, mixing and matching skills as mission parameters required. These Alphas were all Tier One operators recruited from the elite of the elite: Navy SEALs, Army Delta, British SAS, Thai special forces, Ugandan Presidential Guard, El Salvador counterdrug hit squad, the best money could buy. I had worked with some of them for years, others just this month. But we understood each other. In this line of work, danger breeds respect and respect breeds love, faster than a fungus. At this point, they were practically family. But even if they'd been strangers, I trusted Miles. He was my brother-in-arms; he'd been protecting my ass since 1992, when I was fresh meat out of officer training and he was my platoon sergeant. Twenty-two against ten, if it came to that, wasn't particularly dangerous for this team. But it was poor operational planning, and that was on me.

"Move to staggered formation," Miles said. "Alpha Three on overwatch. Alpha Two on me."

The Land Cruisers fanned out, the drivers approaching at a flat angle to face the Tuareg, then turning and stopping in unison with their grills facing the way we had come. In a combat situation, parking mattered. You never wanted to back up. You always chose cover. The embankment would offer protection for our two most important assets: men and engine blocks.

I checked my pistols, being an ambidextrous shooter. Everyone else was kitted out with body armor and heavy weapons. I was wearing mercenary business attire—sunglasses, desert boots, 5.11 cargo pants, a web belt, a super 80 button-down Oxford shirt, and bespoke blue linen sport coat from Jermyn Street in London. No Kevlar vest or assault rifle. A few years ago, I was a Tier One operator, too, but I was corporate now.

I adjusted my earpiece and slid the nine-mils into their dual holsters at the small of my back, the only place my sport coat would hide them. Corporate, but not foolish.

"Ready?" I asked the interpreter. The man nodded weakly. He was in his fifties, dressed in cheap slacks and a short-sleeved button-down shirt. He looked like what he was: a linguistics professor forced into this dangerous job by the ongoing disintegration of Libyan society.

Another weak link, I thought. But what I said was, "Don't worry. You'll be fine. This is a friendly transaction."

I stepped out of the Land Cruiser and walked toward the warehouse, trusting my men enough to keep my eyes on the Tuareg. A few older fighters, but mostly young men. Kalashnikovs slung, but close at hand. There were a few traditional sky-blue robes, beautiful in their simplicity, but most of the men were wearing mismatched desert fatigues. All but one was wearing a black turban. This wasn't religious. The Tuareg weren't zealots. In this climate, turbans were a necessity against sand and sun.

I was disappointed but not surprised they hadn't brought their camels.

"*As-salaam alaykum,*" I said, greeting the Tuareg at the entrance. The building had no ceiling, but faded Italian graffiti was still visible on the walls, probably from the soldiers condemned to live in this hole when Mussolini tried to control this desert.

The man nodded, pulling aside the rug that shielded the empty doorway. I stepped inside. The

Tuareg had swept the room, strung a cloth tarp for shade, and placed five rugs in a circle in the center of the space. Three men in blue robes were sitting on the rugs, watching me. They seemed to have been sitting for days.

"*Marhaba*," the old man in the middle said, and touched his forehead in the traditional greeting. His face was grizzled and his teeth rotten. That was typical of the Tuareg, who drank mostly sugared tea.

The man gestured to an empty rug, and I sat cross-legged before him. The interpreter sat beside me. It was traditional to take off your shoes, but I had no intention of removing my desert boots. I noticed the Tuareg hadn't removed theirs.

We waited, watching each other, saying nothing. These were among the fiercest fighters in the world, but also the most civil. They had survived in this desert for centuries, and their customs were ancient, especially compared with the West. Patience was the Tuareg way.

Finally, the leader nodded. A man appeared from the doorway, carrying a long, slender brass pot. He squatted beside us and lined up four small glass cups on the ground. He placed a lump of sugar in each one, then poured boiling tea slowly over each lump from the long brass spout.

He waited, then poured the tea back into the pot. He repeated the process, this time raising and lowering the ornate kettle as he poured, arcing the tea into the glasses. My interpreter spoke to the Tuareg leader, and the man to his right responded, but there was no need for translation. It sounded like small talk. Perhaps the interpreter was wondering about his lack of a cup. But he wasn't a person here, only a mouthpiece. That was also the Tuareg way.

Finally, after ten minutes of pouring, the teasmith passed out the cups. I took my tea. It was scalding hot, but I drank it without expression. It was sweet and minty.

Sugar cookies followed, then another round of tea. The Tuareg sipped and munched silently, their eyes alert, their battered but well-oiled Kalashnikovs at their sides.

Arms deals are dangerous, I reminded myself. *Arms deals are points of contact. All points of contacts can go wrong . . .*

The teasmith bowed. Then he stood, took his empty pot, and exited. The three Tuareg began speaking softly. I sat silently. I would wait until one of them addressed me, and then enter the conversation.

Don't lose focus. Don't forget the danger . . .

"American?" the Tuareg leader asked.

I nodded solemnly. "A colleague," I replied, stopping to allow the interpreter to repeat my words in Berber. "We have traveled far to meet you."

The Tuareg nodded. They had also traveled far. "Where are you fighting?"

"In the north. Beyond the desert. This is not our fight."

It wasn't the Tuaregs' fight, either. It had been forced on them by European boundaries and the implosion of Gaddafi's regime. This desert was their homeland, and also where the Libyan army dead-enders had withdrawn when there was nowhere else to go. The weapons cache outside had almost surely been Gaddafi's at one time.

The old Tuareg nodded approval. The man on his right spoke.

"Let's go to the trucks," the interpreter said, clearly relieved.

There was no need to negotiate. The terms had been fixed by our mutual friend in Benghazi. No doubt we had overpaid.

Outside, it seemed as if no one had moved, but I spotted Miles in the lead position and surreptitiously extended three fingers on my right hand, telling him all was as planned. Speaking through the earpiece would have raised Tuareg suspicion.

I walked to the two cargo trucks. They were 1960s Soviet, probably taken from Algeria in a past skirmish. I peeked inside the steel cab. The mechanics looked good, and the keys were in the ignition. The doors were rusted, and the canvas over the beds was covered in dust and patches, but the desert tires and metal rims looked new. They would run for miles, even if fragged.

A young Tuareg in an Atlanta Braves baseball cap stepped forward. He was wearing a Bob Marley shirt under his camos, probably thrown in a donation box by a stoner college kid back in Vermont. He dropped the tailgate and smiled, his teeth already rotten. Societies that forbade alcohol, like the Tuareg, were often insatiable for sugar.

The wooden crates were piled two deep, three wide, and four high. I climbed inside and opened two boxes. SA-18 shoulder-launched antiaircraft missiles, known as "Grouse" to NATO and "Iglas" in their country of origin: Russia. With these, amateurs had brought down helicopters in Bosnia, Syria, and Egypt. An SA-18 was rumored to have shot down the Rwandan presidential airplane as it approached Kigali International Airport in 1994, triggering the Rwandan genocide. Throw a few in the trunk of a car, park within a mile of a runway, and a terrorist could bring down a 747 at almost any airport in the world.

The other truck held twelve Soviet KPV-14.5 antiaircraft guns, wrapped in Tuareg blankets. The weapons were used but passable: well oiled, the action unclogged. When mounted on the back of a Toyota HiLux pickup truck to create a "technical"—the workhorse of modern warfare—these guns were devastating. In and out in minutes, killing everything within peripheral vision. I'd seen it in West Africa too many times.

The SA-18s would probably need new coolant units and the AA guns some parts, but they were a great catch. I nodded to Miles as I climbed down from the tailgate and walked over to face the Tuareg leader, a sign of respect, but also a warning. If anything went wrong, I wanted this man to know he wouldn't get away.

"We accept."

The interpreter spoke at surprising length. The Tuareg nodded. Two of my Libyan freelancers emerged from a Land Cruiser, each with a large Pelican case. They walked over and placed the black molded containers on the ground at my feet.

The leader signaled, and the Tuareg in the baseball cap came forward, flashing his brown teeth. He bent down on one knee and popped the top of the nearest case. He lifted out a plastic-wrapped brick of crisp, new hundred-euro notes. The poorer the people, the more they appreciated freshly minted money. He counted the bricks. The leader nodded, and the young man pulled a long, curved knife from his belt.

"Tangos on the east perimeter."

The shout exploded in my earpiece, just as the knife sliced into the plastic. A second later, I heard the *bip-bip-bip* of an Israeli Tavor assault rifle. Our medic Boon's gun.

"Two Tangos"—meaning targets—"at seven o'clock."

"Eight o'clock."

"Taking fire."

I heard Miles's assault rifle firing in controlled bursts, and the flat repeat of a semiautomatic pistol somewhere behind me.

I leapt forward and knocked the young man unconscious with one swing of the collapsible metal baton I kept on my web belt. In an instant, I had his knife. I looked up, locked eyes with the Tuareg leader, and knew he hadn't double-crossed me. This was third party.

I thought about grabbing the closed Pelican case anyway, but turned instead and sprinted for the cab of the first deuce, my earpiece echoing with commands.

"Shooters in the east building."

"Suppressive fire."

"Cover down on Charlie 1."

"Roger."

I grabbed the door handle and swung into the driver's seat, knowing the key was in the ignition. I turned it, and the engine sputtered.

I pumped the gas, the engine revving and then dying. The desert was full of the light popping of automatic fire, never as loud or chaotic as the movies made it seem. I could make out the audio signature of each of my team's weapons, with limited returning shots, mostly AK-47s by the sound of it. We had caught the assailants out of position, probably maneuvering for an ambush, so my men weren't targeting them. They were too well trained for that. This withering barrage was designed to keep enemy heads down, so they couldn't fire back. Only assholes counted kills.

I turned the key again. This time, the engine turned over. I pumped the gas, and the deuce belched smoke. I double-clutched and shifted. The gears ground, but the truck didn't move.

"Where are those shots coming from?"

"Tangos on the southeast dune. No vehicles spotted."

So how did they get here?

"The Tuareg are heading out. I repeat, the Tuareg are on the move."

I looked in my side mirror; both Pelican cases were gone.

"They're taking fire."

I heard the gears grinding on the other deuce, but I didn't look to see which one of my men was behind the wheel. I had one job now, and that was to drive my truck onto the egress route.

I slammed down on the gearshift and heard it

crunch, then muscled it into first and felt the deuce lurch, then start to roll. I shifted to second, cranking the wheel to straighten it on the road. I heard bullets ripping into the wooden crates and cursed my stupidity in trusting the perimeter to the Tuareg. My cargo of SA-18 missiles wouldn't explode in a firefight, but they could be punctured and ruined.

"Fire in the hole," Miles's voice barked in my earpiece, as I shifted into third. I felt the explosion, then heard it, and a moment later, the dust cloud enveloped the truck. That was the end of a hundred-year-old Italian outpost.

"Pop smoke," Miles yelled. That was what I wanted to hear. Behind me, the Alphas were throwing smoke grenades and laying down fire to cover our escape while someone, probably Frank "Wildman" Wild, British ex-SAS, howled over the headset with delight.

At three hundred meters, outside the dust and the effective range of an AK-47, I looked back. The second deuce was straggling behind, two tires shot out, our Thai ex-paratrooper Boon at the wheel. I could still hear the popping of automatic fire.

Then I saw the Toyota pickup angling over the hardscape at the back of the incline. There were four—no five—men in the back, firing AK-47s as they came. Maybe local bandits tipped off to the sale, but more likely Libya Dawn or Dignity, the local jihadist groups.

Nothing dignified or dawning here. Nothing Western but their weapons.

A man stood up and lifted an RPG to his shoulder. It bounced as the truck caromed over the rocks, but the man needed only a second to line it up in my direction. The distance was a hundred meters and closing; there was nothing I could do. Hitting anything with the notoriously imprecise RPG was little more than chance anyway, and this man had probably never fired anything like it in his life.

I pounded the gas pedal and held my breath.

Misfire.

I couldn't hear the click, but I saw the man lower the barrel. *Now*, I thought, jerking the steering wheel toward the hardscape and careening back toward the Toyota. Bullets ripped through the canvas and steel, but I focused on a spot just behind the truck's rear wheel, hit the accelerator, and heard a tremendous crunch as the deuce crushed the rear flank of the Toyota. It spun sideways and flipped, launching the men into the dirt. The deuce sputtered, but I ripped the gear down to second and threw the wheel hard to the right.

A moment later, I was back on the dirt road, the Toyota a worthless hunk behind me. My rear tires were dragging, and blue smoke was spewing from under the hood, but the exit route was clear. Only another truck could catch me now.

"Charlie One clear," I said into my headset.

"Alpha One clear," came the response.

"Alpha Two clear."

"Alpha Three clear."

"What about the Libyans?"

"All clear, Charlie One." It was Miles, confirming the count.

"Even the interpreter?"

There was a pause, then I heard Wildman's

Welsh accent in my ear. "I nabbed 'im, boss. But God, he smells."

Miles laughed. I knew that laugh anywhere, even though I couldn't see his face. I didn't even know where he was for sure. Behind me somewhere, covering my ass. "Number one or number two?" he said.

"Both."

More laughter over the headset, as the tension eased. Everyone shits their pants the first time the bullets start ripping.

"Any more trucks?" I asked.

"One," Miles said, "but it's after the Tuareg. Probably an inside job."

I thought of the Atlanta baseball cap. Maybe.

I eased back on the accelerator. With only one truck, the Islamists, or dissident Tuareg, or whoever they were, wouldn't give chase. It may not have been clean, but we had the weapons we'd come for.

Another victory for the good guys, I thought as I pushed the deuce into third, then fourth. I could barely see the road through the diesel smoke, but there wasn't much to see. It was all dirt and rocks anyway.

Eighty kilometers later the deuce died. Boon's truck, which had been blowing smoke for the last forty kilometers, limped up beside me. It was time to ditch the deuces. The men stripped our three Land Cruisers of excess weight—spare tires, pioneering kit, survival gear—and started to load them with the weapons, while Boon attended to the interpreter, who was in a state of shock. Thai paratroopers as a rule weren't shit, but I'd hired Boonchu "Boon" Tipnant four years ago because he was a combat medic. Turned out, he was an expert at stealth extraction and hand-to-hand combat, and a hell of a good guy, too.

"Lose the crates," I yelled, as the Land Cruisers filled up. "And the 14.5 millimeter ammunition." I could easily source the ammo in Romania.

While the team jammed the weapons into the Land Cruisers—they would enjoy driving the last hundred kilometers with heavy weapons drooping off the tailgate—Miles and I stepped into the desert. I lit a cigar from my portable humidor and activated my sat phone, then lit Miles's cigar, too. It was a ritual we'd picked up in Airborne in the 1990s, half a lifetime ago, and we'd smoked a thousand cigars together since, from Sicily to the drop zone at Fort Bragg to the jungles of Liberia.

"Lucky," I said, walking through my mistakes in my head. Unknown broker. Late arrival. No lookouts. I was getting sloppy.

"It's not lucky if you're good," Miles replied.

"That doesn't make it right."

"That doesn't make it wrong, either," he said. Miles was grinning. He was past fifty, and he looked like a dentist, but if I was in a death cage match with a crocodile and fighting for my life, he was the first man I'd chose to be with me.

The sat phone beeped. I looked down. I was surprised to see I'd missed several calls. I walked away a few paces for privacy, puffed on my cigar, and dialed the familiar number. A familiar voice answered.

"Monday, 0800."

"I'm in the middle of something."

"It's off. Come home."

I straightened my red Hermès tie in the bathroom mirror, then brushed lint from the right shoulder of my dark blue Harvie and Hudson suit, the battle armor of the corporate world. I checked my shave, realized I'd missed a spot on my neck, and dry-shaved the stubble.

Then I went to my closet. On the right were ten suits, blue or gray, and stylishly cut. On the left were a dozen colorful robes and kaftans, gifts from grateful people I'd worked with in Africa. Crammed between them on shelves and utility hooks was my gear. Three sets of boots—black, tan, and olive green. Action slacks in the same three colors. My web belt, my six-inch folding knife, and my collapsible baton, the extendable steel club I'd used to knock the Tuareg unconscious less than thirty hours ago.

I checked my seventy-two-hour "go bag." I always kept two packed—one for the developed world, one for the rest. My third world bag had been depleted in Libya, so I restocked it with sterile syringes, malaria tablets, batteries, codeine, and other items prized in a war zone. Then I packed my personal essentials: the ivory chopsticks I'd picked up as a teenager backpacking around the world, my portable ten-cigar humidor, and an iPod crammed with classical music.

I had arrived home seven hours earlier after a twenty-eight-hour journey that involved driving the weapons to the desert camp, choppering to Tripoli, and buying a ticket to Rome with cash. I'd showered in the first-class lounge, waiting two hours, then bought a ticket to Washington, DC, and slept on the plane. I figured I'd have a day in DC, at most, and then it was back to the grind.

That didn't bother me. It was standard procedure. I was accustomed to flying twelve hours for a two-hour meal with a client or source, and then turning around and flying home. The information shared on such assignments couldn't be written down. It had to be delivered in person, or not at all.

What bothered me, as I locked my apartment and drove my thirty-year-old diesel Mercedes through Adams Morgan, my Washington neighborhood, was the Libyan operation.

I wasn't worried about the firefight. That was a known business risk. And besides, I'd acquired the weapons at the agreed-upon price, losing only two deuce-and-a-halfs in the process, and cargo trucks were essentially worthless. Yet, by the time I got back to base, my desert training camp was already being dismantled by one of the "cleaning" teams my employer, Apollo Outcomes, used to scrub evidence of an operation.

It wouldn't show, and I'd never let the bosses know, but I was pissed. I had spent six months planning the Libyan job. I had been back and forth between Washington and a fashionable conference room in Houston, Texas, a dozen times. Could this job be done? *Should* it be done? How long would it take? How much would it cost?

I had been the Apollo man in Africa for more than a decade: raising small armies for U.S. interests; preventing a genocide in Burundi with twelve competent soldiers; defeating a warlord in Liberia without firing a shot; "shaping the environment" in Sudan to make way for American foreign policy. Standard stuff.

The Libyan operation was different. In Libya, my goal was to seize, protect, and operate major oil fields, on foreign soil, for an American oil company, in the middle of a civil war.

It was un-fucking-precedented.

That was what traditional soldiers never understood, even my old paratrooper mates, the ones who called me merc like it was a dirty word. Working for Apollo wasn't about the money, which was less than most people thought, or the power, which was incidental and fleeting. It was about doing the shit I couldn't do in a uniform. No red tape. No political constraints, like I'd have in the public military. This job wasn't about licking boots in Washington. It was about being assigned mission impossible and getting it done. It was being dropped into the middle of a war zone with my rucksack and my wits and nobody to look over my shoulder . . . and changing the shape of the world.

I understood the geopolitical implications of the Libyan operation. I had sat through endless meetings in top floor conference rooms overlooking Houston, discussing the big question: what if the world found out?

But the circumstances, as I'd arranged them, were airtight. The drilling station had been abandoned for more than two years. The location was remote. The pipeline ran through uninhabited desert or controllable towns. AO, as Apollo was known in the field, even had a long-standing contact inside the port at Zawiyah, where we would load the oil onto tankers, and Zawiyah was truly a city where no questions were asked.

The light turned green, and I turned past the massive brick hotel onto Rock Creek Parkway, slipping out of the urban environment and into the leafy gully of Washington's hidden highway.

The operation was a shit pile, I thought as I passed under arched road bridges reminiscent of Roman aqueducts. It was a box of mismatched puzzle pieces. It should never have fit together. The job had been, by any reasonable estimate, too much to ask.

But I'd done it.

Three weeks in-country, and I'd already seized the drilling station, recruited a few hundred local fighters, and set up a desert camp to train them. We had more than enough light arms and "liberated" black market UN Land Cruisers. Thanks to the Tuareg, we had acquired the firepower to equip helicopters and technical. Already, we could defend a hundred miles of pipeline, and it was still two days before the Houston wildcatters arrived—the craziest bastards on planet earth, even worse than the

Navy SEALs—and slammed the station into working order. If anything, I was ahead of schedule.

So where had it gone wrong?

Not the ground game, I thought, as Rock Creek Parkway bottomed out along the Potomac River. I had gone over every move during my layovers and flights, and my end was clean.

Was the operation compromised? Did someone in Tripoli or Houston leak to the press? Was a major shareholder concerned?

But even if a reporter started sniffing around— and I was sure no reporters had, yet—there was nothing to latch on to. I'd drawn my team from the elite forces of a dozen different nations. My indigenous recruits were loyal to tribal strongmen, who knew nothing of the overall operation. My management group, mere figureheads, were the cousins and other assorted confidantes of connected Libyan businessmen, the type of shady characters paid good money to do nothing more than take the fall, if it ever came to that. All financial transactions were layered through them, then routed through the British Virgin Islands, whose banks were more secretive than Switzerland's. It would be next to impossible to trace anything back to Houston, especially given the cutouts and shell companies I'd created. That was why the Fortune 500 hired Apollo.

What about the U.S. government? I doubted USG was involved, but I knew one phone call from State or Defense could shut down a company operation anywhere in the world. That's the power of handing out thirty billion a year in military contracts.

I downshifted as I passed the Kennedy Center, the giant Kleenex box where I got my opera fix whenever I had the misfortune of being in town, and eased into the bridge traffic. The Washington Monument was behind me, and the Jefferson Memorial off to my left, but the skyscrapers of Arlington, Virginia, rose in front, looming over the low treeline of Roosevelt Island. God, I hated going to Virginia, with its consulting firms and tract mansions and glistening office parks for the military-industrial complex. I distrusted it even now, on a clear morning, at the ass end of rush hour, on a reverse commute, and sure enough, the traffic snarled at the first big bend in U.S. 66. There was only one industry in Washington, and these office jockeys, like everyone here, were policy dependent: consultants, attorneys, think tankers, and advisors, a living army of opinions and analysis.

And yet few of them would understand the Libyan operation. They would insist that we don't seize foreign assets for profit . . . not in the sixty years since the United Fruit Company conquered Central America using the CIA, anyway . . . or since Prescott Bush brokered an oil deal with the Saud family.

But that was merely ignorance. This was the way the world worked. A place like Libya—or Syria or Afghanistan—wasn't a sovereign country in any modern sense. Even before Gaddafi was overthrown, the desert regions had governed themselves. In the end, the self-proclaimed "king of kings of Africa" was little more than the mayor of Tripoli. Now Libya was shattered, and everything from oil fields to "tax stations" along desert camel tracks were run by whatever local racketeer had the muscle and imagination to control them. The Sahara was the American West of 150 years ago: a lawless land where unemployed soldiers, smugglers, natives, and criminals took what they could, sometimes by cunning, usually by force.

Half the world was like that now. West Africa. Congo. Yemen. In South Sudan, I spent four months helping a local strongman with ties to a U.S. congressman destroy a rebellious rival. The strongman's reward was an appointment to the Ministry of Natural Resources. The reward for our client, a large energy firm, was the exclusive right to drill oil in Block 5A—at a hefty price, of course.

I had believed in that operation. The rebels were butchers. I had seen it myself. Then, three months later, I heard the strongman had slaughtered a thousand "Islamic terrorists," most of them women and children.

My Libyan operation cut out the local middleman. A middleman who was most likely a murderer, rapist, and thug. In my opinion, Libya was a step toward a more civilized world, not away from one. It was naïve to think otherwise.

So where had it gone wrong?

Somewhere along this damn interstate, I thought, as someone laid on a horn behind me, and somewhere up ahead another car answered. The traffic was completely stopped, and even the Virginians, who lived with this every day, were getting antsy.

Just get me back to Africa, I thought, as I heard the pounding opening to Verdi's opera *The Force of*

Destiny on the classical station, WETA. It was one of my favorites: two men who fought as mercenary brothers-in-arms, now pitted against each other by fate in a fight to the death. A nice reminder that my occupation was as old as civilization and, like Verdi's opera, often didn't end well.

It wasn't my job to question Apollo or its clients, I reminded myself, as the traffic started moving. I was a high-end fixer. I was paid to solve problems in war zones, using whatever means I could get away with. And for the creative mind there were so many means.

Whatever happened after . . . well, it was only rumors, anyway.

CHAPTER 2

Thirty-eight minutes later, I pulled into the parking lot of a nondescript building in one of the endless office parks near Dulles International Airport. I parked my ancient Mercedes in a long line of similar cars and stared at the man-made pond and the picnic table no one ever used, letting the Verdi wash away my traffic-related stress.

This area was the heart of the mercenary-industrial complex. G4S, a competitor, supplied thousands of security guards to the U.S. military from these buildings, and tens of thousands more to domestic malls. DynCorp pulled down more than three billion a year, although much of that was from military-aircraft maintenance. Blackwater became Xe Services, then Academi, then merged with Triple Canopy, a rival, to beget Constellis Holdings, all in the space of five years. My employer, Apollo Outcomes, had been cleaning latrines on army bases in the 1990s. Now it was a private army with yearly revenues of $3.7 billion, most of it courtesy of Uncle Sam, according to their most recent Securities and Exchange Commission filing.

The mercenary business, to put it in technical terms, was hot. The industry had exploded during the Iraq War, not just because of contracts in Iraq and Afghanistan, although those were massive, of course. Just as important, with every national asset focused on those countries, there was no one left to deal with the other terrible things happening in the world. For the U.S. military, that was the opportunity cost of waging two simultaneous wars. For the mercenary industry, it was a once-every-three-centuries opportunity.

Now, less than fifteen years after the Third Infantry Division rolled into Baghdad, contractors like me were the forward arm of Western power, fighting in every rat hole, brutal dictatorship, and economic backwater in the world. It was, quite simply, the biggest change in the military since the heyday of the *condottieri*, the infamous contract warriors of the Middle Ages. But you wouldn't know it from these shabby surroundings and nondescript office parks, where Apollo and its competitors abutted low-level consulting firms and industrial printers.

And that was all by design. The lack of media attention, the bland buildings in boring locations, the forgettable corporate names and artless logos—it was a strategy. Because to draw attention in this business, even positive attention, was to fail. That was why Blackwater was a pariah, before being sold and renamed three times. The military performed the covert actions the White House would neither confirm nor deny. We took care of the clandestine ones, those the government disavowed if they were ever spoken aloud. Our only competition was the CIA, but we were cheaper. And, in my opinion, far better, because we were so deep undercover that half the time, even the CIA couldn't find us. If you wanted to be a player in the Deep State—the shadowy coterie of big business, politicos, media, and other elites who ruled behind the headlines, beyond government oversight, and across national borders, regardless of who was formally in power, the world where private armies like Apollo thrived—never let them hear or speak your name.

There was a time, five years ago, when I might have been a power player here, a man who contracted operations instead of performed them. I was invited, groomed, *introduced to society* . . . whatever you want to call it. But I hated the DC scene: the economy of favors, the double-dealing, the endless scheming in pursuit of a compromised version of a shining ideal, while the shabby duck on the fetid retention pond shed feathers like the plague.

I was a soldier, not a bureaucrat. I chose Africa.

Now I came back three, maybe four weeks a year. Many mercs in the field never came back at all. We were freelancers, hired by the job: cash on delivery, no health insurance or 401(k)s. Old mercs don't retire, they disappear, maybe to some unknown corner of the world, maybe to an unmarked grave. The ones I knew kept busy, taking job after job, so they wouldn't have to face this life, and the people left behind. But I was a mission leader, the point of contact between the men in the field and the suits in the office. My role was to plan the assignments and assemble the teams, so I came here just barely often enough to recognize the frosty attendant at the front desk, the one who never smiled.

"Hello Jane," I said. It had taken me two years to remember her name. She didn't even pretend to remember mine.

I slid my company ID into the bioscanner and held it for three seconds, waiting for the green light, and then placed my index finger on the fingerprint reader. Jane checked her monitor, confirmed my identity, and waved me to the employee turnstile, the one with the NO TAILGATING placard on it. The thick Plexiglas doors swished open. Next to the doors was a metal detector and X-ray machine, with two armed guards. Typical postterrorism precaution, Apollo always said. Only an expert would notice that the guards changed every few days and carried Heckler & Koch MP5SD6s with integrated suppressor barrels.

Beyond the metal detector was a wall—reinforced steel under plaster—with a huge company logo. I walked through a curved white tunnel called a waveguide, a security measure that emptied into a windowless cubicle farm. Cable trays and monitors hung from the ceiling, as kids in their twenties took phone calls in foreign languages. I had no idea what they did, but they seemed younger every year. When I started here in 2002, the cube dwellers were retired older men from the military and intelligence community, whose pants refused to acknowledge their extra pounds. They were refugees from the great defense layoffs of the 1990s, out here by the airport, playing out the string.

Now the cube ranchers were mostly women, because they make better intelligence analysts, and mostly younger than the Cold War–era coffee stains on the old guys' shirts. I assumed that meant they were going somewhere in life, besides the suburbs.

"Tom Locke. Good to see you. How was the flight?"

The speaker was David Wolcott, my handler for the last five years, lurking as always. Wolcott had the look of those old middle managers, right down to the bald spot and the belt that went underneath his belly instead of around. I figured he had a wife and kids somewhere in the suburbs, a barbecue grill, baseball equipment, and one of those fences with the support poles on the outside so the homeowner can sit in a lounger and look at the pretty side.

"It was first class," I said. As always.

Wolcott had called me home, but that was not something we would discuss. He was a middle manager, and this wasn't a business with postmortem meetings or after-action reviews. If Libya still bothered me a few months from now, I might try to figure out what had happened on my own. Otherwise, I left the past alone.

"Coffee?" Wolcott asked.

"No thanks."

"I don't blame you, Tom. It's garbage. No one has cleaned the pot in a year."

We passed the cube farm and turned down a hallway, where I left my cell phone on a table with twenty others, as required. The next door was steel, with a large combo lock, keypad, and camera. Inside was the Tactical Operations Center, or TOC, a large, windowless room of computer monitors running mission status updates, live team feeds, satellite imagery of areas of interest, and video conferencing with company managers around the world. The TOC was a 24/7 war room, complete with top secret government clearance and immediate access to every operative in the world, and it was the worst job at Apollo: cramped, dark, underventilated and underpaid.

Ten paces further, Wolcott stopped in front of an office suite, opened the door, and motioned me through without a word.

"Brad Winters," I said, as Wolcott closed the door and stayed outside, leaving me alone with my former boss. It wasn't often I was caught by surprise, but this was one of those times.

"Good to see you, Thomas," Winters said, rising from his chair.

I had instinctively straightened and brought my arms to my sides, a military sign of respect, but Winters came around the table to shake hands. This man had recruited me into Apollo Outcomes; we had worked closely together for six years; he had taught me, molded me, broken and invested in me, and then he'd invited me to join him, as his right hand, in Apollo's executive suite.

But I'd gone back to Africa instead, and I hadn't heard from him since.

That was the last anyone had heard from him, really. Brad Winters had transformed Apollo during the gold rush of the Iraq and Afghanistan wars, when the Department of Defense was handing out $300 billion a year to companies with any sort of link to military logistics or firepower. He had almost made a name for himself. And then he had disappeared.

I knew that meant he'd either fallen out of power, or ascended into the realm where only a hundred or so people needed to know your name. Clearly, it was the latter, and I wasn't surprised. Brad Winters was a dinosaur; he would always be around, even if it was just as an oil slick.

And I wasn't surprised that he looked exactly as I remembered him. That was the man's greatest asset: a manner so bland, he could disappear into any crowd. Winters had gotten his start in the 82nd Airborne—that was a big part of our connection, because I'd earned my jumpmaster wings there, too—and had come and gone from Wall Street before coming to Apollo. His grip had gotten firm in his time upstairs, but the only other change I noticed was the stitching on the lapel of his blue suit.

"I have a tailor, from Panama," Winters winked, following my gaze. "I see you're still shopping Jermyn Street."

My first trip with Brad Winters had been to Brussels to brief NATO officials on a security situation in Africa. When we met at Dulles airport, he had eyed my Brooks Brothers suit and tasseled loafers and finally said, "That won't do."

We got off during a stopover at Heathrow and took a cab to Jermyn Street, off Saint James Square, the ground zero of gentlemen's clothing. We walked into several modest-looking shops, where the staff greeted him by name.

Several hours later, I had four bespoke suits on order, nine tailored shirts, an overcoat with a velvet collar, two pairs of John Lobb shoes, a breast pocket wallet, and some Hermès ties and sterling silver cufflinks. It cost me two months' salary, including danger pay, but at least Apollo paid for the connecting flight we'd missed.

Now Winters laughed, and I realized I'd glanced down at his shoes. Most men skimped on footwear, because it was expensive. The shoes I had on this morning cost more than what a Washington bureaucrat takes home in a month. Winters's shoes cost even more.

"I'm glad you haven't turned your back on everything I taught you," Winters said.

I let the remark slide, made a mental note to be more careful with my gaze, and took a seat. If Winters had come down from the mountain, this was important. But I didn't expect to find out a damn thing about it here. In the army, it had been two-hour mission briefings, with a thick PowerPoint presentation and six outside experts. It was death by detail.

At Apollo, it was eight minutes if you were lucky. And no note taking. The company's unofficial motto was: "Figure it out."

"That was solid fieldwork in Libya," Winters said. "I'm sorry it didn't pan out. I know your other recent missions have been . . . less than satisfactory."

It had been a rough few years of muscle work, the kind of cheap intimidation and sudden violence that was beneath a man of my skills. I had started to wonder if I'd been forgotten, or taken for granted. Winters was telling me, straight off, that I hadn't.

"I recently talked to State," he said, tipping his chair back in a show of disdain for that august department. "There's an opportunity in Ukraine.

Short term. Creative. Off the books. Your kind of mission, Thomas."

"Why me?"

I had operated in the Balkans during the '90s as a soldier in U.S. Special Operations Forces, and later transacted arms deals in Eastern Europe for Apollo, but my area of expertise was a thousand miles and a continent away.

"You're the best man for the job," Winters said, like it was a simple statement of fact, which of course it was. "The U.S. and its allies are getting run over by Putin"—*That's an understatement*, I thought, *the man just straight out stole Crimea*—"and clients are being dragged down. This conflict is bad for business."

We must be in a new business, I thought, but I said, "I'm no Putin man, Brad." First name. Power move. You don't intimidate me, old mentor. "Surely you have someone in-country." Vladimir Putin was a field of study. There had to be a dozen company operatives, at least, whose careers were built on him and his cronies. And if I knew Brad Winters, he probably already had a half a hundred Tier One operators in the combat zone.

"This is improvisation, Thomas. I need a military artist. The last thing I want is a Putin man."

I thought of the first time I'd talked to Brad Winters. I was walking across Harvard Yard in the fall of 2001, a year out of special operations forces and a month into my first term as a graduate student at the Kennedy School of Government. "The Army's no place for a young man like you," my commanding officer had advised me. "It's all peacekeeping and politics now. You'll be wasting your career. Go to school. Spend a few years studying. There's a position at State waiting for you." By State, he meant CIA.

A week in, I was bored to tears. I wanted to be where the action was, not doing problem sets for my econometrics class. Then the planes hit the Twin Towers, and all my plans came crashing down. I was outside the Widener library when I received the call.

"You don't know us," Winters said, "but we know you. How would you like to save the world?"

What is this, a joke? I thought.

Two days later, I was drinking cognac in the presidential palace of the Central African country of Burundi. Hutu extremists were massing along the border. They were planning to assassinate the president, the small prim man sitting quietly across from me, and reignite the Hutu-Tutsi conflict that had ravaged neighboring Rwanda years before. I had six weeks, at most, to prevent a genocide, and nobody trusted the Burundian army. Nobody trusted the presidential guard. Nobody, even the U.S. ambassador, thought it could be done. That was why the CIA had turned down the job.

Sometimes, "best man for the job" just meant the least informed. And in Ukraine, I would certainly qualify.

"Who requested me?" I assumed this was a BNR—By Name Request. A client had asked for me.

A slight hesitation. Interesting. "I did, Thomas. This one is important. I'm handling it personally, and you'll be reporting to me directly."

I sat up a little straighter. I didn't care if Winters

noticed, since there was no use pretending I wasn't intrigued. Even if Winters hadn't been my old mentor, he was a powerful man. You don't turn down pet projects. Or complete operational freedom.

"No chain of command?"

Winters nodded. "Just me."

"Nothing through official channels?" That was the telling detail of U.S. government work. On a straight USG contract, even a classified one, everything went through the embassy—cover, communications, money, weapons. I held a top secret clearance for this purpose, even though, these days, most jobs didn't go through the embassy.

"No USG contact. No company contact."

"A kite?" Kites were operatives that could be cut loose in the event of compromise. The riskiest assignments were always the most prestigious.

Winters nodded again.

Given the lack of actual information, company briefings were about understanding the unspoken. This mission was black, outside even Apollo's compartmentalized command structure. I doubted if anyone outside of Winters, Wolcott, and the client would know I was on the ground.

"Who's the client?"

Winters slid a manila folder across the table. It contained one page: a picture of a middle-aged man. He was dressed in a Savile Row suit, with a stylish pocket square and a platinum Lange & Söhne precision watch, but he had questionable teeth. He was either minor British royalty or Slavic nouveau riche.

"Kostyantyn Karpenko," Winters said, "a Ukrainian oligarch and member of parliament. He's been our man in Ukraine for the past ten years." It was unclear who *our* was referring to, although Winters had dropped a mention of the State Department earlier. Still, you could never be sure.

"He's a patriot, Thomas. A believer in freedom. He impressed me during the Orange Revolution in 2004, and we worked with him again during the Euromaidan protests that toppled Putin's puppet government three months ago." Meaning Apollo Outcomes sent organizers, or provided tactical assistance, or both. We were experts at manufacturing so-called color revolutions.

"We expected Karpenko to be minister of energy in the new government. President if everything went right. It didn't. Russia invaded—unofficially, of course—and the place went to shit."

I knew Putin was using strong-arm tactics—fifth-column irregulars, soldiers out of uniform, mercenaries—to destabilize the country. Oligarchs and strong men loved instability; that was why the world was unstable. Putin had done the same thing in Chechnya in 1999 and Soviet Georgia in 2008, and both had almost ended in genocide. Fortunately, Apollo was built for these kinds of shadow wars.

"Our job," Winters continued, "is to reintroduce Karpenko to Kiev power politics. To do this, we need to deliver him a victory. The kind ordinary citizens can rally behind."

A symbolic victory, I thought. *Something public.* It had worked in the Eastern Bloc before. Lech Walesa had freed Poland from Soviet rule with a dock worker's strike. "Storm the palace? Parliamentary assault?" I guessed.

Winters shook his head. "Natural gas."

He handed me another file. It contained a photograph of what must have been a natural gas transfer station. It appeared to be mostly pipes.

"Russia and the West are fighting for energy security, the Pipeline Wars, as we'll phrase it for the press. Ukraine is the battleground. Specifically its liquid natural gas lines. Two days ago, Russian soldiers disguised as a separatist militia occupied the Donbastransgas trunkline station in the eastern Ukrainian city of Kramatorsk. A strategic location. We estimate between ten and twenty men. Karpenko needs help taking it back."

Straightforward enough. "Assets in place?"

"Karpenko has twenty-five loyal men left. And there is a pro-Ukrainian militia twenty kilometers away, the Donbas Battalion. CIA contract, Apollo execution. They're all volunteers, mostly policemen, teachers, the usual patriots. Two hundred men at last count."

More than enough, even if poorly trained. But I could see Winters's hesitation: never trust schoolteachers against trained soldiers, no matter the odds. Especially when the target was filled with a few hundred cubic tons of highly flammable gas. I'd seen it in Africa. Someone taps the wrong pipe, and the explosion levels a hundred huts. You can't even count, much less identify, the bodies. Better for the shooting to be over before the amateurs arrive.

"I want prisoners, not corpses, Thomas. Pretty

pictures for the press. We'll charter two helicopters from Kiev for the media, and lure them with the tagline: evidence of a Russian military invasion."

"And the real story?" I said, knowing that ink was too slim to cut through the clutter of cable news.

"Karpenko's victory speech, which we're writing. It will be his Yeltsin moment."

In 1991, hardliners in the Soviet army surrounded the Russian White House. Boris Yeltsin, then in a power struggle with other reform leaders, stood on a tank and gave a rousing speech against the coup. The troops defected. Four months later, catapulted to a new level of popularity by his speech, Yeltsin became president.

That kind of moment was hard to engineer. I knew, because I'd tried. But it was worth the risk, since leaders mattered. If the Ukrainians lacked a focal point, they needed their own George Washington. But in a pinch, a Boris Yeltsin would do.

"Time frame?"

"Saturday," Winters said.

Five days. Tough.

"I know it's tight. And the window of opportunity is small. There will be less than an hour between the arrival of the Donbas Battalion at 0600 and the press at 0700." If either showed up on time, that is, and militias and reporters rarely did. "This is an active war zone. We don't want to give the Russians time for a counterstrike."

I sat back. This wasn't how Apollo operated. We took our time. We planned things carefully. That was how we stayed out of the news, not to mention the morgue. Someone was running hot on a unique opportunity, as Winters had called it. Maybe the U.S. government. Probably a business client. Someone was willing to gamble on a desperate man sitting on a lot of natural gas. I couldn't quite figure out, though, why it should be me.

"It's doable," I said, "if the Donbas Battalion will follow Karpenko."

"They'll follow him," Winters said, "I can promise you that. He's partially paying them. You just need to get him there."

I didn't like the sound of that. "Karpenko isn't with the Donbas Battalion?"

Winters laughed. "If he was, would I need someone like you?"

He was flattering me. Making me think of whatever he said next as a challenge, instead of a foolish risk. It wouldn't work. Not this time.

"Where is he?"

"In hiding," Winters said. "Bank accounts frozen. Warrant out for his arrest. A bounty on his head from the Kremlin, under the table of course, but enough to keep him on the run."

"Then how can I help him?"

"We have an inside man—"

"And why?"

That was the difference between being a soldier and a merc. In the army, you did what your commanding officer told you to do, no questions asked. A mercenary could turn down work if he didn't like it, logistically, morally, or for any other damn reason he pleased.

So I expected the hard sell: the importance of stopping Putin, Apollo Outcomes as the hand of the West, even Hitler-and-the-Sudetenland. Winters was a master talker, and this was the moment. Closing time. But instead of pumping me up, he stared into the distance. I couldn't tell if he was contemplating what to say next, or chewing a dramatic pause.

"There are children, Thomas," he said finally. "Young ones."

I thought of Burundi. The new president was the ideal leader for a war-ravaged country: a capable man, a humanitarian. That's why the opposition was desperate to assassinate him. The odds were he'd be dead in a month, everyone knew that, especially him, but he was willing to risk his life if it meant a small chance of a better life for his people. Ten years ago, Winters had handed me exactly what I wanted: a chance to make the world a better place. And I was going to turn it down, because keeping this noble man alive *was* impossible.

Then his eight-year-old daughter walked in and gave her father a hug.

Had I told Winters that? I must have—we were inseparable at one time, and I wasn't as careful about revealing myself then as I was now—because Winters was drawing a line: a line visible only to me. Ukraine now is Burundi then. Karpenko is a good man, a *family* man. This is a war-torn nation's best chance.

"Extraction or protection?"

"Extraction. Their passports have been revoked and Interpol is watching. But we have a window, three nights from now, and an An-12 on station in Bucharest."

A military cargo plane, I thought, mulling the possibilities. The Antonov-12 could take a family out, but it could also bring things in. The kind of things difficult to get through customs. The kind of things you needed for an assault on a hardened natural gas facility.

"How do I find them?"

Winters rose and walked to the door. Wolcott was waiting outside. Winters was the pitchman. Wolcott provided the details.

"We've set up a Sherpa," Wolcott said, wasting no time. "John Greenlees. Former CIA station chief in Kiev, retired in place. He'll meet you at the Hyatt Regency in Kiev at 1400 tomorrow."

He placed a box of business cards on the table. "Green Lighthouse Group. Business: facilitation services in frontier markets. You're the president, CEO, and only employee. We've created a legend. Articles on business blogs, old press releases, the usual. The website has been up since yesterday, but it looks like it's been up for months."

Wolcott placed a thick envelope beside the business cards. I knew what was inside: a debit card and €10,000, the maximum allowable without being declared. You broke the law in this business only when you had to. A fake passport meant arrest, a false identity, a hooded car ride to a Siberian prison. You could talk your way out of a two-month-old consulting business.

Besides, there was no hiding from the Internet. If anyone Googled me, it was all there: paratrooper, special warfare training. I even had a blog, the Musical Mercenary, where I wrote opera reviews. I had been interviewed about it on NPR, of all places. It was best, in this day and age, to own your past.

"The debit card is loaded with €50,000, for expenses. Greenlees will have another €50,000 in cash when you arrive. We'll subtract out for your plane ticket and equipment." They were making it look like I paid my own way. That was new. The company always ran cover for action, but not this deep. "Karpenko will pay additional expenses once you link up with him, anything you need."

Wolcott dropped a gold necklace with thick links on the table. It was old school. If things got bad, I could snip off a link at a time and barter my way out of the country.

I didn't like it. Apollo Outcomes was a corporation, not an Old West saloon. They took taxes out of my paycheck. My employment contract was fourteen pages long, for God's sake—and I was a freelancer. You should see my 1099 tax forms.

"You'll get your standard rate," he continued. "Four weeks worth, plus a 50 percent bump up for danger pay, and Mr. Winters is adding a 50 percent completion bonus." That came out to about $80,000 for a week's worth of work. Arguably, my fee should have been higher. But you don't haggle within the company, and if things went pear shaped, I knew Winters would get me out. Trust is worth more than money when your life is on the line.

"And," he continued, "you get a team."

I smiled, thinking of Miles and the boys. Having good men at your side was the only thing in the world more important than trust.

"I know you, Tom," Winters said slowly, stepping

in. He always knew when to step in. "I understand why you stayed in the field."

He didn't. He never had.

"You're right," he said, as if reading my mind. "I don't understand. But I believed you when you said you thought you could do more good there."

He paused again. The man used pauses better than Beethoven. "I know this is unusual. I know it's outside your area of expertise. But it's the big one. The 'good job.' The one we've been waiting for. Forget Africa and look at the big picture. If we shift the balance of power in Ukraine, we stuff Putin back in his box. It's good for our clients and better for the world. Break Russia, Thomas, and we don't just win a victory. We change the future. Even for Africa."

There it was, the Hitler speech, soft-pitched, but unmistakable: *History needs us. We're the chosen ones. This is your purpose.*

He was stroking my ego. Manipulating me, like he always had. But so what? There were pieces missing here, explanations that were incomplete, but my job wasn't to see the forest, it was to cut down trees. If I didn't believe in myself, and my missions, on some deep fundamental level, why had I been risking my life all these years?

Winters rose and knocked on the door. Wolcott entered and handed me a flight itinerary. I glanced at it briefly. One way to Kiev. Three hours from now. Just enough time to head home for warmer clothes and a few appropriate downloads, such as Tchaikovsky's Second Symphony, known as the "Little Russian," after the nickname for Ukraine during the reign of the Czar.

Wolcott handed me another piece of paper. It had my exfiltration data, handwritten: a time, date, and grid square location. I committed it to memory and handed the sheet back. Wolcott put it back into a folder with the photo of Karpenko. They would be in the shredder by lunch.

"A company helicopter will extract your team," he said. "Fifteen-minute window. Don't be late."

And that was it. The operation was set. There would be no file, no photos, no written mission brief. And despite the cubicle gerbils toiling fifty feet away, no useful information. There never was.

"I'll see you in a week," I said, standing up and straightening my suit.

Winters stood up. I thought he was extending his hand for a shake, but instead, he slipped me a phone number. "My personal line," he said. "You'll know when to call."

Three hours later, at almost exactly the time Locke was boarding his flight to Kiev, Brad Winters laid his knife and fork across his plate at the Occidental and pushed away the last of his steak. It was just past one P.M., but he had been here for more than an hour. It was time to get moving.

"You got the talking points?" he said to Tom Hagen, the man sitting across from him. Hagen was the only thing more synonymous with Washington, DC, power than a private government contractor: a law firm partner without a law degree.

Hagen's story was one Winters had heard a hundred times, with slight variations. Undergraduate at Georgetown (sometimes they were Ivy); Senate staffer at twenty-three (after one or two years of "charity work"); chief of staff at thirty; then a permanent member of a prestigious Senate or House committee; and, finally, a filthy rich lobbyist by the time the midlife crisis kicked in at forty. After that—at least in Tom Hagen's case—came the long, slow decline, something Winters had long ago decided was attributable to a lack of both ambition and imagination. He'd seen it too often, from too many people who had cashed out and lost their way. Never make your goal something you can achieve.

"I've got them," Hagen said, knocking back the last of his Sancerre. "It's more than stopping a tyrant. It's energy security. Ukraine has Europe's third largest shale reserves. Putin is imperiling the world economy."

"Freedom gas," Winters said slowly, as you would while teaching a toddler. "Ukrainian gas means freedom from the Soviet threat. Freedom gas."

"I'll start with members from Texas and Louisiana," Hagen said, ignoring the condescending tone. "We'll establish the Friends of Ukraine." Politicians were forever creating informal groups around newsworthy issues—the Friends of the Farmer, the Friends of Coal, the Friends of Real Americans.

"I know a crisis communications firm on K Street for the public angle. We'll create a 501(c)(3) non-profit organization called . . ." Hagen paused, thinking ". . . the U.S.-Ukraine Democracy Alliance."

"Good." Throwing democracy in a name was always a good idea.

"It will be a media platform and attack dog, going after the White House and critics, saying things Congress won't. Don't worry, the firm is clever, founded by ex-CIA. They do oppo research, media hit pieces, muddy reputations. They even infiltrated Greenpeace."

"Make it AstroTurf." Meaning the "nonprofit" should look and feel and, most importantly, sound like a legitimate grass-roots organization. "When's the press conference?"

"When do you want it?"

"Tomorrow afternoon. So we get ahead of any

breaking news. I want four senators, at least." Hagen started to object, but Winters cut him off. "Addison is already onboard."

Hagen nodded. Addison had pull. "Ten and four," he said, meaning at least ten from the lower house—they were easy—and four known names. "And then—"

"I'll see what I can do with Shell."

Shell Oil held the rights to the eastern Ukrainian gas fields, and they were halfway through an estimated infrastructure investment of $410 million, but they had pulled back because of violence in the area. A Putin victory, or a government collapse in Kiev, would put their leases and infrastructure investments at risk. It was a hazard of the modern world economy and, since the pullback in government contracts at the end of the official Iraq War, Brad Winters's main engine of growth. Hagen would kill, almost literally, to have a fat oil company like Shell as a client.

"Are you sure you don't want to go through State?" Hagen said, trying to prove his worth. "I can get you in at the DepSec level." The deputy secretary was the alter ego of the secretary of state and the power behind the policy throne.

"I think it's best if I stay out of it for the moment," Winters said. He had no interest in going anywhere near this political charade until it was safe. That was why he needed Hagen.

"As long as it's for the good of the country," Hagen said with a knowing smile.

Winters figured at one point the phrase had

meant something, but it was so de rigeur by now it had become a punch line.

"Right now," he said, putting his napkin on the table and pushing back from the table, "I'm in the process of saving our asses."

Hagen glanced up, surprised by Winters's serious tone. "You're a patriot, Brad," he said, standing to shake his hand. "Just like the rest of us."

The waiter appeared with the dessert menu, stepping deftly aside as Winters turned. "On my tab," Winters said, as his eyes scanned the room.

"Bodegas Hildalgo Napoleon, thirty-year," Hagen said absently, as he watched Winters glad-hand a few familiar faces as he left, the hundreds of black-and-white portraits of Washington players behind him on the walls, portraits that seemed to retreat farther and farther away the longer Hagen stayed in town.

CHAPTER 4

I'd seen the lobby of the Kiev Hyatt Regency a hundred times in a dozen different countries. The glass façade and square beige furniture were standard business class, the clean, modern lines not fashionable so much as what corporate architects and factories in China churned out to meet the needs of the world's discerning travelers. Even the painting on the wall—red and green interlocking salamanders, either fucking or forming a faux native pattern, I wasn't sure—could have hung on any hotel wall anywhere in the world. The only thing that would be unique, I knew, was the requisite sky bar on the top floor—this one was on the eighth—and then only because of the surrounding city. Fortunately, my suite had a firm mattress, always a pleasant surprise after three weeks on a cot, and a view of the gold onion domes of Saint Sophia's Cathedral (according to the bellboy) to remind me that I wasn't in an upscale area of Juba, South Sudan, or Wichita, Kansas.

The lobby bar was even more comfortably familiar, filled as it was with the usual conflict carrion. People assume upscale accommodations are deserted in war zones, but in the modern world, where economics trumped politics, reliable chain hotels like the Hyatt Regency quickly became de facto embassies. This is the place where conflict entrepreneurs, recently arrived from Lebanon by way of London or, if I had to guess, the more Eastern European sections of Brooklyn, swapped tips on how to "exploit" the situation, a word that wasn't just a positive, but a life mission.

The diplomats, meanwhile, were slumped into their drinks, waiting for whatever it is diplomats spend their lives waiting for. I spotted two squared-off Germans drinking pilsner in the corner; three Frenchmen at the bar with mineral waters and Gauloises; and two Brits in overly wide pinstriped suits with a little coin pocket above the regular pocket on the right side. Only English tailors bothered with that pointless little pocket.

"Woodford Reserve on the rocks," I said, nodding to the Germans and leaning on the bar between the businessmen and the French. Every nationality has a drink, and the bourbon would mark me as American, something I didn't mind. The dozen or so obvious undercover agents hanging around the lobby had already noticed me; the only question was whether they were working for the Ukrainians or the Russians.

Besides, I liked Woodford Reserve.

"Keep it," I said, sliding twenty euros to the bartender and shrugging off the glance of a barfly with blond hair and augmented assets. She was a professional, but she wasn't working for money. In a war zone, information was more valuable, that was what made hotels like these hothouses of intrigue. Everyone wanted a piece of everyone else. She'd probably be outside my room tonight, hoping to catch me in a moment of weakness.

Her, or another one like her.

I sighed. It was 1340 local time, twenty minutes until my meeting with Greenlees, and I'd been traveling for forty-two out of the last fifty-six hours. Despite a nap in my suite and on the Lufthansa overnight, I could feel the fatigue. But it was a virus I'd been living with for years. I was so used to it that I could sit perfectly at ease at a bar in a strange part of the world and use the reflections in the backsplash to pigeonhole everyone in the room.

There were the misfits: maybe tourists caught in the wrong place, maybe missionaries, who always managed to appear awkward. There were a few wealthy locals waiting for visas or other arrangements they needed before leaving the country. They'd probably been here for weeks, holed up inside except for shopping trips on whatever strip was considered the Fifth Avenue of Kiev. Their children looked so bored, I could image them chewing the upholstery. These kids weren't used to slumming it at a four-star hotel.

At the end of the bar, a small group of international journalists was gathered over gimlets and rye. They were all drunks, so it was too early for sloppiness, but I knew they were already telling the same endless war stories they'd been exaggerating for years.

The young reporters were buzzing, chatting each other up or eavesdropping on conversations. There were fewer of the old guys every year, with their set sources and set ideas and focus on the economics of delivering glass to mouth, and more of the young-sters, although *young* was a relative term. The right word was *underemployed*. Most of these reporters were freelancers, either locals or here on their own dimes—the lucky ones were on a daily allowance—hungry for any story they could sell.

That was why they gravitated toward the non-governmental organizations, or NGOs, the swarm that followed modern war like the slatterns followed General Hooker's army. The two groups had a symbiotic relationship: the reporters gave these humanitarian organizations press, and the NGOs showed them suitable horror stories for the websites back home.

Even in the reflection of the bar back, I could smell their self-righteousness: their stylishly unkempt hair; their imperious manner, as if they were here to correct the wrongs men like me inflicted on the world; the colorful shawls they'd picked up in the last conflict. Humanitarian workers had an addiction to third world garb, as if pieces of cloth could make them locals, instead of a "warmonger" like me. Humanitarians liked to wear their internationalism on their sleeve.

Just like being home, I thought as I picked up my drink. A job is a job, and even though Ukraine wasn't my area of expertise, all I really needed to feel comfortable was a quiet corner where I didn't have to worry about eavesdroppers and ten quiet minutes with my bourbon.

And then I saw her, sitting with a group of twenty-somethings, their bags sprawled around them on two lobby sofas. Her curly hair was darker and pulled back; her elegant nose just visible in profile. But I knew it was her. I could feel the heat in the pit of my stomach, just from looking at the curve of her neck. Last I had heard she was in Bulgaria working on one of her sex trafficking stories. But that was a year ago. Now here she was, in Kiev, leaning into one of those good-looking, classically unkempt video-journalists, while staring into the viewfinder of his handheld camera.

Instinctively, I paused, the bourbon coming down to the bar without reaching my lips. I looked down at the glass, collected myself, and looked up. There I was in the backsplash, staring back at myself. The metal was golden, and it gave my face a wavy look, like I was viewing myself through the top of a tanning machine. Even so, I could tell I looked tired.

I grabbed my drink and tipped it back, unsurprised to see her reflection getting larger as she approached, until the only thing I could do was turn around.

"Alie," I said.

"Tom," she said, putting a hand on my shoulder and swinging into the seat next to me. "I hope you weren't planning to ignore me."

"I just got here."

"I know. I saw you come in."

She had lost her roundness and looked harder than the last time I saw her. More sure of herself, maybe, and more fit. I missed her softness, the half inch of give when I caressed her arm, but that didn't mean she didn't look good.

"You look great, Allison. What's it been, eight years?"

"At least," she said, although we both knew exactly how long it had been. "What are you doing here? I thought you'd be in Africa."

"I thought the same about you."

She was sizing me up, and I couldn't help but wonder what she thought of my face, ten years later. What had she expected? Oh right. The way I left, she probably hadn't expected to see me at all.

"Are you still with that little company," she said. "I can't remember the name. Umm . . . Harvard University?" She was digging at me. That had been my cover story, but she knew my real work.

"Are you still with Catholic Relief Services?"

She smiled. "No. I burned that bridge a long time ago."

I wondered if I was part of that.

"You look good," I said, then realized I'd said the same thing thirty seconds before.

She checked me up and down with her legendarily direct stare, but didn't say anything. I hated myself for glancing, but she wasn't wearing a ring.

"Still trying to save the world?"

"You know me," she said, but I didn't. I'd only known her when she was twenty-four, with the life experience of an eighteen-year-old, and nobody is themselves at twenty-four.

"Double vodka," she said to the bartender. "On my friend."

I nodded, to tell him I'd cover the charge.

"So really," she said, glancing around the room, probably to ward off the blonde, who was lingering, no doubt sensing the waft of valuable intel coming off my bourbon and rocks, "what are you doing here, Tom? I'm sure there are plenty of problems in Africa for you to meddle in."

There was an edge in her voice, one I hadn't quite anticipated, and it struck me like a hammer that Alie resented me. Maybe because I left her behind. But maybe because it had been ten years, and while I'd been blowing up oil facilities and killing terrorists, she'd been . . . what? Trying to rescue young girls.

No, that wasn't right. She had gotten famous for those blog entries on Magdelana, a Burundian refugee trying to make it to Europe, but that was six or seven years ago. She'd bumped up to the *Guardian* after that, and she'd made a reputation for herself as a champion of the underclass, especially women. For a while there, she was humming. Sex trafficking. Human slavery. Almost won a Pulitzer, or so I'd heard. But then what? A slowing down, a falling away, followed by a quiet pink slip, or maybe she'd just faded back to the deep Internet and the unsourced pages, the things that would never get past the fact-checkers and lawyers because they were too unspeakable and, therefore, mostly, too true. That was why good-looking college dropouts asked her to look at their unedited documentary film footage— and that was why she did it, even though it was something no sane person would ever do. Out here, with this crowd, Alie was still a groundbreaking reporter.

And I wasn't an ex-lover. I was an exclusive.

"It's not a good time," I said, feeling resentful, as if she was disrespected our past, even though I knew that wasn't fair. She wasn't playing me, not necessarily. She was just leaning on the bar, wearing her confidence like a shawl. I wanted to reach out and touch her shoulder, and tell her I was sorry.

But instead I glanced over her shoulder, ostentatiously checking to see if anyone was eavesdropping. "Let's meet later," I said, knowing she would understand that this conversation, in this bar, wasn't a good idea. The last thing either of us wanted was for someone else to know I was a merc.

"Dinner."

"You choose the place." I handed her my business card, which included one of my real phone numbers. She smirked when she saw it.

"Green Lighthouse Group. Nice." She grabbed a small notebook from her jacket pocket. "Meet me at my room," she said, tearing off a sheet and handing it to me. Number 12, 8:00 P.M.

"First floor? I thought that was all conference rooms."

She laughed. "I'm not staying here. I'm at the Ibis with the rest of the do-gooders. Isn't that what you always called us?"

I thought about inviting her to my suite, with its world-class view, but I'd learned through painful experience never to let an unknown variable into my room. That was why I was meeting Greenlees in the lobby in . . . I glanced at my watch . . . two minutes.

"I have to run," I said.

"It's what you do," she replied.

She downed the double vodka and walked away without looking back, and I couldn't help but watch her go, the roll of her hips just like I remembered it, the heat turning the ice in my bourbon to water.

Then I turned and walked to the farthest corner of the lobby, where it was hardest for others to eavesdrop, and took a seat facing the door. I opened the *Financial Times*, knowing its unique salmon color and English-language format would be a beacon to Greenlees, and let my eyes wander aimlessly over the pages, trying to focus as my mind faded out to the sunset over Lake Tanganyika in Africa, and the French restaurant at the top of the hill, and Alie MacFarlane stepping out of her dress in my little room beneath the palm trees, the freshest girl I'd ever seen, so clean and bright, like they'd taken her out of the package just for me.

CHAPTER 5

Two minutes later, exactly on time, an older gentleman walked through the rotating door of the Hyatt Kiev. He was wearing tan slacks, a golf shirt, a blue blazer, and well-worn loafers, his thin gray hair impeccably combed. He looked like a retiree on a junket, but he was clearly Greenlees. He had an ease most Americans can never pull off when they traveled, especially abroad.

He glanced around, then walked directly toward me. This was a public meeting in a busy hotel. Caution would only draw attention.

"Dr. Locke, I presume."

"That's right."

"John Greenlees," the man said, extending his hand.

"Pleased to meet you sir," I said, folding the *Financial Times* and giving him my Green Lighthouse Group business card, more for show than anything else.

"Call me John," Greenlees said, taking the other seat. "How was the flight?"

"Not bad. I slept."

"And the cab ride? The drivers can be maddening, I know."

He had a vaguely British accent and aristocratic

manner, as if channeling a John le Carré double agent from 1963. Even his teeth had gone British. I had seen it before in Americans who built careers abroad, a subconscious separation from their old lives. It was the CIA's version of wearing an Indonesian shawl.

"Traffic was light," I said.

Greenlees flagged a waiter and ordered in Ukrainian. Turning to me, he said, "I'm having a vodka with lemon. And you?"

I raised my bourbon to show I had a finger to go. A high alcohol tolerance was mandatory in this business.

"To eat?" the waiter asked in English.

Greenlees looked at me, and I shook my head. "No thank you," he said. Then, as the waiter walked away, "How long have you known Dave Wolcott?"

"Five years," I said. "And I've never seen him smile."

"That's him," Greenlees said with a grin. "Droll. But a good man. I served with him in Nicaragua in 1986, before your time, I'm sure."

"I wasn't aware."

"Oh, it's hush-hush, as they say," Greenlees said with a shrug, although no one ever said that. "I was under diplomatic cover. He was military intelligence. Just a title, of course. Nobody ever referred to Dave Wolcott as intelligent."

I laughed. It was true. "You were supporting the Contras?"

"And covertly mining the Nicaraguan harbors." His smile was genuine. It was a fond memory.

"I was in Panama," I said.

"A paratrooper, I hear, then later in a special mission unit in the Balkans." Special mission units, or SMUs, were elite forces trained for the nation's most secret and dangerous work. SEALs. Delta. They were the pinnacle of the military pyramid. Or at least they used to be. Now they served as the Apollo Outcome's favorite recruiting pool.

"82nd Airborne Division," I said with pride.

"What regiment?"

"504th, under Abizaid, McChrystal, and Petreaus, before they made general."

"I remember Abizaid in Grenada," Greenlees mused, referring to the U.S. invasion in 1983. "He ordered his Rangers to drive a bulldozer into a line of Cuban soldiers."

"So I've heard."

"You must know Bernie McCabe from your time in the Balkans." I recognized the tradecraft. It was a question to qualify me. There were no code words or secret signals between colleagues, that was fiction; common points of reference authenticated contacts.

"I know him, but Colonel McCabe wasn't in the Balkans. He commanded Delta Force when I was at Fort Bragg, then went private sector. He ran Sandline International with Tim Spicer, and put down the RUF in Sierra Leone."

"I hear they hired a Hind helicopter for that one," Greenlees said, shaking his head. Hinds were Soviet flying tanks. "Good God, what a mess."

"They got the job done."

"A good man," Greenlees said, perhaps too wistfully. "They were all good men."

I leaned forward, glancing over my shoulder. Alie was across the lobby with a group of charity workers, openly staring at us. So was the blonde. And a couple squared-off local goons. "Do you have somewhere else we can talk?"

Greenlees caught my eye, but didn't turn. An old mission girl, I almost said, meaning a temporary sex partner you pick up in some remote location. But there was no reason to share this information, and besides, I couldn't use that phrase for Alie. Mission girls are women you forget; but with Alie, it had been the opposite. Our time together had grown more important to me, the farther I'd drifted away.

"I have a car," Greenlees said, downing his vodka and rising elegantly from his seat. "Let me show you around."

CHAPTER 6

We bypassed the hotel's parking valets and went straight to the street, where Greenlees had a car waiting. It was a late-model BMW, with tinted windows and evidence of a Berlin green zone sticker scraped off the inside windshield. It was probably stolen in Germany and sold in Eastern Europe, a common fate for luxury cars. Either Greenlees liked to shop the gray market, or someone had given him an expensive gift. A shady-looking local was behind the wheel.

"My wife's brother," Greenlees assured me, sliding into the front seat. Free agents like Greenlees often made their trade a family business to deter enemy infiltration.

"Saint Sophia's Cathedral," he went on, pointing across the plaza. We turned north and passed a pastel-blue palace with golden roofs, straight out of a little girl's fairy princess set. "The Golden Dome, a monastery in a former life. Now, sadly, the oldest building in town."

We passed several nondescript blocks of apartments with the sagging façades of neglected city neighborhoods, then merged onto a major road lined with hotels and businesses. Before long, the Dnieper River was crawling on our left, the hills steep on the far bank. Somewhere over those hills, Putin's hired goons were tearing Eastern Ukraine apart, but from here, Kiev seemed like any other post-Soviet city.

"What do you know about Karpenko?" Greenlees asked, breaking the silence. This was the real conversation, and there was no safer place for it than his personal car.

"Only the name, I'm afraid."

"He's an oligarch," Greenlees said, "but you probably guessed that, or you wouldn't be here. There are perhaps twenty of them in Ukraine, and together they control over 90 percent of the wealth. Factories, natural resources, even chocolate."

The concrete apartment blocks gave way to a large, leafy park, an archlike Soviet-era monument hanging desolately in the background.

"They're all gangsters, born from the ruins of the USSR. Often, they just showed up at a factory with a private army and claimed it."

Our line of work, I thought.

"Who was going to stop them? The locals? They were terrified. The old party officials? They were bought. Or shot."

It was the story of the world. The strong do what they want; the weak suffer what they must. Two decades in the field, and I'd never known a country any different.

"It was a capitalist's dream, Locke. For twenty years, the oligarchs were off-loading duffel bags of cash from private jets into Cypriot banks, until the European Union shut that down. They buy mansions all over the world to keep their money abroad.

That's why London's so bloody expensive." He emphasized the British slang, and talked like it was a personal affront.

"Power makes them daft," he continued. "Igor Kolomoisky keeps a shark tank in his office. When he doesn't like what's being said, he presses a button that drops crayfish meat to his pets."

"Subtle," I replied. It reminded me of Africa. Or James Bond. That was the kind of idea that starts in a movie, then spreads around the world.

"You heard about Yanukovych?" Viktor Yanukovych was the recently deposed president of Ukraine, and was now under Russian protection in Crimea.

"I heard he had a kitchen shaped like a pirate ship."

"Not a kitchen, Locke. A restaurant. At his private compound. With pirate-themed waiters." While half the country starved, I figured he'd say next, but Greenlees surprised me. "While the price of bribes for medicine went through the roof," he said.

That's the difference between Africa and Europe. Here, a fight between billionaires doesn't mean ten thousand starving children.

"What about Karpenko?"

"He's the youngest oligarch at forty-two, the son of a miner in the central city of Poltava. He was a finance student in Kiev when the Soviets collapsed. Two months later, he owned the mine where his father worked. Sasha Belenko, an old-school oligarch, brought him into the upper tier: factories, energy infrastructure, banking. Karpenko is worth $2 billion on the books, probably triple that in reality."

Probably ten times that, if he was like other strongmen I'd known.

"He's second wave, so he's more refined. He's not above aggressive litigation, debt enforcement, hostile takeovers, but he tries to stay clean. The older oligarchs, the ones who spent most of their adult lives under Soviet Russia, wanted to be Robin Hood. Lovable outlaws. Karpenko wants to be Rockefeller. The Karpenko Group, you probably haven't heard of it, but it was the first Ukrainian conglomerate on the London stock exchange. The traders loved him. Until Crimea. Two billion is the new valuation."

And next week, the way things were going, it might be zero. I wondered what percentage Winters was getting for my troubles.

"What happened?" I asked.

Greenlees glanced at me with his head tilted, like a bookstore owner looking over his glasses at a questionable customer.

"Besides the obvious, I mean."

"He bankrolled the democracy movement."

"And Putin wasn't happy."

"Some of his fellow oligarchs weren't happy. Russia has made them rich. Turning toward Europe will make them richer, but why take the risk?"

Because you were never satisfied, I thought, remembering my six months as Winters's protégé in Washington. There was always something more. That's how you became a billionaire—or a president—in the first place.

"Nobody expected Putin's response. After Ukraine's Orange Revolution in 2004, he let the democracy movement destroy itself with infighting. It took him four years to install Yanukovych. But you know what they say about doing the same thing twice?"

"It's for idiots."

"It's for Americans."

Greenlees paused, looking out the window at high-end apartment blocks along the Dnieper. We passed an enormous McDonald's, half a block wide, a beautiful woman sitting in the front window sadly raising a burger to her mouth as we floated by.

"Do you know who benefited most from the Iraq War?"

Apollo and others like it. Within three years, it had gone from cleaning latrines on military bases in the Balkans to a private army powerful enough to overthrow half the countries in the world.

"Vlad Putin, that's who. Ten years ago, he didn't have the courage to conquer Ukraine. Then the world got bogged down fighting medieval Arabs who lop people's heads off in the name of Allah"—I winced at the characterization—"and Putin seized the future. Chechnya, Georgia, Crimea. Those were all . . . groping. Ukraine has always been the goal. And after Ukraine . . ."

He looked at me, and I could see it in his eyes. Greenlees was a lone wolf, a voice crying in the wilderness. He'd probably been giving this speech for the last decade, with nobody to listen. Conspiracy was the last refuge of failures.

So how did we end up in this car together?

Greenlees sighed. He looked tired. "You don't know anything about what's going on here, do you?"

"I'm sorry. I work in Africa."

"Typical," Greenlees muttered, as we turned onto a wide pedestrian street. Several streetlamps were painted blue and yellow, I noticed, and blue-and-yellow Ukrainian flags hung from a few windows. We passed a woman dressed in some sort of peasant garb, clearly traditional, but wearing high heels. The country had reverted to Ukrainian spellings after Euromaidan, I had heard, such as *Kyiv* instead of the Russian *Kiev*. We are a free people, they were saying. Look at our words. Look at our clothes. We have a history that is ours.

"This isn't a war between Russia and Ukraine," Greenlees said, following the patriotic business-woman with his eyes, "so put away your quaint notions of country. It's about economics and oil. ExxonMobil or Gazprom have more power than Belgium ever did."

I didn't bother to tell him I'd put away that notion long ago. Or that Belgium had once slaughtered five million people in Congo.

"Ukraine is a battleground between East and West. The Romans and Slavs; the Polish and Russian empires; Hitler and Stalin; NATO and the Soviet Union. And now, Putin. The oligarchs are taking sides. The people are, as usual, the victims of history."

As they say in Africa: when the elephants fight, the grass gets trampled.

"That's why the world is sitting on its hands, even

as covert Russian troops pour over the border. Because this is nothing but a buffer zone to them." He paused. Sadly. "And because there are no good options. Every leader in Ukraine is crooked."

"Except Karpenko."

"In the most optimistic view, I suppose."

He stopped, staring out the window once again. "The Verkhovna Rada," he said, pointing toward a building strangely reminiscent of the Jefferson Memorial. "The house of parliament. In the West, they use money to buy politicians. Here, it is more honest. Every oligarch simply becomes a parliamentarian."

We turned right, along a street clearly intended by the Soviets as a parade route. The apartment buildings were so massive, they made the lives inside them seem small. I saw more traditional outfits, loose white tops with beadwork and aprons.

"Instytutska Street," Greenlees said. "Yanukovych's police shot forty protesters here. You can still see the bullet holes in the tree trunks. And the videos on the Internet."

I could hear the sadness in his voice. "What happened to Karpenko?"

Greenlees turned with a sigh, as if I'd asked the wrong question. "His mentor, Sasha Belenko, went over to the Russians six days ago. The next night, so-called Ukrainian patriots seized the Donetsk Iron and Steel Works, a centerpiece of Karpenko's empire. They raided the offices of his Financial-Industrial Group in Kiev." Greenlees gave me a knowing look. "Corruption, of course. That's the official charge."

"Belenko sold him out."

"Three days ago, there was an assassination attempt at a house in Poltava. Full frontal assault with RPGs and demo. Nobody claimed responsibility, but it was Spetsnaz." Russian special forces. "The operation was too precise to be anyone else. Rumor has it there was inside help. Fierce fighting amongst his men. Karpenko barely got out alive."

Three days ago, I was buying arms in the Sahara.

"Maidan Nezalezhnosti," Greenlees said, signaling for the driver to double-park in the busy street. "The center of the struggle. Ten thousand gathered here for two months, until Putin's puppet fell."

Maidan Nezalezhnosti was a concrete park, with a pond at the far end and trees along each side. Under the trees were makeshift tents and barricades, occupied by serious young women and older men in off-the-rack camouflage. I could see sand bags, Cyrillic graffiti, the burned remnants of radial tires. I didn't know what war these people thought was being fought, but whatever it was, this wasn't part of it.

"Where are the young men?" I asked.

"At the front. Hundreds have gone."

"But they'll be slaughtered." I had seen it too many times: untrained men and boys run over by trained troops.

"I know that," Greenlees said, "and so do they. I suppose that's why you're here."

He paused. He wanted me to say he was right, that things were being taken care of. But he wasn't right. I was here for five days, to do two jobs. Maybe they would matter in the grand scheme of things. I trusted they would. But either way, by next week I'd be gone.

"The Trade Unions building," Greenlees said, pointing out the car window toward an empty space of blackened debris. "The Russians burned it down with protesters inside. Seventy-seven people gave their lives. Seventy-seven. And what does the world care?"

Count your blessing, old man. It takes one thousand dead Africans before anyone in the West even notices. Ten thousand, at least, before the cavalry arrives.

"Thirty-five years," Greenlees muttered. "Half my life. And this is victory?"

I looked out the window, past the shoddy barricades and piles of golden threadlike wire, the steel belts in burned-off radial tires. I liked Greenlees, and I trusted him, even if his jacket wasn't pressed and his shirtsleeves were showing signs of wear. He was a gentleman, one of those old hands who seemed like a throwback to a more subtle time. But his information was useless, something I could get in half a minute from anyone at the U.S. Embassy. And he was clearly compromised. *Us? We? Our?* The old man had "clientitis." He'd gone native, a cardinal sin for a field operative. I knew the company had to go outside its usual sources for work this black, but if this mission was so important to Winters, why would he saddle me with a sentimentalist?

I looked up. The driver was staring at me in the rearview mirror. Sloppy. He was probably a plumber, before Greenlees brought him onboard.

"We're being followed," I said. "Black car, half-way down the block."

"Don't forget about the tan four-door that passed us thirty seconds ago." Greenlees was right. I had been so focused on the black car, I hadn't looked farther.

"Russian FSB?" The FSB was the new acronym for the KGB.

"One's probably Russian. One Ukrainian. They're following each other as much as they're following us."

"I assume my room will be tossed when I get back."

"At least once, probably twice. For effect, mostly. I assume there's nothing to find."

"Of course," I said, as the car started to roll.

Greenlees handed me three prepaid mobile phones to be used and discarded. I checked them. They were clean. I handed them back. We hadn't used burners in the field in ten years. They were a dead giveaway. My cell phone had been pro-grammed by the company with the right amount and type of contacts.

"I'll stick with a sat phone," I said, not mak-ing a big deal of Greenlees's error. "You have the Berettas?"

Beretta Nanos were my favorite pistols for this type of work, small and easy to conceal. No silenc-ers. Noise suppressors reduced range and accu-racy, changed the gun's balance, and never muffled noise as advertised. If you want to kill silently, get a crossbow.

Greenlees nodded. "And the other supplies."

I had sent the list through Wolcott before leaving Washington. The Berettas were on it, but so were other necessities for an airlift: infrared lights to outline a landing strip, marker beacons, aviation radio, laser range finder, broadband scanners, and night-vision and field glasses. For an operation like this, supplies were often the most difficult part.

He handed me an envelope of euros, probably the €50,000 Wolcott promised. I shook my head and handed it back. "I'm set for now." There was a decent chance the goons would pick me up on suspicion of being suspicious, and I didn't want to give them a reason to detain me.

"I'll pick you up here at 2100," Greenlees said, as we pulled up in front of my hotel. "Wear your fine dining attire."

Nine o'clock. Damn. I thought about the dinner date I'd be missing with Alie and felt a tinge of guilt. I wanted to see her. I wanted to explain myself. Who I was. Why I left. Maybe, if she didn't walk out after the first glass of wine, I'd tell her that I hadn't forgotten her, even after all these years. That she always meant something to me.

But she was a reporter. I was clandestine. I was never really going to meet with her. Was I?

CHAPTER 7

We drove silently through the sparse night traffic, Greenlees's brother-in-law watching me with quiet disdain in the rearview mirror. No trouble with the FSB, Russian or Ukrainian, so I'd had a chance to shower and nap before changing into field clothes, and I was feeling fresh. Greenlees was wearing the same retiree-on-vacation outfit he'd been wearing before, but now with extra wrinkles, both in his shirt and under his eyes. He looked like he'd been at it for an extra ten hours, even though we'd only been apart for six.

Alcoholism, maybe—it was a common malady in the field. Or maybe he'd been compromised. It wasn't unheard-of for these old Cold War warriors to lose their way when the world changed.

"I was visiting with . . . someone," he said, by way of explanation. "I made promises, you see . . ."

"It doesn't matter," I said, not wanting the old man to struggle on. It was clear that his young Ukrainian wife (judging from the age of his brother-in-law) and decade (at least) in retirement had softened the man Ronald Reagan had sent to lay mines with Dave Wolcott in Corinto. We hadn't even left Kiev, and it looked like my Sherpa was coming apart.

What have you gotten me into, Winters?

We took the long route, stopping several times and making several left turns at red lights to see if anyone was following us, which they were. Eventually, we pulled up at a restaurant, walked through the dining room, and out the back door to another car. Old school. Like 1950s old school. So old the goons following us might even be fooled. At least the new driver was a professional. By the time we pulled up to a field somewhere beyond the outskirts of Kiev, even I didn't know what direction we'd gone.

The helicopter appeared less than a minute later, flying low against the dark sky, its lights off. It was an AgustaWestland corporate model, intended to ferry business executives on short commutes. Limited range. Unarmed. Seating for seven at most. It might have been Karpenko's, but more likely, given that Karpenko was a wanted man, it had been rented in the last few hours.

"Grigory Maltov," Greenlees whispered, as a burly man stepped out. "Karpenko's fist."

Maltov was a classic enforcer, maybe a former bodyguard, probably a thug jumped up to the inner circle because of his extreme efficiency at disagreeable tasks. Every organization had a man like this, and twenty more waiting in line to take his place. The key was finding out whether the boss enjoyed his company or treated him like a necessity.

"Grigory," Greenlees said, stepping forward and extending his hand. Maltov didn't shake it. He just frowned at us, clearly unimpressed. But that meant nothing. This kind of man was always unimpressed. That was his job.

"The fixer?" Maltov said, and I knew from the phrase that he was a fan of Western action movies.

"Tom Locke," I said, extending my hand. Maltov tried to crush it. He clearly understood that in America, he would have been cast as the villain. And not without reason.

"Get in," he said.

We retrieved our bags from the trunk of the car. Greenlees had packed lightly, in a 1990s-era stretch-bag that had clearly come out of mothballs.

"We have equipment," Greenlees said, indicating the trunk.

Maltov grunted.

"This wasn't his idea," I muttered to Greenlees, as Maltov packed the radios, beacons, and landing lights without bothering to balance the weight

Within minutes, we were airborne, the ground passing swiftly below us, a dark, endless country-side of flat fields that could have been Kansas or the more fertile upland of Eritrea. I was half asleep by the time we banked steeply and dropped low, a few meters above the treetops. My stomach hit my throat as the pilot skimmed the treeline. It was a common military tactic to fly nap of earth, using natural features to evade radars and missiles, but not like this. The pilot was a cowboy.

"We're near Poltava," Greenlees said into the headset, the first words any of us had spoken for an hour. I wasn't surprised. Karpenko was a wanted man. Contrary to popular wisdom, wanted men usually stayed close to home.

When we swung over the road, I suspected we were close. Even in the dark, I could see it was dead straight with open fields on both sides and a compound at the far end. The edges had been cleared, probably recently. No power lines, meaning they had been buried. We slowed as we approached the compound: a house, a barn, and two outbuildings surrounded by a perimeter fence and six, seven, eight men with AK-47s and dogs.

It would take an army to storm this place, I thought, as we bounced down in the formal garden. I wasn't until I stepped into the mud that I realized this garden wasn't shrubs and flowers, but two-foot-tall weeds.

"Traditional dacha," Greenlees said, sliding up beside me. "Summer home from the Imperial Period, original Russian Empire. Probably abandoned during the late Soviet years. This isn't one of the homes on our list."

Karpenko owned eight homes that Greenlees knew of, including the Poltava mansion that had been assaulted last week. This one was either a recently purchased safe house, or an early purchase on the way up. Karpenko came from a poor background in Poltava; owning this local emblem of wealth was probably the culmination of a childhood dream.

Until reality outstripped that dream a thousand times over.

Now he was a prisoner to that wealth, with two guards at the front door and a keypad security system. Five number. No scrambler. Amateur.

Inside, there was a security room, with two men monitoring camera feeds on laptops, then a second door made of steel. A guard with a handheld metal detector was waved away by Maltov, telling me even

Karpenko's own men were probably being checked. And that this wasn't a job interview. Karpenko hadn't even met me, but I was already hired. He was desperate.

"Captain Locke," a man said, entering the room. He was tall and thin, a generation older than Maltov, wearing forest green fatigues and a 9 mm pistol. I could tell by his bearing he was ex-military, probably Ukrainian special forces. He was almost surely Karpenko's head of security.

"Colonel Sirko," Greenlees whispered, as the man and I shook hands.

The colonel nodded. "Come," he said, like a man who knew three words of English, and had just exhausted his supply.

There were no guards in the inner sanctum, but there wasn't much else to make it feel like home. The rooms were elegant, but damp and musty, with hardly any furniture. The enormous fish tank along one living room wall held dirty water . . . and a large pile of mobile phones. I thought about what Greenlees had hinted at: that the assault in Poltava had been an inside job. So now Karpenko was confiscating cell phones. Good. That meant he was learning.

If the oligarch was paranoid, though, it certainly didn't show. He entered the room moments later, seemingly at ease. He looked like who he was: a businessman. He was wearing a casual suit, tapered cut in the London style, with no tie and unbuttoned cuffs. He was my age, early forties, in Western shape, probably a member of a fancy gym or three, but he wasn't wearing anything flashy except his expensive watch, the same one from the file photo back in DC. Aside from a simple iron wedding band, his hands were clean. I knew he was eaten up inside by the recent turn of events—I wouldn't be surprised if he had ulcers so bad he was shitting blood—but he could have been interviewing a cake decorator for his daughter's birthday party, he was so languid and calm.

I liked him immediately, at least as a client. There was nothing worse than working with a pompous strongman. They had too many ideas, and too much faith in brutality. A man like Karpenko, I suspected, would leave the important work to the professionals. That was probably how he had gotten to the top in the first place.

"Mr. Locke," Karpenko said in a Kensington accent—London School of Economics, perhaps? Hadn't someone mentioned he was an economist by trade? He took the large leather chair; Greenlees took the only other seat in the room. I didn't mind. I preferred to stand. Sirko was standing behind Karpenko, in a protective position. Maltov was standing by the door, a power move, judging by Sirko's sour expression.

"Mr. Karpenko," I said, with proper respect.

"We've been waiting. How was the trip?"

"Long."

"You came from America." He picked up a bottle of translucent brown liquor and poured three glasses. He was checking my connections.

"From Washington, DC," I said, taking a glass.

"You met with Mr. Winters then? He filled you in on the situation?"

"I'm fully up to speed," I lied.

He raised his glass in a toast, *"Bud'mo!"* he said, and I wondered as I knocked back the translucent liquor how he knew Brad Winters by name, since nobody knew Brad Winters by name. But this was a BNR. Winters had named me to Karpenko. Maybe the oligarch was a friend. Or someone with a shared interest, which was as close to a friend as a man like Winters ever had.

"He says you are the best," Karpenko said, watching my reaction to the burning liquid.

"He said the same about you."

Beside me, Greenlees sputtered, then coughed. The liquor really did burn. "Lovely," he muttered, putting down his glass.

Karpenko poured another round. *"Horilka,"* he said. "Homemade herb-infused vodka. A Ukrainian specialty. You won't get anything like it in America."

That's for sure, I thought, as we downed another glass. Greenlees drank in silence this time.

"So what is your plan?" Karpenko asked.

I glanced at Sirko, then Maltov, who were eyeing each other.

"Don't worry," Karpenko said. "I trust these men with my children's lives."

It wasn't an idle phrase. That was exactly what Karpenko was doing.

"I'll exit your family by plane," I said. "Tomorrow night. The plane will come in low, no lights, undetectable by radar . . ."

"Yes, yes," Karpenko interrupted, "I know. But where will it land?"

The question threw me. Had Winters told him the plan already? When? And how?

"We don't have the landing coordinates set. We'll scout the location tomorrow . . ."

Karpenko said something in Ukrainian.

"It's the best way," I said, cutting any objections short. "I have locations in mind based on a map recon and GIS satellite imagery, but I won't commit until I've seen them in person. The plane's landing zone doesn't have to be set until twenty minutes prior to arrival. If the Russians tip their hand, we want to have a backup plan."

This wasn't true. Once we launched the plane from Romania we were committed. It was a one-shot deal. But American military prowess was a power tool. Clients usually believed anything I told them. Enemies usually believed anything they heard.

"Besides," I said, gambling based on the rumor of betrayal and the cell phones in the fish tank, "the longer we wait to commit, the less chance of a security breach."

Karpenko snapped to Colonel Sirko in Ukrainian. "No one has left the compound since they arrived," Greenlees translated. "No one is allowed to leave now."

"Smart," I said. "But that's why Greenlees and I have to scout the landing strips. We need to know what is going on out there. And I need eyes on the landing zone."

Karpenko stared at me quietly, as if waiting for something to sink in. I'd seen that look before, from men accustomed to power, but I never knew what they were thinking. Trusting their gut, I guess. Or seeing if I could be intimidated. It seemed like kindergarten to me.

"Take Maltov," Karpenko said, and I saw a wince cross Sirko's face. He didn't trust Maltov, and he wanted me to know it. Or maybe he just didn't like him. The enforcer and the security chief never liked each other.

"Perfect," I said. "I need your best man. And a car. And a driver."

Karpenko snapped in Ukrainian.

"Maltov has a driver," Greenlees said.

"How many men do you have?" Karpenko asked, looking me in the eyes, something he'd either learned in business school or during a basement torture session. I was guessing business school.

"Just one. How many do you have?"

Karpenko didn't answer.

"Forty," Maltov said, and I wondered how much English he knew. More than Sirko, that was obvious.

"Good. We'll need them tomorrow night."

Maltov nodded.

"What about cars?"

"Fourteen."

"Trucks?"

He looked confused. Greenlees translated.

"Six," Sirko said, butting in.

"What about all-terrain vehicles?"

"What about guns?" Karpenko interrupted. "What about . . . SEALs?" He gestured at Greenlees, then me, then said something in Ukrainian that made the older man drop his eyes. "Do you know how many men Belenko has?"

"More than us," I said, because that was obvious from Karpenko's tone.

"So what are we going to do about it?"

"Stay calm," I said. "And trust each other. Winters sent me for a reason."

Karpenko rose, turned calmly, and said something to Sirko in Ukrainian. Then he turned, looked at me, and walked out of the room.

Typical. Rich men always had unrealistic expectations.

Sirko motioned for us to follow. He took us down a dark back hallway perfect for servants and assassinations. At the end, we entered the servant's kitchen. On a small wooden table were two loaves of brown bread, a bowl of lard, and some cured bacon.

"Eat," the colonel said, turning on his heel.

I was so famished, I fell into the bread, tearing off a huge corner chunk, slathering it with lard, and shoving it into my mouth before I realized I didn't have anything to wash it down.

"What did Karpenko say?" I asked, when I'd finally choked down the crust.

Greenlees looked glum. He hadn't touched his food. "He said he should never have trusted Winters."

"He's right."

"Because I'm old, and you're out of shape, and you don't even speak Ukrainian."

I started to laugh, then tore off another hunk of bread. "Don't worry," I said as I reached for the lard. "I'm definitely not out of shape."

CHAPTER 8

Sirko returned a half hour later, no doubt after a rocky chat with Karpenko. It wouldn't have been his idea to hire Apollo, but he had clearly given his assent, and that was all Karpenko needed to blame him for any problems. Like the cavalry arriving and consisting of a retiree and a guy in a suit.

Fortunately, he had an unmarked bottle of liquor, which turned out to be vodka, so I pushed the last heel of bread aside.

"98th Guards?" I asked, noticing the tattoo on his forearm when he gave me a glass. It was a blue shield featuring a yellow arm, clad in chain mail, holding a sword.

Sirko nodded. The 98th were Soviet paratroopers, but Sirko was pushing sixty, so of course Ukraine had been part of the Soviet Union when Sirko was coming up.

"I'm airborne, too," I said, pounding my right fist on my chest, where I had worn my jumpmaster wings while in uniform.

Sirko smiled and thumped his chest. It was the universal brotherhood of military airborne: paratroopers, rangers, Russian Spetsnaz. Beyond the tough training was the shared suffering, topped off by secret initiation rituals like "Blood Wings" and

"Prop Blast." The U.S. Army put a stop to them in the 1990s after CNN caught Canadian paratroopers pounding jump wing pins straight into new member's chests—thus "blood wings"—but to old dogs like Sirko and me, the rituals would never die.

"Airborne," he said, lifting his glass.

We drank.

"Were you in Bosnia?" I asked. The colonel didn't answer. I doubted he understood. "I was in Srebrenica, summer of 1995."

The images came back to me: the beautiful valleys of northeastern Bosnia, the two Serbian "Red Berets" we captured on the road, the terrible beating we gave them, the first time I'd shattered teeth. It wasn't right, but I was raw and eager, and we were hunting Scorpions, a vicious Russo-Serbian militia that referred to Bosnians as cockroaches. Yugoslavia had shattered into ethnic violence, and the Scorpions, among others on the Serbia side, had elevated that disagreement into ethnic cleansing. Even the Red Berets were more afraid of their allies than they were of us, thus the missing teeth, but they finally gave up a location: Srebrenica. It was only forty clicks away. I radioed in the intel, and requested a change of mission to Srebrenica.

The response from military special ops command was instant and clear.

"Negative, Falcon 2-0. Charlie Mike." Meaning *continue mission*. "Drina Valley is UN safe area and no-go zone."

I locked eyes with Miles, my noncomm. "Your call, Captain," he said.

I made the call. I followed orders. We stayed

away from the valley. The next day, the thunder started to the east, the unmistakable sound of artillery, but headquarters refused our requests to investigate. For the next five days, I ignored the thunder and Charlie Mike'd like a good soldier, sticking to our original mission, my men angry and mutinous, until I finally said, "Fuck it. We're going in."

I will never forget the town of Srebrenica: the smell of smoke and corpses; the burned houses; the destroyed Dutch troop carrier smoldering in the road. It was desolate, even in the center of town, but there were women in the wreckage, traumatized and starving, just as the Serbians intended.

We walked in double-wedge formation with Miles on point, nobody saying a word. On the north end of the town, the destruction was thicker. We saw the back wall of an old zinc factory, covered with blood. The ground was soaked in it, a long line of individual pools. We stayed off the road. Three hundred meters farther, we came to a fresh mound of dirt. Culver, one of the young buck sergeants on my team, started digging. Within seconds, a hand was sticking out. A child's hand.

Culver stopped. He looked up at me. He didn't say it, but he didn't need to. I could see it. *Fuck you, Captain.*

Later, Miles put a hand on my shoulder. "It's all right," he said. "It's my fault. I'm the NCO. I should have told you to fuck that order."

But it wasn't his fault, and it wasn't all right. Eight thousand Bosnians were executed in and around Srebrenica, mostly men and boys, but for me, it only took one. I lasted another four years, but that was the end of my army career. Every time someone asked me why I'd gone merc, I thought of that dead boy, and HQ insisting I stay the course, and how I could have saved him . . . if only I'd had the freedom or the nerve.

"Srebrenica," Sirko said slowly, pronouncing each syllable. He didn't understand English, but any military man in the Eastern bloc understood that word. "Srebrenica. Bosnia. Dah. I was there."

He said something in Ukrainian, and I looked to Greenlees.

"He says that's when he left."

I remembered the calm on the boy's face when we dug him out. There was a bullet hole in his forehead with powder burns around the entry. Barrel on bone. How much worse would it have felt, I wondered, if I had been on the same side as those butchers?

I raised my vodka glass for another round. Sirko poured. We drank in silence, each of us lost in our thoughts, until Sirko put down his glass and spoke.

"He asked if you have a plan," Greenlees translated.

"A thin one," I said. "Mostly assumptions."

Sirko nodded. "That's what he figured," Greenlees said, as Sirko pulled out a worn tactical map case with a faded Soviet star on the front and slapped it on the table. Inside were old Soviet army maps of the Poltava area, complete with an acetate overlay showing military graphics and enemy units. In the side pockets were an orienteer's compass, a map protractor, a small maglite with a red lens for night vision, a few markers for the acetate overlay, and two chem lights. A true soldier's kit.

I pulled out my tablet computer and, while Sirko watched, punched up some GIS satellite maps with movable three-dimensional overlays of the same location: population density, satellite imagery, topography, and militia movements, courtesy of the gerbils. My tablet was security encrypted, ruggedized for field deployment, and completely sterile. I would never use it for writing, and it contained no identifying information. It was simply a traveling reference library. It had its own solar panel and could locate a GPS satellite, but it wasn't Bluetooth or Wi-Fi enabled, and it would never connect to the Internet or a cell phone tower. There was no such thing as cybersafety. I had often tracked prey by remotely locating a smartphone. The only way to stay secure was to stay off the grid: Sirko and I represented two means of doing just that.

"Now," I said, as the maps opened. "Where the hell are we?"

Sirko pointed to a blank spot three kilometers from any road, in the middle of the countryside. He had set up this safe house three years ago, he told us with pride. Hired the old couple in the false farmhouse that fronted the main road. Built the fence and laid in a power supply. Even Karpenko didn't know about it. That caution had probably saved Sirko's job, maybe even his life, when the assassins hit Karpenko's mansion a few days ago. Security chiefs don't usually survive security breaches.

"What happened in Poltava?" I asked.

Sirko grimaced. "Bad partners," Greenlees translated. "But they are dead."

I waited for Sirko to say more.

"He told Karpenko to run after the first night here," Greenlees continued. "Before the enemy could regroup. But Karpenko wouldn't go. He wanted to wait for you."

Not for me, for Winters. At this point, apparently, the oligarch trusted his American friend more than his most trusted security man.

The colonel pushed the map forward, pointing to the Poltava airport. Change the subject, the motion said. Let's talk about the future, not the past. So I did, and for the next two hours, Greenlees earned his money translating between us.

By then, I was exhausted, the last sixty hours finally catching up to me. Or maybe it was the buzzing lights, and the linoleum kitchen, and the dead fly that had somehow burrowed into the lard.

"What should I know about Maltov?" I asked, folding up my tablet. I was reluctant to cut Sirko loose; he was a kindred soul.

But the old colonel smiled, or maybe he grimaced once again. "Maltov is . . . *krysha*," he said. "Only *krysha*. Ho *hrabr*."

"*Krysha* means 'muscle,'" Greenlees translated, knocking back a vodka nightcap. "Maltov is only muscle. But he is brave."

Greenlees looked at me, wondering at the deeper meaning. *Maltov clearly saved his ass during the assassination attempt*, I wanted to explain, but Greenlees looked tired beyond caring, and I felt guilty as I watched the old man shuffle behind Sirko toward one of the outbuildings. The exhaustion was coming over me, though, and my sympathy felt fuzzy and weak. It was dusk, and frogs were calling from the trees, and my mind slipped into the pastoral beauty of "At Night," a song from Delius's *Florida Suite*. The music took me out of Ukraine and back to my childhood home, where I used to sit at my window at five years old and listen to the frogs. That was before the divorce. Before my sister went to live with another family, and I talked my way into Saint Thomas Choir School, a boarding school in Manhattan for musical savants. That was back when I would listen to Beethoven and the frogs, and wonder what it was like to live free, on your own. I knew exactly what it was like now, and it wasn't anything like I had dreamed it would be.

"Oh hell," I said, when I saw the bunks.

Greenlees threw his bag on the bottom. "Too old to climb," he said.

It wasn't even midnight, but I dry-brushed my teeth, jammed the door with a chair, and closed my eyes. This was a plum assignment, I reminded myself. Winters was watching. Six years in the bush, and he'd called me back. I needed to keep quiet and figure it out, to come up with a plan for tomorrow, but instead of focusing on the operation, my mind kept drifting back to my first run in an An-12 cargo plane, more than ten years before.

I was bootstrapping a planeload of weapons from Bulgaria to Liberia with six pilots who were drinking homemade Slivovitz, chain-smoking Caro cigarettes on ammo crates full of RPGs, and using a car GPS suctioned to the windshield to navigate the

Sahara. We stopped for fuel at an unmarked Algerian military base deep in the desert, and a caravan of camels delayed our departure as they meandered across the runway. We were leaking so much hydraulic fluid by then that I figured we were going to crash, and at least three times we almost did. It was one hell of a ride.

For some reason, it made me think of Alie.

But that wasn't right. Alie and I hadn't crashed and burned, like my parents. We hadn't even bootstrapped to a destination. I'd just gotten out in the middle of the journey and walked away.

CHAPTER 9

Chad Hargrove checked himself in the reflection of the china cabinet's glass doors and straightened the tablecloth—*classy touch*, he thought—one last time. He had been out for drinks with the chauffeur of a second-term Kiev city council member, and his half-finished cable for Langley was still on the table.

The doorbell rang again.

Leave it, he thought. He liked the idea of looking busy.

"Allison," Hargrove said with a smile, opening the door to his spacious duplex on the ten-acre U.S. diplomatic compound in Kiev. If he lived in Washington, DC, on his junior CIA salary, he'd be marooned out by Dulles in a cramped one-bedroom. In the field, everyone lived like kings.

"Thanks for meeting me on such short notice, Chad," Alie said, sloughing off his appraising glance at her body, since this happened all the time to every woman she knew. Hargrove had a young man's bulk and a Matt Damon smile, with blazing white teeth he must have bleached twice a month.

"My pleasure," he said, motioning toward his only chair. He was straight out of "the Farm" by way of Colorado State, or so he'd told her the first time they'd met at one of those American gatherings—a bar or an official function, she couldn't remember which. They had been circling each other ever since, but this was the first time she'd had a look at his life. It was clear the CIA had provided this standard-issue Colonial furniture, but he'd probably bought the big television out of his first paycheck. Everything was typically American, except for the ugly shirt, which he'd no doubt bought at some boutique on Khreshchatyk Street to blend in with the locals. But there was no way Chad Hargrove could pass for a local. Not with those aspirational teeth.

"Glass of wine?"

Maybe, if they were both still here in a few months, she'd ask him for a good dentist. She couldn't remember the last time she'd been to the dentist.

"How about Scotch?" she said.

He smiled and grabbed a bottle of Bowmore, a beginner's top-shelf brand. His father had probably introduced him to it back in—where was he from? Suburban Denver?

"Neat," she said, as he dropped a few pieces of ice in a glass.

She checked his bookshelf as he poured. *Clash of Civilizations. The Tragedy of Great Power Politics.* Some well-thumbed Kissinger and a less well-thumbed Stiglitz. York Harding. They were the kind of books young men read in college; the kind that never mentioned a woman, unless it was Margaret Thatcher.

"So what do you need?" Hargrove asked, handing her the Scotch. "I assume this isn't a social call."

She lifted her glass in a toast. "To information," she said.

"You know I can't tell you anything."

She smirked. So FNG—Fucking New Guy. They loved being secretive.

"Don't worry, this is off the record," she said, pulling out her smartphone. "And only a photo. Just wondering if you know this guy."

Hargrove studied the photograph. It was the Hyatt lobby. Two men talking in the corner, distant and out of focus, but recognizable.

"I don't," he said, "but he's American. Must be new in town. Never came to the embassy to check in. Probably a businessman, judging by the suit. I assume he's a douchebag, otherwise you wouldn't be asking." He flashed the teeth. "What did he do, beat up some hookers in Bangkok?"

Alie smiled to hide her anger. She was still known for her investigative reporting on sex slavery and refugees, even if she hadn't broken a story in years. In some circles, that made her a hero. But in others, it was a joke. Women's issues. *Hookers*. Aren't they funny?

"Not him," she said. "The old guy."

Hargrove looked back at the image, relieved that this wasn't competition. The old guy was American, too, probably the younger man's father, maybe on vacation or some sort of find-your-ancestors-before-you-die . . .

"Wait," he said. "That's Greenlees."

"Who's Greenlees?"

"John Greenlees, an old station chief, put out to

pasture ages ago. He comes into the office every so often to talk to Baker, the deputy station chief. They must have worked together, but I don't know, he's in the wind. Nobody has cared about him in years. I only recognize him because I happen to have an office next to Baker."

An office? She almost laughed. She knew Hargrove stamped visas in the morning and spent his afternoons in a cubicle, typing up Baker's cables. It was the fate of all greenhorn case officers who were undeclared.

"What's Greenlees up to?"

"Nothing, as far as I know."

"He doesn't work for, um, your people?"

"Greenlees? No, he's out of the game. But he's got contacts, I'm sure, since he's been around forever. He's burned at the organization, though. Left under a cloud, not too happy about it, I hear. Something about a local mistress."

"Everyone has a mistress," she said.

Hargrove shook his head. "He left his wife for her. A CIA station chief doesn't leave his wife for a sex worker. It's blackmail material. And it's not professional."

She'd heard him use the word before. Professionalism was a sacred concept to earnest young men like Hargrove.

"Sex worker?"

"Whore, I guess. That's the word Baker used."

Which could mean anything. *Whore* was a generic insult used by old glad-handers like Baker, a way to put a woman in her place. Underneath.

"He may have been compromised. That's not

something for print, of course," Hargrove said, "although I can't imagine anyone would care. That was years ago. And I assume nothing was proven, or they would have pulled his passport. But you know how rumors are. They can ruin a career."

She knew he intended to stay clean, but she also knew he wasn't above exploiting a rumor or two, if the timing was right. That's what reporters were for.

"Any idea where to find him?"

Hargrove shrugged. "At the embassy, I suppose. He comes in every now and then. I could ask Baker."

"No," she said too quickly, and saw Hargrove hesitate. He was an ambitious FNG; he wouldn't miss the implication that this was important to her. But there was no use not nailing it down.

"Can you just let me know if he comes in?" she said too casually.

Hargrove reached for the bottle of Scotch. She had been right about him, she thought as she watched him pour. He was well built. Wide, but in a bulldog way, unlike Locke, who was lean. And Hargrove was fresh. Clean. He had good instincts and a sharp eye, and he wanted to learn. He was a young man who could be molded—who *wanted* to be molded—if a woman knew how to handle him.

"So who's the other guy?" he said, handing her a glass.

It was almost too easy.

She handed him Locke's card, with its bullshit consulting business. "It seems legit, but he's ex-military. I knew him years ago. In Africa."

"Knew him?"

She shook her head. "Just because I used to be a nun—"

"I know," Hargrove said.

And I know you love it, Alie thought. She licked her lips and sipped her Bowmore. "Everybody makes bad decisions, right?"

She was laying it on thick, but what the hell. She had been flirting with Hargrove for weeks, practically since he arrived in Kiev, and the longer something like that goes on, the more inevitable it becomes. And besides, she was lonely. It was a hard life on the road, where every story was temporary and every relationship short-lived. If she didn't sleep with sources like Hargrove, who would she sleep with? Those were the only people she knew anymore.

"You don't think he's a merc, do you?" she asked. One of the CIA's new jobs was supervising the contractors hired to do what the Agency used to do.

"You know I can't talk about that."

Which meant he had no idea who Locke was. "I'm just saying, Chad, you wouldn't believe some of the things this guy did in Africa."

"You wouldn't believe some of the things I've done."

Like getting drunk with mistresses and junior staffers? Or taking mental notes at cocktail parties? Or paperwork? First-year agents were so enthusiastic about their paperwork. Spotting new agents to recruit. Running human networks. They never realized the bosses back in Langley didn't read reporting by FNGs.

She let it drop, turning her back and wandering

never occur, and that he would never act
and, he thought, *because* he would never
he would never even ask her name.

," Ivan said with mock surprise, as the
ached the table. Ivan was enormous and
ed, so he never had any use for subtlety.
elenko's enforcer; he came with the oli-
ntract to find the traitor Karpenko. The
ollar reward being offered by Putin's FSB,
as the Wolf's real reason for being here.
utting it down. The club is off-limits."

La Rus?" The Wolf wasn't sure where
heard that phrase for Russians, but it was
"Are we finally going to do something?"
l. Foot soldiers always thought of the fight
rk. It was the part, after all, that was glori-
e old Soviet film footage. The stand outside
ad. The tanks on fire. The endless fistfights
hases of American movies.

was these moments, the maneuvering be-
encounter, when a true soldier thrived. The
d learned that lesson from Sun Tzu and
d it himself, in every battle of the last thirty
om the mountains outside Kandahar to the
d apartment blocks of Grozny and Tbilisi.
as from the lost generation, the foot soldiers
d fought in Afghanistan in the late 1980s, at
end of the world's last great empire, when
lyte commanding officers had plowed relent-
head, in the old Soviet style, leveling villages
ughtering the population to kill a few insur-
He had watched helplessly as men like Andrei
his commanding colonel, turned the tribes

the room, fingering a few of his books. He wasn't
brilliant, but he was a hard worker. Very organized.
Passably neat. Probably bootstrapped himself to top
of his class at the Farm. Even though he spoke Russian and Ukrainian, he probably wanted an assignment to the Middle East, because everyone did, that
was where the promotions were. Europe was over.
Nothing but old-timers. But then he stumbled into
this Ukraine crisis, and all those old movies came
back. Dead drops in Nyvky Park; midnight meetings under bridges; surveillance of Soviet operatives.
There was something romantic about fighting the
Russians. It was the KGB, after all, who killed that
poor man in London with the poisoned umbrella.

And all he had been doing for the past three
months was stamping visas in the consular section
and meeting with schnooks. Then Locke comes
along, and she drops an opportunity right into his
overeager lap.

If she'd stopped to think about it, she would have
realized she was in a similar place: jammed in a career cul-de-sac and latching on to Locke as a way
out. But Alie had stopped thinking about her moti-
vations years ago. It was less painful that way.

"I'm doing you a favor," she said.

"What?"

Wrong tactic. Let him think he's doing the favor.
"I said don't forget me, Chad. When you're in the
field."

"I can't take you into the field, Alie."

We'll see, she thought, setting down her drink.
She knew it was time to leave. There wasn't much
more she could do to set the hook. She already had

the first half of what she'd come for—Greenlees's name—even if, when she'd arrived, she hadn't been acknowledging the second.

Even now, it didn't cross her mind, at least not the conscious part, that her next decision had anything to do with Thomas Locke standing her up three hours ago.

But Hargrove understood. He was grinning behind his Bowmore, contemplating what to say next. She almost rolled her eyes. *You can't let them think everything is their idea*, she thought, as she put down her glass and stepped toward him.

"I've never been with an older woman," he said, sliding his hand around her waist.

Don't blow it, she thought. *I'm only thirty-four.*

Nikolay Balashov, known
as he entered the dark club
Last night, it had been thum
have shaken the radar insta
he thought, with quick nosta
name. This morning, it felt li
try: dreary and depressing, the
the women slumped apathetic

He walked slowly along the
tender not even moving from
saw what he was looking for: t
so short that it barely covered h
in the back, as he knew she wou
two women, drinking *horilka* at

She looked up and saw him.
held his gaze. He didn't change
in and said something to Ivan, w

He didn't care what she thoug
an idea, one that recurred every
dozen different faces. Dark hair,
bones. He didn't care about her
short dress, and he didn't mind
She was a denizen of this world, b
was he. He liked the idea of some r
mance that would shatter that part o

that would
upon. No
act on it.
"La Ru
Wolf app
blockhea
He was
garch's c
million-
though,
"I'm s
"Why
Ivan had
an insult
Typic
as the w
fied in t
Lening
and car
But
fore the
Wolf h
practic
years,
shatter
He
who h
the ta
troglo
lessly
and s
gents
Sirko

against them and good Russian soldiers to heroin, and even now, thirty years later, he hated those incompetent commanders for the humiliation: the greatest country on earth, with the greatest weapons in the history of the world, brought low by primitives with a few Stinger missiles.

And then, a few months after their retreat from Kandahar, the Berlin Wall had come down, and the Soviet Union soon after. He had spent a month on his army base in Bolgrad, getting smashed on vodka and cursing men like Colonel Sirko. He spent the next two months thinking the Soviet Empire was better off dead, and the next two years watching corrupt politicians sell state-owned factories; corrupt senior military officers sell off state munitions; and hardliners in the Red Army stage a coup for the honor of the Motherland . . . only to be upstaged by Boris Yeltsin, the Politburo's drunk.

After the coup, he lost hope. The army was in tatters. The KGB and security systems dissolved. He considered joining the new society, working as a bodyguard for the emerging capitalist class, but Sirko saved him. He had seen one of the new oligarchs on television, not Karpenko but one of the Russian bears, and behind him, for a moment, he had glimpsed Col. Andrei Sirko, with his rigid military bearing, and he knew that world wasn't for him.

So he lit out for the Balkans when Yugoslavia collapsed. He was the Lone Wolf then, *odinokiy volk*, quarrelsome and surly, fighting for the Serbs but fighting, really, without cause or country. He didn't fit it in the new world, he had decided, and he didn't want to. He was a soldier. Fighting was his life.

But he discovered something else in Bosnia, besides the cleansing power of war. He discovered that there were others like him. Thousands of others. Tens of thousands, even, young soldiers cut loose by the collapse of the empire, angry and lost, looking for money and adventure and trained in the rudiments of war.

By Chechnya, five years later in 1999, Nikolay Balashov was the Wolf, a conflict entrepreneur. He had a way of drawing other displaced men to his side: old Soviet soldiers and KGB officers, pro-Moscow Chechyans, fighters from the Caucuses and the "Stans." It was a slaughter in Chechnya; they had shelled Grozny like the Nazi's shelled Stalingrad. They had terrorized the populace and burned the rebel provinces to the ground. But that was what his generation needed. They needed to purge.

That was what Putin understood. That the old structures had to be torn down. That his base of power was a lost generation looking for a hard hand to guide it . . . empower it . . . and turn it loose. It didn't matter anymore that the Russian military was a mess. Russia had Putin now, and Putin knew there were better ways.

Chechnya. Georgia. Crimea. Ukraine. Putin's wars, but also the Wolf's. Together, they would take back their empire, one destroyed country at a time, because that was what they had been born to do.

Young men like Ivan, they would never understand. They weren't soldiers; they hadn't been raised with honor. They were thugs, born into the new world the Wolf had created. They valued nothing but money, worked for no one but the businessmen.

They didn't love the rough, violent romance of war, like true soldiers. They didn't know how to maneuver before a fight.

"Give us an hour, La Rus," Ivan said, calling the Wolf back to this club, this dirty town, this fight. "What can that harm?"

"There's always time for one more," the woman in the red dress said lasciviously.

"Never speak to me," the Wolf snapped. He could feel his heat rising—at the woman for speaking, at Ivan for his ignorance. What was the point of living like this? Without pride or purpose?

"One hour," he said. "Make sure your men are ready."

He turned and walked away. He wasn't worried. Ivan would follow orders. And in the end, he would get his fight. Karpenko was a hunted man. He needed to get out of Eastern Europe, to Vienna at least, and Vienna was 1,300 kilometers away. Even Warsaw, not safe but a doorway to the West, was seven hours. An oligarch would never risk such a drive. He would go by air, by the helicopter that the Wolf's men—his real men, not Belenko's goons—had heard landing somewhere north of Poltava last night. And anything that could be flown out could be shot down.

All it took was professionals, and an intelligent plan. The Wolf was eager to show his old commander, Colonel Sirko, that this former foot soldier had bested him in both.

CHAPTER 11

"Good morning," Karpenko said, as I walked into the kitchen. It was 0600 and not yet full light. I hadn't expected to see him this early. But what was life without surprises?

Maltov handed me a cup of coffee. Karpenko looked sharp, clean-shaven and bright-eyed, dressed in a custom-tailored plaid blazer, English cut. This was the business Karpenko, the man who took meetings in the Square Mile of London and blended in at swank Belgravia restaurants. Or almost blended in. The only people the London upper crust looked down on more than the Eastern European nouveau riche were African princes who bought their Ferraris with humanitarian aid money.

"I apologize for last night," he said, surprising me again. Warlords never apologized. Even Winters never apologized. Unless there was an angle. "I have been under stress, I admit." His slightly stilted English was unnerving, like a serial killer. I glanced at Maltov, but the enforcer didn't blink. "But of course you know that. That's why you're here." He paused. "Are you a father?"

Not in this life. "No."

He smiled. "The sacrifices we make."

We walked outside into the chilly morning air.

In an alley between the barn and an outbuilding, where they would be impossible to see from beyond the perimeter, stood a line of twelve black Range Rovers and two bulletproof black Mercedes, a businessman's motor pool.

"No Maserati, I'm afraid," Karpenko said. "My fleet is built for safety, not speed."

So the Maserati is in London . . .

A young Ukrainian with a Kalashnikov, probably in his teens, opened the barn door. Inside were two beater cars, a winch truck, a tractor, a rusty pickup of Soviet extraction, a three-ton truck, and the AgustaWestland helicopter. A farmer's fleet, plus the bird. If the shit hit the fan, that was the backup plan.

"I'll take that one," I said, pointing to an early 2000s four-door Opel with an eight-cylinder engine and a large trunk. It was the worst car in the lot, meaning it was the car no one would suspect. By the time Greenlees wandered out, looking disheveled in the same golf shirt and loafers, the young Ukrainian—Maltov's driver, as it turned out—had loaded the trunk with our kit. Five minutes later, we headed out, stopwatch in hand.

Three minutes to the iron gate at the end of the entry drive. Click.

Nineteen to the entrance road of the Poltava Airport. Click.

Eighty seconds to the terminal.

We sat in the short-term parking lot. The airport wasn't crowded. In fact, it was almost deserted. Which made it almost perfect.

Too perfect, really.

According to Sirko, Belenko had twenty to twenty-five men in the area. They had moved into a hotel in the center of Poltava, across the street from the city's best brothel. Karpenko's brothel. By two in the morning, any morning, they were mostly drunk. But if they had anti-aircraft missiles, their aim didn't have to be perfect. In fact, it didn't even have to be good.

"Let's check the airbase," I told Maltov's protégé. "Take the back way."

Sirko had pointed out the secondary airfield, a former Soviet air force base. Most people had forgotten it, Sirko told me, but he had checked it himself several months ago, and the runway was usable. I was sure Belenko's men had checked it, too, but the location was still ideal. The airbase was eighteen kilometers from Poltava's town center, and only twelve from the dacha.

We skipped the main entrance—Poltava Museum of Long-Range Aviation, by appointment only, Greenlees translated from a small sign—and found a dirt track that cut through the forest a few hundred meters away. The forest was thick, but it took less than a minute to reach the edge of the parking lot. On the left was a low concrete building, with an abandoned flight tower behind it. On the right was the entry road, a metal gate, and a decrepit guardhouse. There was only one car in the lot, a beat up Soviet-era Lada, but halfway down the entry road, on a blind corner, a Škoda was sitting in the weeds. Belenko's sentries, taking the lazy approach.

As we watched, an old man and an older woman,

themselves relics of the Soviet era, got into the Lada and drove away. Belenko's men watched them go, then walked around the parking lot and checked the lock on the front gate. Three minutes later, their car was filled with cigarette smoke.

"Lucky," Maltov said. "No appointments today."

We circled through the forest to the back of the building, then climbed onto the roof. The parking lot in front was surrounded on three sides by forest. The two-lane entrance was gated, and the two-lane exit emptied onto the landing strip. Nine Soviet aircraft were exhibited in a horseshoe, eight imposing strategic bombers and a lone Antonov-26 cargo plane, the two-engine version of the An-12 Brad Winters had chartered.

I surveyed the surroundings through my field glasses: waist-high weeds, a few abandoned buildings and aircraft bunkers, an obsolete radar array, and decaying gun parapets, presumably for air defense artillery. Weeds poked through cracks in the tarmac, but the runway was long, wide, and serviceable. Winters's An-12 was an antique, even by Soviet standards. It had four turboprops, a glass nose, and 1946 technology, but it was tough and could land almost anywhere, as long as the ground was solid and flat. I'd used the An-12 to ferry guns and other supplies around Africa many times, and we'd landed on worse.

I scanned the open fields. The rusty barbed-wire fence was worthless against vehicles, but the meadows were so rutted that only a ruggedized off-road vehicle could cross.

"You could fly a convoy in here," Greenlees said, staring at the Tupolev 160, a massive Soviet bomber that was the museum's star attraction.

"Flying in isn't the problem," I said. "It's flying out."

Maltov was talking with the teenage Ukrainian, patting the building beneath our feet. "It's good," he said. "Concrete."

"What about the flight tower?" Greenlees asked. It was squatting between the parking lot and the landing strip, as if guarding the bottleneck there.

"Too dangerous for shelter," I said, "but that doesn't make it useless."

It was a good setup: one narrow ingress route from the main road, with a blind corner and thick forests on each side. A sharp turn and a gate at the entrance to the parking lot, which weren't prohibitive, but would slow an attack. Nothing but a narrow road from the parking lot to access the landing strip. Forty men could hold off 150 here, if they were smart.

But Karpenko's men weren't smart.

And there was still the question of antiaircraft missiles. Sometimes, a rutted field was an obstacle, and sometimes it was nothing more than four hundred meters of clear sight lines.

"Let's check the forest," I said. Greenlees's shoulders fell, but Maltov nodded to his protégé. He seemed to understand that, unlike in his line of work, precision was my stock in trade. I needed to understand every angle, calculate every distance. Men were going to die tonight. That was certain. Now was the time to get the details right, because once the shooting started, everything would go wrong.

By the time we finished, the sun was straight overhead, and Belenko's men had been relieved by a second shift. We watched them drive around the airbase once, then park right back where they had been before, as unprofessional as the first crew.

It would be tricky. And dangerous. But it could be done.

"Do you have a friend in the city?" I asked Maltov. "Someone nobody would know to watch."

He nodded.

"What about cargo trucks?"

"I can get what you need."

"C-4?"

He smiled. "How many kilos?"

We drove by an indirect route through the industrial section of Poltava, sticking to residential roads. There were hardly any cars, and steel metal shutters covered the windows. The town was a shithole in the faded industrial style, all rust and concrete and scraggly vegetation, the kind that absolutely refuses to die. No wonder so many people looked back on the Russian years with fondness.

"Here," Maltov said.

Maltov's friend ran a small grocery, with local specialties in front and a counter for beef buns and cabbage rolls in the back. There were a few men lounging on folding chairs, but nobody was eating, and I suspected the greasy beef buns had been sitting under a heat lamp for a month. This wasn't really a restaurant, or even a retail store. The friend hadn't even bothered to stock half of the warmers.

"On the house," Maltov said, as he gave us a plate of buns and took us through to the storage area. The room was half empty and filthy. There were meat hooks hanging from the ceiling, and bloodstains on the floor. I never thought anything would make me long for Karpenko's brown bread and lard, but it had taken only half a day to find something worse.

Twenty minutes later, Greenlees and I exited through the back door with a bag of pork rinds, neither having taken a bite of anything else. We left the car, but took the friend's Škoda Yeti. The Škoda was two years old, while the Opel was fifteen, but it was still a good deal for Maltov's friend.

"Three hours," Maltov said.

We spent the next two hours eating pork rinds and moving around Poltava, circling back a few times to watch Belenko's hotel through my field glasses. There were at least twenty-five men, assuming half on watch, maybe as many as forty, and they weren't trying to hide. They were moving between the building and the parking lot, packing and re-packing two four-by-fours and two cars. It was nervous energy, not professionalism. They were eager. Or overeager.

Forty men. Four vehicles. Probably a few cars on patrol. The leader was a Maltov type: muscle, up from the ranks. They had the numbers, but we would arrive first. We could slow them on the entry road, especially on the curve, and bog them down in the parking lot, but I doubted we could stop them.

So it would all come down to timing.

"Let's go," I said, when the pork rinds were long

gone and fondly missed. We drove slowly, taking extra turns, to a field south of Poltava, far from Karpenko's dacha. Maltov arrived an hour later with two friends and two delivery trucks. The writing on the side of the trucks was in Ukrainian, but the pictures told the story: one had fish on the side, the other potatoes. They weren't exactly what I'd had in mind, but they'd have to do.

"Any trouble?"

Maltov shook his head. "No trouble."

I gave him a stack of euros, and he passed it on to his friends, who left in the Opel. As soon as they were gone, I glanced at the sun, still high in the afternoon sky, and then out across the chaff from last year's wheat. It was a fallow field, unplanted this spring, and the blackbirds were hopping across it in a detestable fashion, their dinosaur claws beneath them. Stravinky's *Rite of Spring* ballet filled my head, with its insistence on grotesque beginnings. The "Harbingers of Spring" scene, especially, always made me feel unclean.

I looked around, trying to shake the unease. Maltov and his driver were leaning against one of the trucks. The driver looked like Maltov's younger brother, but of course all Ukrainian tough guys looked the same. If Maltov wasn't born with a grimace on his face, he'd spent half a lifetime developing one. I doubted he'd see much of the second half.

Greenlees, meanwhile, was slumped in the backseat of the Škoda with the door open and his eyes closed. It was a beautiful mid-May afternoon, sunny and warm, but it was wasted on the three of us.

You get what you get, and you don't throw a fit, I

thought. It was something I'd heard my sister say to her four-year-old son the last time I'd visited her. A few weeks ago, the boy had turned nine.

I picked up the sat phone and called in the landing strip coordinates for the charter plane. The conversation took ten seconds. Ten minutes later, the sat phone rang.

"0215," Wolcott said.

"Done."

"It will work," Greenlees said, as I hung up the phone.

"I know," I said, even though I wasn't sure.

Only fools were sure.

CHAPTER 12

Brad Winters stood in the drizzling rain, driver's license in hand. In front of him stood a two-star army general and his aide-de-camp; behind him were three lobbyists chattering away about their pitch and a former congresswoman whose name he had forgotten. She worked on poverty now—but not in poverty, of course.

Two blocks away, he could hear the squeals of high school kids swarming around the tourist entrance to the White House. For a moment, he envied their ability to see the White House as something other than a pain in the ass, and this line as anything other than undignified. But he knew it was his height, and their puniness, that gave him a more accurate view.

"Brad Winters," he said to the gunny inside the checkpoint, as he showed his driver's license. They checked his name, printed a badge with his picture on it, waved him past the dogs and through the metal detectors, and in less than sixty seconds he was walking on White House grass.

He made his way to the Eisenhower Executive Office Building, a Second Empire colossus with marble floors and fifteen-foot ceilings. The EEOB, as it was called, was a classic signifier of historical importance. Official Washington, DC, from its offices to its bars and hotels, hated anything new. If it didn't look like something Thomas Jefferson would have designed, or even better, Julius Caesar, it wasn't worth taking seriously, so no one but tourists ever did.

Winters made his way up a grand staircase and down a hall lined with huge oak doors, each with a security keypad. He stopped at the one with a small placard, RUSSIA & CENTRAL ASIA, pressed a buzzer, and looked into the small camera.

"Hello?" A woman's voice.

"Hi there. It's Brad Winters for Naveen."

The door buzzed, and he pushed it open. It felt bombproof.

The Old Executive Office Building had once been a nice place to work, back in the 1890s, when it housed the State, War, and Navy Departments, and everyone had a polished wooden desk, a window, and went home for the sunset. But that was when the federal government was a few thousand people, Washington had malaria swamps, and the biggest foreign policy challenge was the western frontier. Now it was cheap cubicles stuffed with senior functionaries, their half desks barely fitting their two computers—one classified, the other unclassified—their half walls obscuring a towering window looking out over traffic. Even though it was lunchtime, the room was more crowded than a think tank intern pit. Nobody here ate, unless they made a dash to the vending machines. National Security Council staffers were vampiric; they worked twenty hours a day for two years straight, tethered to an in-box, and considered it the best two years of their lives.

"Naveen," Winters said, extending his hand as a lean young man in a wrinkled shirt and loosened tie came around the corner of one of the cubicles. Naveen Grummond was the CIA's lead analyst on EurAsia, seconded to the National Security Council to advise the president and other principals, making him one of the ten most powerful individuals in Washington in his area of expertise. It was a rare milestone few ever achieved. And yet, he'd only met the president once, in a receiving line at a White House reception, right behind a Hollywood starlet.

"Brad," Naveen said with a frown.

"They declared a day of mourning in Mariupol," Winters said.

"I saw."

"The local police refused to follow orders from Kiev. They went over to the Russians."

"The Russians want a land bridge to Crimea," Naveen said, searching for something on his desk.

"The Ukrainian military had to intervene," Winters continued. "Seven dead, right in the heart of Europe." Only Naveen would think eastern Ukraine was the heart of anything, but Winters was playing to his audience. "The Russian trolls are saying twenty, killed by Ukrainian tanks rolling down peaceful citizens who only wanted to rejoin their Motherland."

Naveen looked up, bags under his eyes. He'd lost hair, Winters noticed, since being rewarded with this godforsaken job. "What do you want, Brad?"

"Ten minutes with the president."

Naveen smirked. It was their old joke. Naveen was the one that wanted ten minutes, not Winters, even though Naveen was more aware every day how pointless those minutes would be. "What do you really want?"

"Five minutes with the national security advisor."

"Ha, me too," Naveen snorted, flopping into his chair. Winters leaned on a desk for want of a spare chair. The office was buzzing, the incessant noise of the incessantly busy, but they might as well have been at a private spa. Nobody but Naveen's five or six subordinates noticed the conversation, and even they didn't have time to care what was being said.

Winters's expression went from smiles to serious.

"I heard the Hill is forming a Friends of Ukraine coalition," he said. "They're going to ambush the White House during their opening press conference. It's going to be a full-court media blitz demanding military intervention to contain Putin."

Naveen sighed. "Who'd you hear that from?"

"Highly placed sources. I tried to knock them down with the usual talking points. Putin isn't al Qaeda. Putin has nukes and a massive inferiority complex. We're out of the nation-building business."

Naveen pursed his lips. "We're doing all we can," he snapped, "but sanctions take time, and the Germans have their own ideas."

"The Iron Bitch," Winters said, shaking his head. It was their pet name for German chancellor Angela Merkel, who had a soft spot for her neighbors to the east.

"Getting the military involved would make it more dangerous. Can't they see that? What would we do if the Russians sank a destroyer? Draw another line in the sand?"

"I just came to warn you," Winters said, knowing he had his man on the ropes.

"I know, I know," Naveen sighed. "I owe you one. When's the press conference?"

"In two hours. A few congressmen, Senator Addison from Texas . . ."

"Addison," Naveen huffed. It was a button. Naveen hated Addison.

"He's going to say we can't stand by, that we have to do something. He's going to use the term *pussy*, Naveen. Or at least strongly imply it."

"Christ, Brad. We're already at war in Syria."

"They're going to make a congressional campaign out of it. Energy security. Ukrainian pipelines. Freedom gas."

Naveen laughed. Policy wonks never understood propaganda.

"They're comparing Putin to Hitler and the president to Chamberlain. It's Munich '38 all over again. It's going to launch a news cycle and make it to the Sunday news shows."

Especially after Karpenko's heroic moment on Saturday . . .

Naveen didn't say anything. Winters knew what he was thinking. The president was clear: no military interventions that could suck the U.S. into a shooting war with the Russians. The problem was that *any* intervention, beyond sanctions, could do just that.

"I'm sorry, Brad," Naveen said. "You know how it is."

Brad Winters held up his hands in surrender. "Understood." He had groomed Naveen for more than ten years, cleared his way to this so-called prestigious post. Naveen owed him, but the man was a true public servant.

"It's set in stone, Brad," Naveen said. "I'm truly sorry."

"Honesty, Naveen," Winters said. "That's all I ask."

He knew the value of letting Naveen think he let him down. He could use that guilt later. But the truth was, Naveen Grummond had given him exactly what he wanted.

There were wheels outside the government. Wheels with far more power and influence than Naveen could see from his narrow point of view. That was the world Winters was working in. And right now, all he wanted was to make sure that his biggest client, the U.S. government, stayed out of the way.

CHAPTER 13

"Thank you, my friends," Karpenko said. "From my heart, from my wife and daughter, and from my son, I thank you."

He held up his vodka. At the long table before him, set up in the barn with wooden benches for seats, thirty-five men lifted theirs. "God bless you," Karkpenko said.

The men dug into the food. It was a simple meal of brown bread, lard, bacon, and the remnants of everything else, but each place had been set with a candle, a napkin, and a stack of euros.

A last supper, I thought as I tore off a hunk of bread. I had eaten many last suppers. Some were in brocaded dining rooms with formal servants, but most were even more rudimentary than this: tins of sardines or whatever plants had been scrounged, a small group of men eating silently in some remote nowhere place in the hours before dawn. The Romans were wrong: Those about to die don't salute you. They care only about each other.

The plan was a good one. I had gone through it step by step, first with Karpenko and Sirko, then with Maltov. We had laid it out on this very table, using blocks of wood and stacks of euros as cars and buildings, a plank for the runway, hay for the trees.

I knew the colonel didn't like it, so I had walked him through it carefully, noting the pros and cons, the possible evacuation routes and worst-case plans. I let him waver, change a few minor details, but it was too late for new ideas, and I wasn't backing down. The more serious conversation was with Maltov, who would lead the assault. It was a dangerous job, but Maltov didn't hesitate.

"I am Ukrainian," he said with a meaningful glance at Sirko. "This is my fight."

He was right. Everywhere I went, it was a local fight—over freedom and self-government, sure, but also over bread, and beer, and who got to fish which river, and how a society's energy would be spent. Even the evacuation of an oligarch's family, necessitated by a disagreement between rivals, was tied up in nationalism.

So I let Maltov call in the men on the assault team, in small groups, and explain their role in the operation. It was clear immediately that they were loyal to him, even more so than Karpenko; he must have brought them into the oligarch's service. Which was good. Maltov would be their leader tonight; when things went wrong, which they would, the men would have to trust in him. And the more times he explained the operation—the positions, the timing, the intent—the more he owned the plan. I didn't want Maltov to think about what to do when the enemy showed up. I needed him to know. Because I wouldn't be there with him on the front line. My place, as always, was with the principal.

I sliced off a lump of bacon, shoved it into a bit of bread, and stuffed it in my mouth. Maltov had risen

to speak, but when Greenlees bent over to trans-
late, I waved him away. I knew what was being said,
even though I didn't understand the words. This
is the moment. This is what we live for. Or maybe
what we're paid for, I didn't know Maltov that well.
Karpenko is a good man, he would say. He is our
patron. Our future president. But this isn't for one
man, it is for Mother Ukraine, or whatever they
called this place.

There was some pounding on the table, a few
shouts. It was either false bravado, or false ideals.
Death should be respected, not shouted down.

I slipped out into the night and looked up at the
sky, always there, almost empty. It was cold and
clear, with a quarter moon. Too much light.

But this was what we lived for. This was what we
did. And we had to go now.

I pulled out a cigar, an old habit I'd picked up in
the army. I liked the ritual before an op: the snip of
the tip, the careful burn, the slow char of the edges.
It reminded me of General McChrystal, my first and
best commanding officer, and Miles, my right-hand
man, and every Special Operations Forces commander thereafter, until the day I left the organized
world behind and stepped out into this unknown.

I heard a noise behind me, in the direction of the
house. I turned and saw a woman's face framed in a
window. She was holding a baby, so she must have
been Karpenko's wife, but she was younger than
I had expected, with dark hair like Alie's and the
same penetrating eyes, the kind that hinted at other
choices, other lives she might have lived. She didn't
look scared. She didn't look any way at all. She just

stared at me, not moving, and then, slowly, she dis-appeared.

In Kiev, Alie stared at Hargrove's ceiling, wonder-ing how she had ended up here. Not that it was a bad place, this warm bed, and this warm body. It was better than an orphanage in Burundi. Better than a refugee camp in South Sudan or a backwoods cabin in south Alabama, where the screens don't fit the windows and the mosquitos are murder. It was bet-ter than a house in the suburbs, two kids, a yoga class, and a husband who either disappeared for months at a time or resented her for making him stay home and mow the lawn.

She got up and poured herself a drink. At least she was alive. At least she was here, where her ef-forts might matter.

Walk out, Alie, she thought. *Walk now. You still have time.*

The Wolf looked down at the map. He had marked five primary locations: two airfields, an industrial park, a large construction site, and the soccer sta-dium. The stadium was covered by a Chechen mis-sile team. The airfields: too obvious. The industrial park and construction site: a problem.

Where was the helicopter? Where would they hop? Would they risk a short flight to a waiting plane?

"Reinforce the fire team, here," the Wolf said to Ivan, pointing to the airport. Ivan's men were shaky, but then again, they only needed to pin Karpenko down until the Chechens arrived. "Double the watch on the other. And from now until morning, no one is off duty. Everyone must be prepared."

"You think they will go tonight?"

"I would," the Wolf said, and he couldn't think of a better reason to be ready than that.

And Winters? What was he doing, safe in Washington, with his $6,000 suits and two-hundred-year-old townhouse? What was he thinking, now that his plan was on the line?

I stubbed out my cigar and looked up at the stars. *Forget Winters*, I thought. On a mission, the world was an oyster, closed in on itself. Winters was nothing. For the next four hours, this place, and these men, and these guns, were the only things that mattered.

CHAPTER 14

Grigory Maltov sat in the passenger seat of the lead Range Rover, impatient, waiting for the signal. It was after 0130. Enough talking. Enough planning. He hated the plan: too clever. But he had gone along. In fact, when Karpenko balked, and "Colonel" Sirko sat quietly, crapping his fancy pants, he was the one who had spoken up.

He hoped the American appreciated it.

"It's a go," Greenlees said into his earpiece.

"Finally," Maltov muttered in Ukranian, as he signaled the driver.

And then they were moving through the darkness, speeding down Karpenko's private road, a line of twelve Range Rovers and, near the middle, the family's two black armored Mercedes. They hit the main road and turned north. They were in blackout drive, all lights disconnected except the headlamps, which were taped with foil so that only a narrow beam shone on the road ahead. The drivers wore night-vision goggles, and they didn't slow for turns. The convoy would be gone before anyone knew they were there.

Eight minutes to the airbase, the American had estimated. Maltov planned to make it in five.

Let them come, he thought. *Let them bring everything.*

He was happy to be out of the dacha, after days of cowering behind the iron gate. Happy to have been given the most dangerous job. Happy to have been allowed to choose his own men. He had brought most of these men up from the mud with him. They were his brothers, in a way the Communists could never understand. They would follow no one else, at least not as they would follow him. The American understood that much at least.

"Twenty-five mikes." It was Locke, counting minutes.

"Copy." Maltov glanced at his watch: 0148. Twenty-five minutes until the plane was scheduled to arrive. Forty until it could be back in the air.

"0148," Greenlees said on the headset.

Maltov rechecked his kit. He wore a pistol in a chest holster, but he preferred his AK-47, with two magazines taped together at opposite ends for faster reloading. The Kalashnikov had greater firepower and made more noise.

They passed into a forest, the trees thick along both sides of the road. He had been in a firefight before, but not as often as his men assumed. He wasn't an enforcer. He had been the head of the local pipefitter's union at the ironworks in Kramatorsk when Karpenko had taken over the factory. He had fought Karpenko's thugs so brutishly that the boss had finally hired him. The other pipefitters weren't happy—until he brought the best along. Like Romanyuk, in the last car. And Poplavko. And Pavlo, his driver, who he had known as a boy. The rest of the pipefitters never understood. Unionism wasn't a path to better pay; it was a chance to impress the men who could give you a better job.

Now he was one of those men.

The entrance came quickly, with its small museum sign. Eleven vehicles, including the two family Mercedes, turned into the complex; three continued to the gravel road in the forest. Maltov leveled his AK-47. When the parked Škoda appeared, he fired. The Range Rovers behind him did the same as they passed. It was unfortunate. He knew Ivan, who led Belenko's men. He probably knew the two dead men in the car. They were Ukrainian comrades. They drank together, when their bosses had been friends. But their boss was on the wrong side now.

"We're here," he said, when they reached the gate. It was 0159.

"Sixteen minutes," Greenlees replied.

Maltov had argued with the American over the details, but the main components were never in dispute: two Land Rovers stayed to block the entrance from the main road, two stopped to guard the parking lot gate, the rest would form a ring around the parking lot. Locke had insisted on the exact placement of every man, including the ambush team on the entry road and the fire team in the forest. It was too much. Maltov had nodded along, but he had no intention of fussing to that degree. These were his men. They were going to be taking fire. He trusted them to find the place where they felt most comfortable.

He stepped out of the Land Rover and stood

in the middle of the parking lot, directing traffic. "Spread out," he yelled at three vehicles bunched too closely together.

"Block that landing strip access," he yelled, as the family's two armored Mercedes pulled onto the tarmac and edged under the fuselage of the museum's Tu-160, a massive Soviet bomber. Even with the quarter moon, the plane dwarfed the two black cars, making them invisible.

"Set the ambush line there." He pointed with his rifle as armed men poured out of the Land Rovers and found shelter in the tree line. He looked around: he had men on three sides of the parking lot, and the enemy would have to cross between them to get to the landing strip. The American was smart. He had to give him that.

He lifted both arms. "Here is the kill zone," he yelled. "Wait for my shot. No one fires until I do."

"Nine minutes," Greenlees said in his ear.

"In position," Maltov replied, as his men locked the gate and deployed spike strips, covering them in dirt to blend into the ground.

"Is the area secure?" It was Locke.

Maltov looked toward the five Land Rovers parked in front of the runway. Two men were sweeping the grass and tree line with infrared scopes. No sign of trouble.

"Secure," he said.

The headset was quiet. It was 0206. Then: "Light up the landing strip."

Maltov picked up his radio. "*Svititi*," he said.

Two SUVs broke the line and went speeding down the runway, dropping flares every hundred meters or so, making the mothballed war strip come alive.

"Seven minutes," he yelled to his men. "Positions!"

The men disappeared into the shadows, as Maltov slipped into the trees. The base grew silent. No movement. No lights but the parallel lines of red flares. He adjusted his night-vision goggles, as the two SUVs from the runway slipped back into line.

"Six minutes," he said over the radio.

But they didn't have six minutes. They had less than two before he heard automatic gunfire from the main road, and Pavlo yelling "They're here!" into his radio, followed by more fire as the enemy's vehicles passed into the ambush zone on the entry road.

"Wait for them," Maltov yelled, settling behind his Kalashnikov and aiming at the kill zone as a four-by-four careened into sight. It was shot to hell and running scared, the driver not even slowing down as he crashed through the gate. The spikes shredded his tires, the car fishtailed, and then the world burst open, gunfire pouring into the parking lot from three directions, even as a second four-by-four careened through the gate and smashed into the first.

Maltov could feel the AK-47 jerking in his hand. He could hear guns firing around him, a thousand bullets a minute, a deafening roar. It was unreal, as if the bullets exploding into the cars weren't from his gun, as if he wasn't the one tearing apart the men inside.

The fusillade lasted a minute. Maybe two. He

paused, watching for signs of life. He could hear the echo of shots being fired, down by the main road, off to his right, but with no other targets in sight, he fired the rest of his clip into the decimated four-by-fours.

He didn't hear the diesel engine until he stopped to reload. He snapped in the fresh magazine and listened, wondering what was coming, until, *Shit!? How?* he thought, as an armored personnel carrier flattened the spike strip at fifty miles an hour and tore into the parking lot. It was a BTR-80, a tank on wheels with a heavy machine gun turret, firing as it came, splintering trees.

Maltov dove facedown in the dirt. By the time he looked up, a squad of soldiers wearing night-vision goggles were behind the BTR, firing in tight formation.

"They're not Ukrainian," someone shouted.

Maltov unloaded his magazine, half in a panic, the gun muzzle flashing green in his night-vision goggles. More SUVs were pouring in at high speed, swerving around the troop carrier and heading toward the landing strip. Maltov fired wildly, the whole tree line firing with him. An SUV took fire, flipped, and exploded. The SUV immediately behind crashed into it, sending bodies through the windshield.

"Don't let them through," Maltov shouted as he ducked again to reload, but nobody heard him over the gunfire. Another SUV was hit; it fishtailed and smashed into the concrete museum building. The car door opened, blood exploded, and a body fell to the ground.

The BTR lurched forward with a plume of diesel, its turret swinging in Maltov's direction. "Down!" he shouted.

"Kill that thing!" someone yelled. He heard the *fush* of an RPG and saw it zoom over the BTR and explode a tree on the other side.

"Reload!"

The vehicle stopped. The turret turned in the direction of the RPG as two men with AK-47s popped out of hatches on the top. Yuri and Danka, his RPG team, evaporated in a cloud of blood and dirt, the BTR advancing now, firing as it came.

We're being overrun, Maltov thought.

"Fall back," he shouted, wishing he'd gone over the evac plan with his men, as the American had insisted, but it was too late. Most of his men were already running or dead, and to hell with the landing strip, he'd done what he could. He turned to run, but a barrage of well-aimed bullets were slashing toward him. He dropped to the ground, but the man beside him wasn't as fast. Maltov heard the grunt, a thump, and the clattering of the AK-47. It was Poplavko, shot through the chest.

He couldn't look away. He heard the zing of the bullets overhead and the shouting. Chechen. He didn't know the language but he understood the rhythms. Belenko had hired Chechens. Maltov hated Chechens. Every Ukrainian did. But he couldn't see them. All he could see was his old friend, three feet away, lying dead in the leaves.

He started firing, his Kalashnikov propped on a fallen branch, his finger holding down the trigger. He fired through his magazines, two hundred rounds, until they clicked empty. He could feel the heat off the barrel, his hands going numb, but it only made him more determined. He wouldn't run. He would stand his ground. He didn't notice the screaming in his ear until he reached for Poplavko's last magazine.

"The bird is here. The bird is here. Detonate the C-4. Do you copy? Do you copy?"

He heard a plane, maybe, but then something exploded, a grenade, not close, but it knocked him on his ass.

"Detonate the C-4!" the voice was shouting in his earpiece, but he was paralyzed, on his back, there was nothing he could do.

Maltov tore off his night-vision goggles and stared at a sky cut by branches and leaves. He couldn't believe it. The stars were gone. They were overrun. Belenko had come with more than twenty men, a lot more, and an armored troop carrier, and there was no way he could keep them busy, or keep them in this parking lot, any longer.

CHAPTER 15

The Wolf stepped out of his SUV as the machine gun cut into Karpenko's men. He was surprised his old colonel had chosen this airstrip and staged an ambush rather than a classic security perimeter. Pretty cunning for a washed-out relic, and a perfect place for him to die. Here among the old Soviet bombers, in a provincial firefight between amateurs, the kind of men who dove for the nearest cover instead of the best, and emptied their magazines as quickly as possible rather than aim. The Wolf almost felt sorry for them.

Almost.

"Blow them up," he yelled to his Chechens, shooting a line of tracers at Sirko's two remaining SUVs. Two men shouldered RPGs, followed the tracers, and the SUVs exploded.

And then the rabbit bolted. It was a single black Mercedes, hiding under the biggest bomber, now tearing down the landing strip at full speed.

The Wolf leapt back into his vehicle and floored it. He didn't worry about the gunfire; speed would be his cover. Smoke poured from the dead SUVs, obstructing his view, until he cleared the wreckage and was on the access road to the landing strip, following the black Benz.

Wolf saw the BTR's turret turn, tracking its prey.

"No!" he yelled, but the car never stood a chance. The 14.5-millimeter machine gun tore through the Mercedes's "bulletproof" skin with such force that the vehicle flipped on its side and rolled end over end at ninety miles per hour. Two hundred meters later, it burst into flame.

The Wolf lowered his head. The only thing he could do now was hope to find something identifiable as Karpenko, once the car was cool enough to search. He needed DNA proof and pictures of the body to collect his reward.

Maltov heard explosions and saw the branches rattle above him. A twig fell, hitting him in the face, such a pointless thing. He sat up. A hundred meters away, SUVs were on fire, their gas tanks creating secondary explosions, and in the glare, behind the overturned four-by-fours, he could see the armored personnel carrier, its gun turret turning toward the fleeing Mercedes. He could hear screaming in his ear about the plane and the damn C-4, but it was no use, the Mercedes was flipping now, in slow motion, on fire, and the battle was over. They were pinned down, and they were all going to die here, and was there anything worse, really, than dying for a losing cause?

Then he saw it. The potato truck, plowing through the gunfire. For a moment, he didn't understand. Pavlo was supposed to block the exit with this truck bomb. He was supposed to be safe. Of all the men, he was supposed to be safe. He had promised the boy's mother . . . his sister . . . Pavlo was just a teenager. Maltov had been to his christening and bought him his first beer, it seemed like only yesterday. He had promised his sister he would keep her boy safe. But now Pavlo was racing toward the BTR, in a truck full of C-4 and ammonium nitrate . . .

"No, Pavlo," he said, as the truck slammed into the armored troop carrier, it's back end rising into the air with the force of the collision, then smashing down with a massive explosion that sent a pillar of fire into the night sky.

Maltov lay in the leaves, not firing, not moving. Watching. In the silence, he could see men scrambling away from the blast. Some were shot as they fled. Some stumbled, their bodies on fire. It was over now, truly over. It was time to go. He couldn't do anything more. Everyone was dead, including Pavlo, who had given his life for his friends.

"Firing," he said into his earpiece.

He pulled the detonator off his web belt, flipped the safety, and squeezed. He felt the first blast, a shock wave of hot air, and then the deafening bang. Six tall trees fell across the entry road, obstructing the exit. He squeezed a second trigger. The flight tower across the parking lot seemed to lift, then totter, then collapse to the ground, trapping the enemy's SUVs on the landing strip and buying precious time for his men to escape.

CHAPTER 16

I turned away from the radio, the C-4 explosion still ringing in my ears. "It's done," I said, pulling off my headset.

"God be with Maltov," Karpenko said, as he left the dacha's security office, where we'd been listening to the firefight. He hadn't liked the idea of a diversion. I had wondered why, since it was the only plausible plan against overwhelming forces, but I heard the reason in his concern. And it surprised me.

But then again, why should it? A rich man wasn't required to have a cavalier attitude about the deaths of those who worked for him.

I patted Greenlees on the shoulder. He was breathing heavily from the exertion of screaming into the radio. I could hear other explosions in the background, and Maltov ordering his men to fall back. We had twenty-five minutes by my calculations, even if Belenko's men reacted quickly, but I was hoping to be done in ten.

"When the plane lands," I whispered, "recheck the fuses around the house."

I grabbed a pair of night-vision goggles and headed out. Sirko was standing guard outside an open door in the family's private area. He tipped his head as I passed, and I nodded in return. Inside,

I caught a glimpse of Karpenko. He was rocking a young girl, maybe three or four years old, on his lap, singing softly to her in Ukrainian.

Outside, it was cold and empty, but I didn't have time for more than a glance at the sky. I jumped into an SUV, drove down the long driveway, and pulled onto Karpenko's private access road. A kilometer down was a straight section 1,500 meters long and less than ten meters wide, not technically enough room for an An-12, but it was a calculated risk. The company always retained the best flight crews. I trusted them more with a tight landing than I trusted Karpenko's men.

A full kilometer from the gate, I pulled off the road and camouflaged the vehicle in a sea of shadows. I checked my watch: 0217. I did one last wind check and scanned the horizon, holding binoculars to my night-vision goggles. The pilots had radioed their approach twenty-four minutes ago. They should be in visual range.

"This is lima zulu bravo one niner, come in, over." The voice on the aviation radio in my hand had a thick Romanian accent.

"Roger, lima zulu, I read you lima Charlie," I replied. "Wind is twelve knots at two-six-zero. Track is clear."

I held up my infrared strobe to the night sky and gave it three bursts. It was invisible to the naked eye, but a beacon to a pilot wearing night-vision goggles. Then I took a small radio transmitter out of my breast pocket and switched on the infrared beacons that lined the dirt road. Through my goggles, the landing strip came alive.

"Confirm landing strip at three-three-zero."

"Confirmed," I said.

"On final approach," the Romanian replied.

I pulled off my goggles. I could hear the drone of turboprops, but the sound was roaring in my ears before I picked out the dark shape, flying low against the gray night. It looked impossibly large to land on this two-lane road, like a goose trying to land on a fishing line. The wings wobbled as the cargo plane slowed. It veered to the left, far enough to put it over the field, and then corrected and touched down in the road, its propellers churning dirt and rocks out of the fields, its number two engine passing so close over my head that I could feel the engine roar in my chest. The drag chute deployed and the plane pulled against it, slowing gracefully against a backdrop of trees, like a fat ballerina landing a perfect pirouette.

And then the winch truck tore past me, knocking me to the dirt.

"Fuckin' hell!" I said, spitting dust as I leapt to my feet. At least someone had a sense of urgency, even if they drove like shit.

"The bird is in," I yelled to Greenlees, as I raced to the SUV. "The bird is in."

I fired up the vehicle and raced after the winch truck, the plane still rolling along the road toward a soft curve, the engines powering down. In the distance, red star cluster flares arced above Poltava's commercial airport, the second distraction of the night. I was reasonably sure all of Belenko's men had been drawn to the airbase, but it never hurt to provide another false lead. It's amazing what a lone man with a motorcycle and box of flares can achieve.

By the time I arrived, the cargo ramp was lowered and four armed men were jumping out of the bay to form a perimeter around the plane. I recognized Boon, then Wildman . . .

"I thought this was a hot LZ," someone said.

I turned. It was Miles, smiling broadly, his face painted with night camouflage and his night-vision goggles perched on top of his head. He was suited up, but in desert camo instead of green. The team must have come straight from Libya.

"Ten minutes if you're lucky," I said, pointing down the road toward the iron gate just visible in the distance. "A quiet night if you're not."

Miles signaled to Boon and Wildman, who moved down the road. The other two men loosened the cargo netting and prepared to unload, while the flight crew hooked the winch truck's cables to the rear of the plane and began to pull it backward. The plane couldn't turn around on the narrow road; it needed to be hauled back to the airstrip's beginning for take-off. Once there, we unloaded it like a pit crew. Miles's team formed a human chain and passed rucksacks, weapon cases, communications chest, ammo crates, wooden boxes of explosives, and specialty gear illegal in most countries, cramming it into the fish delivery truck Maltov had sourced from his friend. The pilots looked on, smoking and talking among themselves.

"What the hell is that," I yelled, as a flatbed careened past. The truck skidded to a stop and backed up against the airplane's tail ramp. Beyond, in the darkness, I could hear the *chop-chop* of the helicopter, flying in blackout, carrying Karpenko's family from the dacha. It hovered next to the plane and then landed, blowing rock and dirt. One of the pilots ran toward the plane, yelling furiously in Romanian.

At the flatbed, two men had jumped out and were throwing boxes into the back of the plane. What was Karpenko thinking? We didn't have time to load cargo. It was time to go.

"Leave it," I yelled, jumping onto the flatbed as one of the men tore off the canvas cover of the biggest load. Underneath was a five-foot-tall cube of euros, shrink-wrapped in heavy plastic. It was wise to move money out of places like Ukraine, especially the illegal kind, especially if your assets were frozen. I had smuggled some serious stacks of cash in my day. But even I had to gawk at this pile.

"You have to go," someone said.

I heard the words in my head, like a voice from some distant part of my brain.

"I'm sorry, sweetie," the voice said again. "You have to go."

I looked behind me. It was Karpenko. He was crouching by the airplane's side door, his daughter clinging to him with one hand and her stuffed rabbit with the other. A Dora the Explorer backpack was slung over her shoulder, and her face was wet. To my surprise, so was Karpenko's. He didn't try to hide his crying. Instead, he pushed back her hair, hugged her, then kissed her in the center of her forehead.

"Daddy loves you," he said. "I will see you soon."

As I watched her mother take her hand, the baby boy in her other arm, I wondered if that was true.

I knew this deal wasn't just extracting the family, and it wasn't just flying them back to Bucharest, or Berlin, or wherever this plane was headed. It was keeping them somewhere safe, maybe for a week, maybe three, until Winters's plan was complete.

Or we failed.

"We need to go, go, go!" I shouted, tearing myself from the scene. The plane had been on the ground for eight minutes already.

I pushed the men out of the cargo hold, then leapt to the ground as Miles and the flight crew raised the tail ramp. Sirko appeared out of the darkness, pulling Karpenko away as the ramp sealed. The trucks departed and the helo hopped a few hundred meters to the right, to avoid the plane's propblast. The An-12 pilots fired up all four engines simultaneously, and the sound, and the dust, and the pebbles beat against our skin, as the plane rolled down the road, raised its nose, began to lift, slowly, too slowly, and brushed a treetop as it cleared. I imagined a little girl inside, waving good-bye, wondering why her daddy wasn't coming, too.

"You know the coordinates?" I asked Miles, as he shouldered his ruck.

He nodded, lifted one of the SA-18 missile launchers we'd bought in Libya over his shoulder, and smiled.

"See you at the rendezvous," Miles said, climbing into the back of the fish truck and pulling the cargo doors shut behind him.

Three minutes later, the helicopter was in the air, carrying Karpenko, Sirko, Greenlees, and me. We swooped west over the fields, the brake lights flaring beneath us as Miles and the last of Karpenko's men scattered beyond the dacha's front gate, a few muzzle blasts visible off to the east where Belenko's men had broken free of Maltov's trap. There was a risk they would run into Miles's team on the road, but knowing Miles, he probably had a few antitank missiles ready for the Chechens. Miles despised cheap competition.

"Blow it," I said into the headset, as the helicopter peeled off to the north.

Karpenko didn't hear me. He was off in his own world, probably thinking of his family, maybe wishing he'd gotten on that plane. I thought of the woman in the window and realized I probably would have, if I'd had Karpenko's life, and she'd been there for me.

"Blow it," I said again, louder this time.

Karpenko took the detonator and squeezed. The fireball when the dacha exploded turned the night sky orange. There was no coming back. There was never any coming back.

"Winters was right about you," Karpenko said, as we watched his burning compound recede into the distance.

I thought about telling him the same thing, but I didn't know anything about oligarchs or Eastern European power struggles or even fatherhood. I was only an employee, and Karpenko was only my principal.

"Don't celebrate too soon," I said, Buddha calm, although inside, my adrenaline was pumping. I could never tell Karpenko, or Greenlees, or anyone really, even my closest friends, how proud I was pulling off a mission like this. Even if I could, they wouldn't understand.

I picked up my sat phone and punched in the code. Winters would understand. Maybe. He'd respect it, at least. But after this call, we'd never talk about it again. Never even mention that it happened. This was, in the end, a private victory in a private profession. The job was lonely that way.

But what did I care? Fuck the world. I knew what I'd done.

CHAPTER 17

A half hour after Tom Locke's call, Brad Winters pulled up to the security checkpoint. It was the third he had passed through already, each one a step up in prestige. The main purpose of this last one, Winters knew, was to keep out the lower-millionaire riff-raff from the first two rungs.

"Hartley," he said to the guard, showing his identification. "Seven six three."

The guard looked at his notes, then went into his booth and made a call. "Enjoy your visit, Mr. Winters," he said, handing back the driver's license and waving him through.

Inside the third gate, the lots were noticeably larger, with straight rows of trees and large stretches of green lawn. Riding mower territory, even for the full-time lawn crews. It was early evening—the golden hour, photographers called it—but there was nobody out. Hartley's house, number 763, had another gate at the entrance to the driveway, but it opened as soon as Winters pulled up. The mansion was Mediterranean meets *Gone with the Wind*, with white columns, a Spanish tile roof, and poplar trees. He parked in the circular drive beside the fountain. Glenn Hartley was waiting for him in Italian loafers and a bathrobe. Eight o'clock on a Wednesday night, and the man was in a bathrobe.

"Come in, Brad," he said, extending his hand.

They passed through a portico, past a double winding staircase, into a room with six couches. Texas wildcatters like Hartley made and lost more millions than a Vegas casino, so when they were up, they spent.

"Care to sit outside?" Hartley asked. The pool was visible through the floor-to-ceiling windows, with a waterfall at the far end. "The wife and kids are in Dallas for a lacrosse tournament. Saint John's School, they're a powerhouse this year. The boy plays defense and the girl's a cheerleader, if you can believe that."

Winters didn't know what was so hard to believe.

They took seats on the shaded porch overlooking the pool. There was a porch for sunbathing, too. Winters noticed the white sunglasses by the lounge chair and wondered whose they were. There was lipstick on an empty glass.

"Karpenko's in?" Hartley asked, as soon as they sat down. Winters noticed a bar, but Hartley didn't offer him a drink, not even iced tea. He had flown three hours from Washington to Houston for this meeting. He had raced to this godforsaken suburb as soon as he'd gotten the call from Locke, who was conveniently eight hours ahead. All Hartley had done was walk to his door. But the man still seemed inconvenienced.

"Karpenko's a rock," Winters said.

Hartley pursed his lips like he wasn't so sure.

"I've known him for ten years, Glenn. We meet

at the Travellers Club in London. He has a Georgian rowhouse in Kensington. A ski chalet in Vale," though of course he didn't ski, that was for the horse riding, bear shooting, jet-ski-flipping Russians. Ukrainians were still in the acquiring stage. "Sir Gillingham goes way back with him. They own a brewery together."

"It's called a distillery, Brad. They make *artisanal* gin."

God, he hated this about the Houston boys. The way they chewed on words like *artisanal* with disgust. The never-ending kicking of tires. They were all self-made men who distrusted self-made men.

"Do you want to meet with him?"

"No. Of course not."

"If it's a moral issue, I assure you, we've dealt with worse."

"It's not a moral issue."

"Believe me, Glenn. The man is solid. And we have leverage. There's no amount of pressure Putin can apply—"

"It's not about pressure, Brad. It's about rights. International support for basic human rights. I mean, we were neck deep in Venezuela. Neck deep. We'd been working on that project for twenty years. We'd invested billions, Brad. Billions. Chavez took it away in a day. And what did our government do?"

Tried to assassinate him. Funded a rebellion. Undermined his government.

"Nothing," Hartley said.

Venezuela, it was always about Venezuela with these oil boys. What about Ghana? South Sudan? Nigeria? Hadn't Apollo proven itself there? They were pumping pure unadulterated profit by the barrel load, and all it cost was a few million a year and a bit of bad press whenever the starving locals tried to bunker some oil and incinerated their village in the process.

"Full faith and credit, Glenn. Just like I promised. Full United States government backing, guaranteed."

Hartley was agitated, like the very idea of Venezuela gave him hemorrhoids. "Where are we with that?"

"General Roberts is working State. Ray Brayburn, a former national security advisor, is working K Street."

"I know Brayburn," Hartley snapped.

"I've spent the last two days on the Hill. You saw the stories in the papers? Freedom gas. Friends of Ukraine. Elected officials are clamoring for action."

Hartley waved that away with a swipe of his hand. "Did you talk to Addison?"

"He's your senator, Glenn. We know he's onboard. I'm working on the ones who care about what happens in Eastern Europe."

"The idealistic bastards."

The opportunistic bastards.

"Don't worry, Glenn, we have the solution. We can push Putin back, promote democracy, and enrich America in one fell swoop. There's no reason to oppose it."

"My people tell me Addison might not go along. Too risky. Doesn't want America sucked into another war."

"Of course he wants America sucked into another

war, Glenn. He's a hawk. And he's going to run for president."

"He wants cover."

"He wants to sound tough, Glenn, without having to take responsibility if the war goes wrong. That's the best part of being on the outside looking in. Besides, we both know the senators come last. Right now, it's a social call, keep them informed, so they don't complain when we need them."

Like you, Glenn.

It was almost eight thirty, the sun barely clinging to the horizon, but it was still hot. Winters could practically see the humidity hanging above the pool, and he could feel the dampness on the back of his collar. Houston was maybe the only place in America that made the stifling Washington summers seem pleasant. Two world capitals, both carved out of a swamp.

"Look, Glenn," he said. "I'm sorry about Libya. Sometimes you have to cut something loose when a better opportunity comes along."

"You cut fifty million dollars loose, Brad."

"It was only twenty million, Glenn, and half of that was mine—"

Winters stopped. Wrong direction.

He leaned back in his lounge chair and looked out at the swimming pool and the manicured lawn, a lacrosse net hanging limp in the corner. Nobody ever had enough money, especially in River Oaks, but Glenn Hartley came close. This wasn't about money. Hartley was a cowboy. He had loved the *idea* of Libya. But there were ideas he would love even more.

"Every time I come here, Glenn, I think of Prescott Bush, one of your famous oil men."

"He wasn't an oil man, Brad."

"No, Glenn, he wasn't. He was a dealmaker. He saw the opportunity to make a deal with the Saud family in the Middle East and supply oil to the United States for the next fifty years, when everyone else just saw Arabs in the desert. And you know what happened?"

"He made a pile."

"His son became president of the United States. And his grandson, too."

Winters paused to let it sink in. Opportunities to make money were everywhere. Opportunities to change the balance of power in the world for the next hundred years, and get filthy rich doing it, came once in a lifetime, if you were lucky.

"It's not just Ukraine, Glenn. That's a foot in the door. It's Kirkuk, Irbil, Azerbaijan, Turkmenistan. There's a hundred years of oil out there, just waiting to be set free. I can get you in there, and guarantee your safety. But if you aren't interested . . ."

"Brad . . ."

"We need a face, Glenn. Someone legitimate we can trust. If you don't want to be that face, I can find someone else. I can find someone in this very neighborhood—"

"Easy Brad. Easy," Hartley said with a languid smile, turning on the Texas charm. "I told you last year, and I'll tell you again, I like you. I believe in you. And I'm committed, even after Libya. The team is together, and we're ready to go. You give us the call, we'll stick more holes in the ground than you can count." That was life with Glenn Hartley. Like other wildcatters gone corporate, he believed the world was his pincushion, and he wasn't truly happy unless he was driving in the needle. "Don't worry, Brad," Hartley said. "It's going to happen. One way or another, we are going to nail Putin's ass to the ground."

"I'm glad to hear it Glenn, because I've got a favor to ask."

Hartley laughed. "And here I am, licking your ass."

Winters smiled, just to show he was a good sport. "It's just a phone call, Glenn. I have a meeting with Karpenko's London bankers, the day after tomorrow. The ones who backed you in Kirkuk. I need you to put in a good word."

"What kind of word?"

"That you have my back 500 million percent." Five hundred million was the most recent valuation of Hartley's company, Valhalla Energy Group.

Hartley laughed. "Fine. So long as I don't have to sign that statement. Anything else?"

It was Winters's turn to laugh now. "I may have promised Addison you'd be a top backer of his presidential campaign."

"Hell, I practically promised him that fourteen years ago, when I made him a congressman."

Winters stared out across the pool, watching the evaporation burn off into the sky. Tomorrow morning, it would be back as dew. It made him wish for a tall glass of iced tea, one with a lemon wedge on the rim. What had happened to good old Southern hospitality?

"The boy's got a scholarship offer," Glenn said, looking at the lacrosse net in the gathering dusk, "and he's only a junior, if you can believe that. The University of Virginia, up in your neck of the woods. It's a powerhouse, I hear."

Winters felt it, the rush of adrenaline, something almost like joy. If Glenn was thinking of legacies, he was all the way in. All Winters needed now was the general and the bankers. And Locke, of course. All of this depended on Locke.

"Well send him on up, Glenn," he said. "You know we'll take care of him. Washington is always looking for promising young men."

CHAPTER 18

The Wolf wasn't happy. The fallen tower, the mangled gate, dozens of destroyed vehicles. He walked through the gate and down the access road to the blind curve. The Chechens had chained the fallen trees and pulled them from the road, but it had taken time. So had moving the burned remains of the delivery truck. And the Range Rovers blocking the entrance to the main road.

This wasn't Sirko. The Wolf was sure of that. This was too . . . modern. Too carefully planned. Too clever. Karpenko had brought in help. Someone connected. No amateur could fly a plane three hundred miles into Ukrainian airspace and out again. This was a top-flight operation, and the Wolf knew what that meant: the distant enemy. The West.

He wondered, briefly, about Karpenko's story.

Then he put it behind him. The story here, in this wreckage, was more important. He had sent the Chechens out onto the roads, chasing luck, but he knew they wouldn't stick with him for long, not if the bounty and his high-end extraction team had flown beyond his reach. They were in it for the money, nothing more, and there were many opportunities to make money in eastern Ukraine. Hell,

Putin was basically paying mercenaries just to cause trouble.

But if the Wolf could find any proof of what had happened here, he could pay more.

He turned and looked back down the road toward the airbase, running through the operation in his head. Black Range Rovers, two Mercedes. Ambush with AK-47s fired by Ukrainians, not professionals. C-4. Padlock. Delivery truck. Delivery . . .

"Professionals," Ivan said, walking up behind him.

The Wolf wheeled. Ivan was smiling, like this was nothing, even though half his men had been killed. Even though he'd been *beaten*, at the very thing he'd built his life around. Where was the pride? The professionalism?

"There's no way Maltov did this," Ivan said. The Wolf felt the urge to shoot him, right in his big blockhead. But then . . .

"Who's Maltov?" he said.

CHAPTER 19

Alie had gone to Bujumbura in 2004 for the same reason she had gone to the convent: to get away. Africa was as far from Anniston, Alabama, as you could get, after all, and even in Africa, Burundi was a backwater. It was small; it was poor (the fifth poorest country in the world, with a 65 percent Catholic population, Sister Mary Karam told her, a perfect place for mission work), and it was in the middle of the continent, away from lions, elephants, pharaohs, the Sahara desert, Nelson Mandela, and anything else anyone in America had ever heard of.

"Only the Nile River," Sister Mary Karam had said. "It starts there. And genocide. Burundi is the sister country of Rwanda."

Alie had stared at her blankly.

"The Rwandan genocide—where eight hundred thousand people were murdered. With machetes. In ninety days." Alie shook her head no. She hadn't heard of it. She had only been twelve. The sister threw up her hands. Literally leaned back and threw them up in despair. "You do Burundi some good," she said, "and it will return the blessing."

Burundi *had* done her good. She had thought her black grandmother's crumbling farmhouse in Hale County, Alabama, had prepared her for the worst, but Bujumbura was a city of desolate one-story buildings, squalid huts, and anorexic chickens. People were sitting on the side of the dirt road, selling three or four pieces of fruit. A woman pushed a canister of propane in a ratty baby stroller. The huts were cinderblocks or scrap metal, and there were gaunt people in doorless entryways watching their charity's Land Cruisers pass, just as people had watched when they drove their Lexuses down the backroads of Hale County to some shed where her black father had business, or knew somebody, or needed to chat in the backroom while kindly old men fed her pickled pigs' feet long after that Southern delicacy disappeared from the more prosperous gas stations along Route 411.

And Bujumbura was the capital of this country.

Eventually, they pulled up at a checkpoint staffed by two Africans holding clubs. She thought of the genocide in Rwanda, which she'd researched on the Internet, and the extreme violence of death by machete or club.

Barbaric, she thought, and instantly regretted it. She was smart enough to know that was racist, but she couldn't help it. Dear God, she prayed, as they pulled through the gate, have those men actually beaten someone to death?

The neighborhood on the other side of the concrete block wall was a different world. It was still dirt roads and chickens, but now there were electrical poles and oversized American-style houses on tiny lots. The driver stopped in front of a three-story cinderblock and plaster villa, centered on a trim green yard. In the doorway, another African lingered, this one dressed in formal attire, neat as a pin, with his hands clasped behind his back. When he reached for Alie's bags, she saw that he was wearing gloves.

"*Bienvenue à Bujumba*," he said.

The first floor was wide, but through the back doors, open for the breeze, she could see a cinderblock wall with broken glass embedded on top. There were desks, papers, the sounds of activity behind doors, but the man didn't hesitate or inform. He carried her two small bags up the stairs—*I should have carried one of those*, she thought—and into a large room with a balcony and a queen bed. There was a ceiling fan, mosquito netting, African art, even a private bathroom. The air smelled like perfume and mosquito repellent.

"*Votre chambre, mademoiselle*," the man said. Your room, miss.

"*Tout pour moi?*" she asked. All for me?

"*Oui, mademoiselle*," he said, turning on his heels.

She opened the doors, walked onto the balcony, and leaned on the railing. She was looking out over the roofs, water tanks, and backup generators of maybe twenty similar houses, all within the compound walls. Beyond them was a startlingly large blue sky, bracketed by gorgeous green hills.

Africa, she thought, with a thrill.

"The Switzerland of the equator," someone said, and she turned, startled, to find a lean man in a white suit standing in her doorway. "That's what some call it, anyway. I'm not so sure. Maybe Alsace, I think. But the lake is beautiful." He walked onto the balcony beside her and stared at the view. Alie followed his gaze and saw the thin line, right in the middle of the blue. The sky wasn't bigger here; it was reflected in a lake.

"Lake Tanganyika. Over eighteen hundred kilometers long. The second deepest in the world. Over there," he said, pointing toward a hill, "was where Stanley found Livingstone and said, 'Doctor Livingstone, I presume?'"

It was the first story expats told newcomers, something Alie found even stranger now that she knew it probably wasn't true. She must have heard it three dozen times, or maybe three hundred. When she found herself saying it, she knew it was time to leave. But that was years away. On the first day, she was impressed.

"What's over there?" she asked.

"Congo," the man said. "You don't want to go there. It's dangerous." He extended his hand. "I'm Gironoux. I'm the secretary here."

She would see Gironoux almost every day of her stay in Bujumbura, or "Buj" as the expats called it, but never outside the compound walls. He was a sixty-year-old charity professional, tasked with handling the white part of the business: fund-raising, tours, parties.

She was a twenty-four-year-old fallen nun, who spent her days in the community. She sat with the sick and dying in crumbling rooms, quietly terrified of the legendary African maladies: the fly that laid eggs in your eyes and made you go blind, the worms that fed on your organs, HIV. She shopped with a guide at the Central Market (it burned down in 2013, she remembered sadly), where the meat was covered in black flies, and served humble meals out of a community center. She watched babies and filled out forms and helped women set up small market stalls, until she realized she was so ignorant of the local culture that she might actually be setting them back and begged to teach children instead. After that, she spent four days a week in an open-air, mud-walled church that reminded her of the one made out of old tires and broken windshields back in Hale County, watching small girls weave hot pads and pan holders out of scavenged wire.

I'm helping. I'm making a difference. I'm risking myself, she thought, even though every night she was back in the compound, and every Saturday afternoon she was at the embassy beach. It wasn't safe at night, they told her, and she believed it. There was electricity only in the wealthy pockets of town, and most of the city was dark by the time the rebels came out of the hills.

She heard the gunfire on the second night, while she was having dinner with Gironoux and three other natty Europeans at his villa down the road. They were eating goat stew (she was at that precise moment fishing out a few hairs, she recalled) and drinking Bordeaux when the popping started. She put down her spoon, but nobody else seemed to notice.

"Yes, it's gunfire," Gironoux said finally. "You'll get used to it. Now what do you think of Sister Mary Agnes?"

At least guns are better than clubs, she thought, although now, after ten years in war zones, she wasn't so sure. She met Locke two weeks later, right about the time she got bored with the place.

It was the Friday night party at the Marine House, a Buj tradition for young American expats. No, an African tradition. There was a Marine House near every American embassy, she understood now, and while the size and style varied depending on country, they were all the same: young men living in group rooms, in the kind of house none of them would ever be able to afford again. The United States embassy in Burundi was tiny and decrepit, but the twenty Marines sent to guard it lived in a mansion with a swimming pool, large-screen television, pool table, and barbeque. They had a butler for beer duty, a cook for meals, and maids for laundry. The frat boys at Auburn never had it so good.

Or partied so hard. These kids had gone straight into the Marines from high school, and now here they were, in one of the most obscure postings in the armed forces, where they could afford anything, even on their salaries, since everything was cheap. So they created a nonstop beer commercial: BBQ, music, women, satellite television for their favorite sports, a projector to show movies over the pool. She was squeezing through the crowded living room, trying not to spill her margarita, when she saw him, on the other side of the room, in the glow of the neon Budweiser sign.

It wasn't the first time. She had seen him around for at least a week, including that afternoon, at the embassy beach. It was a beautiful day. She was in her pink bikini, enjoying the tropical sun, even though her golden skin never needed a tan. He had been wearing pressed slacks and a linen suit coat; the man he was talking with wore fatigues. He glanced at her, but to her surprise, he didn't seem interested. Her mother always told her she was twenty pounds overweight, her mom told her a lot of terrible things, but she knew men loved her curves.

It was that cursory glance, or maybe just curiosity, that drove her that night. He was handsome, and sure of himself, but more than that, he was mysterious. In a community where everyone had defined roles—military, charity worker, debauched and/or bored diplomat—he didn't fit. He was older, but not old. Martial but not military. He seemed, somehow, to be all three at once, but also none at all.

When he glanced at her this time, she held his stare, and neither of them turned away. Ten seconds later, she was standing in the Budweiser glow.

"I'm Alie," she said.

"Um . . . Locke. Doctor Thomas Locke."

"Médecins sans Frontières?"

He laughed. "No, no. That was stupid. I'm sorry. I'm a doctor of international relations. From Harvard. The Carr Center for Human Rights." He passed her a business card. Who had business cards in Burundi? "I'm studying genocide."

"The civil war?"

"And a few others, all the way back to the Belgians. There's a long history."

"I'm an NGO worker," she said. "Catholic Relief Services."

"I know."

"Really? Did you look me up?"

"The indigenous shawl," he said, pointing to the light wrap she had thrown over her shoulders. "All NGO girls wear them."

She remembered that she and the younger women had gone to the market together, and she and Mary (and the other Mary) had bought similar wraps.

"You have a good eye for detail," she said.

He smiled. "I know what to look for."

Flirtatious. Maybe. "What do you think of Bujumbura?"

"It's a good place to study genocide."

They must have talked. She didn't remember now. She only remembered the end of the night, when she was half in the bag, wearing a sombrero with little tassels along the rim and fending off an overly persistent Marine.

"Let's dance," the Marine insisted, when the piano started. She had agreed. Why not? But the music was odd. It was wild, rhythmic, and toe-tapping, but . . . strange. Not Marine House style. She was about to complain, when she noticed it wasn't the stereo, but Dr. Locke on a battered upright piano covered with half a hundred empty beer bottles. Marine House had a piano? By the time he was finished, she had wandered over to watch.

"What was that?" she asked.

He turned, surprised to see her. "A fandango," he said.

"From Broadway?"

"No, Padre Antonio Soler. Baroque." He was clearly embarrassed. "You'd like him. A Spanish priest who liked to rock the harpsichord. Um . . . can I escort you home?"

She hadn't been thinking about leaving, but once they were outside, she was glad she had. The Marines had full-time staff, but the house was filthy. She had once made the mistake of going into a bedroom. The stench of floor clothes and sweat almost made her sick.

"I can't believe those guys went through Parris Island," Locke said, when they were outside.

She stopped, waiting, but Locke walked on. No one was allowed to travel in Buj after the sun went down without escort from cleared security personnel. Was Dr. Locke cleared? Where was his personal security detail, the one from the beach?

"I thought we might walk," he said, as if he didn't know this was dangerous.

It was a warm August night. The city was dark, so the stars were bright. She always found it odd to live in a city where you could see the stars. They were walking the ridgeline when the gunfire started somewhere in the darkness below. Someone was shouting. She recognized Kirundi, the native language. It was coming from a walkie-talkie hooked to Locke's belt.

"Sorry," he said, lowering the volume but not turning it off. "Someone reporting the shooting."

"Oh," she said. Most people wore walkie-talkies, since there were no landlines and the cell service had an annoying habit of cutting out for hours at a time. But the reports were always in French or English.

"Where did you learn to play piano?"

He blushed. "I was . . . a bit drunk," he said. "I shouldn't have done that." She didn't say anything.

It was three blocks to the Catholic house, and she figured he'd answer eventually, if only to break the silence.

"I'm a classically trained musician," he said finally.

"On the piano?"

"Violin."

"That's an odd skill for a scholar in the middle of Africa."

"I had an odd childhood." He smiled. "How else would I have ended up here?"

She felt the truth in that. It was her own tough childhood that had pushed her into this forsaken part of the world.

"May I take you to dinner?" It was oddly formal, this idea of walking a girl home and asking her for a date, especially here. She wondered if he would give her an old-fashioned good-night kiss on the cheek at the door.

He did.

He arrived in a Land Cruiser the next evening. She hadn't been out of the embassy neighborhood at night, and she was surprised how dark the city felt. The buildings seemed to slink past, their cinder-block frames solid, but everything else sliding toward disarray, or toward the cooking fires fluttering in open windows and doors, like barrel fires in hobo movies. She found it exciting, so much more serene than the bustling days. It took courage to live like this, she knew, and somehow, out here, she felt that courage transferring onto her.

Eventually, they turned into the hills, and she

started to see electrical wires, and then glass windows behind steel bars and lights behind curtains. They wove upward, the houses nicer at every switchback, and stopped in front of a wide brick building with a circular drive. A sign said THE BELVEDERE. The restaurant was mostly empty, but there was a flagstone balcony overlooking the city, the lights of Bujumbura so few and scattered they looked like constellations on the pitch-black lake.

"They say there's a huge crocodile named Leopold in there," Locke said, picking up on the otherworldly darkness of the water, "with a taste for human arms." They sat on the veranda. The hostess lit a candle. "I don't think it's a coincidence that the main form of punishment in the Belgian Congo was to chop off arms. Or that the Belgian king was named Leopold. The bottom of that lake is probably covered with human limbs."

"You are so romantic," she said, laughing, but despite the talk of severed arms, he was. They hovered near the edge of the balcony, the whole continent beneath them, and drank cognac, because that was what he ordered, and red wine, because that was what everyone drank with French food, especially coq au vin, the best she had ever had. She had dreamed of Paris as a teenager—why else would she have spent her Saturday mornings learning French in a strip mall on Choccolocco Road?—and while this certainly wasn't Paris, it was as close as she'd ever come. Paris, after all, wasn't a set of buildings, but an idea, or maybe a feeling, and being a thousand feet above a black lake, with an empty plate of classic French food in front of you and your hands intertwined with a handsome Harvard scholar's, was the essence of that feeling.

They went back to his hotel. It was a quaint guesthouse, twelve rooms around a courtyard, where hidden floodlights lit the undersides of the trees. He had brought a bottle of wine from the restaurant, and they drank it, alone under the branches, and kissed until morning. They hadn't slept together that first night, or even that next week, because when you're that swept up in romance, you don't want to spoil it with rolling and grunting. You want to spread it out, make it last forever.

"Why did you become a nun?" he asked eventually. "You obviously aren't very good at it."

"Simone Weil," she replied, with a laugh. She had always found it embarrassing that a long-dead writer had changed her life—had saved her, really, at the moment her violent, Evangelical mother had almost broken her down.

"Oppression and Liberty?"

She smiled. He knew Simone Weil. He had mentioned the wrong book. It was *Gravity and Grace*, Weill's tour de force on the redemptive power of mysticism, that had converted her, but Thomas Locke had struck closer to her true heart than any man or woman ever had before.

She should have known it was too good to be true.

Maybe she did know. Maybe she just didn't want to admit it at the time.

But no, she knew that wasn't true, either. Back then, she was too wrapped up in her story to worry about his.

And all the little clues? The mysteriousness of his schedule. The way he disappeared at odd times, for days on end. Sometimes he was distant, saying three words in a whole night. He seemed to go out of his way, after that first evening at the Marine House, to avoid the other expats, especially the Americans. And on that special night at the Restaurant Tanganyika, when their table was tucked away in the garden, under a flowering hyacinth, and she had thought, *He's going to tell me he loves me, that he can't live without me*, the words he actually said—"A former president of Burundi was assassinated right there"—should have tipped her off.

Instead, they made her fall in love with him even more.

She remembered the night they went to the street dance with Mary, poor, sheltered Mary, who was living out a fantasy of her own. The event was officially off-limits, and Locke didn't want to go, he was so tight about rules, but she was going, she told him, whether he came or not. So he had come, and she and Mary had danced for hours while he watched, sullen, a nothing night, until she stripped off his jacket on the car ride home and found the guns strapped to his side, and he had looked up at her, hesitated, and then kissed her passionately, truly passionately, until she fell backward on the seat beneath him. That was the first time they had sex, right there in the Land Cruiser, breaking her mother's first rule about boys, the one about never letting the first time be in the back of a car.

She wasn't a virgin, of course. That was obvious. But that was the end of her second chance, the night she took her clean slate and shattered it over her knee.

"You have to meet my family now," she had said, laughing at his shock. "Don't you know how it is with Catholic girls?"

She meant her work family, the twelve of them from Catholic Relief Services and the coterie of UN officials and NGOs who hung around them. All she was doing was inviting him for Sunday dinner, at least that was what she told herself, but he begged off that first week.

To her mild surprise, he showed up the next Sunday unannounced, in a natty suit that he and Gironoux spent five minutes discussing over predinner cognac. Gironoux was the most precise man in Buj (with the possible exception of their valet Prosper, the man who had carried her bags the first day), and he appreciated a sense of style. This dinner was his show, after all, and with Gironoux effort went a long way.

The conversation that evening was about Gatumba, a UN camp between Buj and the Congolese border, where 166 refugees had been massacred the previous day.

"It's not a lack of capacity," Neusberg lamented. "I know that's the official line, but I have to disagree. It's a matter of political will. There are plenty of UN workers here, not to mention our friends in charity, but what is the president willing to do for them?"

"The president is weak," Gironoux confessed.

"The president is lazy. He is holed up in his palace, drinking brandy, while the country slips away.

That's what happens when you have professional politicians. They're like academics. They have no field experience. No offense . . ." he added, as he turned to Locke.

"None taken."

". . . but these are not men of action."

"It's preposterous," Weiss agreed, "that rebels infiltrate almost nightly. This is the capital city, for God's sake. If we can't be safe here, where can we be safe?"

"Perhaps if the military had better training and equipment, they could push back the rebels," Locke suggested. He was politely ignored. Alie looked at him, saw his sincerity, and shrugged, *What can you do?* The humanitarian community would never condone such an idea, even after a massacre.

Later that night, Locke told her he was visiting Gatumba in the morning.

"Take me with you," she said.

"I can't."

"Take me with you," she said again, as she lay naked in his bed that night.

"It's a bad idea," he said.

"So is this. Obviously. But that hasn't stopped me."

He looked at her; it was chilly. "Some ideas are worse than others," he said.

She didn't know why he took her. Maybe it was her charm; maybe he really was in love. What did it matter? Gatumba changed her. The still-smoking remnants of refugee tents; the reek of unburied bodies. She had tried to turn away, but it was too late, she caught a glimpse of corpses being sorted like firewood.

"It's a UN refugee camp. How could this happen?"

"It happens all the time," he said.

"But we said we'd protect them."

Locke looked at his driver, the military man from the beach. He was American, early forties, angry. He hadn't looked at her once on the two-hour drive. He hadn't said a word until he replied, with disgust: "Who's 'we'?"

Locke pulled out a container of Vick's VapoRub. "Put it under your nose," he said. "It kills the smell."

He dropped her off at the Catholic primary school, four cinderblock buildings with a Burundian flag in the courtyard and an African nun, Sister Mary Clementine, to welcome them in French. Had Magdelena been there that day? She was never sure. There were too many girls to remember just one: on the floor, in the desks, standing against the walls. Too many scared and terrified girls staring with empty eyes at the young American from lower Alabama, who had just walked into their hell.

She didn't want to leave. She never wanted to leave. She had told Sister Mary Clementine that. She had told Locke that when he came back hours later, jittery and unnerved, without his companion. But he had insisted, saying he was the last ride, saying it wasn't safe to stay the night.

"If it's safe enough for them, it's safe enough for me."

"It's not safe enough for them," he said. "Get in."

They argued on the way back. She demanded to know what he meant. He refused to tell her. She blew up over his lack of respect. What did he know about refugees? What did he care about altruism? He was an academic. Academics were cold. He saw statistics; she saw souls.

"I'm trying to help," he said.

"What does that mean?"

Silence. It was dusk. He was driving very fast.

"What the hell does that mean?"

He wouldn't say. He wouldn't treat her like a partner. Or an equal. Or an adult. They rode the last half hour in silence, the world darkening around them. They made the compound just as the nightly gunfire started in the hills.

"You don't understand," she said sadly, as she opened the door to leave. "You don't know who I am."

"Alie," he said. "Wait."

"Please . . ." she was fighting back tears ". . . don't . . . don't tell me what to do."

She closed the car door.

Three hours later, the rebels poured out of Congo and attacked Bujumbura in force. She stayed awake all night, locked in the house's safe room with the rest of the Catholic Relief Services workers, listening to the explosions down the hill toward the presidential palace, the gunfire moving back and forth across the city.

By morning, it was over. She slipped out and walked toward the center of town, where the worst of the fighting had occurred. She saw bloodstained streets, bombed-out buildings, burned vehicles. She smelled burned flesh; after Gatumba, she would always know that smell. There were men throwing bodies onto trucks, and others celebrating in the streets. The rebels had lost. Her boyfriend, the so-called scholar, had somehow been involved.

He left before she could ask him anything more. Disappeared. She never saw him again, not until a chance sighting in South Sudan six or seven years later. She had been so deceived, so embarrassed by her gullibility, that she had never even looked for him. She had spent the next nine hours helping the wounded of Bujumbura, and the next nineteen months in Gatumba, at the orphanage, wondering if she was doing any good. She thought she would stay there for the rest of her life, but when Magdelena, only thirteen, told her she wanted a better life in Europe, Alie agreed to help. She traveled with Magdelena and five other female refugees through Rwanda and Uganda, and up into war-torn Sudan. To document their journey, she had told them. To witness for them, so the world would understand.

It had taken almost a year, often on foot, often for weeks at a time in squalid smuggler camps, and for one long stretch on horseback, her whole body a raw wound by then. But she had stuck with it. To tell their story, to give voice to the voiceless. And because she believed somehow that her whiteness—her half-white Western-ness—was protecting them.

"Don't worry, Magdelena, I am with you," she told the girl on the loading dock in Bossaso, Somalia. "I am with you."

Then the boat's fake floor was fitted into place, the darkness descended on that dank hold, and she never saw any of them again. She had tried for years, working through slumlords and other refugees, through NGOs and networks of nuns, but she never found Magdelena, never discovered what had happened to that poor young girl in this civilized new paradise she had tried so desperately to reach . . .

Alie felt a hand on her shoulder and jerked up, her eyes flashing around the grubby hospital room in Kiev. A few feet away, a frail woman lay still on her bed. A nurse was standing between them, with her hand on Alie's shoulder.

"Don't cry," the nurse said in English. "Her pain will end soon. It is for the best."

Alie wiped away her tears. She fished in her pocket. She came up with a twenty-euro note. She held it out, but the nurse waved it away. Health care in Ukraine was free, but doctors and nurses usually required bribes, even if their patients were dying.

"Morphine," the nurse said, plunging the needle into the drip line.

Alie nodded absently. She had gone looking for information on John Greenlees as soon as Chad Hargrove identified him in the photograph. She hadn't expected that search to lead her here, to this dying woman. It was early, barely light outside, but even in the shadows Alie could see the pain. The woman was thin, ancient looking and brittle, but Alie knew that Olena Kravitz was barely a decade older than she was.

She had been a human rights lawyer. A decorated scholar. A lover of life and, apparently, her husband. There was the proof, in the photographs beside the bed: Olena hiking in the mountains, Olena and John Greenlees together. Happy. Healthy. In love. The kind of photographs Alie had never had.

And still those assholes at the U.S. Embassy called her a whore.

The nurse squeezed Alie's elbow and quietly closed the door behind her. The overnight was ending; the next shift would be arriving soon. Alie wondered if there were kind nurses on that shift, too, and if anyone would stay with Olena the rest of the day. *The husband comes every night*, the nurse had told her. *Just wait.*

He hadn't come.

She thought of the ride back from Gatumba, when she had wanted respect, and Locke had refused. When he shut her out. She thought of Olena Kravitz's husband, in the hotel lobby, yesterday afternoon. A man who stayed with his sick wife every evening, until Tom Locke walked into his life.

She touched Olena's hand. It was bones. The woman had days, maybe hours, to live. She crossed herself, the first time she'd done that in years. She thought of Magdelena, another woman left behind.

If there was one thing Alie MacFarlane hated, it was being left behind.

CHAPTER 20

I crouched behind a rusty hulk of machinery with my SCAR assault rifle, watching two boys explore the abandoned factory, a huge complex built in the Soviet heyday and later owned by Karpenko. This was the place, in fact, where he'd found Grigory Maltov, when the enforcer was acting as a union boss. The direct connection to the client was a risk, but worthwhile. The complex was a vouched location in an unknown city, and it was perfectly placed: two kilometers from Kramatorsk's city center, less than a klick from the target. Walking distance.

Besides, it was less than forty-eight hours until the assault, not much time for the enemy to piece together connections. We'd be fine, I was sure, as long as Miles's team arrived on time, and these boys were the only locals who happened to wander in.

As I watched the boys casually breaking glass, my thoughts drifted back to Burundi. I told myself it was the children—that both clients were fathers, that on both missions I had saved young lives—but I knew the connection was Alie. I thought of her confusion that day, when I left her at her doorstep and disappeared. Her effort not to cry, even though I was breaking her heart. That was her innocence, at the moment of being stripped away.

I pictured her three days ago in Kiev, the first time we'd spoken in ten years, and the hardness under her curves. I had dreamed of seeing her again, had followed her career from a distance as it rose and collapsed. I thought we would reconnect, like in the movies, *bam*, we were meant to be together, we've known it all along. I thought she'd remember the good times: my tiny room in the guesthouse, when I'd run my fingers over her scarred backside, and she'd flinched, and shivered, and finally relaxed under my touch. Our night at the Belvedere overlooking Lake Tanganyika, when we talked about Leopold the human-eating crocodile and her personal savior, Simone Weil, the Christian mystic who advocated a life of giving, and who died of self-starvation in 1943.

I should have told her then, that night, when I saw who she was, and who she wanted to be. I should have told her that I was a soldier-for-hire, but still a scholar. That I was in Burundi to stop a genocide. That the country was in danger, even the missionaries, and especially the women and girls.

I should have told her I took her to Gatumba to show her the real Africa, to prove that what I did mattered, to give her a way to access the purity of purpose that drove Simone Weil, who died in solidarity with Nazi victims. But I miscalculated. I thought the massacre at the UN camp was a crime of opportunity, when it was the beginning of the end.

I didn't know that until I dropped her off and crossed the border into Congo, twenty kilometers away. Our mission parameters forbade it, but Miles and I were tagging along with Gaspard, a trusted comrade in the Burundian Presidential Guard. We found the girl half a klick across the border, face-down and silent, with a grown man on top of her and three others laughing. She couldn't have been older than eight or ten.

Miles sensed my anger. My . . . foolishness. He put an arm out to stop me, but it was already done. A slash to a throat, two stabs to a left lung, a cranium crushed with a rifle butt. By the time I reached to help the girl, I was covered in blood. And she woke up. Somehow, she woke up to the pain, when she was safe, and started screaming.

The jungle exploded with shouts, vehicle en-gines, men crashing into underbrush. The FNL rebels were everywhere, in every direction. We ran. What else could we do? This was no raiding party. The FNL was massing for an attack. There were twelve of us, and probably twelve thousand of them.

Eight of us made the Burundian border. "Go to Bujumbura," I yelled at Gaspard, when we reached our SUV. "Raise the alarm. Make sure the men are ready."

"Where are you going?"

"Gatumba."

I saw Miles's mouth drop. I knew what he was thinking. *The white girl? Now?*

"I'll be there," I said.

How could I tell Alie any of this, on that long, rushed drive home? What good would it have done? Honesty would only have led to questions I didn't have time to answer and a conversation I didn't want to have. Not then, anyway.

But what about now? Could I turn our relationship around? Could I make her see that I had no choice, that it was fight that night, right then, or ten thousand people die, or a hundred thousand, or maybe more?

Could I explain that there are no medals for mercs? No celebrations. That I was on a plane out of Bujumbura as soon as the smoke cleared. That . . . that I could have said no to the flight . . . could have taken the time to talk to her, at least . . . but I was inexperienced, in over my head . . . and I've always regretted not saying good-bye.

CHAPTER 21

I was tired. I could feel the heaviness in my limbs, and this fuzzy nostalgia, these thoughts of Alie . . . I knew that was a product of exhaustion, too. The Poltava operation had been stressful, right up until the moment six hours ago when Karpenko's dacha had gone up in flames. We hadn't landed at the factory until four in the morning, and I was running on two hours of sleep. I needed to rest, gather my faculties for the next leg, instead of watching these young boys beating a steel chair to death with a pipe.

My knees hurt from crouching. My back was sore from the two-hour flight in the cramped helicopter, with Greenlees pressed against my side. Time was catching up to me, both in the short sense and the long. When the boys finally wandered away, I stood up, pissed in the bushes, and felt an obscene amount of relief.

I walked back toward our base. The factory complex consisted of eight large buildings with sidewalks between them, surrounded by a chain-link fence. It was a former industrial behemoth, now a rust heap of tendinitis and trash, with a dense forest of weeds and brush closing in. At the corner of our building—the seventh from the entrance—I stopped, scanning the area. The hangar-size front door opened to a paved area, where we had landed the helicopter that morning. There were clear sight-lines for ten meters, to the trees and weeds on the other side.

I walked around the back and inspected the emergency exit, our secondary evac route. There was a building overlooking the exit, and three meters to an eight-foot-high fence crowned with rusty razor wire. First priority: cut an evacuation route through the fence to the forest beyond.

I entered through the emergency exit, bolting the door behind me. The interior of the building was massive, four stories high with floor rails for supply carts, ceiling rails where smelters had hung, and a three-quarters catwalk. The windows started twenty feet up, so dirty they looked like stained glass.

The helicopter looked tiny, sitting in the center of that vast cathedral, the early morning light falling in square patches around it. We had pushed it inside last night before racking, so that wandering kids and scrap scavengers wouldn't see it. The factory had been filthy then, but Sirko had cleared space for our sleeping rolls and scrounged supplies for protective barricades: a few oil barrels, a wooden door, some pieces of rusted metal that had eluded the scavengers. Now he was sitting with his head down, exhausted, Karpenko beside him using a rucksack for a seat.

The only other comfortable seat was the helicopter, where Greenlees was slumped in the cockpit. The pilot was walking toward him yelling in

Ukrainian, and then with the ease of a thousand flying hours he was lifting himself through the door.
He pushed Greenlees out, the old man falling awk-
wardly a few feet to the floor. Greenlees lay there,
not moving. Then he dusted off his sleeves, pushed
himself to his feet, and turned to face the pilot, who
had jumped down beside him. For a moment, the
scene was iconic, two curved men facing off in the
slanting morning light like a George Bellows painting of boxers, until the pilot slugged Greenlees in
the face, knocking him to the ground.

"What's going on?" I said, running toward them.
"What the hell is going on?"

By the time I was halfway there, Sirko had the
pilot by the shoulder and was dragging him away.
He shoved the man against a wall and punched him
hard in the gut. It was the "wall-to-wall counseling"
of an old school military disciplinarian, and I had to
admire the professionalism of his delivery. Effective,
but within reason. Even today's soft army recruits
wouldn't need to flash a stress card for that one.

"I shouldn't be here," Greenlees moaned, as I
pulled him to his feet and dusted off his shirt. He
felt spineless and slack. A welt was already forming
around his right eye. If my back was sore, I could
only imagine how he felt.

"I shouldn't be here," he said again.

"John."

"I'm too old. I've been out of the game ten years.
When Wolcott called, I thought . . ."

He thought it would be like the old days: stiff
vodka and cherries jubilee.

Greenlees was staring at me, as if trying to peer

into my soul. He looked away. "You wouldn't understand," he said. "You don't know . . ." He stopped, sighed. "I should be with my wife."

He looked frail, almost white, and unprepared for hard beds and cold meals. It could have been alcoholism but it was probably age, not to mention a punch in the face. Greenlees was right. I shouldn't have brought him. But it was too late now. A helicopter flight was too risky, and besides, we didn't have enough aviation fuel left to get him more than fifty kilometers. And forget cars. There was no way out of Kramatorsk until Apollo's ex-fil sixty hours from now.

"Do you need a drink?"

Greenlees shook his head no.

"It's only two days," I said. "And it's only radio duty. You'll be fine."

I watched him shuffle off unsteadily, a serious liability to a difficult mission. What was it like, I wondered, to realize your best days were gone?

"What happened?" I snapped, turning to Karpenko. The oligarch was wearing the same suit and pocket square as last night, casually debonair, his hair slicked back. He looked like he was at the races—maybe horses, maybe charioteers. He probably hadn't slept on anything less than a mattress full of money for the past decade, but he seemed no worse for wear. It was clear he had packed his grooming products.

"The pilot said he was trying to use the radio," Karpenko shrugged. He lit a Dunhill blue and offered me one, but I declined.

"Did he?"

Karpenko eyeing me coolly, as if to say, That's

your man, not mine. He exhaled smoothly. "The pilot's an asshole," he said.

Two hours until Miles and his team were scheduled to arrive. Two hours of holding these exhausted, frazzled amateurs together.

"Nobody touches that gentleman," I said to Karpenko. "Nobody."

I turned away. I was exhausted. I needed rack time, but I couldn't risk it until the team arrived. They couldn't come soon enough.

CHAPTER 22

Alie watched Chad Hargrove dig into a plate of pirogis. He wasn't a fan of Ukrainian food, but he had an inordinate fondness for their version of dumplings. Two months ago, when they had first gotten together to swap information and insinuation, Alie had to talk him into trying them. Now he was eating them for breakfast. Like a real Ukrainian, he said. Alie didn't have the heart to tell him these pirogis were Polish.

"So Greenlees's wife is sick?"

"She's dying."

Hargrove bit into a sauerkraut pirogi, his least favorite. He slathered the second half in applesauce. "I wonder what would make him leave when she was like that," he said, with his mouth full. "Money, probably."

"Or the chance to be back in the game." Men always talked like that: gotta be in the game, gotta win the game. Even if I have to leave the woman I love—or say I love—behind. In her experience, men rarely talked about money in the same way. "Sounds like Greenlees missed his old line of work."

"You mean because he hangs around the bureau? I suppose."

Their two nights together seemed to have loosened things up. Hargrove was no longer playing CIA, trying to keep everything just below the surface. Now he was buying her breakfast at her favorite diner, the one with good booths for private conversations.

Hargrove looked around, spy style, then reached into his briefcase and pulled out his laptop. "Came in this morning," he said as he logged on.

He turned the laptop to face her, and she read the report quickly. There had been a firefight at an abandoned airfield outside Poltava. An armored personnel carrier, truck, and multiple SUVs destroyed. Eight or nine trees knocked over, with extreme prejudice. Six dead, officially, all Ukrainians with criminal records. Pretty standard stuff, except . . .

"There was an airplane?"

Hargrove nodded. "Headed west. NATO logged it, and approved it, crossing into Romania."

"Locke," Alie whispered, and her disappointment surprised her. He had flown in for an assassination. To kill six people, not to mention blow up a house. Why did she care about this man again?

"What does Baker think?"

"He's at a meeting, probably will be for hours. But he won't think anything of it. If your friend hadn't been on my mind, I might not have looked closely, either. And that's how I found this." He pointed at the NATO flight report. "I checked back right before I came here. Already wiped from the system."

Our secret, Alie thought. "Good thing I left early, then."

He didn't answer. She had walked out at three

in the morning, while he was asleep, and Hargrove was hurt. Puppy dog hurt.

"I'm joking, Chad," Alie said, reaching for her *pertsovka*. She always drank the local liquor, even when it was hot pepper vodka. Buying local was a point of pride. "I'm sorry about leaving. I just . . . I couldn't get Greenlees off my mind."

"Oh yes. Good old irresistible Greenlees."

Suddenly, she felt annoyed. "I'm not going to apologize."

"I'm not asking you to." He stabbed a pirogi. "And besides, you just did."

Had she really? Jesus. She didn't want to do this: the loaded banter, the relationship probing. She didn't want to have to work to keep this kid with the Colgate grin from feeling like he had the upper hand. He was just a mission boy, right?

She sat back. She realized the operation was probably over, and whatever Locke had come to Ukraine to do, it was done. But that didn't mean it was over for her. She was a reporter. She could find him. Or at least the mess he'd left behind.

"What's your relationship with Thomas Locke?" Hargrove asked.

First name. Official. Hargrove had done his homework.

"We knew each other ten years ago in Africa."

"Knew each other?"

"Slept together."

"Like us."

If you say so. "We left on bad terms. He was posing as a human rights scholar, but . . . he kills people, Chad."

It sounded so stupid when she said it. And worse, she wasn't even sure it was true.

"You saw it happen?"

No, never. "I didn't need to," she said, motioning toward the reports. "You've read about his work."

Hargrove put his hand on top of hers. He wanted to appear sympathetic, but Alie knew he was jealous. Locke was out there doing something. He was in the shit. And that was why Alie loved him, or hated him, or whatever these feelings were. Did she really feel this strongly about Tom Locke, even after all these years?

"What would happen if you saw him now?"

Alie took a sip of her *pertsovka* and eyed Hargrove, wondering what he was fishing for. What had she shown him just now?

"I don't know," she said. It was a stall, but it was also the truth.

Hargrove nodded, chewing his pirogi.

"I talked to Greenlees this morning," he said. "He called for Baker on an aviation channel. His coding was old but still valid. He wants a CIA emergency extraction. It seems he's lost faith in your friend."

Or he missed his wife. "Did he say where?"

"No. He was cut off. But I triangulated his location." Hargrove smiled. "Kramatorsk."

It struck her that Chad Hargrove was breaking his own rules. Just talking with a reporter about mercenaries was, as he'd say, *unprofessional*. Especially if you had feelings for her. But this was an opportunity for both of them. There was something big here: a story, a second chance, a promotion, an adventure, revenge.

"You have a plan?"

Hargrove nodded. "There's a CIA contract in the area. Training and advisement of a militia called the Donbas Battalion. They're overdue for an inspection, and with Baker ass-deep in paperwork.... It's three hours of official oversight work, at most, and then twenty klicks to Kramatorsk."

Klicks. Hargrove already thought he was a soldier. But he was clever, she had to give him that. He hadn't come up with this plan this morning. He must have been working on a way to get into the field for weeks.

"I can get us there, Alie," Hargrove said, the excitement clear in his eyes. "I have Greenlees triangulated to a tenth of a mile. My question is: can you get us inside?"

CHAPTER 23

Jim Miles pulled his sleeping bag up to his eyebrows and tried to stay warm. Usually missions for Apollo Outcomes were top-notch: first-class airfare, five-star hotels, stuff the army would never provide. Stuff you deserved, when you were risking your ass for the bottom line.

On this mission, they'd already flown the military transport "bus" overnight from Romania, after hightailing it from the Libyan desert. Now they were on their way to some industrial facility in some place called Kramatorsk in the back of a fish delivery truck. Most delivery trucks had transparent tops for light, but this one was refrigerated. The cooling unit was off, but it was still cold and dark, and the only reliable light came from four bullet holes Wildman had shot in the side a hundred miles ago, before Miles could stop him.

If not for Locke, he never would have taken the mission, Miles thought, but somebody had to watch out for the kid. Miles had been Locke's platoon sergeant in the 82nd Airborne Division, starting in 1992. Locke was a butter bar then, a month out of ranger school and one of the few officers in Division who hadn't received his commission from West Point. He'd gone to liberal Brown University, of all places. He was an opera zealot. He liked to quote some chick named Michelle Foucault and received an honest-to-God letter of reprimand from the CO ordering him to speak English at a sixth-grade level. Fucking Ivy Leaguers.

Still, the kid had potential, and Miles had wanted to get his claws in before the officer corps lobotomized him. So he took him to the one place they could talk undisturbed, a titty bar on Murchison Road, or "the Murch," as the men called it.

"You heard the term 'fragging'?" Miles asked, as young Locke picked up his Wild Turkey shot, tipped it down his throat, and almost coughed it back up.

"It means getting sabotaged by your own men," Locke said, sucking wind.

Miles ordered another round. "It comes from the Vietnam War," he said, "when arrogant and stupid lieutenants got troops killed." The bourbon arrived. They slugged back another round. "So troops would roll a frag grenade into an officer's tent, and problem solved."

"What are you saying?"

"I'm saying stop listening to Captain Franks."

"But he's the company commander."

"Doesn't mean you suck his ass," Miles said. "I'd hate to see you turn into one of those monkeyclowns." Then he gave Locke the only piece of advice a commander needed to follow every damn day of his life. "Take care of your troops, and they will take care of you."

Nice delivery truck, kid, Miles now thought with a laugh. *Glad you took my advice.*

Truthfully, though, Miles knew there was no place he would rather be. He'd dropped out of the South Hudson Institute of Technology (aka West Point, aka SHIT) after one semester to become a real soldier, sending his TAC officers into apeshit apoplexy, and he'd soldiered for twenty-four years. CAG, also known as "Delta Force." JSOC, *the* task force in Iraq under the legendary Stan McChrystal. Bosnia. Somalia. Afghanistan. Yemen. He knew more about Arabia at this point than he did about America. The only things waiting for him back home were two ex-wives, two kids he didn't know, and the equipment for his beer brewing operation stashed in a storage locker on the outskirts of Phoenix. The only thing he really wanted, at this point, were Rottweilers and the warm thighs of a woman who didn't ask where he was going, or why he couldn't stay. The only thing he cared about were his brothers-in-arms, and most of them were suffering in this truck with him right now.

"Roadblock," Jacobsen said in his earpiece.

Miles sprang out of his bag, his rifle in firing position. There was just enough light coming in through the bullet holes to see Boon, the best damn Thai ex-special forces op in the business, and Charro, El Salvadorean anticorruption death squad motherfucker, kicking out of their fart sacks and hunching over their weapons, too. Charro was a corruption of *Charral*, meaning "bush" in Spanish, because he had Moses' burning bush tattooed on his chest. Charro was a devout Catholic; he'd fled San Salvador after shooting up a drug gang that had taken over his sister's church. He had prayers for mercy tattooed halfway up his neck and all the way down to his boots.

"Lock and load," Wildman whispered, as the delivery truck started to slow. Miles didn't need to see him to know that Wildman was smiling. The man had a darkness in his soul; he'd once sent a goat into the officer's mess hall out of boredom, not to mention fistfighting several of his British 22 Special Air Service Regiment (SAS) comrades and almost killing a guy outside a gay bar late one night while on leave in Aberdeen. Even when not in the combat zone, Wildman was known to sleep with his SA80 assault rifle for a teddy bear and a block of C-4 for a pillow. The man had a serious relationship with det cord.

"Four," Jacobsen said, as the car slowed. "With Kalashnikovs. Two on the driver's side. One on the passenger. Fourth man at the barrier with a radio."

Miles trusted the men with him in the back of the truck. They were outcasts, unfit for ordinary life, but they had found a home in the team, and they'd saved each other's asses so many times they'd stopped keeping count. But he didn't know Jacobsen, the driver, or Reynolds, his partner in the cab. He had needed a Russia-Ukrainian speaker on four hours' notice, and Jacobsen's two-man team was the best qualified available. And Jacobsen, the more experienced of the pair, fit the bill: an ex-Green Beret from Tenth Group, U.S. Army Special Forces, based out of Panzer Barracks in Stuttgart, Germany, meaning he'd been trained by the U.S. government in guerilla warfare against Russia. Plus he was qualified, meaning he'd been through six weeks of Apollo's training at the Ranch, just like the rest of them.

"Shit," Reynolds whispered into his headset, "they're nervous." Miles grimaced. Nerves were bad. Nerves meant amateurs, and amateurs did stupid things.

"Ahoy," Jacobsen said, hailing a man Miles would never see, and Miles couldn't help but think *¿Donde esta?*, the only foreign phrase he knew. The men were speaking rapid Ukrainian now, two voices back and forth. It seemed friendly enough.

Then the light went out of one of the bullet holes, and the tension increased with the darkness. One of the Ukrainians had put his finger over the hole, or maybe his eye, trying to see in. He shouted to his comrade.

It got so quiet, for so long, Miles could hear someone breathing, and knew it as Wildman, gearing up for a fight. The metal sides of the delivery van would never stop a bullet. If the Ukrainians got trigger-happy, the team was sitting ducks. And those ducks were sitting on a truckload of missiles, ammunition, and grenades. Wildman would be out the cargo doors before that happened, Miles knew. It was only a matter of a minute, at most, before he was firing, with orders or without.

A second hole went black, and Miles rocked onto his heels. The men were shouting now, back and forth with each other and Jacobsen, and Miles slowed his breathing, his finger resting a few inches from the trigger. They could shred the Ukrainians right through the walls, and be gone within seconds . . .

"Wait, wait," someone yelled in English. It was Reynolds, and it was a message for Miles. Reynolds knew the team could only sit in the dark so long. *Thirty seconds,* Miles thought, as the men outside grew quiet. *I'll give you twenty-five seconds, and then I'm opening up.*

And when Miles started firing, the rest of the team would start firing, too. And it would all be over then, one way or the other.

CHAPTER 24

Maltov pushed open the door and trudged into the club. It was crowded, especially for a Thursday lunch, but he hardly noticed. These people were insects, bouncing aside as he shouldered his way toward the bar. In the distance, a woman was on-stage, under a bright light, dancing. He didn't turn to look. He didn't feel the halfhearted grip on his shoulder. He didn't care about any of these people. He was here for his nephew Pavlo, who his sister would never be able to bury, nothing more.

He saw the man in a corner beyond the bar and tilted that direction, not changing his speed. He slipped his knife into his palm, shouldered the last few people out of the way, and slid into the booth.

"Ivanych," he said, landing an elbow as he came in.

Belenko's bullheaded mercenary turned. "Grigory," Ivan said, without expression, like he was just taking whatever the world offered, without caring one way or the other. The piece of shit. "Let me buy you a drink."

"I don't think so. I had a rough one last night."

"So did I. That's why I drink today." Beer bottles covered the table, along with cigarette butts and ashes. The two woman across from them looked as strung out as the woman onstage.

"You brought Chechens," Maltov said.

The big man shrugged. "Not by choice."

"You brought a fucking armored personnel carrier."

"You drove a truck into it."

"My friend died in that explosion," Maltov snapped, leaning in.

Ivan stared at him halfheartedly. "That's what you get for having friends."

Maltov felt himself tense. They were only a few inches apart now, and he could taste the man's hot breath. One thrust, and this conversation would be over.

Ivan laughed. "Do you want to compare body counts? Or do you want to compare allies? You were not exactly alone, were you, my friend?"

Maltov eased back, realizing only then how coiled he had been. The knife he had been pressing in Ivan's side slid out farther than he expected.

"It's over, Grisha," Ivan said. He was smiling now. The moment had pulled him out of his stupor. "We are men for hire. Let it go."

Ivan was right. He was being unprofessional. There was the work, and there was the rest of your life. Your enemy in one might be your ally in the other, so you kept them separate. No malice. No revenge. Maltov had lived by that code since walking away from the iron works and into the world of men like Ivan. It was ingrained in him. It had to be, to keep the wolves from tearing each other apart. But he could feel it slipping away, maybe under the Russian military advance, maybe under the dirty squalor of that hooker's smile. Strong things on the surface, he thought, could be rotten underneath.

"Where did the Chechens come from?"

Ivan shook his head. "Chechnya, *urod*." Idiot.

"Why?"

"Because they were paid."

"For what?"

"Karpenko. There's a bounty."

"How much?"

Ivan shrugged. "A half million euros, I hear, although we were offered fifty thousand, as a finder's fee."

Maltov hesitated. A half million euros? That was nothing to men like Karpenko, and Belenko, and Putin, who was no doubt behind the bounty, but big money to a man of fortune. Five hundred thousand was enough to drink and tell stories on for the rest of your life.

"Who offered you the fifty thousand?"

Ivan smiled. "Why are you so interested, Grigory? Are you planning to turn on your boss?"

Maltov didn't answer.

"Oh, that's right, your boss has run away."

Maltov frowned. "Kostyantyn Karpenko would never run. Never. Unlike your traitorous boss Belenko."

Ivan smiled with all his teeth. He reached for his glass and drank half his beer in a long swallow. His hand was huge. Whatever had been pulling him down, he seemed out from under it now.

"It's a job, Grisha. For God's sake, don't take it so seriously. If you can't enjoy yourself—" he looked at the two women, one of whom smiled back "—what is the point?"

Maltov thought of the first job he and Ivan had done together. Ivan had shot a woman in the head—the reason was never clear—and then gone into a bar and sat down, blood on his shirt, and drank four beers. He had left a few-thousand-ruble tip. Generous, but in Russian currency, not the Ukrainian hryvnia.

"He calls himself *volk*," Ivan said. "*Chelovek-volk*. The Wolfman. What an asshole, right?" Ivan was laughing at him now, or maybe not at him, maybe just laughing. To Ivan, this was just another violent encounter in a violent life.

A month ago, it might have been the same to me, Maltov thought. He couldn't see himself drinking with Ivan, not here, not anymore.

"I've heard of him," Maltov said. "He's Russian."

"We're all Russian," Ivan said. "At least a little bit."

Maltov felt the passion flowing back. "No, Ivanych. We're Ukrainian. We're fighting Russia."

Ivan didn't notice the change in his companion's demeanor. "We're fighting death, Grigorivich," he said. "And poverty. And boredom. The rest . . ." The woman across the booth bared her teeth, and Maltov could feel legs at work under the table. ". . . let God sort it out."

Maltov pulled away and closed his knife. There was blood on the booth, but Ivan didn't seem to notice. It didn't matter. One way or another, the man was dead already. He was eaten up, Maltov could see, with disease.

"Good-bye Grigory Maltovovich," Ivan said, as Maltov eased out of the booth. "Say hello to the *americains* for me."

He watched Maltov disappear into the crowd, then turned back to his companions. He had a woman under his arm, whispering to her, by the time the Wolf's shadow fell over his table.

"Do you feel better now, *Chelovek-volk?* I told you he would come."

The Wolf didn't say anything. What did he ever have to say to a man like Ivan? He threw a thousand euros on the table, the agreed-upon price for information.

"Karpenko is still here," Ivan said, tapping the table.

"You are sure?"

"Almost. Follow that man, as I promised, and you will find out."

The Wolf threw another hundred euros on the table.

"What about the girl?" Ivan said, still tapping.

The Wolf rubbed the necklace in his pocket, his souvenir. He could feel his hand throbbing, but that was how it always felt, when his heart was beating this hard. He threw down another hundred euros.

Yes, he felt better, thanks for asking. But only for now.

He wouldn't really feel better until Karpenko was in Moscow, and all his accomplices were dead.

CHAPTER 25

"Any trouble?" I asked, when Miles stepped out of the back of the truck.

He had parked out of sight and sent a buddy team, Boon and Charro, to scout the area and facilitate the linkup. Once operation security was established, his driver, an American merc I'd never met, had pulled the truck into the building and through to the back corner, as far from the helicopter as possible. In case of attack, we didn't want to lose both transports to one grenade.

"Roadblock," Miles said. "About twenty kilometers southwest."

That would explain the delay. "Pay them off?"

"Didn't work."

"Take them out?"

"Almost. At the last second, Reynolds swapped some NYPD badges and a bottle of Johnny Walker Blue for passage."

"Risky," I said, checking out the merc Miles was nodding toward, although *stupid* was the more accurate word. Reynolds was young, probably late twenties, with a skintight buzzcut and monster arms full of tattoos.

"They were teenagers," Reynolds said with a shrug as he humped a chest of tag, track, and locate equipment from the truck. "Just scared recruits. I thought something rare and personal might keep them alive." I knew where he was coming from; I'd done the same many times in Africa, mostly with old airborne patches. "Besides," Reynolds continued, "they were pro-Ukrainian. On our side."

I glanced at Miles. It was one thing to kill; that was often the safest path. It was another to risk your life, and the lives of your team, on nonviolent options. Other commanders might complain about opsec, risk matrixes, blah, blah, but in my opinion Apollo Outcomes, and my missions, could always use a man with that kind of restraint.

"Welcome to the team," I said, extending a hand.

And that was it for small talk. These were my guys, closer than family, and Miles was my best friend, but we weren't the type for sentiments or hugs. This was a deadly business, and the team was already at it, unloading the gear they'd brought with them from Africa: three boxes of grenades, flash and smoke and incendiary; ammunition crates; several blocks of C-4 and four meters of det cord; blasting caps; white phosphorous, or "Willy P," that could create thick smoke screens or burn through bone and metal, depending on your need; night-vision goggles and flares; a case of freeze-dried provisions; a water filter; and six flats of bottled water, Kirkland brand.

"In arms' reach," Miles instructed, as Reynolds and the older new guy, Jacobsen, carried four M90 grenade launchers, which were cheap, abundant, and wickedly effective against armored personnel carriers.

"Back corner," Miles said, as Boon and Charro lifted out a couple of the SA-18 antiaircraft missiles we'd picked up in Libya. Miles had brought himself some toys.

"I could only slip out two," Miles said, smiling, "but it will be enough."

"More than enough," I said, "considering that we're assaulting a natural gas facility holding a hundred trillion tons of explosive gas."

It was a slight exaggeration, but Miles smiled even more. "We'll make sure the helos crash into potato fields," he said.

Wildman had set an old door on two grenade cases, and Boon was positioning two standard-issue Panasonic Toughbook laptops on the "desk." Add the portable generator and an 8 × 11 metal micro-antenna to connect to a satellite, and from there to Apollo's secure mainframe, and we'd be wired and untraceable on a simple system any half-competent Boy Scout troop could rig in an hour. The fancy stuff was the company's proprietary software, like the encryption codes and hyperaccurate three-dimensional maps of Kramatorsk. Many national militaries used Google Earth to plan missions; Apollo Outcomes had a private worldwide grid. The technology was worth millions, which was why a paper-thin layer of C-4 was hidden between the computer components and their hard-shell case. Airport security would never notice it, but insert a pin in the sides of these computers, and all that proprietary coding would be incinerated in an instant, with only the barest hint of visible smoke.

"Up and running," Boon said, as the maps flipped on the screen.

I looked at Karpenko, who was casually smoking another Dunhill, and Sirko, who was trying not to look impressed. It was either the technology, or the fact that my team had done more work in five minutes than he had done in five hours. Of course, none of the other layabouts had offered him any help

"We need to build better barricades?" Charro asked, as he unloaded and distributed ammo magazines and clips. Sirko and I had pulled a few scraps into position, but Charro was right—they wouldn't provide enough cover, and the factory wasn't an ideal defensive position. I'd chosen it for its concealment and proximity to the target.

"Up to you," I said, as Charro turned back to the truck for another load, Mother Mary's hands upraised in bloody tattooed supplication on the back of his neck, "but I'm getting a couple hours of rack. We have thirty-six hours until the Donbas Battalion comes rolling into town, and as of right now, we've never even had eyes on the target."

"If they come rolling into town," Miles said. It was the mercenary's lament, working with amateurs.

"I don't know," Wildman said slowly, as he worked the chambers on his SA-80 assault rifle with a practiced eye. Mercs are mechanics, always tinkering. "I'm happy we're meeting the Donbas lads. Otherwise, this might all be too easy."

CHAPTER 26

It was nearly eight, and almost dark, as Alie crept through the streets of Lozova, Ukraine, looking for the Furshet supermarket. It had been a long drive from Kiev, but she'd kept busy evading the most personal aspects of Hargrove's questions. What had happened in Bujumbura? What had Locke done exactly? Why had he done it? How? Who with? He was excited, she could tell, not to confront Locke, but to meet him. But he was excited, mostly, to be out from behind his desk and in the field. Even if their first stop was a training school for the Donbas Battalion, this was war. Or at least a lot closer to it than Kiev.

"Have you been in a battle?" he asked, his eyes bright and his speech faster and more clipped than normal.

She thought of the villagers she'd seen slaughtered by the Janjaweed militia in South Sudan, and the bodies being stacked like firewood after the Gatumba massacre. She thought of her journey with Magdelena through some of the most violent regions on earth, trying to survive the gray market of human trafficking. She'd seen more rape and starvation than violent death on that underground railroad from African depravation into European slavery, but she'd seen deadly violence, too.

Women's stuff, the old boys scoffed, when she pitched those stories. Actual news, as she put it. About actual human beings.

But it wasn't war, so the old boy's network never understood. They would run those stories, but only two or three times a year at most. Otherwise, it was *too much, Alie. Too much. If you want to write here, write something else.* So she left.

"No. No battles," she said, knowing where Hargrove's sympathies lay.

"What about Locke?"

It was insulting that Hargrove was only scratching the surface of her life—a life more interesting than most, including Tom Locke's—but she didn't mind. She was used to it in military and CIA company, and she didn't want to talk about herself anyway. Nobody who truly lived this life did.

"There it is," Hargrove said, pointing to a store that looked more like a Food-4-Less than a supermarket. Ukraine, especially in the east, was more third world than European. Or maybe it was just more 1963.

They were late. The store was closed. There were only three cars in the parking lot, and a pimply kid pushing the shopping carts inside. At first, Alie thought he was the only person around. Then she noticed a man on the bench, waiting for a bus.

"Pull up next to him," Hargrove said. He rolled down his window. "Which way to the post office?" he asked in Ukrainian.

"Ten blocks as the crow flies. But it's hard to find."

"Perhaps you could show us?"

The stranger got into the back of the car, and Hargrove signaled Alie to drive. "Challenge and response authentication," he whispered.

What is this, 1959? she thought, unfairly. Her nerves, she realized, were frazzled from the drive.

"What's your name?" Hargrove asked the man in the backseat.

"Call me Jessup, sir. Take the right fork here. We're headed east." He paused, sensing Alie eying him in the rearview. "Who's she?"

"Nobody," Hargrove said.

"Nice to meet you," Alie replied.

The man didn't respond. He was her age, early thirties, and clearly military. He was also clearly unhappy. Alie wondered how long he'd been waiting at the Furshet, since Hargrove hadn't made any calls during the drive.

"How's the operation?" Hargrove asked, all smiles.

"I'll let the colonel answer that, sir."

They drove east for half an hour before turning off the main road. Alie assumed they were close, but after another hour, they still hadn't reached their destination.

"There isn't much activity at night," Jessup explained. "It's mostly daytime patrols, especially with the militias. But once you're in the valley, it's wise to stay off the main roads."

Alie was surprised this was the Donbas valley, since the word implied a low space between hills. Even in the dark, she could see this was flat farmland, with a few scattered forests and open-pit mines. Everything in Ukraine, it seemed, was flat farmland. These people were fighting over the Kansas of Europe.

I guess that's why the world doesn't care, Alie thought. But Kansas mattered, of course, if you happened to live in Topeka.

The destination appeared at first glance to be a rural elementary school on a two-lane road. Jessup directed them to a parking lot behind the building, where three cars were parked out of sight. There were six large camouflage-green canvas tents, further back at the tree line. They looked like they'd been bought from a World War II surplus store.

"The locals know we're here," Jessup said, "but there's no reason to advertise."

They walked to the front of the building. There was artwork on the walls and a long central hallway with doors along each side. Alie saw a monster with a misshapen head and five terrifying claws coming out of each forearm. The face next to it was perfectly round with no mouth.

Jessup turned into a small anteroom. The desk had a typewriter on it. The chart on the wall featured little gold stars. There was a door leading to another office. The principal's office. This *was* an elementary school. Or at least it had been before the uprising.

Colonel Barkley was standing behind the desk with his hands behind his back. He was in his late fifties, over six feet tall with white hair, a beer belly, and the ramrod bearing of a military lifer. He wore an olive-drab baseball cap, military fatigues with a wide black leather belt and brass buckle, and spit-polished Corcoran jump boots. When he reached to shake Hargrove's hand, Alie noticed an enormous Citadel class ring on the same finger as his wedding band. Behind him, on the top of a low bookshelf, was an old-fashioned slicer used to cut the edges off school projects and the fingers off people who double-crossed the mob.

"Welcome to the Dumb-ass," Barkley said in a thick Southern accent. "Take a seat."

Hargrove sat, and Barkley did too, his belly rolling over his belt buckle. He looked like a grandfather, and in fact, he was. Barkley had three messed-up kids back home in South Carolina—he hadn't been there for them, he had realized too late, but that was no damn excuse—and six grandkids he figured he was going to have to put through college himself. That was why he took a few of these six- to twelve-week jobs with Apollo every year, preferably when it wasn't Clemson football season. An operation would pay for a year of college. Twenty-four tours, and he might get them all through.

"No offense," he said, holding up his hand to Alie, "but who's the girl?"

"She's with me, sir," Hargrove said.

"Well, I know that, son."

Alie expected Hargrove to back down. Colonel Barkley talked like Foghorn Leghorn and looked like the executive vice president of a small-town rotary club, but he had served twenty-five years in Special Forces, and that was obvious, too.

"You can trust me, Colonel," Hargrove said. "I'm on your side."

Alie noticed Hargrove's slight Southern drawl and stiff back. He looked like he'd grown a spine. The colonel was rubbing off on him. Hargrove was so young he was still bending to the characters around him.

"All right," the colonel said, dropping the request. "What do you want to know?" He didn't say it with respect, but with a slight air of annoyance. He wanted to pass this spot inspection quickly, like a kidney stone.

Jessup arrived with a chair. Alie thanked him and sat down.

"So how's it going?" Hargrove said. He looked calm, but he couldn't quit looking around, as if there was something to see.

"What do you mean?"

"In general. How's the war going?"

"There is no war, son. There is an armed insurrection by pro-Russian forces, aided and abetted by little green men, courtesy of Comrade Putin. I hope you didn't come all this way to ask me about that, because that is not my job. I am not here to fight. I train men."

"That's true, sir," Hargrove said, taken aback. "But that doesn't mean you don't know how the . . . um, insurrection . . ."

Barkley did everything short of sighing. "You'll have to ask the Ukrainians. Or your CIA bosses. I don't do intel. I do combat. Next question."

Hargrove hesitated. This wasn't going as planned.

Barkley was disrespecting the partnership between the CIA and the men in the field. And even worse, making him feel like a kid. "How many men have you trained?"

"Fifty a week, for five weeks, that's two hundred fifty, give or take. About twenty percent wash out—" he paused "—and that's a conservative number."

"You don't know how many men you've trained?"

"Not exactly."

"But you get paid by the head."

"I get paid by the hour."

"But the Apollo Outcomes contract—"

"Son, my name is William Bedford Barkley. I am fifty-eight years old. I am a former full-bird colonel in the United States Army, Special Forces, and I have been training men in foreign lands to fight for their freedom since before you were born. And I don't count heads."

"But that's not what your contract says," Hargrove said. He wasn't challenging the colonel, Alie could tell, he was trying to gather his thoughts. This wasn't, as he would say, the *professionalism* a young go-getter had been led to expect.

"Jessup," the colonel barked. The soldier was in the doorway so fast it was like he'd been standing there all along. Barkley had his own five-man team. Jessup was the youngest, and thus the gofer, but he was valuable, because he knew his place.

"Yessir."

"Get this *operative* the numbers on how many men we've trained."

"Yessir."

Jessup left. Barkley stared at Hargrove. Waiting.

"I guess there's not any paperwork on the battle-field, right?" Hargrove joked, smiling weakly.

Alie rolled her eyes. "How about a drink?" she said, nodding toward the half-empty bottle of Bulleit Bourbon on a shelf behind Everly. "To show that we're all friends."

Barkley looked at her, then Hargrove. When the man didn't object, Barkley figured he had to oblige. He wouldn't be surprised if the woman was the boss. It was like that these days.

"What training are you providing?" she asked, when she'd knocked back a tumbler of Kentucky's eighth finest bourbon.

Barkley pursed his lips to show his distaste, but he figured he had to answer. "Physical fitness, marksmanship, individual movement techniques, battle drills, squad formations, first aid. The basics. That's why we call it basic training."

"You provide the weapons?"

"For those that don't bring their own," he said. "Who'd a thunk we'd be smuggling Kalashnikovs *into* Ukraine?" He let out a belly laugh as he poured himself another. He waved the bottle in midair, offering to refresh their glasses. No one declined.

Alie could see the headline: UNITED STATES ARMS MILITIA IN UKRAINE. But she wasn't going to write it. That was small beer. And besides, it was a good idea. She'd heard Ukraine was a munitions desert, and the government was desperate for arms.

"How do you recruit?" Hargrove asked, having found his second wind.

"We don't. They've been coming since Crimea went red. Young, old, everybody. The paramilitary leaders split them into groups of fifty and send them here. Two weeks later, I send them back."

Hargrove gulped. "You think that will make a difference?"

The colonel sighed. He'd spent his career in "white SOF," covertly training indigenous forces to fight for U.S. interests. These two probably didn't even know the concept. It was all "black SOF" now, hallelujah for the scalp hunters. If these forever wars were to be won, Barkley believed, it wouldn't be through Americans martyring bad guys. It would be through men like him training others to fight for their God-given rights so that we didn't have to fight for them. Otherwise, it was terrorist whack-a-mole till the end of time.

"Young man," he said, "I believe not only in the right to bear arms, but the obligation to bear arms. I believe in the power of those arms, rightly respected and rightly used. A polite society is an armed society."

"I'm not sure I believe that," Alie said.

"I didn't ask what you believe. You asked what *I* believe. And I believe we are making a difference. Will it be enough in this particular case? I do not know. It would help if the United States government would provide additional funds, so that I can train twice as many men."

This was the standard line. Apollo Outcomes was a business; contractors were taught to always ask for additional funds to elongate the operation or widen the scope. Hargrove wasn't biting. He hadn't even seen the training grounds, and he was already worried he was going to have to write this colonel up.

Barkley shrugged. "The efficiency of my actions is not a calculation I have been tasked to make."

Hargrove started to object, but Barkley rose from his seat, his beer belly accosting them from across the desk.

"It's late," he said. "We start early. And we had very little notice of your arrival. We did not have the time to requisition a feather bed, I am afraid, but I can offer you a bunk in a classroom with my instructors. If the girl wants private quarters, she will have to sleep in a closet."

Hargrove looked appalled, but before he could object, Alie jumped in. "We can share quarters," she said.

Barkley stared at her, and he didn't look like a grandfather anymore, at least not the kind she remembered. He looked like a man who had tolerated enough.

"I bet you can," he said.

"I'm not going to give him a blowjob, if that's what you're implying," Alie said. She snatched the bottle of Bulleit and poured herself a glass. Then she laughed, and Bill Barkley did too.

"I have to admit, I'm disappointed," Hargrove said, raising his glass for another drink. It was a joke, but Alie knew there was some truth in there, too.

CHAPTER 27

Half a world away, and seven time zones behind, Brad Winters walked into the scallop-pink lobby of 1050 Connecticut Avenue, with its oversized plastic plants, and took the escalator to the second floor. He was wearing his civilian "dress blues"—a boxy suit with an American flag lapel pin, the exact same kind that had become a conservative cause célèbre during the 2012 presidential debates. He knew empty gestures were never as empty as they seemed.

He entered Morton's steakhouse, adjusting quickly from the overly bright atrium with the four-story American flag to the darkness of the steakhouse interior. There was a Morton's in every city in America. There were five in Washington, DC, alone. This was the only one that mattered.

"Your locker, Mr. Winters?" the hostess asked.

The restaurant had a long narrow vestibule, with wine bottles forming one wall and polished wooden lockers forming the other. Each locker was a square foot and featured a small silver nameplate. The hostess unlocked the one with "B. W." etched on the plate and stepped back. There was no one else in the vestibule, and if anyone had glanced around the corner, they would have seen that there was nobody in the dining room. There never was.

Winters removed a small box. "Thank you, Sheila," he said.

Sheila smiled. That was her job: to recognize and smile. "Your guest is here, on the balcony."

She walked through the crowded bar and toward a small glass door. Winters followed her onto the patio, a thin strip of concrete covered by a black awning. The patio was only one floor above Connecticut Avenue, so it was loud. The view was upscale chain stores and nondescript offices. For a high-end steak restaurant, the tables and chairs were cheap. Nobody came here for the ambiance, but everybody came. Even at 4:30 on a Wednesday, the tables were full of men in suits, puffing away on cigars. They came because it was a tradition. And because it was off K Street, and three blocks from the White House. And because, in a city that had banned almost all forms of smoking, this patio was one of the few refuges where you could indulge.

The general, Winters noticed, was already well into his indulgences, a half-smoked stogie protruding from his lips—a Cuban, for Christ's sake—and an empty glass of what used to be Scotch in front of him.

"General Raimy," Winters said, extending his hand. "Thanks for meeting me on such short notice."

"It's my pleasure," the general said, without standing. Normally he wore his uniform with all his pins and medals, including his four stars. Today it was a suit. His security detail sat three tables away, drinking soda water.

"Well, I know you're a man who loves his country."

"And his steak." The general smiled. It was true. The man liked his perks.

"Macallan 18, neat. Another round," Winters said, as the hostess slid the menu in front of him. "So how is the Pentagon?"

"Large," the general said.

"I spent half the week in the Capitol building," Winters said. "I could say the same thing." He opened the small box from his locker. "But it would be a lie. That place gets smaller every year."

He removed the cushion from the box and chose a cigar. Nicaraguan tobacco with a Connecticut wrapper. He was a patriot, and Cubans were over-rated anyway.

"What were you doing on the Hill?"

"Meeting friends, specifically the Friends of Ukraine. You saw their press statements, I presume?"

The general laughed. "I should have known you were involved."

"That doesn't mean they lack conviction, General. This is Russia, after all. There are plenty of important people on our side." *Important*, of course, was a relative term. He was only talking about congressmen.

He worked the cigar, rolling the end in his fingers, loosening the tobacco. Then he worked his fingers down the shaft, squeezing delicately. Then he turned it around and sliced off the tip with the cutter.

The Scotch arrived, and he held up a finger. Wait. He dipped the end of the cigar in the whiskey and held it there for twenty seconds. "Bring me another, please," he said, handing the glass back to the waiter.

"You're a decadent bastard," the general said admiringly, puffing dramatically on his Cuban. Below him, cars honked. The light at L Street had turned red, and someone had refused to run it.

"You are what you smoke," Winters said as he toasted the end of the cigar with the torch lighter, turning it slowly, so that it darkened and dried evenly all the way around. He blew on the end, causing it to glow a hot red. Finally, he sucked in smoke and blew it out, satisfied.

"Let's order," the general commanded.

They ordered porterhouses, with a precracked lobster to share, and a bottle of 2009 Bordeaux, but not before another two rounds of Scotch while they finished their cigars. Winters asked the general about this family. He had been working with the general for a decade, and he still didn't know his wife's name. But he knew the general had a daughter up for promotion as a below-the-zone major, and his fatherly pride would keep the conversation going until the lobster arrived.

Eventually, the talk turned to business: Putin's next move, the future of NATO, al Qaeda, Pakistan, and how Apollo Outcomes could solve such problems. The usual. The general had been stationed in Germany for much of the 1980s, and was the commanding officer of the 66th Military Intelligence Brigade at Darmstadt when the Wall came down. That fortuitous posting had gotten him promoted to the Eastern European section of the Pentagon, just as its importance was being torpedoed by the Butcher of Baghdad. He'd been hiring Apollo ever since. Winters had all but promised him a seat on the board of directors, whenever the general decided he'd be of more use in the civilian world. It was a typical unspoken quid pro quo. Every four-star either had one or was angling. Air Force generals go to Lockheed; Navy admirals to Raytheon; Army generals to the mercenary companies. Federal law said they had to wait two years after retirement, but everyone was willing to wait, usually at some think tank.

"How deep are you in Ukraine?" the general asked finally, pushing away the last few bites of his steak. If you finished a meal, you hadn't ordered enough. Winters had barely touched his porterhouse.

"Training and equipping the Ukrainian army, as well as militias on the ground in the eastern oblasts and some intel collection," Winters said casually, as if this wasn't what he'd come here to discuss.

"Contract?"

"CIA." He actually had four contracts, all with different agencies, but honesty was no asset here.

"For counterinsurgency?"

"For peacekeeping operations. But the Russians have three times as many."

"Can we beat them?"

"Yes, if it was only pro-Russian militias. But it's not."

The general had read the top secret reports, and

Winters, of course, had seen them, too. The resistance was homegrown, but the Russians had supplemented it with several brigades of professional soldiers. It was indisputable. They were even showing state funerals for fallen troops on Russian television, under the flimsy excuse that the soldiers had died in training exercises, just like in the old days of Afghanistan. The West wasn't in denial; Putin was openly daring them to act. The West was afraid. That was why patriots like the general were so important.

"Fucking Obama," the general said.

"Fucking Germans."

"Merkel has more dick than Obama and the French put together," the general snapped. Merkel was beloved for her economic austerity, but she had grown up behind the Berlin Wall, and she had a blind spot for Eastern totalitarianism.

"Too bad she's swinging it the wrong way," Winters replied smoothly, knowing the general would agree.

The general took a sip of his fourth Macallan. "What do you need?"

Winters shrugged. "Depends on where you want to draw the line."

The general took another sip. "We're willing to give them the two eastern provinces . . ." He wouldn't on principle use the Soviet term *oblast*.

Winters leaned in. "I didn't ask where our government's line was, General. I asked where *your* line was." He could tell the alcohol was working, although not enough that the general would, on reflection, find anything amiss.

"My line is where the damn line was three months ago," Raimy said.

Winters leaned back and sipped his drink, changing conversational gears. The ice had been broken. It was time for a deep dive.

"We can drive them back from Mariupol, General. That's Putin's immediate objective, to secure a land bridge from Russia to Crimea. We can drive them all the way back to the border, if that's what you want. But it's a commitment. The Ukrainian army isn't ready. Yanukovych spent seven years hollowing it out."

"Sabotage."

"Of course. But the core is solid. Good fighters. Disciplined. And most important, they believe in the cause."

This was the kind of talk generals liked. The kind that implied there was something right in the West and wrong in the East. It wasn't that American flag officers didn't respect the Russians. They did. The Russians were fierce adversaries. If you had said, "The just will prevail," the generals would have scoffed. History had proven that wrong a thousand times. And yet they always believed that, through some inherent defect in their belief system, the Russians were doomed.

"The problem is timing. The volunteers can't fight a trained army, and the Ukrainian army won't be ready for an offensive until June. The Russians are there now, looting the place. We can push them back in July, maybe, but by then, it might be too late. The eastern oblasts are historically Russian.

Given a reason, or inevitability, they will revert to their old ways. And once the people are loyal, or at least not resisting . . ."

He shrugged. It was so obvious, even a general could see it. The Russians would use the popular sentiment as an excuse. They would bite off another part of the continent, and they would never let it go.

"What are you suggesting?"

"We cede Mariupol, but fight them like hell for the rest of the East. That gives Putin the land bridge that he wants and keeps the rest under the control of the West."

Including the shale gas fields. After all, a smart deal meant everyone got what they wanted, and Winters wanted the shale.

The general shook his head. "That means giving up territory."

"For now. But I've talked with Naveen at the NSC. The diplomats are working behind the scenes. Sanctions are coming, full sanctions, including freezing the SWIFT accounts for the Kremlin elite. They're going to work."

"As long as the Russians aren't in Kiev."

"If Putin had any balls, he'd be there already."

The general nodded. Winters was right. They were lucky Putin had lost his nerve. If Russia had steamrolled Ukraine, the Europeans would have folded like 1938.

"I'm not selling you on a war, General. Or a two-month solution. We all know how those promises turn out. I'm talking long-term containment."

"What do you need?"

"One hundred million for the eastern oblasts. To hold the line. Not at the border, but a reasonable compromise."

It was a concession. A new Cold War, with the line drawn west a few hundred kilometers. The general hated it. He even felt sorry for the bastards behind the line. But without a real commitment from above, it was the best he could do.

"Fifty million," he said, even though Winters's one hundred million was only a rounding error for the Pentagon's budget. Apollo Outcomes had an annual IDIQ umbrella contract for a billion. They didn't necessarily get a billion, but they were cleared for that much each fiscal year without having to get specific authorization, and it was only May. The general doubted they were at more than two hundred million this quarter.

"For one year, with two optional years," Winters said. "Scalable to, say, two hundred and fifty million."

"Two hundred."

"I have to stick to my number, General," Winters said. He knew the first number wasn't nearly as important as the second. Once Apollo men were on the ground, he could always find a way to expand or lengthen the contract to the maximum level. "I can't leave men behind. I have to be able to get them out."

The general understood. He was an army man; he believed in loyalty above all. "How long to be up and running?"

"Ten days?"

The general looked shocked. Winters laughed. "Do you think I've been sitting around waiting for your candy ass to come around?" he said with a smile, knowing the general would appreciate his aggressive braggadocio. "All I need is your word on the contract."

"It will have to be Title 10," the general said.

Title 10 contracts had a few more rules than CIA Title 50 work, which didn't appear on public records, even the ones Apollo filed with the Securities and Exchange Commission. Title 50 profits could be declared without any more explanation than "top clearance government work." It was Winters's preferred contract, by far. But his company already had four in Ukraine alone; he supposed he shouldn't be greedy.

Besides, Title 10 offered what everyone wanted: cover. Apollo received official government sanction for almost any and all actions in the area; the Pentagon brass received "plausible deniability." If caught, the generals would deny specific knowledge and blame a "rogue" company for breaking the law.

"I'll have our lawyer contact you in the morning," Winters said.

"Quietly," the general said. "I don't want this getting to the State Department."

Of course, Winters thought. That was always understood. "Just give us the tools, General, and we'll get the job done."

The general raised his glass. So did Winters. Once Churchill was quoted, a deal was struck. Everyone in the military-industrial complex knew that.

"To the last superpower," the general said.

"To the shield of the west."

The general looked around: at the other men, at the suits, at the waiters. His wife was waiting at home. It was bridge night.

"How about some cordials?" he asked.

"I'm sorry, sir," Winters said, "I can't. I have a plane to catch."

CHAPTER 28

Miles lay prone on a rooftop, covered by canvas he had scrounged from the factory, peering through binoculars. It was 0300, almost exactly twenty-four hours before the scheduled assault, and it was quiet. Two hundred meters in front of him was the pipeline trunk station, two nondescript brick buildings and a spaghetti of yellow and blue pipes, each about a meter in diameter. Heavy machinery pumped the liquefied natural gas from Russia through the eastern oblasts of Ukraine. At this station it was compressed and consolidated before moving on to Europe, making it a strategic choke point.

It also meant one stray bullet, and the entire facility would blow. They had to be precise, which was why Apollo sent a Tier One team. And the Russians had sent real troops instead of locals.

"I count three," Miles said. "Probably more inside the control room."

"Roger. Three echos."

"Carrying Vals"—an assault rifle with built-in noise suppressor, issued primarily to Russian Spetsnaz special forces units for undercover or clandestine operations. "Sexy, sexy."

"Roger," I replied. "Sexy arms."

I was hunched over the makeshift desk, with Greenlees beside me. Strewn across the desk were two Toughbooks, my GIS tablet, radios, a flashlight, a half-eaten protein bar, water bottles, maps, my equipment vest, and my FN SCAR-H assault rifle, which I favored for its stopping power. Greenlees sat next to me, manning the radios. I was sketching the facility on butcher-block paper, and I didn't like what I was seeing. The facility's main defense was openness. It was on the edge of Kramatorsk, surrounded by open fields on three sides. The fourth side had fifty meters of standoff area between the facility wall and the closest building. An alert enemy would see us coming.

At least it will keep the civilians safe, I thought. Contrary to reputation, real mercs like to minimize collateral damage. It's cleaner and more professional, and I hated innocent people getting hurt.

"Alpha Two, what are you seeing?"

"Open ground," Charro said. "Too soft for wheeled vehicles. A few sniper holes." He was scouting the field behind the facility. I marked it off as no-go. We hadn't brought any sniper teams qualified for low-visibility operations.

"Alpha Five?"

"Quiet," Jacobsen replied. He was walking the mixed industrial and residential area near the facility, reconnoitering possible avenues of approach. For most of the night, the streets had been vacant, a sure sign of an active war zone. Even in the early morning, there should have been taxis, teenage lovers sneaking out, men coming off the late shift. Jacobsen had even wondered if the power grid was knocked out, until he noticed a few lights in apartment windows.

"Shit," he muttered.

Four men with guns slung over their shoulders appeared at the corner two blocks up. Local militiamen, out for a stroll. Jacobsen turned right, stopping in front of a window to watch them in the reflection. He could pass for Ukrainian, with his stubble and worker's jacket, but a good look and locals would know he was not from around here.

Best, then, to avoid closer examination.

"Four echos, 150 meters northeast of my position," he whispered. "Repeat four echoes, militia I think. Copy?"

"Roger that Alpha Five. Alpha Four, do you have eyes on?"

"Negative. Moving," Wildman replied. He was driving a four-door Škoda, hotwired several hours ago.

"Boon?"

"En route," Boon said. He was standing a few feet away from me in the warehouse, piloting one of AO's proprietary quadcopter drones. It was small, virtually silent, and could be flown from up to a kilometer away with a remote control and electronic glasses that allowed the operator to see through its camera.

"Got them," Boon said, as Jacobsen appeared on the second computer screen. Boon was a Buddhist, and a man of contemplation, at least until the Myanmar military junta came over the mountains and started burning monks alive, and he was still a man of few words.

But God Almighty, if he didn't have a steady hand.

I watched the live feed on the laptop as Boon took the quadcopter below the roof line, so it wouldn't be silhouetted against the sky, then hovered it in the shadow of a chimney. The copter was only a few feet wide, so an unflappable pilot like Boon could fly it almost anywhere: up walls, through windows. *Boon could probably drop it on a dragonfly*, I thought, as the copter's camera zoomed in on the militia.

"Yep, that's four local gang members," I said to Jacobsen. "Ugly, too."

"Moving out," Jacobsen said, slipping out of view as Boon kept the camera on the thugs. They had probably been a small-time criminal enterprise, drugs and protection, but as soon as the shooting started, those kinds of men always found politics. And became more aggressive. These "military patrols" were the reason the street activity was dead.

Sirko said something. He was watching over my shoulder.

"Pro-Russian," Greenlees interpreted, "at least until it becomes more profitable to be pro-Ukrainian."

Wildman's Škoda turned into view, driving slowly to avoid suspicion. By the time Wildman passed them, one of the men was peeing on the side of a building while the others lit cigarettes.

"Confirmed, four local muscle, inebriated," Wildman said.

"Solid copy, Alpha Two," I said. "Charlie mike."

Wildman turned onto the road that dead-ended at the facility's front gate. He had already placed two surveillance cameras. The first was eight feet up a pole, hidden in a tangle of dangerous-looking wires. It watched the facility's pedestrian door. The second was buried in debris on a ledge above a trash container, with eyes on the front gate.

The last camera needed to be high enough to see over the wall into the facility itself. The quadcopter drone could take clear footage inside the walls, but only at night, otherwise it would be detected. They needed to know the movement of men, inside and outside, at all times of day.

He slowed the car and examined the building on his right. It was an apartment tower, two stories taller than any nearby building, and only three blocks from the entrance to the facility. *Perfect.*

He eyed the fire escape. It was an older style: ten feet above the street and not connected to an alarm. He took a right into the alley and parked underneath it. He got out, climbed on top of the car, and pulled himself onto the ladder.

The rooftop was flat, but there were air conditioners and an old pigeon coop for cover, so he wouldn't be highlighted against the sky. From the back, he could see the downtown square in the distance, where militants had set up tire barricades and were flying the flag of the breakaway Donetsk People's Republic. The flag was blue, red, and black, with a two-headed bird holding a shield in the center, but Wildman couldn't have identified it on a dartboard. From this distance, it looked like a rag.

He turned back to the pipeline facility. There were two small buildings, but most of the space inside the wall was open ground, pipes, or pumping equipment. He saw the three sentries smoking behind the larger building—he was close enough to see the flare of their cigarettes—and, less than ten meters away, dozens of pipes full of highly flammable natural gas.

The fools might blow themselves up, he thought, *before I have the chance. That would suck.*

Lying on his back, he pulled the small camera and transmitter from his bag, removed the adhesive tape from the bottom, and stuck it to the edge of the roof. He sighted it in on the facility, switched it on, and held his middle finger in front of the lens.

"How do you read me?"

"Fuck you, too."

He grinned and crawled back to the fire escape.

"Bollocks," Wildman said, looking down. Three armed men, weaving like drunks and singing what sounded like old Soviet marches, had stumbled into the alley and spotted the Škoda. The singing stopped, as they peered inside the car. One took his mobile phone from his pocket.

Not good, Wildman thought.

He crawled to the roof's center, where there was a trap door. It was unlocked. Thank God for teenagers smoking cigarettes. He dropped into the stairwell and ran down, leaping three or four steps at a time. Before he got to the exit, he unholstered his 9 mm pistol and screwed on the large noise suppressor. He concealed it behind his body, then walked out the front door.

The men were arguing when he appeared in the mouth of the alley, but they stopped when they saw him. They spoke, but he kept walking toward them. The first yelled and raised his weapon. Wildman drew and squeezed off three rounds so fast it sounded like automatic gunfire, but a thud rather than a bang.

Two bodies fell to the pavement. The third man stumbled backward in a pink mist of blood. Wildman's shot had gone wide and struck him under his right clavicle, rather than at his center of mass.

"*Ey! Chto yebat!*" the man yelled in Ukrainian as he fumbled with his rifle.

Wildman corrected his mistake, and the man slumped forward, landing on his AK-47, then clattering to the ground. Wildman looked around. Nobody yet. Casually, he walked toward the car.

"Fuck," he said, as he stared down at the dead men. How was he going to fit all three bodies in the trunk?

CHAPTER 29

Brad Winters straightened his red Hermès tie in the bathroom mirror, then brushed lint from the right shoulder of his Brioni suit. He checked his shave. He hadn't missed a spot. He never did.

He brushed his teeth. He combed his hair to the point it looked sculpted, and put an American flag pin on his lapel. He walked into the bedroom of his Manhattan apartment—a one-bedroom on Sutton Place, owned by Apollo Outcomes, of course—then into the living room. There was a bar and a piano, but he hadn't touched either. He didn't turn on the lights. He never did. It was 8:30 P.M. EST. 3:30 A.M. EBS: Eastern Bloc Standard. He wondered, for a moment, what Locke and his team were doing. So much, after all, depended on them. He went to the window and saw, one hundred blocks down, the Freedom Tower. It looked like his mother's favorite cut-glass vase. It was ugly, but he didn't think it an embarrassment, or a sign that America had lost its way. The things that made America great were intangible, and always had been. But was there anything worse than spending billions of dollars for something that looked cheap?

Half an hour later, the town car pulled up to a skyscraper on Park Avenue, a few blocks north of

Grand Central. The guards were still manning the desk, since it was only 9:00 P.M., and everyone here was putting in late hours. Occupy Wall Street had gotten it wrong; the banks had abandoned Wall Street for midtown decades ago. The hedge fund guys thought this hilarious. Dumb hipsters.

He gave the guards the name of the company. They called upstairs. A minute later, he was in the elevator, where he took off his security sticker and crumbled it in his pocket.

Blyleven was waiting for him when the doors opened. He was twenty-seven and thought he was Matthew McConnaughy. His coat and tie were off, his white shirttail was hanging out, and he had an extra button undone for chest effect. He was handsome, and confident, and rich, but he couldn't quite pull off the look. And his wingtips were out of style.

"Bradley," he said. Brad wasn't short for Bradley, but Winters ignored it. "Welcome home."

They passed through the small lobby. There was new art: two white squares on white walls. Winters knew the firm had paid a few hundred thousand at least, or they wouldn't be here. The corner office—his old office—featured a painting of a nurse by Richard Prince. He knew that because Blyleven pointed at it and said, "That's a Richard Prince." Winters didn't know or care who that was.

"Brad. Good to see you."

"Nice to be here, David." He shook hands with David Givens, his old partner, and took a seat in the most expensive piece of plastic money could buy. Hatcher was there as well. The venture capital firm had four hundred million dollars invested at ten times leverage, and this was half the staff. The other half was under twenty-five and in the cubicles thirty feet away, talking with Hong Kong or Singapore. Only Givens was over forty.

There were the usual pleasantries, and a bottle of Japanese whiskey, but it didn't take long to get down to business.

"What happened in Libya?"

"Growing pains."

"Just like Guinea."

"Not like Guinea at all."

"But with the same results."

"Process over product," Winters said, sipping his Yamazaki 18, the upper echelon's whiskey of the moment. "You know that."

"And what is the process?"

"We're putting the right team together: engineers, drill crews, suppliers, security. We're testing methods for staying off the grid. We're practicing for the right hole. We haven't found it yet."

"It's been three years."

Three years was nothing, but it was a dog's life on Wall Street. Three years ago, two of these partners were at Goldman Sachs, and three years before that, Wharton. Patience wasn't their deal, and he wasn't their mentor. Everything old was out, and here, Winters knew, he was old. So was Givens, if it came to that. They probably called him Yoda.

"We talked about a five-year time frame..." Winters started.

"So we're still two years away from striking gold."

"I was hoping for another five."

"Brad," Givens said, shaking his head.

"Thirty-eight million," Hatcher said. Hatcher was the numbers guy. He looked like a momma's boy, but he had a kink for BDSM. Winters wondered if he was wearing latex underwear.

"It's only twenty-five," Winters said.

"Up front, yes. But we've done the numbers. That's our opportunity cost."

That was what this was about. Hatcher, or more likely Blyleven, wanted to fund his own project, but this ancient investment was clogging the balance sheet.

"It's a lottery ticket," Winters said. "You pay a little for the chance to make a lot."

"It's not a lot. Not compared to Uber. It's just a lot riskier."

Kids. They had never lived in a world of ordinary valuations. They were always chasing the next technology, willing to pay a billion even before it netted a million. Except it wasn't even technological advancement anymore. That moment had passed. It was just business models now.

"I'm sorry, Brad," Givens said, and Winters could tell it was true. "It's a legacy investment in a legacy business. No one invests in oil anymore." That was clearly untrue, but Winters understood the point. He was moving too slowly. Or more apt, the firm was trying to move too fast.

"We appreciate the investment in Apollo Outcomes," Hatcher said.

Damn right, you insufferable ass. I made that investment, then moved over to the company and grew it a hundred times over. Apollo Outcomes was no software bubble. It was real. It was boots on the ground.

"If you were willing to take a little more of the company public . . ."

"I'm not." Ten percent already meant too much scrutiny.

"Then we're out of this side venture."

That was all. It was over in fifteen minutes. Hatcher shook his hand, Blyleven expressed his regrets, and the relationship was done.

"I'm sorry, Brad," Givens said, as they walked to the elevator. "But it's the right thing. No free rides. You would have done it yourself."

"No hard feelings. I knew it was coming." It was half the reason he had pulled out of Libya. To force their hand.

"If you want a personal investment—"

"I don't."

"Do you want to get dinner?"

Winters looked at his former friend, but he knew that wasn't quite the right word. More like former colleague. Or understudy. "I can't. I'm on my way to London."

"Well, tell Josey I said hi. And . . . I'm sorry."

Winters stepped onto the elevator. Givens wasn't so bad, he thought, as the doors closed. He was simply an idiot, only forty and desperate to keep up with the younger crowd.

CHAPTER 30

Alie stared at the enormous, pajama-clad ass of the man on the jungle gym. They weren't really pajamas, more like an ill-fitting ninja suit, solid black with a blue-and-gold ribbon tied around the upper right arm, symbolizing independent Ukraine. This was the uniform of the Donbas Battalion, although *uniform* wasn't exactly accurate, since every man was supplying his own. The sloppiness was not instilling Alie with confidence, but she'd seen worse. She'd seen half-naked kids with broken mirrors for jewelry charging tanks with machetes.

The man in the ninja suit swung for the next rung, missed, and went down in the sand, screaming and grabbing his balls.

"I don't know what to say," Hargrove said. "I seriously, swear to God, do not know what to say."

The trainers had set up a tire course for agility drills and six-foot wooden walls for the recruits—no, volunteers—to scale, but otherwise the operation was one officer in sunglasses watching thirty grown men on a playground. Jump the swings. Climb the ladder. Slide down the slide. Low crawl. High crawl. Make a circuit. Do it again.

Off to the side, a group of six was drinking water, two of them bent over with their hands on their knees. Behind them, another group of six was sitting on their rucks with their boots off. Alie recognized the squad assigned to march with their fifteen-pound rucks. Five miles, Colonel Barkley had said. It had taken them an hour and half.

"I don't know what to say," Hargrove said again.

It was the only thing he'd said all morning, but he must have said it a hundred times. Americans had seen videos of al Qaeda recruits training like this in the run-up to the Gulf War and laughed. We were going to fight these dogs? What a joke. And yet, right here, in front of him, American trainers were doing the exact same thing.

"Honestly, Bill," Hargrove said. "To say this isn't what I expected would be such a vast understatement, that I can't even say it. So what is left to say?"

Colonel Barkley didn't respond. He'd been around the world a dozen times, from Indonesia to Latin America, and this was how it was done. Every method had been tested; every exercise had a purpose. Even with the Iraqi security forces, this was the way it was done. The difference was time. In Iraq, the trainers had six months, and that still wasn't enough.

"I have to work with what I have," he said. "I have two weeks to train whatever comes my way."

"But these guys aren't even in shape."

Some were, some weren't. This was a representative cross-section of a modern society, not a Cross-Fit class. There was nothing substantially different about these Ukrainians than any other army Barkley had trained, and there was nothing substantially different about the way he was training them. He wasn't a scientist. He was a mechanic. It amazed him that the bureaucrats still hadn't figured this out.

"My job is not to get them into shape, *Officer*," Barkley said, emphasizing Hargrove's unearned title. "That is not going to happen in fourteen days. I assumed that would be self-evident. My job is to strengthen their minds. To give them the spirit of the bayonet, by which I mean the will to persevere. When I am through with these men, they may not be able to run a mile, but they will have the intestinal fortitude to fight."

"What are you talking about?" Hargrove asked.

"I'm talking about the warrior spirit, son."

"With bayonets?"

"With your bare hands, son, if that's what it takes." The colonel could feel himself getting hot. This was the mission: the lesson that had been taught to him in 1981, when he enlisted, and that he had taught to thousands around the world. Harden the mind. Control the fear. Trust the team. When you lived it, you understood. If you lived like a pussy, it could not be explained.

"I need to see your results," Hargrove said coldly. He'd lost the *sir*, and the respectfulness, of the night before. "Where is the Donbas Battalion?"

"At the front. *Sir*."

Hargrove waited for more.

"Five miles up the road," Barkley spat. "Jessup will show you the way."

They argued halfway to the Donbas Battalion headquarters before Alie gave up. Hargrove insisted the training was a travesty, a swindle, a gross injustice to the American taxpayer and the CIA. She understood; this wasn't the world you imagined when you were at Camp Peary, running obstacle courses and reading field manuals. This wasn't how the military was portrayed in all those history books back in Hargrove's room. But it was how the world actually was. Alie had seen it before: in Sudan, in Kenya, in Niger.

"Locke trained security forces in Burundi, Chad. They prevented a genocide," she said.

"And?"

"They don't even have playgrounds. Three years in that country, and I never saw a single slide."

Hargrove stared out the car window. The guards for the Sloviansk Battalion appeared briefly, waving them through. Jessup, driving in front, had vouched for them. "I don't want to hear about Locke," Hargrove said.

She knew it was trouble when she saw the camp: men in mismatched black fatigues packing trucks, gear being tossed haphazardly, small groups of wandering militiamen. There were far fewer men than she had anticipated, maybe eighty at most, but that could be for tactical security. These days, nobody concentrated troops in camps. Too easy for the enemy to count, capture, or bomb. Except for traditional armies, most forces operated in small units now.

Twenty minutes later, they were gearing up to head out with a patrol. And Hargrove was fuming. The militia was sloppy, he said. The mercenaries— *his* mercenaries, the ones the CIA hired—had been curt. There was no respect for authority. His authority. The CIA's authority. The authority of being . . . right and proper in your work environment. Of being fucking professionals.

"They're going to Kramatorsk," Alie said. She had seen it in the master sergeant's eyes when she mentioned the city. It was only twenty kilometers away. That was why the men were gearing up. "They're going early in the morning," she said, when Hargrove didn't answer. "Mission early. Assault on the enemy early."

Hargrove wasn't listening. He was staring at a group of men smoking cigarettes and cutting up for a militiaman with a cell phone camera. This was the unit they'd been assigned to shadow.

"We're going to Kramatorsk," Alie said, grabbing Hargrove's arm. "That's why we're here."

"I'm going to do my job," Hargrove snapped. "I'm going to make sure these men get what's coming to them. And then, and only then, are we going to Kramatorsk."

Alie watched him stalk off. Of all the macho bullshit . . . of all the wrong times. Locke was out there, twenty kilometers away. How could this patrol possibly matter?

"I suppose you're a soldier," Alie said to the man beside her. His name was Shwetz, and he was their interpreter. He was dressed in black, with blue and yellow cloth tied around his upper right arm. A Kalashnikov was slung incompetently over his shoulder.

"I've been trained," Shwetz replied, handing her something black.

"At the school?"

"Yes. For two weeks. Two weeks ago."

She took the black item. It was a full-face ski mask, with only the eyes and mouth cut out. She shivered involuntarily, remembering the docks in Bosaso, Somalia, when they'd put her in a hood, when she'd lost Magdelena . . . there was no way she was putting it on.

"What did you do before?" she said, handing it back.

Shwetz smiled from inside his ski mask. "I was a teacher. Third grade." Alie could see it. He had a gentle disposition and fearful eyes. "But I guess, really, we are all soldiers now."

CHAPTER 31

Miles and I were sitting on our rucks, eating cold French field rations. One of the best perks of being a private sector soldier was that you didn't have to choke down American MREs—Meals Ready to Eat, aka Meals Rejected by Everyone. It was embarrassing, as an American, that the French version was so much better.

"Reminds me of Tamanrasset," Miles said, in the way other people might reminisce about their anniversary dinner at the Olive Garden or hearing Pachelbel's *Canon* yet again. I knew why he was thinking of Algeria. It was only Miles and me on that mission, and we had played backgammon for three days, while our local contact became increasingly unhinged with worry. We ignored him, and in the end, our man walked right into the line of fire and was killed, as we knew he would. If I recall correctly, I beat Miles 213 games to 62, although I wasn't convinced he was trying.

"Reminds me of Guinea-Bissau," I said, picking up a bite of freeze-dried navarin d'agneau with my ivory mission chopsticks, "when we left Tailor in the jungle." We were hunting a Colombian drug lord that had taken over this West African country, making it a transit point for cocaine going to

Europe. Tailor had made the mission a living hell, constantly bitching about the local prostitutes and his scrotal infection, so when we accidently lost him on an all-night op, we weren't in a hurry to reunite.

"We tracked him for three damn hours," Miles laughed.

"We were a hundred meters away, and he never heard us."

"Because he kept bitching out loud about his scrotum, even though he was the only one there!"

"What a bonehead," I said, working the chopsticks with practiced ease, a calming ritual I'd been using for almost twenty years. Every outfit has boneheads, even the elite.

"I'm glad he washed out," Miles said. "But I feel sorry for his wife. She probably has the clap."

Greenlees came over and sat. "We're just talking about dick infections," Miles said to him, "but don't worry, Johnny, it's nothing you can catch from giving blowjobs."

Greenlees chuckled unconvincingly.

"What did he say?" I said, nodding toward Karpenko.

The helicopter pilot was the one reminding Miles of Tamanrasset, because he was becoming increasingly unhinged. He was a civilian. My guess was that Maltov had claimed to be hiring him for a corporate flight.

"He wants extra money," Greenlees said. "Hazard pay."

"What did Karpenko say?"

"He threw out a number, a good one, but he won't negotiate."

At least he had some spine. Karpenko was too willing to compromise, if you asked me, especially with assholes. Never compromise with assholes.

"Sirko should just punch him in the face," I said, thinking of the effective violence of their last encounter, after the pilot had gone gorilla on Greenlee's eye.

"Agreed," Greenlees said.

But Sirko wasn't going to do it. Not without word from Karpenko. I could tell the old colonel disagreed with his boss's generosity, but he'd spent a lifetime following the chain of command, and if this was how the boss wanted it, this was how Sirko would act. It was disappointing. I thought old-school Russian commanders were bolder than that.

"*Mierda*," Charro said. "Two more."

Miles and I looked at each other, then pushed our meals away and swung around to the Toughbook screens. We'd gotten lucky. The edge of one of our surveillance feeds showed the industrial building where the local toughs hung out. The club was on the ground floor, front corner. It had probably been a workingman's club when the factories were flourishing, a place where shift workers gathered to knock off the rust. But the area had fallen into disrepair as the factories closed, and this protomilitia had taken over.

The club had been quiet, at least for a while, but since 0800 the members had been out in force, harassing passersby and looking for the three missing men. Around ten, they had congregated outside, smoking and arguing. Eventually most of them left, probably to sleep off their drunks. For two hours, almost nothing.

Then, five minutes ago, a low-end Mercedes had pulled up and two goons in ill-fitting, off-the-rack suits had gotten out. One went inside. One, with an AK-47, stood by the door. The second Mercedes, the one Charro had just spotted, was almost identical to the first.

"War council," Miles said.

"How many?"

"Five in the front door," Charro said. "Inside unknown. They've been in and out all day. And there's a back door."

I didn't like it. The muscle had gone home, but chances were, they were simply resting up for tonight.

"What do you think?" I asked Miles. He knew the calculus: leave them and hope for the best, or knock them out now. If we chose the latter, the next hour was our window of opportunity.

"It's a risk either way. When the dead men don't turn up for afternoon cocktails, they'll go looking for them. If they find the bodies in the Dumpster"— damn the Škoda and its small trunk, Wildman really hadn't had a choice—"this place will be crawling with ants. But take them out now, and the Russians may arrive, asking questions."

It was a matter of timing. We needed only a few hours without interference, but we needed them early tomorrow morning.

"Maybe we can distract them . . ." I started, when I caught sight of Boon, who was standing guard on the catwalk, raising his Israeli Tavor-21 assault rifle. Instantly, the FN SCAR was off my shoulder and aimed at the door. By the time we heard the car crunching on the gravel, the entire team was in firing position.

The sound stopped. Ten seconds later, there was a pounding on the door and shouting in Ukrainian. Karpenko relaxed. It was Maltov. When Charro opened the door, the enforcer walked in like a conquering hero, trailing seven tough-looking Ukrainians. The last of his loyal men.

I started to say something. It was ridiculous for Maltov to drive up unannounced, even if he was the one who had suggested this facility. What if he had been followed? What if someone else had been here? His lack of opsec was staggering.

But Sirko beat me to it. He was on Maltov in a second, yelling in his face, and I didn't need a translator to know that he was up his ass about professionalism.

Maltov didn't care. He brushed Sirko off with a wave of the hand and went directly to Karpenko, who gave him a hug. They hadn't seen each other since before the assault, I realized. Until this moment, Karpenko might have thought he was dead. And I hadn't even given the Ukrainian a second thought.

Sirko started to say something else, but Karpenko turned away, his arm on Maltov's shoulder. Maltov was his guy. It was Maltov and his men, I was sure, who had saved Karpenko from the palace coup three days before my arrival in Poltava. Maybe Maltov had always been the inside man; maybe that moment had thrust him there. Either way, Sirko was out. Maltov was Karpenko's man now.

"Double the watch," I snapped to Jacobsen, since we'd still been compromised by the enforcer's stupidity. No sense taking our operational security for granted. But there was a positive side here, too, because I could always use extra muscle, and because Maltov had proven adept at sourcing supplies from locals, and he knew Kramatorsk . . .

I turned to Miles with a smile, thinking of the club. "Third option," I said.

CHAPTER 32

They passed into a town, Alie driving in the rear, following two sedans and a minivan that comprised the official vehicles of the Donbas Battalion patrol. The town was scattered houses, then apartment blocks and small businesses, and finally, a one-story building next to a park.

"We're here," said Shwetz, the teacher, taking a deep calming breath.

He jumped out of the car and started toward the building, as twelve men jumped out of the other cars, their weapons drawn. Several stopped behind a planter, a few against the front wall of the building, while three rushed to the door and burst through. Alie could hear yelling from inside, and then gunfire, and then all the militiamen began to converge, swiftly, as if they were being sucked through the front door.

Alie followed the teacher, figuring it was safer that way. Inside the small building, it was a scrum of bodies. Men were swinging guns, and screaming, and one man was down on the floor holding a wad of bloody paper to his face. A police officer was rushed by, two militiamen holding his arms behind his back, his face covered with blood. Two policemen were on the floor, their hands on their heads.

Two more were cornered in a front room, where a man without a hood was yelling in their faces, spittle flying, the militiaman with the cell phone camera close enough to capture the veins bulging as he barked. One of the two policemen was nodding absently. The other was staring out the window.

Alie grabbed the teacher, who was on the edge of a scrum. "What's he saying?"

"That they are prostitutes," the teacher translated. "That Ukrainian citizens have been paying them with taxes. That they are not getting what they paid for because the police have gone over to the separatists. That he is an unhappy customer."

A complicated message, Alie thought, as more men surged into the room holding policemen, knocking her against the wall. She could see a dozen fresh bullet holes in the ceiling. Intentional? Or was someone about to get accidently shot in the face?

She saw Hargrove in the crowd, recognizable under the hood, as two policemen were knocked aggressively to their knees. The cell phone cameraman caught the triumph, then switched to another corner. There were eight policemen in the front room now, their hands behind their heads. They were not resisting. They had experienced this kind of harassment before, Alie figured, probably from the other side.

The mission leader stepped forward, berating and lecturing along with the civilian, whose voice was starting to crack. The militiamen nodded along. The policemen had their heads down, avoiding eye contact.

"They are shamed," Shwetz said.

They are waiting it out, Alie thought.

The speech seemed interminable, but eventually the men started to chant. "Putin is a motherfucker," the teacher translated with a smile.

The leader chose two policemen, and the militia moved into the street, shoving the policemen before them with their AK-47s. Hargrove made eye contact with her as he passed, but Alie couldn't tell what he was thinking. At this point, after the disappointments of the last twelve hours, his brain might be totally fried.

"Where are they going?"

"To victory," Shwetz said gleefully, heading out the door.

The street was quiet. There was no one on the block except a few militiamen swinging their AK-47s and the knot of men leading the policemen toward the park. It was a few hours after noon, and the sun was shining. Three trees were in bloom. The police station had felt claustrophobic, but out here, the operation was a stroll. A block away, a small crowd of people on foot and bicycles had stopped to watch.

Really? Alie thought when she saw the Ukrainian flag.

The flagpole was in the middle of the park, but the cord was too high. *It must have been cut by the militia that raised the Donetsk Republic flag*, Alie thought. After a few leaps, the Donbas men stopped and stared. They signaled for an older man, who was wearing an antique World War II infantry helmet, and tried to lift him. No good. Finally, someone ran back to the police station for a table. It took a moment to get it straight. Then the old man—

now the symbolic everyman of the group—climbed on top and hauled down the Donetsk Republic flag. Another man tore it off the cord, stepped on the corner, and ripped it in half, or tried to—flags are hard to tear. When three men couldn't do it, they stomped on it, kicked it into the street, and lit it on fire as the man with the cell phone tried to direct them for his propaganda piece. The fire also failed to take. The spectators at the intersection started to fidget.

The cameraman turned to the park. The new flag was on the cord, but the leader wanted to make sure the ceremony was filmed. The man in the antique helmet gave a thumbs-up, then started to raise the flag. The Donbas militiamen began to sing the Ukrainian national anthem, while the cameraman zoomed in on the limp flag as it inched its way bravely toward the top.

And then something cracked, loud enough for Alie to hear it from half a block away, where she'd stopped outside the police station. Even from that distance, she could see the old man totter. A leg had snapped off the table, but the men were holding him steady now, the group precariously balanced.

The singing started again. The flag started to move. And then another crack, and this time the whole group went down in a heap.

It's gunfire, Alie realized, as a third bullet struck the table. The old man was lying on the ground, his crazy helmet beside him, the other three men crawling and tumbling backward to get out of range.

They're beaten, Alie thought.

But then a man stepped forward from the body of

the militia, walking in the direction of the hidden gunman. There was one more shot, but it banged off the flagpole with a resounding gong. The spectators scattered, and Alie saw a man with a deer rifle slide out from behind a parked car and start to run.

The militiaman pointed, waved for his colleagues to join him, and started to run. Behind him, the militia poured out of hiding, following him into the breach. It was the sands of Iwo Jima, on some unnamed Ukrainian square.

The lead runner fired. It was a tinny shot, because he wasn't carrying a Kalashnikov. He was carrying a pistol.

Oh Christ, Alie thought. It was Hargrove.

CHAPTER 33

Maltov stepped up to the door of the club at precisely 1700 hours. It had taken him more than three hours to assemble the equipment the American needed, but he had done it gladly, thinking through each request, so that he would understand how the pieces fit. He was even the one to suggest the garbage truck—a stroke of genius, the American had to admit.

"*Davaite pohkovorymo*," he said calmly, as two guards leveled their AK-47s. Let's talk.

Inside, the club was dank. There was one room with a hallway, clearly leading to a back door, and two windows: one in the front to the left of the door, one on the right wall looking out on a side street. A few lightbulbs hung overhead, throwing a feeble light. Three men sat at a table in the center of the room. One was Vadim, a local tough Maltov had known since childhood. The second was the Russian who had arrived ten minutes ago in the bulletproof Mercedes. The third was simply in the way. Behind them, three bodyguards had their guns drawn. There were cigarettes and glasses scattered on the table.

"*Da?*" the Russian said.

Maltov continued to look around. Bar in the back

left corner with a man behind it. A pool table blocking access to the side window. Empty right front corner.

"*Chto ty khochesh?*" the man continued in Russian. He turned to Vadim and said, again in Russian, the prick: "Is this your man?"

Maltov placed his hands in his pockets and the three guards raised their guns (they already had rounds chambered, the muscle always had rounds chambered), even though he'd been searched for weapons outside. Two more men came from the back hallway, rubbing their noses and pointing their guns like amateurs. That would be all of them.

"I am Maltov," he said in Ukrainian. "Vadim knows me, and he knows my reputation. I am from Kramatorsk."

Vadim nodded. They had been a few years apart in school, and they had run in similar circles ever since, sometimes as enemies, sometimes as friends. Maltov hadn't seen him in almost a decade, but he wasn't worried about Vadim. The man was small. He always had been. This filthy club must have been his, because it was about his speed.

"I hear your boss went down," Vadim said. It was almost a sneer. After years of watching his old acquaintance rise, Vadim thought he had the upper hand.

"I have a new boss. He sent me to apologize."

The Russian looked up with interest. He was young. Too young to be somebody. His guards were young, too. Even if they were connected in Moscow, they were nothing more than thugs on the make.

"We mean you no harm," Maltov said. "We have

a long-term interest in this city, and a long-term interest in your friendship. The three men last night, that was an accident."

Let them think what they want: drugs, arms, as long as it was lucrative.

"Are they dead?" Vadim asked.

"How much?" the Russian said.

"I am authorized to give you five thousand euros."

The Russian snorted. "Not enough."

"Per man."

Vadim tried to hide his smile. He would sell out for too little. The small-timers always did.

The Russian sneered. "Why should we settle?"

Why should you *get a piece?* Maltov thought. *You just got here.*

"This country is at war," the Russian continued. "That's an opportunity. If you have operations here, cut us in. We can protect you from the separatists."

It was what the Americans wanted. They had sent him to cut a deal that would buy them one day of peace. That was all. But Maltov had a longer interest in Kramatorsk. And he still wanted revenge for Pavlo.

"I won't cut you in," Maltov said. "And I won't give you the money. The payment is off the table. I deal with Ukrainians, not pig fuckers."

"Maltov . . ." Vadim said, always a coward. "Be reasonable. We don't want trouble."

But I do, Maltov thought.

"I will be back in three hours," he said. "If the Russian mercenary is gone, I will give you ten thousand euros, as a peace offering. If he's not . . ."

Maltov shrugged. "I apologize again, this time in advance."

He turned and walked out. Behind him, he could hear the Russian laughing. Outside were the three Mercedes and two guards. He scratched his pen, then pushed down on his lapel to switch the microphone on. *Too bad the Americans didn't hear what was said inside*, he chuckled to himself.

"Eight," he whispered, without lowering his head or changing his stride. "Two on the door. Target is young. Black hair. Black tracksuit. Table inside the door."

CHAPTER 34

Hargrove sat down on the curb. Collapsed onto it, really, his muscles already starting to seize up. He could feel his blood pounding in his head. He needed water, but he didn't have any, so he stared at the street beneath his feet, sucking wind.

How far had he chased the man? Maybe half a mile. Not far.

But it wasn't the distance that exhausted him. He could run half a mile in his sleep. It was the firefight. The zigzagging and sprinting. The tension. The excitement.

He hadn't expected that. The compulsion to keep going. The excitement, once the enemy turned their backs. How many had there been? Maybe five. Six. He had only seen them in glimpses, hiding behind cars, running up the street. Militiamen without uniforms but heavily armed. Like his men. Like *these* men, the Donbas Battalion, the ones who followed him.

"Good work, guys," he said. "Great work."

Eight militiamen had joined him on the corner, but none responded.

"They don't speak English," someone said finally.

It was the interpreter. The man from the car. He was a teacher, right? He had a baby . . . a baby girl, was it? It didn't matter. Whatever his life had been, it didn't matter here. They were strangers, heaving on a corner with their guns in their hands. Because of the hoods, he had never seen most of their faces. But they were his brothers. *Blood brothers*, Hargrove thought. First blood. His first firefight. He hadn't hit anybody, but nobody on his side had been hit. Had they?

"Is anybody hit?"

Nobody responded, even Shwetz. The one in the back, the short one, was filming. He wondered if the man had filmed the whole battle—how long did it last, half an hour? He looked at his watch. Eleven minutes! He would have loved to get a copy, but he wasn't supposed to be here, and he wasn't supposed to engage the enemy. It was a serious breach of protocol. But it was spontaneous. An intuitive act. They had shot first. It was self-defense.

He felt for his hood. Still on. Good.

He took a deep breath, his pulse slowing. It had been a while since the last shot was fired, so he could relax. Take a moment. The hostile militia had been driven off. People were starting to drift back into the street. An old man shuffled past, a bag over his arm. Going shopping.

A kid on his bicycle rode by, looked, circled back. Twelve. Maybe seven. Hargrove couldn't tell his age, only that he was young. The boy stopped and stared. He looked nervous, until one of the militiamen started chatting with him—the older man with the antique helmet who had led the chant about Putin.

The man stood up and went into the shop. They

were sitting in front of a shop. Hargrove was surprised he hadn't realized that. He looked around. They were in a residential neighborhood in a small town . . . what town were they in?

He heard yelling, and instantly, he was alert, clutching his pistol.

It was only the militiamen, saying good-bye to the boy on the bicycle. The boy was pedaling away, waving, a smile on his face. *An odd kid*, Hargrove thought. He hadn't said much. But then Hargrove realized what they must have looked like, nine men in masks with AK-47s, sitting on a neighborhood corner. It had taken courage to come up to them. He never would have done it when he was a boy. But then again, he never would have seen masked gunmen in Centennial, Colorado.

A bell rang, causing Hargrove to jerk his pistol into firing position. It was the chime on a door, the old man coming out of the store. One of the militiamen was following the kid, shouting for him. The man was holding a bag, but the boy was gone. It was a backpack, the kind Hargrove had carried himself, in elementary school. The boy must have been in elementary school. Was it a school day? No. There was no school. School was cancelled.

"Is that the kind of kid you taught?" he asked the interpreter-teacher.

"I can't tell," Shwetz said sadly.

They were doing the right thing. The boy was proof. The Donbas Battalion may have seemed out of shape and poorly trained, but they had charged into gunfire. They had cleared this neighborhood of separatists. He watched the man with the backpack.

He watched the older man look down at the bottle of Coke in his hand, obviously intended for the boy, but all that was left of him was the backpack and a cell phone. The boy had left his cell phone.

They would give it back, Hargrove decided. They would find the boy and return his backpack and cell phone, because they weren't just fighters. They were liberators. They were fighting for these people. Not for ideology, or politics, but for the ordinary people and their ordinary lives.

He looked up at the Soviet-style apartments. The buildings were dull, yes, but the people were proud. He could see their colorful curtains. Their freshly painted shutters. There were flags, mostly Donetsk Republic, but that was to be expected, they had only five minutes ago liberated this block, using the spirit of the bayonet, of course, Sergeant Barkley had been on to something there, but also the spirit of compassion. And freedom. And self-determination. Everything he had learned in his CIA training program.

He never saw the missile. He saw the old man with the antique helmet holding the cell phone, walking toward him. Then a shock wave, a huge noise, and the man was gone, and Hargrove was rolling on the pavement, covered in glass and blood, the ringing in his ears erasing the cacophony of car alarms.

He never made the connection: the tracking function on the cell phone, the targeting mechanism of the missile. He felt the blast, saw blood spray a building. The windows were blown out. He was lying in blood. There was blood on the sidewalk, blood in his hand, and a hand under the curb.

How could a severed hand be under a curb, and what had happened to the curb? He looked away. The top of the Coke bottle had been torn off, and it was lying in the street, the liquid pouring out, foamy and brown.

He sat up. There was a man screaming into a radio. The car alarms were pummeling. There was a car, its tires flattened by shrapnel, with five men crouched behind it. His men. The Donbas Battalion. They were firing, and there were bullets coming back, but his men were in a perfect firing formation, holding their ground. They were real soldiers, brave men who stood and fought for their country.

The old man was dead. So was the teacher. He was lying on his back in the road, with a hole in his head.

No, it wasn't Shwetz. Shwetz was behind the car, firing at the enemy. It was some other teacher. Or butcher. Or baker. Someone else whose family would receive a video of their last moments. If the cameraman made it out alive.

And he would, Hargrove was sure of that. The Donbas men were disciplined. They were *right*. There was no way a separatist militia could push these soldiers back.

Then he saw the T-72 tank come around the corner, crumpling a car in its path.

"Get outta here!" he yelled in English to no one in particular, frantically searching for something to take out the tank. He tried to grab an assault rifle from the dead man, but it slipped out of his hands. He tried again, and again it was jerked away. It was still strapped to the man's shoulder.

He tried to run. He tried to pull away and get the hell out, but his feet kept slipping on the blood, and then he was falling backward, falling . . .

No. He was being dragged backward. Someone was pulling him. He could feel the hand on his throat, and he couldn't breathe, until he was in a car, in the backseat, being taken away. Kidnapped. Tortured because he was an American, because he was CIA . . .

He kicked the door, but his knees buckled. He tried to grab the seat, but his hands were slick. He grabbed for his CIA service pistol but fumbled it. His shirt was slick. His stomach was covered in blood. He'd been shot.

"I've been shot," he screamed. "I'm covered with blood."

He heard the brakes, and he was thrown violently forward, then bounced back onto the seat. He had time to see the fist a half second before it hit his face.

"Shut the fuck up," the man said. Then they were moving again, faster this time. Hargrove didn't know what to do. He couldn't move. He was too stunned to talk, or think, or even make a sound . . .

"Quit screaming. You're not hurt."

Hargrove complied. He didn't even know he'd been screaming. He felt his stomach. He didn't know what he was feeling for, a hole maybe, but there was no hole. He was sore, but not split. *It's someone else's blood*, he thought.

"Alie," he said.

"Shut up," the driver said again.

"You speak English."

"Don't be an asshole."

Hargrove sat up. The driver spoke English. The driver was . . . Sergeant Barkley's go-fer, what was his name? Jesus. No, Jessup. What was Jessup doing here?

"You're Jessup?"

The man didn't answer.

"What are you doing here?"

"Rescuing you."

What about the other men? "What about the other men? The Ukrainians."

Jessup shook his head. "Can't be done. Only you."

"But I'm not an asset . . ."

"No shit. You're a liability."

They drove in silence, Hargrove wasn't sure for how long. He kept thinking of the old man with the bag. The kid on the bicycle. The missile. The Coke.

"Good men got killed because of you," Jessup said.

It was true. Hargrove knew that, and he felt ashamed. "And Alie?"

Jessup didn't say anything for three or four blocks, until the town started to recede. Hargrove was sure the man wanted to punch him again. Was it the ambushed men? The botched mission? Or was it him? Was he asking the wrong questions? Was Alie dead?

"Your girlfriend left you fifteen minutes ago," Jessup said.

CHAPTER 35

"It's a go," I said into my headset, as I watched Maltov walk away from the club. I had hoped the payment would work. Truly, it was the best option. But luck wasn't on our side. At least we had given them a chance.

I started humming Verdi's *Requiem* as I moved into position. It was an instinct, a desire to find something that calmed me. For some guys, it was heavy metal. For others, the Lord's Prayer. For me, today, it was the terrifying "Dies Irae" from Verdi's death mass, a work that defined the relationship between man and his mortality, and thus his maker. This music, like so many classical works from my violin playing days, was etched into my soul. It made me feel like death incarnate.

I lifted my SCAR rifle and prepared to run. On the eighth note, the garbage truck accelerated past Maltov, who was a block from the club and still walking away, and then past my position in the alley, one of Maltov's boys at the wheel. The guards had their eyes on Maltov; by the time they realized the garbage truck wasn't stopping, it was too late. Twelve seconds into the *Requiem*, the truck smashed the club like a battering ram, collapsing half the front wall.

We were shock and awe before the dust could settle, throwing flashbangs and smoke grenades of various colors as we poured into the breech. Charro pounded a guard in the head, Boon high-kicked the second in the solar plexus, and we leapt inside as the music frenzied at thirty seconds, our gas masks on and laser scopes dancing in the smoke. *Pop. Pop. Pop.* I could hear precision shooting, incapacitating the guards.

I looked for the black tracksuit, my laser scope flashing through the smoke, the violent music in my head focusing my mind. I found the Russian on his back behind an overturned table and put a bullet in his shoulder, close enough that the muzzle flash would sear. I stomped his shoulder, snapping his clavicle, and he shrieked in pain. Killing the leader would incite the pack; hearing him screaming in pain would terrify them. I dropped a playing card on his chest. The King of Hearts. It didn't mean anything; it was just meant to confuse. And it was some badass shit.

"Nastupnoho razu," I said. Next time. The only two words I knew in Ukrainian, taught to me by Sirko an hour ago.

I stepped past the Russian. The smoke was thick, the music in my head winding down. It was time to go. I looked for my team, found them, and fired one more shot at a bodyguard moving in the smoke. Then I was in the back hallway and out the back door and running down the street, following my evac route.

Two minutes, and everything was finished. Death had passed, the shadow moving on. The entire team was at the rally point, safe and accounted for. I nodded to Miles; he nodded back. We moved out in formation, silently, down the alley and out of sight, and before anyone could figure out what had happened, we were gone.

CHAPTER 36

Winters picked up the phone. "Yes," he said.

It was Wolcott. It was 1000 EST, so Wolcott was in. That was a rule at Apollo: Wolcott was always in. "It's getting ragged," Wolcott said. "Extracurricular activity a few blocks south."

"Is everything on schedule?"

"For now."

"Let me know."

Winters hung up. That was another rule of the company. Winters hung up whenever he felt like it.

1500 London time, *two hours until the meeting*, he thought, instinctively straightening his tie, cobalt blue with yellow parachutes, in honor of this club. He had flown overnight from New York to London, five hours' time difference, and he was feeling the lack of adequate rest. He should be napping. But he couldn't sleep, not with this much on the line, so he had fallen back on his familiar routine, and that meant a drink at the Special Forces Club.

There was a time when gaining admittance to this redbrick row house on a quiet street in central London was an honor. It was the social hub of the international mercenary community, and at that time, he had enjoyed the exclusivity. The history. Now he could see how shabby it was: threadbare furniture, a stain on the carpet. Imperial decrepitude.

He looked up. There on the wall, staring down from his portrait, was Sir David Stirling, the father of them all. The founder of the SAS in 1941 and, more important, Watchguard, the first modern mercenary company. Under the portrait was the SAS motto: "Who Dares Wins." It was catchy, but he preferred the photo in the entry lobby of Churchill giving his famous "set Europe on fire" speech. As the Navy SEALs said: "The only easy day was yesterday."

1800 Ukrainian time, Winters thought, counting time zones. Ten hours until the Donbas Battalion arrived. Eleven until the press junket flew in.

Eleven hours, he thought. Eleven hours until Karpenko's victory speech, and then he could leave this fraying place behind. For a higher place. A more powerful place. Or maybe he should say, a deeper state.

CHAPTER 37

It wasn't hard to find Kramatorsk, since it was only about twenty kilometers from the little town with the police station. Alie had expected roadblocks and soldiers, but the road was empty, the farmland punctured by two rusty factories with grasping pipes and defiant smokestacks, like south Alabama without the mosquitos. Actually, she wasn't sure about the mosquitos.

She rubbed her temples, fighting the headache. She felt cotton in her mouth, and she wondered about the last time she'd eaten. Early morning at the elementary school, she remembered, long before Hargrove had gone cowboy in the park. He was a good guy. Smart. A true believer. He wanted to work his way up in his country's service: recruit spies, defeat enemies, and defend the flag in the pat way history books and novels portrayed.

But he was impatient, as young men often are. He wanted to be Bill Donovan, the legendary head of the OSS during World War II, but act like Tom Locke, the mercenary, because he thought Locke was changing the world. *Maybe he is*, Alie thought, although she wasn't so sure.

To be like Locke, though, you had to understand where he came from. You had to know the scars, the bullet hole in the back of his left shoulder and the cut across his ribs, and all those fucked-up places in his soul. Hargrove was too fresh and innocent. His only scar was the tooth he'd chipped doing a keg stand in college, and even that had been immaculately repaired.

She hated leaving him behind. It felt like Locke and innocent Alie in Burundi, with the roles reversed. But she knew that wasn't true. She'd see Hargrove again, probably tonight, after he'd gotten his cowboy fix and rejoined the main body of the Donbas Battalion.

She could have waited with the milita for whatever was coming. She could have found Locke that way, she was sure of it. But she had a feeling the militiamen were on the outside of whatever was really happening here, and she wanted to be inside. She wanted to find Locke before the action went down. It was the only way to get the real story, and that was what she was here for, right?

Maybe she was impatient, too. Maybe she should have waited. After all, Hargrove knew where Locke was. He had him triangulated to within a hundred meters. But he had refused to tell her the location, even on their long drive together. Maybe Hargrove suspected that, with enough information, Alie would take the car and run.

Funny, because she didn't realize that herself, until it was already done.

She pulled into a bar. Bars were a good place to collect information, but this one was mostly empty, even at 5:30 on a Friday afternoon. It was tidy, with strings of yellow flags advertising Obolon, a local beer. There was an unused Obolon dartboard, and two pensioners drinking out of Obolon glasses. The bartender cheerfully wiped a spot with an Obolon towel, chatting in rapid Ukrainian, but his smile didn't diminish the depression that hung over the place.

She ordered a pint of Obolon with a *horilka* back. When in Ukraine, drink as the locals drink. She drank. The bartender had lost his enthusiasm when he realized she didn't speak Ukrainian, but she called him over for a second round.

"Food?" she said, miming the act of eating.

The bartender pointed to a display of Lay's potato chips.

"Ukrainian?" She moved her hands like she was holding an assault rifle. "Militia?"

He didn't understand. Some people, when they don't know a language, don't even try. The formerly cheerful bartender was one of them.

She made the motion of a gun again. "Kiev?"

He shook his head. "Donetsk."

She showed him the picture of Locke on her phone, taken in the Kiev hotel bar two days ago.

"American?" she said, motioning to ask if he had seen him.

The bartender shook his head no.

Alie drank her second round of local beer and liquor and ate the bag of chips. She left hryvnias on the counter along with her contact information—in case he saw "the Americain"—and got back in her car.

She drove, trusting her instincts. Kramatorsk was a midsize city of five-story apartment blocks, but off to the west she could see larger apartments, and off to the east, a bristling black factory. The train station bridge, crossing ten tracks and several abandoned red and green engines, afforded a perfect view of the smoking colossus. No pedestrians, the town was quiet, the billowing smoke the closest thing to a social life.

Beyond the train station, the pavement was scorched and windows blown out. At the river, she turned north. The trees were yellow and white, the green grass broken up with black mud. Monet would have loved the waterlillies, but Alie could see slag in their tendrils. She imagined the fish, nibbling at the corners of plastic bottles. The river made her sad for the people who lived here, although she couldn't say why, it just made her feel like nothing would change, like this would go on and on until it was forgotten. But the white church with the gold metal onion domes, the one she caught only in glimpses— that was lovely.

A few blocks later, she saw a mortared building, the front sloughing off like a rockslide. She passed a burned bus left in the street, the electric wires cut or blown off their supports. More shattered windows, more scorch marks, more metal hanging perilously off façades.

She pulled off the road near a makeshift memorial, dying flowers and a photo of a young man. The damage here was extensive. Three burned buses were flopped down on their bellies, their melted tires stolen. A block ahead, she saw a barricade, mostly tires held in place by barbed wire. The two men at the barricade were wearing skeleton ski masks.

She turned into a package store and bought a bottle of vodka in a brown plastic bag. It was the only open store on the block. She showed the photo of Locke as she paid. "Americain?" No. She left the man her card.

Outside, she turned back the way she had come and went down a side street, avoiding the barricade. There was a barricade on the next street as well. She saw the handle of a baseball bat sticking up from the pile—how strange, did they play baseball here?—and men in masks, mostly stocky, with bushy beards. They were wearing camouflage, as if they were in a forest, even though they were standing in front of a coffee shop. It seemed to be open. She wondered if the Cossacks paid for their coffee.

There was a small park, like the one Hargrove had charged across. There was a flagpole flying the colors of the Donetsk Republic and a statue of Stalin, which was surprising—she thought they had all been torn down decades ago. An armored troop carrier was sitting on the far edge, no doubt stolen by separatists from the Ukrainian army, and men were wandering around with guns. A young woman was sitting against Stalin's pedestal, a sandwich in her hand, a handheld video camera beside her.

"Reporter?" Alie asked, handing her the brown paper bag.

"Doing my best," she said. Alie had thought she was American, but she was European, Dutch or a Scandi probably, judging by the accent and glasses. "Who do you work for?"

"Independent," Alie replied.

"The *Independent*?"

"No, I'm independent. I work for myself. I've had some stuff in the *Guardian*." Three years ago.

"A liberal," the woman said crookedly. She took a sip from the vodka bottle and grimaced, handing back the bag.

"I publish anywhere that will take me. What about you?"

"*Vice*."

"The website?"

"YouTube channel. More traffic that way. We file dispatches under the heading Russian Roulette."

Alie took a long pull and settled in beside her. "Anybody else around?"

"A couple Germans. One Brit. Locals, of course, they have a thriving press here. Professional and independent." She smiled at the word. In this context an independent meant anyone with a cell phone and the ability to upload to the Internet.

"Any Americans?"

"You're the first I've seen."

Alie wasn't surprised. The American news agencies never came this deep. They were barely even in Kiev.

She showed the girl the picture of Locke. "How about him?"

The kid shook her head no. "Is he in town?"

Alie took a drink. "Probably." The bearded Cossacks were intimidating, but they weren't even looking at her. It was tough to stay on alert. "If he is, he doesn't want to be found. I figure if I make enough noise, show his picture around, he'll have to find me."

Silence me, in other words. It wasn't much of a

plan, and it had its risks, but it had worked before, in much worse places and with much worse men.

The young woman understood. Maybe. She didn't ask any questions.

"It's quiet," Alie said, taking another drink.

"The fighting has moved on. The separatists have held this part of town for a week. The battle is out at the airport and the television tower."

She had read about the Ukrainian army offensive at the airport. The one runway had been rendered useless by the first mortar attack last month. It was purely symbolism now. Not Locke's type of gig.

"Television tower?" she said.

"I know," the young woman said. "Crazy, right? But television still matters here."

"Military or militias?"

"Official Ukrainian military," she said. "We're going this afternoon, if you want a lift."

Alie drank and handed back the bottle. That didn't sound like Locke's spot, either. The U.S. wouldn't send a merc for a television tower, would it? There must be something else. "What about local militia?"

"Which side?"

"Ukrainian."

The vice reporter shrugged. "There's the Donbas Battalion about twenty minutes away, if you have a car."

Alie shook her head. "I want something here, in Kramatorsk."

"Well, it's mostly Donetsk."

"What do you mean?"

"Most people are for the separatists. I'd say 75 percent."

"Seriously?" Kiev was running 90 percent the other way, from what she could tell.

The young woman pointed across the street. "See the holes in that building? And the apartments with the front blown off? That was the Ukrainian military firing mortars toward these barricades." Poor propaganda. Bad for winning hearts and minds. "I doubt the support lasts long, though. It's going to get worse for these people before it gets better."

The young woman was maybe twenty-two, younger than Hargrove, but she knew what she was talking about. The idea of an insurrection was easy to support, especially in a poor region, because there were always legitimate grievances, and nothing bad had happened yet, and the future was sunshine and lollipops. The reality of an insurrection was usually hell.

"If you want pro-Ukraine," the kid said, pointing to her left, "take that road. Keep going until you see the flags. It's about a kilometer." She took a long drink of the vodka and wiped her mouth. "Or you could try that," she said, pointing in the other direction.

Alie looked behind her. Smoke was rising from the west. "When did that happen?"

"About an hour ago." The young woman smiled. She looked exhausted, filthy, but convinced this was her calling, because it was the greatest experience of her life. Alie envied her youth.

"Be careful," the young woman said. "The separatists kidnapped a female reporter a few days ago. They let her go, *untouched*"—an emphasis on the word Alie understood too well—"but she was local, so it's not necessarily a precedent."

"Don't worry. I've done this before."

"In Ukraine?"

"In Africa."

"I knew it," the young woman said. "You're Alie MacFarlane, right?"

Alie looked at her. Who was this girl?

"I saw you speak at a refugee conference in the Hague a few years back. You're a legend. Sort of. To a few of us diehards anyway." Okay kid, *legend* was nice. Quit qualifying it. "That refugee series, when you traveled with those women from Burundi to Bosaso. . . . It's obscure, sure. You have to take a deep dive to find it. But that's where the good stuff is, right? Down in the depths."

It's not down there to be cool, Alie thought. *It's down there because I couldn't verify it. Because I didn't organize my sources, some of whom might have killed me. Because I lost my subjects and lost the ending and didn't bring it home with a bang.*

"That series was brilliant," the young woman continued. "I read it when I was a junior in upper school. It changed my life."

That series was a failure, in every way.

"How is Magdelena?" The young woman sat up even straighter. "Is she here? In Ukraine?"

Alie felt the lump in her throat. She couldn't say it. Magdelena is missing. It hurt for her to even think it: Magdelena is almost surely dead.

"I'm working on a bigger story," Alie said, and

she wished she hadn't. Why did she need to impress this kid?

"About Ukraine?"

"Nobody cares about Ukraine. This is about the USA."

She knocked back another gulp of vodka, then handed the young woman the last of the bottle. She felt tired. "I'm going to check on that smoke," she said.

It wasn't even a decision. At this point in her life, what else could she do?

CHAPTER 38

The Wolf stood outside the smoking building, staring at the back end of the garbage truck, the only part not buried in the wall. There were policemen on the scene, but they seemed mostly intent on extricating the stolen city property and getting it back on duty.

It's a tank, he thought, as he stared at the hard metal frame.

"It's a miracle no one was killed," an older man was saying.

It's not a miracle, the Wolf thought. *It was intentional.*

Eight wounded, none dead. It would have been easier to wipe them out. One incendiary device, fired or planted. Boom. Nothing. No worries, no risk. Killing people was the simplest act in modern warfare, if you simply wanted them dead. That was why the world had spent the last hundred years figuring out how to make better munitions. No, this was specialized, like a laser-guided missile.

"They were pro-Russians," the old man is saying. "They were wearing separatist uniforms."

Unlikely, the Wolf thought. This was a professional team. The combination of brutality and precision. The spectacle of the garbage truck and the staged "clumsiness" of the shooting. They missed from point-blank range! No, they didn't. This was a message.

Or a distraction.

"Why here?" the old man was lamenting to no one in particular, or maybe to the Wolf, who wouldn't even turn toward him. "Why in my building?"

Good question, old man, the Wolf thought.

He walked around the side of the building. Witnesses had seen six men run this way. They had been wearing gas masks, the old-fashioned Soviet kind with the greenish-brown face cover and the alien-like breathing hose. Masks that could be sourced locally, and were ghoulish enough to distract from any other details.

Maybe they were separatists. Maybe. But he didn't know anyone else at his level working the area.

He thought of the Ukrainian. Maltov. He had tracked the man to Kramatorsk, where his henchmen had dropped him off for the night. Somehow, he had slipped out during the night. The safe house turned out to be his mother's apartment. Nice lady. Excellent blinis. Far too trusting for this day and age.

Karpenko was here, and so was his hired team. There were too many coincidences to think otherwise. But why? What was their objective in this nothing town?

The Wolf walked the side street, checking the surroundings. He walked to the front of the building. A gas facility was five hundred meters away, its pipework visible behind the surrounding walls and two low houses. The guards were wearing militia uniforms, but the Wolf knew them immediately for Russian Spetsnaz. He had worked with them for decades, all the way back to Afghanistan. They had stormed the Crimean parliament, in a similar disguise. They were the tip of the spear. The pressure point . . .

"Americain?" he heard someone say.

"No, no." It was the same old man, muttering, still in his pajama bottoms, the Wolf noticed, at four in the afternoon.

"Americain?" the foreign woman said, turning to him and holding out her phone for him to see.

CHAPTER 39

"Shit," I said, as I watched the surveillance feed of the crowd outside the club.

"What?" Miles said, appearing at my shoulder.

In America, there would have been a crowd of news crews and gawkers. Here, two months into the street fighting, there was already a weary acceptance. If the insurrection lasted another year, this kind of tragedy would be so commonplace, even this sparse crowd wouldn't bother.

I pointed to Alie.

"An American." Miles said, leaning in. "What's she doing? Charro, can we get a closer look?"

The camera zoomed in, but I didn't need to see what was on her cell phone. I knew it had something to do with me. Why else would she be in Kramatorsk?

"She's looking for me," I said.

Miles looked up, confused. I could tell he was trying to put this together.

"You know this woman," Karpenko said. It didn't sound like a question. For a boss, he had a way of slipping into the edges of conversations. Dangerous.

"From an old job," I muttered, glancing at Miles, wondering if he remembered her from Burundi. It had been ten years, after all. "I ran into her in Kiev four days ago. She knows what I do."

"How does she know you're here?"

Exactly what I was wondering. "I don't know," I admitted, "but I think we need to find out."

Miles was shaking his head no. I tried to turn away, but he pulled me aside. "Is that who I think it is?" he hissed. "The white girl from Burundi?"

"Half white," I said.

"The one you risked everything for at Gatumba?" I knew by *everything*, he really meant everything: the mission, the country, thousands of lives, his respect. He hadn't forgotten.

"She's a reporter," I said. "We can't leave her on the street."

"She's an emotional attachment," he snapped. "You have to let her go. We've already risked too much."

He was right. The operation at the club looked like a success, at least in terms of spooking the local thugs back into their holes. But if it brought too much attention, if it spiraled into other loose ends I needed to tie up . . .

"Mission focus," Miles said, his arm on my shoulder, his head close so no one else could hear. "I don't care about your past. That's over. You know that."

It should have been over. I promise, Miles, I thought it was.

"She's smart, Miles. She's making noise. She knows I can't have my picture shown around."

"Ten hours," he said. "And we're done. We're out of here."

But it wasn't done. And I wasn't out.

"Actioning her isn't personal," I said.

"It isn't professional," Miles countered with bite. "We're warriors, Locke. We're here for a mission. We don't do damsels in distress."

She wasn't a damsel, I wanted to say. And she wasn't in distress.

"I determine the mission parameters," I said, turning to the computer monitor to let him know this discussion was over. Miles was my NCO, my second, but I was still the unit commander.

Miles didn't like it, but he took it. Like a professional. I almost turned to say something to him, to say I appreciated his support and his trust, not in a dickish way, but sincerely, because it really did mean everything to me.

But I didn't. I let it go. I leaned in toward the monitor, watching my old love show her cell phone to a stream of Ukrainian men. *Are you thinking about opsec, Locke?* I asked myself. *Is this about maintaining secrecy?*

Or is it about Alie?

The Wolf stepped into the shadows, where he could keep an eye on the attractive American without being seen. You never knew, after all, who was watching. He took out his cell phone. One of his Chechens answered.

"He is here. Yes. Karpenko. Kramatorsk. It's a town. No. With a gas facility." The Wolf looked at his watch, a Soviet military model he had been wearing since Afghanistan. It was 1923. "Yes. Fine. The whole million. For as many as you can bring, but only if you can get them here by midnight."

The Wolf hung up. He would give the Chechens the entire FSB million-dollar bounty on Karpenko's head, assuming the oligarch was actually in Kramatorsk. Karpenko didn't concern him, as long as it got the Chechen hunter-killers here.

He wanted the American special forces team, the one that had outmanuevered him in Poltava. He wanted the reward for them, and for proof of an American invasion, and knew it could set him up for life.

And revenge? Well . . . there was nothing wrong with that, either. Once a mercenary reached the age of the Wolf, everything felt like revenge for something.

CHAPTER 40

Now this is a room, Brad Winters thought, as he eased into a large leather chair next to a massive fireplace mantel, probably Renaissance Venetian. Across from him was a huge carved desk from the 1700s with the ancient crest of England carved into its front. An old-fashioned brown globe in a ponderous metal stand sat nearby. The walls were dark red silk damask, with old paintings hung by wire from the ornate crown molding. The ceiling was coffered, with gold leaf detailing; palatial Persian carpets overlapped to cover the floor. The leather club couch was so deep you could knife a wayward assistant (or willing secretary) without disturbing the adjacent office.

The building, like the Special Forces Club, was a row house, but not the American kind, a hundred years old and built for the upper middle class. In the London neighborhood of Belgravia, the stone buildings were three hundred years old and built by those in the process of conquering the world. Nothing in the New World could compare. This, after all, was the real thing: the seat of Empire. It was what the inhabitants of Washington, DC, aspire to, and what New York hedge fund managers had never understood. To them, the world was now. How can I make unfathomable money, and spend unfathomable money, before I die? In America, three months was a window.

For these men, three decades was a first step. They were connected to power, and wielded power, in ways Winters could only imagine. Their bank was not listed in any phone directory; its true holdings not recorded in any database. Most of its clients' wealth was older than the desk. If you worked here, you thought in generations and centuries, not quarterly reports.

He had stepped out of the gutter, Winters felt, when he started to think that way, too. But he had no illusions. He was little more than a curiosity here, an ambitious nouveaux man on the rise. Still . . . he was here.

"Mr. Winters," a man said, extending his hand as he entered the room.

"Mr. Cavendish," Winters said. The great irony, he supposed, was that Eastern European oligarchs, who made American hedge fund managers seem like long-term thinkers, were now these bankers' richest clients, because they were now the richest men in England. It was through Karpenko, in fact, that Winters had entered their circle, albeit on the fringe. That was how he knew Ukraine mattered: because these men cared.

"My associates," Cavendish said.

Winters shook hands with the other two men. One was classically British, Sir Hyphen-Something, no doubt followed by a string of letters for arcane knighthoods. The other was Indian subcontinent by race, English by every other measure. No doubt his ancestors had been among the collaborators who made the Empire possible. Despite his dark skin, he was as British as Cavendish, from his facial expressions to his pointy shoes.

The last man in the group, who didn't seek or receive a handshake, was younger than the others, but impeccably groomed and attired. No doubt he was next in a line of private bankers that stretched back to the Glorious Revolution of 1688 and forward as far as London's existence. He took a seat in the back. He was empty-handed, without a pad of paper or cell phone. Winters hadn't noticed electronics anywhere, even though he knew this bank was connected.

"Have you given up on North Africa?" Cavendish asked.

"Temporarily."

"Why?"

Winters shifted, already off guard. How did the bankers know about his North African operation? "There's more opportunity in Eastern Europe," he said.

"I doubt that."

"A better opportunity, anyway. For me. And you." He had to be careful here.

Cavendish turned and walked past the large brown globe to his desk. Winters could taste the skepticism, but then again, it could have been the British mannerisms. These men had a way of looking down their noses at everything, including their own noses. He wouldn't have brought his partners, Winters assured himself, if he wasn't interested.

"I know you have interests in Ukraine," Winters said.

"We have interests everywhere."

"Yes, but Ukraine is special. There's enough shale gas there to power Europe until Putin retires, and enough infrastructure to get it here within six months." It wasn't the right word, men like Putin never *retired*, but he had shied away from *expires*. Look how long Castro had held on. Putin would outlive Sir Hyphen for sure, and probably a few others.

The bankers weren't impressed. They hadn't agreed to meet him for his philosophy. It was time to be American.

"I know you secretly backed the Nabucco pipeline," Winters said, shifting into direct mode. "It was a smart idea. Bring gas directly from Turkey into Europe, castrating Gazprom and dimming Russia's influence. I know that, in retaliation, Putin began a pipeline of his own, South Stream, from Russia through the Black Sea. It was an old-fashioned arms race, with pipes instead of nukes, and it killed Nabucco. You took a haircut. A big one. Do you know why he did it?"

Nothing.

"Because he could."

Cavendish breathed deeply. Or maybe he just breathed. "Your point, sir."

"I can change the dynamic. I can put Putin on his heels, and Europe in the driver's seat." He was mixing metaphors, losing his edge. *Jesus, Brad, get a hold of yourself.* "But it's more than that," he said, moving quickly past the momentary stumble. "It's more than business deals or a few billion dollars." Let them chew that number. "It's victory, gentlemen. I'm talking about taking Russia off the world stage and snuffing out its last chance to rival the West. The end of an era." He glanced around the room for effect. "The end of an enemy."

The bankers stared at him in silence, but Cavendish must have signaled for the meeting to proceed, because after a few seconds the younger man rose from his seat and walked to the credenza, where an ornate crystal decanter of Scotch was perfectly positioned on a silver tray. He poured four glasses, and added a few drops of water to each. Winters took his with a nod. Nobody else acknowledged the young man's existence.

"Tell us," Cavendish said.

It was a blunt statement, but Winters could read the significance. *We are listening.* These men knew war. They had profited off everything from the Boer War to Afghanistan. He wouldn't be surprised if they had backed the winners at the Battle of Hastings. But they rarely started wars; they finished them. That was why they endured. He was going to have to make them stretch.

"We have the power, gentlemen," Winters said. "The West is distracted by the Arabs, and our citizens are tired, but Russia is worse. It is hollow. Their economy is one-dimensional, dependent on oil and gas, and any rupture—supply, transport, price drops—will cripple them. Their military has spent a decade feasting on children—Georgia, Chechnya, Azerbaijan—to hide its inadequacy, but their officer corps is thin and their soldiers poorly trained.

They couldn't even control a third-tier shithole like Georgia without the help of mercenaries."

"And America couldn't control a second-tier shithole like Iraq, even with mercenaries," Sir Hyphen huffed, but for business purposes—the business purposes only—Winters let it slide.

"They are a paper tiger, gentleman, fatally flawed on two fronts. All we need is a spark, and they will go up in flames."

"And the invasion of Ukraine is that spark," Cavendish said, in the dry British way that made it impossible to tell questions from answers.

"My firm has three hundred top military professionals operating in the Balkans. I've trained hundreds of fighters in the region. Within three months, I could have an army of thousands, well trained, heavily armed, and under elite command. And that doesn't include the official Ukrainian army. With minimal effort, we could hold Russia in a stalemate for years. That's not an opinion. That's a fact. But why settle for that? It gains us little. Why not destroy them instead?"

"How?"

"First, we break their military in Ukraine. It is easier than you imagine, and more effective than you might think. Putin has wrapped Russia in the symbolism of strength. A proud nation resurgent, a northern bear reborn. When we shatter that image, we shatter the people's faith. Then we break them economically."

"With oil."

Winters nodded. "Once we roll back the Russians, I will install my own man as the Ukrainian

Minister of Energy. We will control their shale gas reserve in the East, which only the violence has kept Shell from exploiting. We will control the pipelines between Putin and the West. Ukraine has enough untapped natural gas reserves to become Europe's main supplier of energy within two years. That will make you powerful, gentlemen. And better, it will make Putin poor."

"It could also cause a devastating spike in energy prices," Sir Hyphen said with unprofessional fluster. He was probably a legacy. "Just the threat of all-out war could cause a market panic that could crater the world economy."

"That's the fear Putin counts on," Winters said calmly. "It's his currency of power. But the window here is small: only two years before the East—*our* East—is pumping enough oil to make Gazprom dispensable. There is easily enough oil output amongst our other suppliers: Norway, Venezuela, Nigeria, Saudi Arabia . . ."

"The Saudis hate Putin," Cavendish said thoughtfully, "because Putin is propping up Syria and Iran."

"Exactly. It's to the Saudis' advantage to fill the supply gap. And you have the contacts"—Winters glanced quickly from man to man—"to show them why."

Cavendish nodded. Winters was coming to them with a different kind of proposal: a request to use their influence, instead of their cash. At least, Winters assumed it was a new kind of proposal, because it was unlike any he had made before.

"This all hinges on your man in Ukraine," the Indian said languidly, speaking for the first time.

Exactly, Winters thought, hoping the change of direction meant they had bought the oil argument. "As you probably know," he said, "I have been grooming Kostyantyn Karpenko for some time."

The Indian sipped his Scotch, as if he'd never heard the name. But these men not only knew Karpenko, they owned him, or at least the part of him not currently listed on the London Stock Exchange. Karpenko had told Winters as much.

"You are invested in him, I believe, to the tune of a billion or more. So am I, but in sweat equity and personal reputation. Right now, in fact, his future is in my hands. Which practically makes us partners."

The Indian scowled, and Winters regretted his flippancy.

"Tomorrow morning, Karpenko will lead an assault on a Russian army unit that has taken over a strategic natural gas facility in the city of Kramatorsk. Karpenko's forces are Ukrainian patriots, all men who have volunteered, a citizen army . . . with a bit of professional help, of course. It will be a small battle, but an enormous symbol. These are Russian troops, threatening a major energy hub, a hundred miles from the Russian border. When Karpenko climbs on a troop carrier to proclaim his victory, he will show the world not just proof of an invasion, but his personal resolve to fight for Ukrainian freedom. This will be his Yeltsin moment."

"You have press, I assume?"

"Two helicopters, thirty passengers each. Reporters, photographers, video, Internet and traditional outlets, from Europe and the United States. We will manufacture a CNN effect, and drive the news cycle until it gets enough airlift. After Kramatorsk, it is a short drive to the next pipeline trunk station, and an even shorter one to the next. Within a week, Karpenko will become a national hero, my army will make sure of that."

"And then?"

"Ukraine will rally to him, and so will the West."

Another long pause. The Brits were masters of feigned disinterest. "The Americans will never go for it," Cavendish said.

"Do you think I would come," Winters said slowly, "if I didn't have that angle covered?"

He saw Sir Hyphen squirm. Was he impressing them, or had he gone too far? The only way to find out was to plunge on.

"If you've seen the news from our Congress, you know the United States is looking for a point of entry"—this wasn't true, they were looking for a way out, but there were layers under the administration with more insight and courage. "The congressional resolution in support of Ukraine introduced this week; the war hawks on the talk circuit. Freedom gas. The timing is not an accident. There are many who agree with my plan, even if they don't know the details, and we have been carefully amplifying their voices. Karpenko's triumph will prove they were right to demand action, and give them a way to respond."

"Obama will never agree to military action."

"He doesn't have to. I have Houston, gentleman. I have the Pentagon and cover in Congress. I have five current contracts with the United States government that can be rolled into a private military offensive under Ukrainian army cover. All Obama has to do is stand aside and let me work, and he will, because he always avoids hard choices, and that is the easiest choice."

In the silence, Winters realized he was leaning forward, and that he'd spoken with more passion than he'd intended. He wanted to say, Fuck it, this was years of work, this is my big chance, I'm not going to come in half-cocked. But instead, he sat back and adjusted his cuffs, to signal his casual reserve.

"You're absolutely right," Winters said. "The U.S. won't intervene to help us. But they won't stop us either"—as long as we're winning—"not with my business, military, and Congressional co-alition. If you can simply rally the EU, publicly or privately . . ."

He left them the opening, but the bankers didn't respond. They could rally the British—they could make the British government do almost anything—but they wouldn't commit. Yet.

"Are you sure Karpenko will do as you ask?" It was the Indian again.

Winters nodded. "We're partners. He has agreed to everything."

"And when he starts to believe his own press?"

"I have leverage." Personal leverage. Family leverage. The best kind.

"What about the current government of Ukraine?" Sir Hyphen asked. "What if they don't want him to be the Minister of Energy?"

"Why would they refuse? It is a low profile position for a national hero. It strengthens their government, instead of threatening it."

"And when Karpenko is in place?" It was the Indian, cutting to the crux.

Winters smiled. "Pipelines, oil fields, leases in the Black Sea, anything you want. Anything you have desired. It must be a fair price, of course, but gentlemen . . . how can you place a price on a country's freedom?"

The Brits didn't even nod. They simply looked at him, as if they'd never seen him before. Winters had heard of stiff lips, but this made concrete look like Silly Putty.

"And if Putin returns?"

"That's part of my fee, gentleman, a long-term lease on a private military base in eastern Ukraine: airstrip, training grounds, fortified installations. From that base, I will not only keep your investments in Ukraine safe, I will keep Putin on the defensive, and I will keep the peace from Belarus to the Balkans. Think of it, gentlemen, a new Eastern Europe, free from Russian tyranny. And all of it, or at least the military portion, paid for by the United States government."

"You have that guaranteed?"

Winters shook his head. "No, but that is the least of my concerns." Once he had sent Putin scurrying, he'd be up to his elbows in Title 10 contracts. He would be so in demand, he could write them himself. And he would.

The Indian leaned back, as if trying to see him at a new angle. He had a regal nose, and bushy eyebrows, and a stare that told Winters this was the man he needed to impress. And that he was listening.

"You've split with your New York bankers," the Indian remarked.

Winters swallowed his surprise. Of course they knew. "I think you know why."

Cavendish nodded. Everyone understood this room was an upgrade over New York. "What is the other part of your fee?" he asked. Sharp. These men never missed anything.

"A partnership with you, on a gas field in Eastern Ukraine. Preferably a big one." Winters had no intention of stealing oil leases from potential allies in Houston, but there were fields still available, especially just across the border in Russia, because why would he stop at the border, gentlemen, once he had Putin on the run?

"We secure the lease for your congolomerate—"

"—and you share the profits as silent partners."

Cavendish sniffed. "At what percentage?"

"I need 40 percent. The rest is unimportant to me."

"That is a remarkably poor negotiating technique."

It wasn't about negotiating. In New York, yes. But not at this level.

"It's enough to keep our mutual friends in Houston happy *and* heavily invested in the democratic future of Ukraine. I'll make my stake on the security contracts." With a tidy taste off the top of the shale profits, of course. "It's not just the Balkans, gentlemen," he said, lifting his glass. "A base in Eastern Ukraine is the perfect staging area for the Middle East, Russia, the Caucuses, Iran. As I said at the top:

from Ukraine, together, we can"—he almost said *control*, but caught himself—"change the world."

He sipped his Scotch. It was strong and smoky, straight out of a peat bog. Fifteen years in a barrel, at least. In the scope of things, that wasn't long.

"You are asking for nothing up front," Cavendish said.

"Nothing," Winters confirmed, "until Karpenko is in Kiev. Then I will need your influence, as well as your money, to make sure Europe and the markets go along."

"What are the chances of success?" the Indian asked.

Winters grimaced, but only to hide a smile. "It depends on *your* determination," he said. "With your help, greater than 90 percent. And that's to secure Ukraine for a generation."

Or plunge Europe into war. Those were the stakes. And still, the bankers didn't react. Was there anything that could make them flinch? What if he told them their wives had been murdered? Or their mistresses?

"And if the assault on the gas facility fails? That is the first step, is it not?"

Winters smiled. "The assault won't fail."

Cavendish and the Indian glanced at each other, but Winters couldn't read their expressions. He hated not being able to read expressions.

"You said tomorrow, if I'm not mistaken," Cavendish said.

"That's right."

"Okay," the Indian said slowly. "What time?"

He hadn't known how the bankers would react. They had kept him waiting, alone in the office, for an eternity, and beneath his cool nonchalance, Winters was nervous and cold. The world on a string, and he was sitting in a London office, counting the minutes until these starched-collared bankers returned. Was his plan too bold? Had he chosen the wrong partners? He didn't worry if the plan would work. He only worried that he wouldn't get the chance.

A half an hour. An hour. And then, finally, Cavendish and the Indian returned, this time without Sir Hyphen. "We need you to meet an associate of ours," Cavendish said. "Now. Before your operation."

Inside, Winters relaxed. He had thought, only half in jest, that they were going to have him arrested for off-the-books ballsiness. Or worse, exiled to Virginia.

"An honor," he said.

"A car is downstairs. It will take you to Farnborough."

Winters hid his shock. Farnborough was the corporate airport where London's superrich stowed their private jets. Maybe they were going to take him to a secret CIA prison in Poland after all.

"Who am I to meet?"

"All will be made plain soon enough," the Indian said.

Winters bowed. "Thank you, Mr. Beckham."

The Indian smiled. "Please. Call me Kabir."

CHAPTER 41

Alie tried not to panic. She tried to think straight. How had this happened?

She had stayed outside the shattered social club for an hour, maybe more, making notes and talking with citizens, trying to piece together what had happened. She had seen the Ukrainian, or Russian, maybe he was Russian, as she walked back to her car three blocks away. He was big, scowling, watching her. But it had only been, what? Two minutes since she'd left the site of the attack. God, they were fast.

Which meant Locke, right? Wasn't that what she wanted? To force him to grab her and get her off the street.

But the hood. Why did they need the hood?

She took a breath. She felt the cloth clogging her mouth, and she tried to slow herself down, tried to focus on her breathing. She thought of people with hoods over their heads: those being led to executions, their anonymous executioners. She thought of the ship captain all those years ago in Somalia, when she was trying to escape with the girls . . .

She jerked her shoulder, trying to chase away the memory, but her hands were tied. They hadn't tied on the hood, but her hands were tight behind her back, and she couldn't reach it. She couldn't move more than a few inches. She had known that, but feeling it was different.

Breathe, Alie, she thought, trying not to panic. *Alie, you have to breathe.*

The captain's face came to her, unwanted. The beautiful green eyes, the filthy brown teeth. She felt the warmth of his room in the Bosaso flop house. "Sorry to pull you aside, sister, we don't get many white women here," he had said, as he shoved goat into his mouth with his fingers. "We can't let you ride with the others, of course, we aren't savages, we'll give you a room on deck, my second mate's cabin, he had an accident anyway, here, have some of this." It was the worst liquor she had ever tasted. Why had she kept drinking it? Why had she listened to him lying, saying, "Don't worry, we'll take care of the women. We always do."

Breathe, she thought. *Alie, you have to breathe.*

She had to focus on these men, here, now, the ones who had grabbed her off the streets of Ukraine, not the ghosts from Bosaso. There were three of them. The big Russian who met her on the street, and the two who jumped out, grabbed her, and tossed her, literally, onto the delivery truck's cold metal floor.

Forget the hood, Alie. Forget the African captain and his teeth, and your stupid relief when he laughed and said, "We'll take you to the ship now, you can see your friends, they have to hide in the hold, but they will be fine."

She jerked again, trying to wrench her hands out of the cuffs, but a hand was on her shoulder. "Be calm," someone barked in accented English.

She thought of the hood back in Africa, her dizziness as the sailors covered her, and the captain saying, "For secrecy, you understand." Then the short walk to the docks in total darkness, or so she had thought, until she felt the blow to the back of her head, and the ground rushed upward to meet her, and then the captain was leaning over her, saying, "We cannot take you, we must leave you here, but don't worry, sister, I won't rape you. I am a Christian, just like you."

She screamed, the sound muffled by the hood and the truck. She jerked wildly, an animal instinct. Something was grabbing at her. Something was holding her face down, pressed into the floor, *and you can't breathe*, her mind told her, *when your mouth is facing the floor*.

"We're not going to hurt you," the voice said.

But she was losing consciousness, losing her ability to understand.

"Your friend sent us," the voice said, as a hand pulled her up.

Locke, she thought, but distantly, because the darkness was rushing in, and she could feel it filling the hood like blood, and the last thing she remembered was the foul goat breath of the captain, whispering, "I'm not going to rape you, sister," *but when you wake up tomorrow, alone, in a filthy bed in a Bosaso boardinghouse, you are going to wish that you had died.*

CHAPTER 42

I hardened myself when I saw the Ukrainian carrying the unconscious body like a cord of firewood. I needed to keep cool, like Karpenko or my first commanding officer, General McChrystal, the epitome of grace under pressure. This was not the time for dissent in the ranks.

"She fell," Maltov said, laying her down.

I pulled off the hood. It was Alie, all right, her curly hair damp with sweat and plastered to her face, blood in her mouth where she'd bitten through her lip. A bruise was forming on her forehead, distending her golden skin.

"Crazy bitch," Maltov said.

I couldn't stop myself. I lashed the man for his cruelty, as savagely as I could. Maltov simply looked down from six inches above me, his eyes uninterested, waiting for me to finish. It was thirty seconds before I was back in control.

"Bad ju-ju, American," Maltov said, something he must have heard in a third-rate movie. "You told us to use the hood."

That stung, because I couldn't argue.

"Leave her to me," I snapped, signaling for Miles. We carried her to a far corner of the warehouse, for relative privacy, and laid her gently on the ground.

"Increase the watch," I said.

Miles nodded. He was thinking the same thing. Maltov had only been gone twenty-three minutes. He should have driven around for at least half an hour after snatching Alie to see if he was being tailed. Instead, he must have come straight home.

I should have sent Colonel Sirko. But no, this was proper thuggery, not a military operation, and Kramatorsk was Maltov's turf. He had the local knowledge and the respect of his men, both things Sirko lacked. Besides, I could sense the colonel's distaste for kidnapping women. He would do it if ordered by Karpenko, but he wouldn't like it. I admired his honor, but it saddened me, too. His rigidity wasn't practical for this world; he was a man outside his time.

Alie groaned, and I bent a knee beside her. She started to retch, so I turned her onto her side, so that she wouldn't choke, and put a hand on her hip, hoping my touch would calm her. Her body was shaking.

Seven hours, at most, until we had to be on our way. And shit tons of work left to do.

Bad ju-ju indeed.

CHAPTER 43

Alie started to come around thirty minutes later, so Greenlees and I propped her on the ammo crate against the back wall of the warehouse. Greenlees had taken care of her while I went over the final details of the operation with Miles. The older man, it turned out, was a natural nursemaid. He'd wiped the grime from her forehead, and the blood and vomit from her lips, with a surprisingly delicate touch.

Now he gave her a shoulder to lean on, as she rolled her head, trying to lift it. Her curly hair was matted from the hood, her eyes closed, and I felt strangely nervous as I watched her coming around, not daring to touch her. I had rarely seen Alie in repose. Only once, in my bed in Bujumbura, when I was alerted to the slaughter at Gatumba at 0200, and I had taken a moment to relish her before strapping on my guns and heading out . . .

Eventually, her eyes opened, and she began to look around. Greenlees gave her a sip of water, then stood back to give her space. Alie's eyes roamed the warehouse, resting on everything briefly, before finding me. For a moment, I thought she was still in a daze. Then she tried to tear her hands out from behind her, as if she expected them not to be bound, and her momentum threw her off balance. Before I could grab her, she crumpled to the floor. Greenlees started to rush to her aid. I signaled him to stand down. Let her lie there, undisturbed.

"You son of a bitch," she muttered.

"What are you doing here, Alie?" I said coolly—professionally—as Greenlees and I lifted her onto the ammo crate.

"What are *you* doing here?" she said, as her eyes flicked to Miles and a few others who were gathering behind me.

"Work."

She was angry. Of course. She was lost, bruised, no doubt worried, and shaking from the physical exertion of the last few hours. She'd be sore in the morning, but by then, sadly, I'd be gone.

"I need a drink," she said.

Greenlees offered her water. She laughed and refused it.

"Does anyone know you're here?" I said.

"You can't shoot me, Tom."

Of course I could. But she was the last person I'd shoot, and I was surprised she didn't know it. "I'm not going to shoot you, Alie, but we're leaving, and we can't take you with us. Do you have someone to pick you up?"

She looked past me, at the helicopter, the hasty defensive positions we'd made out of piles of metal scrap, the drone. She looked up at the roof of the warehouse, at the cracked windows, the rusted beams. "So this is what it's like," she said, "on the inside."

She checked me up and down with her fiercely direct stare. I could see Alie coming back. Not the girl I knew in Africa, but the woman I had met three days ago in Kiev.

"You look like shit," she said.

It was true. I'd ditched my action slacks and blazer in Poltava, and my fatigues and ballistic vest were carrying three days of grit and sweat. I hadn't washed since Kiev, and I had mission stubble from my chin to the bottom of my neck. I smelled like the rest of the team: body odor and gun oil. It probably hung over the place like a fog. But I was sporting duel thigh holsters for my nine mils, with my SCAR slung over my shoulder, and my Gerber knife strapped upside down over my left pectoral. Four grenades were rigged to my vest, so I could pull and throw with one hand. And I was jacked, like you get before a mission, when the adrenaline is pounding, even though on the surface you're calm. I looked like a motherfucking badass, come to think of it, because only backbenchers went into battle looking like a recruitment poster.

"Hello, Mr. Greenlees," Alie said, turning to him. "I bet you're wishing you never had that drink in Kiev. I should have warned you that Locke leaves people behind."

Greenlees looked sick, and I almost pitied him. He was wearing his same retiree-casual attire, but it was as filthy as my battle gear, and surprisingly frayed. He was coming apart seam by seam, and Alie could always sense a weakness.

"Let it go," I said.

"Who's he?" Alie said, nodding toward Karpenko.

"None of your business."

She smirked. "Then he must be yours." She turned to the oligarch. "I hope he kills the right man."

I felt a hand on my shoulder, and I knew it was Miles. "That's enough," he said, stepping toward Alie. "I guess you think you're a reporter now . . ."

"And you're his bodyguard?" She paused. "Even now. Ten years later."

Miles never lost his cool. Never. But he was close. "This isn't the job, Alie. This isn't what reporters do, flashing photographs around, attracting attention. You don't endanger people. You don't compromise the mission . . ."

"And what is the mission, Miles, if that's even your real name? Secret warfare? Targeted assassination? Stealing oil rights?"

I flinched. Was that really what Alie thought I did? But the shot seemed to have missed with Miles, who looked calmer now.

"The mission is what we are sent here to do," he said.

"And I'm endangering that mission?"

"You're endangering men's lives. *My* men's lives," I said.

"Good. Then I'm probably saving someone on the other side."

Out of the corner of my eye, I saw Karpenko shift his weight and Maltov reach for his gun. Alie was lucky the other Ukrainians didn't speak English, because she had gone too far. She knew it, I could tell, but she was moving now, letting go, so she pivoted and pressed forward, too stubborn to turn back.

"I know this man," she yelled, so everyone in the

warehouse could hear her. "I knew him in Africa. In Burundi. He will not bring you peace."

I wanted to say I stopped a genocide in Burundi. I stopped a fucking genocide. What have *you* ever done? But I breathed deep and swallowed the Apollo line. "I was never in Burundi," I said.

"What about Darfur then? Were you ever there?"

I could see Miles out of the corner of my eye, ushering people away. It was no one's business what we did for the company, and the less people that knew anything, the better.

"I was never in Darfur," I said, stepping closer so that no one but Alie could hear me.

"I saw you, you lying bastard," she hissed. "Outside Garsila." I could see the emotion in her face, and it surprised me, because it wasn't anger, it was . . . disappointment. "I know you could have stopped it. You had the men. But you watched. You watched as an entire village was slaughtered by the Janjaweed. You watched children being chopped down, men shot for sport, women stolen on horseback never to be seen again."

"It wasn't the mission."

"It wasn't the mission to save innocent people?"

I didn't answer. I'd already said too much, and Alie was rolling, maybe with stuff she'd been saving up for years, maybe from the adrenaline rush of surviving death in a black hood, maybe because she realized she had a moment, only a moment, before she was gone from my life, maybe for good.

"The mission," she scoffed, like it was a dirty word. "Do you only save innocent people when someone pays you to do it?"

"I saved that orphanage," I said.

"Don't you take my—"

"I gave you Gatumba, I gave you those girls, because they were in war's way, and without me they would have been dead before you even arrived, them and their nuns, too."

She hesitated. Never hesitate. "So who have you really saved?" I pressed. "Not those orphan girls. Not those women in Darfur. Not those refugee families you wrote those articles about so many years ago."

"You don't know anything about that."

"I know everything about that," I said. "I know you went with them to Bosaso. I know you bribed a UN official to find a worthy ship captain, and paid him a thousand American dollars to smuggle the girls out. And I know you wouldn't go any further, Alie. In the end, you wouldn't submit your white girl virtue to the hold. You booked passage above deck, over dinner with the captain."

"You've been following me."

"And you still missed the boat. You missed the fucking boat—" I was snarling now, and she knew it was coming, I could see the horror in her eyes "—because you were drunk."

"I wasn't . . ." she tried.

And then she broke. I could see it. And it only made me more vicious. "It was your idea, wasn't it? You wanted to take them to Europe. You wanted that story, as a memorial to your own past: two women and three little girls escape lives of abuse by crossing the ocean in a sweltering hold. But they didn't make it, did they, Alie? Did they?"

She cracked. She would never admit it, she would fight like hell to deny it, but I'd beaten her.

"Or even worse," I said slowly, "you don't know. You don't know what happened to them. And that's why you're here. You're looking for penance. You're trying to rescue all the lost girls, in Darfur, Somalia, Ukraine. But being a reporter fixes nothing."

"You've been spying on me."

"I've been protecting you," I snapped. "I'm protecting you now." It wasn't true. Ten years, and I'd never done shit for Alie, never had the balls to be anything to her, except for tonight.

"I don't want your protection," she said, rising out of her self-loathing, like I knew my Alie would. "I hate your fucking protection."

I leaned even closer, I don't know why. Maybe to punch her. Maybe to comfort her. Maybe, I don't know, to kiss her. But before I could figure any of that out, Miles stepped in and slammed me in the shoulder, knocking me back. It was more of a shove than a tackle, I'm sure, but it felt like stones colliding.

"Take it easy, brother," Miles said as he pulled me away, his arm around my shoulder, his head close to mine. "Take it easy."

He punched my chest, hard, like he was giving me airborne bloodwings. He was reminding me who I was, reminding me to breathe, which I did, slowly.

"Mission girl," I said, even though both of us knew it wasn't true.

He smacked me, flat hand, even harder this time. "Mission focus," he said.

He was right. I couldn't lose control. Ever. But especially now, with men's lives on the line, and only a few hours left. "Mission focus," I said.

I looked back at Alie. She was slumped on the ammo case, exhausted, and Karpenko was talking to her almost like Miles was talking to me. Close, with his arm over her shoulder.

"I'm going to tell her," Karpenko said, looking up at Miles, but talking to me, "what this man has done for my family."

His children. Poltava. Whatever. What was done was done, what was coming was coming fast.

Miles nodded his approval.

Karpenko turned to me. "I will take care of her," he said.

Fuck her, I thought. But I didn't mean it. I didn't know what I meant. None of this had gone like I'd expected. On this mission, nothing had.

Alie felt the Ukrainian's arm around her, soft as a habit, hard as a rosary. She thought of her time in the cloth, weeping before the statue of a virgin. She was a fraud, she thought, as the Ukrainian led her away, saying, "Let me tell you a story" quietly into her ear. She'd chickened out. Sold women and children out. Then wrote the story like that part, the dark hood in the alley in Somalia and everything after, had never happened at all.

She was a fraud, she thought, as the Ukrainian took her under his arm. But so what? Everybody was a fraud. Everybody.

CHAPTER 44

Brad Winters sipped orange juice from a champagne flute and eased back in his off-white leather seat. The whole airplane was off-white and gold, except for the teak, but in true *ancien régime* style it managed to be understated. The attendant rose when he swiveled the teak table to the side, but he waved her away. He only wanted to stretch his legs. In the last twenty-four hours, he'd flown from DC to NYC to London, with an eight-hour time zone change and only three hours of sleep. Now he was heading east. But he wasn't tired. Luxury like this will do that for a man. But so will adrenaline, and the pressing need to figure out the next move.

The bankers hadn't even bothered to ask him any questions, not important ones anyway, like how much natural gas went through Kramatorsk? What percentage was that of the total that passed through Ukraine into Europe? Who would be affected? What effect would taking the facility offline have on the broader economy? Could Europe be wounded? How badly? For how long? Could he guarantee any of this, or was he playing a hunch?

He could have given answers confidently. Cited numbers proficiently. Yes, this was the right pipeline station. Yes, this was the right time. He'd done his homework, that was why he had spotted the opportunity. He knew the cubic liters of gas involved, of course, but he was much less clear on the ramifications on the interlocking global market and industrial infrastructure of a postunification austerity EU, not to mention the internal politics of an oligopoly like Ukraine, where only money mattered. The bankers knew that. They kept a spectacularly stiff upper lip, but they were men of the world. They knew any numerical discussion was speculative at best, so they didn't bother.

It was the idea that mattered. The idea on a broad level, not in the specifics.

Ukraine was a Gordian knot, an interlooping factional hive of actions, threats, and consequences. The West had been trying to unravel it for years, decades in fact, even before the Cold War or the Russian Revolution. And what do you do with a Gordian knot?

You don't untie it. You slice through it, as quickly as possible.

The idea had come to him two days ago, like that legendary sword through that mythical rope. He knew Karpenko was only half an answer on his own, but he had seized the opportunity after the assassination attempt in Poltava. It was a time-tested strategy: bring in the player, put him in motion, figure out how to use him later. Bringing in Locke from outside the conflict zone was equally orthodox. Locke was the perfect combination of excellent at his job and unknown, at least in Russia and the Eastern Bloc.

Align the pieces. Apply pressure. Look for the

angles, as he had always done. Push with a steady hand. He had engineered the assault on the facility, the Donbas Battalion, Karpenko's press. He had done the same many times before. He was doing it in other parts of the world right now.

But then, for the first time in his life, he had burst through. He had flashed onto a masterstroke and gambled on intuition.

Why were the Russians guarding the pipeline facility? To protect it. From whom? *From everybody.* And what your enemy fears most: that is your greatest asset.

Anyone can play the odds. But you can grasp the moment, Winters thought, only when you've mastered the game. When you've studied all the moves; when you understand them in your bones.

It was a long rise from being the only white kid in that poor black neighborhood in south Baltimore, with his broken family and his hippy single mom. Altar boy, even though he wasn't religious. Principal's pet and "special project," even though he wasn't well behaved. Then the army. It broke his mother's heart, but she signed the enlistment papers when he was sixteen, and that was when he lost respect for her, when she supported him in something she despised. Officer School. Airborne. Wall Street. Private banking. Ivy League MBA, even without an undergrad degree. The Pentagon. Back to Wall Street. He caught a lucky break when the planes hit the Twin Towers, because he was already in the private military business, but he had worked it from there, making himself not just a beneficiary of government largesse, but a creator of it. He devised the policies, through the K Street two-step, that put armed contractors on the ground. Then he cashed the checks.

But this was different. This was beyond money, beyond the place where people were impressed by billions. He had felt it the moment Karpenko introduced him to the London bankers. There was another layer, a deeper level of power. Anyone could turn a billion dollars into ten billion. But how many could shape the next century? Rothschild. Carnegie. Rockefeller. Prescott Bush, but not his offspring. Jobs . . .

The bankers were insiders, workers for those who moved the world. And like all employees, they had expected a business plan. Instead, he had given them a solution. Ukraine can struggle on for a generation, savage and inefficient, or we can change the dynamic. Force the pussies in Europe to act, as self-preservation. Force the Americans to strike the death blow to Russia they should have delivered in 1992. He would break Eastern Europe, he might break the continent, but in the end, he would remake it, exactly as it always should have been.

And then, as he neared the final moment, the bankers had changed the game.

Winters sipped his orange juice, feeling the jet throttle back for its initial descent. He looked out the window, past the blinking light on the tip of the wing. It was dark, but beneath that darkness, and those clouds, was the place he had never anticipated going, at least not on this trip.

Russia. The home of the enemy.

Great men develop great plans, he thought. *Truly*

great men can improvise in the arena, even when they don't know the rules. Are you a truly great man, Brad Winters?

He laughed to himself. *You're about to find out.*

At least he'd been smart enough to hide an ace up his sleeve.

CHAPTER 45

The rusty fishing boat bobbed in the Black Sea, which on this night wasn't living up to its name. The moon was waning gibbous, almost full, and it threw a bright path of light from the boat to the horizon. It was so bright, Jacob Ehrlich could see the patterns of their nets in the water, rocking on a gentle breeze.

The moon didn't matter. There wasn't anyone else out, not this deep. Ehrlich had been out here every night for the past twenty days, and there never was. He had taken this job for the adventure, but he had quickly realized it was even more boring than sitting in a motor pool, changing the oil on Stryker combat vehicles. At least it was thirty days on and thirty days off, with twice the pay of a warrant officer.

He turned back to his work, running his scanner over the wing of the drone, then the body. Usually, his primary duty was to make sure the cameras were in place and working. They were worth more than the drones, and besides, it wasn't any good to send spy drones over Ukraine and the Balkans if the cameras weren't in proper order. Apollo Outcomes had some sort of overlook contract, tracking troop movements, probably, although Ehrlich didn't know. He didn't even fly the things. That was done thousands of miles away in Michigan, if the rumors were true, or maybe Minnesota. He never even saw the footage. He just maintained, launched, and recovered them from this rusty scupper.

Six a night, every night. Always the same: except for this one.

"It's a banger," Johnson said, as he finished his inspection. Johnson was the other tech, and the only other company man on the job. The six fishermen were locals, hired for cover and trained in firearms. Ehrlich didn't entirely trust them, but he assumed Apollo paid them well. More than they could make fishing, anyway.

"Previous generation," Ehrlich said. "Not as fast, but at eight thousand feet, still invisible. And I guess they don't have to worry about pretty pictures." There were no cameras on this drone, but it had a special nose cone, bulkier than any he had ever seen.

"I wonder what's up?" Johnson said, nodding to the cone.

"None of my business," Ehrlich shrugged. "I just get them in the air. You clear?"

"Clear," Johnson said, stepping back.

Ehrlich looked at his watch. They were eight miles south of a remote stretch of Ukrainian coast, and it was midnight on the dot, as specified. He punched in the launch code, telling the boys back in Michigan the bird was ready to fly. Maybe if he had realized the nose cone was a blasting cap filled with a pound of C-4, and that almost fifty pounds of C-4 were laced through the interior of the drone, making it a bomb big enough to blow up a building, or an entire factory, especially one filled with natural gas, he would have paid closer attention.

But he didn't, so Jacob Ehrlich didn't think anything of it as he watched the massive drone bomb lift into the air. Thirty seconds later, it was invisible, even in a moonlit sky.

"Bring up the next one," Ehrlich said.

CHAPTER 46

Almost three thousand miles away, the Gulfstream-V corporate jet touched down at Pulkovo Airport outside St. Petersburg. It was 0100 local time, three hours ahead of London and one hour ahead of Ukraine.

The door opened, and Brad Winters stepped off. He had never been to Russia. He'd never done business on this side. The Berlin Wall had come down decades ago; Wall Street had arrived five seconds later; but in the mercenary business, there was a barrier between East and West. Apollo would work for almost anyone, anywhere, if the mission and money were right, but it had never worked for the East. Putin was an ex-KGB officer; he had his own private armies. And he was the enemy.

But Russia was warmer than he expected, at least for May.

Below him, a black sedan pulled onto the tarmac and parked four feet from the airplane stairs. Winters walked down and got inside. There was a man in the backseat. Early forties, neat as a military bedsheet, clearly British from the cut of his hair to the lack of a chin.

"Welcome, Mr. Winters," the young man said. Young for private banking, old for private equity.

He must be out here in the hinterlands, Winters figured, working his way toward the London office.

"Thank you, Mr. . . ."

"Everly." They didn't shake hands. As soon as Winters's bag was loaded into the trunk, they started moving.

"I've been briefed on your plan," Everly said. "You are here to communicate it to our contact on the other side, Mr. Gorelov. Have you ever dealt with Russians?"

No comment on the plan, Winters noticed. Everly knew the company rules. "I've met a few," he said.

"They are tough," Everly said. "Blunt, even by American standards. You are not here to finesse the details. Nor are you here to negotiate. You are here to break legs. I understand you are a military man . . ." Everly looked at him for the first time and smiled, although it looked pained, due to his lack of chin. ". . . I assume you know what I mean."

Ambush him. Keep him in the kill zone. "No offense, but what are you expecting from this?"

Everly side-eyed him. It was as close to an emotion as the banker's had ever given him. "You're the first person that's ever presented a plan for Ukraine that might work. That has . . ." the banker searched for the right word ". . . testicular fortitude. We expect you to convince them, just as you've convinced us. Do you understand?"

"I understand." He didn't. Not entirely. But he was working on it.

"Good. The meeting is at 5:00 A.M. It is 1:09 A.M.

local time. I will take you to a room. I advise you to get some sleep."

0500 St. Petersburg time. 0400 in Kramatorsk. That left only two hours before the Donbas Battalion was scheduled to arrive and four, maybe, before he lit his secret weapon and blew Russia's excuses, not to mention her precious gas lines, into a fireball half a mile high. If it came to that. And Brad Winters was finding that, increasingly, he hoped it did.

"Not much time," he said.

Everly smiled, sort of. "Pressure," he said, "is our ally."

CHAPTER 47

I stood over the sand table, a five-by-eight-foot mock-up of the gas facility and surrounding area that Miles and I had created on the warehouse floor, as Miles gathered the team. As the noncom, it was his role to call the men to order. As officer, it was my role to devise and brief the plan. We weren't strict about protocol in Apollo, but the team was former military, and old ways die hard.

It was a big group. The seven men on the team: myself, Miles, Charro, Wildman, Boon, Jacobsen, and Reynolds. Then Greenlees, looking a thousand years old. And the three Ukrainians: Colonel Sirko, Maltov, and Karpenko, who had come out of the back of the warehouse, where he had been talking with Alie for most of the last hour.

He'd convinced me not to cuff her and, reluctantly, I'd agreed. Now, with Maltov's men on guard duty and Alie falling toward an exhausted three-in-the-morning nap, I was happy he'd talked me out of it. He was taking care of her, just like he'd promised, so I could keep her off my mind. I wasn't particularly happy to have Karpenko at the sand table, but it was the client's prerogative to sit in on the plan meeting, and we had a good working relationship. I knew he'd respect my authority on military matters. But . . .

"Only the principal and team members," I said, pointing my broken broomstick at the pilot, who was skulking over Karpenko's shoulder.

Karpenko turned and snapped something in Ukrainian. The pilot started to object, but Karpenko took him by the collar, pulled him close, and muttered something that made the man turn pale.

"'One more word, one finger,'" Greenlees translated in a whisper to Miles and me, as the pilot backed away.

I locked eyes with Miles, and I could tell he was impressed. Karpenko knew when it was time to get down to business, and he could swing the hammer. If I wasn't mistaken, that hammer was Maltov. Maybe Winters was on to something. Maybe Karpenko *was* the right man for Ukraine.

"This is the target," I said, pointing with my broomstick to the bricks and cardboard that denoted the facility. The sand table looked haphazard—bricks or concrete chunks for buildings, cardboard and other scraps for walls, copper wire for the tangle of natural gas pipes—but Miles and I had rendered every distance and size as carefully as possible, since lives depended on accuracy. Of course, when I wasn't looking, Wildman had painted the words "slags KIA" at the spot where he took down the three thugs and tricked up one of the wooden block "cars" with a racing stripe. I had to laugh. Soldier humor was puerile, but important. Every unit needed a clown.

"This is north," I said in my command voice, pointing. "East. West. South." I touched each one.

"North is fallow fields. No good avenues of approach, if they have thermal imagers. East is the same. On the south is the industrial park and two entry points, each with a metal security door: one vehicle, one pedestrian. Parking lot in the southeast corner. Road along the front." I traced it out. "Fifty meters of open space between the road and two industrial buildings, here and here. Two-story industry buildings along these three blocks. Apartment buildings here, including the tall one where Wildman set the camera. Good for overwatch, but be alert for slags."

I glanced at Wildman. He was nodding, looking serious, as if I was simply recounting useful information, but a couple of the other guys laughed.

"You all know about the pub thugs here," Miles said, taking the broomstick and pointing to the club we had hit a few hours ago. "So far, they are scared back into their hole, but we should avoid this part of the AO." Area of operation.

I took back the stick. He who has the stick has the floor. "Inside the facility are pipes, a small equipment warehouse, and a control building. They are surrounded by a six-foot brick wall, with embedded broken glass and rusty concertina wire on top." I traced the wall with my pointer. "The entry points are monitored by closed-circuit cameras and floodlights here, here, and here. We are ghosts. We are not here. We avoid the entry points and lights unless our lives depend on it."

Only Karpenko nodded. It was standard operating procedure for the rest of us.

"The enemy are Spetsnaz." I paused and looked at the men. That word had gotten their attention. No joking now, except for Wildman, who was smiling like this was the funny part. "Random three-person foot patrols inside the facility, no discernable time or pattern. Single-man overwatch from this roof." I tapped the control building. "Also random times. It's designed to look sloppy, right down to the fake militia uniforms, but it's highly professional. Miles and I estimate a squad-size element, as many as twelve men, although only three have ever appeared outside at the same time. They are heavily armed and well trained, but bored and not expecting us. Those not on patrol will be here"—the control building—"probably on the first floor, but that's best guess. We have no eyeballs inside."

Nodding. Half blind was not ideal, but common.

"There are two civilians on the overnight shift. Engineers. They are monitoring the pipeline from here, the control building. They are to be unharmed and incapacitated. We'll hand them over to the Donbas Battalion on linkup, and they won't see the light of day until the operation is over." Meaning the press has departed and Karpenko is a national hero.

"Got it boss, no molesto," Wildman affirmed. "Civilians sleep like babies tonight."

What did Wildman know, I wondered, about babies?

"The facility operates 24/7 and the day shift starts at 0700. Workers arrive as early as 0630, so we need to have the little green men flex-cuffed by then or we're fucked. Questions?"

Silence.

"Good. Our objective is to capture Russians. I repeat, capture not kill." I tapped the copper wires. "Fire discipline is paramount. One stray bullet here, and . . ."

"Kaboom," Wildman whispered, like it was a forbidden love.

"Kaboom," I agreed.

I looked around. Everyone was alert, especially Karpenko. His eyes were gleaming, and he was grinning like a carnivore.

"At 0430"—I looked at my watch—"that is two hours and thirty-three minutes from now, we move out on foot, and approach the facility here." I traced our route from the factory to the facility's northwest corner. "Use available concealment from the surrounding forest and BMNT." Before Morning Nautical Twilight, military speak for twilight, a good time to catch unaware soldiers in their rack.

"We scale the wall here," Miles said, taking over the tactical portion of the briefing, "on the far side, where the pipes come out of the ground. Locke and Charro carry the folding ladder. Charro, once the ladder is up, I want you to cut the wire and lay the blanket over the glass." Miles tossed him a thick wool blanket, scrounged by Maltov's crew.

"Boon will fly the drone, so we're not blind." Earlier, we'd had tryouts to see who could walk and fly at the same time. Boon smoked everyone. Jacobsen almost flew the damn thing into a tree.

I took back the stick. "Object is to catch all men

inside, so we maintain cover through the pipes to here." I pointed. "It's cover, but it's also insurance. Spetsnaz aren't stupid enough to shoot at us in the pipes." I hope.

The team nodded. Incineration would be excruciating, but instantaneous.

"If we mistime, and there's a patrol, we hunker down in the shadow. Whoever is closest, take them out. Silently. Assume one Spetsnaz on deck at the control building, so hug the dark."

"The drone's noise may alert them. I'll park it here," Boon said, pointing to the center of the maze of pipes. "Once the op is finished, I . . . or someone else," Boon said calmly, at peace with the idea that he might be killed tonight, "can fly it out before the workers arrive."

I could feel it now, like I always could at some point during the briefing. I could see the movement in my mind, and I was walking the steps, picturing myself there. The adrenaline was pumping, but I knew how to control that. Movement to contact would take seven to eight minutes, the same length as "Mars: The Bringer of War" from Holst's symphonic odyssey *The Planets*. I could already hear the rhythmic beat of the music, its trajectory toward total obliteration. By the time we were on the ground, it would be an inferno in my mind.

"We split into three teams," Miles said, pointing at the control building with the stick. "Jacobsen and Reynolds provide overwatch. Sniper anything that moves. If shit gets bad, use the M90 rocket launchers." We had five, tough enough to kill tanks and blast through walls, but we could realistically only carry two. "Civilian collateral damage is authorized but discouraged. And don't forget the drone. We'll rig a block of C-4 to it, as a backup kamikaze, if the shit gets thick."

Everyone nodded. They were feeling it, too.

"Wildman and I will breach the building's east door," Miles said. This was the most dangerous part. Close-quarters combat was the trench warfare of the modern world. But Wildman held up his det cord and duct tape with a grin, like it was a gift, and this mission was Christmas morning.

"Boon and Charro, take the west door. I'll synchronize detonation over comms. I leave it up to each team how you stack and sector for room clearance. Watch your corners, and clear room by room. Hit tangos, spare civvies, and don't bother with sensitive site exploitation. This is a snatch-and-grab, with prejudice."

"Nonlethal takedowns?" Boon asked.

Easy for him, I thought. Boon was fast as a cat and could break black belts like he was swatting mosquitos. He was so quiet, they usually didn't know he was there.

Me? No so much. Not anymore.

Miles nodded. "Nonlethal if possible, but no unnecessary risks. Locke and Sirko will be backup . . ."

Wildman and Charro fidgeted. Sirko wasn't one of us; they weren't comfortable with an outsider. I could see Maltov scowl, and Sirko smirk. The enforcer wanted to be there, but he was going to man the radio with Greenlees back here in the warehouse.

I guess you shouldn't have manhandled Alie, I told him telepathically.

"Sirko and Locke will be second in the east door," Miles said, raising his voice to drown out any objections, "providing firepower where needed. Sirko will be our interpreter. You can talk to each other, but only Sirko talks to the prisoners."

"Remember the mission," I said. "The more live Russian special operators Karpenko can parade before the cameras in flex-cuffs, the better."

"What do I do?" Karpenko asked. He was no doubt thinking of his moment standing in front of the world, imagining himself there, the impending king of Ukraine. It always seemed so clean and easy on the sandtable.

"We'll call Greenlees when the facility is secure. You walk down with Maltov and his men and scale the wall. If this all goes down right," I said, turning back to the team, "we lock it down in eight minutes, and hold the objective until the Donbas Battalion arrives, expected 0600. The press birds arrive at 0700."

More than two hours inside. It was a risk, especially in an active war zone.

"And if it goes sideways?" Jacobsen asked.

I pointed to the fish truck in the corner of the warehouse. Maltov's men had welded scraps of steel to its side for protection, like something from Mad Max, and loaded it with three drums of gasoline wired to a few kilos of C-4 and a blasting cap.

"Maltov drives the truck," I said, "and blows the front gate. We improvise from there."

Wildman smiled. I hadn't noticed before that he was missing teeth. "Now you're talking, boss," he said.

CHAPTER 48

It took another ten minutes to finish the briefing—almost fifteen minutes total—but only because Maltov and Karpenko had to be walked through their part three times, even though it was straight-forward.

If I call Greenlees and say "green," walk down and act like you just kicked Russian ass.

If I say "red," drive the fish truck to the front entry gate of the facility as fast as you fucking can. Park it there. Light the fuse. Run.

No shooting. That was the hard part for Maltov to understand: that the last thing I wanted was a Ukrainian cowboy running into a gas facility with guns blazing. That was why the Russians had sent Spetsnaz, their best-trained troops. That was why Winters was sending a Tier One team before the militia arrived.

"And if the Russians send reinforcements?" Jacobsen asked.

A good question, and a distinct possibility, given that the camera crews weren't scheduled to arrive until 0700 and would probably be late.

"If the Russians roll in, I call the boss," I said, meaning Winters. "I'll see how far he wants to take this."

"And if that doesn't work, we blow the place up," Wildman exclaimed, clearly liking the idea. Thank God Apollo provided a place for men like Wildman. Thank God he was here to cover my ass. But there was no way I was blowing the place up. I'd have rather run than take that chance.

"It's 0213 zulu time," I said. Shit, it was late. "Rack out. We're up at 0415 to sanitize this place, and then move out. Let's hit it."

The team dispersed. They had two hours for last preparations and personal rituals before sleep: pray in the case of Charro, meditate in the case of Boon, listen to music in my case, sculpt bunny rabbits out of C-4, if you were a certain Welsh ex-SAS son of a bitch.

I kicked the sand table apart, making sure that no one could figure out later what had been planned here. I piled the few things we would leave behind on top—rations, spent batteries, ammo crates, excess equipment. One of Maltov's men would burn it with white phosphorus after the op was done. Take only the objective; leave nothing behind, not even footprints. That was our mission, every time.

I needed rack, but instead of heading to my sleeping bag, I found myself drifting to the far corner, where the Ukrainians were holding Alie. She was asleep near a crate of smoke grenades, and even from across the warehouse I could see the curve of her neck, the soft golden skin of her cheek.

I heard angry voices and turned toward them. Maltov was shoving the pilot, who was gesturing toward Boon, who was siphoning helicopter fuel into one of the truck's barrel bombs. Smart. Aircraft fuel was extremely explosive.

When I turned back, Alie was watching me. I expected her to get up, the better to confront me, but she only pushed herself to a seated position as I approached. Behind me, the loud Ukrainian curses crescendoed, until they turned into a single voice. It sounded like the pilot pleading.

"Hello again, Alie," I said, as a scream ripped through the warehouse. Someone had lost a finger.

"Asshole," she muttered to me, without her previous conviction.

"How do you like Karpenko?"

"I like him, of course," she said wearily. "He's a rich man. That's how rich men get rich, by being smooth. Telling you what you want to hear. It's called manipulation." She paused. "He seems to have taken a genuine shine to you, though."

I shrugged. "Nobody's perfect."

"You saved his children. Or at least that's what he thinks. He told me he doesn't know where they are."

"They're safe," I said, but I could tell she wasn't convinced. Who did she think I was working for? The mafia? "I don't know where they are, but I know who they are with. They are safe."

"I guess you have to think that way . . ."

She trailed off. She was tired. Her hand was shaking. I noticed Karpenko's label-less bottle of booze from Poltava, now empty. Perhaps they had been toasting better times. But the better times were in the past, and all we had was right now.

"We're leaving before dawn. You're staying here

with Greenlees. It will be your job to get yourself to . . . wherever it is you want to go." I felt bad for her, and I felt lost, although I wasn't sure why. Perhaps because, after this was over, I didn't have anywhere else I wanted to be. "You can take the bird, but I wouldn't advise it. There are antiaircraft batteries between here and . . . everywhere. And the pilot . . . I think he's lost some blood."

She didn't question me on that.

"I'd take the Škoda, since it won't attract attention. Drive with Greenlees back to Kiev. I can't guarantee your safety, but it's the best I can offer."

I stopped. I was tired. I knew she would write about what had happened here, but I also knew it wouldn't matter. We had her cell phone, so there were no photographs, and no one would corroborate what she'd seen. It would just be more rumors from the front lines, on an Internet already swimming with them. Worse things could happen. People were "disappeared" in war zones everyday.

"You shouldn't have come," I said, more tenderly than I expected.

She looked up at me. She was fierce, and then she wasn't.

"I'm sorry," I said. "For . . . you know."

She wouldn't take her eyes off mine, so I was the one who stood up and turned away, giving her a last small victory. It was the least I could do.

"Tom," she said after I'd taken a few steps, causing me to turn. She was smaller than I had ever seen her before, but she was still everything I wanted . . . in some other life. "Don't leave me here."

Bam. A frag grenade to my heart.

"You can't come with me," I said.

She didn't argue, so I turned around, started walking, and didn't look back. What else could I have said? She couldn't break me. I was far too hard for that, no matter how much she meant to me. I needed this mission to work, and she had to know that. I needed to do it right, so that everyone would walk away alive—including Alie.

Karpenko caught up with me a minute later, as I was pulling my sleeping bag over me like a blanket. He pulled up an ammo crate and lit one of his blue Dunhills. He crossed his legs, so that his $5,000 shoes were hovering near my face. I knew he had worked on this pose, maybe for years. It was his signature move: dominant indifference.

"I'll take care of her," he said. "I'm going to take her with me."

He was the client. Fine.

"I've told her my story. I want her to write it."

"Leave me out of it. And the team."

"She knows. This was Ukrainian, purely Ukrainian. It is better for both of us that way. Especially me."

He smoked his cigarette slowly. He was the only man in the warehouse who still looked clean. Never let them see you sweat.

"What is your father like?" he said.

"My father was Miniver Cheevy," I said. Cheevy was a character in a poem I'd read in sixth grade, a hopeless romantic who dreamed about the past.

"He was a minister," Karpenko said, nodding, as if that explained something.

My father was a drunk and an amateur historian,

a lover of the doomed romance of the Confederate cause, not slavery but chivalry, for which our ancestors fled south across the Maryland border to fight with the Army of Virginia. He always wished he'd been born then, he said, but if he had, he'd just have pined for some other, earlier cause. The time period didn't matter. You were either a man of action or you weren't. Or as his hero Teddy Roosevelt once said, a "man in the arena," or a nobody. That was why he pushed me, in his absentee-father, show-up-once-every-six-months way, into military service. Or maybe I'd done it to show him I wasn't going to be the loser he'd always been.

"He named you Thomas after the prophet?" Karpenko mused, still misunderstanding.

Thomas was a disciple, and a doubter, not a prophet.

"He named me Jubal, after an American Confederate general" and patron saint of lost causes. "Thomas is my middle name."

Karpenko puffed his Dunhill and recrossed his legs. "You have no doubt heard about my father," he said. I hadn't. "How I came back from college in Kiev after the Soviet Union collapsed and liberated the steel plant were my father worked. How he came out, covered in slag, and I handed him a check like all the other men, six months of unpaid wages. How we hugged, the first time since I was a boy. And then every worker hugged me, a long line of dirty men, crying as they poured out of that hole."

"Yeah, something like that," I lied. I had never heard a word about his past.

"It isn't true," he said, flicking away his butt. "It is

propaganda. I don't know who started it, maybe me, I honestly can't remember."

He lit another cigarette. It was his way of creating drama. Or calming his nerves.

"My father died when I was eight, soon after the Russians moved him to the steel plants in Poltava. It was a promotion, perhaps. Or a punishment. He may have been a nationalist. We were ethnic Cossacks, and the Soviets didn't trust us. I hated the Russians after that, because my father never recovered. He only lived six months. He was sick, and the foreman never allowed him to go to hospital, even on the day he died."

I thought of what Alie had said, about Karpenko being smooth, about his ability to manipulate you into liking him. I admit it. I liked him.

"I want my son to know me," he said, blowing a big lungful of smoke. "I want him to understand that I did this for my country. For our country, because Ukraine is his, too. Is that too much to ask?"

I didn't know. I didn't have a son. "Your children are safe," I said, eyes closed.

"Yes, but I am not."

I was tired. I had a mission to run in less than two hours, and time was ticking down. Besides, he wasn't asking if he should risk his life for his cause. He'd already made up his mind.

"You shouldn't smoke," I said. "Nobody smokes anymore. It will kill you."

CHAPTER 49

They met in a restaurant, one with a bare concrete façade and burgundy curtains closed over the windows, a type very common in the East. The inside was ornate, burgundy and gold, with abundant curlicues and lurking cherubs in the old Russian style. Even in the deserted quiet of 4:45 A.M., or maybe because of it, Winters felt like he'd stepped inside a Fabergé egg.

But if the restaurant décor was delicate (and it was), their contact seemed designed to counteract it. The Russian sat heavily in the back corner of a back room as if made of a thousand pounds of lead, his neck bulging over the collar of his too-small Italian suit. He was sixty, perhaps, and rough, with loose jowls and a shock of unnaturally black hair, a cigarette between fat gold-ringed fingers, a five o'clock (A.M.) shadow crusted onto his slumping face. On the table in front of him were a pack of cigarettes, a bottle of vodka, espresso in a glass cup with an ornate metal holder, and six cell phones.

I always expect Russians to look different from the stereotype, Winters thought, *but they never do.*

"Mr. Gorelov," Everly said, extending his hand.

Winters had studied Putin's inner circle, and a few outer ones too, but he'd never heard the name.

He didn't like that. It put him on shaky ground. Who was this man?

"This better be good," Gorelov grumped. Behind him, a couple of bodyguards were frowning. Winters had counted eight in the restaurant, all armed, smoking on the job.

"I don't know if it's good," Everly said. "But it's important."

"I hope this isn't about the transfer agreements again," Gorelov grumbled. No formalities, Winters noted. And no espresso for his guests.

"Any change in your position?"

"No change."

"Have you discussed it with your superiors?"

"I have no superiors," Gorelov said.

"Of course," Everly replied, dipping his nonexistent chin. "But I assume the right people know of our proposition. Our clients expect . . ."

"I don't give a damn about your clients," Gorelov said, burying his head in his coffee. He was stonewalling. Winters wondered if it was personal, or personality. About 110 Russians owned 40 percent of the country's wealth. Winters suspected more than a few were Everly's clients, and Gorelov's enemies. Stereotypes suggested that Russians were men of titanic grudges.

"So who is he?" Gorelov sniffed, jerking his head.

"This is Mr. Winters."

"Pleased to meet you," Winters said, extending his hand.

The Russian drank vodka from a short glass. He looked anything but pleased. "An American," he said.

"An expert on Ukraine," Everly replied, only slightly exaggerating.

Gorelov turned toward him for the first time, his eyes bloodshot. "You have something for me?" he asked in gruff, accented English. He was a man, Winters could tell, who liked to dominate the conversation.

"I have an opportunity," Winters shrugged, almost as if he regretted it, "created by you." There was no point in being coy.

"Let me guess. You think you can use Little Russia for your advantage." A derogatory Czarist term for Ukraine, meant to irritate him.

"We must protect Western interests," Winters said.

"And expand them, because you are takers. But Ukraine is ours, Mr. Winters. It always has been, and it always will be. When the czars ruled, Ukraine was a province, just like your California. When the Soviets came to power, they marched through Kiev, just like Moscow. *Ukraine* means 'meadow' in Russian—did you know that?—because they grow our grain. They feed our mothers. They nourish our factories with coal. They speak our language, with an atrocious accent, yes. They are not our most sophisticated region, but they are ours."

"That's not what the international community says."

"International community. What does that mean? The West? What is the West, in the face of hundreds of years of history?"

"What about the will of the people?"

Gorelov scoffed. "The people want to be Russian. That is why they fight."

"They want to be free."

Gorelov waved the suggestion away. He drank vodka, then coffee, then dragged on his cigarette. One of his phones buzzed. He ignored it. "They want to be happy. They want to be free of this violence brought on by the meddling of the West."

"The West didn't create the crisis."

"But you believe you can exploit it."

"I know I can," Winters said, switching to the first person.

Gorelov laughed, one of the least joyous sounds Winters had ever heard. It sounded like a cat choking on a brick of coal. "You think a businessman," the Russian said with disgust, "can face down the greatest nation on earth."

That's our phrase buddy, Winters thought, and no kleptocratic petrostate is going to steal it. But he wasn't offended. He was intrigued. It was going to be brass balls and bullshit, he could see that. No wonder France buckled like a Peugeot under a tractor-trailer when Putin dared them to intervene.

"It's not a matter of facing down," Winters said. "This isn't intimidation. I plan to beat you at your own game."

"And what game is that?"

"Military exploitation."

Gorelov grunted, or maybe it was another laugh. "I am a bureaucrat, Mr. Winters."

Good to know, Winters thought. "And I'm a military man, with a private army."

The Russian glanced at Everly and frowned. This was new. Winters saw his advantage and moved in, cornering the Russian with his eyes.

"For years, you have counted on our passivity," he said. "On our refusal to meet you with force. No please, don't insult me by objecting, you know it's true. You support our enemies—Iran, Syria, even Afghanistan—in order to grind us down, to make our Deep State interests weary of war. But I am different, Mr. Gorelov. I feast on war. Conflict is my business, and business is booming. But it can be better. My dream, unlike the men you bully, isn't peace. It is war. The type that grinds you back, the way you have subdued Georgia and Chechnya, the way you will try to grind down Ukraine. In other words, I am what you fear most, without knowing it. I am a Putin of the West."

Gorelov visibly recoiled, as Winters knew he would. "You are no Putin," he grunted.

"No. I am not a monster."

Gorelov pounded the table, making his vodka glass rock. He curled his hand around a cellphone, his weapon of choice. "You insult me, Mr. Winters."

Winters smiled. He had hit the big man where it hurt. At this level, every Russian worked for the state, and that meant Vladimir Putin, because in Russia, Putin *was* the state. He had reined in the oligarchs with ex-KGB muscle and crushed all political opposition. If you opposed him you died, went to prison, or, if you were lucky, into exile. If you worked with him, he gave you whole cities or entire segments of Russia's economy, bringing unfathomable wealth and power. It was institutionalized mafia—Nigeria with nukes and snow. It wasn't much different, in all honesty, from how the country had been ruled for the last thousand years, except for brief interludes from 1917 to 1921, and most of the 1990s. At those points, the country was chaos.

Putin created his order, Winters had to admit, as he watched the Russian fume. Too bad he was such a shit.

"Don't worry," Winters said, when he'd stretched out the silence and Gorelov was sufficiently rattled, "I am not merely talking. I will show you how like Vladimirivich"—he used the honorific for Putin, a serious breach of etiquette for outsiders—"I truly am."

"You're going to attack Ukraine," Gorelov snorted.

"Only the parts you want."

"We'll stop you."

"At what cost?"

"It doesn't matter the cost," Gorelov said smugly, "because we control it all, and the Russian people are with us. The Russian people, the ones you call Ukrainians, will never accept you. They will curse your name."

"Do you know who I am?" Winters said smoothly.

"I know everyone, Mr. Winters," Gorelov said, leaning forward. He looked ready to bite. "And I have never heard of you."

"And the Ukrainians won't either, Mr. Gorelov. Even when my man is king of Kiev."

Gorelov blinked. He sat back in his chair, his hand cradling a cell phone. He hadn't considered the power of anonymity as a choice, and now it was his turn to be thrown off balance, to think, as Winters had only minutes before: who is this man?

CHAPTER 50

I grabbed my SCAR and rolled into position. Miles was laying prone a few feet away, his Bushmaster ACR up and aimed, the safety unlocked. I dropped my weapon to my side and kicked out of my sleeping bag beside him.

"There's someone at the gate," Miles said. I looked at my watch: 0352. I'd lost only a few minutes of sleep.

"Ukrainian?"

Miles shook his head. "He looks homeless, but he's speaking English. Yelling in English, actually."

"Grab him."

"We already have. There will be blood."

"Good," I said as I slipped on the earpiece of my headset. From the way Miles was looking at me, I knew he was worried about my breakdown with Alie. Poor form, and not just in front of the troops. As the old commercial said, never sweat. "Mission focus," I assured him, as I strapped on my pistols.

"Warrior spirit," Miles said, fist thumping his chest. Meaning: For the mission, for your brothers. Get your head on straight.

The prisoner looked terrible. Boon had zip-cuffed his hands in front of him, and he'd taken a few "shut the fuck up" punches to the face, but I doubted he'd looked much better when he arrived. He had a crusted bandage circling his head, half-covering one eye, and dried blood on his clothes. His hair was matted from blood and sweat. He didn't look like a threat, unless he was rabid. But he was here, and that was dangerous.

"Who are you?" I said.

"CIA."

"What does that mean?"

"Central Intelligence, Kiev, Operations Officer Chad Hargrove." Like he was reading off a dog tag. Was this what they taught at the Farm these days?

"How did you get here, Hargrove?"

"Stole a car. From Jessup."

"You parked on the road?" Miles exclaimed in disbelief.

The man nodded. He didn't seem to understand the implication of the highly visible car. I punched him in the face, for his stupidity. He took it pretty well.

"What are you doing here?" I said.

"Looking for Alie."

Miles glanced at me, but he didn't need to worry. Mission focus. "Who is Alie?"

"Alie MacFarlane." The man looked around. Wildman kneed him in the back of the leg. He buckled. No looking around, asshole. Eyes front.

"Who is Alie MacFarlane?" I said, my voice rising. This was a serious problem. This was becoming a compromised operation an hour short of the assault.

Nothing.

"Why the fuck are you here?" I yelled, resisting the urge to punch him again.

He looked up. "Are you Locke? The mercenary? She was looking for you."

I drew my pistol. I never drew my pistol unless I planned to use it.

"Don't," Miles said, just as Alie's "Shit" echoed through the warehouse. She was coming out of the shadows, Karpenko beside her. They were probably best friends by now.

"Alie," Hargrove muttered with relief.

"What the hell happened?" she said, taking in the bandages.

"Jumped. By Russians . . ."

"What the hell?" I said, lowering my weapon. "Alie, what is going on?"

I watched as she walked toward us, everyone on edge. She knelt beside the prisoner. He looked up at her tenderly. Thankfully. He was missing a tooth, a recent loss judging by the amount of blood on his gums, but he was no Wildman. "Let him go," she said.

I laughed, but nothing about this was funny.

"He's a CIA officer, Locke." She was speaking softly, as if that would make her sound more serious. "He's a United States government employee."

"Don't care."

"He's been injured."

"Don't care."

"He's a kid." She looked at me. I looked at the so-called CIA officer. She was right; he was young, maybe midtwenties. And he was scared.

"He's not here on Company business," she said, meaning the old company, the CIA. "He was just trying to find me. Make sure I was safe."

"Why?"

"I ditched him."

He was in love with her. I could see it in his face. "You used him."

Alie frowned. The truth hurt. "Would it help if I said yes?"

No, it wouldn't.

I turned back to the kid. "Is there anybody else?"

He took his time, probably contemplating his odds, or maybe his relationship with Alie. Not as easy as you thought, is it?

I punched him again, right in his Aryan nose. "Is anybody else coming?"

He shook his head no. I could tell he had settled on the truth.

"Does anybody else know you are here?"

"I'm an American," he said. "I'm on your side."

It doesn't work like that, asshole. "Does anyone else know you are here?"

He hesitated, then sadly: "No."

I put the gun to his head. "How did you know we were here?"

This was the big one, but Hargrove wasn't answering. He was a coward who hoped his silence made him a hero. I turned to Alie and put the gun to her head. "How the fuck did you know we were here?"

"I told him."

I turned. It was Greenlees, of course it was Greenlees, looking more pathetic than usual, looking exactly, in fact, like the man he was: a relic. If this was a le Carré novel, he'd be the hero, but that was what had gotten him in trouble. Too much faith in the power of the past.

"I called for an evac," Greenlees said. "That first morning. After I was punched." He glanced at Karpenko, as if to apologize. To Karpenko. Not to us.

"You gave up our position over a punch?"

He shook his head. It wasn't the punch, I could see that, but Greenlees knew that didn't matter, because right now I didn't give a fuck.

"I know that kid," Greenlees said. "He's a newbie, still on a leash and answering phones for the Deputy Chief of Station. He must have intercepted my radio call—"

"I never told anyone," the kid said frantically. He was starting to get it now. "Except Alie, I swear. I never told Baker."

Who is Baker? I wanted to scream. Who the fuck is Baker?

Miles must have sensed my frustration. "You don't want to shoot him," he said calmly.

The hell I didn't. Hargrove was young, a hell of a lot younger than Alie. Maybe he was just a kid in over his head, in love with an older woman, the possibility of an adventure, an ideal. But he was a kid who knew my name.

"Gag him." I looked around. "Attach him to that pipe," I said, pointing to the far end of the warehouse. "If he gives you any problems, kill him. We'll leave the body." Let the CIA sort it with the Russians.

"Tom," Alie started. Since when did she think she could use my first name?

"Don't worry, Alie, you can cut him out when we're gone. If you can find a strong enough blade."

I could see Greenlees slump. He'd mined harbors in Central America; he knew the game. The kid was resigned. Alie was going to fight, I could see that in her face, even before she grabbed me.

"Tom," she said quietly, really looking me in the eye for the first time, or at least for the first time since that night in Burundi when we'd fallen in love.

And that was when my world exploded.

My ears pressurized. Then I felt the shock wave, like a physical assault. Time stopped, and I saw the windows above me blowing inward, glass shards and debris hanging in the air. I sensed, but didn't hear, the *crack* of the explosion, and then time caught up with the RPG, and the glass shattered against the far wall.

Instinctively, I pushed Alie down and rolled flat, groping for my weapon. My vision was blurry, my breathing hard in my ears.

Two more RPGs slammed through the front wall, the concrete exploding toward me, and I buried my head in the floor as the shock waves passed above me.

Another rocket came through the breach, hissing across the factory and blowing out a chunk of the back wall, leaving a thick smoke trail hanging in the middle of the room.

My senses came back.

"Cover!" I heard Miles shout, as Boon vaulted from the catwalk.

Two grenades hurtled through the smoke into the center of the warehouse. I heard a *clink clink*, as they bounced off the concrete floor a few meters away. I pushed Alie behind our makeshift barricade and leapt on top of her. Successive blasts shook the building, and automatic gunfire raked the room, shredding the computer workstation and exploding a box of smoke grenades.

It had only been seconds since the windows blew out, but I'd already lost Miles in the smoke. I'd lost most of the team. Half the front wall was gone, sections of the ceiling were collapsing, but the building was holding together. This was a commando raid: fast and vicious. *Survive the first minute*, I thought, as the first man leapt through the blasted wall. *Must. Survive.*

"Tangos East wall!" I shouted into my headset, as a second man leapt a pile of shattered concrete, moving like a pro.

I glanced at Alie, crouched beside me. Behind her sat Hargrove, his eyes wide in terror. A few feet away I saw a body on the ground. It was Greenlees. It looked like he'd taken one in the head.

Get off the X, I thought. *Escape the ambush zone.*

"Suppressing fire," I yelled. "Everyone out."

Alie nodded, but I wasn't talking to her, I was talking to the team. They were already at it, laying down a wall of lead and tossing grenades, adding to the chaos. I swiveled. A figure rose on my right— Boon, I think—and headed toward the back. A third man appeared through the hole in the front wall. I leveled my SCAR, acquired the target in my sight picture, exhaled, and squeezed the trigger twice. Target down.

I took my time, finding the space in the fury of my team's massive counterbarrage. Slow is smooth, and smooth is fast. I melted behind a pile of metal scrap and slowed my breathing, steadying my nerves. Buddha calm. My SCAR was a precision weapon, unlike their AK-47s, and it shot 7.62 mm body-armor-piercing rounds. So I waited for a silhouette, and dropped it with a double shot, center of mass. Two more came through the crumbling wall, and I took them down, buying time for my team. The goal was to withstand the first wave of an assault, but this first wave was withering.

"Fall back," I barked, this time at Alie, but she wasn't there, only Greenlees, still dead.

I turned back to the attack, as the familiar smell of gunpowder filled the factory. The Škoda was on fire. My barrel was hot from too many rounds, making precision shooting difficult, so I flipped to automatic and fired three-round bursts. There were plenty of targets now, but most were behind cover. I tossed a grenade toward the breach point and ducked behind the barricade to reload, wishing I'd taken the time to build it right, as Charro had suggested.

Two more explosions rocked the building and put me on my ass. The first was an RPG. The second was the Škoda's gas tank. I looked up. Half the roof was blown out. The corner of the warehouse had collapsed. I could see the sky through the smoke, with only one blinking star, maybe a planet out there on the edge. I followed the cracks along the metal ceiling. It was safe. For now. I turned to fire again, as two figures rose from our side of the barricade and started to run. I spotted the Ukrainians on the left. Sirko was laying down impressive lead, holding his field of fire, but Karpenko was still crouched beside him. He should have fallen back.

Too bad. Too late now.

I shot another magazine on semiauto as two hostiles jumped the barricade. Someone—Charro—was in hand-to-hand combat. I ran without thinking, leapt into the void, and plunged my knife into the enemy's back, slamming him to the ground. Charro was under him, struggling, but my knife was an eight-inch blade; it didn't penetrate all the way through the chest cavity.

I pulled out the knife and rolled off into firing position, as Charro rolled the dead man onto his back. We locked eyes, he nodded, and then, as he popped into a firing position, a bullet ripped into his throat, and right out the back through Mother Mary's tattooed hands.

"Watch out," someone yelled.

A gunburst, close enough to shatter my hearing, and a man fell dead on top of me. I could hear the bullets whistling over me from both directions, and I knew I was in no-man's-land, so kept my head down. I could see hostiles—Russians? Spetsnaz?—struggling to hold their positions. *Get up. Get up now*, I thought. *Move to the evac route*. And then, just as I was about to run, a figure leapt up and sprinted through the fire. It was the pilot, racing for the helicopter. What was he doing? Where did he think he was going, up through the hole in the ceiling?

Time slowed, as the pilot loped across the last five meters, leapt over a pile of debris, and exploded. It was as if the door handle had been rigged, but it was an RPG, screaming in from beyond the breach, hitting the helicopter and hurling body parts and aluminum through the back wall a moment before the concussion caught up with the carnage and knocked everyone down.

"Pop smoke!" I heard Miles shout over the headset, as three smoke grenades plunked onto the factory floor, filling the warehouse with colored smoke. I crouch-ran for the back door, following someone—Reynolds—to the evac route. We passed Boon, hunkered behind a broken smelter, and laid down suppressing fire while Reynolds kicked the exit door at a full run, almost taking it off its hinges, and burst out into the open space beyond.

The air lit up, the lead ricocheting off the warehouse wall, as Reynolds danced a foot in front of me, the bullets tearing him apart. I grabbed him by the upper arm and hurled myself back through the door. My face was coated with Reynolds's blood; his shoulder was disintegrating in my hands. The enemy had all the exits covered. The enemy had a machine gun trained on the alleyway, the fucking pros.

"Alpha Four down. Alpha Four down. Back alley a no-go," I shouted, dropping Reynolds's body and making a throat-slashing gesture at Boon. The smoke grenades had done their work, and visibility was zero in the red-and-purple haze. The enemies' laser sites danced in the smoke, marking our targets. No time to reload the SCAR. I reached for my twin pistols and moved down the factory floor, popping skulls. A nine-millimeter pistol can sound like an air gun in battle, but it packs stopping power at close range, and three hostiles didn't get up. I missed two more, as they slipped behind cover and turned off their laser sights.

"Fire in the hole!" someone shouted, as a satchel charge thrown from the Russian side landed in the center of the storm.

I leapt behind the smelter with Boon and covered my ears. Several kilos of C-4 cratered the floor and sent a shock wave that knocked the smelter over and stunned and deafened everyone within thirty meters. I stumbled away, right into a Russian, his muzzle pointed at my chest, and it was over, all over, until someone opened up on automatic—it was Jacobsen's M249 SAW machine gun—and the Russian collapsed.

"Thanks Jake," I said as I turned, still stunned, but it wasn't Jacobsen. It was Alie, gasping for air and staring at the body, holding Jacobsen's gun.

"I fucking pissed myself," she said.

I looked down. She had. I almost said it was a good look, but instead I told her to fall back, this isn't over. "Is Jacobsen dead?"

"I think so."

The gunfire had stopped. In the smoke, the hostiles were falling back, consolidating their position outside, using the remains of the front wall as cover. Five meters in front of me, a wounded Russian attacker lay on his back, breathing heavily. His head swiveled toward me, and I put a bullet through his brain.

"Who's hit?" I screamed into the headset, my ears aching and hearing mostly gone.

"Charro, Jacobsen, Reynolds," Wildman said. "KIA."

"The old man, Greenlees. KIA."

"A couple Ukrainians . . ."

"Three dead," Maltov said, crawling up next to me. "One wounded."

I could see a young man a few feet away, slumped against the wall, sucking air. The other three living Ukrainians were near him, along with Sirko and Karpenko.

"Fuck." The voice snapped from the back of the warehouse. "Holy fuck, get me out of here. Get me out of these." I couldn't find the voice. I was looking but . . .

"It's me . . . It's Hargrove."

He was lying on his side ten meters away, breathing heavily. "Get me out of these cuffs," he said. He smelled like shit, and his eyes were wild with fear.

"Miles is wounded," someone said.

"Get me out," Hargrove said.

I turned away.

"Locke. Please. Locke . . . don't leave me."

"Shut the fuck up," I said, resisting the urge to smash his skull in with the butt of my rifle. This was his fault. The enemy had followed his car.

I surveyed the scene before me. We were cornered in the back of the warehouse. Smoke clung to the air, and half the building was on fire. Bodies littered no-man's-land, piles of broken concrete and glass, but no movement; the enemy had withdrawn to the other side of the flames. But they were out there, waiting. They had the tactical advantage, because they had the only exits covered, and we were stuck inside a burning building going down like a torpedoed ship.

Think fast, Locke. Think. These motherfuckers won't wait long.

"Call your dogs," I said to Maltov, tossing him my sat phone. "Anybody you know. Get them here."

I scrambled to Miles. He was on his back, gasping. He had taken three shots to the ballistic vest; its ceramic plates had been destroyed, saving his life but breaking ribs. Another shot in his left arm had missed the bone but rendered the arm useless. But the real problem was his left leg, torn and soaked with blood, a tourniquet tied around his thigh.

"Femoral artery," said Boon, our medic, as he tied on a second tourniquet. "He's bleeding out."

I'm not going to let him fucking die, I thought.

But a hospital was out of the question. Even if we got him there, anonymously, the FSB would pick him up, interrogate him by torture, and dump his body in a beet field. The Geneva Conventions didn't extend to mercenaries, not that modern soldiers benefitted much either.

"Morphine," Miles gasped.

He clenched his teeth. He knew the bargain: no extraordinary measures that could get others killed. But I had one chance. A desperate one: Winters. We just had to get out of here first.

"Ten minutes," Maltov said, handing me back the sat phone.

Shit. Too long. I figured we had two, at the most, before the Russians came knocking again.

"Two teams," I said, as Boon jammed the morphine into Miles. "Out the back and into the woods. Get far away, and get there fast. We'll link up in town, on the roof of the building where Wildman killed the slags. If I'm not there by 0700, head to the extraction point and wait. I'm taking Jimmy"—I could see Miles shaking his head, but I ignored it—"and the Ukrainians and the girl—"

"We're not going."

I turned. It was Maltov, his three healthy men crouched behind him. "We're not leaving," he said. "We're here to hang Russians."

"Chechens," Sirko snapped. Of course. The Colonel was right. They were mercs, not Spetsnaz.

Maltov turned and barked something in Ukrainian. Sirko spat back, then raised his rifle and stepped toward the enforcer, his finger on the trigger. I could feel the tension in his glare and the ferocity of his voice. Sirko had been pushed too far by Maltov. Sirko hated the man's recklessness and lack of finesse. But we were part of it too: Hargrove, Alie, and me. From Sirko's perspective, and it was a fair one, our carelessness was about to get him and his client killed.

"Enough," I said, cutting through the heated exchange.

Sirko didn't lower his bullpup, but Maltov laughed, even with the rifle in his face. He turned to the three men beside him, who laughed in turn. The Ukrainians were young and hard, but I could tell only Maltov's force of will kept them together. They were terrified.

"True Ukrainians will fight," Maltov said, turning toward me. "This . . . Russian will follow you."

"He follows me," Karpenko said.

The oligarch stepped forward and whispered something to Maltov. It looked like a business tip, not a good-bye. If Maltov survived, Sirko was out. He was probably out anyway. But I doubted either would survive.

Focus, Tom, I thought, looking around.

The fish truck was in the corner, untouched. It was packed with high-octane helicopter fuel.

"Please . . ." someone said.

The drone was next to the truck, also untouched. "The SA-18s?" I asked.

"Punctured," Boon said, shaking his head. Useless.

But still, a thought was coming together. Maybe even a plan. It wasn't much, but it was something, and I'd lived through worse . . . or almost as bad.

"Please," the voice pleaded again.

It was Hargrove.

"Please," he said.

He was on his back, crying and holding up his zip cuffs. What was I going to do with Hargrove? What was I going to do with the man who had brought this down on us, our extra baggage, our bad-luck charm?

Alie grabbed my arm. "He's CIA," she said. I had seen her vicious, and I had seen her passionate, but I had never seen her this determined. "He's a walking international incident, Tom, not to mention congressional investigation."

She was right. I had to bury Hargrove deep. The Russians could never find him, dead or alive. I knew which option I preferred. So I pulled out my knife, thinking through the steps—and at the last moment, decided to cut him loose.

"Wallet," I said with my hand out. "Keys. Badge. Anything that can identify you."

Hargrove emptied his pockets. I ripped off his dog tags. Why would a Case Officer have dog tags? He probably bought them at the mall. Everybody thought they were soldiers now.

"Find a gun," I said, reaching for my ruck.

It wasn't his fault. He didn't kill the guys on my team. He didn't kidnap Alie. He didn't hurt Miles.

I did.

CHAPTER 51

The Wolf stood in a copse of trees thirty meters from the front of the warehouse, watching it burn. The Chechen machine gun crew had reported only one kill behind the building; the rest had gotten the message and retreated. Part of the front wall had collapsed, enough to glimpse the wreckage inside: a shoddy barricade, a burning car. He could see five or six bodies scattered inside the building, the KIA of his first assault. The survivors were outside, surrounding the building.

He was glad it wasn't Colonel Sirko, his old commander, who had snatched the American girl in Kramatorsk. The Wolf might not have been able to resist shooting him on the spot. Instead, it was the Ukrainian Maltov, and he had been able to follow the fool straight back here. He had scouted the warehouse quickly, planning the assault in his head. He had gone in blind, as soon as the Chechens arrived, but there hadn't been a choice. He couldn't afford a "wait and see" strategy with quarry this elusive, or this good. He'd been burned that way in Poltava, and he wanted payback. These Chechens were hardened fighters, men who had hunted Islamists door to door, like dogs, from Damascus to Tbilisi.

This time, the plan had been pure firepower, the old Soviet way. Hit hard, hit fast. Leave corpses.

He had made two errors. The first was not killing the loud American when he arrived in the car. The second was not attacking the mercs when they opened the door to pull him inside. But his men weren't in position, and launching a raid prematurely could have been disastrous. The Westerners could have slipped the noose.

As things stood, the Wolf wasn't worried. He hadn't lost. He had taken casualties, but so had they. Now they were trapped in a burning building, with wounded, and their exits were covered.

The Wolf slid the action on his twenty-year-old Steyr AUG bullpup assault rifle, his life's true friend and companion. He stared down the scope and saw movement in the depths of the warehouse, men crouching and moving, but no clear shots.

He dropped the rifle to his side. "Be ready," he said to the ten-man secondary assault force around him in the trees.

The enemy was cornered, and they would either roast or run. It was that simple. All the Wolf had to do now was wait.

A thousand miles away, Gorelov put down his phone. Another was already ringing. "We have no troops in Little Russia," he said with the arrogant bravado of a man used to lying in the face of clear evidence. The Russians were even showing funerals for "martyred" soldiers on state television.

"You have a brigade in Severdonetsk," Winters replied calmly. "Three units outside Sloviansk. Not to mention the Spetsnaz near Mariupol, and the brigade helping the separatists hold the line to the west."

"They are volunteers," Gorelov growled, spouting the party line. "Patriots on holiday."

The man was grasping. Winters could see it. Gorelov didn't know military strategy. He didn't know mud—not the business variety, but the actually stinking, bloodstained dirt. If Winters could keep the battle on this terrain, guns not numbers, then he was confident he could break his man.

"They are Russian military units, under Russian command," he said, slowing down as Gorelov quickened his pace, "and I'm going to prove it. By this time tomorrow, the whole world will see you with your dick in the cookie jar."

Gorelov spoke abusive Russian into one cell phone, grabbed another, shouted, then put it down. He stubbed out a cigarette and lit another. Smoke was circling his head. He grinned.

"You think a private militia can defeat us?" He laughed. "You think a man like you can defeat Russia? The mightiest empire on earth?"

Wrong move. You already said that, my friend.

"No," Winters replied, "nor do we need to. I simply have to break you, at the point where you are weakest."

Gorelov refused to look away, staring his opponent down as he spoke rapidly into one cell phone after another. Winters didn't know what the Russian was saying, but he knew he was relaying threats to others further up the line, government officials, maybe military men. Good. He was probably trying to confirm the positions of Russian troops, and whether there was a Western private military company operating in east Ukraine. Let him try.

"My man will break you once, two hours from now, and then he will break you again, and again, until the world knows his name," Winters said, feeling it now, watching the military and media campaign unfurl in his mind. "By tomorrow, he will be Nikolay Karpenko, the savior of Ukraine."

Winters saw Everly swallow, then hesitate, and he knew he'd made a mistake, even before Gorelov slammed down his phone. He had become overconfident, Winters realized. He'd swerved back onto Gorelov's terrain, names, and power structures, when he should have stayed in the mud.

"Karpenko?" Gorelov snorted, with a laugh that sounded like a cat caught in an industrial crushing machine. "Kostyantin Karpenko? The baby oligarch? The so-called businessman of the West? *That* is your man?"

Winters started to answer, but Gorelov stubbed out his cigarette, violently, snapping off the unsmoked barrel. "Karpkeno is *nichego*," he barked. Nothing.

"He is a leader," Winters said, pressing forward, knowing it was all he could do. "He is a symbol . . ."

"He is, what, maybe the sixtieth most powerful man in Ukraine?"

"Who was Stalin, before he changed his name to Joe Steel?" Winters barked, with more confidence than he felt. *Press on. Right the ship.* "Who was Lenin, before he murdered the czar? Who was Putin before the Wall fell? Who were you, for that matter, before your godfather lifted you to this position?"

"I was a violinist," Gorelov smiled. He was a good one, in fact, trained at the Saint Petersburg Conservatory. "Karpenko is *zhaba*." A toad.

But Gorelov was the toad, squatting in his smoky backroom, puffing out his chest. "And besides," the Russian croaked, knocking back a short glass of vodka for effect, "Karpenko is dead."

CHAPTER 52

We moved fast and stayed low, throwing Hargrove's personal effects onto the burn pile of equipment we were leaving behind. Then we gathered the bodies—Greenlees, Jacobsen, Reynolds, and Charro—and tossed them on top. We left the dead Ukrainians for the police, or whoever came next. Those bodies would tell the right story and, if the dead men were lucky, maybe even find their way home to their mothers for last rites.

I thought about saying a few words, but there was nothing to say. Boon took Charro's cross and kissed it, as Charro often did, but nobody knew Jacobsen or Reynolds. They didn't have anything that would identify them, and they didn't seem to be carrying mementos. They were strangers.

I turned away and scrambled over to the fish truck, where the Ukrainians were gathered. "Ready?" I said.

They had been slamming vodka from the bottle, particularly the injured man, who was strapped into the driver's seat. He was half drunk and half delirious, and he was saying something slurry and serious to each man in turn. His wound wasn't fatal, but apparently he didn't know that. I wondered if Maltov knew. If this was the sacrifice required.

"Good luck," I said to Maltov, as the driver finished the bottle and smashed it on the factory floor.

"No luck necessary," he said. "Only pride."

The driver started the engine. I noticed he was crying. Fuck pride.

"Take her up," I said to Wildman. He nodded, and our drone-copter whirred up through the roof and into the night. It was met immediately by gunfire.

I walked to the pile. "Adios, brothers," I said.

"Wait," Alie said, running from the back of the factory, where the team was waiting at the evac door. She stopped at the pile, reached in, and carefully removed Greenlees's wedding ring, as if she didn't want to pull his finger too hard. She touched his cheek, then slipped it into her pocket. "Okay," she said. She wasn't crying. She wasn't showing any emotion. It only made her look sadder.

"Diving," Wildman said.

I signaled to Maltov—go time—lit the fuse, and ran. The white phosphorous, or "Willy P," would eat through the bodies and the equipment and wouldn't stop until it had eaten two feet into the concrete floor. In ten minutes, there wouldn't even be a tooth.

"Let's go," I said, as the truck crashed through the front wall, the driver's desperate scream disappearing into the void.

The Wolf heard the motor, then saw the small quadcopter slip through a shattered window and bank upward, losing itself in the sky. It was a spy drone, probably used to scout their objective. Now it was scouting his positions. So what.

"*Yego sbit*'," The Wolf said. Shoot it down.

The first barrage missed, as the copter zigzagged across the dark sky. Lousy Chechens.

"Take it down," he said more forcefully, as the drone dipped toward them.

A kamikaze run, the Wolf thought. *Or a decoy.*

"*Oni idut*," he yelled. They are coming.

A flash from the warehouse. A blinding white starburst. Phosphorous fire. The Wolf grabbed a rocket-propelled grenade launcher. The whirring of the drone faded to gunfire, the world faded into ten men firing, but he kept his eye on the target and his finger on the trigger and, just as he anticipated, a truck burst out of the warehouse. What he hadn't anticipated, as he lined up his shot, was the explosion a few feet above them, right in the middle of his men.

Everly sucked in his breath, a small sound, but from the London banker, it might as well have been a gasp. He had seen the look on Gorelov's face, too, Winters realized. For the second time that morning, Gorelov had blinked.

He was bluffing about Karpenko being nothing. He had either been told Karpenko was dead, or he had created the lie himself and forgotten. There was no reason for either to be the case, unless the Ukrainian mattered, not just in Kiev, but in Moscow, too. Gorelov had been cocky as he gloated over Karpenko's death, until he saw the look on Winters's face, and knew that he was wrong.

Winters pounced. "Call your friends," he said and gestured to the Russian's phone bank. "Tell them that Karpenko is alive. Tell them he is coming."

Gorelov grabbed two cell phones, as if on impulse.

"Call someone important," Winters laughed. "By all means, call someone who matters. I hope they are early risers."

Maltov opened up with Jacobsen's M249 SAW machine gun as soon as the white phosphorus grenade strapped to the drone exploded. He was behind a barricade near the center of the warehouse, too far away to target with any hope of accuracy, but close enough that he could see, through the burning front wall, the Russians squirming in the starburst of the blast, like earthworms in bleach. He kept firing, pointing the gun toward anything that moved, as the fish truck barreled through the hole in the front wall of the warehouse, Yevgeny at the wheel. Poor Yevgeny, who had once played three consecutive games of eight ball without missing a shot. Who always received a card from his mother on Valentine's Day, meaning he was a perverted bastard, sure, but also that his mother knew where he was, and what he was doing, but not that he was already dead, that even now, as Maltov fired, a Russian RPG was ripping into the truck, exploding the fuel drums and C-4, making the kamikaze drone look like mere fireworks.

The SAW machine gun clicked dry, out of ammo. Maltov let go and grabbed the AK-47 from his shoulder. He ran toward the Chechens and their Russians overlords. He didn't think of death or country or burning to nothing, not even ash, in unholy flames. He simply got to work.

Gorelov slammed down a phone. "You don't have the men," he said brusquely.

He had been talking with military commanders. Winters heard the name Karpenko several times. Good.

"Stalin said there's a certain quality in quantity," Winters replied slowly, with affected ease. "I disagree. I believe in actual quality. That's why my soldiers are the best."

"Even the best soldier is nothing when the ammo runs out. How many could you possibly have?"

"Almost a hundred," Winters lied.

"We have thousands," Gorelov lied in return. "We have troops in every oblast in eastern Ukraine. We can be anywhere in minutes."

"It will take an hour," Winters said confidently, "once you factor in the time to mobilize."

Gorelov shrugged. "An hour is nothing. You can't change the world in an hour with a hundred men."

"Maybe," Winters said, "but in an hour, it will be too late for either of us to turn back."

"You're bluffing," the Russian said dourly, but Winters could almost taste the fear.

Winters smiled. "Go on. Make calls. Waste time. I'm a conflict entrepreneur. I have spent years planning this operation. It is my life's work. But if you wish to gamble on my incompetence, be my guest."

The Wolf lifted his head. His men were burning around him, the white phosphorous eating through their flesh as they screamed. The truck was a crater, its fire burning hot, but he had been ready. He had blown it apart before it reached the trees, and there wasn't much firepower behind it, only four men with Kalashnikovs, if his count was right. The rear guard, clearly untrained, fighting a hopeless delaying tactic out of adrenaline and pride. No Colonel Sirko, his old commander, no oligarch, and certainly no Western mercenaries.

The Wolf shook his head. He lowered his rifle, considering his next move. *Ukrainians*, he thought with contempt, as one of the rear guard fell. *History's fools.*

CHAPTER 53

Wildman lunged into the back alley, wheeling three steel doors on a truck dolly in front of him as a makeshift shield. Behind him, Boon bent to a knee with the first M90 rocket launcher. The M90 could take out tanks, not to mention a machine gun crew on a roof only fifty meters away. Within seconds, Boon had pulled the trigger. The rocket's backblast scorched the pavement behind him. The shot went high, over the heads of the gun crew.

"Next!" Boon yelled, and I tossed him the other M90. Machine gun fire rained around him, slamming into Wildman's steel shield with thudding force, but Boon sighted calmly, adjusted for the weapon's arc of fire, and squeezed the trigger. *Fwoosh.* The rocket hit just below the machine gun nest, collapsing the wall.

Wildman screamed and tossed aside the shield in favor of his British SA-80. Sirko jumped through the door beside him, letting rip with his bullpup ASh-12 as the enemy struggled to right themselves and return fire. Next came Karpenko, then Alie and Hargrove, pulling Miles behind them on an improvised litter. The Chechens were scrambling, pulling the machine gun from the pile of bricks and bodies and readying it for firing. *Ten seconds*, I thought. I kicked Hargrove like a mule to get his ass in gear, practically knocking him across the open area and through the hole we'd cut in the fence directly beyond the door.

Within seconds, we were in the forest, with Boon and Wildman laying down cover behind us. I sprinted past Karpenko ten meters into the twilight and underbrush, then dropped to a knee in the leaves, signaling the group to pass me, then cut to the left.

I knelt, breathed deep, and scoped the Chechens through the trees, their guns up now and firing, but raggedly. I squeezed the trigger and laid down heavy covering fire. Seconds later, Sirko sprinted passed me and cut left. Boon and Wildman cut the other way, heading right into the forest. They were the diversion. If they couldn't draw the enemy off, they'd circle back to cover us.

"Pick up the pace," I whisper-yelled, moving past Hargrove and Alie as they struggled through the underbrush.

"The blood . . ." Alie huffed.

Jimmy Miles was delirious and bleeding through his bandages; Hargrove's incompetent jostling of the litter was killing him; but it was the best I could do for him. My gun was worth more than Alie and Hargrove put together.

"Fuck the blood," I said. "We have to move."

I heard Maltov's machine gun fall silent in the distance, out of ammo. I heard his AK-47. It was met by a vicious barrage. The Chechens had survived Maltov's best shot, which had always been a long shot at best, and they were hammering him.

"Move fast," I said. "Light and noise discipline." No shots, unless lives were on the line. We needed to move silently and rely on stealth, not firepower.

"Don't stop," I said, turning to Alie and Hargrove before double-timing ahead to take point. "No matter what."

"Thanks," Alie said, but I didn't know what she was talking about.

There was a gully a hundred meters to the east. I'd scouted it as a possible evac route the first morning, and I was heading for it now. It was first light, bright enough to silhouette us against the horizon. If we could make the dry creek bed, we'd have some cover to run or, more likely, find an ambush spot for a last stand.

I dropped into the gully and paused, the rest of the group filing in behind me, Miles grunting as the litter slipped down the short incline into the rocky ravine. In the distance, Boon and Wildman were firing, drawing the enemy away from us. Beyond the warehouse, Maltov and his men were still in a firefight, but for how long? We had passed five of the seven buildings in the complex, dark squares behind a fence, blocking our access to the road, but even here, I could see the warehouse fire lighting the sky.

The road.

I moved quickly to Hargrove. "Do you have your keys?"

"What?" He was huffing. It had been a long day.

"Do you have your car keys?"

"What?" He grimaced. Behind him, Jimmy grunted. I didn't dare look.

"Can we take your car?" Alie snapped.

"I think so," Hargrove said. "I think . . . Yes. I have the keys. I left it at the front gate."

I moved past Karpenko to Sirko, who was crouched behind a fallen tree, listening for hostiles. I heard an Israeli Tavor, Boon's gun. Then Wildman's SA-80. Then half a dozen AK-47s. They were a few hundred meters away.

"Around the incinerator," I said to Sirko, pointing toward the small building on the far edge of the factory complex, "then left toward the road." The fence was done at the far end of the complex. If we could get past the incinerator, we would have cover all the way to the road. I just hoped Hargrove's abandoned car was unguarded and in one piece.

I heard Boon's Tavor, closer now, but not Wildman's SA-80. I heard gunfire from the direction of Maltov's men. Somewhere, something exploded. Something large collapsed. My ears were ringing, but I felt attuned. I tried not to think of Miles bleeding out. He had half an hour; that was what I had told myself when we left. I couldn't doubt now.

"Now," I said, signaling Sirko to lead. He bolted up and crouch-ran toward the incinerator, trailed by Karpenko, Alie, Hargrove, and Miles on his litter. As I'd hoped, the old colonel was a skilled operator in the right conditions, so I waited six beats. I expected the enemy to come quickly, if they came, and I might be able to catch a few before they knew I was there.

No one came, so I moved out. The others were halfway to the incinerator, fifty meters to go at the most. There was an open area in our direct path, so Sirko skirted the widest part and hit a narrower clearing at speed, his ASh-12 bullpup rifle level before him. I saw Alie pass into the open area and, suddenly, I knew she would be gunned down—almost anticipated it, already feeling the shock—but she was through before I could react, with Hargrove beside her and Miles's litter dragging at their heels and me a few paces behind, my SCAR rifle ready. *Not much farther now*, I thought, as Sirko passed into the partial concealment of high weeds.

And then the guns opened up, *pop, pop, pop*, and the dirt danced. Something struck me, and I fell headlong, my shoulder slamming into Miles, and then my face into the ground.

Reflexively, I pulled my Beretta pistols and rolled. I wasn't hit. It wasn't a bullet that knocked me down. It was Hargrove, spinning backward, knocking me onto Miles. I saw Alie falling, pulled down by the force of my weight on the litter. The SCAR was gone, lost in the tall weeds, but I had my pistols, one for each hand, siting for targets, when I heard someone bark: "Kapitan Sirko."

"Leytenant Balashov," Sirko hissed, jerking his bullpup upward as a shadow stepped out from behind the incinerator and shot him in the face.

I sighted the man's head with the Beretta in my right hand. Five meters. High percentage shot. I started to squeeze the trigger, but Karpenko stepped into my line of fire. His back was to me, his arms partially raised in supplication. Fuck. I twisted around, trying to get an angle with the Beretta in my left hand, but a Chechen appeared to my right, his AK-47 trained on my head, his finger on the trigger.

Silence. The world was silence, except for gunfire in the distance, meaningless to us now. There was no motion, there was nothing at all, until Sirko's killer spoke in Russian, first to the corpse, then to Karpenko.

"I knew that man," he said in rough English, for my benefit, and I knew then he was my counterpart, the mercenary leader who had engineered this ambush.

"Do you who I am?" Karpenko said in English. The Russian merc's Steyr AUG laser sight was dancing on his heart.

Nothing. No reply.

"I am Nikolay Karpenko," he said calmly, again in English. That was smart, to use a secondary language. It forced the Russian to focus on his words. "I believe there is a half million euro bounty . . ."

"One million," the Russian interrupted.

"I will pay you two . . ." Karpenko stopped. "No. I will pay you five million euros for safe passage to Vienna."

The Russian didn't say anything.

"To Krakow then. No . . . Lviv."

"Vilnius," the Russian said. Lithuania. Due north. He must have friends there.

"Fine . . ."

"*I ihk?*" the Russian said. And them?

Karpenko hesitated, and in his silence, I heard death.

I lunged hard, clearing my lines of fire, and squeezed. I felt the recoil of both pistols and heard two shots. The left, aimed at the Russian, went wide, but that was my weak hand. The right connected and spun the Chechen sideways, causing him to spray his fire above our heads as Boon leapt from the trees, a savage ghost, and plunged his knife into the man's sternum, burying it in his heart.

I ducked and turned hard, trying to find the next shot, trying to locate the Russian merc, but nothing was moving. No shadows. No sounds. Even the shooting in the distance had stopped.

Then I saw him, dead on the ground, with one blue hole in his chest. I followed the direction of entry and saw Karpenko, standing motionless, holding a six-shot Glock.

He turned and looked at me. He wasn't stunned or shaken by what had happened, at least as far as I could tell. He dropped his gun hand to his side, his arm steady. His hair was barely mussed.

"I've sacrificed too much," he said slowly. "For my children. For my country. For *their* country, because they are Ukrainian, too. I'm not going to fucking Vilnius."

He stopped. He glanced at Miles. Suddenly, I could see the strain, not just of this moment, but of everything.

"*You've* sacrificed too much," he said, turning toward me, and I didn't care if it was manipulation or sincerity, I knew he was right.

"Charlie Mike," I said, nodding. Continue mission.

I turned to Boon, who was crouching over the dead Chechen, wiping his knife clean. "Out of ammo?"

He nodded.

"Where's Wildman?"

"In the wind."

They must have gotten separated in the firefight. At least Wildman wasn't KIA. Maybe.

I looked at the Russian merc. He was old, that was the first thing I noticed. Older than me. Jimmy Miles's age. And this was a young man's world. I thought about throwing his body in the incinerator, out of respect. I knew he didn't have anyone who would miss him. After a certain point, very few of us did.

I looked at Jimmy. He was thrashing, delirious and in pain, probably spiking a fever. His leg was covered with blood down to his boot.

"We've got to go," I said. "Now. We've got to make the car."

"Hargrove's down," Alie said. I looked. He'd been clipped in the shoulder, nothing more.

"Leave him. I got it," I said, grabbing Miles's litter and moving out. Ten steps, and Miles and I were into the shadows behind the incinerator, putting distance between ourselves and whoever might be following. Ten more steps, and I was gasping. *Hang in there, Jimmy.* Twenty more to the road. But the car wasn't there. The car wasn't fucking there.

"The car isn't here," Alie said. She had her arm under Hargrove's shoulders, and she was carrying him, dragging him out of the dark, when only his will was broken, not his legs.

We moved to the tree line, and I laid Miles down. I pulled out my sat phone and dialed Apollo's twenty-four-hour tactical operations center. They picked up without a ring. They always picked up without a ring.

"Man down," I said. "Mission abort. Need immediate medevac."

"Authenticate."

I didn't have a password. "This is Locke. Thomas Locke. My team is down, mission fail. I have a man bleeding out. I need a dust-off."

"I have no Locke on record."

You fucker. You know me. "I need an extraction. Now!"

"Authenticate."

I tried a few passwords from old missions, but I knew they wouldn't work. This was a kite. No calls. No records. They hung up. I dialed Winters. He had given me his private number.

He'd said I would know when to call.

CHAPTER 54

Brad Winters reached into his pocket and put his cell phone on the table without taking his eyes from Gorelov. He knew who was calling. Only two people in the world had this number. It would be gone by tomorrow. "That's my guy," he said. "That's the man who is right now setting this whole thing in motion. So tell me, have you figured it out yet?"

Gorelov's jowls quivered, as much from rage as confusion. *Pressure*, Winters thought, *is our ally*. The Russian took a slug of vodka. He hadn't touched the coffee since Karpenko's name had come up, but he'd smoked through half a pack of filterless Marlboros.

"Suddenly, ten thousand men doesn't seem like so many, does it?" Winters said. "Not to cover a thousand miles."

He was toying with him, daring the Russian to figure it out, and it was crushing him. An unsolvable puzzle wasn't pressure. When the answer was in your grasp, but you couldn't put the pieces together: that was when you broke down.

"Here's a hint. Tell them you already have Russian troops in disguise on location," Winters said with a smirk, as Gorelov snapped rapid Russian into his cell phone. By now, he had no doubt reached high up into the Kremlin and the FSB.

"Why would you tell me this?" Gorelov said. He was agitated, and not hiding it. "Do you think we won't reinforce our position?"

"I know you will. You might even bring more Spetsnaz, since they were recently spotted only twenty kilometers away."

Gorelov barked in Russian, relaying the latest information.

"Of course," Winters said casually, "there are Spetsnaz all over Eastern Ukraine, so that might not help much."

Gorelov slammed down the phone and poured more vodka. "We won't fall for a trap," he said, knocking back an unhealthy slug, "especially not one based on threats."

The cell phone rang again.

"Do you even know what the trap is?" Winters said, placing his hand over Gorelov's phone so that he couldn't answer. He knew Gorelov didn't. The Russian had no idea what a man on the cusp of his dream was capable of. Time to push this confrontation to its conclusion and see what happened.

"Bring too few men, and I'll capture them, parade them on camera, and show the world who you really are," Winters said. "Bring too many, so many that the world media will see without a doubt that the Russian army is attacking a Ukrainian natural gas station . . . and I will blow it up."

Everly's chin disappeared entirely, like a turtle retreating into its shell. Gorelov looked stunned.

"That's right," Winters said, nodding, as he saw the light coming on in Gorelov's weary eyes. "The big bang."

"You're going to blow up a transfer station."

"And your invasion will be blamed."

"But that would cripple the European economy . . ."

"And make the world realize what a threat you are," Winters said. "Isn't that what you fear? Not that this little invasion of yours blows up in your face, but that it blows up in Western Europe's face, in a way they can't ignore."

Gorelov didn't know what to say. Was this man, this Mr. Winters, really crazy enough to escalate the confrontation between Russia and the West into outright war?

"That's mutually assured economic destruction," he muttered, buying time.

"The West can weather it," Winters shrugged. "But you can't, not with an energy-dependent economy."

"The Russians will do what they must," Gorelov said. "They always do."

"No Yuri," Winters replied calmly, using Gorelov's first name for the first time. "I'm afraid you misunderstood me. When I said 'you,' I didn't mean Russia, although that certainly applies. I meant you, Yuri, the man who has been waking up half of Putin's senior advisors at dawn to tell them how badly you're mishandling this situation. When they see this story fire-hosed across international media, and they realize that you knew and could have stopped it . . ."

Three or four of the Russian's cell phones were ringing, as they had been for the last twenty minutes. Now Winters's phone joined in again, and Gorelov glanced at it, almost with dread.

"Pick up your phone," Winters whispered, ignoring his own call. "Figure it out. But remember: I don't need a military victory to defeat you. All I need is . . . testicular fortitude."

"These men," Gorelov said, nodding his fat jowls toward Winters's ringing phone. "They must be fanatics, to blow themselves up for this crazy plan."

"Oh Yuri," Winters chortled, shaking his head. "I said the assault and explosion would be linked, in the media, in the eyes of politicians and Deep State players around the world. I never said they'd happen at the same transfer station."

Winters felt a hand on his arm, pulling him gently backward, and Everly leaned forward into his line of sight for the first time.

"You can't stop him, Yuri," the banker said calmly. "I think you see that now."

Gorelov looked beaten, slumped into his Italian suit, a cigarette turning to ashes in his fist.

"Yuri . . ." Everly said, getting him to focus. "Yuri . . . don't you think it's time we made a deal?"

CHAPTER 55

Somewhere out there, eight thousand feet beyond the clouds, in the cold upper reaches of the atmosphere, the drone was cruising on its appointed path. It was nothing more than a cold machine, invisible to eyes and instruments, transporting a large amount of explosives inside its protective shell.

There were other ways to destroy a natural gas transfer station. You could send a Tier One team, or a sniper with an incendiary round, but odds of human error were higher and tracks were harder to cover. You could destroy it with a cyberattack without leaving your command center, but every cyberaction was traceable, no matter how much you covered your tracks.

That was why when Apollo Outcomes wanted to send a confidential message, it sent a man to deliver it verbally, even when that meant a trip halfway around the world. When that wasn't an option, for whatever reason, the company sent a fax. The fax system was so out of date that no one bothered to monitor it, and so low-tech it was untraceable after the fact.

It was the same thinking that made the kamikaze drone work. Who would suspect? Who would be able to trace it? The drone was an emotionless piece of equipment with no cybertrail, designed to incinerate on impact, and that made it the perfect weapon to set off a chain reaction that would be felt around the world.

The Russians were prepared for atom bombs. Brad Winters had thrown a stone.

CHAPTER 56

I almost threw the sat phone into the undergrowth. Winters was supposed to answer. Winters always answered. That was the bare minimum of his guarantee: I risk my life, he answers the phone. Why would he give me the number, if he wasn't going to answer the phone?

I stared at the forest, frustrated and betrayed. We were in a thicket of bushes, half a klick from the warehouse, the trees providing some cover and concealment, even as the deep purple sky made dark spikes of the branches and leaves. The mission was a kite. I knew that. This was how kites worked. I knew that, too. But this wasn't how our kite was supposed to turn out. Jimmy Miles wasn't supposed to bleed out in a scrubby forest in Eastern Europe. Jimmy was supposed to die in a bar fight in Juba, or on the African savannah wrestling lions, or behind a Vulcan machine gun, mowing down a legion of machete-wielding fanatics. Or jumping on a grenade to save his team. Or with a wife, goddammit, one of those after-sex heart attacks that we always joked about, what a way to go. Not that either of us had a wife, but still . . .

I pushed past Karpenko, who was quietly sitting on his heels, and examined Miles's side with my

Maglite. The bandages were soaked through, and blood was pulsing from his artery. But weakly. Too weakly. I shone my light on his face. His eyelids fluttered involuntarily, but his eyes didn't open. He was alive, but he wasn't going to make it, and it was going to be a painful death. It might take an hour, but out here, without an evac, it was death, guaranteed.

I started walking, pulling Miles behind me on the litter, Boon moving ahead to walk point and Hargrove leaning on Alie in the rear. Hargrove murmured, every now and then, but otherwise, no one made a sound.

I stopped twenty minutes later on the edge of a potato field a half klick north of our intended route. It was almost sunrise, the first blue tinge on the horizon, and the world was quiet. Nobody was following; we'd left the firefight behind. Alie was behind me in the trees. Hargrove was in the shadows. But this was our hour, Jimmy's and mine. We'd watched the sun come up on dozens of successful missions. We'd smoked a hundred cigars in tight-lipped triumph. We'd told a million stories of these mornings over bourbon, while I played the "Toreador" aria, the macho bullfighter's song from Bizet's opera *Carmen*, to celebrate being alive—I mean really alive, not lives of quiet desperation—for another day.

But not today.

I signaled to Alie. She nodded. She understood that this was Miles's last stop, and she knew I wanted to be alone. She rounded up the company and moved off into the morning. I waited until I couldn't hear anything but Jimmy's shallow breathing, and the hundred thousand legs crawling out of the forest, coming for Jimmy, coming for all of us.

I remembered the way my grandfather signaled for me to come closer. He was ninety-eight, laid up in a hospital bed with a broken hip. He whispered, "I'm done." I helped him pull the oxygen tube out of his nose, because he was too weak to remove it on his own. He died that night.

How do you kill a friend?

We were out of morphine, so I did it with my bare hands on his neck, in the classic style, choking him out.

Then I knelt beside him, not wanting to wipe the blood off my hands. I unbuttoned his shirt pocket. Jimmy always carried a heavy metal ring; he'd picked it up on a patrol in Bosnia, a lifetime ago. It was industrial, made for some broken off bolt-hole, but Jimmy used it to rap skulls and open beer bottles. The perfect piece for the perfect job, he'd say, but now there were no more skulls to rap. Nobody would ever use that brewing equipment in his storage locker outside Phoenix. They'd just, some day soon, stop paying the rent.

"*Vive la mort! Vive la guerre! Vive le sacré mercenaire!*" I whispered over his body. The mercenary's battle cry, or maybe his lament.

I put the metal ring in my pocket. Then I pulled the pin on the white phosphorous grenade and gently placed it on Jimmy's chest. A funeral pyre, the Viking way. The enemy would see it from a kilometer away, especially in this dim light, but by the time they got here, if they got here, we'd be gone, and so would Jimmy Miles.

This wasn't supposed to matter. None of it. None of us. That was how we did this job, by believing we would beat the odds. I'd seen a thousand men die violent deaths, many at my own hand. I shot a man in the head in Nigeria because he wouldn't sell land to an oil company, and I couldn't remember his face. Alie was right. I'd watched a village full of women and children gunned down from the back of Toyota trucks for sport, the gunners laughing and counting kills, something I'd sworn I'd never do again after the massacre in Srebrenca. I had burned four good mercs and a retiree less than an hour ago, and left three Ukrainian allies dead in the dirt, and who was going to remember them, or know what happened to them, or care? We were walking tombs of unknown soldiers, trying to make a difference, trying to do some good in the world.

By the time I reached the others, the rim of the earth was blue. They were standing in shadow, in a canebrake, looking out on a field of cow manure and crops.

"Charlie mike," I told the team, or whatever was left of it. "Let's move. We have a mission to complete."

It would have been what Miles wanted, because he was a soldier. But more important, I didn't know what else to do.

CHAPTER 57

Brad Winters listened closely, as Everly and Gorelov hammered out their deal, sometimes in Russian, other times in English. Everly's first concern seemed to be transfers from Bank Rossiya, Putin's bank. Bank Rossiya had gone from $1 million in assets in the 1990s to more than $100 billion in 2011 by serving the needs of the Russian Deep State. Now it was a pariah institution, locked out of SWIFT, the international banking consortium, by sanctions imposed after Russia's annexation of Crimea two months ago. Everly wasn't trying to skirt those sanctions, not explicitly, but the Londoners clearly had clients and projects caught up in the mess, and they needed Gorelov's reluctant help to free them.

Half the conversation—the half in Russian—went over Winters's head. The other half mostly bored him. He was more intent on watching the men and understanding their relationship. When he and Everly had arrived, Gorelov was arrogantly dismissive, the man in control. Even now, he appeared the same, gruffly rebuffing his more urbane counterpart between slugs of vodka, rejecting aspects of every request.

But Winters could see the shift in power. He could tell that in his stiff, unflustered way, Everly was a bar brawler, and he was pounding the Russian into submission, piece by piece. He could see it in the way Gorelov shifted in his chair, in his reluctance to make the phone calls required to seal certain deals, in the way he grimaced at odd moments like acid reflux was tearing his insides apart.

Ukraine was, in the end, little more than incremental business opportunities. Everly was less concerned with the fate of the country, Winters soon realized, than in making sure that current agreements—especially for the big energy companies, but for other clients, too—were honored no matter what happened in Kiev. Winters had offered the London bankers the chance to change Eastern Europe; they had chosen the status quo.

He daydreamed, briefly, about upending the relationship. During one long exchange in Russian, he even pictured the drone, floating downward out of the heavens, and then accelerating into the massive chamber where natural gas was compressed into liquid for concentrated delivery, the C-4 ripping the drone's skin apart like so many treaties and alliances and exploding it into a million worthless burnedout shards.

But Brad Winters was practical. He had seen this coming when the Indian banker called him on the private jet and told him his destination was Saint Petersburg. So when Everly and Gorelov offered him minor shale oil fields on the edge of Eastern Ukraine and free passage to operate, he accepted gracefully and then said, "And Azerbaijan."

Gorelov scoffed. "That's not our country."

Winters ignored the obvious lie. "I'm not talking

ownership of the oil fields. I'm talking about a partnership, with one of your smaller national subsidiaries. My people will explore and extract the oil, and your people will ship it."

"It's a dangerous region, an unstable investment."

"I'll build a private military base, for the protection of your shipping lines, and for other work in the region. I'll keep you apprised of our activities, of course, and rest assured, you will find our services profitable."

Gorelov squinted.

"And Georgia and Armenia, too," Winters said, offhandedly, although he was not going to walk away without a piece of all three. "If we are going to be working together in the region, we might as well dominate it, right, Yuri?"

Those three countries formed the bottleneck between Russia and Southwest Asia. They had been a battleground between Deep States, dating back to the "Great Game" between Russia and England for control of central Asia in the 1800s.

"The Kremlin would never agree to that," Gorelov snapped.

"Yes they will," Winters said, "if you explain it to them correctly. It's better to have me inside the tent pissing out, after all, then outside pissing in."

Gorelov stammered, but Winters held up his hand. When a man was beaten, there was no point in indulging his concerns. "I must insist," he said. "That is my price, and it's a onetime offer."

He was thinking of the drone, and of Thomas Locke and his men, no doubt creeping up on the facility right now. He tapped his watch. *Time is running out, Gorelov. I'm not a patient man.*

"I require proof of your goodwill," Gorelov said, squatting like a toad. He seemed to have spent the last hour sinking into his chair, as if it were mud. The air was foul with his smoky stench. "The Near East for Karpenko."

"No."

"And your men."

CHAPTER 58

I lay prone on the roof of the apartment building where Wildman had planted the last camera, watching the pipeline facility through my scope. It was a clear blue morning, almost full light, and I was pinpointing heads, trying to grab that rush you feel when you have a man's life in your hands and he doesn't know it, but it wasn't coming. I had been angry after Miles died, and then brokenhearted. Now I wanted to feel angry again, but I couldn't muster it. I felt wrung out. Not just exhausted, but empty. The only thought that kept running through my head was, *What am I doing here? How did it come to this?*

I wasn't surprised the Donbas Battalion didn't show at 0600. Everything had gone to shit so far, and besides, militias were notorious for being late. By 0630, I was agitated. My body was locking down, my brain curling up on itself, my stomach wanting to vomit, except I hadn't eaten anything but a single energy bar since Miles and I ate MREs in the warehouse twelve hours ago and talked about old times.

Then three military trucks screamed up to the facility gate, and dropped their tailgates.

Whiskey Tango Foxtrot. What the fuck?

Russian reinforcements poured out, shouting and

gesturing, and my heart dropped into my boots as they covered the exit points and swarmed into the facility, fanning out in search formation. I scoped the Spetsnaz commander, and I could practically read his lips when he saluted the officer in charge. *No one is here but us, sir!* Of course, he was speaking Russian, so that piece was in my head. But I could read the signs. We'd been sold out.

If the militia had been hit, prisoners might have been captured and interrogated. Had someone, under duress, given up the location of the assault? But no one outside my team knew about the mission, except for the Apollo men with the Donbas Battalion. They wouldn't crack. And they wouldn't have told the Ukrainians. This mission was blacker than black.

Two minutes later, a call came in on my sat phone. I hit Talk on my earpiece, still scanning the facility through my rifle scope.

"Mission abort. What's your sitrep?" Winters's voice.

"Three hundred meters south southeast of the objective," I said, giving him a false locale. "We ran into trouble. I called—"

"Is the client with you?"

"Affirmative."

Winters paused, long enough for me to sight the Spetsnaz leader's head in my crosshairs. It was a clean shot.

"Roger," Winters said. "Make your way to the extraction point ASAP. Bird en route. Watch your fourth point of contact, and wait for the signal."

Two seconds later, the Spetsnaz commander

reached for his radio, listened, then frantically waved his men to get into one of the trucks. *We have them!* I imagined him saying, as I watched his lips move. The vehicle belched black smoke and lurched forward, heading east, toward the extraction point. That was the signal.

"Wilco out," I said, ending transmission.

Brad Winters had done the worst thing any commander could do: he'd betrayed his men.

Maybe. Because he was also trying to save us. The five points of contact for landing after a parachute jump are (1) balls of feet, (2) heels of feet, (3) thighs, (4) ass, and (5) shoulder blades. So when Winters said "fourth point," he was telling me to watch my ass, in a way that no one without jump wings would understand. Somebody outside the military had been listening, forcing him to make the call.

Maybe. Because if everything had gone as planned, and Alie and Hargrove hadn't screwed the pooch, we'd have been inside the facility, waiting for the Donbas Battalion, when the Russian reinforcements arrived. There was no way Winters could have anticipated the Chechen mercs . . . or contacted them . . .

Don't get crazy, Locke, I thought, scoping the Russian commander's right cheekbone to calm my nerves. Winters didn't know where we were holed up. He thought we'd be in the facility as planned. The Chechens had followed Hargrove. In a way, Hargrove had saved our lives . . .

"What now?" Alie whispered, sliding up beside me on her belly so the Russians wouldn't see her silhouetted against the morning sky.

There were only five of us left: me, Boon, Karpenko, Alie, and Hargrove, who was wrapped in bloody bandages and nearly comatose from shock and exhaustion. I thought about what I had in my ruck: field jacket, night-vision goggles, a small amount of ammo, four nutrition bars, water. Around my neck was the gold chain Wolcott had given me last week in Washington, so I could snip links if I needed funds. In the map pocket of the ruck was about thirteen thousand euros in a Ziploc bag, the last of my Apollo cash. Boon and I could escape and evade, but what about the rest?

The smartest move was to leave them and run. They were war tourists, after all. Alie and Hargrove, at least, would probably survive. Karpenko, though, was wanted by all sides.

"We wait," I said, without taking my eye from my scope. One shot to the cheekbone, and the Russian commander's head would blow out like a Jackson Pollock painting. I breathed deep and thought about the shot, the trajectory, the windage. I probably wouldn't hit him from this distance, at least not a clean kill, and I was glad. For the first time in a long time, the thought of killing made me sick.

I didn't realize Alie was still beside me, until she put her hand on my back and started rubbing it gently. I had a scar; I don't know if she remembered that. Maybe she could feel it. I had a brief, horrible thought that I might have been crying, but my scope was clear. My eyes were dry. Mercs don't fucking cry.

"I'm sorry," she said, but it didn't move me. She'd said that before. "I'm sorry I compromised your mission. I didn't realize it would be like that. I didn't realize that people would die."

Did she mean Miles? Or did she mean everyone?

"I'm sure you've seen it before," I whispered.

Alie was tough. She'd been in back alleys and slave brothels and God knew where else in pursuit of her truth, places even I wouldn't go. Anyone who thought she wasn't a hardened warrior was a fool. But I knew she hadn't seen anything like the last four hours before. I had never been in a worse battle, or on a more devastating mission, so how could she have been? We were lucky to be alive.

"I don't understand what you do," she said. "I don't see how you can live like this." She paused. The carnage was catching up to her. "But I respect it, Tom. No one would go through that if they didn't believe in the cause. Right? I didn't realize that before. I guess that makes you think I'm naïve."

It made me wonder what I think. It made me wonder why it had come to this, why I made all the decisions I'd made—leaving grad school for Burundi, turning down Winters's offer to climb the executive ladder, walking away from the one woman I never wanted to forget. Why bother, if all my choices only led me here?

"I would have married you, Alie," I said without turning from my scope. "In some other life. I would have taken an office job, and bought a minivan, and we would have raised our children on ice cream and spy novels, even the girl. We would have been happy."

I felt Alie's hand moving down my back, and then

falling away. "Oh Tom," she said sadly, "what makes you think I would ever have wanted that?"

I thought she'd leave me then, alone with my weariness and regret. But she didn't. She lay beside me, not touching me, not moving. Was she watching the Russians below us loading their trucks, getting ready to ambush us at the extraction point? Or was she thinking what I was thinking: that there was still a place for us, a bed somewhere and happiness, at least for a night, until one or both of us left to save the world. Maybe Paris. Why not? The place didn't have to be large or fancy, it just had to be there. One bed and one window would do.

"What do we do now?" Alie asked again.

"We keep waiting," I said. "Play for the breaks. Something will come up. Something always does."

Twenty minutes later, we heard the helicopters, two Mi-17s, each capable of carrying thirty people. At first, I thought they might be Spetsnaz reinforcements, about to fast-rope into the facility from a hover. But the Russians were screaming and scurrying out of sight, like roaches when the kitchen light flicks on. *The choppers are with us*, I thought.

"News crews," I said, as the two birds came into view, black against the morning blue. "My boss lined them up for Karpenko's victory speech. It must have been too late to recall them back to Kiev."

"So they'll be going back soon," Alie said.

I took my eye away from the rifle scope and looked at her. She was smiling.

"I can talk my way on," she said.

I believed her. Alie could talk her way out of a

sunburn. "What about them?" I said, nodding toward the others.

Alie looked over her shoulder, at Hargrove with his bandages, and Karpenko, lying faceup in the sun, smoking a cigarette. "Are you asking if I'd risk my life for Hargrove?"

I laughed. "You already have."

"Then it's my call."

I heard it then, even above the blades of the choppers setting down two blocks away in front of the gas facility. It was a jaunting whistling, "God Save the Queen." I turned, knowing exactly what that meant. *Don't shoot my head off, assholes.* Sure enough, Wildman appeared at the top of the fire escape thirty seconds later, carrying his SA-80, a rucksack, and an RPG. Splattered blood stained the front of his shirt.

"It's a proper shit show down there," he said with a twisted smile.

"I have to go," I said to Alie. This was no time for moping, and no time for regret. We had miles to go, hundreds of miles, and most of it would be on foot.

"Call of the wild," Alie said, but she was smiling.

CHAPTER 59

"They aren't going to find them, are they?" Everly asked, as the black Benz limo pushed through Saint Petersburg's early morning traffic.

"Unlikely."

Everly pursed his lips, pushing his lackluster chin deeper into his neck. "Did you warn them?"

"I didn't have to."

Winters had come up through army airborne, and he'd kept his military mind-set: never leave a man behind. Not an Apollo man. It was a guiding principle behind Apollo Outcomes. It was literally chiseled into a stone that someone had given him as a paperweight, which he'd passed down to the man who replaced him as the leader of the paramilitary wing of the firm. He felt wrong about what he had done, deeply wrong, but maybe, he reasoned, that was the price of success: to lay down a few of your core convictions in pursuit of the greater good. At least he had warned Locke.

"It wasn't necessary," Winters said, with steel in his voice. "Karpenko, maybe. But my team?"

"It was currency," Everly replied bluntly. "Gorelov needed to save face in order to pitch our deal to his superiors."

They were quiet. Brad Winters was hardly ever quiet.

"I admit," Everly said, with a snuffling laugh, "I enjoyed seeing Yuri so . . . incontinent. I'd like to thank you for that."

"It was my pleasure. Sincerely." Winters liked sticking it to a Russian, any Russian. He was Cold War that way.

"He may try to use this . . . escape as an excuse," Everly frowned. "To back out on your part of the deal."

"I don't think so," Winters said. "They had their chance at the facility, they have no one to blame but themselves. And this is a smart deal for the Russians." Winters had planned it that way. He knew the power of mutual benefit. "That's the real way Gorelov will save face. And besides—" he smiled at Everly "—I have the same protection as everyone else you negotiated for today: your bank and its backers."

Winters had long known the game. He knew the Deep State wasn't a powerful cabal. It was a ruthless jungle of apex-predators in a zero-sum contest of conquest and annihilation, where every alliance was temporary, and everyone, even the largest players and power brokers, could be destroyed. Gorelov could fall out of favor with Putin all the way to a prison cell, or a grave. Karpenko could be sold for assassination. The London bank could fail, if it stopped being useful to the right people at the highest levels of influence. At the Deep State level, everyone was both predator and prey. That wasn't a defect in the system, but its survival mechanism; competition kept everyone's claws sharp.

What Winters hadn't realized was that East and West no longer mattered. The Deep State, as seen through the bankers, penetrated across the great divide, from London to Moscow. Its interests didn't track with normal geopolitics, or even official government positions. He had been raised a patriot, always believing that it was us versus them; that national interests trumped business; that flags were, in the end, more than cloth.

But that was twentieth-century thinking, and as he'd just learned, the modern world was much bigger than states, and much more dangerous and profitable, too. Yes, there was negotiation left to do, but Glenn Hartley and his partners were now looking at three times as much drillable land as he'd promised in Ukraine. The security environment was worse, sure, but Apollo would roll its Ukrainian security contracts into Azerbaijan, either with the financial backing of the U.S. government or some other partner. Within a few years, his conglomerate would be pumping millions of barrels, and Apollo would be the best military force in the hot zone between Russia, Iraq, and Iran. And then, if and when the time was right, Gorelov would learn what Winters had taken to heart: that all strategic alliances are temporary, until the next opportunity comes along.

"I hope you're not disappointed," Everly said, misinterpreting the silence. "It was a brilliant plan, in its way. Expose the Russian military invasion. Blow up our energy network. Pressure the world into war. Jolly good as bluffs."

If you say so.

"But the world doesn't work that way, I'm afraid,"

Everly said. "It is not remade, all in one whack. History is a series of carefully applied pressures, moving things incrementally toward where you want them to go. It's managing crises, not creating them. That is our business, Mr. Winters. The steadying hand. That's how we'll push Putin into line. And you gave him a mighty big push today."

Everly was wrong. History didn't work like that. It was a constant collision, a series of catastrophic breaks and long repairs. Bin Laden had changed the world in a moment, when his men flew airplanes into the World Trade Center. George Bush had remade the world in three weeks, when he blitzkrieged Baghdad. Bush had intended to break the Middle East so that he could build back: newer, modern, and better than before. The first part worked; the second part . . . not so much. But that was a failure of execution, not vision. It didn't mean the idea was wrong.

"Cheer up, old chap," Everly said with a knock on the shoulder and fresh British pip. "We did a good thing today. *You* did a good thing. It was impressive indeed."

"Thanks," Winters said, without much conviction. They were approaching the airfield. He could see the private jet on the tarmac.

"We'd like to express our appreciation," Everly said, turning serious. "We'd like to buy back your firm's stock and take you private, through a shell company, of course. You'll have complete managerial control, and once your firm meets our clients' needs, you'll never have to depend on another government contract again. The possibilities are greater, Mr. Winter, than even you can imagine."

He was talking about a 10 percent stake in a $1.8 billion company at current valuations, probably more once the hedge funds got wind of the rumors and drove the stock through the roof. It was more than payment in full. And it would correct Winters's most foolish error, when he had listened to his New York banker friends and decided fifty million in his pocket was better than the anonymity of being privately held.

"Take your time. It's a big decision, I know. We don't expect an answer right away."

"I accept," Winters said.

Everly raised an eyebrow. "To our partnership, then."

"To our future."

Winters smiled, and whether the smile was false or how he truly felt, even he wasn't sure. This wasn't how he had hoped his Ukrainian gambit would turn out; but maybe, if he played this opportunity right, it was better. The London bankers thought they were buying him, but Winters knew that if you were going to climb a man to power, you had to stand close.

Everly snuffled his nasal laugh, and Winters realized that, in his way, the man was truly enjoying himself. Today was a major victory; maybe even bigger than Winters understood.

"It was clever, you know, what you said about nobody knowing you."

"It's the truth," Winters said. "It's my code."

"It's *our* code," Everly correctly him, "but you can rest assured, my friend, Vladimir Putin is going to know you now."

CHAPTER 60

The pilots were back in the cockpit by the time Alie burst onto the scene. The helicopters had been on the ground for more than forty minutes, and the reporters were eager to leave this dry hole in a dangerous war zone. They had been up since 5:00 A.M.; they had four-star food and expense accounts waiting for them back in Kiev; and the only people going in or out of this pipeline facility were employees.

Alie took advantage of their eagerness to slip past the thin line of spectators that news cameras always attract and grabbed one of the women by the arm, a low-level on-air personality, although Alie didn't recognize her, since she had long ago given up watching American television news. She was risking a pistol-whipping from the so-called protection, but Alie knew her looks would save her. She wasn't a desperate damsel in distress, but she knew how to play it for TV.

"Please," she begged. "Take me with you."

The newswoman turned, startled. She was young and beautiful, the right kind of woman for the post-Internet news, and Alie knew she'd have no sympathy for a freelancer in a bind.

"I'm an American," Alie said, with flagrant despair. "Take me with you. Please. My husband. He's hurt."

The woman looked at the bloody rags covering the man's face and his staggering steps. He looked like he was about to fall over.

"My name is Alie . . . Alie Jenson. I'm from Missouri, USA. My husband . . . he's a minister. We're Christian missionaries. We've been stranded for a month. Please. My husband needs medical attention. The Russians . . . they beat him. They beat everyone at the mission . . . even the children."

The woman eyed her, but not with compassion. With greed. Behind her, a cameraman was calling for her to get onboard.

It took her only a second to decide.

"It's against the rules," the reporter whispered as she ushered them into the helicopter. Alie knew the woman smelled a story, but she was going to be disappointed when they got back to Kiev, because there was no story to be had.

"What's his name?" the reporter shouted over the rotors, as they rose into the air, but Alie tapped her ear, pretended she couldn't hear her. The reporter turned away. Alie leaned into her husband, settling into the flight.

"It's only Kiev," she said into his ear, "but it will have to do."

Karpenko smiled, although nobody could see it under the filthy bandages. "Better than Vilnius," he said.

———

Eight hundred miles away, the drone eased out of the blue sky and came to rest on the deck of a rusty scupper in the middle of the Black Sea. Jacob Ehrlich sighed and began the postflight inspection. This was the last one of the night, so he went quickly, like a Hertz employee looking over a just-returned rental car at the end of a long shift. Fifteen minutes later, the drone was packed up and hidden in the hold.

Ehrlich took off his hat and wiped the sweat from his forehead. The sun was up, the deck was rolling beneath his feet, and there was nothing in any direction but water, as far as the eye could see.

Just another boring nothing day in paradise, he thought, as the engines kicked in for the long boat ride home. *But at least I'm getting paid.*

British Virgin Islands

July 4, 2014

I should have known, I thought, as I watched him take a seat at the beachside bar, like a man who owned the world. He was wearing a Panama hat and Bermuda shorts, and was puffing a nice cigar, like the ubiquitous middle-aged white man on vacation that crowded every beach north of the equator, and quite a few south of it, too.

But he wasn't on vacation; he was here for me.

After Boon, Wildman, and I had humped it out of Ukraine, we spent a few weeks on the run, watching our six for an Apollo hit team, but it never materialized. Maybe Winters had decided we weren't a threat; maybe we were just that good. By the time we reached Ankara, Turkey, my money was running low, so I saddled up and flew to the British Virgin Islands with the last of our stash. I knew the company would find me if they wanted to, since I was flying on my real passport, using my real name. So when I didn't see anyone at the airport, I thought they might let me go, and I was disappointed. Was that all I meant to them? Then I spotted a stiff loitering across from my bank. Apollo Outcomes knew everything, apparently, including where I kept my secret emergency cash and safety deposit box.

So I pulled back and waited to see what happened. Two days later, the boss arrived and hit a bar at the beach. He wasn't hiding or planning an operation. He was here to be found. There was nothing to do but oblige.

"Wolcott," I scoffed, as my shadow fell over his table.

Wolcott lowered his *Financial Times* and squinted. He hadn't even bothered to watch if anyone was coming. "Thomas Locke," he said, as if I was expected, which of course I was. He gestured to the empty seat. He could tell I was angry. "I know you were hoping for someone else."

"I thought he might want to apologize."

Wolcott laughed. "Our friend doesn't apologize or explain. You know that." No names. Fine.

"He burned me, Wolcott."

"I don't think so."

"He sabotaged the mission. He tried to have me killed."

"I don't know what you're talking about," Wolcott said, "but I assure you, Thomas, whatever happened, it wasn't personal."

"Men died, Wolcott. My friend Miles. Your friend Greenlees . . ."

"I know. I am sorry."

Sorry meant nothing, especially from an empty suit. I needed to talk with the man himself.

"Why are you here?"

"To close the loop," Wolcott said. "To make sure we're square."

He really had a way with words. "We're not square."

"Don't make this hard."

My hands wanted to reach for my Berettas, holstered in the small of my back under my Tommy Bahama shirt and linen blazer, but I restrained myself. "You think this is hard? Sitting on the beach drinking . . . what? A cherry margarita?"

"It's a Singapore Sling. You should try one." Wolcott called the waiter. I glared at the young man, which wasn't fair, he was just doing his job.

"Fine," Wolcott huffed, turning to the waiter. "A piña colada for my friend."

He drank. I've always had issues with multicolored drinks garnished with tiny umbrellas, but this one looked right in Wolcott's chubby hand.

"I assume you're not coming back," he said between slurps.

"No."

"Then take this as a severance package." He slid the folded *Financial Times* across the table. Inside was a sealed envelope thick with cash. "Consider this your exit interview."

There was an old joke at Apollo Outcomes: the exit interview was the funeral. I looked out at the water. It was strikingly blue. There were a few white sailboats bobbing on the swell.

"You going to the competition?"

Half of me wanted to hunt Winters down, figure this out, and deliver the kind of moral justice my job at Apollo had always promised, but rarely produced. The other half wanted to disappear.

"Tell him I'm going solo. Low-key. Starting a company with a couple of friends. Preventing genocide. Taking down tyrants. Disrupting the disrupters." That was a Brad Winters phrase, from our time in management together. "Tell him not to worry about competition because this will only be missions worth killing and dying for." I thought of Miles. We should have done this years ago, together. "Tell him Ukraine was the last time I work for someone I don't trust."

Wolcott let the trust issue slide. He was a corporate jockey, a company man, but he was sympathetic, I think. "Then you're definitely going to need this," he said, shoving the envelope of money closer.

I looked out at the harbor and thought, *I like white boats.* I used to make them out of scrap paper when I was a kid. Sometimes they'd float a few feet, before they sank.

"Did you see the article?"

He meant Alie's article about Karpenko, "The George Washington of Ukraine." Apparently, the oligarch was holed up somewhere in London, in a town house whose windows were two-way glass. Most of the article was standard hagiography, but part five was a detailed account of his family's rescue and the "Russian aggression" in Kramatorsk, from the point of view of the client. It read like a *New York Times* puff piece on Navy SEALs, as if my team was all supermen, especially Miles. I appreciated that.

"Cut her some slack, Wolcott. Everything was true. And she didn't include names, including

Apollo Outcomes, and you know she could have. Our employment records can be found."

"We killed it, anyway. That's why it ended up on a website out of Amsterdam, with no office and no assets, instead of the *Atlantic*. We had it taken down, of course, but not before it had been copied into the ether a hundred times. It's still causing us grief."

Not enough, considering.

"But our litigators will find her." He switched gears, but not artfully. "Have you had any contact? I hear you two used to be close."

He knew I hadn't. But did he know that was why my return flight was routed through Amsterdam? "No."

"Did you hear about the CIA kid, the one that stumbled back from Kramatorsk?"

"No."

"He got a tongue-lashing. Then he got a medal for bravery. He was promoted to Islamabad."

My piña colada arrived, but I ignored it. Wolcott noisily sucked up the last of his Singapore Sling. He was sunburned on his nose and the back of his neck. Why was he even bothering to wear the hat?

"Am I free?" I asked. Boon and Wildman were waiting in Bosaso, and I needed to get back. For the sake of the local Somalis, of course. You don't want Wildman haunting your bar district for long.

"We forgive you, if that's what you mean. Assuming you forgive us."

Nothing forgiven, Wolcott. Nothing forgotten. The loop wasn't closed, and the circle wasn't squared.

"Look, Thomas," Wolcott said, leaning forward

confidentially as another Singapore Sling appeared on his cocktail napkin. The Breezy Point Inn, the napkin said. "This isn't right. I know that. But there's nothing I can do. Men like Brad Winters . . . we spend a lot of time wondering about them. What are they doing? Why are they doing it? Why are they doing this to me? But the fact is, guys like Winters, they never think about guys like us."

"He asked for me, Wolcott."

"And you think you're the only one? He asks for everyone, every now and then."

Wolcott sat back. He looked out at the boats. He took a deep drink, like he was on a long weekend with the family at the Jersey Shore.

"You might be right, Locke," he said finally. "You might be special. That might be why I'm here. He's never sent me, he's never sent anyone, like this before. Usually, it's just adios, and a burn notice or a body bag. Sign the confidentiality agreement and get off my lawn. But for some reason, he cares about you."

I took the money.

"Tell him I'm . . . disappointed."

I almost said, *Tell him I'll see him soon.* But why let him know I'm coming? Winters would understand my message, just as I understood his. He would know I wasn't going to let this lie. And now I knew he wouldn't, either. That was what made us different from men like Wolcott, I suppose, and the billion other middle managers slugging it out in an office every day.

"I have to go," I said, standing up.

I left the bar and didn't look back. What would

be the point? I had a world to save, and two friends to meet in Ankara. And before that, a small bed in a small room in the Jordaan neighborhood of Amsterdam, and a single night, for now, when I knew it would be warm.

ACKNOWLEDGMENTS

Thank you to Jessica, my wife, whom I met while writing this book. I'm sorry I spent so many late nights laboring over these pages.

Thank you to my agent, Peter McGuigan and everyone at Foundry, including Emily Brown, Kirsten Neuhouse, and Richie Kern. And to all the great people at HarperCollins: my editor, David Highfill, Chloe Moffett, Mumtaz Mustafa, Kaitlin Harri, Danielle Bartlett, David Palmer, and Mark Steven Long. And, of course, my co-conspirator, Bret Witter. None of this would have happened without you guys.

This book is a result of what seems like a lifetime in combat, and I am grateful to all those who served with me and helped along the way, especially Gifford Miles, my platoon sergeant from the 82nd Airborne Division, who has always been a big brother to me.

Thanks as well to those who helped me get it right. A CIA friend (you know who you are). Fred Kagan, a great muse of international intrigue. Henry Escher, a seasoned thriller reader, who showed me what good dialogue looks like. Elena Pokalova, my Russian/Ukrainian friend who helped with the slang and feel of the place. Deanne and Jim Lewis,

Jay Parker, Corinne Bridges, Brett Duke, Elizabeth Butler, and Robert "the firewood guy," who read my drafts with keen eyes.

Lastly, I wish to acknowledge all those professional warriors out there who serve in the complicated shadows of world politics. You will never be left behind or forgotten.